A Dance to the Music of Time
II

Summer

Anthony Powell was born in 1905. After working in publishing and as a scriptwriter, he began to write for the *Daily Telegraph* in the mid-1930s. He served in the army during World War II and subsequently became the fiction reviewer on the *TLS*. Next came five years as literary editor of *Punch*. He was appointed a Companion of Honour in 1988. In addition to the twelve-novel sequence, *A Dance to the Music of Time*, he is the author of seven other novels, and four volumes of memoirs, *To Keep the Ball Rolling*. Anthony Powell died in March 2000.

ANTHONY POWELL

A Dance to the Music of Time
II

Summer

At Lady Molly's

Casanova's Chinese Restaurant

The Kindly Ones

ARROW

Reprinted in Arrow Books 2000

1 3 5 7 9 10 8 6 4 2

At Lady Molly's first published in Great Britain 1957
by William Heinemann Ltd
Copyright © 1957 by Anthony Powell
Casanova's Chinese Restaurant first published in Great Britain 1960
by William Heinemann Ltd
Copyright © 1960 by Anthony Powell
The Kindly Ones first published in Great Britain 1962
by William Heinemann Ltd
Copyright © 1962 by Anthony Powell

This edition first published in the United Kingdom
in 1997 by Mandarin and reprinted 4 times

Arrow Books
The Random House Group Limited
20 Vauxhall Bridge Road, London SW1V 2SA

Random House Australia (Pty) Limited
20 Alfred Street, Milsons Point, Sydney, New South Wales 2061, Australia

Random House New Zealand Limited
18 Poland Road, Glenfield, Auckland 10, New Zealand

Random House (Pty) Limited
Endulini, 5a Jubilee Road, Parktown 2193, South Africa

The Random House Group Limited Reg. No. 954009

www.randomhouse.co.uk

A CIP catalogue record for this book is available from the British Library

Papers used by Random House are natural, recyclable
products made from wood grown in sustainable forests. The
manufacturing processes conform to the environmental
regulations of the country of origin

Printed and bound in the United Kingdom by
Cox & Wyman Ltd, Reading, Berkshire

ISBN 0 09 941687 5

At Lady Molly's

For J.M.A.P.

1.

WE had known General Conyers immemorially not because my father had ever served under him but through some long-forgotten connexion with my mother's parents, to one or other of whom he may even have been distantly related. In any case, he was on record as having frequented their house in an era so remote and legendary that, if commission was no longer by purchase, regiments of the line were still designated by a number instead of the name of a county. In spite of belonging to this dim, archaic period, traces of which were sometimes revealed in his dress and speech—he was, for example, one of the last to my knowledge to speak of the Household Cavalry as 'the Plungers'—his place in family myth was established not only as a soldier with interests beyond his profession, but even as a man of the world always 'abreast of the times'. This taste for being in the fashion and giving his opinion on every subject was held against him by some people, notably Uncle Giles, no friend of up-to-date thought, and on principle suspicious of worldly success, however mild.

'Aylmer Conyers had a flair for getting on,' he used to say, 'No harm in that, I suppose. Somebody has got to give the orders. Personally I never cared for the limelight. Plenty of others to push themselves forward. Inclined to think a good deal of himself, Conyers was. Fine figure of a man, people used to say, a bit too fond of dressing himself up to the nines. Not entirely friendless in high places either. Quite the contrary. Peacetime or war, Conyers always knew the right people.'

I had once inquired about the General's campaigns.

'Afghanistan, Burma—as a subaltern. I've heard him talk big about Zululand. In the Soudan for a bit when the Khalifa was making trouble there. Went in for jobs abroad. Supposed to have saved the life of some native ruler in a local rumpus. Armed the palace eunuchs with rook rifles. Fellow gave him a jewelled scimitar—semi-precious stones, of course.'

'I've seen the scimitar. I never knew the story.'

Ignoring interruptions, Uncle Giles began to explain how South Africa, grave of so much military reputation, had been by Aylmer Conyers turned to good account. Having himself, as a result of his own indiscretions, retired from the army shortly before outbreak of war in the Transvaal, and possessing in addition those 'pro-Boer' sentiments appropriate to 'a bit of a radical', my uncle spoke always with severity, no doubt largely justified, of the manner in which the operations of the campaign had been conducted.

'After French moved over the Modder River, the whole Cavalry Division was ordered to charge. Unheard of thing. Like a gymkhana.'

'Yes?'

For a minute or two he lost the thread, contemplating the dusty squadrons wheeling from column into line across the veldt, or more probably assailed by memories of his own, less dramatic, if more bitter.

'What happened?'

'What?'

'What happened when they charged?'

'Cronje made an error of judgment for once. Only sent out detachments. Went through to Kimberley, more by luck than looking to.'

'But what about General Conyers?'

'Got himself into the charge somehow. Hadn't any business with the cavalry brigades. Put up some excuse. Then, day or two later, went back to where he ought to have been in the first place. Made himself most officious among the transport wagons. Line of march was like Hyde Park at the height of the Season, so a fellow who was in the advance told me—carriages end to end in Albert Gate—and Conyers running about cursing and swearing as if he owned the place.'

'Didn't Lord Roberts say something about his staff work?'

'Bobs?'

'Yes.'

'Who said that, your father?'

'I think so.'

Uncle Giles shook his head.

'Bobs may have said something. Wouldn't be the first time a general got hold of the wrong end of the stick. They say Conyers used to chase the women a bit, too. Some people thought he was going to propose to your Great-aunt Harriet.'

Other memories, on the whole more reliable, gainsay any such surmise regarding this last matter. In fact, Conyers remained a bachelor until he was approaching fifty. He was by then a brigadier-general, expected to go much further, when—to the surprise of his friends—he married a woman nearly twenty years younger than himself; sending in his papers about eighteen months later. Perhaps he was tired of waiting for the war with Germany he had so often prophesied, in which, had it come sooner, he would certainly have been offered high command. Possibly his wife did not enjoy following the drum, even as a general's lady. She is unlikely to have had much taste for army life. The General, for his own part, may have felt at last tired of military routine. Like many soldiers of ability

3

he possessed his eccentric side. Although no great performer, he had always loved playing the 'cello, and on retirement occupied much of his time with music; also experimenting with a favourite theory that poodles, owing to their keen natural intelligence, could profitably be trained as gun dogs. He began to live rather a social life, too, and was appointed a member of the Body Guard: the role in which, from early association of ideas, I always think of him.

'Funny that a fellow should want to be a kind of court flunkey,' Uncle Giles used to say. 'Can't imagine myself rigged out in a lot of scarlet and gold, hanging about royal palaces and herding in and out a crowd of young ladies in ostrich feathers. Did it to please his wife, I suppose.'

Mrs. Conyers, it is true, might have played some indirect part in this appointment. Eldest daughter of King Edward VII's friend, Lord Vowchurch, she had passed her thirtieth birthday at the time of marriage. Endless stories, not always edifying, are—or used to be—told of her father, one of those men oddly prevalent in Victorian times who sought personal power through buffoonery. His most enduring memorial (to be found, with other notabilities of the 'seventies, hanging in the damp, deserted billiard-room at Thrubworth) is Spy's caricature in the *Vanity Fair* series, depicting this high-spirited peer in frock-coat and top hat, both grey: the bad temper for which he was as notorious at home as for his sparkle in Society, neatly suggested under the side whiskers by the lines of the mouth. In later years Lord Vowchurch grew quieter, particularly after a rather serious accident as a pioneer in the early days of motoring. This mishap left him with a limp and injuries which seem to have stimulated that habitual banter, rarely good-natured, for which he had often been in trouble with King Edward, when Prince of Wales; and, equally often,

4

forgiven. His daughters had lived their early life in permanent disgrace for having, none of them, been born a boy.

My parents never saw much of the General and his wife. They knew them about as well as they knew the Walpole-Wilsons; though the Conyers relationship, with its foundations laid in a distant, fabled past, if never more intimate, was in some way deeper and more satisfying.

Like all marriages, the Conyers union presented elements of mystery. It was widely assumed that the General had remained a bachelor so long through conviction that a career is best made alone. He may have believed (like de Gaulle, whom he lived to see leading the Free French) in a celibate corps of officers dedicated like priests to their military calling. He wrote something of the sort in the *United Service Magazine*. This theory rested upon no objection to the opposite sex as such. On the contrary, as a young officer in India and elsewhere he was judged, as Uncle Giles had indicated, to have enjoyed a considerable degree of quiet womanising. Some thought that ambition of rather a different sort—a feeling that he had never fully experienced some of the good things of life—had finally persuaded him to marry and retire. A few of the incurably romantic even supposed him simply to have 'fallen in love' for the first time on the brink of fifty.

General and Mrs. Conyers seemed to 'get on' as well, if not better, than many married couples of a similar sort united at an earlier age. They moved, on the whole, in a circle connected, it might be said unpretentiously (because nothing could have been less 'smart', for example in Chips Lovell's use of the term, than the Conyers ménage) with the Court: families like the Budds and Udneys. In the limited but intense—and at times ornamental—preoccupations of these professional courtiers, the General seems to have found an adequate alternative to a life of command.

They had an only daughter called Charlotte, a rather colourless girl, who married a lieutenant-commander in the Navy. I used sometimes to have tea with her when we were both children.

In 1916, towards Christmas, at a time when Mrs. Conyers was assembling 'comforts' for troops overseas (still at this period in more amateur hands than the organisation that employed Uncle Giles after America came into the war) I was taken—passing through London on the way home from school—to her flat near Sloane Square. My mother paid the call either to add some knitted contribution to the pile of socks, scarves and Balaclava helmets lying about on chairs and sofas, or to help in some matter of their distribution. In the corner of the room in which all these bundles were stacked stood the 'cello in a case. Beside it, I at once noticed a large photograph of the General, carrying a halberd and wearing the plumed helmet, swallow-tailed coat and heavy gold epaulettes of a Gentleman-at-Arms. That is why I always think of him as a statuesque figure at levées and court balls, rather than the man of action he must for the greater part of his life have been. Retired from the army too long for any re-employment of the first importance, he had acquired soon after the outbreak of war some job, far from momentous, though respectably graded in the rank of major-general.

We had finished tea, and I was being shown the jewelled scimitar to which Uncle Giles had referred, which was kept for some reason in the London flat instead of the small house in Hampshire where the poodles were trained. This display was made by Mrs. Conyers as some amends for the fact that Charlotte was in the country; although no apology was necessary as it seemed to me more amusing without her. I was admiring the velvet-covered scabbard, wondering whether to draw the steel from its sheath would be permissible, when the maid showed someone into the room. This new arrival was a young woman wearing V.A.D. uniform, who strode in like a grenadier. She turned out to be Mildred Blaides, youngest sister to Mrs. Conyers.

Difference of age between the two of them must have been at least that of Mrs. Conyers and her husband. This Miss Blaides, indeed, represented her parents' final, unsuccessful effort to achieve an heir, before Lord Vowchurch's motor accident and total resignation to the title passing to a cousin. She was tall, with a long nose, no more handsome than her sister, but in my eyes infinitely more dashing than Mrs. Conyers. Her face was lively, not unlike the mask of a fox. Almost immediately she took from her pocket an ornamental cigarette-case made of some lacquer-like substance and lit a cigarette. Such an act, especially in one so young, was still in those days a sign of conscious female emancipation. I suppose she was then about twenty.

'Mildred is at Dogdene now,' explained Mrs. Conyers, 'You know the Sleafords offered their house as an officers' hospital when the war broke out. They themselves live in the east wing. There are huts all over the park too.'

'It's absolute hell having all those blighters in huts,' said Miss Blaides. 'Some of the tommies got tight the other night and pushed one of the stone urns off the Italian bridge into the lake. It was too bad of them. They are a putrid unit anyway. All the officers wear "gorblimeys".'

'What on earth are those, Mildred?' asked Mrs. Conyers, nervously.

I think she feared, after asking the question, that they might be something unsuitable to mention in front of a small boy, because she raised her hand as if to prevent the exposure of any too fearful revelation.

'Oh, those floppy army caps,' said Miss Blaides, carelessly. 'They take the stiffening out, you know. Of course they

7

have to do that when they are up at the Front, to prevent bits of wire getting blown into their cocoanuts, but they might try and look properly turned out when they are over here.'

She puffed away at her cigarette.

'I really must check all these gaspers,' she said, flicking ash on to the carpet. 'By now it's got up to about thirty a day. It just won't do. By the way, Molly Sleaford wants to come and see you, Bertha. Something about the distribution of "comforts". I told her to look you up on Wednesday, when she is next going to be in London.'

For some reason this announcement threw Mrs. Conyers into a state of great discomposure.

'But I can't possibly see Lady Sleaford on Wednesday,' she said, 'I've got three committee meetings on that day and Aylmer wants me to have five Serbian officers to tea. Besides, dear, Lady Sleaford is Red Cross, like you—and you remember how I am rather wedded, through Lady Bridgnorth, to St. John's. You see I really hardly know Lady Sleaford, who always keeps very much to herself, and I don't want to seem disloyal to Mary Bridgnorth. I——'

Her sister cut her short.

'Oh, I say, what a bally nuisance,' she remarked. 'I quite forgot about beastly old St. John's. They are always cropping up, aren't they? I really think they do more than the Germans to hold up winning the war.'

After voicing this alarming conjecture, she paced up and down the room, emitting from each nostril a long eddy of smoke like the trail of a ship briskly cutting the horizon. Throughout the room I was increasingly aware of the hardening of disapproval, just perceptible at first even on the immediate arrival of Miss Blaides: now not by any means to be denied. In fact a sense of positive disquiet swept through the small drawing-room so powerfully that mute condemnation seemed to rise in a thick cloud above the 'comforts', until its disturbing odour reached the ceiling and hung about the whole flat in vexed, compelling waves. This disapproval was on the part not only of Mrs. Conyers, but also—I felt sure—of my mother as well, who now began to make preparations to leave.

'A blinking bore,' said Miss Blaides, casting away her cigarette-end into the grate, where it lay smouldering on the tiles. 'That's what it is. So I suppose I shall have to tell Molly it's a wash-out. Give me another cup of tea, Bertha. I mustn't stay too long. I've got plans to scramble into some glad rags and beetle off to a show tonight.'

After that, we said good-bye; on my own part with deep regret. Later, when we were in the train, my mother said: 'I think it a pity for a girl like Miss Blaides to put on such a lot of make-up and talk so much slang. I was rather interested to see her, though. I had heard so much about her from different people.'

I did not mention the fact in reply, but, to tell the truth, Miss Blaides had seemed to me a figure of decided romance, combining with her nursing capacity of a young Florence Nightingale, something far more exciting and perhaps also a shade sinister. Nor did I realise at that time the implications contained in the phrase to 'hear a lot about' someone of Miss Blaides's age and kind. However, the episode as a whole—the Conyers' flat, the General's photograph, the jewelled scimitar, the 'comforts' stacked round the room, Miss Blaides in her V.A.D. uniform—all made a vivid impression on my mind; although, naturally enough, these things became soon stored away, apparently forgotten, in the distant background of memory. Only subsequent events revived them in strong colours.

That afternoon was also the first time I ever heard Dogdene mentioned. Later, of course, I knew it as the name of a 'great house' about which people talked. It came into volumes of memoirs like those of Lady Amesbury, which I read (with some disappointment) at an early age after hearing some grown-up person describe the book as 'scurrilous'. I also knew Constable's picture in the National Gallery, which shows the mansion itself lying away in the middle distance, a faery place set among giant trees, beyond the misty water-meadows of the foreground in which the impastoed cattle browse: quite unlike any imaginable military hospital. I knew this picture well before learning that the house was Dogdene. By then the place was no longer consciously associated in my mind with Miss Blaides. I was aware only vaguely that the owners were called Sleaford.

Then one day, years and years later, a chance reference to Dogdene made me think again of Miss Blaides in her original incarnation as a V.A.D., a status become, as it were, concealed and forgotten, like relics of an early civilisation covered by an ever-increasing pile of later architectural accretion. This was in spite of the fact that the name of Mildred Blaides would sometimes crop up in conversation after the occasional meetings between my parents and General or Mrs. Conyers. When she figured in such talk I always pictured a person somehow different from the girl chattering war-time slang on that winter afternoon. In fact the original memory of Miss Blaides returned to me one morning when I was sitting in my cream distempered, strip-lighted, bare, sanitary, glaring, forlorn little cell at the Studio. In that place it was possible to know deep despondency. Work, sometimes organised at artificially high pressure, would alternate with stretches of time in which a chaotic nothingness reigned: periods when, surrounded by the inanities and misconceptions of the film world, a book conceived in terms of comparative reality would to some extent alleviate despair.

During one of these interims of leisure, reading a volume of his Diary, I found Pepys had visited Dogdene. A note explained that his patron, Lord Sandwich, was connected by marriage with the then Countess of Sleaford: the marquisate dating only from the coronation of William IV.

'So about noon we came to Dogdene, and I was fain to see the house, and that part newly builded whereof Dr. Wren did formerly hold converse with me, telling me here was one of the first mansion houses of England contrived as a nobleman's seat rather than a keep moated for warfare. My Lord Sleaford is yet in town, where 'tis said he doth pay court to my Lady Castlemaine, at which the King is not a little displeased, 'tho 'twas thought she had long since lost her place. The Housekeeper was mighty civil, and showed us the Great Hall and stately Galleries, and the picture by P. Veronese that my Lord's grandfather did bring with him out of Italy, a most rare and noble thing. Then to the Gardens and Green Houses, where I did marvel to see the quickening of the Sensitive Plant. And so to the Still Room, where a great black maid offered a brave glass of metheglin, and I did have some merry talk with her begging her to show me a painted closet whereof the Housekeeper had spoken, yet had we not seen. Thither the bold wench took me readily enough, where I did kiss her twice or thrice and toyed wantonly with her. I perceive that she would not have denied me *que je voudray*, yet was I afeared and time was lacking. At which afterwards I was troubled, lest she should speak of what I had done, and her fellows make game of me when we were gone on our road.'

Everyone knows the manner in which some specific name will recur several times in quick succession from different quarters; part of that inexplicable magic throughout life that makes us suddenly think of someone before turning a street corner and meeting him, or her, face to face. In the same way, you may be struck, reading a book, by some obscure passage or lines of verse, quoted again, quite unexpectedly, twenty-four hours later. It so happens that soon after I read Pepys's account of Dogdene, I found myself teamed up as a fellow script-writer with Chips Lovell. The question arose of some country house to appear in a scenario.

'Do you mean a place like Dogdene?' I asked.

'That sort of thing,' said Lovell.

He went on to explain, not without some justifiable satisfaction, that his mother, the current Lord Sleaford's sister, had been brought up there.

I was then at the time of life when one has written a couple of novels, and moved from a firm that published art books to a company that produced second-feature films. To be 'an author' was, of course, a recognised path of approach to this means of livelihood; so much so, indeed, at that period, that to serve a term as a script-writer was almost a routine stage in literary life. On the other hand, Lovell's arrival in the Studio had been more devious. His chief stock in trade, after an excellent personal appearance and plenty of cheek, was expert manipulation of a vast horde of relations. Much more interested in daily journalism than in writing scenarios, he coveted employment on the gossip column of a newspaper. I knew Sheldon slightly, one of the editorial staff of the evening paper at which Lovell aimed, and had promised to arrange, if possible, a meeting between them.

Lovell delighted in talking about his relations. His parents had eloped on account of family opposition to their marriage. There had not been enough money. The elder Lovell, who was what Uncle Giles used to call 'not entirely friendless in high places', was a painter. His insipid,

Barbizonish little landscapes, not wholly devoid of merit, never sold beyond his own circle of friends. The elopement was in due course forgiven, but the younger Lovell was determined that no such grass should grow under his own feet. He was going to get on in life, he said, and in a few years make a 'good marriage'. Meanwhile, he was looking round, enjoying himself as much as business permitted. Since there were few enough jobs going about for young men at that time, his energies, which were considerable, had brought him temporarily into the film business; for which every one, including himself, agreed he had no particular vocation. Something better would turn up. The mystery remained how, in the first place, he had been accepted into an overcrowded profession. Our colleague, Feingold, hinted that the American bosses of the company dreamed of some intoxicating social advantage to be reaped by themselves, personally, through employing an eligible young man of that sort. Feingold may have been right: on the other hand, he was not wholly free from a strain of Jewish romanticism. Certainly it would have been hard to think of any fantasy too extraordinary for the thoughts of these higher executives to indulge.

One night, not long after we had talked of Dogdene, I had, together with Lovell, Feingold and Hegarty, unwillingly remained later than usual at the Studio in an effort to complete one of those 'treatments' of a film story, the tedium of which is known only to those who have experienced their concoction. On that particular evening, Feingold, in his mauve suit and crimson tie, was suffering from an unaccustomed bout of depression. He had graduated fairly recently from the cutting-room, at first full of enthusiasm for this new aspect of his craft. The pink skin of his plump, round face had begun to sag, making pockets around his bluish chin, as he lay back in a chair with an enormous pile of foolscap scribblings in front of him. He looked like a highly-coloured poster designed to excite compassion for the sufferings of his race. Hegarty was also in poor form that day. He had been a script-writer most of his grown-up life—burdened by then with three, if not four, wives, to all of whom he was paying alimony—and he possessed, when reasonably sober, an extraordinary facility for constructing film scenarios. That day, he could not have been described as reasonably sober. Groaning, he had sat all the afternoon in the corner of the room facing the wall. We were working on a stage play that had enjoyed a three-weeks West End run twenty or thirty years before, the banality of which had persuaded some director that it would 'make a picture.' This was the ninth treatment we had produced between us. At last, for the third time in an hour, Hegarty broke out in a cold sweat. He began taking aspirins by the handful. It was agreed to abandon work for the day.

Lovell and I used to alternate in which of us brought a car (both vehicles of modest appearance) to the Studio. That night it was Lovell's turn to give me a lift. We said good night to Feingold, who was moving Hegarty off to the pub at the end of the road. Lovell had paid twelve pounds ten for his machine; he started it up, though not without effort. I climbed in beside him. We drove towards London through the mist, blue-grey pockets of cloud drifting up ominously from the river.

'Shall we dine together?'

'All right. Let it be somewhere cheap.'

'Of that I am strongly in favour,' said Lovell. 'Do you know a place called Foppa's?'

'Yes—but don't let's go there.'

Although things had been 'over' with Jean for some time by then, Foppa's was still for some reason too reminiscent of her to be altogether comfortable; and I was firmly of the opinion that even the smallest trace of nostalgia for the immediate past was better avoided. A bracing future was required, rather than vain regrets. I congratulated myself on being able to consider the matter in such brisk terms. Lovell and I settled on some restaurant, and returned to the question whether Sheldon would be able to arrange for the job to be offered at just the right moment: the moment when Lovell's contract with the film company terminated, not before, nor too long after.

'I'm going to look in on an aunt of mine after making a meal,' Lovell said, tired at last of discussing his own prospects, 'Why not come too? There are always people there. At worst, it's a free drink. If some lovely girls are in evidence, we can dance to the gramophone.'

'What makes you think there will be lovely girls?'

'You may find anything at Aunt Molly's—even lovely girls. Are you coming?'

'I'd like to very much.'

'It's in South Kensington, I'm afraid.'

'Never mind. Tell me about your aunt.'

'She is called Molly Jeavons. She used to be called Molly Sleaford, you know."

'I didn't know.'

Confident that Lovell would enjoy giving further information, I questioned him. He had that deep appreciation of family relationships and their ramifications that is a gift of its own, like being musical, or having an instinct for the value of horses or jewels. In Lovell's own case, he made good practical use of this grasp, although such a talent not uncommonly falls to individuals more than usually free from any desire for personal advancement: while equally often lacking in persons rightly regarded by the world as snobbish. Lovell, almost as interested in everyone else's family as his own, could describe how the most various people were in fact quite closely related.

'When my first Sleaford uncle died,' said Lovell, 'his widow, Molly, married a fellow called Jeavons. Not a bad chap at all, though of rather unglamorous background. He couldn't be described as particularly bright either, in spite of playing quite a good game of snooker. No live wire, in fact. Molly, on the other hand, is full of go.'

'What about her?'

'She was an Ardglass.'

'Any relation of Bijou Ardglass?'

'Sister-in-law, before Jumbo Ardglass divorced Bijou—who was his second wife, of course. Do you know her—probably slept with her? Most of one's friends have.'

'I've only seen her about the place. No other privileges.'

'Of course, you wouldn't be rich enough for Bijou,' said Lovell, not unkindly. 'But, as I was saying, Bijou got through what remained of the Ardglass money, which wasn't much, and left Jumbo, who'd really had enough himself by that time. Since then, she has been keeping company with a whole string of people—Prince Theodoric —God knows who. However, I believe she still comes to see Molly. Molly is like that. She will put up with any-one.'

'But why do you call him your "first" Sleaford uncle?'

'Because he died, and I still have an uncle of that name—the present one is Geoffrey—the first, John. Uncle Geoffrey was too poor to marry until he succeeded. He could only just rub along in one of the cheaper cavalry regiments. There were two other brothers between him and the title. One was killed in the war, and the other knocked down by a bus.'

'They don't seem much good at staying alive.'

'The thing about the Sleafords,' said Lovell, 'is that

they've always been absolutely mad on primogeniture. That's all very well in a way, but they've been so bloody mean to their widows and younger children that they are going to die out. They are a splendid example of upper-class stinginess. Geoffrey got married at once, as people do when they come into a peerage, however dim. Of course, in this case—with Dogdene thrown in—it was something worth having. Unfortunately they've never managed to knock up an heir.'

Lovell went on to describe his 'first Sleaford uncle', who seems to have been a chilly, serious-minded, competent peer, a great organiser of charitable institutions, who would have done well for himself in any walk of life. For a time he had been taken up with politics and held office under Campbell-Bannerman and Asquith.

'He resigned at the time of the Marconi scandal,' said Lovell. 'He hadn't been making anything on the side himself, but he thought some of his Liberal colleagues had been a bit too liberal in the ethics of their own financial dealings. He was a selfish old man, but had what is called an exaggerated sense of honour.'

'I think I've seen Isbister's portrait of him.'

'Wearing the robes of the Garter. He took himself pretty seriously. Molly married him from the ballroom. She was only eighteen. Never seen a man before.'

'When did he die?'

'Spanish 'flu in 1919,' said Lovell. 'Molly first met Jeavons when Dogdene was a military hospital in the war. He was rather badly wounded, you know. The extraordinary thing was they didn't start a love affair or anything. If Uncle John hadn't died, she would still be—in the words of an Edwardian song my father hums whenever her name is mentioned—"Molly the Marchioness."'

'Where did she re-meet her second husband?'

'At the Motor Show. Went to Olympia in her widow's weeds and saw Jeavons again. He was acting as a polisher on one of the stalls. I can't remember which make, but not a car anyone would be proud to own. That represented just about the height of what he could rise to in civil life. They were married about six months later.'

'How does it go?'

'Very well. Molly never seems to regret the Dogdene days in the least. I can't think what they use for money, because, if I know the Sleafords, she didn't get much in the way of a jointure—and I doubt if she has a hundred a year of her own. The Ardglass family have been hopelessly insolvent since the Land Act. However, she manages to support herself—and Jeavons—somehow. And also get some fun out of life.'

'Doesn't Jeavons bring in anything?'

'Not a cent. I think he feels pretty ill most of the time. He often looks like death itself. Besides, he is quite unemployable. As a matter of fact, it isn't true to say he does nothing. Once in a way he has some appliance he is marketing—an automatic bootjack or new cure for the common cold. Something he gets a commission on, or perhaps some firm is paying him a trifle to recommend the thing.'

The description made an impression on me. The picture of Jeavons took on a more positive shape: not a particularly attractive one. 'Realism goes with good birth,' Lovell used to say, and he himself certainly showed this quality where his own relations were concerned. The statement might be hard to substantiate universally, but, by recognising laws of behaviour operating within the microcosm of a large, consanguineous network of families, however loosely connected, individuals born into such a world often gain an unsentimental grasp of human conduct: a grasp sometimes superior to that of apparently more perceptive persons whose minds are unattuned by early association· to the constant give and take of an ancient and tenacious social organism. Of course, it does not always work that way, but Lovell, with his many limitations, was himself a good example of the principle.

'The chief reason I want to visit Aunt Molly,' he said, 'is to take another look at Priscilla Tolland, who is quite often there.'

'A sister of Blanche Tolland?'

'Yes. Do you know Blanche?'

'Only by sight, and years ago. She is rather dotty, isn't she?'

'Quite dotty,' said Lovell. 'Lives in a complete world of her own. Fairly happy about it though, I think.'

'Then there is one called Norah, isn't there, who set up house with a rather strange girl I used to know called Eleanor Walpole-Wilson.'

'That's it. She is rather dotty too, but in a different way. That couple are said to be a *ménage*. Then there is Isobel. She is rather different. Priscilla is the youngest. She isn't really "out" yet.'

I was about twenty-eight or twenty-nine at that period, to Lovell's twenty-three or twenty-four, and through him had become aware for the first time that a younger generation was close on my heels. I told him I felt much too old and passé to take an interest in such small fry as young ladies who were not yet 'out'.

'Oh, I quite realise that,' said Lovell indulgently. 'There will certainly be elder persons there too for chaps like you who prefer serious conversation. You might like Isobel. I believe she is a bit of a highbrow when she isn't going to night clubs.'

We drove precariously down Gloucester Road, the car

emitting a series of frightening crepitations and an evil fume, while Lovell artlessly outlined his long-term plans for the seduction of Priscilla Tolland. We turned off somewhere by the Underground station. I liked the idea of going to this unknown place for an hour or so, surroundings where the cheerless Studio atmosphere might be purged away. Lovell stopped in front of a fairly large house of dark red brick, the architecture of which sounded a distant, not particularly encouraging, echo of the High Renaissance. After waiting on the doorstep for some time, the door was opened by a man of indeterminate age in shirt sleeves and carpet slippers. He might have passed for a butler. Pale and unhealthy looking, he had the air of having lived for months at a time underground in unventilated, overheated rooms. He brought with him odours of beer and cheese. Closer examination of this unkempt, moody fellow revealed him as older than he had appeared at first sight.

'Good evening, Smith,' said Lovell, rather grandly.

' 'Evening,' said Smith, speaking without the smallest suggestion of warmth.

'How are you, Smith?'

Smith looked Lovell up and down as if he considered the enquiry not merely silly, but downright insulting. He did not answer.

'Is her Ladyship upstairs?'

'Where do you think she'd be—in the basement?'

The tone of Smith's voice made no concession whatever towards alleviating the asperity of this answer. Lovell showed no sign of surprise at being received so caustically, passing off the retort with a hearty laugh. Smith shambled off down the stairs, muttering to himself. He seemed thoroughly fed up, not only with Lovell, but also with his own job.

'Smith is wonderful, isn't he?' said Lovell, as we mounted the staircase. 'Aunt Molly sometimes borrows him from Erridge, when, for one reason or another, Thrubworth is closed down. I should warn you there is never an electric light bulb in the downstairs lavatory here and sometimes no bromo.'

I followed him to the first floor; and into a double drawing-room in which eight or nine persons were standing or sitting. A general though never precisely defined suggestion of chinoiserie, sustained by a profusion of Oriental bowls and jars, pervaded the decoration. Some of the furniture was obviously rather valuable: the rest, gimcrack to a degree. Pictures showed a similar variation of standard, a Richard Wilson and a Greuze (these I noted later) hanging among pastels of Moroccan native types. A dark, handsome woman, now getting a trifle plump by the emaciated standards of the period, came towards us.

'Why, Chips,' she said. 'Here you are at last. We thought you would be earlier.'

'Couldn't get away, Aunt Molly,' said Lovell. 'This is Mr. Jenkins. He and I slave away writing films together.'

'What will you drink?' she asked. 'Teddy, get them something to drink quickly. They must be in dire need.'

She smiled at me as if she were rather proud of that last phrase. Jeavons now appeared before us and began to make some rather hopeless gestures in the direction of several bottles and decanters standing on a table at the far end of the room. It was at once apparent that he was something left over from the war. I found it almost impossible to believe that he would so much resemble the mental picture conjured up by Lovell's earlier description of him. Like one of those mammoths—or, in Jeavons's case, somewhat less gigantic form of primeval life—caught in a glacier and physically preserved into an age when his very kind was known only from fossilised bones, or drawings on the walls of subterranean caves, he somehow managed to look just as he must have looked in 1917: hardly a day older. Perhaps a better simile to indicate the effect of remoteness he gave, standing there with a vacant expression and both hands in his pockets, would be that of some rare insect enclosed in amber. He wore a minute Charlie Chaplin moustache, his dark, shiny hair, in which there was a touch of red, rolling away from his forehead like the stone locks of a sculpted head of Caracalla.

At this point I became suddenly aware that at least one of the guests present was already well known to me. This was my family's old friend, Mrs. Conyers. Although I had not seen her at all recently, we had met from time to time— usually at intervals of several years—since the distant day when I had been taken to her flat and shown the scimitar. The last occasion had been the wedding of her daughter, Charlotte, to the lieutenant-commander. Evidently Mrs. Conyers had been dining with the Jeavonses. However, it appeared that she did not know them well, and, perhaps not greatly at ease in their society, she was clearly much relieved at finding, in myself, someone she knew of old. I was not sure that I myself was equally pleased, for, although I liked Mrs. Conyers well enough, I thought it preferable to explore new ground like the Jeavons house unobserved by old friends of my parents. However, nothing could have been less admonitory than Mrs. Conyers's manner towards myself; if admonition properly defines the attitude threatened, when one is young, by the presence of old family friends.

In appearance Mrs. Conyers retained, no doubt from her childhood, the harassed, uncertain expression of those who have for many years had to endure close association with persons addicted to practical joking. Like the rest of her sisters, she must have suffered in no small degree from her father's love of horse-play. One of six daughters, she had been regarded as 'on the shelf' by her parents when the General proposed to her. She herself had probably abandoned thought of marriage, because she was by then devoting most of her time to attending an elderly, intractable relation, Sybil, Lady Amesbury, whose memoirs I mentioned earlier. One of her father's exploits had been recorded in this book, the occasion when Lord Vowchurch, in his younger days, had loosed half a dozen monkeys wearing tail-coats and white ties at an ambassadorial ball: a casual relic of innumerable similar anecdotes that have passed into oblivion.

Although never exactly handsome, Mrs. Conyers was not without a look of sad distinction. In public she deferred to her husband, but she was known to possess a will of her own, displayed in that foxy, almost rodent-like cast of feature, which, resembling her sister's in its keenness, was not disagreeable. It was said that she had entirely reorganised the General's life after he had left the army; and much for the better. When I went across the room to speak with her, she raised her eyebrows slightly to indicate, if not precise disapproval, at least a secret signal that she felt herself not altogether at home. The message read that she required any support she could get.

Lovell had made for a red-faced, grey-moustached, elderly man, who seemed, like Mrs. Conyers, to have been a member of the dinner-party. This person possessed a curiously old-world air, suggesting an epoch considerably more remote than the war-time span conveyed by his host's outward appearance. Although not so old, he seemed to belong more, at least in spirit, to the vintage of General Conyers. I caught the words 'Uncle Alfred'. Lovell called so many men uncle that one could not be sure how closely related to him, if at all, any of them might be. This uncle acknowledged Lovell's greeting fairly curtly. There was something familiar about that red face, white moustache and muffled, uneasy manner. Then I realised that he was Tolland, that lonely, derelict character accustomed to frequent the annual Old Boy dinner of Le Bas's house. In fact, I had myself once sat next to Tolland at one of those functions: an occasion when I had made up my mind never to attend another.

It was a surprise to find Mrs. Conyers and Tolland here, but there was no reason why they should not both be friends of Lady Molly Jeavons. Mrs. Conyers was now engaged by her hostess, and led up to a swarthy young man, also wearing a dinner-jacket, who was standing by the gramophone turning over the pages of a book of records. They all began to talk French together. At that moment my eye caught Tolland's. He stared back, not without a certain apprehension in his look. Then he cleared his throat and advanced towards me.

'I didn't see you at the Le Bas dinner this year,' he said.

He spoke with reproach, as if to mention such a breach of faith was an embarrassing duty his conscience laid upon him. In these surroundings, evidently his own ground, I felt less ability to cope with his peculiarities than at the Le Bas dinners. It seemed better to conceal the decision never to attend another one.

'I didn't manage to get there.'

'It went off all right,' said Tolland slowly, as if ghastly failure had been a matter of touch and go. 'I always accept when the card comes round. It makes a pleasant evening. Got to keep in touch. Of course Le Bas always says that in his speech.'

Molly Jeavons, after talking for a minute or two with

Mrs. Conyers and the young man with the black moustache, now rejoined Tolland and myself.

'I couldn't keep it up any longer,' she said. 'French is too exhausting. My governess said I was the worst pupil she'd ever had at the irregular verbs. All the same, I wanted to hear if there was anything new about Theodoric.'

She pointed her finger at me.

'Is he another of your relations, Alfred?' she asked.

Her tone suggested that potential relationship with Tolland might explain everything: why I had come to the house: why I looked as I did: why we were talking together. I attempted to reduce my appearance to something as negative as possible, so that no one might be unduly committed by the enquiry, which had thrown Tolland into an appalling access of embarrassment.

'Really, I believe you have more relations than I have myself,' she went on. 'My grandfather had ninety-seven first cousins, and he was only three up on my grandmother on my mother's side.'

'No—no—no,' said Tolland, hurriedly. 'At least I don't think we are, are we? Never know—perhaps I oughtn't to have been so definite—quite on the cards, I suppose, as a matter of fact. Shouldn't speak hastily about such things. Certainly got a lot of 'em. Some people might think too many, as you say, Molly. No—no—no. Perhaps you can tell better than me. Are we related? No? Thought not. Always try to keep track of 'em. Hard to manage sometimes. Go abroad and get married and get divorced and into debt, glad to see the back of 'em sometimes. But where you and I meet is at the Le Bas dinner. That's where *we* meet.'

He gasped a bit after all this, as if not only breathless from speaking at such length, but also overcome with confusion at the predicament into which he had been thrown

25

by the question. Yet, even in spite of this floundering, he seemed to feel himself on much surer ground in this house than at our previous meetings. He might be temporarily at a disadvantage here with his hostess, even on guard against attack from her (a minute or two later I found he had good reason to fear that), but at least his credentials were known and freely accepted in the Jeavons drawing-room. I was by no means sure that I felt myself equally at ease. The atmosphere of the house was not exactly restful. The other persons who made up the party were nondescript enough, but there was also the feeling that one had penetrated the outskirts of a secret society. Mrs. Conyers had seemed as subject as myself to this sense of disquiet. Perhaps it was merely that she had passed on to me her own agitation; for I was sure she was agitated about something. Lovell had certainly tried to prepare me for an unusual household, but to absorb such antecedent descriptions is never easy. Molly Jeavons's noisy, absolutely unrestrained directness of manner was of a kind that suggested both simplicity of nature and certainty of her own position: both characteristics that can stimulate that streak of social cruelty that few lack. There could be no doubt that Tolland was showing signs of preparing himself for some onslaught. The reason for his fears soon became apparent.

'I didn't know you ever met anyone but your own relations, Alfred,' she said, evidently determined to pursue that subject. 'You always pretend to me that you never go anywhere. I only got you here tonight because you wanted to hear from her own lips Mrs. Conyers's story about the Empress Frederick. I believe your quiet evenings at home are all make-believe and that you live a disgracefully fast life—the gayest of gay bachelors.'

Tolland denied this imputation emphatically. He did not seem in the least flattered at the suggestion that he might be, so far as social life was concerned, a dark horse. He was patently without the smallest personal vanity, open or secret, on the matter of cutting a dash in life. He came at last to the end of his protests.

'Alfred was talking about his family all through dinner,' said Molly Jeavons, turning once more to me. 'You know they are all in trouble—every blessed one of them.'

'It's too bad of you to say that, Molly. I only asked for your advice about some of my nephews and nieces.'

Now he sounded thoroughly aggrieved, although at the same time unwilling to withdraw voluntarily from a conversation devoted to his relations.

'What's the matter with the Tollands this time, Aunt Molly?' asked Lovell.

He had been making a tour of the room, ending with our group.

'Oh, it's Erridge again,' she said.

She spoke as if the question were hardly worth asking.

'What's Erridge's latest?'

Lovell, for his part, spoke as one expecting to hear an enjoyable piece of gossip about a character always to be relied upon to provide a good story.

'Living as a tramp,' said Molly Jeavons. 'So I'm told at least. Somewhere in the Midlands. Grew a beard. He has still got it, they say. I don't think he actually slept in casual wards. The other tramps must have had an awful time if he did. As a child he used to talk in his sleep and bawl the house down with night terrors.'

'Is he doing that now?' asked Lovell. 'Being a tramp, I mean, not bawling the house down—though I shouldn't wonder if he doesn't have night terrors still.'

'He is back at Thrubworth. Getting cleaned up after his adventures—as much as Erry ever gets cleaned up. Smith goes back tomorrow. I am more and more coming to think

27

that Smith is more trouble than he is worth. It's convenient to have a manservant in the house, but I found this morning we were completely out of gin, and I know at least two inches remained in the bottle left when we went to bed last night.'

Lovell was obviously disappointed that nothing more sensational about Erridge was to be revealed.

'Feingold had some story about "a lord" who was doing "social research",' he said. 'I thought it might be Erridge. I don't expect the dumps he stopped at were any more uncomfortable than he has made Thrubworth by now. The whole place has been under dust-sheets since he succeeded, hasn't it? Do you know Erridge, Nick? He must be about a contemporary of yours.'

'He is a year or two older. I used to know him by sight. His brother, George Tolland, was nearer my age, though I didn't know him either. But he isn't "Erridge" any longer, is he?'

'No, no, he is "Warminster" now, of course,' said Molly Jeavons, impatiently. 'But Alfred's family always call their eldest son by the second title. I don't even know what Erry's Christian name is. Perhaps he hasn't got one.'

'Nonsense, of course he has,' said Tolland, quite angrily. 'His name is Alfred, like my own. You know that perfectly well, Molly. Besides, to call him "Erridge" is perfectly usual, isn't it? In fact, off-hand, I can't think of a single family that does differently.'

'We always used to think it rather pompous,' said Molly Jeavons. 'I can't imagine myself ever addressing Jumbo as "Kilkeel" when he was alive. It would sound like a race-horse.'

'Well, "Jumbo" sounds like an elephant to me,' said Tolland.

This retort must have struck him as one of unusual

subtlety, since he looked round at Lovell and myself in an appeal for applause; or at least for sympathy.

'That's just it,' said Molly Jeavons, now speaking almost at the top of her voice. 'My poor brother did look like an elephant. Nobody denied that, not even himself. But he did not look like a race-horse. Not one I would have put my money on, anyway.'

'Bijou put her shirt on him,' said Lovell.

'Rubbish, she didn't,' said Molly Jeavons, beginning to laugh. 'He put his shirt on her, you idiot—and lost it, too.'

I remembered, then, that Tolland had spoken of 'my nephew, Warminster', at the Le Bas dinner where we had met; at the same time mentioning that this young man had succeeded his father some years before. Tolland had added that his nephew was 'a funny boy'. Erridge (as it seems simplest—like his parents—to continue to call him, anyway for the time being) remained in my mind as a gloomy, cadaverous schoolboy, trudging along the road close to the wall, his hands in his pockets and a pile of books slipping from under his arm. Angular, sallow and spotty, he was usually frowning angrily to himself, weighed down with anxiety, as if all the troubles of the world rested on his shoulders. The only time I could recall seeing him in later life was, years before, at a dance given by the Huntercombes. On that occasion, Erridge had looked so hot, cross and untidy that only the fact that he was wearing a tail-coat and white tie—neither in their first freshness—prevented him from resembling, even then, a harassed young tramp. His appearance that night had certainly borne out this recent account of him. The ball at the Huntercombes' remained always with peculiar clarity in my mind as the night Barbara Goring had poured sugar over Widmerpool's head.

'Does Erridge often do this sort of thing?' I asked. 'Go off on "social research", I mean?'

'Oh yes,' said Molly Jeavons. 'He has the oddest ideas. All your family have, haven't they, Alfred? The whole blessed lot of them.'

Tolland made a nervous movement with his head, as if attempting to deny the principle of the accusation while at the same time regretfully having to admit, anyway in part, some of its immediate justice.

'Warminster was not like that,' he said. 'I'm not like that. Not in the least. Nor are Frederica and George. And I trust the younger ones will turn out different from Erridge. They all seemed all right when they were children. Ran about and made a lot of noise. Just can't tell, I suppose. Just—can't—tell.'

If he expected this exhibition of philosophic resignation in some manner to appease Molly Jeavons, he was mistaken.

'Certainly Frederica is not strange,' she said, laughing uproariously at the idea. 'Frederica is ordinary enough for anyone. Got to be in her job. Frederica is as ordinary as you like.'

This agreement with his conclusion—the complete, the absolute ordinariness of his niece, Frederica—seemed to bring some temporary alleviation to Tolland's feelings. He nodded several times with satisfaction. I had some vague idea as to Frederica's identity. She had married one of the Budds, brother or cousin of a 'beauty' called Margaret Budd, and her husband had been killed in a hunting accident only a few years later. People had talked about his death in the days when I used to dine with the Walpole-Wilsons. I remembered Anne Stepney talking about the accident.

As I was by then committed to this conversation about a lot of people regarding whom I knew little or nothing, I decided to take an active part by seeking further information. I asked what Frederica Budd's job might be that required such extreme correctness of behaviour.

'She is Lady-in-Waiting,' said Molly Jeavons. 'Or she may be an Extra Woman of the Bedchamber. Something like that. Anyway, she has to behave herself jolly well. I'm surprised you haven't met her, if you are an old friend of Mrs. Conyers. She and Frederica are great cronies.'

At that period, as I have said, I knew little of the Tollands, although increasingly during the past few years I had been hearing scraps of information about one or other of them, as happens when a large family, close to each other in age, begin in quick succession to appear in the world. Lovell had given some account of them at dinner. Molly Jeavons's sister, Katherine, a childless widow, had married the late Lord Warminster as his second wife. 'As a result,' Lovell had said, 'she possesses a dozen step-children.' It turned out, in fact, that Erridge had only nine brothers and sisters. Even that number seemed preposterously large to an only child like myself. There is something overpowering, even a trifle sinister about very large families, the individual members of which often possess in excess the characteristics commonly attributed to 'only' children: misanthropy: neurasthenia: an inability to adapt themselves: all the traits held to be the result of a lonely upbringing. The corporate life of large families can be lived with severity, even barbarity, of a kind unknown in smaller related communities: these savageries and distillations of egoism often rendered even less tolerable if sentimentalised outside the family circle. The Tollands, from what Lovell reported of them, sounded no exception to this prejudiced judgment.

'Of course it was hard for them losing their mother—being left orphans, in fact,' said Tolland. 'Though of course Katherine has always done her best—been splendid, really.'

By introducing the name of the second Lady Warminster

into the conversation, he may have hoped to carry the war into the enemy's country. By then his face was more flushed than ever. His hostess was determined to let him off nothing. I had the impression that she was teasing him, not precisely for my especial benefit, but, at the same time, that my presence as a newcomer to the house afforded a particularly favourable opportunity for the application of torments of this sort. I found later that she was indeed what is called 'a tease', perhaps the only outward indication that her inner life was not altogether happy; since there is no greater sign of innate misery than a love of teasing. Later, too, I understood how much that night Alfred Tolland must have been torn between a pride that made him hesitate to discuss his relations in front of a stranger, and a taste for talking about his family, too rarely satisfied in his lonely life. It was a treat to visit someone who understood the niceties of family gossip, even if Molly Jeavons required her pound of flesh by ragging him. His face, completely masculine in cast, had at the same time that air of being quite untouched by sexual passion : a look noticeable sometimes among men of his generation. Lovell explained to me later that Tolland had always had a taste for good works and had been much used by the late Lord Sleaford in connexion with his charities. He was a fine example of my friend Barnby's observation that 'melancholy is the curse of the upper classes'.

'And what about Norah?' said Molly Jeavons.

She had to repeat the question twice, for the first time Tolland made no attempt to reply. He seemed completely knocked out. The challenge was apparently unanswerable. He could only nod his head. There was no spirit left in him. To bridge the silence, I asked if it were not true that Norah Tolland shared a flat with Eleanor Walpole-Wilson.

'She does, she does,' cried Molly Jeavons, laughing loudly

again at my question, as if I had shown myself to have missed the whole point of what was being said. 'Do you know them? I didn't think they ever saw any young men. I'm jolly glad to hear they do. Tell me about them. Is it true that Eleanor has been seen in a green pork-pie hat and a bow tie?'

Mrs. Conyers, escaped from the man to whom French must be talked, now joining our group, nodded her head and pursed her lips, as if to emphasise the depths to which Eleanor had fallen.

'As a matter of fact, I haven't seen Eleanor for years,' I said. 'I used to dine with them once in a way. I saw Sir Gavin Walpole-Wilson at the Isbister Retrospective Exhibition when it was on, and he said something about Norah Tolland. I've never met her.'

'They look like a couple of stable-boys,' said Molly Jeavons. 'And talk like stable-boys, too. I hear they swear like troopers.'

From the way she spoke, I suspected she knew very little about these two young women, and was, in fact, anxious to learn more. Finding me unable to offer a closely observed report on their activities, she abandoned the subject and renewed her general attack on Tolland.

'And then Hugo,' she said. 'What about Hugo?'

She spoke as if Hugo clinched every other argument. If the name of Norah had knocked Tolland out, that of Hugo reduced him to the position of an army not only defeated in the field, but also forced to join as an ally its victorious adversary.

'I hear his clothes are—well, awful,' he muttered, almost inaudibly.

So far as Hugo was concerned, he seemed to agree absolutely with Molly Jeavons in thinking the situation could scarcely be worse.

33

'But all undergraduates are like that,' said Mrs. Conyers, unexpectedly. 'I mean they all wear extraordinary clothes, don't they? They always have—and say things to try and shock people. My father used to say they were like that even in his day. I know he himself, just after he had been sent down from Oxford, said some terrible thing to Mr. Gladstone when he was introduced to him at Holland House. My father had to write and apologise, or I don't know what would have happened. I am not sure the Ministry might not have fallen.'

'Well,' said Molly Jeavons, 'I've known some under-graduates in my time—Jumbo, for instance, you should have seen him in his young days—but I've never met one who dressed like Hugo. I was talking to the Bridgnorths' boy, John Mountfichet, when he was here the other day. He is at the same college as Hugo. He told us some things that would make your hair stand on end. They made Teddy laugh, and you know how difficult that is.'

'Even Sillery says Hugo goes too far,' said Lovell. 'He drives all the other dons quite mad, of course, but I should have thought Sillery would have stuck up for him. The other undergraduates are very disapproving too. Apart from anything else, æsthetes have gone completely out of fashion at both universities these days. I told Hugo when I saw him the other day that he was hopelessly out of date.'

'What did he say?'

' "My dear, I love being *dated*. I hate all this bickering that goes on about politics. I wish I'd lived in the *Twenties* when people were *amusing*." '

Lovell spoke the words with the mannerism he judged appropriate to such an impersonation.

'He'll grow out of it,' said Mrs. Conyers, surprising me with this repeated display of toleration. 'Lots of nice young men go through a stage of being rather silly.'

'Let's hope so,' said Alfred Tolland, with a sigh.

He did not sound very confident.

'At any rate, George is all right,' he added a moment later.

I had the impression he was playing his last card, but that this card was a trump.

'What is George Tolland doing now?' I asked. 'He was the one of the family who was my contemporary, though I never really knew him.'

'In the Coldstream for some years,' said Alfred Tolland. 'Then he thought he ought to try and make some money, so he went into the City. He has done fairly well, so they say. Never know what people mean by that—but they say pretty well.'

'Oh, yes,' said Molly Jeavons. 'I am sure that George has done well. But what a correct young man—*what a correct young man*! I don't think I ever met a young man who was so correct. I can't see how we are ever going to get him married, he is so correct—and even if we found a correct wife for him, I am sure they would both be much too correct to have any children. And even if they did, what frightfully correct children they would have to be.'

'You can't have it both ways, Molly,' grumbled Tolland. 'You blame some of them for misbehaving themselves. Perhaps you are right. But then you don't approve of George because he is what you call "correct". Can't understand it. There is no pleasing you. It isn't reasonable.'

'Well, now I'll tell you about the rest of them,' said Molly Jeavons, turning to me. 'Of course I really adore them all, and just say these things to make Alfred cross. There is Susan, who is showing every sign of getting engaged to a nice young man, then there is Blanche——'

'I've seen Blanche, though I don't know her.'

'Blanche is dotty. You must know that much, if you've seen her. But she's not a bad old thing.'

'Of course not.'

Alfred Tolland showed no disposition to deny the 'dottiness' of his niece, Blanche.

'Robert is a bit of a mystery. He is in some business, but I don't know whether he will stay there. Isobel—well, she is a bit different too. I'm not sure she isn't going to get engaged soon herself. Then there is Priscilla, who is on the point of coming out, and was to have been here tonight, but she doesn't seem to have turned up yet.'

I made an effort to take in this bird's-eye view of the Tollands, who now seemed to surround me on all sides after this vivid exposition of their several characters. Instinctively, I felt the greatest interest in Isobel, who was 'different'; and also an odd feeling of regret that she might be about to become engaged in the near future. While I was brooding on this, Jeavons joined us. He stood there, scanning everyone's face closely, as if hoping for some explanation of the matter in hand; perhaps even of life itself, so intense was his concentration: some reasonable interpretation couched in terms simple enough for a plain man to understand without undue effort. He also gave the impression of an old dog waiting to have a ball thrown to retrieve, more because that was the custom in the past than because sport or exercise was urgently required. However, no one enlightened him as to the subject under discussion, so he merely filled up my glass, and then his own. His wife and Alfred Tolland had now embarked on some detailed aspect of Tolland life, too esoteric for an outsider to follow.

'In the film business like Chips?' Jeavons asked, in a low husky voice, as if he had a cold coming on, or had drunk too much whisky the night before.

'Yes.'

'Ever met any of the stars?'

'Not so you'd notice. I'm on the scenario side. The studio only makes English pictures for the quota. They wouldn't be likely to employ anyone very grand in the way of an actor or actress.'

Jeavons seemed disappointed at this answer.

'Still,' he urged, 'you must see some beauties sometimes, don't you?'

'I've sat next to Adolph Menjou,' said his wife, suddenly abandoning the subject of the Tollands, and breaking in with her accustomed violence, though not, I think, with any idea of preventing him from pursuing the question of film actresses and their looks. 'He had such nice manners. Of course Garbo is the one I should really like to meet. I suppose everyone would. Wouldn't you like to meet Garbo, Alfred?'

'Never heard of him,' said Tolland.

Inevitably there was some laughter at this.

'It's a *she*,' said Molly Jeavons. 'It's a *she*, Alfred.'

'An actress, I suppose,' said Tolland, 'or you wouldn't be using that tone of voice. I don't think I particularly want to meet Miss Garbo—or perhaps it is Mrs. Garbo.'

There was more laughter at that. I was not sure—I am not sure to this day—whether he was feigning ignorance of the famous film star, whose name at that moment, the zenith of her fame, was a synonym for mysterious, elusive, feminine beauty; or whether he had, in truth, never heard of her.

'I once met Mrs. Patrick Campbell when I was a young man,' he said, speaking as if the statement was an afterthought. 'Heard her read aloud *High Tide on the Coast of Lincolnshire*. Wonderful experience. Felt different all the evening. Couldn't sleep after it. Lay awake—well—till the morning, nearly.'

Possibly Molly Jeavons felt that for a brief second the tables had been turned on her, because she now returned to the charge in the game of baiting him about his family, probably feeling in that activity on safer ground.

'Tell us more about the stained-glass window, Alfred,' she said.

This request galvanised him once again to the point of anger. She seemed to have touched some specially sensitive nerve.

'I've told you already, Molly,' he said, 'the window has never been put up as it should have been. Erridge isn't interested.'

'Surely somebody in the family can tell him to do it,' she said. 'Why can't you tell him to get on with the job yourself? He must do it, that's all.'

She spoke as if her own decision made the matter final. Alfred Tolland shook his head gloomily.

'As well ask him to lead the glass himself,' he said. 'Better, in fact. He might have a try at that. Dignity of labour or something. But as for taking an interest in his own grandfather's memorial——'

Tolland shook his head, finding metaphor, as applied to Erridge, impotent.

'Can't George take it on?' insisted Molly Jeavons. 'You think so highly of George.'

Tolland shook his head again.

'Difficult for George,' he said. 'Delicate, with Erridge the eldest son. George doesn't want to be snubbed.'

'Oh, goodness,' said Molly Jeavons, throwing up her hands, 'you Tollands drive me mad.'

Some new guests came into the room at that moment, so that her own plan for solving the problem of the stained-glass window was never revealed. In the reshuffle of places, I found myself *tête-à-tête* with Mrs. Conyers. After a few preliminary enquiries about my parents, she explained that the General was indisposed, though not seriously, having fallen headlong from the stable loft where the poodles' food was stored. He must at that time have been a few years short of eighty.

'But I did not remember you knew Lady Molly,' said Mrs. Conyers in a low voice.

'I did not, until tonight.'

'Rather a happy-go-lucky household. That very extraordinary butler. One does not know what is going to be said next.'

'So I should think.'

'Too much so for me. I am old-fashioned, I'm afraid. I do not at all mind admitting it.'

I was reminded of Hugo Tolland, said to like being 'dated', but thought it wiser not to remind Mrs. Conyers of the parallel. I wondered why she had agreed to dine with the Jeavonses if she felt so inimical to them.

'But you yourself must have known Lady Molly for a long time?'

'Of course we have known her for years and years. But never well. When she was Lady Sleaford my youngest sister, Mildred, knew her, and we used to meet sometimes. I have hardly seen her since her second marriage. We know the present Sleafords, but I don't think Lady Molly ever sees anything of them. That is to be expected, perhaps.'

'You dined here?'

'It was really on account of my sister. I can't remember whether you have ever met Mildred.'

'Only when I was a child. When you showed me the sword the sultan gave the General.'

Mrs. Conyers smiled.

39

'That was a long time ago,' she said. 'Then you really do not know her.'

Some of the subsequent history of Mildred Blaides was, in fact, familiar to me from occasional talk on the part of my parents. Considered rather 'fast' in her early days—as might be expected from my memory of her—she had married a Flying Corps officer called M'Cracken, who had been killed not long after the wedding in a raid over Germany. Then there had been a period of widowhood, when her behaviour had been thought 'flighty'. From the manner in which this interlude in her career used to be discussed, I imagine that my parents' generation supposed her to be about to go to the bad in a spectacular manner. However, this very generally prophesied débâcle never took place. Mildred Blaides married again: the second time to an Australian business-man, a Mr. Haycock, retired, fairly rich, who owned a villa in the South of France and spent a good deal of his time travelling round the world. Mr. Haycock, who was said to possess sterling virtues in addition to his comfortable income, was also agreed to be 'rather rough'. The marriage, so far as I knew, had been quite a success. There were children, but I did not know how many.

'As a matter of fact, my sister Mildred is a very old friend of our hostess,' said Mrs. Conyers, as if the ·matter was weighing on her mind. 'As I say, she knows Lady Molly far better than I do. Mildred nursed at Dogdene during the war.'

'I remember her in nurse's uniform.'

'She is coming here tonight. She was to have dined, but at the last moment she was unable to be at dinner. She is—more or less engaged to a friend of Lady Molly's. As I expect you know, Mildred's husband died about a year ago. Unfortunately a business engagement prevented her—I suppose I should say—fiancé from dining. He is a very busy man. He just could not get away tonight in time. Then Mildred herself is always changing her plans. Goodness knows why she herself could not come here without him. However, she couldn't, so there it was. They are both looking in later.'

There could be no doubt now that the matter which worried, or at least unusually preoccupied, Mrs. Conyers was connected with her sister's arrival. I could not at first decide exactly what had upset her.

'This is not the first time you have met him—the fiancé?'

'As a matter of fact, I haven't seen him yet,' she said, almost apologetically, as if that was the least I could expect of her. 'You see, it only happened yesterday. That was why Lady Molly arranged the dinner. She didn't seem to mind their not turning up in the least. Of course, she is much more used to people changing their arrangements than I am.'

It seemed probable that she was merely suffering some anxiety regarding the potentialities of the man who was to be her sister's third husband. I knew enough about the reputation of Mildred Blaides to realise that anxiety was reasonable enough.

'He is a good deal younger than Mildred,' she said.

After announcing this fact, Mrs. Conyers decided to abandon the subject, perhaps fearing that in her own over-wrought state she might say too much. She gave a sigh.

'If I must talk French,' she went on, with rather forced gaiety, 'I do so much prefer not to have to talk the language to a Frenchman. They are so terribly severe. I always tell them that they will never admit that any other Frenchman speaks correct French, so how can they possibly expect me to do so. That young man over there actually complimented me on my French accent.'

'Who is he?'

'From one of the Balkan Legations. I think his father was Minister over here, and used to stop at Dogdene. He was invited about rather more than you might expect because he was an unusually good shot. In the end the poor fellow was shot himself by an anarchist in his own country. The son had news of Prince Theodoric. In fact, I think he has just ceased to be a member of the Prince's personal household. As you probably know, Theodoric was rather a special friend of the divorced wife of Lady Molly's brother, Lord Ardglass, who died some years ago. Our hostess always likes to hear about him on that account. Between you and me, I am afraid she is a tiny bit of a gossip, but don't say I said so.'

Mrs. Conyers smiled a little slyly.

'Who are the two girls who have just come in and are talking to Chips Lovell?'

'He is the young man you arrived with, isn't he? The nearest is one of the Tolland girls, Priscilla, I think. She was going to see a film with a former school friend of hers whose name I was not told.'

Priscilla Tolland looked more than seventeen: even so, she had not entirely lost a long-legged, childish awkwardness in the manner in which she stood with her legs crossed. I could see she bore a strong likeness to the 'dotty' Blanche, though certainly free herself from any such disability. The girl with her, prototype of all school friends, was small and dark with horn-rimmed spectacles and an air of bossing everyone about. I thought I would have a word with them in a minute or two; when Mrs. Conyers had finished speaking of the misty past, into which she was now making a deep excursion. However, opportunity to approach the girls never came, because a second later, just as Mrs. Conyers had invited me to tea with herself and the General the following Sunday, two more persons, a man and woman, entered the room.

'Ah, there is Mildred at last,' said Mrs. Conyers, fumbling with her lorgnette, her thin hands, almost pale mauve in colour, shaking with excitement and anxiety.

I myself was curious to see what Mildred Blaides—or rather Mildred Haycock—might look like after all these years, half expecting her to be wearing her V.A.D. outfit and smoking a cigarette. But when my eyes fell on the two of them, it was the man, not the woman, who held my attention. Life is full of internal dramas, instantaneous and sensational, played to an audience of one. This was just such a performance. The fiancé was Widmerpool. Scarlet in the face, grinning agitatedly through the thick lenses of his spectacles, he advanced into the room, his hand on Mrs. Haycock's arm. He was wearing a new dark suit. Like a huge fish swimming into a hitherto unexplored, unexpectedly exciting aquarium, he sailed resolutely forward: yet not a real fish, a fish made of rubber or some artificial substance. There was something a little frightening about him. That could not be denied. Molly Jeavons, this time supported by her husband, closed in on these new arrivals immediately.

'Well, he is no beauty,' said Mrs. Conyers.

She spoke with such deep relief at her discovery of the unpleasingness of Widmerpool's features that she must have feared the worst of her sister's choice on account of the reported difference of age. Probably she had pictured some golden-haired gigolo of altogether unacceptable personal appearance. The truth was a great consolation to her. Certainly, to look at them, they seemed on the score of age to be a couple very reasonably to be associated together. Mrs. Haycock was in the neighbourhood of forty, and looked no younger, but Widmerpool, although only a year or so over thirty, had always appeared comfortably middle-aged even as a boy.

'I know him.'

'Who is he?'

'He is called Kenneth Widmerpool. I was at school with him as a matter of fact. He is in the City.'

'I know his name of course. And that he is in the City. But what is he like?'

Mrs. Conyers did not attempt to conceal her own impatience. The reason of her anxiety was now made plain. She had no confidence in her sister's choice of husband. She wanted to know the worst as soon as possible. Her first, and most serious, fears were passed; she wished to move on to a later stage of enquiry. Widmerpool, although giving her reason to be thankful that the outlook was not more threatening, had evidently made no very captivating impression.

'Is he nice?'

'I've known him a long time——'

By then we were both involved in general introductions taking place round the room, so that I was not forced to answer the question. Afterwards, when I got home, I pondered what I should most properly have said in reply. The fact was that Widmerpool could hardly be described as 'nice'. Energetic: able: successful: all kinds of things that had never been expected of him in the past; but 'nice' he had never been, and showed little sign of becoming. Yet, for some reason, I was quite glad to see him again. His reappearance, especially in that place, helped to prove somehow rather consolingly, that life continued its mysterious, patterned way. Widmerpool was a recurring milestone on the road; perhaps it would be more apt to say that his course, as one jogged round the track, was run from time to time, however different the pace, in common with my own. As an aspect of my past he was an element to be treated with interest, if not affection, like some unattractive building or natural feature of the landscape which brought back the irrational nostalgia of childhood. A minute later I found myself talking to him.

'No, I haven't seen you for a long time,' he said, breathing heavily as usual, 'I've been trying to get hold of you, as a matter of fact, to tell you I was getting married.'

'Many congratulations.'

'Time to settle down,' he said.

This remark was fatuous, since he had never been anything but 'settled down', at least in my eyes. I could not imagine why he should specially wish to tell me about his marriage, although there could be no doubt from his manner that he was in a great state of excitement at the thought of being engaged. His nose and lips, beneath the huge headlamps of his now rimless spectacles, were twitching slightly. Lunging out towards Mrs. Haycock, who stood not far from him, he seized her arm and drew her in our direction.

'This is Nicholas Jenkins, my dear. An old friend of mine. He was somewhat my junior at school.'

Mrs. Haycock, who had been talking to her sister, now turned and faced me, so that for the first time since she had entered the room I had an opportunity of observing closely the woman he hoped to make his wife. I could at once appreciate the strong impression she might have made on him the moment she showed herself prepared to accept him as an admirer. Tall, elegant, brassy, she was markedly of the same generation as Molly Jeavons, without personally at all resembling her. Mrs. Haycock's moral separateness from Widmerpool, immediately noticeable, was not on account of any difference of age, as such, for—as I have said —Widmerpool had never looked young. It was a separateness imposed upon her by the war. Like Jeavons, that was the epoch to which she belonged by some natural right. Life on the Riviera had no doubt left its mark too: a society in which Widmerpool was unlikely hitherto to have participated. She retained some of her sunburn from the previous summer, and, although dressed quite normally—indeed, rather well—her clothes seemed in some indefinable manner more adapted to a *plage* or casino than the Jeavons drawing-room.

I had always felt an interest in what might be called the theoretical side of Widmerpool's life: the reaction of his own emotions to the severe rule of ambition that he had from the beginning imposed upon himself: the determination that existence must be governed by the will. However, the interest one takes in the lives of other people is, at best, feeble enough, so that, knowing little of his affairs in recent years, I had in truth largely forgotten about him. Now, for the second time that evening, I recalled the night when that noisy little girl, Barbara Goring, had poured sugar over his head at the Huntercombes' dance. He had been in love with her; and I, too, for that matter, or had thought so at the time. Then there had been his brief, painful association with Gipsy Jones, the grubby Left Wing nymph, whose 'operation' he had defrayed unrewarded. After the Gipsy Jones business, he had told me he would never again have anything to do with a woman who 'took his mind off his work.' I wondered whether Mrs. Haycock would satisfy that condition: whether he had proposed to her under stress of violent emotion, or had decided such a marriage would help his career. Perhaps there was an element of both motives; in any case, to attempt to disengage motives in marriage is a fruitless task. Mrs. Haycock took my hand, smiling absently, and gave it a good squeeze; the clutch of a woman pretty familiar with men and their ways.

'One always has to meet such crowds of people when one gets married,' she said, 'It is really too, too exhausting. Did you say we had met before? Was it at Cannes? I seem to know your face.'

She spoke breathlessly, almost asthmatically, in which she resembled Widmerpool, but using that faint hint of cockney, an accent in part bequeathed by the overtones of the Prince of Wales to the world to which she belonged. I tried, quite unsuccessfully and perhaps not very tactfully, to explain the circumstances of our infinitely distant former meeting. It was plainly years since she had listened to any remarks addressed to her, either serious or trivial, so that perhaps deservedly—for the exposition was a formidable rigmarole upon which to embark at that moment—she swiftly disengaged herself from its demands.

'I'm absolutely longing for a drink, Molly,' she said. 'Oh, thank you so much, Mr. Jeavons, what an angel you are. I have been having the most awful time tonight. You know I abominate making plans.. Never make them, as a matter of fact. I just won't. Well, this evening I got caught up by one of the most awful bores you ever met.'

She drank deeply of the glass brought by Jeavons, and began telling him the story. Widmerpool took me aside.

'Did I hear you say you had met Mildred before?'

He spoke anxiously.

'When I was about nine or ten.'

'What on earth do you mean?'

He sounded quite angry at this statement of mine, intended to set his mind at rest. He supposed I wanted to tease him.

'Just what I said. It was years ago—with her sister, Mrs. Conyers, to whom you were introduced a second ago. My family have always known General Conyers.'

I hardly knew why I added this last piece of information

which sounded somehow a trifle absurd and unnecessary, emphasing the fact that Widmerpool and the General would become brothers-in-law. However, Widmerpool was appeased by this amplification.

'Quite so,' he said. 'Quite so.'

All at once he became abstracted in manner.

'Look here,' he said. 'Come and have luncheon with me. We haven't had a talk for a long time. What about next Sunday—at my club?'

'All right. Thanks very much.'

The name of the club surprised me a little. There was no reason at all why he should not belong there, yet its mild suggestion of cosmopolitan life and high card stakes evoked an environment seemingly unsuited to his nature. When employed at Donners-Brebners, Widmerpool must have spent a fair amount of his time with foreign business-men. Indeed, his professional background at that time might well have been described as international. There was nothing against him on that count. Equally, if he ever played cards, he might, for all I knew, venture high stakes. He could presumably afford such a risk. Neither of these aspects of the scene altered the sense of incongruity. To eyes that had known him as a boy, even the smallest pre-tension to swagger appeared, for Widmerpool, out of place. That was the point. The verdict was inescapable. Only an atmosphere of quiet hard work and dull, serious conversa-tion were appropriate to him. Such a demand on my part, even though unvoiced, was, of course, absurd. Widmer-pool's conduct was, in any case, no concern of mine. Besides, these sentiments were utterly at variance with Widmerpool's own view of himself; a view that would obviously play the chief part in his choice of club—or, for that matter, of wife. If such a club was inappropriate to him, how much more incongruous would be a wife like

Mrs. Haycock. I could not help thinking that. We talked for a time of general matters. Later on Lovell came across the room.

'I am giving Priscilla Tolland and her friend a lift home,' he said. 'Do you want to be taken as far as your flat?'

I had no difficulty in perceiving the reason for this offer and resigned myself to sitting in the back with the friend.

'Come and see us again,' said Molly Jeavons, when saying good-bye. 'Make Chips bring you, or just drop in.'

'So long, old man, come again,' said Jeavons.

He had been standing for a long time by the drink tray, plunged in deep thought, perhaps still contemplating the subject of film stars and their varied, disturbing charms. Now he took me by the hand, as if his thoughts were far away. I followed Lovell and the girls downstairs to the car. Outside there was a hint of fog in the air. The river mist seemed to have pursued us from the Studio. Nothing of note happened on the way home. The school friend talked incessantly of the visit she was going to pay to Florence. We dropped her at an address in Wimpole Street, after disposing of Priscilla Tolland at her stepmother's house in Hyde Park Gardens.

2.

'WE might go straight in to lunch,' said Widmerpool, when we met a day or two later. 'If you so wish, you can drink a glass of pale sherry at the table. We are sometimes crowded at the luncheon hour. Incidentally, you will probably see the Permanent Under-Secretary of the Home Office at one table. He honours us with his presence most days—but I forgot. It is Sunday today, so that he may not be with us. I am afraid, now I come to think of it, that it is a long time since I went to church. I shall attend a service next week when I stay with my mother in the country.'

'How is your mother?'

'Better than ever. You know she literally grows younger. A wonderful woman.'

'Does she still have the cottage near Hinton?'

'It is a little small, but it suits us both. We could well afford something larger nowadays, but she loves it. Her roses are the admiration of the neighbourhood.'

'You still see something of the Walpole-Wilsons and Sir Magnus Donners?'

'The Walpole-Wilsons I have lost all touch with,' said Widmerpool. 'Sir Magnus is, of course, an old friend. Whatever his faults—some of which it would be foolish to disregard—he has rendered me in the past inestimable service. As it happens, he has not asked me over to Stourwater recently. I must ring him up. But come along. To lunch, to lunch.'

He spoke with that air of bustle that infected all his dealings. During the few seconds in which we talked he had managed to convey the sensation that we were physically too close together. More than once I edged away. He seemed all the time pressing at one's elbow, like a waiter who breathes heavily over you as he irritably proffers a dish awkward to handle. Widmerpool, too, gave the impression of irritation, chronic irritation, as if he felt all the time that the remedy to alleviate his own annoyances lay in the hands of the people round him, who would yet at the same time take no step to relieve his mounting discomfort; for his manner conveyed always a suspicion that he knew only too well that things were almost as bad for those who were with him as for himself.

He swept me forward into the dining-room. The club steward, no doubt familiar with Widmerpool's predispositions, indicated a table by the window, flanked on one side by two yellow-faced men conversing in stilted, sing-song French: on the other, by an enormously fat old fellow who was opening his luncheon with dressed crab and half a bottle of hock. One of the men talking French I thought I recognised as the Balkan diplomatist seen at the Jeavonses and said to be of Prince Theodoric's entourage.

'Have anything you like to eat or drink,' said Wimerpool. 'Consult the menu here. Personally I am on a diet—a little gastric trouble—and shall restrict myself to cold tongue and a glass of water.'

He handed me the card, and I ordered all I decently could in the face of this frugality.

'You are still—publishing—advertising——?' he asked. 'Was it not something of the sort?'

His manner of asking personal questions was of that kind not uncommonly to be found which is completely divorced from any interest in the answer. He was always prepared to embark on a lengthy cross-examination of almost any-one he might meet, at the termination of which—apart from such details as might chance to concern himself—he had absorbed no more about the person interrogated than he knew at the outset of the conversation. At the same time this process seemed somehow to gratify his own egotism.

'I was in publishing. Art books. Now it is the film business.'

'Indeed? What unusual ways you choose to earn a living. Not acting, surely?'

'Hardly. I am on what is called the "scenario side". I help to write that part of the programme known as the "second feature". For every foot of American film shown in this country, a proportionate length of British film must appear. The Quota, in fact.'

'Ah, yes, the Quota, the Quota,' said Widmerpool, cutting short any further explanation, which would certainly have been tedious enough. 'Well, I never expected to sit at the same table as host of a man who wrote films for the Quota. Do you like the work?'

'Not greatly.'

'It may lead to something better. If you are industrious, you get on. That is true of all professions, even the humblest. You will probably end up in Hollywood, or somewhere like that. But tell me, do you still see those friends of yours, Stringham and Templer?'

'Stringham I haven't seen since the night he got so tight, and you and I helped to put him to bed. I rang up a day or two later and found he had gone abroad. From what I hear, he is drinking enough to float a battleship. There was even a question of taking a cure.'

'And Templer?'

'I see him occasionally. Not for rather a long time, as it happens. You know his marriage broke up?'

'Like Stringham's,' said Widmerpool. 'Your friends do not seem very fortunate in their matrimonial ventures. I

52

run across Templer sometimes in the City. We have even done a little business together. I was able to fix up a job for Bob Duport, that rather disreputable brother-in-law of his.'

'So I heard.'

'Oh, he told you, did he?' said Widmerpool, gratified at this action of his being so widely known. 'I believe there were various repercussions from that good turn I was able to do him. For instance, Duport was living apart from his wife. He had behaved rather badly, so people say. When he got this job, the two of them patched things up again, and she went back to him. I was glad to have been the cause of that. We all three had dinner together. Rather an odd woman. Moody, I should think. She didn't seem particularly pleased at the reunion. Not at all grateful to me, at least.'

'Why not?'

'I couldn't say. She hardly spoke a word throughout the course of an extremely good dinner at the Savoy. I may say it cost me quite a lot of money. Not that I grudge it. They are in South America now, I believe. Did you ever meet either of them?'

'Met him once with Templer when I was an undergraduate.'

'And her?'

'I knew her a bit. In fact I first met her ages ago when I stayed with the Templers. Peter's father was still alive then.'

'Not unattractive.'

'No.'

'Quite elegant in her way too.'

'Yes.'

'Too good for Duport, I should have thought.'

'Possibly.'

Widmerpool could not have had the smallest notion of

53

anything that had taken place between Jean Duport and myself; but people are aware of things like this within themselves without knowing of their own awareness. In any case, conscious or unconscious, Widmerpool had the knack of treading on the corns of others. His next question seemed to show the extraordinary telepathic connection of ideas that so often takes place in the mind when anything in the nature of being in love is concerned.

'You are not married yourself, are you, Nicholas?'

'No.'

'Not—like me—about to take the plunge?'

'I haven't properly congratulated you yet.'

Widmerpool bowed his head in acknowledgment. The movement could almost have been called gracious. He beamed across the table. At that moment the prospect of marriage seemed all he could desire.

'I do not mind informing you that my lady mother thinks well of my choice,' he said.

There was no answer to that beyond agreeing that Mrs. Widmerpool's approval was gratifying. If Mrs. Haycock could face such a mother-in-law, one hurdle at least—and no minor one, so it seemed to me—had been cleared.

'There are, of course, a few small matters my mother will expect to be satisfactorily arranged.'

'I expect so.'

'But Mildred will fall in with these, I am sure.'

I thought the two of them, Mrs. Widmerpool and Mrs. Haycock, were probably worthy of the other's steel. Perhaps Widmerpool, in his heart, thought so too, for his face clouded over slightly, after the first look of deep satisfaction. He fell into silence. When pondering a matter of importance to himself, his jaws would move up and down as if consuming some immaterial substance. Although he had finished his slices of tongue, this movement now began. I guessed that he intended to pose some question, the precise form of which he could not yet decide. The men with yellow faces at the next table were talking international politics.

'*C'est incontestable, cher ami, Hitler a renoncé à son intention d'engouffrer l'Autriche par une agression directe.*'

'*A mon avis—et d'ailleurs je l'ai toujours dit—la France avait tort de s'opposer à l'union douanière en '31.*'

The fat man had moved on to steak-and-kidney pudding, leeks and mashed potato, with a green salad. Widmerpool cleared his throat. Something was on his mind. He began in a sudden burst of words.

'I had a special reason for inviting you to lunch today, Nicholas. I wanted to speak of my engagement. But it is not easy for me to explain in so many words what I desire to say.'

He spoke sententiously, breaking off abruptly. I had an uneasy feeling, unlikely as this would be, that he might be about to ask me to act as best man at his wedding. I began to think of excuses to avoid such a duty. However, it turned out he had no such intention. It seemed likely, on second thoughts, that he wanted to discuss seriously some matter regarding himself which he feared might, on ventilation, cause amusement. Certainly I found it difficult to take his engagement seriously. There is, for some reason, scarcely any subject more difficult to treat with gravity if you are not yourself involved. Obviously two people were contemplating a step which would affect their future lives in the most powerful manner; and yet the outward appearance of the two of them, and Widmerpool's own self-sufficiency, made it impossible to consider the matter without inner amusement.

'Years ago I told you I was in love with Barbara Goring,' said Widmerpool slowly.

55

'I remember.'

'Barbara is a thing of the past. I want her entirely forgotten.'

'Why not? I shan't stand up at your wedding and say: "This ceremony cannot continue—the bridegroom once loved another!".'

'Quite so, quite so,' said Widmerpool, grunting out a laugh. 'You are absolutely right to make a joke of it. At the same time, I thought I should mention my feelings on that subject. One cannot be too careful.'

'And I presume you want Gipsy Jones forgotten too?'

Widmerpool flushed.

'Yes,' he said. 'She too, of course.'

His complacency seemed to me at that time intolerable. Now, I can see he required only to discuss his own situation with someone he had known for a long period, who was at the same time not too closely associated with his current life. For that rôle I was peculiarly eligible. More than once before, he had told me of his emotional upheavals—it was only because of that I knew so much about Barbara Goring and Gipsy Jones—and, when a confessor has been chosen, the habit is hard to break. At the same time, his innate suspicion of everyone inhibited even his taste for talking about himself.

'Mildred is, of course, rather older than I,' he said.

I felt in some manner imprisoned by his own self-preoccupation. He positively forced one to agree that his own affairs were intensely important: indeed, the only existing question of any real interest. At the same time his intense egoism somehow dried up all sympathy for him. Clearly there was much about his present circumstances that made him nervous. That was, after all, natural enough for anyone contemplating marriage. Yet there seemed more here than the traditionally highly-strung state of a man who

56

has only lately proposed and been accepted. I remembered that he had never asked Barbara Goring to marry him, because in those days he was not rich enough to marry. He read my thoughts, as people do when their intuition is sharpened by intensity of interest excited by discussing themselves.

'She was left with a bit of money by Haycock,' he said. 'Though her financial affairs are in an appalling mess.'

'I see.'

'How long have you known Lady Molly?'

'That was the first night I had been there.'

'I wish I had known her in the great days,' he said. 'I cannot say that I greatly care for the atmosphere of her present home.'

'You would prefer Dogdene?'

'I believe that in many ways Dogdene was far from ideally run either,' said Widmerpool curtly. 'But at least it provided a suitable background for a *grande dame*. Mildred is a friend of the present Lady Sleaford, so that I dare say in due course I shall be able to judge how Lady Molly must have looked there.'

This manner of describing Molly Jeavons somehow affronted me, not so much from disagreement, or on account of its pretentious sound, but because I had not myself given Widmerpool credit for thus estimating her qualities, even in his own crude terms. I was, indeed, surprised that he did not dismiss her as a failure, noting at the same time his certainty of invitation to Dogdene. From what Chips Lovell used to say on that subject, I was not sure that Widmerpool might not be counting his chickens before they were hatched.

'It is because of Dogdene, as you know yourself, that Mildred is such an old friend of Lady Molly's. Perhaps not a very close friend, but they have known each other a long time.'

'Yes?'

I could not guess what he was getting at.

'In fact we first met at Lady Molly's.'

'I see.'

'Mildred is—how shall I put it—a woman of the world like Lady Molly—but—well—hardly with Lady Molly's easy-going manner of looking at things—I don't mean that exactly—in some ways Mildred is very easy-going—but she likes her own way—and—in her own manner—takes life rather seriously——'

He suddenly began to look wretched, much as I had often seen him look as a schoolboy: lonely: awkward: unpopular: odd; no longer the self-confident business-man into which he had grown. His face now brought back the days when one used to watch him plodding off through the drizzle to undertake the long, solitary runs across the dismal fields beyond the sewage farms: runs which were to train him for teams in which he was never included. His jaws ceased to move up and down. He drank off a second glass of water.

'Anyway, you know General and Mrs. Conyers,' he said.

He added this rather lamely, as if he lacked strength of mind to pursue the subject upon which he hoped to embark.

'I am going to tea with them this afternoon as it happens.'

'Why on earth are you doing that?'

'I haven't seen them for a long time. We've known them for ages, as I told you.'

'Oh, well, yes, I see.'

He seemed disturbed by the information. I wondered whether Mrs. Conyers had already shown herself 'against' the marriage. Certainly she had been worried about her

58

sister at the Jeavons house. I had supposed the sight of Widmerpool himself to have set her worst fears at rest. Even if prepared on the whole to accept him, she may have let fall some remark that evening unintentionally wounding to his self-esteem. He was immensely touchy. However, his present uneasiness appeared to be chiefly vested in his own ignorance of how much I already knew about his future wife. Evidently he could not make up his mind upon this last matter. The uncertainty irked him.

'Then you must have heard all about Mildred?' he persisted.

'No, not much. I only know about Mrs. Conyers, so to speak. And I have often been told stories about their father, of course. I know hardly anything about the other sisters. Mrs. Haycock was married to an Australian, wasn't she? I knew she had two husbands, both dead.'

'Only that?'

Widmerpool paused, disappointed by my ignorance, or additionally suspicious; perhaps both. He may have decided that for his purposes I knew at once too much and too little.

'You realise,' he said slowly, 'that Mildred has been used to a lot of her own way—her own way of life, that is. Haycock left her—in fact even encouraged her—so it seems to me—to lead—well—a rather—rather independent sort of life. They were—as one might say—a very modern married couple.'

'Beyond the fact that they lived on the Riviera, I know scarcely anything about them.'

'Haycock had worked very hard all his life. He wanted some relaxation in his later days. That was understandable. They got on quite well so far as I can see.'

I began to apprehend a little of what Widmerpool was hinting. Mrs. Haycock's outline became clearer. No doubt she had graduated from an earlier emancipation of slang and cigarettes, to a habit of life with threatening aspects for a future husband.

'Did they have any children?'

'Yes,' said Widmerpool. 'They did. Mildred has two children. That does not worry me. Not at all. Glad to start with a family.'

He said all this so aggressively that I suspected a touch of bravado. Then he paused. I was about to ask the age and sex of the children, when he began to speak hurriedly again, the words tumbling out as if he wanted to finish with this speech as quickly as possible.

'I should not wish to appear backward in display of affection,' he said, developing an increased speed with every phrase, 'and, in addition to that, I don't see why we should delay unduly the state in which we shall spend the rest of our life merely because certain legal and religious formalities take time to arrange. In short, Nicholas, you will, I am sure, agree—more especially as you seem to spend a good deal of your time with artists and film-writers and people of that sort, whose morals are proverbial—that it would be permissible on my part to suppose—once the day of the wedding has been fixed—that we might—occasionally enjoy each other's company—say, over a week-end——'

He came to a sudden stop, looking at me rather wildly.

'I don't see why not.'

It was impossible to guess what he was going to say next. This was all far from anything for which I had been prepared.

'In fact my fiancée—Mildred, that is—might even expect such a suggestion?'

'Well, yes, from what you say.'

'Might even regard it as *usage du monde*?'

'Quite possible.'

Then Widmerpool·sniggered. For some reason I was conscious of embarrassment, even of annoyance. The problem could be treated, as it were, clinically, or humorously; a combination of the two approaches was distasteful. I had the impression that the question of how he should behave worried him more on account of the figure he cut in the eyes of Mrs. Haycock than because his passion could not be curbed. However, to have released from his mind these observations had clearly been a great relief to him. Now he cheered up a little.

'There is a further point,' he said. 'As my name is an uncommon one, I take it I should be called upon to provide myself with a sobriquet.'

'I suppose so.'

'In your own case, the difficulty would scarcely arise—so many people being called "Jenkins".'

'It may surprise you to hear that when I embark on clandestine week-ends, I call myself "Widmerpool".'

Widmerpool laughed with reasonable heartiness at that fancy. All the same, the question of what name should cover the identity of Mrs. Haycock and himself when first appearing as husband and wife still worried him.

'But what surname *do* you think should be employed?' he asked in a reflective tone, speaking almost to himself.

'"Mr. and Mrs. Smith" would have the merit of such absolute banality that it would almost draw attention to yourselves. Besides, you might be mistaken for the Jeavonses' borrowed butler.'

Widmerpool, still pondering, ignored this facetiousness, regarding me with unseeing eyes.

'"Mr. and the Honourable Mrs. Smith?" You might feel that more in keeping with your future wife's rank and station. That, in any case, would strike a certain note of originality in the circumstances.'

At this suggestion, Widmerpool laughed outright. The pleasantry undoubtedly pleased him. It reminded him of the facts of his engagement, showing that I had not missed the point that, whatever her shortcomings, Mildred was the daughter of a peer. His face lighted up again.

'I suppose it should really be quite simple,' he said. 'After all, the booking clerk at an hotel does not actually ask every couple if they are married.'

'In any case, you are both going to get married.'

'Yes, of course,' he said.

'So there does not seem much to worry about.'

'No, I suppose not. All the same, I do not like doing irregular things. But this time, I think I should be behaving rightly in allowing a lapse of this kind. It is expected of me.'

Gloom again descended upon him. There could be no doubt that the thought of the projected week-end worried him a great deal. I could see that he regarded its achievement, perhaps rightly, as a crisis in his life.

'And then, where to go?' he remarked peevishly.

'Had you thought at all?'

'Of course it must be a place where neither of us is recognised—I don't want any——'

His words died away.

'Any what?'

'Any jokes,' he said irritably.

'Of course not.'

'The seaside, do you think?'

'Do you play any games still? Golf? You used to play golf, didn't you? Some golfing resort?'

'I gave up golf. No time.'

Again he looked despairing. He had devoted so much energy to achieving his present position in the world that even golf had been discarded. There was something impressive in this admission. We sat for a time in silence. The fat man was now enjoying the first taste of some apple-pie liberally covered with cream and brown sugar. The yellow-faced couple were still occupied with the situation in Central Europe.

'*La position de Dollfuss envers le parti national-socialiste autrichien serait insoutenable s'il comptait sur une gouverne-ment soi-disant parlementaire: il faut bien l'avouer.*'

'*Heureusement le chancelier autrichien n'est pas accablé d'un tel handicap administratif.*'

Widmerpool may have caught some of their words. In any case, he must have decided that the question of his own immediate problems had been sufficiently ventilated. He, too, began to speak of international politics; and with less pessimism than might have been expected.

'As you probably know,' he said, 'my opinions have moved steadily to the left of late years. I quite see that there are aspects of Hitler's programme to which objection may most legitimately be taken. For example, I myself possess a number of Jewish friends, some of them very able men—Jimmy Klein, for example—and I should therefore much prefer that item of the National Socialist policy to be dropped. I am, in fact, not at all sure that it will *not* be dropped when matters get straightened out a bit. After all, it is sometimes forgotten that the National Socialists are not only "national", they are also "socialist". So far as that goes, I am with them. They believe in planning. Every-one will agree that there was a great deal of the old Germany that it was right to sweep away—the Kaisers and Krupps, Hindenburgs and mediatised princes, stuff of that sort—we want to hear no more about them. Certainly not. People talk of rearming. I am glad to say the Labour Party is against it to a man—and the more enlightened Tories, too. There is far too much disregard, as it is, of the

63

equilibrium to be maintained between the rate of production and consumption in the aggregate, without the additional interference of a crushing armaments programme. We do not want an obstacle like that in the way of the organised movement towards progressive planning in the economic world of today. People talk of non-aggression pacts between France, Belgium and ourselves. The plain consequence of any such scatter-brained military commitments would be merely to augment existing German fears of complete encirclement. No, no, none of that, please. What is much more likely to be productive is to settle things round a table. Business men of the right sort. Prominent trade unionists. Sir Magnus Donners could probably play his part. If Germany wants her former colonies, hand them back to her. What is the objection? They are no use to anyone else. Take a man like Goering. Now, it seems pretty plain to me from looking at photographs of him in the papers that he only likes swaggering about in uniforms and decorations. I expect he is a bit of a snob—most of us are at heart—well, ask him to Buckingham Palace. Show him round. What is there against giving him the Garter? After all, it is what such things are for, isn't it? Coffee?'

'Yes, black.'

'You can have it downstairs. I never take coffee.'

'Talking of uniforms, are you still a Territorial?'

'I *am* still a Territorial,' said Widmerpool, smiling with some satisfaction. 'I hold the rank of captain. I can perfectly follow your train of thought. You suppose that because I am opposed to sabre-rattling in the direction of our Teutonic neighbours, that therefore I must be the sort of man incapable of holding his own in an officers' mess. Let me assure you that such is not the case. Between you and me, I am by no means averse from issuing orders. An army—even an amateur army—is no bad school in which to learn to command—and you must know how to command in business, my dear Nicholas, as much as in any army. Besides that, one has in a battalion opportunity for giving expression to one's own point of view—a point of view often new to the persons I find myself among. These young bank clerks, accountants and so on, excellent Territorial officers, are naturally quite unfamiliar with the less limited world inhabited by someone like myself. I make it my business to instruct them. However, I dare say I may have to give up my Territorials when I get married. I do not know about that yet.'

At last it was time for me to go on my way.

'So you are off to have tea with some of my future inlaws, are you?' said Widmerpool, at the door of the club. 'Well, you mustn't repeat to them some of the things we have talked about. I am sure the General would be greatly shocked.'

He sniggered once again, making one of his awkward gestures of farewell that looked as if he were shaking his fist. I went down the steps feeling strangely dejected. It was a sunny afternoon and there was time to kill before the Conyers visit. I tried to persuade myself that the gloom that had descended upon me was induced by Widmerpool's prolonged political dissertations, but in my heart I knew that its true cause was all this talk of marriage. With the age of thirty in sight a sense of guilt in relation to that subject makes itself increasingly felt. It was all very well mentally to prepare ribald jokes about Widmerpool's honeymoon for such friends who knew him, and certainly nothing could be more grotesque than his approach to the matter in hand. That was undeniable. Yet one day, I knew, life would catch up with me too; like Widmerpool, I should be making uneasy preparations to 'settle down'. Should I, when the time came to 'take the plunge', as he had called it, feel inwardly less nervous about the future than he? Should I cut a better figure? This oppression of the heart was intensified by a peculiar awareness that the time was not far distant; even though I could think of no one whose shadow fell across such a speculation.

Dismissing my own preoccupations and trying to consider Widmerpool's position objectively, I found it of interest. For example, he was about to become brother-in-law of General Conyers, now little short of an octogenarian. I did not know whom the remaining Blaides sisters had married—one, at least, had remained single—but their husbands must all have been years senior to Widmerpool, even though they might be younger than the General. I attempted to find some parallel, however far-fetched, to link Widmerpool with General Conyers; thereby hoping to construct one of those formal designs in human behaviour which for some reason afford an obscure satisfaction to the mind: making the more apparent inconsistencies of life easier to bear. A list could be compiled. Both were accustomed to live by the will: both had decided for a time to carve out a career unburdened by a wife: both were, in very different ways, fairly successful men. There the comparison seemed to break down.

However, the family connexions of Mrs. Conyers had been thought by some to have played a part in bringing her husband to the altar; similar considerations might well be operating in the mind of Widmerpool where her sister was concerned. That would not be running contrary to his character. Alternatively, any such estimate of his motives—or the General's—might be completely at fault. In either case, love rather than convenience might dominate action. Indeed, such evidence as I possessed of Widmerpool's former behaviour towards women indicated a decided lack of restraint, even when passion was unsatisfied.

Then there was Mrs. Haycock herself. Why on earth—so her circumstances presented themselves to me—should she wish to marry Widmerpool? Such an inability to assess physical attraction or community of interest is, of course, common enough. Where the opposite sex is concerned, especially in relation to marriage, the workings of the imagination, or knowledge of the individuals themselves, are overwhelmed by the subjective approach. Only by admitting complete ignorance from the start can some explanation sometimes slowly be built up. I wondered, for example, whether she saw in Widmerpool the solid humdrum qualities formerly apparent in her Australian husband: although no evidence whatever justified the assumption that her Australian husband had been either solid or humdrum. For all I knew, he might have been a good-for-nothing of the first water. Once again, it was possible that Mrs. Haycock herself was in love. The fact that Widmerpool seemed a grotesque figure to some who knew him provided no reason why he should not inspire love in others. I record these speculations not for their subtlety, certainly not for their generosity of feeling, but to emphasise the difficulty in understanding, even remotely, why people behave as they do.

The question of love was still apt to be associated in my own mind with thoughts of Jean; additionally so since Widmerpool had spoken of her brother, Peter Templer, and her husband, Bob Duport: even making enquiries about Jean herself. Evidently she had impressed him in some way. Could I safely assure myself that I was no longer in love with her? I had recently decided, at last with some sense of security, that life could proceed on that assumption. All the same, it was not uniformly easy to state this decision to myself with a feeling of absolute confidence; even though

I found myself dwelling less than formerly on the question of whether we could have 'made a success of it'. For a moment the thought of her reunited to Duport had brought to the heart a touch of the red-hot pincers: a reminder of her voice saying 'that was rather a wet kiss.'

Some people dramatise their love affairs—as I was doing at that moment—by emphasis on sentiment and sensuality; others prefer the centre of the stage to be occupied by those aspects of action and power that must also play so prominent a part in love. Adepts of the latter school try to exclude, or at least considerably to reduce, the former emotions. Barnby would rarely admit himself 'in love' with the women he pursued: Baby Wentworth was believed never to speak another civil word to a man after taking him as a lover. The exhibitionism of publicity is necessary to one, just as to another is a physical beauty that must be universally acknowledged. Peter Templer liked to be seen about with 'obvious beauties': Bijou Ardglass, to be photographed in the papers with her lover of the moment. Most individual approaches to love, however unexpected, possess a logic of their own; for only by attempting to find some rationalisation of love in the mind can its burdens easily be borne. Sentiment and power, each in their way, supply something to feed the mind, if not the heart. They are therefore elements operated often to excess by persons in temperament unable to love at all, yet at the same time unwilling to be left out of the fun, or to bear the social stigma of living emotionally uninteresting lives.

I thought of some of these things as I made my way, later that afternoon, towards Sloane Square, the neighbourhood where General and Mrs. Conyers still inhabited the flat which I had visited as a small boy. I felt, to tell the truth, rather out of practice for paying a call of this sort. I was usually away from London on Sunday, certainly un-

accustomed to spend the afternoon at tea with an elderly
general and his wife. Even tea at the Ufford with Uncle
Giles would take place only a couple of times within a
period of about three years. However, this seemed one of
several hints of change that had become noticeable lately,
suggesting those times when the ice-floes of life's river are
breaking up—as in that scene in *Resurrection*—to float
down-stream, before the torrent freezes again in due course
into new and deceptively durable shape.

Although I used to see the General or Mrs. Conyers once
in a way when I was younger, usually with my parents at
the Grand Military (the General himself had formerly done
some steeplechasing) or at some point-to-point at Hawthorn
Hill, the last of these meetings between us had taken place
years before. The Conyers's flat, when I arrived there,
appeared considerably smaller than I remembered. Otherwise the place was unchanged. There on the bookcase was
the photograph of the General with his halberd. The 'cello
I could not immediately locate. The reason for this became
apparent a moment or two after I had been greeted by Mrs.
Conyers, when a low melancholy wailing began all at once
to echo from somewhere not far off, persistent, though
muffled by several doors: notes of a hidden orchestra,
mysterious, even a shade unearthly, as if somewhere in the
vicinity gnomes were thumbing strange instruments in a
cave. Then the music swelled in volume like a street band
coming level with the window, so that one felt instinctively
for a coin to throw down.

'Aylmer will be with us in a minute,' said Mrs. Conyers.
'He always practises until five o'clock when we are in
London. As you were coming this afternoon he agreed
to finish a little earlier. He is never satisfied with his
execution.'

'The piece seems familiar.'

'*Ave Maria.*'

'But, of course.'

'When it isn't Gounod, it is Marcello's sonatas.

The thought of the General at his 'cello conjured up one of those Dutch genre pictures, sentimental yet at the same time impressive, not only on account of their adroit recession and delicate colour tones, but also from the deep social conviction of the painter. For some reason I could not help imagining him scraping away in the uniform of the Bodyguard, helmet resting on a carved oak chest and halberd leaning against the wall. Mrs. Conyers dismissed her husband's cadences, no doubt only too familiar.

'What a strange household that is of Lady Molly's,' she said. 'I don't mind telling you that I find *him* rather difficult. He seems to have nothing whatever to talk about. He once told me of a wonderfully cheap place to buy white cotton shirts for men. Of course, Aylmer was glad to know of the shop, only you don't want to go on discussing it for ever. So tedious for his wife, it must be, but she doesn't seem to mind it. All the Ardglass family are very odd. I believe you come across all kinds of people at the Jeavonses —some of them decidedly what my father used to call "rum". Of course that was where my sister first met Mr. Widmerpool. How funny you should know him already.'

She spoke with some show of indifference, but there could be no doubt that her unconcern was simulated and that she longed to discuss the engagement exhaustively: probably hoping to hear special revelations about Widmerpool before her husband joined us.

'I know him quite well. In fact, I have just been lunching with him.'

Mrs. Conyers was enchanted at this news.

'Then you can really tell us what he is like,' she said. 'We have heard some—of course I don't believe them—not exactly flattering accounts of him. Naturally you don't want to listen to everything you hear, but Mildred *is* my youngest sister, and she *does* do some rather reckless things sometimes. Do describe him to me.'

At that moment tea was brought in by the maid, and, before Mrs. Conyers could further insist upon a reply, the General himself appeared. He was still limping slightly from his fall. He grasped my arm near the elbow for a second in a grip of steel, as if making a sudden arrest. Generals, as a collective rank, incline physically to be above, or below, average stature. Aylmer Conyers, notably tall, possessed in addition to his height, much natural distinction. In fact, his personality filled the room, although without active aggression. At the same time he was a man who gave the impression, rightly or wrongly, that he would stop at nothing. If he decided to kill you, he would kill you; if he thought it sufficient to knock you down, he would knock you down: if a mere reprimand was all required, he would confine himself to a reprimand. In addition to this, he patently maintained a good-humoured, well-mannered awareness of the inherent failings of human nature: the ultimate futility of all human effort. He wore an unusually thick, dark hairy suit, the coat cut long, the trousers narrow, a high stiff collar, of which the stud was revealed by the tie, and beautifully polished boots of patent leather with grey cloth tops. He looked like an infinitely accomplished actor got up to play the part that was, in fact, his own. At the same time he managed to avoid that almost too perfect elegance of outward appearance to be found in some men of his sort, especially courtiers. The hairiness of the suit did that. It suggested that a touch of rough force had been retained as a reminder of his strenuous past, like ancient, rusty armour hanging among luxurious tapestries.

'Never get that last bit right,' he said. '. . . *Nunc et in hora mortis nostrae* . . . always a shade flat on that high note in *hora* . . .'

He slowly shook his head, at the same time lowering himself into an arm-chair, while he straightened out his left leg with both hands as if modelling a piece of delicate sculpture. Evidently it was still rather painfully stiff. After achieving the best angle for comfort, he began to conduct through the air the strokes of an imaginary baton, at the same time allowing himself to hum under his breath:

> 'Tum, tumtitty, tum-te-tum
> Te-tum te-titty tum-tum-te-titty, tum-te-titty
> Amen, A-a-a-ame-e-e-en . . .'

Mrs. Conyers, throughout these movements and sounds, all of which she completely ignored, could scarcely wait for the maid carrying the tea-tray to leave the room.

'Too late to learn at my age, much too late,' said the General. 'But I go on trying. Never mind, I'm not getting on too badly with those arrangements of Saint-Saëns.'

'Aylmer, you remember I told you Nicholas knows Mr. Widmerpool?'

'What, this Nicholas?'

'Yes.'

'You know the fellow who is going to marry Mildred?'

'Yes.'

If Mrs. Conyers had already told her husband of my acquaintance with Widmerpool, the General had entirely forgotten about that piece of information, for it now came to him as something absolutely new, and, for some reason, excruciatingly funny, causing him to fall into an absolute paroxysm of deep, throaty guffaws, like the inextinguishable laughter of the Homeric gods on high Olympus, to whose characteristic faults and merits General Conyers's own nature probably approximated closely enough. A twinge of pain in his leg brought this laughter to an end in a fit of coughing.

'What sort of a fellow is he?' he asked, speaking now more seriously. 'We haven't heard too satisfactory an account of him, have we, Bertha? Is he a good fellow? He'll have his hands full with Mildred, you may be sure of that. Much younger than her, isn't he?'

'I was at school with him. He must be about——'

'Nonsense,' said the General. 'You can't have been at school with him. You must be thinking of someone else of that name—a younger brother, I expect.'

'He is a year or two older than me——'

'But you couldn't have been *at school* with him. No, no, you couldn't have been at school with him.'

Mrs. Conyers, too, now shook her head in support of her husband. This claim to have been at school with Widmerpool was something not to be credited. Like most people who have known someone as a child, they were unwilling to believe that I could possibly have arrived at an age to be reasonably regarded as an adult. To have ceased, very recently, to have been an undergraduate was probably about the furthest degree of maturity either of them would easily be inclined to concede. That Widmerpool's name could be put forward as a contemporary of myself was obviously the worst shock the General had yet sustained on the subject. His earlier attitude suggested the whole affair to be one of those ludicrous incidents inseparable from anything to do with his wife's family; but the news that he might be about to possess an additional brother-in-law more or less of an age with myself disturbed him more than a little. He began to frown angrily.

'I met a young fellow called Truscott last week,' he said.

'There was a question of his coming on to a board from which I retired the other day. He is connected with the by-products of coal and said to have a good brain. I asked him if by any chance he knew Widmerpool—without divulging the nature of my interest, of course—and he spoke with the greatest dislike of him. The greatest dislike. It turned out they had been in Donners-Brebner together at one time. Truscott said Widmerpool was a terrible fellow. Couldn't trust him an inch. Now that may be a pack of lies. I've never been in the habit of listening to gossip. Haven't got time for it. Naturally I didn't tell Truscott that, in case it made him dry up. Thought it my duty to hear whatever he had to get off his chest. I must say he produced a whole string of crimes to be laid at Widmerpool's door, not the least of which was to have got him—Truscott—sacked from Donners-Brebner. Now what I say is that a man who marries Mildred must be a man with a will of his own. No good marrying Mildred otherwise. Now a man with a will of his own is often a man to make enemies. I know that as well as anyone. Evidently Widmerpool had made an enemy of Truscott. That isn't necessarily anything against Widmerpool. He may be an excellent fellow in spite of that. Getting rid of Truscott may have been a piece of first-class policy. Who am I to judge? But what I do know is this. Bertha's sister, Mildred, has been used to a lot of her own way. Do you think that Mr. Widmerpool is going to be able to manage a woman some years older than himself and used to a lot of her own way?'

I had not thought of Truscott for years. At the university he had been billed for a great career: prime minister: lord chancellor: famous poet: it was never finally decided which rôle he would most suitably ornament; perhaps all three. Now I remembered being told by someone or other that Widmerpool, before himself leaving the firm, had contrived to have Truscott ejected from Donners-Brebner. The General had certainly brought a crisp, military appraisal to the situation. I was wondering what to answer—since I saw no way of giving a simple reply to a subject so complicated as Widmerpool's character—when the maid reappeared to announce another guest.

'Lady Frederica Budd.'

The niece whose condition of unassailable rectitude had given such satisfaction to Alfred Tolland, and at the same time caused some unfriendly amusement to Molly Jeavons, was shown into the room. This crony of Mrs. Conyers, widow with several children and lady-in-waiting, was a handsome woman in her thirties. She was dressed in a manner to be described as impregnable, like a long, neat, up-to-date battle-cruiser. You felt that her clothes were certainly removed when she retired for the night, but that no intermediate adjustment, however minor, was ever required, or would, indeed, be practicable. This was the eldest of the Tolland sisters, formed physically in much the same mould as Blanche and Priscilla; though I could see no resemblance between her and her brothers as I remembered them. She kissed Mrs. Conyers. The General greeted her warmly, though with a touch of irony in his manner. I was introduced. Lady Frederica looked at me carefully, rather as if she were engaged upon an army inspection: a glance not unfriendly, but extensively searching. I could see at once that she and Molly Jeavons would not be a couple easily to agree. Then she turned towards the General.

'How are you feeling after your fall?' she asked.

'A bit stiff. A bit stiff. Took a fearful toss. Nearly broke my neck. And you, Frederica?'

'Oh, I've been rather well,' she said. 'Christmas was

spoiled by two of the children developing measles. But they have recovered now. All very exhausting while it lasted.'

'I spent Christmas Day cleaning out the kennels,' said the General. 'Went to Early Service. Then I got into my oldest clothes and had a thorough go at them. Had luncheon late and a good sleep after. Read a book all the evening. One of the best Christmas Days I've ever had.'

Frederica Tolland did not seem greatly interested by this account of the General's Christmas activities. She turned from him to Mrs. Conyers, as if she hoped for something more congenial.

'What have you been doing, Bertha?' she asked.

'I went to the sales yesterday,' said Mrs. Conyers, speaking as if that were a somewhat disagreeable duty that had been long on her mind.

'Were you nearly trampled to death?'

'I came away with a hat.'

'I went earlier in the week,' said Frederica. 'Looking for a cheap black dress, as a matter of fact. So many royalties nearing their century, we're bound to be in mourning again soon.'

'Have they been working you hard?' asked the General.

I had the impression that he might be a little jealous of Frederica, who, for her part, was evidently determined that he should not be allowed to take himself too seriously. There was just a touch of sharpness in their interchanges.

'Nothing really lethal since the British Industries Fair,' she said. 'I had to throw away my best pair of shoes after *that*. You are lucky not to have to turn out for that sort of thing. It will finish me off one of these days.'

'You come and carry my axe at the next levée,' said the General. 'Thought I was going to drop with fatigue the last time I was on duty. Then that damned fellow Ponsonby trod on my gouty toe.'

'We saw your Uncle Alfred the other night, Frederica,' said Mrs. Conyers.

She spoke either with a view to including me in the conversation or because habit had taught her that passages of this kind between her husband and Frederica Budd might become a shade acrimonious: perhaps merely to steer our talk back to the subject of Widmerpool.

'He was looking well enough,' she added.

'Oh no, really?' said Frederica, plainly surprised at this. 'Where did you meet him? I thought he never went out except to things like regimental dinners. That is what he always says.'

'At Molly Jeavons's. I had not been there before.'

'Of course. He goes there still, doesn't he? What strange people he must meet at that house. What sort of a crowd did you find? I really must go and see Molly again myself some time. For some reason I never feel very anxious to go there. I think Rob was still alive when I last went to the Jeavonses'.'

These remarks, although displaying no great affection, were moderate enough, considering the tone in which Molly Jeavons herself had spoken of Frederica.

'That was where I found Nicholas again,' said Mrs. Conyers.

She proceeded to give some account of why they knew me. Frederica listened with attention, rather than interest, again recalling by her manner the checking of facts in the course of some official routine like going through the Customs or having one's passport examined. Then she turned to me as if to obtain some final piece of necessary information.

'Do you often go to the Jeavonses'?' she asked.

The enquiry seemed to prepare the way to cross-questioning one returned from the remote interior of some little-

77

known country after making an intensive study of the savage life existing there.

'That was the first time. I was taken by Chips Lovell, whom I work with.'

'Oh yes,' she said vaguely. 'He is some sort of a relation of Molly's, isn't he?'

She showed herself not at all positive about Lovell and his place in the world. This surprised me, as I had supposed she would know him, or at least know about him, pretty well. A moment later I wondered whether possibly she knew him, but pretended ignorance because she disapproved. Lovell was by no means universally liked. There were people who considered his behaviour far from impeccable. Frederica Budd might be one of these. A guarded attitude towards Lovell was only to be expected if Molly Jeavons was to be believed. At that moment the General spoke. He had been sitting in silence while we talked, quite happy silence, so it appeared, still pondering the matter of Widmerpool and his sister-in-law; or, more probably, his own rendering of Gounod and how it could be bettered. His sonorous, commanding voice, not loud, though pitched in a tone to carry across parade-ground or battle-field, echoed through the small room.

'I like Jeavons,' he said. 'I only met him once, but I took to him. Lady Molly I hardly know. Her first husband, John Sleaford, was a pompous fellow. The present Slea-ford—Geoffrey—I knew in South Africa. We see them from time to time. Bertha tells me Lady Molly was teasing your Uncle Alfred a lot the other night. People say she always does that. Is it true?'

The General laughed a deep ho-ho-ho laugh again, like the demon king in pantomime. He evidently enjoyed the idea of people teasing Alfred Tolland.

'I think she may rag Uncle Alfred a bit,' said Frederica,

without emotion. 'If he doesn't like it, he shouldn't go there. I expect Erridge came up for discussion too, didn't he?'

I suspected this was said to forestall comment about Erridge on the part of the General himself. There was a distinct rivalry between them. Men of action have, in any case, a predisposition to be jealous of women, especially if the woman is young, good looking or placed in some relatively powerful position. Beauty, particularly, is a form of power of which, perhaps justly, men of action feel envious. Possibly there existed some more particular reason: the two of them conceivably representing rival factions in their connexion with the Court. I supposed from her tone and general demeanour that Frederica could hardly approve of her eldest brother's way of life, but, unlike her uncle, was not prepared to acquiesce in all criticism of Erridge.

'Do you know my brother, Erridge—Warminster, rather?' she asked me, suddenly.

She smiled like someone who wishes to encourage a child who possesses information more accurate, or more interesting, than that available to grown-ups; but one who might be too shy or too intractable to impart such knowledge.

'I used to know him by sight.'

'He has some rather odd ideas,' she said. 'But I expect you heard plenty about that at Molly Jeavons's. They have hardly anything else to talk about there. He is a real blessing to them.'

'Oh, I think they have got plenty to talk about,' said Mrs. Conyers. 'Too much, in fact.'

'I don't deny that Erridge has more than one bee in his bonnet,' said the General, unexpectedly. 'But I doubt if he is such a fool as some people seem to think him. He is just what they call nowadays introverted.'

'Oh, Erry isn't a fool,' said Frederica. 'He is rather too

clever in a way—and an awful nuisance as an eldest brother. There may be something to be said for his ideas. It is the way he sets about them.'

'Is it true that he has been a tramp?' I asked.

'Not actually been one, I think,' said Frederica. 'Making a study of them, isn't it?'

'Is he going to write a book about it?' asked Mrs. Conyers. 'There have been several books of that sort lately, haven't there? Have you read anything else interesting, Nicholas? I always expect people like you to tell me what to put down on my library list.'

'I've been reading something called *Orlando*,' said the General. 'Virginia Woolf. Ever heard of it?'

'I read it when it first came out.'

'What do you think of it?'

'Rather hard to say in a word.'

'You think so?'

'Yes.'

He turned to Frederica.

'Ever read *Orlando*?'

'No,' she said. 'But I've heard of it.'

'Bertha didn't like it,' he said.

'Couldn't get on with it,' said Mrs. Conyers, emphatically. 'I wish St. John Clarke would write a new one. He hasn't published a book for years. I wonder whether he is dead. I used to love his novels, especially *Fields of Amaranth*.'

'Odd stuff, *Orlando*,' said the General, who was not easily shifted from his subject. 'Starts about a young man in the fifteen-hundreds. Then, about eighteen-thirty, he turns into a woman. You say you've read it?'

'Yes.'

'Did you like it? Yes or no?'

'Not greatly.'

'You didn't?'

'No.'

'The woman can write, you know.'

'Yes, I can see that. I still didn't like it.'

The General thought again for some seconds.

'Well, I shall read a bit more of it,' he said, at last. 'Don't want to waste too much time on that sort of thing, of course. Now, psychoanalysis. Ever read anything about that? Sure you have. That was what I was on over Christmas.'

'I've dipped into it from time to time. I can't say I'm much of an expert.'

'Been reading a lot about it lately,' said the General. 'Freud—Jung—haven't much use for Adler. Something in it, you know. Tells you why you do things. All the same, I didn't find it much help in understanding *Orlando*.'

Once more he fell into a state of coma. It was astonishing to me that he should have been reading about psychoanalysis, although his mental equipment was certainly in no way inferior to that of many persons who talked of such things all day long. When he had used the word 'introverted' I had thought that no more than repetition of a current popular term. I saw now that the subject had thoroughly engaged his attention. However, he wished to discuss it no further at that moment. Neither of the two ladies seemed to share his interest.

'Is it true that your sister, Mildred, is going to marry again?' asked Frederica. 'Someone told me so the other day. They could not remember the name of the man. It hasn't been in the papers yet, has it?'

She spoke casually. Mrs. Conyers was well prepared for the question, because she answered without hesitation, allowing no suggestion to appear of the doubts she had revealed to me only a short time earlier.

81

'The engagement is supposed to be a secret,' she said, 'but, as everybody will hear about it quite soon, there is really no reason to deny the rumour.'

'Then it is true?'

'It certainly looks as if Mildred is going to marry again.'

No one, however determined to make a good story, could have derived much additional information on the subject from the manner in which Mrs. Conyers spoke, except in so far that she could not be said to show any obvious delight at the prospect of her sister taking a third husband. That was the farthest implication offered. There was not a hint of disapproval or regret; on the contrary, complete acceptance of the situation was manifest, even mild satisfaction not openly disavowed. It was impossible to withhold admiration from this façade, so effortlessly presented.

'And he——?'

'Nicholas, here, was at school with him,' said Mrs. Conyers, tranquilly.

She spoke as if most people must, as a matter of course, be already aware of that circumstance; for it now seemed that, in spite of her husband's doubts, she had finally accepted the fact that I was within a few years of Widmerpool's age. The remark only stimulated Frederica's curiosity.

'Oh, do tell me what he is like,' she said. 'Mildred was just that amount older than me to make her rather a thrilling figure at the time when I first came "out". She was at the Huntercombes' once when I stayed there not long after the war. She was rather a dashing war widow and wore huge jade ear-rings, and smoked all the time and said the most hair-raising things. What is her new name to be, first of all?'

'Widmerpool,' I said, since the question was addressed to me.

'Where do they come from?' asked Mrs. Conyers, anxious

to profit herself from Frederica's interrogation.

'Nottinghamshire, I believe.'

This reply was at worst innocuous, and might be taken, in general, to imply a worthy family background. It was also—as I understood from Widmerpool himself—in no way a departure from the truth. Fearing that I might, if pressed, be compelled ultimately to admit some hard things about Widmerpool, I felt that the least I could do for an old acquaintance in these circumstances was to suggest, however indirectly, a soothing picture of generations of Widmerpools in a rural setting: an ancient, if dilapidated, manor house: Widmerpool tombs in the churchyard: tankards of ale at The Widmerpool Arms.

'You haven't said what his Christian name is,' said Frederica, apparently accepting, anyway at this stage, the regional superscription.

'Kenneth.'

'Brothers or sisters?'

'No.'

I admired the thoroughness with which Frederica set to work on an enquiry of this kind, as much as I had admired Mrs. Conyers's earlier refusal to give anything away.

'And he is in the City?'

'He is supposed to be rather good at making money,' interpolated Mrs. Conyers.

She had begun to smile indulgently at Frederica's unconcealed curiosity. Now she employed a respectful yet at the same time deprecatory tone, as if this trait of Widmerpool's —his supposed facility for 'making money'—was, extraordinary as this might appear, a propensity not wholly unpleasant when you became accustomed to it. At the same time she abandoned her former position of apparent neutrality, openly joining in the search. Indeed, she put the next question herself.

'His father is dead, isn't he?' she said. 'Nottinghamshire, did you say?'

'Or Derbyshire. I don't remember for certain.'

Widmerpool had once confided the fact that his grandfather, a business man from the Scotch Lowlands, had on marriage changed his name from 'Geddes'; but such an additional piece of information would sound at that moment too esoteric and genealogical: otiose in its exactitude. In a different manner, to repeat Eleanor Walpole-Wilson's remark made years before—'Uncle George used to get his liquid manure from Mr. Widmerpool's father'—might strike, though quite illogically, a disobliging, even objectionably facetious note. Eleanor's 'Uncle George' was Lord Goring. It seemed best to omit all mention of liquid manure; simply to say that Widmerpool had known the Gorings and the Walpole-Wilsons.

'Oh, the Walpole-Wilsons,' said Frederica sharply, as if reminded of something she would rather forget. 'Do you know the Walpole-Wilsons? My sister, Norah, shares a flat with Eleanor Walpole-Wilson. Do you know them?'

'I haven't seen Eleanor for years. Nor her parents, for that matter.'

The General now came to life again, after his long period of rumination.

'Walpole-Wilson was that fellow in the Diplomatic Service who made such a hash of things in South America,' he said. 'Got unstuck for it. I met him at a City dinner once, the Mercers—or was it the Fishmongers? Had an argument over Puccini.'

'I don't know the Gorings,' said Frederica, ignoring the General. 'You mean the ones called "Lord" Goring?'

'Yes. He is a great fruit farmer, isn't he? He talked about fruit on the only occasions when I met him.'

'I remember,' she said. 'He is.'

She had uttered the words 'Lord Goring' with emphasis on the title, seeming by her tone almost to suggest that all members of that particular family, male and female, might for some unaccountable reason call themselves "Lord": at least implying that, even if she did not really suppose anything so absurd, she wished to indicate that I should have been wiser to have steered clear of the Gorings: in fact, that informed persons considered the Gorings themselves mistaken in burdening themselves with the rather ridiculous pretension of a peerage. When I came to know her better I realised that her words were intended to cast no particular slur on the Gorings; merely, since they were not personal friends of hers, to build up a safe defence in case they turned out, in her own eyes, undesirable.

'I think Widmerpool *père* was mixed up with the fruit-farming side of Goring life.'

'But look here,' said General Conyers, suddenly emerging with terrific violence from the almost mediumistic trance in which he had sunk after the mention of Puccini. 'The question is simply this. Can this fellow Widmerpool handle Mildred? It all turns on that. What do you think, Nicholas? You say you were at school with him. You usually know a fellow pretty well when you have been boys together. What's your view? Give us an appreciation of the situation.'

'But I don't know Mrs. Haycock. I was only nine or ten when I first met her. Last night I barely spoke to her.'

There was some laughter at that, and the necessity passed for an immediate pronouncement on the subject of Widmerpool's potentialities.

'You must meet my sister again,' said Mrs. Conyers, involuntarily smiling to herself, I suppose at the thought of Widmerpool as Mildred's husband.

After that, conversation drifted. Mrs. Conyers began once more to talk of clothes and of how her daughter, Charlotte, had had a baby in Malta. The General relapsed once more into torpor, occasionally murmuring faint musical intonations that might still be ringing the changes on '. . . *nunc et in hora* . . .' Frederica rose to go. I gave her time to get down the stairs, and then myself said good-bye. It was agreed that so long a period must not again elapse before I paid another visit. Mrs. Conyers was one of those persons who find it difficult to part company quickly, so that it was some minutes before I reached the hall of the block of flats. In front of the entrance Frederica Budd was still sitting in a small car, which was making the horrible flat sound that indicates an engine refusing to fire.

'This wretched car won't start,' she shouted.

'Can I help?'

At that moment the engine came to life.

'Shall I give you a lift?' she said.

'Which way are you going?'

'Chelsea.'

I, too, was on my way to Chelsea that evening. It was a period of my life when, in recollection, I seem often to have been standing in a cinema queue with a different girl. One such evening lay ahead of me.

'Thank you very much.'

'Jump in,' she said.

Now that she had invited me into her car, and we were driving along together, her manner, momentarily relaxed while she had been pressing the self-starter, became once more impersonal and remote; as if 'a lift' was not considered an excuse for undue familiarity between us. When the car had refused to start she had seemed younger and less chilly: less part of the impeccable Conyers world. Now she returned to an absolutely friendly, but also utterly impregnable outpost of formality.

'You have known Bertha and the General for a long time?'

'Since I was a child.'

'That was when you met Mildred?'

'Yes.'

'You probably know all the stories about their father, Lord Vowchurch?'

'I've heard some of them.'

'The remark he is said to have made to King Edward just after Bertha's engagement had been announced?'

'I don't know that one.'

'It was on the Squadron Lawn at Cowes. The King is supposed to have said: "Well, Vowchurch, I hear you are marrying your eldest daughter to one of my generals", and Bertha's father is said to have replied: "By Gad, I am, sir, and I trust he'll teach the girl to lead out trumps, for they'll have little enough to live on". Edward VII was rather an erratic bridge-player, you know. Sir Thomas Lipton told me the story in broad Scotch, which made it sound funnier. Of course, the part that appealed to Sir Thomas Lipton was the fact that it took place on the Squadron Lawn.'

'How did the King take it?'

'I think he was probably rather cross. Of course it may not be true. But Lord Vowchurch certainly was always getting into trouble with the King. Lord Vowchurch was supposed to be referring to some special game of bridge when he had been dummy and things had gone badly wrong with King Edward's play. You said you'd met my Uncle Alfred, didn't you?'

'A couple of times.'

'And you know whom I mean by Brabazon?'

'The Victorian dandy—"Bwab"?'

'Yes, that one.'

'Who said he couldn't remember what regiment he had exchanged into—after leaving the Brigade of Guards because it was too expensive—but "they wore green facings and you got to them by Waterloo Station"?'

'That's him. How clever of you to know about him. Well, when Uncle Alfred was a young man, he was dining at Pratt's, and Colonel Brabazon came in from the Marlborough Club, where he had been in the card-room when the game was being played. According to Uncle Alfred, Colonel Brabazon said: "Vowchurch expwessed weal wesentment while his Woyal Highness played the wottenest wubber of wecent seasons—nothing but we-deals and wevokes." '

'I had no idea your uncle had a fund of stories of that kind.'

'He hasn't. That is his only one. He is rather a shy man, you see, and nothing ever happens to him.'

This was all very lively; although there was at the same time always something a shade aloof about the manner in which these anecdotes were retailed. However, they carried us down the King's Road in no time. There was, in addition, something reminiscent about the tone in which they were delivered, a faint reminder of Alfred Tolland's own reserve and fear of intimacy. Amusing in themselves, the stories were at the same time plainly intended to establish a specific approach to life. Beneath their fluency, it was possible to detect in Frederica Budd herself, at least so far as personal rather than social life was concerned, a need for armour against strangers. Almost schooled out of existence by severe self-discipline, a faint trace of her uncle's awkwardness still remained to be observed under the microscope. There could be no doubt that I had scored a point by knowing about 'Bwab'.

'I met your sister, Priscilla, at the Jeavonses the other night—only for a minute or two. Chips Lovell drove us both home.'

She did not seem much interested by that, hardly answering. I remembered, then, that she probably did not care for Lovell. However, her next words were entirely unexpected.

'I am on my way to call on my sister, Norah, now,' she said. 'It seemed rather a long time since I had set eyes on her. I thought I would just look in to see that she is behaving herself. Why not come and meet her—and see Eleanor again.'

'Just for a second. Then I shall have to move on.'

At the sound of this last statement I was aware of a faint but distinct disapproval, as if my reply had informed her quite clearly—indeed, almost grossly—that I was up to no good; yet made her at the same time realise that in a locality where so much human behaviour commanded disapprobation, minor derelictions—anyway, in a man—must, in the interest of the general picture, be disregarded. However, together with that sense of constraint that she conveyed, I was by then also aware of a second feeling: a notion that some sort of temporary alliance had been hurriedly constructed between us. I could not explain this impression to myself, though I was prepared to accept it.

By that time we had arrived before a dilapidated stucco façade in a side street, a house entered by way of a creaking, unlatched door, from which most of the paint had been removed. The hall, empty except for a couple of packing-cases, gave off that stubborn musty smell characteristic of staircases leading to Chelsea flats: damp: cigarette smoke: face powder. We climbed the uncarpeted boards, ascending endlessly floor after floor, Frederica Budd taking the steps two at a time at a sharp pace. At last the attics were reached; and another battered door, upon which was fastened a brass knocker, formed in the image of the

Lincoln Imp. Attached with four drawing-pins to the panel below this knocker was a piece of grubby cardboard inscribed with the names:

TOLLAND
WALPOLE-WILSON

Frederica, ignoring the claims of the Lincoln Imp, clenched her fist and banged on the door with all her force, at the same time shouting in an unexpectedly raucous voice:

'Norah! Eleanor!'

There was a sound of someone stirring within. Then Eleanor Walpole-Wilson opened the door. She was wearing a very dirty pair of navy blue flannel trousers and smoking a stub of a cigarette. Apart from her trousers and cigarette, and also a decided air of increased confidence in herself, she had changed very little from the days when, loathing every moment of it, she used to trail round the London ball-rooms. She still wore her hair in a bun, a style which by then brought her appearance almost within measurable distance of 'the mode'; or at least within hail of something that might, with a little good will, be supposed unconventionally chic. Square and broad-shouldered as ever, she was plainly on much better terms with herself, and with others, than formerly.

'I've brought an old friend to see you,' said Frederica.

Eleanor showed no surprise at my arrival. There was even a slight suggestion of relief that Frederica Budd had not to be entertained singly; for towards Frederica Eleanor displayed a hint of her old aggressiveness, or at least gave indication that she was on the defensive. This sense of quiet but firm opposition became more positive when we moved into the sitting-room.

'How are you, Nicholas?' said Eleanor. 'Fancy your turning up here. Why, you've got a grey hair. Just above your ear.'

The place was horribly untidy, worse than the Jeavonses, and the furniture struck an awkward level between boudoir and studio: an ancient sofa, so big that one wondered how it could ever have been hoisted up the last flight of stairs, stood covered with chintz roses among two or three unsubstantial, faintly 'Louis' chairs. The walls had been distempered yellow by some amateur hand. A girl was lying prone on the ground, her skirt rucked up to her thighs, showing a strip of skin above each stocking. This was Norah Tolland. She was pasting scraps on to the surface of a coal-scuttle.

'Hullo, Frederica,' she said, without looking up. 'I shan't be a moment. I must finish this before the paste runs out.'

She continued her work for a few moments, then, wiping the paste from her hands with a red check duster, she rose from the ground, pulled her skirt down impatiently, and gave her sister a peck on the cheek. Eleanor presented me, explaining that we had known each other 'in the old days'. Norah Tolland did not look very enthusiastic at this news, but she held out her hand. She was dark and very pale, with a narrow face like her sister's, her expression more truculent, though also, on the whole, less firm in character. The coltishness of her sister, Priscilla, had turned in Norah to a deliberate, rather absurd masculinity. Frederica glanced round the room without attempting to conceal her distaste, as if she felt there was much to criticise, not least the odour of turpentine and stale cake.

'I see you haven't managed to get the window mended yet,' she said.

Her sister did not answer, only flicking back her hair from her forehead with a sharp, angry motion.

'Isobel is supposed to be coming in to see us some time today,' she said, 'with her new young man. I thought it was her when you arrived.'

'Who is her new young man?'

'How should I know? Some chap.'

'I saw her last night at Hyde Park Gardens.'

'How were they all?' said Norah, indifferently. 'Would you like a drink? I think there is some sherry left.'

Frederica shook her head, as if the idea of alcohol in any form at that moment nauseated her.

'You?'

'No, thank you. I must really go in a moment.'

The sherry did not sound very safe: wiser to forego it.

'Don't leave yet,' said Eleanor. 'You've only just arrived. We must have a word about old times. I haven't seen the Gorings for ages. I always think of you, Nicholas, as a friend of Barbara's.'

'How is Barbara?'

It seemed extraordinary that I had once, like Widmerpool, thought myself in love with Barbara. Now I could hardly remember what she looked like, except that she was small and dark.

'You know she married Johnny Pardoe?' said Eleanor.

'I haven't set eyes on either of them since the wedding.'

'Things have been a bit difficult.'

'What?'

'There was a baby that went wrong.'

'Oh, dear.'

'Then Johnny got awfully odd and melancholy after he left the Grenadiers. You remember he used to be an absolutely typical guardee, pink in the face and shouting at the top of his voice all the time, and yelling with laughter. Now he has quite changed, and mopes for hours or reads books on religion and philosophy.'

'Johnny Pardoe?'

'He sits in the library for weeks at a time just brooding. Never shoots now. You know how much he used to love shooting. Barbara has to run the place entirely. Poor Barbara, she has an awful time of it.'

Life jogs along, apparently in the same old way, and then suddenly your attention is drawn to some terrific change that has taken place. For example, I found myself brought up short at that moment, like a horse reined in on the brink of a precipice, at the thought of the astonishing reversal of circumstances by which Eleanor Walpole-Wilson was now in a position to feel sorry for Barbara Goring—or, as she had by then been for some years, Barbara Pardoe. The relationship between these two first cousins, like all other relationships when one is young, had seemed at that time utterly immutable; Barbara, pretty, lively, noisy, popular: Eleanor, plain, awkward, cantankerous, solitary. Barbara's patronage of Eleanor was something that could never change. 'Eleanor is not a bad old thing when you get to know her,' she used to say; certainly without the faintest suspicion that within a few years Eleanor might be in a position to say: 'Poor Barbara, she does have a time of it.'

While indulging in these rather banal reflections, I became aware that the two sisters had begun to quarrel. I had not heard the beginning of the conversation that had led to this discord, but it seemed to be concerned with their respective visits that summer to Thrubworth, their brother's house.

'As you know, Erry always makes these difficulties,' Frederica was saying. 'It is not that I myself particularly want to go there and live in ghastly discomfort for several weeks and feel frightfully depressed at seeing the place fall to pieces. I would much rather go to the seaside or abroad. But it is nice for the children to see the house, and they enjoy going down to talk to the people at the farm, and all that sort of thing. So if you are determined to go at just that moment——'

'All right, then,' said Norah, smiling and showing her teeth like an angry little vixen, 'I won't go. Nothing easier. I don't particularly want to go to the bloody place either, but it is my home, I suppose. Some people might think that ought to be taken into consideration. I was born there. I can't say I've had many happy moments there, it's true, but I like walking by myself in the woods—and I have plenty of other ways of amusing myself there without bothering either you or Erry or anyone else.'

Eleanor caught my eye with a look to be interpreted as indicating that high words of this kind were not unexpected in the circumstances, but that we should try to quell them. However, before dissension could develop further, it was cut short abruptly by the door of the room opening. A small, gnarled, dumpy, middle-aged woman stood on the threshold. She wore horn-rimmed spectacles and her short legs were enclosed, like Eleanor's, in blue flannel trousers —somewhat shrunk, for her largely developed thighs seemed to strain their seams—into the pockets of which her hands were deeply plunged.

'Why, hullo, Hopkins,' said Norah Tolland, her face suddenly clearing, and showing, for the first time since I had been in the room, some signs of pleasure. 'What can we do for you?'

'Hullo, girls,' said the woman at the door.

She made no attempt to reply to Norah's question, continuing to gaze round the room, grinning broadly, but advancing no farther beyond the threshold. She gave the impression of someone doing a turn on the stage.

'If you take to leaving your front door on the latch,' she said at last, 'you'll find a *man* will walk in one of these days, and then where will you be, I should like to know? By Jove, I see a man has walked in already. Well, well, well, never mind. There are a lot of them about, so I suppose you can't keep them out all the time. What I came up for, dear, was to borrow an egg, if you've got such a thing. Laid one lately, either of you?'

Norah Tolland laughed.

'This is my sister, Lady Frederica Budd,' she said. 'And Mr. ——'

'Jenkins,' said Eleanor, in answer to an appeal for my name.

Eleanor was, I thought, less pleased than Norah to see the woman they called Hopkins. In fact, she seemed somewhat put out by her arrival.

'Pleased to meet you, my dear,' said Hopkins, holding out her hand to Frederica; 'and you, my boy,' she added, smirking in my direction.

'Miss Hopkins plays the piano most nights at the Merry Thought,' said Eleanor.

This explanation seemed aimed principally at Frederica.

'You ought to look in one night,' said Hopkins. 'But come soon, because I've got an engagement next month to appear with Max Pilgrim at the Café de Madrid. I'll have to make sure that old queen, Max, doesn't hog every number. It would be just like him. He's as vain as a peacock. Can't trust a man not to try and steal the show anyway, even the normal ones, they're the worst of all. Now the other thing I wanted to remind you girls about is my album. You've still got it. Have you thought of something nice to write in it, either of you?'

It appeared that no good idea had occurred either to Eleanor or Norah for inscription in the album.

'I shall want it back soon,' said Hopkins, 'because another girl I know—such a little sweetie-pie with a little fragile face like a dear little dolly—is going to write some *lovely* lines in it. Shall I repeat to you what she is going to write? You will love it.'

Frederica Budd, who had been listening to all this with a slight smile, imperceptibly inclined her head, as one might when a clown enquires from his audience whether they have understood up to that point the course of the trick he is about to perform. Eleanor looked as if she did not particularly wish to hear what was offered, but regarded any demur as waste of time. Hopkins spoke the words:

'Lips may be redder, and eyes more bright;
The face may be fairer you see tonight;
But never, love, while the stars shall shine,
Will you find a heart that is truer than mine.'

There was a pause when Hopkins came to the end of her recitation, which she had delivered with ardour. She struck an attitude, her hand on her hip.

'Sweet, isn't it?' she said. 'This friend of mine read it somewhere, and she memorised it—and so have I. I love it so much. That's the sort of thing I want. I'll leave the album a little longer then, girls, but remember—I shall expect something really nice when you do, both of you, think of a poem. Now what about that egg?'

Norah Tolland went into the kitchen of the flat. Hopkins stood grinning at us. No one spoke. Then Norah returned. On receiving the egg, Hopkins feigned to make it disappear up the sleeves of her shirt, the cuffs of which were joined by links of black and white enamel. Then, clenching her fist, she balanced the egg upon it at arm's length, and marched out of the room chanting at the top of her voice:

'Balls, Picnics and Parties,
Picnics, Parties and Balls . . .'

We heard the sound of her heavy, low-heeled shoes pounding the boards of the uncarpeted stairs, until at length a door slammed on a floor below, and the voice was cut off with a jerk.

'She really plays the piano jolly well,' said Norah.

It was a challenge, but the glove was not picked up.

'Rather an amusing person,' said Frederica. 'Do you see much of her?'

'She lives a couple of floors below,' said Eleanor. 'She is rather too fond of looking in at all hours.'

'Oh, I don't know,' said Norah. 'I like Heather.'

'So you've made up your mind about Thrubworth?' said Frederica, as if the merits of Hopkins were scarcely worth discussing.

I explained that I must now leave them. Frederica, at the moment of saying good-bye, spoke almost warmly; as if her conjecture that I might be a support to her had been somehow justified. Norah Tolland was curt. It was agreed that I should ring up Eleanor one of these days and come to see them again. I had the impression that my departure would be the signal for a renewed outbreak of family feuds. Anxious to avoid even their preliminary barrage, I descended the rickety, fœtid stairs, and proceeded on my way.

Later that evening, I found myself kicking my heels in one of those interminable cinema queues of which I have already spoken, paired off and stationary, as if life's co-educational school, out in a 'crocodile', had come to a sudden standstill: that co-educational school of iron discipline, equally pitiless in pleasure and in pain. During the eternity of time that always precedes the termination of the 'big picture', I had even begun to wonder whether we should spend the rest of our days on that particular stretch of London pavement, when, at long last, just as rain had begun to fall, the portals of the auditorium burst open to void the patrons of the earlier performance. First came those scattered single figures, who, as if distraught by what they have seen and seeking to escape at whatever the cost, hurry blindly from the building, they care not how, nor where; then the long serpentine of spectators to whom expulsion into the street means no more than a need to take another decision in life; who, accordingly, postpone in the foyer any such irksome effort of the will by banding themselves into small, irregular, restless groups, sometimes static, sometimes ineffectively mobile. As the queue of which we formed a link stumbled forward towards the booking office, I discerned through the mist of faces that must dissolve before we could gain our seats, the features of J. G. Quiggin. Our eyes met. He shook his head sharply from side to side, as if to express satisfaction that we should run into each other in so opportune a manner. A moment later he was near enough to make his small, grating tones heard above the murmur of other voices.

'I've been trying to get hold of you,' he said.

'We must meet.'

'There were some things I wanted to talk about.'

Since we had been undergraduates together my friendship with Quiggin, moving up and down at different seasons, could have been plotted like a temperature chart. Sometimes we seemed on fairly good terms, sometimes on fairly bad terms; never with any very concrete reason for these improvements and deteriorations. However, if Quiggin thought it convenient to meet during a 'bad' period, he would always take steps to do so, having no false pride in this or any other aspect of his dealings with the world. After such a meeting, a 'good' period would set in; to be dissipated after a time by argument, disagreement or even by inanition. This periodicity of friendship and alienation had rotated, almost like the seasons of the year, until a year or two before: a time when Quiggin had 'run away' with Peter Templer's wife, Mona. This act threatened to complicate more seriously any relationship that might exist between Quiggin and myself.

As things turned out, I had seen nothing either of Templer or Quiggin during the period immediately following the divorce. Templer had always been out or engaged when I had telephoned to him; and, as we had by then little left in common except having been friends at school, our intermittent meetings had entirely ceased. There was perhaps another reason why I felt unwilling to make more strenuous efforts to see him. He reminded me of Jean. That was an additional reason for allowing this course to prevail. I heard quite by chance that he had sold his Maidenhead house. It was said, whatever his inner feelings about losing Mona, that outwardly he was not taking things too hard: demonstrating a principle he had once expressed: 'Women always think if they've knocked a man out, that they've knocked him out cold—on the contrary, he sometimes gets up again.' However, no husband enjoys his wife leaving the house from one day to the next, especially with someone like Quiggin, in Templer's eyes unthinkable as a rival. Quiggin, indeed, belonged to a form of life entirely separate from Templer's, so that gossip on the subject of the divorce was exchanged within unconnected compartments; Templer's City acquaintances on the one hand: on the other, the literary and political associates of Quiggin.

'You are script-writing now, aren't you?' Quiggin asked, when we came within closer range of each other, and without any preliminary beating about the bush. 'I want to have a talk with you about films.'

My first thought was that he hoped to get a similar job. To be a script-writer was at that period the ambition of almost everyone who could hold a pen. There was no reason why Quiggin should prove an exception to the rule. So far as I knew, he had yet to make the experiment. I noticed that he had almost discarded his North Country accent, or perhaps thought it inappropriate for use at that moment. In his university days, one of his chief social assets had been what Sillery used to call 'Brother Quiggin's Doric speech'. He looked well fed, and his squat form was enclosed in a bright blue suit and double-breasted waistcoat. He was hatless, such hair as remained to him carefully brushed. I had never before seen him look so spruce.

'We've had a cottage lent us,' he said. 'I'd like you to come down for the week-end. Mona wants to see you again too.'

My first instinct was to make some excuse about weekends being difficult owing to the oppressive manner in which the film business was organised: in itself true enough. However, as it happened, an electricians' strike had just been called at the Studio, with the result that work was likely to be suspended for at least a week or two. I was unwilling to seem to condone too easily the appropriation of an old friend's wife; although it had to be admitted that Templer himself had never been over-squeamish about accepting, within in his own circle, such changes of partnership. Apart from such scruples, I knew enough of Quiggin to be sure that his cottage would be more than ordinarily uncomfortable. Nothing I had seen of Mona gave cause to reconsider this want of confidence in their combined domestic economy. It was generally supposed by then that they were married, although no one seemed to know for certain whether or not any ceremony had been performed.

'Whereabouts is your cottage?' I asked, playing for time. The place turned out to be rather further afield than the

destination of the usual week-end visit. While this conversation had been taking place, the queue had been
moving forward, so that at that moment my own turn
came at the booking office; simultaneously, the crowd behind Quiggin launched themselves on and outwards in a
sudden violent movement that carried him bodily at their
head, as if unwillingly leading a mob in a riot.

'I'll write the address to you,' he bawled over his
shoulder. 'You must certainly come and stay.'

I nodded my head, fumbling with tickets and money.
Almost immediately Quiggin, driven ahead by his seemingly fanatical followers, was forced through the doors and
lost in the night.

'Who was that?' asked the girl accompanying me.

'J. G. Quiggin.'

'The critic?'

'Yes.'

'I think he has gone off rather lately.'

'I expect he goes up and down like the rest of us.'

'Don't be so philosophical,' she said. 'I can't bear it.'

We passed into the darkness and *Man of Aran*.

3.

CURIOSITY, which makes the world go round, brought me in the end to accept Quiggin's invitation. There was, indeed, some slight mystery about its origin, for after our last meeting—late one evening in the days before he had gone off with Mona—there had been disagreement between us either about Milton as a poet, or (various writers had been discussed) Meredith as a novelist, as a result of which I thought myself finally in disgrace. Of recent years, so everyone agreed, Quiggin had become increasingly dogmatic on such subjects, unable to bear contradiction, and almost equally offended by verbal evasion that sought to conceal views differing from his own. Although publication of his long-promised work, *Unburnt Boats*, had been once more at the last moment postponed, Quiggin's occasional writings were at this time much in evidence. The subject matter of *Unburnt Boats*, thought to be largely autobiographical, remained, in spite of a good deal of speculation on the part of his friends, a closely guarded secret. His journalism was chiefly contributed to papers in which politics and literature attempted some fusion; and letters signed by him appeared with regularity in the 'weeklies' on the subject of public liberties or unworthy conduct on the part of the police. In private, Quiggin considered that there was too much freedom in modern life; but he was a great champion of individual liberty in his letters to the Press.

Accustomed, like so many literary men of that decade, to describe himself as a communist, he may indeed have been a member of the Communist Party. Later, at different stages of his career, he disseminated such contradictory statements on the subject of his own political history that card-holding membership remains uncertain. Most of his acquaintances inclined to think that at one moment or another he had belonged to some not very distinguished grade of the communist hierarchy. Certainly he pertained to the extreme Left and subscribed to several 'anti-fascist' organisations. He himself tended to cloak his political activities in mystery in so far as they took practical form: occasionally hinting that these activities might be more important, even more sinister, than persons like myself supposed.

'The Lewis gun may be sounding at the barricades earlier than some of your Laodicean friends think,' he had announced in a rasping undertone at the climax of our controversy about Milton—or Meredith.

'I can never remember what the Laodiceans did.'

'They were "neither hot nor cold".'

'Ah.'

Such revolutionary sentiments, as I have said, were common enough then, especially in the verse of the period, on which Quiggin was an authority. However, he had seemed rather unusually annoyed that evening, so that in spite of his friendliness in the foyer of the cinema I was not at all sure what sort of a reception I should get when I arrived on his doorstep. I went by train, and found a taxi had been sent to meet me at the station. We drove a mile or two through pretty country and by the low stone wall of a large estate. Quiggin was living in a small, grey, comparatively modern house, hardly a cottage in the sense that comes immediately to the mind—the cottage in a forest inhabited by a peasant in a fairy story, or the gabled, half-timbered sort of the Christmas card by which a robin sits in the snow—but, although the building itself was bleak, the situation was pleasant enough, in fact enchanting: overlooking woods, fields and distant hills, not another house in sight.

Quiggin was in a mood to be agreeable. When he set out to please, he was rarely unable to keep the most unpromising people amused; or at least quiet. He would assume his North Country accent, together with an air of informed simplicity, that would charm all kind of unexpected persons, normally in hearty disagreement with his literary or political opinions. He was particularly accomplished at effecting a reversal of feeling in the case of those who, on introduction, had taken an immediate dislike to his face or his clothes. Probably with that end in view, he cultivated a certain irregularity of dress. For example, when he opened the door on my arrival he was wearing a dark-grey woollen garment with a zip-fastener down the front, which, in conjunction with rope-soled canvas shoes, made him look like an instructor in some unusual sport or physical exercise.

'Come in,' he said, 'Mona is blonding her hair. She will be along soon.'

Mona's hair had been black in the days when I had first set eyes on her at Mr. Deacon's birthday party above the antique shop off Charlotte Street, but, even before she had married Templer—when her Cupid's bow mouth was still advertising toothpaste on the hoardings—it had already taken on a metallic honey colour. She looked distinctly sluttish when at length she appeared, far less trim than when married to Templer, a reversion to the Charlotte Street period when she had been an artists' model. However, she had not returned to the style of dress of her bohemian days, trousers and sandals or whatever was then the fashion. Instead, wearing an old black coat and skirt, an outfit not much suited to the country, she retained a kind of shabby smartness of appearance. I had not seen her for some time, and had forgotten the formal perfection of her face. Her skin was coarse, it was true, and her fixed smile recalled the days when her photograph was on the front of every London bus; yet, even admitting such defects, the detail of every feature insisted upon admiration. She was like a strapping statue, Venus conceived at a period when more than a touch of vulgarity had found its way into classical sculpture.

I could not help thinking how odd it was that, having once married Templer, she should have deserted him for Quiggin. In the general way of gossip she had the reputation of a beautiful girl not particularly attractive to men. Naturally, with looks like hers, she had been accustomed to all the outward paraphernalia of male attack; certainly at what might be called the 'picking-up' level. In a railway carriage, or on board ship, there had always been a man to approach her with greater or lesser delicacy; but Templer and Quiggin (my informant was Templer) were the only men to have taken her 'seriously'. It had even been suggested (by Quiggin's old friend and rival, Mark Members, probably without much truth) that in her early days Mona had had emotional leanings towards her own sex. Latterly, there had been no talk of that sort. Her manner usually suggested that she was interested in no one except herself; although the fact remained that she had abandoned a comfortable home, and relatively rich husband, to share Quiggin's far from destitute, though not particularly luxurious existence.

To Templer, accustomed to easy success with women, she had perhaps represented the one absolutely first-rate example of the goods he had been for so long accustomed to handle—in the manner that a seasoned collector can afford to ignore every other point in any object he wishes to acquire provided it satisfies completely in those respects most difficult to attain. In some way, for Templer, Mona must have fulfilled that condition. Dozens of girls not very different from her were to be found in dress shops and art schools, but Templer, like a scholar who can immediately date a manuscript by the quality of the ink, or the texture of the parchment, had seen something there to crown his special collection: a perfect specimen of her kind. At least that seemed, on the face of it, the only reason why he should have married her.

To Quiggin, on the other hand, himself not particularly adept with girls, Mona must have appeared a wholly unexpected triumph, a 'beauty' at whom passers-by turned to gaze in the street, who had positively thrown herself at his head—leaving her 'boring' stockbroker husband to live with a writer and a revolutionary. Here was a situation few could fail to find flattering. It was clear from his demeanour that Quiggin still felt flattered, for, although sulky that afternoon, there seemed in general no reason to suppose that Mona regretted her past. Like Molly Jeavons, in such a different context, she appeared—so I had been told—to accept her completely changed circumstances. Her air of temporary dissatisfaction was no doubt merely the old one implying that insufficient attention was being paid to her whims. Perhaps for that reason she spoke of Templer almost at once.

'Have you been seeing anything of Peter?' she asked, without any self-consciousness.

'Not for some time, as it happens.'

'I suppose he has found a new girl?'

'I shouldn't wonder.'

She did not pursue the subject. It was just as if she had said: 'Have you change for a pound?'; and, on learning that I had no silver, immediately abandoned the matter. There was no question of emotion; only a faint curiosity. That, at least, was all she allowed to appear on the surface. Quiggin, on the other hand, looked a trifle put out at this early mention of Templer's name.

'By the way, ducks,' he said, 'I forgot to tell you I tried to get the bath-lotion when I was last in London. The shop was out of it. I'll try again next time.'

Mona compressed her lips in displeasure. Merely to have remembered to enquire for the bath-lotion she evidently considered insufficient on Quiggin's part. She began to hum to herself.

'You have a nice landscape here,' I said. 'Is there a house behind those trees? It looks as if there might be.'

'Do you think it nice?' said Quiggin, his previous tone of harsh geniality somewhat impaired by Mona's mood. 'You know these days I scarcely notice such things. Once I might have done—should have done, certainly, in my romantic period. I suppose by "nice" you mean undeveloped. Give me something a bit more practical. You can keep your picturesque features so far as I am concerned. If English agriculture was organised on a rational —I do not even say a just—basis, I dare say there might be something to be said for the view from this window. As it is, I would much rather be looking at a well-designed power station. Perhaps, as being more rural, I should say a row of silos.'

He smiled to show that he did not mean to be too severe. This was, after all, the kind of subject upon which we had often disagreed in the past. There was something about Quiggin that always reminded me of Widmerpool, but, whereas Widmerpool was devoid of all æsthetic or intellectual interests, as such, Quiggin controlled such instincts in himself according to his particular personal policy at any given moment. Widmerpool would genuinely possess no opinion as to whether the view from the cottage window was good or bad. The matter would not have the slightest interest for him. He would be concerned only with the matter of who owned the land. Perhaps that was not entirely true, for Widmerpool would have enjoyed boasting of a fine view owned by himself. Quiggin, on the other hand, was perfectly aware that there might be something to be admired in the contours of the country, but to admit admiration would be to surrender material about himself that might with more value be kept secret. His rôle, like Widmerpool's was that of a man of the will, a rôle which adjudged that even here, in giving an opinion on the landscape, the will must be exercised.

'No,' he said. 'What I like in this place, as a matter of fact, is the excellent arrangement that the bath is in the scullery. Now that is realistic. Not a lot of bourgeois nonsense about false refinement. The owner had it put there quite recently.'

'Does he live here himself?'

Quiggin smiled at this question as if it displayed an abyss of ignorance.

'No, he doesn't. He keeps it for lending friends— usually people with views similar to my own—*our* own, I should say.'

He slipped his arm round Mona's waist. She was not won over by this attention, disengaging his hand, and making no effort to assume the comportment of a woman gifted with keen political instincts. An extreme, uninhibited silliness had formerly been her principal characteristic. Now I had the impression she had become more aware of life, more formidable than in her Templer days.

'Your landlord is an active Leftist too, is he?'

'Of course.'

'You speak as if all landlords belonged automatically to the Left.'

'We are expected to do a bit of work for him in return for living here free,' said Quiggin. 'That's human nature. But everything he wants is connected with my own political life, so I did not mind that.'

'Who is the owner?'

'You wouldn't know him,' said Quiggin, smiling with a kind of fierce kindliness. 'He is a serious person, as a matter of fact. You would not come across him at parties. Not the sort of parties you go to, at least.'

'How do you know the sort of parties I go to?'

'Well, he wouldn't go to the sort of parties I used to see you at.'

'Why? Does he go to parties only frequented by his own sex?'

Quiggin laughed heartily at that.

'No, no,' he said. 'Nothing of that kind. How like you to suggest something of the sort. He is just a politically conscious person who does not enjoy a lot of gallivanting about.'

'I believe he is going to turn out to be Howard Craggs, after all this mystery you are making.'

Quiggin laughed again.

'I still see a certain amount of Craggs,' he admitted. 'His firm may be launching a little scheme of mine in the near future—not a book. Craggs is politically sound, but I prefer a publishing house of more standing than Boggis & Stone for my books.'

Since Quiggin's books remained purely hypothetical entities, it seemed reasonable enough that their publisher should exist hypothetically too. I was tempted to say as much, but thought it wiser to avoid risk of discord at this early stage. Quiggin was evidently enjoying his own efforts to stir up my curiosity regarding his landlord and benefactor.

'No, no,' he said again. 'My friend, the owner—well, as a good social revolutionary, I don't quite know how I should describe him. He is a man of what used to be regarded—by snobs—as of rather more distinction, in the old-fashioned sense, than poor Craggs.'

'Poor Craggs, indeed. That just about describes him. He has the most loathsomely oily voice in the whole of Bloomsbury.'

'What has been happening in London, talking of Bloomsbury?' asked Mona, bored by all this fencing on Quiggin's part. 'Have there been any parties there, or anywhere else? I get a bit sick of being stuck down here all the time.'

Her drawling, angry manner showed growing discontent, and Quiggin, clearly foreseeing trouble, immediately embarked upon a theme he had probably intended to develop later in the course of my visit.

'As a matter of fact there was something I wanted specially to ask you, Nick,' he said hurriedly. 'We may as well get on to the subject right away. Mona has been thinking for some time that she might make a career as a film star. I agree with her. She has got champion looks and champion talent too. She made more than one appearance on the screen in the past—small rôles, of course, but always jolly good. That gives the right experience. We thought you ought to be able to hand out some useful "intros" now that you are in the business.'

To emphasise his own enthusiasm for Mona's talent, Quiggin renewed in his voice all the force of his former rough honesty of tone. The enquiry revealed the cause of my invitation to the cottage. Its general application was not unexpected, though I had supposed Quiggin, rather than Mona, hoped to launch out into the fierce, chilling rapids of 'the industry'. However, since Mona was to be the subject of the discussion, we began to talk over possibilities of introductions to those who might be of use. Her previous employment in films seemed to have been of scarcely higher grade than superior crowd work, or the individual display on her part of some commodity to be advertised; although, at the same time, it could be said in her favour that when, in the past, she had belonged to the advertising world, she could have claimed some little fame as a well-known model.

Quiggin, whose grasp of practical matters was usually competent enough, must have known that I myself was unlikely to be any great help to an aspiring film star. As I had explained to Jeavons, I had little or no contact with the acting side of the business. But people of undoubted ability in their own line are often completely lost in understanding the nature of someone else's job. It was possible that he pictured nothing easier than introducing Mona to some famous director, who would immediately offer her a star part. Alternately, there was, of course, the possibility that Quiggin himself wished merely to allow the matter free ventilation in order to supply Mona with some subject upon which happily to brood. He might easily have no thought of practical result, beyond assuming that a prolonged discussion about herself, her beauty and her talents, held between the three of us over the course of the weekend, would have a beneficial effect on Mona's temper. This might even be a method of scotching the whole question of Mona's dramatic ambition, of which Quiggin might easily be jealous.

On the other hand, the film business, always unpredictable, might envisage Mona as a 'discovery'. Perhaps, after all, the change from the time when she had been married to Templer was not so great as physical and financial circumstances might make it appear. She was still bored: without enough to do. A woman who could 'cook a bit' had been provided by the mysterious personage who had lent them the cottage. It was natural that Mona should want a job. Chips Lovell, always engaged in minor intrigue, would be able to offer useful advice. We were still discussing her prospects later that evening, sitting on kitchen chairs drinking gin, when a faint tapping came on the outside door. I thought it must be a child come with a message, or delivering something for the evening meal. Mona rose to see who was there. There was the noise of the latch; then she gave an exclamation of surprise, and, so it seemed to me, of pleasure. Quiggin, too, jumped up when he heard the voice, also looking surprised: more surprised than pleased.

The man who came into the room was, I suppose, in his early thirties. At first he seemed older on account of his straggling beard and air of utter down-at-heelness. His hair was long on the top of his head, but had been given a rough military crop round the sides. He wore a tweed coat, much the worse for wear and patched with leather at elbows and cuffs; but a coat that was well cut and had certainly seen better days. An infinitely filthy pair of corduroy trousers clothed his legs, and, like Quiggin, his large feet were enclosed in some form of canvas slipper or *espadrille*. It seemed at first surprising that such an unkempt figure should have announced himself by knocking so gently, but it now appeared that he was overcome with diffidence. At least this seemed to be his state, for he stood for a moment or two on the threshold of the room, clearly intending to enter, but unable to make the definitive movement required which would heave him into what must have appeared the closed community of Quiggin and myself. I forgot at the time that this inability to penetrate a room is a particular form of hesitation to be associated with persons in whom an extreme egoism is dominant: the acceptance of someone else's place or dwelling possibly implying some distasteful abnegation of the newcomer's rights or position.

At last, by taking hold of himself firmly, he managed to pass through the door, immediately turning his sunken eyes upon me with a look of deep uneasiness, as if he suspected —indeed, was almost certain—I was plotting some violently disagreeable move against himself. By exercising this disturbed, and essentially disturbing, stare, he made me feel remarkably uncomfortable; although, at the same time, there was something about him not at all unsympathetic: a presence of forcefulness and despair enclosed in an envelope of constraint. He did not speak. Quiggin went towards him, almost as if he were about to turn him from the room.

'I thought you were going to be in London all the week,' he said, 'with your committee to re-examine the terms of the Sedition Bill.'

He sounded vexed by the bearded man's arrival at this moment, though at the same time exerting every effort to conceal his annoyance.

'Craggs couldn't be there, so I decided I might as well come back. I walked up from the station. I've got a lot of stuff to go through still, and I always hate being in London longer than I need. I thought I would drop in on the way home to show you what I had done.'

The bearded man spoke in a deep, infinitely depressed voice, pointing at the same time with one hand to a small cardboard dispatch-case he carried in the other. This receptacle was evidently full of papers, for it bulged at top and bottom, and, since the lock was broken, was tied round several times with string.

'Wouldn't you rather deal with it another time?' Quiggin asked, hopefully.

He seemed desperately anxious to get rid of the stranger without revealing his identity. I strongly suspected this to be the landlord of the cottage, but still had no clue to Quiggin's secrecy on the subject of his name, if this suspicion proved to be true. The man with the beard looked fairly typical of one layer of Quiggin's friends: a layer which Quiggin kept, on the whole, in the background, because he regarded them for one reason or another—either politically or even for reasons that could only be called snobbish—to be bad for business. Quiggin possessed his own elaborately drawn scale of social values, no less severe in their way than the canons of the most ambitious society hostess; but it was not always easy for others to know where, and how, he drew his lines of demarcation. Possibly the man with the beard was regarded as not quite at a level to be allowed to drink with Quiggin when friends were present. However, he was not to be expelled so easily. He shook now his head resolutely.

'No,' he said. 'There are just one or two things.'

He looked again in my direction after saying this, as if to make some apology either for intruding in this manner, or, as it were, on behalf of Quiggin for his evident wish that we should have nothing to do with each other.

'I haven't butted in, have I?' he said.

He spoke not so much to Quiggin as to the world at large, without much interest in a reply. The remark was the expression of a polite phrase that seemed required by the circumstances, rather than anything like real fear that his presence might be superfluous. My impression of him began to alter. I came to the conclusion that under this burden of shyness he did not care in the least whether he butted in on Quiggin, or on anyone else. What he wanted was his own way. Mona, who had gone through to the kitchen now returned, bringing another glass.

'Have a drink, Alf,' she said. 'Nice to see you unexpectedly like this.'

She had brightened up noticeably.

'Yes, of course, Alf, have a drink,' said Quiggin, now resigning himself to the worst. 'And sorry, by the way, for forgetting to explain who everybody is. My rough North Country manners again. This is Nick Jenkins— Alf Warminster.'

This, then, was the famous Erridge. It was easy to see how the rumour had gone round among his relations that he had become a tramp, even if actual experience had stopped short of that status in its most exact sense. I should never have recognised him with his beard and heavily-lined face. Now that his name was revealed, the features of the preoccupied, sallow, bony schoolboy, with books tumbling from under his arm, could be traced like a footpath lost in the brambles and weeds of an untended garden: an overgrown crazy pavement. Examining him as a perceivable entity, I could even detect in his face a look of his sisters, especially Frederica. His clothes gave off a heavy, earthen smell as if he had lived out in them in all weathers for a long time.

'Alf owns this cottage,' said Quiggin, reluctantly. 'But he kindly allows us to live here until the whole place is turned into a collective farm with himself at the head of it.'

He laughed harshly. Erridge (as I shall, for convenience, continue to call him) laughed uneasily too.

'Of course you know I'm frightfully glad to have you here,' he said.

He spoke lamely and looked more than ever embarrassed at this tribute paid him, which was certainly intended by Quiggin to carry some sting in its tail: presumably the implication that, whatever his political views, whatever the social changes, Erridge would remain in a comfortable position. When Quiggin ingratiated himself with people —during his days as secretary to St. John Clarke, for example—he was far too shrewd to confine himself to mere flattery. A modicum of bullying was a pleasure both to himself and his patrons. All the same, I was not sure that Erridge, for all his outward appearance, might not turn out a tougher proposition than St. John Clarke.

'I don't know that farming is quite my line,' Erridge went on, apologetically. 'Though of course we have always done a bit of it here. Incidentally, is the water pumping satisfactorily? You may find it rather hard work, I am afraid. I had the hand pump specially put in. I think it is a better model than the one in the keeper's cottage, and they seem to find that one works all right.'

'Mona and I take our turn at it,' said Quiggin; and, grinning angrily in my direction, he added: 'Guests are expected to do their stint at the pump as a rule. Pumping is a bit of a bore, as you say. You can't do it any better, or any quicker, or any way that makes the tank last longer. The pump movement is just short of the natural leverage of the arm from the elbow, which makes the work particularly laborious. But we get along all right. Pumping is a kind of image of life under the capitalist system.'

Erridge laughed constrainedly, and took a gulp of gin, involuntarily making a grimace as he did so. This seemed to indicate that he belonged to the class of egoist who dislikes the taste of food and drink. He would probably have abstained from alcohol entirely had not his special approach to life made a duty of mixing on equal terms with people round him. He seemed now a little put out by Quiggin's lack of affection for the pump. Having installed the equipment himself, like most innovators or, indeed, most owners of property, he did not care for the disparagement of his organisation or possessions; at least on the part of persons other than himself.

'I met some of your sisters the other day,' I said.

Erridge's face clouded at these words, while Quiggin gritted his teeth in irritation. This, as intended, was nothing short of a declaration that I knew more about Erridge and his background than Quiggin might think desirable, and also was not prepared to move solely upon lines laid down by Quiggin himself. Indeed, Quiggin may have hoped that the name 'Warminster' inarticulately mumbled with the emphasis on the prefix 'Alf', would in itself at the time convey little or nothing; later, he could please himself how much he revealed about his current patron. There was a moment's pause before Erridge answered.

'Oh, yes—yes——' he said. 'Which—which ones——?'

'Priscilla and then Frederica, who took me to see Norah.'

'Oh, yes,' said Erridge. 'Priscilla—Frederica—Norah.'

He spoke as if he had now begun to remember them quite well. The manner in which he screwed up his face, while making this effort of memory recalled his uncle, Alfred Tolland. Although, at first sight, it would have been difficult to think of two men whose outward appearance was superficially more different, something deeper remained in common. If Alfred Tolland had grown a beard, dressed in rags and slept out all night, or if Erridge had washed, shaved and assumed a stiff collar and dark suit, something more than a passing resemblance might have become evident. Indeed, Erridge's features had assumed some of that same expression of disappointment which marked his uncle's face when Molly Jeavons teased him; with the contrast that, in Erridge, one was reminded of a spoilt child, while Alfred Tolland's countenance was that of a child resigned from an early age to teasing by grown-ups. There could be no doubt that Erridge recoiled from the invocation of his immediate family. The world of his relations no doubt caused him chronic dissatisfaction. I saw no reason, for my own part, why he should be let off anything. If he lent Quiggin the cottage, he must put up with Quiggin's guests; especially those invited primarily to help Mona become a film star.

Silence fell. Erridge looked out towards the uncurtained window beyond which night had already fallen. Unlike his uncle, he had no wish to discuss his family. After all, it was perhaps hard that he should be forced to talk about them merely to plague Quiggin, though to try the experiment had been tempting. Quiggin himself had become increasingly restive during this interchange. Mona had spoken little, though undoubtedly cheered by the visit. Quiggin seemed to judge, perhaps correctly, that Erridge was displeased by all this chit-chat, and began to mention tentatively executive matters existing between them; although at the same time unquestionably anxious that Erridge should leave the cottage as soon as possible. However, Erridge in spite of his own unwillingness to make conversation, showed equally no desire to move. He took an ancient leather tobacco-pouch from one of his coat pockets and began to roll himself a cigarette. When he had done this—not very successfully, for a good deal of tobacco protruded from each end of the twist of rice-paper—he licked the edge to seal it and lit the rather flimsy result of these labours. The cigarette seemed not to 'draw' well, so after a minute or two he threw it into the grate. Sipping the drink Mona had given him, he again made a face, tipping back the kitchen chair upon which he sat until it cracked ominously. He sighed deeply.

'I was wondering whether it would be better for you to be secretary instead of Craggs,' he said.

'What makes you think so?' asked Quiggin cautiously.

'Craggs always seems to have something else to do. The fact is, Craggs is so keen on running committees that he can never give any of them the right amount of attention. He is on to German refugees now. Quite right, of course, that something should be done. But last week I couldn't get hold of him because he was occupied with Sillery about the embargo on arms to Bolivia and Paraguay. Then there's the "Smash Fascism" group he is always slipping off to. He would like us to pay more attention to Mosley. He wants to be doing the latest thing all the time, whether it's the independence of Catalonia or free meals for school-children.'

'Anti-fascism comes first,' said Quiggin. 'Even before pacifism. In my opinion, the Sedition Bill can wait. After all, didn't Lenin say something about Liberty being a bourgeois illusion?'

Quiggin had added this last remark in not too serious a tone, but Erridge seemed to take it seriously, shifting about uncomfortably on his hard wooden seat as if he were a galley-slave during an interval of rest.

'Of course,' he said. 'I know he did.'

'Well, then?'

'I don't always think like the rest of you about that.'

He rose suddenly from his chair.

'I want to have a talk about the magazine some time,' he said. 'Not now, I think.'

'Oh, that,' said Quiggin.

He sounded as if he would have preferred 'the magazine' not to have been so specifically named.

'What magazine?' asked Mona.

'Oh, it's nothing, ducks,' said Quiggin. 'Just an idea Alf and I were talking about.'

'Are you going to start a magazine?'

Mona sounded quite excited.

'We might be,' said Erridge, moving his feet about.

'It is all very vague still,' said Quiggin, in a voice that closed the matter.

Mona was not to be so easily silenced. Whether her interest had been genuinely aroused or whether she saw this as a means expressing her own views or teasing Quiggin was not clear.

'But *how* thrilling,' she said. 'Do tell me all about it, Alf.'

Erridge smiled in an embarrassed way, and pulled at his beard.

'It is all very vague, as J.G. has explained,' he said. 'Look here, why not come to dinner tomorrow night? We could talk about it then.'

'Or perhaps later in the week,' said Quiggin.

'I've got to go away again on Monday,' Erridge said.

There was a pause. Quiggin glared at me.

'I expect you will have to go back to London on Sunday night, won't you, Nick?' he said.

'Oh, do come too,' said Erridge, at once. 'I'm so sorry. Of course I meant to ask you as well if you are staying until then.'

He seemed distressed at having appeared in his own eyes bad mannered. I think he lived in a dream, so shut off from the world that he had not bothered for a moment to consider whether I was staying with Quiggin, or had just come in that night for a meal. Even if he realised that I was staying, he was probably scarcely aware that I might still be there twenty-four hours later. His reactions placed him more and more as a recognisable type, spending much of his time in boredom and loneliness, yet in some way inhibited from taking in anything relevant about other people: at home only with 'causes'.

'The trains are not too good in the morning,' said Quiggin. 'I don't know when you have to be at the Studio——'

'The Studio is closed all this week owing to the strike,' I said. 'So I had thought of going up on Monday morning in any case—if that is all right.'

'Oh, are you on strike?' asked Erridge, brightening up at once, as if it were for him a rare, unexpected pleasure to find himself in such close contact with a real striker. 'In that case you simply must come and have a meal with me.'

'I'd love to, but it is not me on strike, I am afraid—the electricians.'

'Oh, yes, the strike, of course, the·strike,' said Quiggin, as if he himself had organised the stoppage of work, but, in the light of his many similar responsibilities, had forgotten about its course. 'In that case we would all like to come, Alf. It's an early supper, as I remember.'

So far as Quiggin was concerned, it had been one of those great social defeats; and, in facing the fact squarely, he had done something to retrieve his position. Presumably he was making plans for Erridge to put up the money to install him as editor of some new, Left Wing magazine. It was perhaps reasonable that he should wish to keep their plans secret in case they should miscarry. However, now that the dinner had been decided upon, he accepted the matter philosophically. Erridge seemed to have no similar desire to discuss matters in private. He was, I think, quite unaware of Quiggin's unwillingness to allow others to know too much of their life together. I could see, too, that he was determined not to abandon the idea that I was myself a striker.

'But you support them by not going,' he said. 'Yes, come early. You might possibly like to look round the house—though there really is nothing to see there that is of the slightest interest, I'm afraid.'

He moved once more towards the door, sunk again in deep despair, perhaps at the thought of the lack of distinction of his house and its contents. Shuffling his *espadrilles* against the stone floor, he caught his foot in the mat, swore gently and a trifle self-consciously, as if aspiring to act as roughly as he was dressed, and left with hardly a further word. Quiggin accompanied him to the door, and shouted a farewell. Then he returned to the room in which we sat. No one spoke for a minute or two. Quiggin slowly corked up the gin bottle, and put it away in a cupboard.

'Alf is *rather* sweet, isn't he?' said Mona.

'Alf is a good fellow,' agreed Quiggin, a shade sourly.

'Where does he live?' I asked.

'Thrubworth Park. It is a big house beyond the trees you see from our windows.'

Quiggin had been put out by this sudden appearance of Erridge. It had been a visit for which he was unprepared : a situation he had not bargained for. Now he seemed unable to decide what line he himself should take about his friend.

'How much do you know about him?' he asked at last.

'Hardly anything, except that he is said to have been a tramp. And, as I said just now, I met some of his sisters the other day.'

'Oh, yes,' said Quiggin, impatiently. 'I am not at all interested in the rest of his family. He never sees anything of them, anyway. A lot of social butterflies, that's all they are. Just what you might expect. Alf is different. I don't know what you mean by being a tramp, though. Where did you get that story? I suppose you think everyone is a tramp who wears a beard.'

'Aren't they? Some of his relations told me he had been experimenting in life as a tramp.'

'Just the sort of thing they would put about,' said Quiggin. 'Isn't it like people of that class? It is true he has been making some study of local conditions. I don't think he stayed anywhere very luxurious, but he certainly didn't sleep in casual wards.'

'His relations suppose he did. I think they rather admire him for it.'

'Well, they suppose wrong,' said Quiggin. 'Alf is a very good fellow, but I don't know whether he is prepared to make himself as uncomfortable as that.'

'What did he do then?'

'Useful work collecting information about unemployment,' Quiggin conceded. 'Distributed pamphlets at the same time. I don't want to belittle it in any way, but it is absurd to go round saying he was a tramp. All the same, the experience he had will be of political value to him.'

'I think he is rather attractive,' said Mona.

For some reason this did not seem to please Quiggin.

'Did you ever meet a girl called Gypsy Jones?' he said. 'A Communist. Rather a grubby little piece. I'm not sure Alf may not be a bit keen on her. I saw them sitting together at a Popular Front meeting. All the same, he is not a man to waste time over women.'

'What do you mean, "waste time over women"?' said Mona. 'Anyway, nobody could blame you for that. You think about yourself too much.'

'I think about you too, ducks,' said Quiggin mildly, no doubt judging it advisable to pacify her. 'But Alf is an idealist. Rather too much of one sometimes, when it comes to getting things done. All the same, he has most of the right ideas. Shall I get that bottle out again? Supper doesn't seem to be nearly ready.'

'Yes, get it out,' said Mona. 'I can't imagine why you put it away.'

All this was reminiscent of the Templer household before Mona left her husband. During the twenty-four hours that followed, this recollection was more than once repeated.

Quiggin, too, had begun to placate her with 'treats', the impending dinner with Erridge certainly grading in that class. In fact Quiggin began to talk as if he himself had arranged the invitation as an essential aspect of the weekend. Although its potentialities had been reduced for him by my inclusion, there was, I think, nothing personal in that. He would equally have objected to any other friend or acquaintance joining the party. Dinner at Thrubworth was an occasion not to be wasted, for Mona had remarked: 'We don't get invited every day of the week.' I asked how long they had known Erridge.

'In the days when I was secretary to St. John Clarke,' said Quiggin, smiling to show how distant, how incongruous, he now regarded that period of his life. 'St. J. went one afternoon to a bookshop in Charing Cross Road, where he wanted to cast his eye over some of Lenin's speeches. As you know, St. J. was rather careful about money, and he had suggested I should hold the bookseller in conversation while he looked up just as much as he needed. This was at the beginning of St. J.'s conversion to Marxism. We found Alf pottering about the shop, trying to get through the afternoon. Old habits die hard, and, of course, up to the time I met him, St. J. had been a champion snob—and he wasn't altogether cured of his liking for a high-sounding name. He often said afterwards, when we knew each other well, that I'd saved him from snobbery. I only wish I could also have saved him from Trotskyism. But that is another story. It happened that St. J. had met Alf quite a time before at the home of one of Alf's relatives—is there a woman called Lady Molly Jeavons? There is—well, it was at her house. St. J. had a word or two with Alf in the bookshop, and, in spite of his changed view of life, forgot all about Lenin's speeches and asked him back to tea.'

And you have known him ever since?'

'Alf turned up trumps when St. J. behaved so foolishly about myself and Mona. Since then, I've done my best to canalise his enthusiasms.'

'Has St. John Clarke still got his German boy as secretary?'

'Not he,' said Quiggin. 'Guggenbühl is a shrewd young man, Trotskyist though he be. He has moved on to something more paying. After all, he was smart enough to see Hitler coming and clear out of Germany. I hear he is very patronising to the German refugees arriving now.'

'He is probably a Nazi agent.'

'My God,' said Quiggin. 'I wouldn't wonder. I must talk to Mark about that when he comes back from America.'

The possibility that Mark Members and himself had been succeeded in the dynasty of St. John Clarke's secretaries by one of Hitler's spies greatly cheered Quiggin. He was in a good mood for the rest of the day, until it was time to start for Thrubworth. Then, as the hour approached, he became once more nervous and agitated. I had supposed that, having secured Erridge for a patron some years before, Quiggin must be used by then to his ways. The contrary seemed true; and I remembered that in his undergraduate days he used to become irritable and perturbed before a party: master of himself only after arrival. He had changed into his suit of that cruel blue colour when at last we set off across the fields.

'What date is the house?'

'What house?'

'Where we are going.'

'Oh, Thrubworth Park,' said Quiggin, as if he had forgotten our destination. 'Seventeenth century, I should say, much altered in the eighteenth. Alf will tell you about it. Though he doesn't really like the place, he likes talking about it for some reason. You will hear all you want about its history.'

Passing into the wood to be seen from the windows of the cottage, we went through more fields and climbed a stile. Beyond was a deserted road, on the far side of which, set back some distance from the highway, stood an entrance —evidently not the main entrance—to a park, the walls of which I had already seen from another side on my way from the station the day before. A small, unoccupied lodge, now fallen into decay, lay beside two open, wrought-iron gates. We went through these gates, and made our way up a drive that disappeared among large trees. The park was fairly well kept, though there was an unfriended, melancholy air about the place, characteristic of large estates for which the owner feels no deep affection.

'I hope there will be something to drink tonight,' said Mona.

'Is it a bit short as a rule?' I asked.

'Doesn't exactly flow.'

'Why didn't you have a pint of gin before you came out then,' asked Quiggin, gratingly, 'if you can't ever get through an evening without wanting to feel tipsy at the end of it? There always seems enough to me. Not buckets but enough.'

His nerves were still on edge.

'All right,' said Mona. 'Don't bite my head off. You grumbled yourself the last time you came here.'

'Did I, ducks?'

He took her arm.

'We'll have a nice drink when we get back,' he said, 'if Alf should happen to be in one of his moods.'

I felt apprehensive at the thought that Erridge might be 'in one of his moods'. Quiggin had not mentioned these 'moods' before, although their nature was easy to imagine from what had been said. I wished we could continue to walk, as we were doing, through glades of oak and chestnut trees in the cool twilight, without ever reaching the house and the grim meal which now seemed to lie ahead of us. We had continued for about ten minutes when roofs came suddenly into view, a group of buildings of some dignity, though without much architectural distinction: a seventeenth-century mansion such as Quiggin had described, brick at the back and fronted in the eighteenth century with stone. The façade faced away from us across a wide stretch of lawn, since we had arrived at the side of the house amongst a network of small paths and flower-beds, rather fussily laid out and not too well kept. Quiggin led the way through these borders, making for a projection of outbuildings and stables. We passed under an arch into a cobbled yard. Quiggin made for a small door, studded with brass nails. By the side of this door hung an iron bell-pull. He stopped short and turned towards me, looking suddenly as if he had lost heart. Then he took hold of himself and gave the bell a good jerk.

'Does one always come in this way?'

'The front of the house is kept shut,' he said.

'What happens inside?'

'The state rooms—if that is what you call them—are closed. Alf just lives in one corner of the place.'

'In the servants' quarters?'

'More or less. That is probably what they used to be.'

We waited for a long time. Quiggin appeared unwilling to ring again, but, under pressure from Mona, at last decided to repeat his wrench at the bell. There was another long pause. Then steps could be heard moving very slowly and carefully down the stairs. Inner fumbling with the door-knob took place, and the door was opened by a man-servant. I recognised Smith, the butler temporarily employed by the Jeavonses on my first visit to their house.

'Lord Warminster?' muttered Quiggin, interrogatively.

Smith made no answer. A kind of grimace had crossed his features when he saw Quiggin and Mona; naturally enough, he gave me no sign of recognition. Apart from this brief, indeed scarcely perceptible contraction of nose and lips—perhaps merely a nervous twitch—he expressed no further welcome. However, he stood aside to allow us to enter. We trooped in, finding ourselves in a kind of back hall where several passages met. There was an impression of oak chests, shabby bookcases full of unreadable books, mahogany dressers and other huge pieces of furniture, expelled at one time or another from the central part of the house; the walls covered with large oil paintings of schools long fallen out of fashion. Smith, as if suffering from some painful disease in the lower half of his body, strode uncertainly before us towards a narrow flight of stairs. We followed in silence. Even Mona seemed overawed by the cavernous atmosphere of gloom. Passing through corridors, and still further corridors, all lined with discredited canvases and an occasional marble bust, Smith stopped before a door. Then he turned almost savagely upon us.

'Mr. and Mrs. Quiggin—and what other name?'

Fancy made him seem to emphasise the word 'Mrs.', as if he wished to cast doubt on the legal union of the two of them. Quiggin started, then mumbled my name grudgingly. Smith threw open the door, bawling out his announcement, and propelled us within.

Erridge was sitting at a desk, the upper part surmounted by a glass-fronted bookcase filled with volumes enclosed for the most part in yellow paper wrappers. He jumped up immediately we entered, removing his spectacles and stumbling forward confusedly, as if our arrival was totally unexpected. He had been writing, and the open flap of the desk was covered with letters and papers which now cascaded to the floor; where they lay in a heap for the rest of the time we were in the house. A dark wall-paper and heavy mahogany furniture, not very different in style to that exiled to the back parts of the house, made the room seem smaller than its real extent, which was in fact considerable. There were no pictures, though rectangular discoloured patches on the walls showed where frames had once hung. Over the fireplace hung a chart which I took to be the Tolland pedigree, but on closer examination proved to illustrate in descending scale some principle of economic distribution. Shelves holding more books—classics, Baedekers and a couple of bound copies of the *Boy's Own Paper*—covered the far wall. At the end of the room stood a table littered with current newspapers and magazines. Another smaller table had been laid with four places for a meal.

It was clear that Erridge lived and moved and had his being in this room. I wondered whether he also spent his nights there on the sofa. Such rough and ready accommodation might easily be in keeping with his tenets: except that the sofa looked rather too comfortable to assuage at night-time his guilt for being rich. Still embarrassed, so it seemed, by the unexpectedness of our arrival, he had now begun to walk quickly up and down the room, as if to give expression and relief to the nervous tension he felt. Quiggin, his own self-possession completely restored by contact with his host—like the warm glow that comes after a plunge in cold water—must have recognised these symptoms in Erridge as normal enough. He took Mona by the arm and drew her towards the window, where the two of them stood side by side, looking down at the gardens and the park beyond. They began to discuss together some feature of the landscape.

Left by myself in the middle of the room, I was at first uncertain whether to join Quiggin and Mona in their survey of the Thrubworth grounds, or, by interrupting his pacing with some conventional remark, to follow up Erridge's vague but general greeting to the three of us on arrival. The latter course threatened to entail an attempt to march up and down the room beside him: like officers waiting for a parade to begin. On the other hand, to move away towards Quiggin and the window would seem ineffective and unfriendly. I decided to glance at the economic chart for a minute or two in the hope that the situation might assume a less enigmatic aspect; but when a moment later Erridge paused by his desk, and began laboriously to straighten some of the few papers that remained there, I saw that he and I, sooner or later, must establish some kind of host-guest relationship, however uneasy, if we were to spend an evening together. The quicker this were done the better, so far as my own peace of mind was concerned. I therefore tackled him without further delay.

'I saw your butler some months ago at the Jeavonses'.'

Erridge started, at last coming to himself.

'Oh, did you, yes,' he said, laughing uncomfortably, but at least putting down the pages of typescript which he was shuffling together. 'Smith went there while I was—while I was away—doing this—this—sort of investigation. He has been with me for—oh, I don't know—several years. Our other butler died. He had something ghastly wrong with his inside. Something really horrible. It was quite sudden. Smith is rather a peculiar man. He doesn't have very good health either. You can never guess what he is going to say. You know Aunt Molly, do you?'

Erridge's face had begun to work painfully when he

130

spoke of his earlier butler's unhappy state of health and subsequent death. It was easy to see that he found the afflictions of the human condition hard even to contemplate; indeed, took many of them as his own personal responsibility.

'I've been there once or twice.'

'You seem to know a lot of my relations,' said Erridge.

He made this remark in a flat, despondent tone, as if interested, even faintly surprised that such a thing should happen, but that was all. He appeared to wish to carry the matter no further, uttering no warning, but certainly offering no encouragement. It would probably have been necessary to discover a fresh subject to discuss, had not Quiggin at that moment decided that the proper period of segregation from Erridge was at an end—or had been satisfactorily terminated by my own action—so that he now rejoined us.

'I was showing Mona the place where I advise you to have those trees down,' he said. 'I am sure it is the right thing to do. Get them out of the way.'

'I'm still thinking it over,' said Erridge, again using an absolutely flat tone.

He did not show any desire to hear Quiggin's advice about his estate, his manner on this subject contrasting with his respectful reception of Quiggin's political comments. Mona sat down on the sofa and gave a little sigh.

'Would you—any of you—like a drink?' asked Erridge.

He spoke enquiringly, as if drink at that hour were an unusual notion that had just occurred to him. It was agreed that a drink would be a good idea. However, Erridge seemed to have little or no plan for implementing his offer. All he did further was to say: 'I expect Smith will be back in a minute or two.'

Smith did, indeed, return a short time later. He added a large jug of barley water to the things on the table.

'Oh, Smith,' said Erridge. 'There is some sherry, isn't there?'

'Sherry, m'lord?'

It was impossible to tell from Smith's vacant, irascible stare whether he had never before been asked for sherry since his first employment at Thrubworth, or whether he had himself, quite simply, drunk all the sherry that remained.

'Yes, sherry,' said Erridge, with unexpected firmness. 'I am sure I remember some being left in the decanter after the doctor came here.'

Erridge said the word 'doctor' in a way that made me think he might add hypochondria to his other traits. There was something about the value he gave to the syllables that emphasised the importance to himself of a doctor's visit.

'I don't think so, m'lord.'

'I know there was,' said Erridge. 'Please go and look.'

A battle of wills was in progress. Clearly Erridge had little or no interest in sherry as such. Like Widmerpool, he did not care for eating and drinking: was probably actively opposed to such sensual enjoyments, which detracted from preferable conceptions of pure power. Quiggin, of course, liked power too; though perhaps less for its own sake than for the more practical consideration of making a career for himself of a kind that appealed at any given moment to his imagination. Quiggin could therefore afford to allow himself certain indulgences, provided these did not endanger the political or social front he chose to present to the world. In supposing that Erridge, like most people who employ eccentric servants, was under Smith's thumb, I now saw I had made an error of judgment. Erridge's will was a strong one. There could be no doubt of that. At his words Smith had bowed his head as one who, having received the order of the bowstring, makes for the Bosphorus. He turned in deep dejection from the room. Erridge's sallow cheeks had almost taken on a touch of colour. In this mood his beard made him look quite fierce.

'You would like some sherry, wouldn't you?' he repeated to Mona.

He was suffering a twinge of conscience that to the rest of us his demeanour to Smith might have sounded arrogant: out of keeping with his fundamental beliefs.

'Oh, *yes*,' said Mona.

She adopted towards Erridge a decidedly flirtatious manner. Indeed, I wondered for a moment whether she might now be contemplating a new move that would make her Countess of Warminster. Almost immediately I dismissed such a speculation as absurd, since Erridge himself appeared totally unaware that he was being treated to Mona's most seductive glance. Turning from her he began to discuss with Quiggin the economics of the magazine they hoped to found. The Quiggin plan was evidently based on the principle that Erridge should put up the money, and Quiggin act as editor; Erridge, on the other hand, favoured some form of joint editorship. I was surprised that Mona showed no sign of dissatisfaction at Erridge's indifference to her. I noted how much firmer, more ruthless, her personality had become since I had first met her as Templer's wife, when she had seemed a silly, empty-headed, rather bad-tempered beauty. Now she possessed a kind of hidden force, of which there could be no doubt that Quiggin was afraid.

Smith returned with sherry on a salver. There was just enough wine to give each of us a full glass. I remarked on the beauty of the decanter.

'Are you interested in glass?' said Erridge. 'Some of it is rather good here. My grandfather used to collect it. I don't know, by the way, whether you would like to look

133

round the house by any chance. There is nothing much to see, but some people like that sort of thing. Or perhaps you would rather do that after dinner.'

'Oh, we are more comfortable here with our drinks, aren't we, Alf?' said Quiggin. 'I don't expect you want to trudge round the house, do you, Nick? I am sure I don't.'

I think Quiggin knew, even at this stage, that there was no real hope of sabotaging the project, because Erridge was already determined to go through with it; but he felt at the same time, in the interests of his own self-respect, that at least an effort should be made to prevent a tour of the house taking place. Erridge's face fell; looking more cheerful again at the assurance that, after we had dined, I should like to 'see round'. Smith appeared with some soup in a tureen, and we ranged ourselves about the table.

'Will you drink beer?' asked Erridge, doubtfully. 'Or does anyone prefer barley water?'

'Beer,' said Quiggin, sharply.

He must have felt that the suggested tour of the house had strengthened his own moral position, in so much as the proposal was an admission of self-indulgence on the part of Erridge.

'Bring some beer, Smith.'

'The pale ale, m'lord?'

'Yes, I think that is what it is. Whatever we usually drink on these occasions.'

Smith shook his head pessimistically, and went off again. Erridge and Quiggin settled down to further talk about the paper, a conversation leading in due course to more general topics, among these the aggressive foreign policy of Japan.

'Of course I would dearly like to visit China and see for myself,' Quiggin said.

It was a wish I had heard him express before. Possibly he hoped that Erridge would take him there.

'It would be interesting,' Erridge said. 'I'd like to go myself.'

Soup was followed by sausages and mash with fried onions. The cooking was excellent. The meal ended with cheese and fruit. We left the table and moved back to the chairs round the fireplace at the other end of the room. Mona returned to the subject of her film career. We had begun to talk of some of the minor film stars of the period, when the sound of girls' voices and laughter came from the passage outside. Then the door burst open, and two young women came boisterously into the room. There could be no doubt that they were two more of Erridge's sisters. The elder, so it turned out, was Susan Tolland; the younger, Isobel. The atmosphere changed suddenly, violently. One became all at once aware of the delicious, sparkling proximity of young feminine beings. The room was transformed. They both began to speak at once, the elder one, Susan, finally making herself heard.

'Erry, we were passing the gates and really thought it would be too bad mannered not to drop in.'

Erridge rose, and kissed his sisters automatically, although not without some shade of warmth. Otherwise, he showed no great pleasure at seeing them; rather the reverse. I had by then become familiar with the Tolland physical type, to which Susan Tolland completely conformed. She was about twenty-five or twenty-six, less farouche, I judged, than her sister, Norah; less statuesque than Frederica, though resembling both of them. Tall and thin, all of them possessed a touch of that angularity of feature most apparent in Erridge himself: a conformation that in him became a gauntness recalling Don Quixote. In the girls this inclination to severity of outline had been bred down, leaving only a liveliness of expression and underlying sense of melancholy: this last characteristic to some extent masked by a great pressure of high spirits, notably absent in Erridge. His eyes were brown, those of his sisters, deep blue.

Would it be too explicit, too exaggerated, to say that when I set eyes on Isobel Tolland, I knew at once that I should marry her? Something like that is the truth; certainly nearer the truth than merely to record those vague, inchoate sentiments of interest of which I was so immediately conscious. It was as if I had known her for many years already; enjoyed happiness with her and suffered sadness. I was conscious of that, as of another life, nostalgically remembered. Then, at that moment, to be compelled to go through all the paraphernalia of introduction, of 'getting to know' one another by means of the normal formalities of social life, seemed hardly worth while. We knew one another already; the future was determinate. But what —it may reasonably be asked—what about the fact that only a short time before I had been desperately in love with Jean Duport; was still, indeed, not sure that I had been wholly cured? Were the delights and agonies of all that to be tied up with ribbon, so to speak, and thrown into a drawer to be forgotten? What about the girls with whom I seemed to stand nightly in cinema queues? What, indeed?

'Aren't we going to be told who everyone is?' said Susan, looking round the room and smiling.

Although her smile was friendly, charming, there could be no doubt that, like her sister, Norah, Susan was capable of making herself disagreeable if she chose.

'Oh, sorry,' said Erridge. 'What am I thinking of? I am not used to having so many people in this room.'

He mumbled our names. Isobel seemed to take them in; Susan, less certainly. Both girls were excited about something, apparently about some piece of news they had to impart.

'Have you come from far?' asked Quiggin.

He spoke in an unexpectedly amiable tone, so much muting the harshness of his vowels that these sounded almost like the ingratiating speech of his associate, Howard Craggs, the publisher. Quiggin had previously named Erridge's family in such disparaging terms that I had almost supposed he would give some outward sign of the disapproval he felt for the kind of life they lived. He would have been capable of that; or at least withholding from them any mark of cordiality. Now, on the contrary, he had wrung the girls' hands heartily, grinning with pleasure, as if delighted by this opportunity of meeting them both. Mona, on the other hand, did not trouble to conceal traces of annoyance, or at least disappointment, at all this additional feminine competition put into the field against her so suddenly and without warning.

'Yes, we've come rather miles,' said Susan Tolland, who was evidently very pleased about something. 'The car made the most extraordinary sounds at one point. Isobel said it was like a woman wailing for her demon lover. I thought it sounded more like the demon lover himself.'

'Anyway, here you are in "sunny domes and caves of ice",' said Quiggin. 'You know I get more and more interested in Coleridge for some reason.'

'Do you—do you want anything to eat, either of you?' Erridge enquired, uneasily.

He pointed quite despairingly at the table, as if he hoped the food we had just consumed would, by some occult processs, be restored there once more; as if we were indeed living in the realm of poetic enchantment adumbrated by Quiggin.

'We had a bite at the Tolland Arms,' said Isobel, taking

a banana from the dish and beginning to peel it. 'And very disgusting the food was there, too. We didn't know you would be entertaining on a huge scale, Erry. In fact we were not even certain you were in residence. We thought you might be away on one of your jaunts.'

She cast a glance at us from under her eyelashes to indicate that she was not laughing openly at her brother, but, at the same time, we must realise that the rest of the family considered his goings-on pretty strange. Quiggin caught her eye, and, with decided disloyalty to Erridge, smiled silently back at her: implying that he too shared to the fullest extent the marrow of that particular joke. Isobel threw herself haphazard into an armchair, her long legs stretched out in front of her.

'Where have you come from?' asked Erridge.

He spoke formally, almost severely, as if forcing himself to take an interest in his sisters' behaviour, however extraordinary; behaviour which, owing to the fortunate dispensations of circumstance, could never affect him personally to the smallest degree. Indeed, he spoke as if utter remoteness from his own manner of life, for that very reason, made a subject otherwise unexciting, even distasteful, possess aspects impossible for him to disregard. It was as if his sisters, in themselves, represented customs so strange and incalculable that even the most detached person could not fail to allow his attention to be caught for a second or two by such startling oddness.

'We've been at the Alfords',' said Isobel, discarding the banana skin into the waste-paper basket. 'Throw me an orange, Susy. Susan had an adventure there.'

'Not an adventure exactly,' said her sister. 'And, anyway, it's my story, not yours, Isobel. Hardly an adventure. Unless you call getting married an adventure. I suppose some people might.'

'Why, have you got married, Susan?' asked Erridge.

He showed no surprise whatever, and very little interest, at the presentation of this possibility: merely mild, on the whole benevolent, approval.

'I haven't yet,' said Susan, suddenly blushing deeply. 'But I am going to.'

She was, I think, suddenly overwhelmed at the thought of marriage and all it implied. The announcement of her engagement, planned with great dash, had not been entirely carried off with the required air of indifference. I even wondered for a moment whether she was not going to cry. However, she mastered herself immediately. At the sight of her sister's face, Isobel began to blush violently too.

'To whom?' asked Erridge, still completely calm. 'I am so glad to hear the news.'

'Roddy Cutts.'

The name clearly conveyed nothing whatever to her brother, who still smiled amiably, unable to think of anything to say.

'There was a Lady Augusta Cutts who used to give dances when I was a young man,' he said, at last.

He spoke as if he were at least as old as General Conyers. No doubt the days when he had occasionally gone to dances seemed by then infinitely distant: indeed, much further off, and no less historic, than the General's cavalry charge.

'Lady Augusta is his mother.'

'Oh, yes?'

'She is rather a terror.'

There was a pause.

'What does he do?' asked Erridge, as if conscious that it might seem bad-mannered to drop the subject altogether, however much he himself hoped to move on to something more interesting.

'I can't tell you exactly,' said Susan. 'But he has something he does. I mean he doesn't absolutely beg his bread from door to door. He looks into the Conservative Central Office once in a way too.'

Erridge's face fell at the mention of this last establishment. Quiggin, however, came to the rescue.

'Much as I hate the Tories,' he said, 'I've heard that Cutts is one of their few promising young men.'

Everyone, including Susan Tolland herself, was surprised by this sudden avowal on the part of Quiggin, who was showing at least as much enthusiasm on the subject of the engagement as might have been expected from Erridge himself.

'I grant it may not be my place to say so,' Quiggin went on, switching at the same time to a somewhat rougher delivery. 'But you know, Alf, you really ought to celebrate rightly in a bottle of champagne. Now, don't you think there is some bubbly left in that cellar of yours?'

This speech astonished me, not because there was anything surprising in Quiggin's desire for champagne, but on account of a changed attitude towards his host. Erridge's essentially ascetic type of idealism, concerned with the mass rather than the individual, and reinforced by an aristocratic, quite legitimate desire to avoid vulgar display, had no doubt moved imperceptibly into that particular sphere of parsimony defined by Lovell as 'upper-class stinginess'. To demand champagne was deliberately to inflame such responses in Erridge. Possibly Quiggin, seeing unequivocal signs of returning sulkiness in Mona, hoped to avert that mood by this daring manœuvre: equally, as a sheer exercise of will, he may have decided at that moment to display his power over his patron. Neither motive would be out of keeping with his character. Finally, he might have hoped merely to ingratiate himself with Susan Tolland—certainly a pretty girl—whom he possibly cast for some at present unrevealed rôle in his future plans. Whatever his reason, he received a very encouraging smile from her after making this proposal.

'What a jolly good idea,' she said. 'As a matter of fact I was waiting for Erry to suggest it.'

Erridge was undoubtedly taken aback, although not, I think, on the ground that the suggestion came from Quiggin. Erridge did not traffic in individual psychology. It was an idea that was important to him, not its originator. The whole notion of drinking champagne because your sister was engaged was, in itself, obviously alien to him; alien both to his temperament and ideals. Champagne no doubt represented to his mind a world he had fled. Now the wine was presented as a form of rite or observance, almost, indeed, as a restorative or tonic after hearing dangerously exciting news, he seemed primarily concerned with the question whether or not any champagne remained in the house. The fact that Quiggin had put forward the proposal must at least have disposed of any fears as to whether in this manner a coarse display of his own riches might be symbolised. However, even faced with this utterly unforeseen problem, Erridge was by no means thrown off his guard. I could not help admiring the innate caution with which he seasoned his own eccentricity. Even in Erridge, some trace of that 'realism' was observable of which Chipps Lovell used to speak; among the rest of the Tollands, as I discovered later, a characteristic strongly developed.

'I really cannot reply to that question offhand,' Erridge said—and one caught a faint murmur of ancestral voices answering for the Government some awkward question raised by the Opposition—'As you know I hardly ever drink anything myself, except an occasional glass of beer—

141

certainly never champagne. To tell the truth, I hate the stuff. We'd better ask Smith.'

Smith, as it happened, appeared at that moment with coffee. Already he showed signs of being nervously disturbed by the arrival of the girls, his hands shaking visibly as he held the tray; so much so that some of the liquid spilled from the pot.

'Smith, is there any champagne left in the cellar?'

Erridge's voice admitted the exceptional nature of the enquiry. He asked almost apologetically. Even so, the shock was terrific. Smith started so violently that the coffee cups rattled on the tray. It was evident that we were now concerned with some far more serious matter than the earlier pursuit of sherry. Recovering himself with an effort, Smith directed a stare of hatred at Quiggin, at once revealed by some butler's instinct as the ultimate cause of this unprecedented demand. The colourless, unhealthy skin of his querulous face, stretched like a pale rubber mask over the bones of his features, twitched a little.

'Champagne, m'lord?'

'Have we got any? One bottle would do. Even a half-bottle.'

Smith's face puckered, as if manfully attempting to force his mind to grapple with a mathematical or philosophical problem of extraordinary complexity. His bearing suggested that he had certainly before heard the word 'champagne' used, if only in some distant, outlandish context; that devotion to his master alone gave him some apprehension of what this question—these ravings, almost—might mean. Nothing good could come of it. This was a disastrous way to talk. That was his unspoken message so far as champagne was concerned. After a long pause, he at last shook his head.

'I doubt if there is any champagne left, m'lord.'

'Oh, I'm sure there is, Smith, if you go and look,' said Susan. 'You see it is to celebrate my engagement, Smith. I'm going to get married.'

Another twitch passed quickly, almost like a flash of lightning, over Smith's face. I had by no means taken a fancy to him, either here or at the Jeavonses', but it was impossible not to feel some sympathy for his predicament: forced at short notice to adapt himself to the whims of his different employers; for it was unlikely that his Thrubworth routine was anything like that at the Jeavonses'.

'Very pleased to hear the news, m'lady,' he said. 'Wish you the best of luck. I expect it will be Lady Isobel's turn soon.'

These felicitations were handsome on Smith's part, although Isobel, in spite of being several years younger than her sister, evidently had no wish for comparison between them to be drawn in a manner which made her, by representing, as it were, those girls not yet engaged, seem to come out second best. However, if Smith hoped by drawing attention to engagements in general to dispose of the question of champagne, he was disappointed.

'Anyway, Smith, do go and have a look,' said Isobel. 'My throat is absolutely parched.'

Erridge might have no wish to drink champagne, even if available, but he had also clearly decided that things had gone too far for the idea to be abandoned without loss of face on his own part. Smith, too, must finally have realised that, for he now set down the coffee tray and abandoned the room in full retreat, moving like a man without either enthusiasm or hope.

'Smith doesn't seem to get any soberer,' said Susan, when he had shut the door.

'As a matter of fact, Smith hasn't had one of his real bouts for a long time,' said Erridge.

He spoke reprovingly.

'So drink is Smith's trouble, is it?' said Quiggin, with great geniality. 'You never told me that. I often thought he might be one over the eight. That explains a lot.'

'Smith sometimes takes a glass too much,' said Erridge, shortly, perhaps beginning to notice, and resent, the change in Quiggin's manner since the arrival of the girls. 'I usually pretend not to notice. It must be an awful job to be a butler anyway. I don't really approve of having indoor men-servants, but it is hard to run a house this size without them, even when you live, like me, in only a small part of it. I can't get rid of the place, because it is entailed—so there it is.'

He sighed. There was rather an awkward pause. Erridge was perhaps getting cross. It was possible that the entail was not a popular subject in the family.

'What sort of luck will he have in the cellar?' asked Isobel. 'I must say champagne is just what I need.'

'I really don't know,' said Erridge. 'As I told you, I hardly drink anything myself.'

'Do you keep it locked?' asked Susan.

Erridge coloured a little.

'No,' he said. 'I like trusting people, Susan.'

Susan showed no disposition to accept this observation as a snub, although her brother was obviously displeased by her flippancy. It was natural that anyone should be annoyed whose evening had been so radically altered by force of circumstance. He had been looking forward to some hours of discussing plans for the magazine, discussion which my own presence would not have hindered. A third, and unconcerned, party might even have made Quiggin more tractable, for a certain amount of patron-protégé conflict clearly took place between them. Now, the arrival of his sisters had transformed the room into a place not far removed from one of those haunts of social life so abhorrent to him. Instead of printing charges, advertising rates, the price of paper, names of suitable contributors, their remuneration, and other such matters which, by their very nature, carried with them a suggestion of energy, power and the general good of mankind, he was now compelled to gossip about such a trifle as Susan's engagement, a subject in which he could not feel the smallest interest. This indifference was not, I felt sure, due to dislike of Susan, but because the behaviour of individuals, consanguineous or not, held, as such, no charm whatever for him. His growing vexation was plain: not lessened by Quiggin's manifest betrayal of principles with the two girls.

'Do you like driving, Lady Susan?' asked Quiggin.

'Oh, all right,' she said. 'We rattled along somehow.'

'Have you had your car long?'

When he asked that, she began to blush furiously again. 'It is a borrowed car,' she said.

'It's Roddy's,' said Isobel. 'Just to show him what married life is going to be like, Sue took his car away from him, and made him go back by train.'

'Oh, shut up,' said her sister. 'You know it was the most convenient arrangement.'

This cross-fire continued until the return of Smith. He brought with him a bottle, which he banged down quite fiercely on the table. It was Mumm, 1906: a magnum. Nothing could have borne out more thoroughly Erridge's statement about his own lack of interest in wine. It was, indeed, a mystery that this relic of former high living should have survived. Some latent sense of its lofty descent must from time to time have dominated Smith's recurrent desire, and held him off. I could not help reflecting how different must have been the occasions when its fellows had been consumed; if, in truth, we were to consume this, which seemed not yet absolutely certain.

'Just the one left,' said Smith.

He spoke in anguish, though not without resignation. Erridge hesitated. Almost as much as Smith, he seemed to dislike the idea of broaching the wine for the rest of us to drink. A moral struggle was raging within him.

'I don't know whether I really ought not to keep it,' he said. 'If there is only one. I mean, if someone or other turned up who——'

He found no individual worthy enough to name, because he stopped suddenly short.

'Oh, *do* let's, Alf,' said Mona.

She had hardly spoken since the arrival of Susan and Isobel Tolland. Her voice sounded high and strained, as if she were suffering strong nervous tension.

'Oh, yes,' said Erridge. 'You're right, Mona. We'll break its neck and celebrate your engagement, Sue.'

He was undoubtedly proud of fetching from somewhere deeply embedded in memory this convivial phrase; also cheered by the immediate, and quite general, agreement that now was the moment to drink so mature—so patriarchal— a vintage. Smith disappeared again. After another long delay he returned with champagne glasses, which had received a perfunctory rub to dispel dust accumulated since at least the time of Erridge's succession. Then, with the peculiar deftness of the alcoholic, he opened the bottle. The explosion was scarcely audible. He poured the wine, a stream of deep dull gold, like wine in a fairy story, at the same time offering an almost inaudible, though certainly generous, appreciation of the occasion by muttering: 'I'll be drinking your ladyship's health myself later this evening.' Susan thanked him. Erridge, who had himself refused a glass, shifted his feet about uneasily. Traces of the Mumm's former excellence remained, like a few dimly remembered words of some noble poem sunk into oblivion, or a once famous statue of which only a chipped remnant still stands.

'Have you informed Hyde Park Gardens yet?' asked Erridge.

He spoke as if that were a new thought; one that worried him a little.

'I rang up,' said Susan.

The champagne had perhaps helped her to recover casualness of tone.

'What was said?'

'Great delight.'

I knew this reference must be to their stepmother, Katherine, Lady Warminster, of whom Lovell had given me some account, describing her as 'frightfully amusing'. Invalid and somewhat eccentric, she was, I suspected, a less easy-going figure than Lovell's words might lead one to suppose. There seemed indications that her stepchildren regarded her as formidable. She had always hated the country, so that her husband's death had provoked none of those embarrassments, not uncommon, in which an heir has to apply pressure to enjoy sole rights in his inheritance. On the contrary, the difficulty had been to persuade Erridge to take over Thrubworth when Lord Warminster, a traveller and big-game hunter of some celebrity, died abroad. That had been five or six years before, when Erridge's political views were still comparatively undeveloped. Lovell's picture of Erridge's early days depicted a vague, immature, unhappy young man, taking flats and leaving them, wandering about on the Continent, buying useless odds and ends, joining obscure societies, in general without friends or interests, drifting gradually into his present position.

'I'm glad the news was well received,' said Erridge.

'So was I,' said Susan. 'Jolly glad.'

This interchange on the subject of their stepmother was somehow of a much closer intimacy than anything said previously about the engagement. In relation to Lady War-minster, the Tollands presented a united front. Their sentiments towards her were not, one felt, at all unfriendly; on the contrary, rather well disposed. They were at the same time sentiments charged with that powerful family feeling with which no outward consideration, not even love or marriage, could compete, except upon very unequal terms.

'Have you been over the house?' asked Isobel, beside whom I was sitting on the sofa.

We had drunk the champagne, and the atmosphere had become more relaxed. Erridge heard the question, and spoke himself, before I could answer. Although he had had nothing to drink, he had not been able to withstand the increased warmth of relationship that the rest of us had drawn from the wine.

'Why, no, you haven't seen the house yet,' he said. 'Would you by any chance like to go round, Jenkins? There is really little or nothing of any interest to see, I must warn you, except a hat that is supposed to have belonged to the younger Pitt.'

'I should like to go round very much.'

'I expect you will prefer to stay where you are, J.G.,' said Erridge, who may have decided to take this opportunity of making a tour of the house as a kind of counterblast to Quiggin's demand for champagne. 'And I don't expect you will want to go round either, Mona, as you have seen it all several times. Jenkins and I will walk through the rooms very quickly.'

However, both Quiggin and Mona insisted that they would like to take part in the tour, in spite of its repetitive character, so far as they themselves were concerned; and the Tolland girls agreed, rather loudly, that there was nothing they enjoyed more than their eldest brother's showmanship in this particular undertaking.

'Those anti-fascist pamphlets will have to wait for another night,' Quiggin muttered to Erridge.

He spoke, as if to salve his conscience, as he rose from his chair.

'Oh, yes,' said Erridge testily, as if he wished to be reminded of the pamphlets as little as Quiggin. 'Anyway, I want to go through them carefully—not with a lot of people interrupting.'

He strode firmly in front of us. We followed down several passages, emerging at last at the head of a broad staircase. Erridge descended. Half-way down, where the wall of the landing faced the hall, hung the full-length portrait, by Lawrence, of an officer wearing the slung jacket of a hussar. Erridge stopped in front of the picture.

'The 4th Lord Erridge and 1st Earl of Warminster,' he said. 'He was a very quarrelsome man and fought a number of duels. The Duke of Wellington is supposed to have said of him: "By God, Erridge has shown himself a greater rake than Anglesey and more damn'd a fool than ever was Combermere. It is my firm belief that had he been present on the field of Waterloo we should never have carried the day." '

'But that was only when the Duke was cross,' said Isobel. 'Because he also remarked: "Erridge spoke out last night when Brougham extolled the virtues of Queen Caroline. I never saw a man so put out of countenance as was Brougham by his words." I always wonder what he said. Of course, one knows in a general way, but it would be nice to know the actual phrases.'

'I think he probably used to score off Wellington,' said Susan. 'And that was why the Duke was so sharp with him. Erridge was probably the more cunning of the two.'

'Oh, rot,' said Isobel. 'I bet he wasn't. Dukes are much more cunning than earls.'

'What makes you think so?' said her brother.

Not greatly pleased by this opinion, he did not wait for an answer, but moved on down the stairs. Denigration of ancestors was more agreeable to him than banter regarding the order of peerage to which he belonged. Not for the first time that evening one was conscious of the bones of an old world pomposity displayed beneath the skin of advanced political thought. However, he soon recovered from this momentary discomposure.

'Of course the Tollands were really nobody much at the beginning of the fourteenth century,' he said. 'That is when they first appear. Lesser gentry, I suppose you might call them. I think they probably made their money out of the Black Death.'

As such a foundation of the family fortunes seemed of interest, I enquired further. Erridge was taken back by the question.

'Oh, I don't know for certain,' he said. 'There was a big industrial and social upheaval then, as you probably know. The Tollands may have turned it to good account. I think they were a pretty awful lot.'

He appeared a little disturbed by this perhaps over close attention on my own part to the detail of the history he provided. The girls giggled. Quiggin came to the rescue.

'When did these *kulaks* begin their career of wholesale exploitation?' he asked.

He sweetened the enquiry with some harsh laughter. Erridge laughed too, more at home with Quiggin in his political phraseology than in domestic raillery with his sisters.

'*Kulaks* is the word,' he said. 'I think they first went up in the world when one of them was knighted by

Edward IV. Then another was Esquire of the Body to Henry VIII, whatever that may have been, and lost his job under Bloody Mary. They've been an awfully undistinguished lot on the whole. They were Cavaliers in the Civil War and got a peerage under Queen Anne. John Toland, the deist, was no relation, so I've been told. I should rather like to have claimed him.'

We entered a long room hung with portraits. The younger Pitt's hat stood within a glass case in one corner by the window. The furniture, as described by Lovell, was under dust-sheets.

'I never use any of these rooms,' said Erridge.

He pulled away the dust-sheets without ceremony; leaving in the centre of the room a heap of linen on the floor. The furniture was on the whole mediocre; although, as at the Jeavonses', there was a good piece here and there. The pictures, too, apart from the Lawrence—the bravura of which gave it some charm—were wholly lacking in distinction. Erridge seemed aware of these deficiencies, referring more than once to the 'rubbish' his forbears had accumulated. Yet, at the same time, in his own peculiar way, he seemed deeply to enjoy this opportunity of displaying the house: a guilty enjoyment, though for that reason no less keen.

'We really ought to have my Uncle Alfred here,' said Erridge. 'He regards himself as rather an authority on family history—and, I must say, is a very great bore on the subject. Nothing is worse than someone who takes that sort of thing up, and hasn't had enough education to carry it through.'

I recalled Alfred Tolland's own remarks about his nephew's failure to erect a memorial window. Erridge, whose last words revealed a certain intellectual arrogance, until then dormant, probably found it convenient to diminish his own scrutiny of family matters where tedious negotiation was concerned. In any case, however much an oblique contemplation of his race might gratify him, there could be no doubt that he regarded any such weakness as morally wrong.

'It makes a very nice museum to live in,' said Quiggin.

We had completed the tour and returned to the room where we had dined. No trace seemed to remain of Quiggin's earlier objections to the tour. His inconsistencies, more limited by circumstance than those of Erridge, were no less pronounced. Erridge himself, entirely at ease while displaying his possessions, now began once more to pace about the room nervously.

'How are you and Isobel getting back, Susy?' he asked.

He sounded apprehensive, as if he feared his sisters might have come with the idea of attempting to stay for several months: perhaps even hoping to take possession of the house entirely, and entertain at his expense on a huge scale.

'Well, I've got Roddy's car,' said Susan, blushing again at mention of her future husband. 'We thought if you could put us up for the night, we'd start early for London tomorrow morning.'

Erridge was not enthusiastic about this proposal. There was some discussion. However, he could not very well turn his sisters out of the house at that hour of the night, so that in the end he agreed; at the same time conveying a warning that the sheets might not be properly aired.

'All right,' said Isobel. 'We'll get rheumatic fever. We don't mind. I can't tell you how smart Roddy's car is, by the way. If we get up reasonably early, we shall reach London in no time.'

'It is rather a grand car,' said Susan. 'I don't know whether anyone would like a lift in the morning.'

This seemed an opportunity not to be missed. I asked if I might accept the offer.

'Yes, do come,' said Isobel. 'It will be too boring otherwise, driving all the way to London with Susy talking of nothing but arrangements for her wedding.'

'We will pick you up when we come past the cottage, which we do, anyway,' said Susan. 'I warn you I am frightfully punctual.'

Quiggin did not look too pleased at this, but, having enjoyed his evening, he was by that time in a mood to allow such an arrangement to pass. Erridge, already suppressing one or two yawns, seemed anxious now that we should go, and give him an opportunity to make for bed. Mona, too, had been silent for a long time, as if lost in thought. She looked tired. It was time to say good-night.

'See you in the morning,' said Isobel.

'I will be waiting at the gate.'

Erridge came to the door and let us out. We passed once more through the dim glades of the melancholy park, now dramatised by moonlight. It was a warm night, damp, though without rain, and no wind stirred the trees. There was a smell of hay and wet timber in the air. The noise of owls came faintly as they called to each other under the stars.

'Alf is a champion lad,' said Quiggin. 'His sisters are grand girls too. You didn't take long to press your company on them, I must say.'

'I've got to get back to London somehow.'

'I didn't think the girls were up to much,' said Mona. 'They behaved as if they owned the place. I hate those tweed suits.'

'You know, Alf is rather like Prince Myshkyn in *The Idiot*,' said Quiggin. 'A Myshkyn with political grasp. You wouldn't believe the money spent on good causes that he has got through, one way and another.'

'What sort of thing?'

'He has helped a lot of individual cases that have been recommended to him from time to time. Howard Craggs got quite a bit out of him a year or two back, which I bet he never repaid. Then Alf has founded several societies and financed them. Refugees, too.'

'Mind he doesn't meet Guggenbühl.'

'I'll see to that,' said Quiggin, laughing sourly.

'He ought to marry a nice girl who would teach him to look after his money instead of handing it out to all these wasters,' said Mona.

One of her bad moods seemed on the way.

'All very good causes,' said Quiggin, who seemed to enjoy contemplating this subject. 'But sums that would make you gasp.'

'Bloody fool,' said Mona.

4.

IN the Jeavonses' house everything was disposed about the rooms as if the owners had moved in only a week or two before, and were still picknicking in considerable disorder among their unsorted belongings. Whether the better pieces were Sleaford spoils, or derived from Molly's side of the family, Lovell was uncertain. Certainly Molly herself had not bought them; still less, Jeavons. Lovell said the only object the two of them were known to have acquired throughout their married life together was a cabinet made of some light, highly polished wood, designed—though never, I think, used—to enclose the wherewithal for mixing cocktails. In practice, bottles, glasses and ice were always brought into the drawing-room on a tray, the cabinet serving only as a plinth upon which to rest the cage enclosing two budgerigars. You could never tell who would carry in this drink tray; or, for that matter, who would open the front door. Regular servants were employed only spasmodically, their duties on the whole undertaken by such temporary figures as Erridge's Smith, or super-annuated nurses and governesses of the Ardglass family, whose former dependants were legion. Even personal friends of Molly's, down on their luck for one reason or another, would from time to time lend a hand on the domestic side, while a succession of charwomen, gloomy or jocular, haunted the passages by day.

No one was ever, so to speak, turned away from the Jeavons table. The place was a hinterland where none of the ordinary rules seemed to apply and persons of every sort were to be encountered. Perhaps that description makes the company sound too diverting. Certainly Lovell was less complimentary. 'Of course you hardly ever meet intelligent people there,' he used to say, for some reason cherishing in his mind that category of person, without too closely defining means of recognition. 'And you rarely see anyone whom *I* would call really smart.' Then he was accustomed to relent a little, and add: 'All the same, you may find absolutely anybody at Aunt Molly's.'

In making this practical—even brutal—analysis, I think Lovell merely meant that individuals deeply ambitious of receiving a lot of grand invitations would never dream of wasting time among the rag, tag and bobtail normally to be found at the Jeavonses'; but he probably intended at the same time to imply that such over-eager people might sometimes be surprised—possibly even made envious—by the kind of visitor from Molly's past—or, for that matter, her unconformable present–who was the exception in the house rather than the rule. A powerful substratum of relations was usually to be found there, Ardglass and Sleaford connexions, as a rule: not, on the whole, the most eminent members of those families. Jeavons, certainly no snob in the popular and derogatory sense (although he had acquired for everyday purposes a modicum of lore peculiar to his wife's world) would from time to time produce a relation of his own—for example, a nephew who worked in Wolverhampton—but, even had he so desired, he could never have attempted to compete in point of number with the ramifications of Molly's family: the descendants of her grandfather's ninety-seven first cousins. It was at the Jeavonses' that I met the Tolland sisters again.

Lovell, probably unreliable, I thought, upon such a point, said that Jeavons used occasionally to kick over the traces of married life.

'He goes off by himself and gets tight and picks up a woman,' Lovell said. 'Just once in a way, you know. One evening he brought an obvious tart to the house to have a drink.'

'Were you there?'

'No. Someone told me. One of the Tollands, I think.'

I questioned the truth of the story, not so much because I wholly disbelieved it, as on account of the implications of such behaviour, suggesting additionally mysterious avenues of Jeavons's life, which for some reason I felt unwilling, almost too squeamish, to face. However, Lovell himself agreed that whichever Tolland sister had produced the story was probably no very capable judge of the degrees of fallen womanhood, and might easily have used the term without professional connotation: admitting, too, had any such incident taken place, that the girl was unlikely to have been remarked as someone very unusual in such a social no man's land as the Jeavons drawing-room. He conceded finally that Molly would be more than equal to dealing with an intrusion of just that sort, even had she decided—something very unlikely—that the trespassing guest had unexpectedly passed beyond some invisible, though as it were platonically defined, limit as to who might, and who might not, be suitably received under the Jeavons' roof.

All the same, the story, even if untrue, impressed me as of interest in its bearing on a sense of strain suffered, perhaps continuously, by Jeavons himself. At worst, the supposed introduction of a 'tart' into his house was a myth somehow come into existence, which represented in highly coloured terms a long since vanquished husband's vain efforts publicly to demonstrate his own independence from a wife's too evident domination. The legend itself was a kind of tribute to Molly's strength: a strength of which her first husband too, for all I knew, might in his time have been made equally aware; although Lord Sleaford, at least outwardly, was better equipped to control a wife of Molly's sort.

'I don't think she was unhappy when she was married to Uncle John,' Lovell used to say. 'Of course, he was rather a dull dog. Still, lots of women have to put up with dull dogs—not to say dirty dogs—without the advantage of lots of money and a stately home. Besides, Ted is a dull dog, too. I suppose Aunt Molly prefers husbands like that.'

My own feeling was that Jeavons could not be described as 'dull': even though he had appeared so, in that very phrase, to Widmerpool equally with Lovell. On the contrary, Jeavons seemed to me a person oddly interesting.

'Molly never really got on with her contemporaries,' Lovell said. 'The kind of people one associates with Lady Diana—and all that. She knew some of them, of course, very well, but she couldn't be called one of that, or any other, set. I dare say Uncle John was afraid of his wife being thought "fast". She was very shy, too, I believe, in those days. Quite different from what she is like now.'

A picture of Molly Jeavons was beginning to emerge: separateness from her 'young married' contemporaries: perhaps a certain recoil from their flamboyance: in any case, nothing in common with the fleeting interest in the arts of that new fashionable world. She might have the acquisitive instinct to capture from her first marriage (if that was indeed their provenance) such spoils as the Wilson and the Greuze, while remaining wholly untouched by the intellectual emancipation, however skin-deep, of her generation: the Russian Ballet: the painters of the Paris School: novels and poetry of the period: not even such a mournful haunt of the third-rate as the Celtic Twilight had played a part in her life. She had occupied a position many women must have envied, jogging along there for a dozen years without apparent dissatisfaction or a breath of scandal; then contentedly taking on an existence of such a very different kind, hardly noticing the change. All that was interesting. The fact was, perhaps, that her easy going, unambitious manner of life had passed unremarked in a vast house like Dogdene, organised in the last resort by the industrious Sleaford, who, according to Lovell, possessed rather a taste for interfering in domestic matters. While married to him, Molly remained a big, charming, noisy young woman, who had never entirely ceased to be a schoolgirl. When the Dogdene frame was removed, like the loosening of a corset of steel, the unconventional, the eccentric, even the sluttish side of her nature became suddenly revealed to the world.

So far as 'getting on' with her second husband was concerned, the strongest protest she ever seemed to make was: 'Oh, Teddy, dear, do you ever catch hold of the right end of the stick?', spoken kindly, and usually not without provocation; for Jeavons could be slow in grasping the point of a story. Some husbands might certainly take even that rebuke amiss, but Jeavons never seemed to question Molly's absolute sway over himself, the house and all those who came there. I heard her say these words on subsequent visits after Lovell had introduced me there. Neither Widmerpool nor Mrs. Haycock had turned up again since that first night, and I made some enquiry about them.

'Oh, you know Mr. Widmerpool?' said Molly, at once beginning to laugh. 'How extraordinary that you should know him. But perhaps you said so before. He has got jaundice. What a thing to happen when you are going to get married.'

'How disagreeable for him. But I am not altogether surprised. He always makes a great fuss about his health. I think he has had jaundice before.'

'You know him well then?'

'Fairly well—though I don't often see him.'

'He is rather amusing, isn't he?' said Molly. 'Quite a wit in his way. But he must look awful now that he is bright yellow.'

I agreed that the disease would give Widmerpool an un-attractive appearance. It seemed to me extraordinary that she should have thought him 'amusing'. I sometimes found his company enjoyable, because we had experienced much in common; but I could never remember him making an entertaining remark. I wondered what he could have said to cause that judgment: learning in due course that she was quite reckless in the characteristics she attributed to individuals. A chance remark would have the effect of swaying her entirely in favour of one person, or of arousing the bitterest opposition to another. She was very critical of many of the people who came to see her, and hoarded an accumulation of largely unfounded inferences about their character. These inaccuracies seemed to cancel each other out in some manner, so that in the last resort Molly was no worse informed, indeed in point of acuteness often better placed, than what might be regarded as 'the average'.

'Do you think he is in love with Mildred?' she asked sharply.

'I really don't know. I suppose so. If he wants to marry her.'

I was not at all prepared for the question.

'Oh, that doesn't necessarily follow at all,' she said. 'I feel rather sorry for him in some ways. Mildred is not an easy person. I've known her such a long time. She isn't a bit easy. But now you simply must come up to my bed-room and see the monkey. I bought him today from a man in Soho, where I went to get some pimentos.'

A good deal of the life of the Jeavons' household was, in fact, lived in Molly's bedroom, either because a sick animal was established there (with the budgerigars, four principal dogs and at least as many cats inhabited the house), or simply because Molly herself had risen late, or retired early to rest, in either case holding a kind of reception from her bed, a Victorian fourposter that took up most of the room. On a chest of drawers beside the bed stood a photograph of Jeavons in uniform: breeches: puttees: at the back of his head a floppy service cap of the kind stigmatised by Mrs. Haycock in her youth as a 'gorblimey'. He held a knotted bamboo swagger cane under one arm, and, wearing on his tunic the ribbon of the M.C. (awarded after the action in which he had been so seriously wounded), he looked the complete subaltern of war-time musical comedy.

'Come along, all of you,' said Molly. 'You must all see the monkey. You too, Tuffy. You simply must see him.'

I had already recognised the tall, dark, beaky-nosed woman to whom she spoke as Miss Weedon, former secretary of my old friend Charles Stringham's mother, Mrs. Foxe. Miss Weedon, now in her late forties, had been his sister Flavia's governess. After Flavia grew up, she had stayed on to help with Mrs. Foxe's social engagements and charities. I had been waiting an opportunity to have a word with her. I reintroduced myself as we climbed the stairs with the other people who wished—or were being compelled—to visit the monkey. Miss Weedon, wholly unchanged, still sombrely dressed, gave me a keen look.

'But of course I remember,' she said. 'Charles brought you to luncheon in the London house before he went to Kenya to stay with his father. They had forgotten to get a ticket for Charles in a theatre party that had been made up—the Russian Ballet, I think. I was put to all kind of trouble to produce the extra ticket. However, I got it for him in the end.'

I, too, remembered the incident; and also the look of

adoration Miss Weedon had given Stringham when she entered the room. I well recalled that passionate glance, although even then—that night at the Jeavonses'—I had not yet guessed the depths of her devotion. I wondered what she did with herself now. Stringham, when last we had seen something of each other, had told me: 'Tuffy has come into a little money,' and that she was no longer his mother's secretary. I found in due course that Miss Weedon was a close friend of Molly's; in fact that she re-enacted at the Jeavonses' many of her former duties when in the employment of Mrs. Foxe, although, of course, in a household organised on very different terms. It was impossible to know from her manner how unexpected, or the reverse, she found the fact that we had met again at this place. In her profound, though mysterious, dimness, she was typical of the background of Jeavons gatherings.

'I always regret that Charles ever made that journey to Kenya,' she said.

She spoke severely, as if I had myself been in part to blame for allowing such a thing ever to have taken place; even though at the same time she freely forgave me for such former thoughtlessness.

'Why?'

'He was never the same afterwards.'

I had to admit to myself there was some truth in that. Stringham had never been the same after Kenya. It had been a water-shed in his life.

'Perhaps it was just because he became a man,' she said. 'Of course, his upbringing was impossible—always, from the beginning. But he changed so much after that trip to Africa. He was a boy when he went—and such a charming boy—and he really came back a man.'

'People do grow up. At least some do.'

'I am afraid Charles was not one of them,' she said

gravely. 'He became a man, but he did not grow up. He is not grown up now.'

I hardly knew what to answer. It was one of those head-first dives into generalisation that usually precedes between two persons a greater conversational intimacy. However, Miss Weedon made no attempt to expand her statement; nor, so to speak, to draw closer in her approach to the problem of Stringham. She merely continued to look at me with a kind of chilly amiability; as if, by making an immediate confession that I was a former friend of his, I had, so far as she was concerned, just managed to save my bacon. When a boy, I had regarded her as decidedly formidable. I still found her a trifle alarming. She gave an impression of complete singleness of purpose: the impression of a person who could make herself very disagreeable if thwarted.

'Do you ever see Charles now?' I asked.

She did not answer at once, as if waiting a second or two in order to make up her mind how best to deal with that question; perhaps trying to decide the relative merits of plain statement and diplomatic evasion. Finally she came down on the side of bluntness.

'Yes, I do see him,' she said. 'Quite often. You probably know he drinks too much—really much too much. I am trying to help him about that.'

She stared at me very composedly. Once more I hardly knew how to reply. I had not expected our conversation to take this unreservedly serious turn; especially as we had by then reached the bedroom, and were only delayed in our introduction to the ape by the concourse of people who surrounded him, offering homage and applauding Molly's particularisation of his many charms of character.

'Charles had certainly had rather too much the last time I saw him,' I said, trying to pass off the matter of Stringham's drunkenness as if it were just a question of getting rather tight once in a way, which I knew to be far from the truth. 'That was at a dinner he and I went to—two or three years ago at least.'

'You have not seen him since then?'

'No.'

'It still goes on. But I think I shall be able to help him.'

I had no clear idea of how she would set about 'helping' Stringham, but the way she spoke made me conscious of her undoubted strength of will. In fact, her voice chilled my blood a little, she sounded so firm. However, at that moment we found ourselves confronted by the monkey— named by his owners 'Maisky', after the then Soviet Ambassador—and were introduced by Molly to shake hands with him. He was sitting thoughtfully among the cushions of a spacious basket, from time to time extending a small, dry paw in greeting to Molly's guests as they came into his immediate presence. A saucer of nuts stood beside him. There was something of Quiggin in his seriousness and self-absorbtion: also in the watchful manner in which he glanced from time to time at the nuts, sometimes choosing one specially tempting to crack.

'Have you known Lady Molly long?' asked Miss Weedon, after we had taken leave of Maisky, and were returning down the stairs.

'Only a short time.'

'I thought I had never seen you here before.'

'I was brought by Chips Lovell.'

'Oh, yes. One of her nephews. Rather a pushing young man. She was very good to him when he was a boy and his parents did not take much trouble about him. She is a very kind-hearted woman. Quite exceptionally kind-hearted. The house is always full of people she is doing good turns to. Children stay here while their parents are fixing up a divorce. Penniless young men get asked to meals. Former servants are always being given help of one sort or another. There is an old cousin of her husband's ill in one of the upper bedrooms now. She has nowhere else to go, and will certainly never leave the house alive. I really cannot think how Lady Molly stands some of the people who come here. Many are quite dreadful.'

'They certainly seem a mixed bag.'

'They are worse than that, some of them.'

'Really?'

'At the same time, you may find yourself talking to someone like Charles's former father-in-law, Lord Bridgnorth—whom Charles detests and thinks the most conceited, pompous man in the world—who eats out of Lady Molly's hand. He even takes her advice about his horses. Lady Plynlimmon was here at tea the other day. She really seemed quite interested in what Mr. Jeavons was saying about Germany, although usually she won't speak to anyone who is not in the Cabinet. Not long ago Lord Amesbury looked in on his way to a court ball, wearing knee breeches and the Garter. Lady Molly was giving the vet a meal she had cooked herself, because everyone else was out for one reason or another and she had made him come in from miles away in the suburbs to see a cat that had fever. I happened to drop in, and found all three of them eating scrambled eggs together.'

By that time we had once more reached the drawing-room. Miss Weedon ceased to enlarge upon these occasional —indeed, very occasional—glories of the Jeavons' salon; which were, as it happened, in marked contrast to the company gathered together that evening. I asked if she knew Mrs. Haycock.

'Certainly I do,' said Miss Weedon. 'Do you remember a boy called Widmerpool who was at school with Charles and yourself? I think you were all in the same house together, were you not? Charles used to give imitations of him. I am sure you must remember. Well, Mrs. Haycock is going to marry Mr. Widmerpool.'

She nodded her head sharply, to emphasise what she had said. I was amazed that she should be familiar with Stringham's mimicry of Widmerpool. I could have found it within the bounds of possibility that she had heard of Widmerpool, but that Stringham should have shared with her such jokes as his brilliant, though essentially esoteric, Widmerpool imitations, I should never have guessed. This new light on Stringham's relationship with Miss Weedon suggested quite a different sort of intimacy to any I had previously surmised. I told her that I already knew of Widmerpool's engagement. That had been my reason for enquiry. Miss Weedon smiled her thin freezing smile.

'I think Mildred Haycock was quite glad to find someone to marry,' she said. 'Especially a man with such a good future in front of him. Of course he is a bit young for her. All the same, it is *easier* for a woman like Mrs. Haycock—who has two children, both quite old now—to be married. Then, also, although she is not badly off, she is very extravagant. Everyone says so.'

'She has been living in the South of France?'

'Where she made herself rather notorious, I believe.'

'Meanwhile, her fiancé is suffering from jaundice.'

'Indeed,' said Miss Weedon, smiling thinly again. 'I expect she will find someone to console her. Commander Foxe, for example.'

'Buster? How is he?'

'He might begin to take her out again. He retired from the Navy some years ago. He has got rather fat. It worries him terribly. He does all kinds of things for it. Every sort of diet. Cures at Tring. It is really his sole interest now.'

'And you thought Mrs. Haycock might take his mind off the weighing machine?'

Miss Weedon's mouth stiffened. I saw I had gone too far. She probably regretted her own indiscretion about Buster's past with Mrs. Haycock. I had not thought of Buster Foxe for years. Stringham had never cared for him. It sounded from Miss Weedon's tone as if Buster had been reduced—like Jeavons—to a purely subordinate position. There was a certain parallel in their situations. I wondered if they had ever met.

'And how is Mrs. Foxe herself?'

'Very well, I understand. As social as ever.'

'What does Charles do about money now?'

'Money is rather a difficulty,' said Miss Weedon, abandoning her air of cold malice, and now speaking as if we had returned to serious matters. 'His father, with that French wife of his in Kenya, has not much to spare. Mrs. Foxe has the Warrington money, but it is only for her lifetime. She spends it like water.'

At that moment Jeavons himself approached us, putting an end to any explanation Miss Weedon was about to offer on the subject of Stringham's financial resources.

'What do you make of Maisky?' asked Jeavons.

He spoke in a preoccupied, confidential tone, as if Miss Weedon's reply might make all the difference by its orientation to plans on foot for Maisky's education.

'I don't care for monkeys,' said Miss Weedon.

'Oh, don't you?' said Jeavons.

He stood pondering this flat, forthright declaration of anti-simianism on Miss Weedon's part. The notion that some people might not like monkeys was evidently entirely new to him; surprising, perhaps a trifle displeasing, but at the same time one of those general ideas of which one can easily grasp the main import without being necessarily in agreement. It was a theory that startled by its stark simplicity.

'Molly has taken a great fancy to him,' he said, at last.

'I know.'

'Oh, well,' said Jeavons. 'These fancies come and go.'

Miss Weedon made no attempt to deny the truth of that observation. Nor did she elaborate her dislike of monkeys. She continued to smile her arctic smile. Jeavons slowly strolled off again, as if to think out the implications of what Miss Weedon had said. I was aware once more of my strong disagreement with those—amongst whom I suspected Miss Weedon might be numbered—who found Jeavons without interest. On the contrary, he seemed to me, in his own way, rather a remarkable person. An encounter with him away from his own home confirmed that there existed more sides to him than might be apparent in the Jeavons drawing-room.

This episode took place a month or two later, on an evening that had begun with having a drink with Feingold in the pub near the Studio. Feingold had plans to write a satirical novel about life in the film business. He wanted to tell me the plot in the hope that I might be able to suggest a suitable ending to the story. Returning to London later than usual as a result of Feingold's unwillingness to treat the subject in hand briefly (he himself lived in the neighbourhood of the Studio), I decided to dine off a sandwich and a glass of beer at some bar. The pubs in the neighbourhood of my own flat had not much to offer, so, quite fortuitously, I entered an establishment off the south side of Oxford Street, where an illuminated sign indicated an underground buffet. It was the kind of place my old, deceased friend, Mr. Deacon, used to call a 'gin palace'.

At the foot of the stairs was a large, low-ceilinged room filled with shiny black-topped tables and red wicker arm-chairs. The bar, built in the shape of an L, took up most of two sides of this saloon, of which the pillars and marbled wall decoration again recalled Mr. Deacon's name by their resemblance to the background characteristic of his pictures: *Pupils of Socrates*, for example, or *By the Will of Diocletian*. No doubt this bar had been designed by someone who had also brooded long and fruitlessly on classical themes, determined to express in whatever medium available some boyhood memory of *Quo Vadis?* or *The Last Days of Pompeii*. The place was deserted except for the barman, and a person in a mackintosh who sat dejectedly before an empty pint tankard in the far corner of the room. In these oppressively Late Roman surroundings, after climbing on to a high stool at the counter, I ordered food.

I had nearly finished eating, when I became obscurely aware that the man in the corner had risen and was making preparations to leave. He walked across the room, but instead of mounting the stairs leading to the street, he came towards the bar where I was sitting. I heard him pause behind me. I thought that, unable at the last moment to tear himself away from the place, he was going to buy himself another drink. Instead, I suddenly felt his hand upon my shoulder.

'Didn't recognise you at first. I was just on my way out. Come and have one with me in the corner after you've finished your tuck-in.'

It was Jeavons. As a rule he retained even in his civilian clothes a faded military air, comparable with—though quite different from—that of Uncle Giles: both of them in strong contrast with the obsolete splendours of General Conyers. A safety pin used to couple together the points of Jeavons's soft collar under the knot of what might be presumed to

be the stripes of a regimental tie. That night, however, in a
somewhat Tyrolese hat with the brim turned down all the
way round, wearing a woollen scarf and a belted mackintosh, the *ensemble* gave him for some reason the appearance
of a plain-clothes man. His face was paler than usual.
Although perfectly steady on his feet, and speaking in his
usual slow, deliberate drawl, I had the impression he had
been drinking fairly heavily. We ordered some more
beer, and carried it across the room to where he had been
sitting.

'This your local?' he asked.

'Never been here before in my life. I dropped in quite by
chance.'

'Same here.'

'It's a long way from your beat.'

'I've been doing a pub crawl,' he said. 'Feel I have to
have one—once in a way. Does you good.'

There could be no doubt, after that, that Jeavons was
practising one of those interludes of dissipation to which
Lovell had referred, during which he purged himself, as it
were, of too much domesticity.

'Think there is going to be a war?' he asked, very unexpectedly.

'Not specially. I suppose there might be—in a year or
two.'

'What do you think we ought to do about it?'

'I can't imagine.'

'Shall I tell you?'

'Please do.'

'Declare war on Germany right away,' said Jeavons.
'Knock this blighter Hitler out before he gives further
trouble.'

'Can we very well do that?'

'Why not?'

'No government would dream of taking it on. The country wouldn't stand for it.'

'Of course they wouldn't,' said Jeavons.

'Well?'

'Well, we'll just have to wait,' said Jeavons.

'I suppose so.'

'Wait and see,' said Jeavons. 'That was what Mr. Asquith used to say. Didn't do us much good in 1914. I expect you were too young to have been in the last show?'

I thought that enquiry rather unnecessary, not by then aware that, as one grows older, the physical appearance of those younger than oneself offers only a vague indication of their precise age. To me, 'the Armistice' was a distant memory of my preparatory school: to Jeavons, the order to 'cease fire' had happened only the other day. The possibility that I might have been 'in the war' seemed perfectly conceivable to him.

'Some of it wasn't so bad,' he said.

'No?'

'Most of it perfect hell, of course. Absolute bloody hell on earth. Bloody awful. Gives me the willies even to think of it sometimes.'

'Where were you?'

'Joined up at Thirsk. Started off in the Green Howards. Got a commission after a bit in one of the newly-formed battalions of the Duke of Wellington's Regiment. I'd exchanged from the Duke's into the Machine-Gun Corps when I caught it in the tummy at Le Bassée.'

'Pretty unpleasant?'

'Not too good. Couldn't digest anything for ages. Can't always now, to tell the truth. Some of those dinners Molly gives. Still, digestion is a funny thing. I once knew a chap who took a bet he could eat a cut-off-the-joint-and-two-veg at a dozen different pubs between twelve o'clock and three on the same day.'

'Did he win his bet?'

'The first time,' said Jeavons, screwing up his face painfully at the thought of his friend's ordeal, 'someone else at the table lit a cigarette, and he was sick—I think he had got to about eight or nine by then. We all agreed he ought to have another chance. A day or two later he brought it off. Funny what people can do.'

Conversation could be carried no further because at this point 'closing time' was announced. Jeavons, rather to my surprise, made no effort to prolong our stay until the last possible moment. On the contrary, the barman had scarcely announced 'Time, gentlemen, please,' when Jeavons made for the stairs. I followed him. He seemed to have a course for himself clearly mapped out. When we reached the street, he turned once more to me.

'Going home?'

'I suppose so.'

'Wouldn't like to prolong this night of giddy pleasure with me for a bit?'

'If you have any ideas.'

'There is a place I thought of visiting tonight. A club of some sort—or a 'bottle party' as they seem to call it these days—that has just opened. Care to come?'

'All right.'

'A fellow came to see Molly some weeks ago, and gave us a card to get in any time we wanted. You know, you buy a bottle and all that. Makes you a member. Chap used to know Molly years ago. Gone the pace a bit. Now he is rather hard up and managing this hide-out.'

'I see.'

'Ever heard of Dicky Umfraville?'

'Yes. In fact I met him once years ago.'

'That's all right then. Umfraville is running the place. Molly would never dream of going near it, of course. Thought I might go and have a look-see myself.'

'Is Dicky Umfraville still married to Anne Stepney?'

'Don't think he is married to anyone at the moment,' said Jeavons. 'That would make his third or fourth, wouldn't it?'

'His fourth. She was quite young.'

'Come to think of it, Molly did say he'd had another divorce fairly recently,' said Jeavons. 'Anyway, he is more than usually on the rocks at the moment. He used to stay at Dogdene when Molly's first husband was alive. Gilded youth in those days. Not much left now. First-class rider, of course, Umfraville. Second in the National one year.'

While we talked, Jeavons had been making his way in a south-easterly direction. We continued in silence for some time, threading a path through a tangle of mean streets, past the plate-glass windows of restaurants opaque with steam.

'I think we must be close now,' said Jeavons, at last. 'I know more or less where the place is, and Dicky has drawn a sort of map at the back of the card.'

By that time we were in the neighbourhood of the Trouville Restaurant, a haunt of Uncle Giles, where one night, years before, I had joined him for a meal. The entrance to the club was concealed in an alleyway, by no means easy to find. We discovered the door at last. The name of the place was inscribed upon it on a minute brass plate, as if any kind of display was to be avoided. At the end of a narrow, dimly-lit passage a villainous-looking fellow with watery eyes and a nose covered with blue veins sat behind a rickety table. On the mention of Umfraville's name and production of the card, this Dickensian personage agreed that we might enter the precincts, after he had with his own hand laboriously inscribed our names in a book.

'The Captain's not in the club yet,' he said, as he shut this volume, giving at the same time a dreadful leer like that of a very bad actor attempting to horrify a pantomime audience. 'But I don't expect he'll be long now.'

'Tell him to report to the Orderly Room when he comes,' said Jeavons, causing the blue-nosed guardian of the door to reveal a few rotting teeth in appreciation of this military pleasantry.

The interior of the club was unimpressive. An orchestra of three, piano, drum and saxophone, were making a deafening noise in the corner of the room. A few 'hostesses' sat about in couples, gossiping angrily in undertones, or silently reclining in listless attitudes against the back of a chair. We seemed to be the first arrivals, not surprisingly, for it was still early in the evening for a place of this kind to show any sign of life. After a certain amount of palaver, a waiter brought us something to drink. Nothing about the club suggested that Umfraville's fortune would be made by managing it.

'Anyway, as I was saying,' remarked Jeavons, who had, in fact, scarcely spoken for some considerable time, except for his negotiations with the doorkeeper and waiter. 'As I was saying, you did have the odd spot of fun once in a while. Mostly on leave, of course. That stands to reason. Now I'll tell you a funny story, if you'll promise to keep it under your hat.'

'Wild horses won't drag it from me.'

'I suppose it's a story a real gent wouldn't tell,' said Jeavons. 'But then I'm not a real gent.'

'You are whetting my appetite.'

'I don't know why I should fix on you to hear the story,' said Jeavons, speaking as if he had given much thought to the question of who should be his confidant in this particular matter, and at the same time taking a packet of Gold Flake from his trouser pocket and beginning to tear open the wrapping. 'But I've got an idea it might amuse you. Did I see you talking to a fellow called Widmerpool at our house some little while ago—I believe it was the first night you ever came there?'

'You did.'

I was interested to find that new arrivals at the Jeavonses' were so accurately registered in the mind of the host.

'Know him well?'

'Quite well.'

'Then I expect you know he is going to marry someone called Mildred Haycock, who was also there that night.'

'I do.'

'Know her too?'

'Not really. I met her once when I was a small boy.'

'Exactly. You were a small boy and she was already grown up. In other words, she is quite a bit older than Widmerpool.'

'I know. She was a nurse at Dogdene when your wife was there, wasn't she——?'

'Wait a moment—wait a moment;' said Jeavons. 'Not so fast. Don't rush ahead. That's all part of the story.'

'Sorry.'

'Well, as I was saying, you did occasionally have a spot of fun in those days. Especially on leave. That's the point. No good going too fast. Had to dodge the A.P.M., of course. Still, that's by the way. Now I happened to get ninety-six hours' leave at short notice when I hadn't time to make any arrangements. Found the easiest thing was to spend the time in London. Didn't know a soul there. Not a bloody cat. Well, after I'd had a bit of a lie-up in bed, I thought I'd go to a show. The M.O. had told me to look in on Daly's, if I got the chance. It was a jolly good piece of advice. *The Maid of the Mountains*. Top-hole show. José Collins. She married into the aristocracy like myself, but that's nothing to do with the story. I bought myself a stall, thinking I might catch a packet in the next 'strafe' and never sit in a theatre again. Hadn't been there long before a large party came in and occupied the row in front of me. There were a couple of guardsmen in their grey great-coats and some ladies in evening dress. Among this lot was a nurse—a V.A.D.—who, as I thought—and it subsequently proved correct—began to give me the glad eye.'

Jeavons paused to gulp his drink. He shook his head and sighed. There was a long silence. I feared this might be the termination of the story: a mere chronicle of nostalgic memory: a face seen on that one occasion, yet always remembered: a romantic dream that had remained with him all his life. I spurred him gently.

'What did you do about it?'

'About what?'

'The nurse who gave you the glad eye.'

'Oh yes, that. In the interval we managed to have a word together in the bar or somewhere. Next thing I knew, I was spending my leave with her.'

'And this was——'

'Mrs. Haycock—or, as she then was, the Honourable Mildred Blaides.'

Jeavons's expression was so oracular, his tone so solemn, when he pronounced the name with the formal prefix attached, that I laughed. However, he himself remained totally serious in his demeanour. He sat there looking straight at me, as if the profound moral beauty of his own story delighted him rather than any purely anecdotal quality, romantic or banal, according to how you took it.

'And you never saw her again from that time until the other night?'

'Never set eyes on her. Of course, I've often heard Molly speak of Mildred Blaides and her goings-on, but I never knew it was the same girl. She and Molly used to meet sometimes. It so happened, for one reason or another, I was never there.'

'Did she say anything about it the other night?'

'Not a word. Didn't recognise me. After all, I suppose I've got to take my place in what must be a pretty long list by now.'

'You didn't say anything yourself?'

'Didn't want to seem to presume on a war-time commission, so I kept mum. Besides, it's just as well Molly shouldn't know. If you gas about that sort of thing too much, the story is bound to get round. Silly of me to tell you, I expect. You'll keep your trap shut, won't you?'

'Of course.'

'Just thought it might interest you—especially as you know Widmerpool.'

'It does—enormously.'

'That's the sort of thing that happens in a war. Happens to some chaps in peace-time too, I suppose. Not chaps like me. Haven't the temperament. Things have changed a lot now anyway. I don't mean people don't sleep with each other any longer. Of course they do. More than ever, if what everyone says nowadays is true. But the whole point of view is different somehow. I expect you were too young to have seen *The Bing Boys*?'

'No, I wasn't too young. I saw the show as a schoolboy.'

The band had momentarily ceased its hubbub. Jeavons leant forward. I thought he had something further to say which he wished to run no danger of being overheard. Instead, he suddenly began to sing, quite loud and in an unexpectedly deep and attractive voice:

'I could say such—wonderful things to you,
There would be such—wonderful things to do . . .'

Taking this, perhaps not unnaturally, as a kind of sum-
mons, two of the girls at a neighbouring table rose and
prepared to join us, a tall, muscular blonde, not altogether
unlike Mona, and a small, plump brunette, who reminded
me of a girl I used to know called Rosie Manasch. (Peter
Templer liked to say that you could recognise all the girls
you had ever met in a chorus: like picking out your friends
from a flock of sheep.) Jeavons immediately checked this
threatened incursion before it could take serious form by
explaining that we were waiting for the 'rest of the party'.
The girls withdrew. Jeavons continued the song as if there
had been no interruption:

'If you were the only—girl in the world,
And I was the only boy . . .'

He had only just time to finish before the band broke out
again in a deafening volume of sound, playing some tune
of very different tempo from that sung by Jeavons.

'People don't think the same way any longer,' he bawled
across the table. 'The war blew the whole bloody thing up,
like tossing a Mills bomb into a dug-out. Everything's
changed about all that. Always feel rather sorry for your
generation as a matter of fact, not but what we haven't all
lost our—what do you call 'em—you know—somebody used
the word in our house the other night—saying much what
I'm saying now? Struck me very forcibly. You know—
when you're soft enough to think things are going to be a
damned sight better than they turn out to be. What's the
word?'

'Illusions?'

'Illusions! That's the one. We've lost all our bloody

illusions. Put 'em all in the League of Nations, or somewhere like that. Illusions, my God. I had a few of 'em when I started. You wouldn't believe it. Of course, I've been lucky. Lucky isn't the word, as a matter of fact. Still people always talk as if marriage was one long roll in the hay. You can take it from me, my boy, it isn't. You'll be surprised when you get tied up to a woman yourself. Suppose I shouldn't say such things. Molly and I are very fond of each other in our own way. Between you and me, she's not a great one for bed. A chap I knew in the Ordnance, who'd carried on quite a bit with the girls, told me those noisy ones seldom are. Don't do much in that line myself nowadays, to tell the truth. Feel too cooked most of the time. Never sure the army vets got quite all those separate pieces of a toffee-apple out of my ribs. Tickles a bit sometimes. Still, you have to step out once in a way. Go melancholy mad otherwise. Life's a rum business, however you look at it, and—as I was saying—not having been born to all this high life, and so on, I can't exactly complain.'

It was clear to me now that, if Molly had had her day, so too in a sense had Jeavons, even though Jeavons's day had not been at all the same as his wife's: few days, indeed, could have been more different. He was one of those men, themselves not particularly aggressive in their relations with the opposite sex, who are at the same time peculiarly attractive to some women; and, accordingly, liable to be appropriated at short notice. The episode of Mildred Blaides illustrated this state of affairs, which was borne out by the story of his marriage. It was unlikely that these were the only two women in the course of his life who had decided to take charge of him. I was hoping for further reminiscences (though expecting none more extraordinary than that already retailed) when Dicky Umfraville himself arrived at our table.

Wearing a dinner jacket, Umfraville was otherwise un-changed from the night we had met at Foppa's. Trim, horsey, perfectly at ease with himself, and everyone around him, he managed at the same time to suggest the proximity of an abyss of scandal and bankruptcy threatening at any moment to engulf himself, and anyone else unfortunate enough to be within his immediate vicinity when the crash came. The charm he exercised over people was perhaps largely due to this ability to juggle with two contrasting, apparently contradictory attributes; the one, an underlying implication of sinister, disturbing undercurrents: the other, a soothing power to reassure and entertain. These incom-patible elements were always to be felt warring with each other whenever he was present. He was like an actor who suddenly appears on the stage to the accompaniment of a roll of thunder, yet utterly captivates his audience a second later, while their nerves are still on edge, by crooning a sentimental song.

'Why,' he said, 'this is a surprise. I never thought we should persuade you to come along here, Ted. Why didn't you bring Molly with you? Are they treating you all right? I see they've brought you a bottle. Apply to me if there is any trouble. Would you like to meet any of the girls? They are not a bad crowd. I can't imagine that you want any-thing of the sort.'

Jeavons did not answer. He barely acknowledged Um-fraville's greeting. Once more he was lost in thought. He had undoubtedly had a fair amount to drink. Umfraville was not at all put out by this reception. He pulled a chair up to the table and glanced across at me.

'We've met before somewhere,' he said.

'At Foppa's two or three years ago. You had just come back from Kenya. Hadn't you been racing with Foppa?'

'My God,' said Umfraville, 'I should think I do remember. Foppa and I had been to Caversham together. We are both interested in trotting races, which many people aren't in this country. You came in with a very charming young woman, while Foppa and I were playing piquet. Then your friend Barnby appeared with Lady Anne Stepney—and before you could say Jack Robinson, the next thing I knew was that the Lady Anne had become my fourth wife.'

I laughed, wondering what he was going to say next. I knew that his marriage to Anne Stepney had lasted only a very short time.

'I expect you heard that Anne and I didn't manage to hit it off,' he went on. 'Charming child, but the fact was I was too old for her. She didn't like grown-up life—and who shall blame her?'

He sighed.

'I don't like it much myself,' he said.

'Where is she now?'

I hardly knew whether the question was admissible. However, Umfraville had apparently achieved complete objectivity regarding his own life: certainly his matrimonial life.

'Living in Paris,' he said. 'Doing some painting, you know. She was always tremendously keen on her painting. I fell rather short on that score too. Can't tell a Sargent from a "Snaffles". She shares a flat with a girl who also walked out on her husband the other day. Come on, Ted, you mustn't go to sleep. I agree this place is pretty boring, but I can't have it turned into a doss-house. Not for the first week or so, anyway.'

Jeavons came too with a jerk. He began to beat time thoughtfully on the table.

'How are you doing here?' he asked.

He spoke severely, as if he had come to audit the accounts. Umfraville shrugged his shoulders.

'Depends how people rally round,' he said. 'I don't picture myself staying at this job long. Just enough to cover my most urgent needs—or rather my creditors' most urgent needs. These joints have a brief vogue, if they're lucky. We haven't been open long enough yet to see how things are going. I look upon your arrival, Ted, as a very good omen. Well, I suppose I must see everything about the place is going all right. Ought to have turned up earlier and done that already. I'll look in again. By the way, Max Pilgrim and Heather Hopkins are coming in later to do a turn.'

He nodded to us, and moved away. People were now arriving in the club by twos and threes. The tables round us began to fill up. The girls lost some of their apathy. These newcomers offered little or no clue to the style of the place. They belonged to that anonymous, indistinct race of night-club frequenters, as undifferentiated and lacking in individuality as the congregation at a funeral. None of them was in evening dress.

'Rum bird, Umfraville,' said Jeavons, thickly. 'Don't like him much. Knows everybody. Wasn't a bit surprised when it turned out you'd met him before. Molly used to see quite a lot of him in the old days when he was a johnny about town.'

'He married a girl much younger than himself as his fourth wife. They parted company, I hear.'

'I know. The Bridgnorths' second daughter,' said Jeavons. 'She has been to the house. Badly brought up. Been taken down a peg or two, I hope. Bad luck on Eddie Bridgnorth to have a girl like that. Done nothing to deserve it.'

Earlier in the evening, Jeavons had expressed only the vaguest knowledge of Umfraville's last marriage. Now, he seemed familiar with all its essential aspects. His awareness seemed quite unpredictable from one moment to another. The compassionate tone in which he had named

Lord Bridgnorth clearly voiced regret for a member of a caste rather than an individual, revealing for a split second a side of Jeavons on the whole concealed, though far more developed than might be supposed on brief acquaintance; the side, that is to say, which had by then entirely assimilated his wife's social standpoint. Indeed, the words might have been uttered by Alfred Tolland, so conventional, yet at the same time so unaffected, was the reflection that Eddie Bridgnorth had done nothing to deserve a rackety daughter.

'I think I'll make a further inspection of these quarters,' said Jeavons, rising. 'Just as well to know your way about.'

He made at first towards the band, but a waiter redirected him, and he disappeared through a small door. He was away a long time, during which two fresh elements were added to the composition of the room.

The first of these new components, a man and a woman, turned out to be Max Pilgrim and Heather Hopkins. They entered with the animation of professionals, almost as if their act had already begun, at once greeted by Umfraville who led them to a table near the band. I had never met Pilgrim, although I had more than once watched his performances at restaurants or cabarets, since that night, years before, when he had quarrelled so bitterly with poor Mr. Deacon at Mrs. Andriadis's party. Tall and stooping, smiling through large spectacles, there was something mild and parsonic about his manner, as if he were apologising for having to draw peoples' attention to their sins in so blatant a manner. He wore tails. Hopkins had cleaned herself up greatly since her application for the loan of an egg from Norah Tolland and Eleanor Walpole-Wilson. Her black coat and skirt, cut like a dinner jacket, had silk lapels above a stiff shirt, butterfly collar and black bow tie. Her silk stockings were black, too, and she wore a bracelet round her left ankle.

This couple had scarcely appeared when another, far less expected party came in, and were shown to a table evidently reserved for them. Mrs. Haycock led the way, followed by my old friend, Peter Templer; then Widmerpool, walking beside an unusually good-looking girl whose face I did not know. They were in evening dress. From the rather stiff way in which Templer carried himself, I guessed that he felt a shade self-conscious about the company he was keeping. By that time I was used to the idea that he no longer regarded Widmerpool with derision. After all, they did business together, and Widmerpool had helped Bob Duport to get a job. All the same, there remained something incongruous about finding Templer and Widmerpool embarked upon a *partie carrée* at a night club. Night clubs were so much to be regarded as Templer's natural element, and so little Widmerpool's, that there seemed even a kind of injustice that Widmerpool should in this manner be forced to operate in a field so inappropriate to himself; and, on top of that, for Templer to be covertly ashamed of his company.

In addition to his air of being—almost literally—a fish out of water, Widmerpool looked far from well. Still yellow from his jaundice, he had grown thinner. His dinner jacket hung on him in folds. His hair was ruffled. His back was bent like that of an elderly man. Perhaps it was this flagging aspect of Widmerpool's that made Templer seem more elegant than ever. He, too, was thinner than when I had last seen him. His habitual tendency was to look just a little too well dressed, and that evening he gave the appearance of having walked straight out of his tailor's wearing an entirely new outfit. This glossy exterior, in juxtapositior with Widmerpool, could hardly have been more sharply emphasised. The unknown pretty girl was wearing an unadventurous frock, but Mrs. Haycock was dressed to kill. Enclosed within a bright emerald-green dress with huge leg-of-mutton sleeves, she was talking with great vivacity to Templer, whose arm from time to time she took and squeezed. She looked younger than when I had last seen her.

Before any sign of recognition could take place between the members of this party and myself, the band withdrew from their position at the end of the room, and settled down at one of the tables. A moment later Pilgrim and Hopkins mounted the dais, Hopkins appropriating the pianist's stool, while Pilgrim lounged against the drum. He glanced at his nails, like a nervous don about to lecture a rowdy audience of undergraduates. Hopkins struck a few bars on the piano with brutal violence. By that time Jeavons had returned.

'Found it all right,' he said.

'Have you seen who has arrived?'

'Saw them on my way back. You know Mrs. H. doesn't look a bit different from what she looked like in 1917.'

This comment on Mrs. Haycock seemed to me an extraordinary proposition: either crudely untrue, or most uncomplimentary to her earlier appearance. In due course one learns, where individuals and emotions are concerned, that Time's slide-rule can make unlikely adjustments. Angular and flamboyant, Mrs. Haycock was certainly not without powers of attraction, but I doubted whether Jeavons saw in those severe terms. It was impossible to say. That side of her may, indeed, have constituted her charm for him both at that moment and in 1917. On the other hand, both then and in Umfraville's night club, she may have been equally no more than a romantic dream, a figure transcending any mere question of personal appearance. At that moment Pilgrim advanced a little way in front of the drum, and, in a shrill, hesitant voice, like that of an elderly governess, began to sing:

185

'Di, Di, in her collar and tie,
Quizzes the girls with a monocled eye,
Sipping her hock in a black satin stock,
Or shooting her cuffs over *pernod* or *bock* . . .'

'I've a damn good mind to ask her for a dance,' said
Jeavons. 'Who are they with? Do you know them?'

'The man is called Peter Templer. I've known him for
years.'

'And the other girl?'

'I don't know.'

'Who is Templer?'

'A stockbroker. He was divorced not so long ago from a
very pretty model, who then married a writer called
Quiggin. Templer is like your friend in the Ordnance, a
great one with the girls.'

'Looks it,' said Jeavons.

When Pilgrim and Hopkins had left their table, Umfraville had moved to the party of which Templer seemed
to be host. He was talking to Mrs. Haycock. Templer
began to gaze round the room. He caught sight of me and
waved. I signalled back to him. Meanwhile, Pilgrim was
continuing his song, while Hopkins thumped away vigorously, with a great deal of facility, at the piano.

'Like a torpedo, in brogues or tuxedo,
She's tearing around at Cap Cod, or the Lido;
From Bournemouth to Biarritz, the fashion parades
Welcome debonaire Di in her chic tailor-mades . . .'

'You see this sort of song, for instance,' said Jeavons.
'Who the hell wants to listen to something like that? God
knows what it is all about, for one thing. Songs were quite
different when I was younger.'

The song came to an end and there was a little clapping.

Templer crossed the dance floor to our table. I introduced him, explaining that Jeavons had brought me; and also that Jeavons knew Widmerpool and Mrs. Haycock. I told him that at once, to forestall comments that might easily be embarrassing in the mood to which Jeavons had abandoned himself.

'So you already know that Widmerpool is getting married?' said Templer. 'I was hoping to break the news to you. I am disappointed.'

For someone in general so sure of himself, he was a shade self-conscious at being caught entertaining Widmerpool in a haunt of this kind, hardly a routine place to take a business acquaintance. He had probably hoped that the news of Widmerpool's engagement, by its broad humour, would distract attention from his own immediate circumstances.

'The old boy behaved rather well about my brother-in-law, Bob,' he said, rather hurriedly. 'And then Dicky kept on pestering me to come to this dive of his. Do you know Dicky?'

'Just met him once before.'

'And then the girl I'm with loves to be taken to places she thinks "amusing". It seemed a chance of killing several birds with the same stone.'

'Who is your girl?'

'She is called Betty. I can never remember her married name. Taylor, is it? Porter? Something like that. We met at a dreadful bridge party the other day. Her husband is only interested in making money, she says. I can't imagine what she finds amiss in that. Rather a peach, isn't she?'

'Certainly.'

'Why don't you both come over and join us?'

Templer addressed the question to me, but he turned in the direction of Jeavons as if to persuade him.

'As you know our friend Widmerpool already,' said

Templer. 'I need not explain what he is like. I know he'll be glad to see both of you, even though he is a bit under the weather tonight.'

Rather to my surprise, Jeavons at once agreed to join the Templer party. I was not nearly so certain as Templer that Widmerpool would be glad to see us. Jeavons bored him; while Templer and I were such old friends that he might suspect some sort of alliance against himself. He was easily disturbed by such apprehensions.

'What is wrong with Widmerpool?'

'Feeling low generally,' said Templer. 'Mildred had to drag him out tonight. But never mind that. It is extraordinary those two should be engaged. Women may show some discrimination about whom they sleep with, but they'll marry anybody.'

Templer was already, so it appeared, on Christian name terms with Mrs. Haycock. We moved across, bearing our bottle with us. Widmerpool, as I could have foretold, did not look too well pleased to have us at the same table, but his state of health disposed him to show this no more than by offering a rather sour greeting. Mrs. Haycock, on the other hand, was delighted by this increase in numbers. Flushed in the face, she looked as hard as nails. She could hardly be called handsome, but there was a dash about her that Widmerpool could justly feel lacking in his own life as a bachelor. It was surprising to me not merely that he should be alarmed at the prospect of becoming her husband, but that he should ever have had the courage to propose; although, at the same time, plenty of reasons for his doing so presented themselves. Probably he was prepared—for he did most things rationally—to accept, even to welcome, attributes in a wife other men might have approached with caution. At the same time, the notion that he was entirely actuated by 'rational' motives was also no doubt far from the truth. He was possibly not 'in love', but at the same time impelled by feelings, if less definable than 'love', no less powerful. It was perhaps his imagination which had been captured; which is, after all, something akin to love. Who can say? Mrs. Haycock turned a dazzling smile upon us.

'I'm Molly's husband,' said Jeavons gruffly.

'But, of course.'

She held out her hand, cordially, but without any suggestion that she knew him apart from her recent visit to the Jeavons house. It was certain, I had no doubt on that point, that she remembered nothing of having met him on the earlier occasion. I was curious to see how he would conduct himself. Mrs. Haycock faced me.

'I know you are an old friend of Kenneth's,' she said. 'As you can see, the poor boy is still as yellow as a guinea, isn't he? It was over-eating that did it.'

'But he is always so careful about his food.'

'Of course, he fusses all the time,' she said. 'Or used to. That is just it. I won't stand any nonsense of that sort. I like my food. Naturally, if you are banting, that is another matter. What I can't stand is people who pick at carrots and patent foods and never have a drink.'

This description sounded a fairly exact definition of the meals Widmerpool enjoyed.

'I have been making him take me to some decent restaurants—such as there are in this country—and showed him how good food can be. I suppose some of it must have disagreed with him. He is back having his own way now, dining off a sardine and a glass of Malvern water.'

Widmerpool himself smiled feebly at all this, as if making no attempt to deny the truth of the picture presented by her of his medical condition. All the time she was speaking, I could think of nothing but the story Jeavons had told me of his former adventure with her. Conversation became general, only Widmerpool continuing to sit in bleak silence. Templer's girl had large, liquid eyes, and a drawl reminiscent of Mona's. She was evidently very taken with Templer, gazing at him all the time, as if she could not believe her luck. I asked her what she thought of the Pilgrim–Hopkins turn.

'Oh, they were good, weren't they?' she said. 'Didn't you think so, Peter?'

'A frightfully old-fashioned couple,' said Templer. 'The only reason they are here is because their act was a flop at the Café de Madrid. Still, I'm glad you liked them, darling. It shows what a sweet nature you have. But I don't want you to wear clothes like Miss Hopkins. You won't do that, will you?'

She found this dissent from her own opinion delicious, darting excited, apprehensive glances at him from under her eyelashes. I saw that it was no good attempting, even conversationally, to compete. Mrs. Haycock would make easier going. I asked whether she and Widmerpool had decided where they were going to live after they were married.

'That's rather a big question,' she said. 'Kenneth's business keeps him most of the time in London. I like the idea of making our headquarters in Paris. We could have a small flat over there quite cheaply—in some dingy neighbourhood, if necessary. But I've lived too long in France to want to live anywhere else now. Anyway, for most of the year. Then there are the boys. That's another problem.'

I thought for a second that she must refer to a personal obligation she owed to some male group living probably on the Riviera, to be generically thus classified. Seeing that she had not made herself clear, she added:

'My two sons, you know.'

'Oh, yes.'

'They are always cropping up.'

'Are they at school?'

'Yes, of course they are,' she said, as if that were a foolish question to ask. 'That is, when they haven't been expelled.'

She stared at me fixedly after saying this, still seeming to imply that I should already know about her sons, especially the fact that they were continually being expelled from school. Uncertain whether or not she intended to strike a jaunty or sombre note, I did not know whether to laugh or commiserate. In fact, so peculiar was her tone that I wondered now whether she were entirely sane. Although in most respects impossible to imagine anyone less like Mrs. Conyers, a change of expression, or tone of voice, would suddenly recall her sister. For example, when she spoke of her children, I was reminded of Mrs. Conyers invoking the General. There was, however, one marked difference between them. Mrs. Conyers bestowed about her a sense of absolute certainty that she belonged—could only belong—to the class from which she came, the world in which she lived. Mrs. Haycock, on the other hand, had by then largely jettisoned any crude certainties of origin. She may even have decided deliberately to rid herself of too embarrassing an inheritance of traditional thought and behaviour. If so, she had been on the whole successful. Only from time to time, and faintly, she offered a clue to correct speculation about herself: just as Jeavons would once in a way display the unmistakable action of his marriage on his point of view. On the whole, Mrs. Haycock's bluff manner suggested long association with people who were rich, but rich without much concern about other aspects of life.

'Of course I know they are dreadfully badly behaved,' she said. 'But what am I to do?'

She had that intense, voluble manner of speaking, often characteristic of those who are perhaps a little mad: a flow of words so violent as to give an impression of lack of balance.

'How old are they?'

'Fourteen and fifteen.'

Widmerpool, who at that moment looked in no state to shoulder such responsibilities as a couple of adolescent step-sons habitually expelled from school, leant across the table to address Mrs. Haycock.

'I think I'll retire for a minute or two,' he said, 'and see what taking a couple of those pills will do.'

'All right, my own, off you go.'

Widmerpool scrambled out from where he sat in the corner next to the wall, and made for the door.

'Isn't he priceless?' said Mrs. Haycock, almost with pride. 'Do you know his mother?'

'I've met her.'

'Do you know that she suggested that she should live with us after we were married?'

Again she spoke in that strange, flat voice, looking hard at me, so that I did not know how to reply; whether to express horror or indulge in laughter. However, she herself seemed to expect no answer to her question. Whatever her feelings about Widmerpool's mother, they lay too deep for words. Instead of continuing to discuss her personal affairs, she pointed to Jeavons.

'Your friend seems to be going to sleep,' she said. 'You know I have always heard so much about him, and, although I've known Molly for years, I only met him for the first time the other night.'

Her observation about Jeavons's state was true. Templer and his girl had risen to dance, and Jeavons had fallen into a coma similar to those in which General Conyers would sometimes sink. Jeavons seemed to have lost all his earlier enthusiasm to dance with Mrs. Haycock, a change of heart due probably to the amount of beer he had drunk earlier in the evening, before we met. I roused him, and he moved to the other side of the table, into the seat next to Mrs. Haycock.

'How is Molly?' she asked him.

'Molly is all right.'

He did not sound too bright. However, he must have understood that something was expected of him, and made an effort.

'Where are you staying?' he asked.

'Jules's.'

'In Jermyn Street?'

'I always have a suite there when I come over.'

Jeavons suddenly straightened himself.

'Come and dance,' he said.

This surprised me. I had supposed him to be speaking without much serious intention, even when he had first said he wanted to dance with her. After he had all but gone to sleep at the table, I thought he had probably found sufficient entertainment in his own reflections. On the contrary, he had now thrown off his drowsiness. Mrs. Haycock rose without the smallest hesitation, and they took the floor together. I was sure she had not recognised Jeavons; equally certain that she was aware, as women are, that some disturbing element was abroad, involving herself in some inexplicable manner. She danced well, steering him this way and that, while Jeavons jogged up and down like a marionette, clutching her to him as he attempted the syncopated steps of some long-forgotten measure. I remembered that he himself never danced when the carpet was rolled back and the gramophone played at the Jeavonses' house. I was still watching them circle the floor when

Widmerpool returned from his absence in the inner recesses of the club. He looked worse than ever. There could be no doubt that he ought to go home to bed. He sat down beside me and groaned.

'I think I shall have to go home,' he said.

'Didn't the pills work?'

'Quite useless. I am feeling most unwell. Why on earth have you come here with that fellow Jeavons?'

'I ran across him earlier in the evening, and he brought me along. I've met Umfraville before, who runs this place.'

I felt, I did not know why, that it was reasonable for him to make this enquiry in an irritable tone; that some apology was indeed required for my appearance there at all. It was clear that the sooner Widmerpool left, the better for his state of health. He looked ghastly. I was going to suggest that he should make some sign to recall Mrs. Haycock to the table, so that they might leave immediately, when he began to speak in a lower voice, as if he had something on his mind.

'You know what we were talking about when we last met?'

'Yes—your engagement, you mean?'

'I—I haven't had an opportunity yet.'

'You haven't?'

I felt unwilling to reopen all that matter now, especially in his present state.

'But we've been asked to stay at Dogdene.'

'Yes?'

In spite of his malaise, Widmerpool could not keep from his voice a note of justifiable satisfaction.

'You know the house, of course.'

'I've never stayed there.'

'No, no,' he said. 'I mean you know about it. The Sleafords' place.'

'Yes, I know all that.'

'Do you think it would be—would be the moment?'

'It might be a very good one.'

'Of course it would make a splendid background. After all, if any house in the country has had a romantic history, it is Dogdene,' he said.

The reflection seemed to give him strength. I thought of Pepys, and the 'great black maid'; and immediately Widmerpool's resemblance to the existing portraits of the diarist became apparent. He had the same obdurate, put-upon, bad-tempered expression. Only a full-bottomed wig was required to complete the picture. True, Widmerpool shared none of Pepys's sensibility where the arts were concerned; in the æsthetic field he was a void. But they had a common preoccupation with money and professional advancement; also a kind of dogged honesty. Was it possible to imagine Widmerpool playing a similar rôle with the maid? There I felt doubtful. Was that, indeed, his inherent problem? Could it be that his love affairs had always fallen short of physical attack? How would he deal with Mrs. Haycock should that be so? I wondered whether their relationship was really so incongruous as it appeared from the exterior. So often one thinks that individuals and situations cannot be so extraordinary as they seem from out-side: only to find that the truth is a thousand times odder.

While Widmerpool sat in silence, and I pondered these matters, there came suddenly a shrill burst of sound from the dance floor. I saw Mrs. Haycock break away violently from Jeavons. She clasped her hands together and gave peal after peal of laughter. Jeavons, too, was smiling, in his quiet, rather embarrassed manner. Mrs. Haycock caught his hand, and led him through the other dancing couples, back to the table. She was in a great state of excitement.

'Look here,' she said. 'We've just made the most marvellous discovery. Do you know that we both knew each other in the war—when I was a nurse?'

'What, when you were at Dogdene?' asked Widmerpool.

His mind, still full of the glories of that great house, remained unimpressed by this news. To him nothing could be more natural than the fact that Mrs. Haycock and Jeavons had met. She had been a V.A.D. at Dogdene: Jeavons had been a convalescent there. There was no reason why Widmerpool should even speculate upon the possibility that their Dogdene interludes had not overlapped. He was, in any case, not at all interested in the lives of others.

'I never recognised him, which was quite mad of me, because he looks *just* the same.'

'Oh, really?' said Widmerpool.

He could not see what the fuss was about.

'Isn't it absolutely marvellous to meet an old friend like that?'

'Why, yes, I suppose it is,' said Widmerpool, without any great conviction.

'It's scrumptious.'

Widmerpool smiled feebly. This was plainly a situation he found hard to envisage. In any case, he was at that moment too oppressed by his own state of health to attempt appreciation of Mrs. Haycock's former friendships.

'Look here, Mildred,' he said, 'I am still feeling far from well. I really think I will go home. What about you? Shall I take you back?'

Mrs. Haycock was appalled.

'Go back?' she said. 'Why, of course not. I've only just arrived. And, anyway, there are millions of things I want to talk about after making this marvellous discovery. It is too priceless for words. To think that I never knew all these years. It is really *too* extraordinary that we should never have met. I believe Molly did it on purpose.'

Widmerpool, to do him justice, did not seem at all surprised at this not very sympathetic attitude towards his own condition. There was something dignified, even a little touching, about the manner in which he absolutely accepted the fact that his state of health did not matter to Mrs. Haycock in the least. Perhaps by then already inured to indifference, he had made up his mind to expect no more from married life. More probably, this chance offered to slip away quietly by himself, going home without further trouble—even without delivering Mrs. Haycock to her hotel—was a relief to him. In any case, he seemed thankful, not only that no impediment had been put in his way of escape, but that Mrs. Haycock herself was in the best possible mood at the prospect of her own abandonment.

'Then I can safely leave you with Peter Templer and Mrs. Taylor—or is it Mrs. Porter?' he said. 'You will also have Nicholas and Mr. Jeavons to look after you.'

'My dear, of course, of course.'

Widmerpool rose a little unsteadily. Probably the people round thought, quite mistakenly, that he had had too much to drink.

'I shall go then,' he said. 'I will ring you up tomorrow, Mildred. Make my apologies to Peter.'

'Night, night,' she said, not unkindly.

Widmerpool nodded to the rest of us, then turned, and picked his way through the dancers.

'But this is too, too amusing,' said Mrs. Haycock, taking Jeavons by the arm. 'To think we should meet again like this after all these years.'

She poured out another drink for himself, and passed the bottle round the table, so delighted by the discovery of Jeavons that Widmerpool seemed now dismissed entirely from her mind. The sentiments of Jeavons himself at that moment were hard to estimate; even to know how drunk he was. He might have reminded Mrs. Haycock of their former encounter with some motive in his mind, or merely on impulse. The information could even have emerged quite fortuitously in the course of one of his long, rambling anecdotes. No one could predict where his next step would lead. Outwardly, he gave no impression of intoxication, except for those intermittent bouts of sleepiness, in which, for that matter, he probably often indulged himself at home when dead sober. Templer and his girl returned to the table.

'This is really rather a grim place,' said Templer. 'What do you say to moving on somewhere else—the Slip-in, or somewhere like that?'

'Oh, but darling Peter,' said Mrs. Haycock, who had, so it appeared, met Templer for the first time that evening. 'I've just begun to enjoy myself so much. Kenneth decided he wasn't feeling well enough to stay, so he has gone home —with many apologies—and now I have just found one of my oldest, my very oldest, friends here.'

She pointed to Jeavons.

'Oh, yes,' said Templer.

He looked a bit surprised; but there was, after all, no reason why Jeavons should not be one of her oldest friends, even if, in Templer's eyes, he was rather an oddity. If Templer's first predisposition had been embarrassment at being caught in a party with Widmerpool, his mood had later changed to one of amusement at the insoluble problem of why I myself was visiting a night club with Jeavons. Jeavons was not an easy man to explain. Templer had none of Chips Lovell's appreciation of the subtleties of such matters. The Jeavons house, irretrievably tinged, in however unconventional a manner, with a kind of life against which he had rigidly set his face, would have bored Templer to death. Mrs. Haycock was, for some reason, another matter; he could tolerate her. · Patently rackety, and habituated to association with what Uncle Giles called 'all sorts'—different, for some reason, from Molly Jeavons's 'all sorts'—she presented no impediment to Templer. He sat down beside her and began to discuss other places that might be more amusing than Umfraville's club. Umfraville himself now returned, bringing with him Max Pilgrim and Heather Hopkins.

'May we join you for a moment?' he said. 'You know, Mildred, I don't believe we have met since that terrible night at Cannes in—what was it?—about 1923, when Milly Andriadis gave that great party, and we walked round the port together and watched the sunrise.'

We made room for them. Hopkins and Pilgrim were on their best behaviour. Templer's girl seemed for the moment almost to have forgotten him in the excitement of sitting with such celebrities. I found myself next to Templer and we had a moment to talk.

'How are you, Nick,' he said. 'I haven't seen you for centuries.'

'No worse—and you?'

'Not too bad,' said Templer. 'Family worries of various kinds, though there is a lot to be said for no longer being married. The usual trouble is raging with Bob and that sister of mine. No sooner does Bob get a good job than he goes off with some girl. All men are brothers, but, thank God, they aren't all brothers-in-law. I believe Jean has left him again, and gone to stay in Rome with Baby Wentworth—or whatever Baby Wentworth is now called after marrying that Italian.'

It was quite a good test, and I came out of it with flying colours; that is to say, without any immediate desire to buy an air ticket to Rome.

'You did know my sister, Jean, didn't you?' he said. 'I

mean I haven't been telling you a long story about someone you've never met?'

'Of course I knew her. And your other sister, too. I
met her ages ago.'

'Baby Wentworth is a cousin of mine,' said Mrs. Haycock, suddenly breaking off an argument with Hopkins
regarding the private life of the barman at the Carlton
Hotel at Cannes. 'What a pretty girl she is. When my
father died, he hadn't managed to produce a son, so Baby's
father succeeded. Her brother, Jack Vowchurch, is rather
hell, I believe. I've never met him. They were quite distant
cousins, and we never saw anything of them. Then one
day at Antibes someone pointed out Baby to me. Didn't
Sir Magnus Donners have rather a fancy for her? She was
with him then.'

'Wasn't your father the chap who rode his horse upstairs
after dinner?' asked Jeavons, wholly unexpectedly.

'Yes, of course he was,' said Mrs. Haycock. 'His favourite
hunter. That was before I was born. I think he was supposed to be celebrating something. "Peace with Honour",
would it have been? That kind of thing. I believe that was
the story. We had a hunting-box at Melton Mowbray that
season. They had to demolish the side wall of the house to
retrieve the animal. It cost the hell of a lot of money, I
know.'

Once again, when she spoke of her father, I was reminded of Mrs. Conyers, even though the phraseology of
the narrative was so different from any her sister would
have employed.

'And then there was some other story,' insisted Jeavons.
'Setting fire to a fellow's newspaper in a train. Something
like that.'

This interest in Lord Vowchurch on the part of Jeavons
I found astonishing.

'There are absolutely hundreds, darling,' said Mrs. Haycock. 'Do you know about when he squirted mauve ink over an archbishop at a wedding?'

'I met such a sweet archbishop at the Theatrical Garden Party last year,' said Pilgrim. 'Perhaps he wasn't an archbishop, but just a bishop. He wore a hat just like one of Heather's.'

'I might get a clerical hat,' said Hopkins. 'That's not a bad idea. There is a place off Oxford Street where they sell black boaters. I've always wanted one.'

I asked if she had been seeing much of Norah Tolland and Eleanor Walpole-Wilson.

'Oh, those two girls,' she said. 'I thought I'd met you before somewhere. No, I haven't been seeing them. I found out Eleanor had said a very unkind thing about me. I thought she was a friend, but I see I made a mistake.'

'Look here,' said Jeavons, who had cast off inertia and was now in his most lively mood. 'Do you remember how that song used to go:

> "He ran a pin
> In Gwendolyn,
> In Lower Grosvenor Place . . ."

I can't remember the exact words.'

By this time I was becoming tired of Umfraville's night club. Like Widmerpool, I wished to go home. Jeavons's companionship demanded an almost infinite capacity for adaptation to changed moods and circumstances. In many ways sympathetic, he lacked any of that familiar pattern of behaviour to be found, say, in Quiggin, so that in the last resort his company was exhausting rather than stimulating. Umfraville went off to attend to the club's administration. Discussion began once more as to whether the party should move elsewhere.

'I'll tell you what,' said Mrs. Haycock. 'If you all want to go to the Slip-in, why not leave me here with Ted. He and I will talk about old times for a bit. Then he can see me home.'

That was agreed. There was still a lot of talk. I left before the final plan was put into execution. Out in the passage, Umfraville was instructing the villainous, blue-nosed custodian as to who could, and who could not, wisely be admitted to the club.

'Not going?' he said. 'It's early yet.'

'I've got to get up early tomorrow and write filmscripts.'

'Good God,' he said. 'But, look here, just before you go, what's happened to Mildred Haycock these days? I hadn't seen her in an age. She seems to be holding up pretty well. I know Peter Templer, but who was the other chap who left the party early on?'

'He is called Widmerpool. She is engaged to him.'

'Is she, indeed? What does he do?'

'A bill-broker.'

Umfraville nodded his head sagely.

'Come again,' he said. 'Now that you know the way.'

I passed through empty streets, thinking that I, too, should be married soon, a change that presented itself in terms of action rather than reflection, the mood in which even the most prudent often marry: a crisis of delight and anxiety, excitement and oppression.

5.

A BACKGROUND of other events largely obscured the steps leading up to my engagement to Isobel Tolland. Of this crisis in my life, I remember chiefly a sense of tremendous inevitability, a feeling that fate was settling its own problems, and too much reflection would be out of place. Marriage, as I have said, is a form of action, of violence almost: an assertion of the will. Its orbit is not to be charted with precision, if misrepresentation and contrivance are to be avoided. Its facts can perhaps only be known by implication. It is a state from which all objectivity has been removed. I shall say something, however, of the incident which at this juncture chiefly distracted attention from my own affairs.

Although that evening when we had dined at Thrubworth had been by no means the sole occasion when Quiggin had announced that he wanted to 'see China and judge for himself', no one among his acquaintances supposed him at all likely to set sail at once for the Far East. The words were generally—and, as it turned out, correctly—assumed to be in the main rhetorical: merely buttressing opinions already propagated by him about the ominous situation in Asia. There was, for example, the matter of fare. High as his reputation stood as a critic, it was doubtful whether any publisher would be prepared to advance enough on a projected travel book, with a political bias, to transport Quiggin so far; while Erridge, sympathetic to the wish, had at the same time shown no impulse to foot the bill. Doubts had been maliciously expressed by Mark Members, just returned from his lecture tour in America, as to whether, when it came to the point, Quiggin would be impatient to enter an area in which the Japanese Army was at that time engaged in active operations. Members may have been unjust. He was certainly applying to Quiggin the heartless criticism of an old friend. All the same, I should have been surprised to hear that Quiggin had set out upon that journey.

On the other hand, when Erridge for the same reason—'to see for himself'—turned out to be on his way to China, there was less to wonder at. Erridge had already shown himself prepared to undergo uncomfortable forms of travel; he was undoubtedly in a restless state of mind; he was interested in the political implications of the situation: finally, he could afford to buy a ticket. The enterprise might be the result of Quiggin's advocacy, or his own gnawing sense of moral obligation. The motive was almost immaterial. There was another far more absorbing aspect of his departure when it came about. He did not go alone. He took Mona with him.

Naturally this affair was discussed at great length at houses such as the Jeavonses', where no details were available, beyond the fact that Erridge and Mona were together on a P. & O. liner bound for the East; while Quiggin had been left in England. Their precise destination was unknown. The immediate Tolland family were, naturally, in a ferment of interest. Even so, the story made on the whole less stir than might be thought; for Erridge had by then so firmly established a reputation for eccentricity that those who knew him personally were prepared for anything. Since he inhabited no particular social milieu, his doings affected few individuals directly. Such persons were chiefly a small group of hangers-on, like Quiggin or Howard Craggs, the Left Wing publisher, and the members of some of Erridge's committees. For the rest of the world, those to whom his name alone was familiar, his behaviour as usual took on the unsubstantial shape of a minor paragraph in the newspaper, momentarily catching the attention, without at the same time giving a conviction of its subject's existence in 'real life'. Uncle Giles, with his very different circumstances, was in much the same case, in that no one knew, or, for that matter, greatly cared what he would do next, provided he made no disastrous marriage and kept out of prison. In Erridge's position, the question of marriage now loomed steeply for his relations, a matter of keen speculation, particularly since this was the first occasion when he was known to have been closely associated with any woman.

All this had considerable bearing on my own life at the time, because my engagement was made public in the same week that the Erridge–Mona story broke, and was naturally overshadowed—especially upon my first meeting with Katherine, Lady Warminster—by this far more striking family convulsion. Some people considered Mona's abandonment of Quiggin less remarkable than the fact that she should have stayed with him for several years. Others took the opportunity to recall that, after crossing the Rubicon of leaving Templer, further changes of partner were inevitable. That was all very well, but I had to admit to myself that, when I had seen them together at Thrubworth, I had never guessed they were about to run away together. Erridge had shown no sign whatever of having any so desperate a plan in view, while Mona's interest in him had appeared to be no more than the natural product of her own boredom at the cottage. Possibly at that time neither had contemplated any such development. All at once the urgency of action had swept irresistibly down upon them: a sudden movement that altered the value of every piece on the board. This would deal a serious blow to

Quiggin. Even if he had never gone through the ceremony of marriage with Mona (which now seemed probable), his close relations with Erridge would scarcely survive such conduct; or would, at best, take some little time to repair on Erridge's return from China.

This escapade of Erridge's—at present it was spoken of merely as an escapade, because any question of marriage must in the first instance depend upon whether or not Mona was already Quiggin's wife—very considerably magnetised the atmosphere when for the first time I came to see his stepmother. No one yet knew how much Lady Warminster, on the whole alarmingly well informed on all topics connected with her relations, had up to that time been able to discover about Erridge and Mona. She was suspected, as usual, of possessing more information than she was prepared to admit. Like a foreign statesman, who, during important international negotiations, insists upon the medium of an interpreter in spite of his own familiarity with the language in which discussion is being conducted, she preferred every approach to be devious, and translated into her own idiom.

Although, by then, I had often visited the house in Hyde Park Gardens, she and I had not met on those earlier occasions, chiefly because Lady Warminster's health kept her for weeks at a time confined to her room. Views differed as to the extent to which hypochondria governed her life, some alleging that no one enjoyed better health, others taking her side in insisting that, delicate since childhood, she bore her ailments courageously. Smaller, older, quieter in manner and more handsome than Molly Jeavons, she was also much more awe-inspiring. Something of the witch haunted her delicate, aquiline features and transparent ivory skin: a calm, autumnal beauty that did not at all mask the amused, malicious, almost insane light that glinted all the time in her infinitely pale blue eyes. When young, she must have been very good-looking indeed.

Unlike her sister, who was entirely detached from intellectual interests of any sort, Lady Warminster lived largely in a world of the imagination. Her house, a complete contrast to the Jeavonses', reflected the more ordered side of her nature, surprising by the conventionality of its taste and air of stylised repose; at least until the rooms given over to her stepchildren were reached. These quiet, rich, rather too heavy decorations and furniture were deceptive. Little about the house could be thought quiet, or conventional, when closely examined. Perhaps, after all, when closely examined, no sort of individual life can truly be so labelled. However, against this formal background, when her health allowed, Lady Warminster wrote her books, historical studies of the dominating women of the past: Catherine the Great: Christina of Sweden: Sarah, Duchess of Marlborough: volumes rarely mentioned in the press, though usually kindly treated by such critics as noticed them, on account of their engaging impetuosity of style and complete lack of pretension to any serious scholarship.

This literary preoccupation with feminine authority had come to Katherine Warminster, so it appeared, only after her second widowhood. Like her sister, Molly, she had no child by either husband, the first of whom had been one of those 'well-born' City men for whom Peter Templer used to express such aversion. He had been a fairly successful stockbroker, fond of hunting and shooting, a man, so far as could be judged, with no salient characteristic. His wife had spent most of her days with friends who belonged to a world quite other than his own; latterly submitting to him in their marriage only to the extent of living in the country, where she was bored to death. She can have seen little more of Lord Warminster, when married to him, much of whose time was spent abroad unaccompanied by his wife, fishing in Iceland or pig-sticking in Bengal. This status of having twice married, without, so it might seem, great attachment to either husband, perhaps gave Lady Warminster the mysterious, witch-like quality she dispensed so pervasively about her.

The second marriage was said—quite unexpectedly—to have improved, on the whole, Erridge's relations with his father, with whom, without any open quarrel, he had never been on good terms. Lord Warminster had accepted his son's idiosyncrasies stoically, together with anything else of which he disapproved in his children, attributing everything to their mother's Alford blood. The rest of the Tolland brothers and sisters had lived—Norah was an exception—amicably with their stepmother: the younger ones entirely brought up by her. Lady Warminster, eccentric herself, showed a decent respect for eccentricity. She had no wish to interfere with other people, her stepchildren or anyone else, provided her own convenience was not threatened, so that the Tollands were left largely to their own devices. Life at Hyde Park Gardens might be ruthless, but it was played out on a reasonably practical basis, in which every man was for himself and no quarter was given; while at the same time a curtain of relatively good humour was usually allowed to cloak an inexorable recognition of life's inevitable severities.

I was fortunate enough already to have established myself to some small extent in Lady Warminster's good graces by a book written a year or two before which she happened to have enjoyed, so that my own reception might have been a worse one. Even so, with a person of her sort that was not a matter upon which to presume. For a time we discussed affairs personal to Isobel and myself, and then, as soon as these could be politely, and quite kindly, dismissed, Lady

Warminster gave a smile that showed plainly we should turn to more intriguing topics.

'I think you are one of the few people, either in or out of the family, who have met Erridge lately,' she said. 'So that you must now tell me what you think about this trip of his to China.'

I assured her that I knew little or nothing of Erridge and his movements, but that the journey seemed a reasonable one for him to make in the light of his interests and way of life. I admitted that I had heard him discuss a visit to China.

'I agree with you,' she said. 'Erridge is much too much by himself. He will not be alone on the voyage, I think, will he?'

That was not easy to answer. I did not wish, at this early stage in our relationship, to be detected telling, or, indeed, implying, a deliberate lie. I hoped equally to avoid revealing all that was known about Erridge and Mona, scanty as that might be. I said that I knew no details about the arrangements made by Erridge for his journey.

'There are always plenty of people to talk to on boats,' I suggested, with a sense of descending into banality of the most painful kind.

'Of course,' she said, as if that notion had never before been so well presented to her. 'Do you like the sea?'

'Not at all.'

'Nor me,' she said. 'There is nothing I detest more than a sea voyage. But surely he is taking a secretary, or some-one of that sort. I think he will. It will be so lonely other-wise. Especially as he is used to living by himself. You are never so lonely as when among a lot of people you do not know.'

It was impossible to tell whether the reference to 'a secretary' designated Mona, or some new figure in Erridge's life;

or was merely a random shot to draw information.

'I don't think I know about a secretary.'

'Perhaps I am mistaken. Someone may have said something of the sort. What did you think of Thrubworth? Erridge does not take much interest in the house, I am afraid. Still less in the grounds.'

I commented on Thrubworth and its surroundings, again aware that banality had not been avoided. Lady Warminster sighed. She moved her thin, pale hands, covered with a network of faint blue veins, lightly over the surface of a cushion.

'You were staying in the neighbourhood, I think.'

'Yes.'

'Not, by any chance, with the writer, J. G. Quiggin?'

'Yes—with J. G. Quiggin. I have known him a long time. Do you read his articles?'

'I was so interested when I heard Erridge had him living in that cottage. I enjoy Mr. Quiggin's reviews so much, even when I do not agree with them. They have not been appearing lately.'

'No. I haven't seen any of them lately.'

'Is there a Mrs. Quiggin?'

'Yes, she——'

'But I do not know why I am asking you this, because Susan and Isobel told me how they met you and the Quiggins, both of them, at Thrubworth. She is a great beauty, is she not?'

'I think she might certainly be called a great beauty.'

'An actress?'

'No, a model. But she thinks of going on the films.'

'Does she? And what does Mr. Quiggin think about that?'

'He seemed quite to like the idea.'-

'Did he?' she said. 'Did he? How strange.'

She paused for a moment.

'I like his articles so much,' she went on, after a few seconds. 'He is such—such a broad-minded man. So few critics are broad-minded. You know I want to talk to you about the new book I am writing myself. Will you give me your advice about it?'

For the time being the subject of Erridge was abandoned. I was glad of that. Lady Warminster had either learnt enough, or decided that for the moment, whatever her available knowledge, she would pursue the matter no further. Instead she talked for a time about Frederica, explaining that she had been so named on account of a Tolland great-uncle, a secretary of legation in Prussia, who, sharing an interest in painting, had been on friendly terms with the Empress Frederick. That was how the name had come into the family; that explained why Alfred Tolland had wanted to hear Mrs. Conyers's anecdote about the Empress, the night we had met at the Jeavonses'. Lady Warminster represented to a high degree that characteristic of her own generation that everything may be said, though nothing indecorous discussed openly. Layer upon layer of wrapping, box after box revealing in the Chinese manner yet another box, must conceal all doubtful secrets; only the discipline of infinite obliquity made it lawful to examine the seamy side of life. If these mysteries were observed everything might be contemplated: however unsavoury: however unspeakable. Afterwards, thinking over the interview when I had left the house, I knew something of what Alfred Tolland could feel after one of Molly Jeavons's interrogations. Lady Warminster might be outwardly quieter than her sister: her capacity for teasing was no less highly developed. A long time later, when the subject of Erridge and Mona had become a matter of common talk at the Jeavonses'—gossip which she must have known from her sister, even though they met rather rarely—Lady Warminster continued to refer to the association under enigmatic pseudonyms.

This mannered obscurity of handling the delicate problems of family life had nothing in common with the method of Chips Lovell, who, as I have indicated, spent a good deal of his time at the Studio telling the other scriptwriters about his relations. It would be easy to imagine a community in which this habit might have given offence, since many people feel disquisitions of that kind in some manner to derogate their own importance, few being interested in how others live. Lovell's material was presented with little or no editing, so it was for the listener to decide for himself whether the assumption in him of a working knowledge of the circles in which Lovell moved, or liked to think he moved, was complimentary or the reverse. Feingold, I think, considered the whole of these Lovell annals a fabrication from start to finish, a dream life legitimate in one exercising the calling of script-writer. He treated Lovell's stories of duchesses and grand parties like brilliantly improvised accounts of a brush with gangsters or Red Indians, narrated as if such florid adventures had not been in the least imaginary. Hegarty, on the other hand, on the rare occasions when he listened to anything anyone else said, would immediately cap all Lovell's anecdotes with stories of his own, sometimes sharp enough in their own way, but at the same time petrified into that strange, lifeless, formalised convention to illustrate human experience, particularly current among persons long associated with films. For my own part, I always enjoy hearing the details of other people's lives, whether imaginary or not, so that I found this side of Lovell agreeable.

When someone repeatedly tells you stories about their relations, pictures begin at last to form in the mind, tinged always in colours used by the narrator; so that after listening day after day to Lovell's recitals, I had become not only well versed in the rôle of each performer, but also involuntarily preoccupied with their individual behaviour. This concern for Lovell's relations had grown into something like a furtive interest in the comic strip of a daily paper, a habit not admitted to oneself. Lovell covered a good deal of ground. He was as ready to contemplate the doings of some distant cousins of his, whose only claim to fame seemed to be that they had emigrated to Vancouver and returned to live at Esher, as to recount the more splendid aspects of ancestral archives, for example, the epic of his mother's elopement with his father at a moment when her parents supposed her all but engaged to his more eligible cousin.

In these sagas, Lovell's 'second Sleaford uncle' (to give him his nephew's initial label) played a surprisingly small part. That was altogether unexpected. Lovell liked talking about Dogdene, but not about his uncle. The fact was that Lord Sleaford lived a very secluded life there, undertaking in the neighbourhood a bare minimum of such duties as were expected of a landowner of his magnitude. He would give a small shooting party from time to time ('shepherd's pie for luncheon,' Lovell said, 'and not enough sprouts'), existing on the whole outside, or at best on the edge of any given world of recognisable social activity; especially that of a kind to be treated at any degree of sensationalism in print. In quite a different way, he sounded almost as much a recluse as Erridge.

Lovell himself was in a manner proud of this honourable, uncorrupted twilight in which Lord Sleaford had his being, infinitely removed from the gossip-column renown so dear to his own heart; but he also felt, perhaps reasonably enough, that the historical and architectural magnificence of Dogdene was all the time being wasted as a setting for great events.

'I know there is a lot to be said for a peer being quiet and well behaved,' he used to say. 'But really Uncle Geoffrey goes too far. When you think of the house parties they used to have at Dogdene, it is a bit depressing. You know, when George IV came to stay, they painted the place white and gold from top to bottom, including the Chinese Chippendale commodes. Even Aunt Molly, who never showed the slightest desire to cut a dash, quite often used to entertain royalty there. Then there was the occasional literary lion too. I believe Henry James was at Dogdene once. St. John Clarke was there just before the war. It wasn't the complete morgue it is now. The fact is, Uncle Geoffrey is a very dull man. Aunt Alice, though she does her best, isn't much better. If Uncle John hadn't died, I don't believe either of them would have married anybody— Uncle Geoffrey wouldn't have been able to afford a wife, anyway. As it is, they just potter about and read the newspapers and listen to the wireless—and that is the extent of it.'

The general impression of Lord Sleaford that emerged from these fragments of information was certainly that of a person rather unusually lacking in any quality of liveliness or distinction. Dispiriting years as a younger son had destroyed in him any enterprise or geniality he might once have possessed. That was Lovell's theory. Like Alfred Tolland, he had consistently failed to make a career for himself, while at the same time lacking the philosophic detachment which gave Alfred Tolland a certain moral dignity: even a kind of saintliness. Inheritance of Dogdene had come too late to alter his routine, set, no doubt congenially, in an unimaginative mould. Such was the portrait painted by Lovell, in which Lord Sleaford lived in my

214

imagination with a certain rugged reality of his own; although I sometimes wondered whether, in this individual case, the uncompromising monochrome of Lovell's pigment might be tinged by the possibility that Lord Sleaford himself did not greatly care for his nephew: perhaps openly disapproved of him. That was a contingency to be borne in mind.

Lady Sleaford, as depicted by Lovell, possessed for me, on the other hand, none of her husband's clarity of outline. She was given no highlights, except the crumb of praise that she 'did her best'. Lovell had contrived to afford her no separate existence. She was simply the wife of Lord Sleaford. I pictured her as embodying all the unreality of a dowager on the stage: grey-haired: grotesquely dressed: speaking in a stiff, affected manner: possibly gazing through a lorgnette: a figure belonging to Edwardian drawing-room comedy. Armed with this vision of the Sleafords, I could not help wondering how Widmerpool had been asked to their house, according to Lovell, so rarely visited.

'Easy to explain,' said Lovell. 'Aunt Alice, the most conventional woman alive, is also one of those tremendously respectable people who long to know someone they regard as disreputable. To have Mildred Haycock as a friend has been the great adventure of Aunt Alice's life.'

'And she includes Mrs. Haycock's husbands?'

'Not necessarily,' said Lovell. 'You've got something when you ask that. I very much doubt whether Haycock ever reached Dogdene. However, as the Widmerpool engagement took place over here—and Mildred, in any case, coming to England so rarely—I suppose an invitation to both of them was hard to refuse. You see, Mildred almost certainly invited herself. She probably took the opportunity of asking if her young man could come too.'

This was a credible explanation.

'It is just like the Sleafords,' said Lovell, 'that Aunt Alice should disapprove of Molly Jeavons, who is really so frightfully well behaved, in spite of the ramshackle way in which she lives, and take to her bosom someone like Mildred, who has slept with every old-timer between Cannes and St. Tropez.'

'What will the Sleafords think about Widmerpool?'

'He sounds just the sort of chap Uncle Geoffrey will like. Probably talk stocks and shares all day long, and go to bed every night at half-past ten sharp, after one glass of port. The port is quite good at Dogdene, I must admit. Only because no one has ever bothered to drink it. All the same, I am a bit surprised myself by their both getting an invitation. It is not so easy to penetrate Dogdene these days. I know. I've tried.'

I was, naturally, much occupied at this period with my own affairs, so that was all I heard about Widmerpool going to Dogdene before learning from Lovell—quite by chance one day at the Studio—that Mrs. Haycock's engagement had been broken off. Lovell hardly knew Widmerpool. He would have had no particular concern with the engagement had not Dogdene provided the background for this event. He had no details. I learnt more of the story as a result of Molly Jeavons announcing: 'I shall have a few people in next week, Nicholas, a sort of party for yourself and Isobel. Something quite small.'

When I had next been to the Jeavonses' house after the visit to Umfraville's night club, Jeavons himself had made no reference whatever to that excursion. Indeed, he hardly talked at all during the course of the evening, striding aimlessly about the room as if lost in thought. It was possible that his wound was giving him trouble. However, Molly spoke of the matter, pretending to be cross with me.

'You are a very dissipated young man,' she said. 'What do you mean by keeping poor Teddy up till all hours in the way you did? I never heard such a thing. Do you know he had to spend a whole week in bed after going out with you?'

I tried to make some apology, although at the same time feeling not greatly to blame for the way Jeavons behaved when he went out on his own. As a matter of fact, I had not been at all well myself the following day, and was inclined to blame Jeavons for having caused me to sit up so late.

'Just as well he found Mildred Blaides to look after him,' said Molly. 'I always thought they had known each other for ages, but it turned out they had only met once, a long time ago. You know she was a nurse at Dogdene during the war. Lucky she didn't turn up when Teddy was there, or she would have scalded him to death with hot-water-bottles, or something of that sort. She was the worst nurse they ever had there—or in the whole of the V.A.D., for that matter.'

Molly spoke with more than a touch of acrimony, but at the same time it was impossible to guess how much she knew, or suspected, of Jeavons's night out; impossible, if it came to that, to know with any certainty how that night had ended, even though the nostalgic mood of Jeavons's and Mrs. Haycock's impetuous nature might, in unison, give a strong hint.

'If Mildred is not careful,' said Molly, 'she will polish off Mr. Widmerpool before she has time to marry him. I hear he had to go home, he was feeling so ill.'

I thought the sooner the subject of that night was abandoned, the better. While we had been talking, Jeavons had listened in silence, as if he had never before heard of any of the persons under discussion, including himself. I admired his detachment. I wondered, too, whether at that very moment his head was seething with forgotten melodies, for ever stirring him to indiscretion by provoking memories of an enchanted past.

'I can't have all the Tollands at this party,' Molly had said. 'So I had better have none of them. Bound to be jealousy otherwise. Just like Erridge to go to China when one of his sisters gets engaged.'

Smith was again on duty with the Jeavonses on the day of the party. He looked haggard and more out of sorts than ever.

'You're late,' he said, taking my hat. 'It has all started upstairs. Quite a crowd of them arrived already. Hope her ladyship hasn't invited every blessed soul she knows.'

The guests seemed, in fact, to have been chosen even more at random than usual. Certainly there had been no question either of asking people because they were already friends of Isobel or myself; still less, because Molly wanted either of us specifically to meet them. All that was most nondescript in the Jeavons entourage predominated, together with a few exceptional and reckless examples of individual oddity. I noticed that Alfred Tolland had not been included in the general prohibition against the Tolland family of my own generation. He was standing in the corner of the room, wedged behind a table, talking to—of all people—Mark Members, whom I had never before seen at the Jeavonses', and might be supposed, in principle, beyond Molly's normal perimeter, wide as that might stretch; or at least essentially alien to most of what it enclosed. To describe the two of them as standing looking at one another, rather than talking, would have been nearer the truth, as each apparently found equal difficulty in contributing anything to a mutual conversation. At the same time, the table cut them off from contact with other guests.

'I know you are interested in books, Nicholas,' said Molly. 'So I asked a rather nice young man I met the other day. He also writes or something. You will like him. A Mr. Members.'

'I know him of old.'

'Go and talk to him then. I don't think he is getting on very well with Alfred Tolland. It is a great compliment to Isobel that Alfred has come. As you know, he never goes out. At least that is what he says. I always tell him I believe he leads a double life of great wickedness. He tried to get out of coming tonight, but I told him he would never be asked to the house again if he did not turn up. Then he didn't dare refuse. Isobel, dear, there is someone I want you to meet.'

Both Alfred Tolland and Mark Members showed relief at the arrival of a third party to break up their *tête-à-tête*. They had by then reached a conversational standstill. This was the first I had seen of Alfred Tolland since the announcement of my own engagement. I was aware that he could no longer be regarded merely as the embarrassed, conscience-stricken figure, vaguely familiar in the past. Now he fell automatically into place in the profusion of new relationships that follow an organic change of condition. He began at once to mutter incoherent congratulations. Members watched him with something like hatred in his beady eyes.

'Expect you've heard that Erridge has gone East,' said Alfred Tolland. 'Just heard it myself. Not—a—bad—idea. They are in a mess there. Perhaps the best thing. Might do him a lot of good. Get experience. Good thing to get experience. Ever been East?'

'Never.'

'Got as far as Singapore once,' he said.

It seemed incredible. However, there appeared to be no

reason why he should invent such a thing. I said a word to Members, who stood there looking far from pleased.

'I shall have to be going now,' said Alfred Tolland, snatching this offer of release. 'I expect I shall see you at the dinner next . . .'

'I'm not sure yet. Don't know what our circumstances will be.'

'Of course, of course. You can't say. I quite understand. Pity you weren't at the last one. Nice to feel that we . . .'

Exact expression of what it was nice for both of us to feel either evaded him, or was too precarious a sentiment to express in words. He merely nodded his head several times. Then he made for the door. Members sighed. He was in a bad humour.

'What on earth is this party?' he said in a low voice. 'Did that man say something about your being engaged?'

'Yes. I am engaged.'

'To whom?'

'Isobel Tolland—over there.'

'Congratulations,' said Members, without any exaggerated effusiveness, as if he disapproved of any such step in principle. 'Many congratulations. I was stuck with that appalling bore for about twenty minutes. It was impossible to get away. Is he absolutely right in the head? What a strange house this is. I met Lady Molly Jeavons quite a long time ago at the Manaschs'. She asked me to come and see her. I called once or twice, but no one answered the bell, though I rang half a dozen times—and knocked too. Then she suddenly telephoned this invitation to me yesterday. She never mentioned your name. I did not think it would be quite like this.'

'It is often different. You never know what it is going to be.'

'Have you met her husband?' said Members, quite plaintively. 'I talked to him for a while when I first arrived. He asked me if I ever played snooker. Then he introduced me to the man you found me with.'

By then Members had several jobs of a literary kind which, since he was still a bachelor, must bring him in a respectable income. His American trip was said to have been a success. He no longer wrote verse with Freudian undertones, and he had abandoned anything so extreme as Quiggin's professional 'communism', in the wake of which he had for a while half-heartedly trailed. Now he tended to be associated with German literature. Kleist; Grillparzer: Stifter: those were names to be caught on the echoes of his conversation. Latterly, he was believed to be more taken up with Kierkegaard, then a writer not widely read in this country. Members, no fool, was always a little ahead of the fashion. He was a lively talker when not oppressed, as at that moment, by a party he did not enjoy. His distinguished appearance and terse manner made him a popular spare man at intellectual dinners. 'But one really does not want to eat amateur *paella* and drink Chelsea Médoc for ever,' he used to say: a world into which he felt himself somewhat rudely thrust immediately after losing his job as secretary to St. John Clarke. For a time now Members had been reappearing, so it was said, in the rather more elegant of the circles frequented by the famous novelist before his conversion to Marxism. In the light of this effort to maintain and expand his social life, Members found the Jeavons house a disappointment. He had expected something more grandiose. I tried to explain the household, but was glad when he brushed this aside, because I wanted to ask if he knew further details about Erridge and Mona. Members turned almost with relief to this subject.

'Of course I knew J.G. had got hold of Lord Warminster,' he said impatiently. 'Surely everyone has known

that for a long time. We had dinner together before I went
to America. J.G. told me about the magazine he hoped to
persuade Warminster to start. I saw at once that nothing
would come of it.'

'Why not?'

'Warminster is too much of a crank.'

'Do you know him?'

'No, but I know of him.'

'How did the Mona situation arise?'

All at once Members was on his guard.

'But there is every prospect of Warminster becoming your
brother-in-law, isn't there?'

'Most certainly there is.'

Members laughed, not in his most friendly manner, and
remained silent.

'Come on—out with it,' I said.

We had by then known each other for a long time. It
was not an occasion to stand on ceremony, as Members was
well aware. He thought for a second or two, pondering
whether it would be preferable to circulate a good piece of
gossip, or to tease more effectively by withholding any information he might himself possess. In the end he decided
that communication of the news would be more pleasurable.

'You know what Mona is,' he said.

He smiled maliciously; for although, so far as I knew,
there had never 'been much' between them, he had known
Mona years before her association with Quiggin; in fact I
had first set eyes on Mona in the company of Members at
Mr. Deacon's birthday party.

'She was altogether too much for Erridge, was she?' I
asked. 'When she struck.'

'Erridge?'

'For Warminster, I mean—his family call him Erridge.'

'Yes, Mona was too much for him. I don't think things

got very far. Some sort of an assignation. J.G. found out
about it. The next thing was the two of them had gone off
together.'

'How has J.G. taken it?'

'He was full of *gêne* at first. You know she had a strangle-
hold on him, I am sure. Now that he has cooled down, he is
really rather flattered, as well as being furious.'

'Were they married?'

'No.'

'Is that certain?'

'Absolutely.'

I should have liked to hear more, but at that moment
Jeavons came up to us. He took an unfamiliar object from
his coat pocket, and held it towards me.

'A present?'

'No,' he said. 'That reminds me we'll have to get you
one, I suppose. Anyway, that's Molly's job. This is just for
you to see. You might even want to buy one for yourself.'

'What is it?'

'Guess.'

'I don't like to say the word in company.'

Jeavons extended his clasped fist towards Members, who
shook his head angrily and turned away.

'For your car,' urged Jeavons.

'I haven't got a car,' said Members.

He was thoroughly cross.

'What do you really do with it?' I asked.

'Fix it on to the carburettor—then you use less petrol.'

'What's the point?'

'Save money, of course. Are you a bloody millionaire, or
what?'

Molly drew near our group as she crossed the room to
refill one of the jugs of drink. She saw what Jeavons was
doing and laid a hand on his arm.

'You'll never sell Nicholas one of those things,' she said. 'Nor Mr. Members, either, I'm sure. I don't myself think you will sell it to anyone, darling.'

She moved on.

'It is called an atomiser,' said Jeavons, slowly, as if he were about to lecture troops upon some mechanical device. 'It saves thirty-three and a third consumption per mile. I don't expect it really saves you that for a moment, as a matter of fact. Why should it? Everybody would have one otherwise. It stands to reason. Still, you never know. It might do some good. Worth trying, I suppose.'

He spoke without great conviction, gazing for a time at the object in his open palm. Then he returned it to his coat pocket, fumbling about for some time, and at last bringing out a tattered packet of Gold Flake. He nicked up one of the cigarettes with his thumb, and offered it to each of us in turn.

'Well,' he said to me, 'so you are going to get married.'

Members watched him with absolute horror. Jeavons, I was sure, was wholly unaware of the poor impression he was making. Members could stand it no longer.

'I think I must go now,' he said. 'I have another party I have to look in on. It was kind of Lady Molly and yourself to ask me.'

'Not at all,' said Jeavons. 'Glad to see you. Come again.'

He watched Members leave the room, as if he had never before seen anyone at all like him. His cigarette remained unlighted in his mouth.

'Odd bloke,' he said. 'I feel shocking this afternoon. Had too much lunch. Red in the face. Distended stomach. Self-inflicted wounds, of course.'

We talked together for a minute or two. Then Jeavons wandered off among the guests. By then General and Mrs. Conyers had arrived. I went across the room to speak to them.

They had come up from the country the day before. After making the conventional remarks about my engagement, Mrs. Conyers was removed by Molly to be introduced to some new acquaintance of hers. I was left with the General. He seemed in excellent form, although at the same time giving the impression that he was restless about something: had a problem on his mind. All at once he took me by the arm. 'I want a word with you, Nicholas,' he said, in his deep, though always unexpectedly mild, voice. 'Can't we get out of this damned, milling crowd of people for a minute or two?'

The Jeavonses' guests habitually flowed into every room in the house, so that to retire to talk, for example in Molly's bedroom, or Jeavons's dressing-room, would be considered not at all unusual. We moved, in fact, a short way up the stairs into a kind of boudoir of Molly's, constricted in space and likely to attract only people who wanted to enjoy a heart-to-heart talk together: a place chiefly given over to cats, two or three of which sat in an ill-humoured group at angles to one another, stirring with disapproval at this invasion of their privacy. I had no idea what the General could wish to say, even speculating for an instant as to whether he was about to offer some piece of advice—too confidential and esoteric to risk being overheard—regarding the conduct of married life. The period of engagement is one when you are at the mercy of all who wish to proffer counsel, and experience already prepared me for the worst. The truth turned out to be more surprising.

As soon as we were alone together, the General sat down on a chair in front of the writing-table, straightening out his leg painfully. It still seemed to be giving trouble. Alone with him, I became aware of that terrible separateness which difference of age imposes between individuals. Perhaps feeling something of this burden himself, he began at first to speak of his own advancing years.

225

'I'm beginning to find all this standing about at Buck House a bit of a strain,' he said. 'Not so young as I was. Dropped my eyeglass not so long ago in one of the ante-rooms at St. James's and had to get a fellow who was standing beside me to pick it up for me. Secretary from the Soviet Embassy. Perfectly civil. Just couldn't get down that far myself. Afraid I'd drop my axe too, if I tried. Still, although I'm getting on in life, I've had a good run for my money. Seen some odd things at one time or another.'

He moved his leg again, and groaned a bit. I always had the impression that he liked talking about his appearances at Court.

'I'm a great believer in people knowing the truth,' he said. 'Always have been.'

Without seeing at all clearly where this maxim would lead us, I agreed that truth was best.

'Something happened the other day,' said the General, 'that struck me as interesting. Damned interesting. Got on my mind a bit, especially as I had been reading about that kind of thing. Odd coincidence, I mean. The fact is, you are the only fellow I can tell.'

By that time I began to feel even a little uneasy, having no idea at all what might be coming next.

'When you came to tea with us not so long ago, I told you I had been reading about this business of psycho-analysis. Don't tie myself down to Freud. Jung has got some interesting stuff too. No point in an amateur like myself being dogmatic about something he knows little or nothing about. Just make a fool of yourself. Don't you agree?'

'Absolutely.'

'Well, a rather interesting illustration of some of the points I'd been reading about happened to come my way the other day. Care to hear about it?'

'I should like to very much indeed.'

'In connexion with this fellow you say you were at school with—this fellow Widmerpool—who wanted to marry my sister-in-law, Mildred.'

'I hear the engagement is off.'

'You knew that already?'

'I was told so the other day.'

'Common knowledge, is it?'

'Yes.'

'Know why it's off?'

'No. But I wasn't altogether surprised.'

'Nor was I, but it is an odd story. Not to be repeated, of course. Happened during their stay at Dogdene. Perhaps you've heard about that too?'

'I knew they were going to Dogdene.'

'Ever stopped there yourself?'

'No. I've never met either of the Sleafords.'

'I was once able to do Geoffrey Sleaford a good turn in South Africa,' said the General. 'He was A.D.C. to the Divisional Commander, and a more bone-headed fellow I never came across. Sleaford—or Fines, as he was then—had landed in a mess over some mislaid papers. I got him out of it. He is a stupid fellow, but always grateful. Made a point of trying out our poodle dogs at his shoots. Then Bertha knew Alice Sleaford as a girl. Went to the same dancing class. Bertha never much cared for her. Still, they get on all right now. Long and the short of it is that we stop at Dogdene from time to time. Uncomfortable place nowadays. Those parterres are very fine, of course. Alice Sleaford takes an interest in the garden. Wonderful fruit in the hot-houses. Then there is the Veronese. Geoffrey Sleaford has been advised to have it cleaned, but won't hear of it. Young fellow called Smethyck told him. Smethyck saw our Van Troost and said it was certainly genuine. Nice things at Dogdene, some of them, but I could name half a dozen houses in England I'd rather stop at.'

None of this seemed to be getting us much further so far as Widmerpool was concerned. I waited for development. General Conyers did not intend to be hurried. I suspected that he might regard this narrative he was unfolding in so leisurely a manner as the last good story of his life; one that he did not propose to squander in the telling. That was reasonable enough.

'I was not best pleased,' he said, 'when Bertha told me we had been asked to Dogdene at the same time as Mildred and her young man. I know the Sleafords don't have many people to stop. All the same it would have been quite easy to have invited some of their veterans. Even had us there by ourselves. Just like Alice Sleaford to arrange something like that. Hasn't much tact. All the same, I thought it would be a chance to get to know something about Widmerpool. After all, he was going to be my brother-in-law. Got to put up with your relations. Far better know the form from the beginning.'

'I've been seeing Widmerpool on and off for ages,' I said, hoping to encourage the General's flow of comment. 'I really know him quite well.'

'You do?'

'Yes.'

'Now, look here,' he said. 'Have you ever noticed at all how Widmerpool gets on with women?'

'He never seemed to find them at all easy to deal with. I was surprised that he should be prepared to take on someone like Mrs. Haycock.'

We had plunged into an intimacy of discussion that I had never supposed possible with an older man of the General's sort.

'You were?'

228

'Yes.'

'So was I,' he said. 'So was I. Very surprised. And I did not take long to see that they were getting on each other's nerves when they arrived at Dogdene. She was being very crisp with him. Very crisp. Nothing much in that, of course. Engaged couples bound to have their differences. Now I know Mildred pretty well by this time, and, although I did not much take to Widmerpool when I first met him, I thought she might do worse at her age. What?'

'So I should imagine.'

'Not every man would want to take her on. Couple of step-children into the bargain.'

'No.'

'All the same Widmerpool seemed to me rather a trying fellow. Half the time he was being obsequious, behaving as if he was applying for the job as footman, the other half, he was telling Geoffrey Sleaford and myself how to run our own affairs. It was then I began to mark down his psychological type. I had brought the book with me.'

'How did he get on with Lord Sleaford?'

'Pretty well,' said the General. 'Pretty well. Better than you might think. You know, Widmerpool talks sense about business matters. No doubt of it. Made some suggestions about developing the home farm at Dogdene which were quite shrewd. It was with Mildred there was some awkwardness. Mildred is not a woman to hang about with. If he wanted to marry her, he ought to have got down to matters and have done it. No good delaying in things of that sort.'

'He has been having jaundice.'

'I knew he'd been ill. He made several references to the fact. Seemed rather too fond of talking about his health. Another sign of his type. Anyway, his illness was beside

229

the point. The fact was, Mildred did not think he was paying her enough attention. That was plain as a pikestaff. Mildred is a woman who expects a good deal of fuss to be made over her. I could see he was in for trouble.'

'What form did it take?'

'First of all, as I told you, she was a bit short with him. Then she fairly told him off to his face. That was on Saturday afternoon. Thought there was going to be a real row between them. Alice Sleaford never noticed a thing. In the evening they seemed to have made it up. In fact, after dinner, they were more like an engaged couple than I'd ever seen 'em. Now, look here, where would you put his type? Psychologically, I mean.'

'Rather hard to say in a word—I know him so well——'

'It seems to me,' said the General, 'that he is a typical intuitive extrovert—classical case, almost. Cold-blooded. Keen on a thing for a moment, but never satisfied. Wants to get on to something else. Don't really know about these things, but Widmerpool seems to fit into the classification. That's the category in which I'd place him, just as if a recruit turns up with a good knowledge of carpentry and you draft him into the Sappers. You are going to say you are a hard-bitten Freudian, and won't hear of Jung and his ideas. Very well, I'll open another field of fire.'

'But——'

'You haven't heard the rest of the story yet. I came down to breakfast early on Sunday morning. I thought I'd have a stroll in the garden, and have another look at those hot-houses. What do you think I found? Widmerpool! in the hall, making preparations to leave the house. Some story about a telephone call, and being summoned back to London. Fellow looked like death. Shaking like a jelly and the colour of wax. Told me he'd slept very badly.

Hardly closed his eyes. I'm quite prepared to believe that. Alice Sleaford won't use the best bedrooms for some reason. Never know where you are going to be put.'

'And did he go back to London?'

'Drove off, there and then, under my eyes. Whole house had been turned upside down to get him away at that hour on Sunday morning. Left a message for the host and hostess to say how sorry he was, neither of them having come down yet. Never saw a man more disgruntled than the Sleafords' chauffeur.'

'But what had happened? Had there really been a telephone call? I don't understand.'

'There had been some telephoning that morning, but the butler said it had been Widmerpool putting the call through. Only heard the true story that afternoon from Mildred when we were walking together in the Dutch garden. She didn't make any bones about it. Widmerpool had been in her room the night before. Things hadn't gone at all well. Made up her mind he wasn't going to be any use as a husband. Mildred can be pretty outspoken when she is cross.'

The General said these things in a manner entirely free from any of those implied comments which might be thought inseparable from such a chronicle of events. That is to say he was neither shocked, facetious, nor caustic. It was evident that the situation interested, rather than surprised him. He was complete master of himself in allowing no trace of ribaldry or ill nature to colour his narrative. For my own part, I felt a twinge of compassion for Widmerpool in his disaster, even though I was unable to rise to the General's heights of scientific detachment. I had known Widmerpool too long.

'Mildred told me in so many words. Doesn't care what she says, Mildred. That's what young people are like nowadays. Of course, I don't expect Mildred appears young to you, but I always think of her as a young woman.'

I did not know what comment to make. However, General Conyers did not require comment. He wished to elaborate his own conception of what had happened.

'Widmerpool's trouble is not as uncommon as you might think,' he said. 'I've known several cases. Last fellows in the world you'd suppose. I don't expect the name Peploe-Gordon means anything to you?'

'No.'

'Dead now. Had a heart attack in the Lebanon. I remember it happened in the same week Queen Draga. was murdered in Belgrade. At Sandhurst with me. Splendid rider. First-class shot. Led an expedition into Tibet. Married one of the prettiest girls I've ever seen. Used to see her out with the Quorn. He had the same trouble. Marriage annulled. Wife married again and had a string of children. This is the point I want to make. I saw Peploe-Gordon about eighteen months later at the yearling sales at Newmarket with another damned pretty girl on his arm. Do you know, he looked as pleased as Punch. Didn't give a damn. Still, you don't know what neuroses weren't at work under the surface. That is what you have got to remember. Looking back in the light of what I have been reading, I can see the fellow had a touch of exaggerated narcissism. Is that Widmerpool's trouble?'

'It wouldn't surprise me. As I said before, I've only dipped into these things.'

'I don't set up as an expert myself. Last thing in the world I'd pretend to do. But look here, something I want to ask—do you know anything of Widmerpool's mother?'

'I've met her.'

'What is she like?'

I felt as usual some difficulty in answering directly the

232

General's enquiry, put in his most pragmatical manner.

'Rather a trying woman, I thought.'

'Domineering?'

'In her way.'

'Father?'

'Dead.'

'What did he do?'

'Manufactured artificial manure, I believe.'

'Did he . . .' said the General. 'Did he . . .'

There was a pause while he thought over this information. It was undeniable that he had been setting the pace. I felt that I must look to my psycho-analytical laurels, if I was not to be left far behind.

'Do you think it was fear of castration?' I asked.

The General shook his head slowly.

'Possibly, possibly,' he said. 'Got to be cautious about that. You see this is how I should approach the business, with the greatest humility—with the *greatest* humility. Widmerpool strikes me as giving himself away all the time by his—well, to quote the text-book—purely objective orientation. If you are familiar with tactics, you know you can be up against just that sort of fellow in a battle. Always trying to get a move on, and bring off something definite. Quite right too, in a battle. But in ordinary life a fellow like that may be doing himself no good so far as his own subjective emotions are concerned. No good at all. Quite the reverse. Always leads to trouble. No use denying subjective emotions. Just as well to face the fact. All of us got a lot of egoism and infantilism to work off. I'd be the last to deny it. I can see now that was some of Peploe-Gordon's trouble, when I look back.'

'I'm sure Widmerpool thought a lot about this particular matter. Indeed, I know he did. He spoke to me about it quite soon after he became engaged to Mrs. Haycock.'

'Probably thought about it a great deal too much. Doesn't do to think about anything like that too much. Need a bit of relaxation from time to time. Everlastingly talks about his work too. Hasn't he any hobbies?'

'He used to knock golf balls into a net at Barnes. But he told me he had given that up.'

'Pity, pity. Not surprised, though,' said the General, 'Nothing disturbs feeling so much as thinking. I'm only repeating what the book says, but I didn't spend thirty odd years in the army without discovering that for myself. Got to have a plan, of course, but no use knotting yourself up in it too tight. Must have an instinct about the man on the other side—and the people on your own side too. What was it Foch said? War not an exact science, but a terrible and passionate drama? Something like that. Fact is, marriage is rather like that too.'

'But surely that was what Widmerpool was trying to make it? To some extent he seems to have succeeded. What happened sounded terrible and dramatic enough in its own way.'

'I'll have to think about that,' said the General. 'I see what you mean. I'll have to think about that.'

All the same, although I had raised this objection, I agreed with what he said. Marriage was a subject upon which it was hard to obtain accurate information. Its secrets, naturally, are those most jealously guarded; never more deeply concealed than when apparently most profusely exhibited in public. However true that might be, one could still be sure that even those marriages which seem outwardly dull enough are, at one time or another, full of the characteristics of which he spoke. Was it possible to guess, for example, what lay behind the curtain of his own experience? As I had never before conceived of exchanging such a conversation with General Conyers, I thought this an

234

opportunity to enquire about a matter that had always played some part in my imagination since mentioned years earlier by Uncle Giles. The moment particularly recommended itself, because the General rarely spoke either of the practice or theory of war. The transient reference he had just made to Foch now caused the question I wanted to ask to sound less inept.

'Talking of the army,' I said. 'What did it feel like when you were in the charge?'

'In where?'

'The charge—after French's cavalry brigades crossed the Modder River.'

The General looked perplexed for a moment. Then his expression altered. He grasped the substance of my enquiry.

'Ah, yes,' he said. 'When the whole cavalry division charged. Unusual operation. Doubted the wisdom of it at the time. However, it came off all right. Extraordinary that you should have known about it. That was the occasion you mean? Of course, of course. What was it like? Just have to think for a moment. Long time ago, you know. Have to collect my thoughts. Well, I think I can tell you exactly. The fact was there had been some difficulty in mounting me, as I wasn't officially attached to the formation. Can't remember why not at this length of time. Some technicality. Ride rather heavy, you know. As far as I can remember, I had the greatest difficulty in getting my pony out of a trot. I'm sure that was what happened. Later on in the day, I shot a Boer in the shin. But why do you ask?'

'I don't know. I've always wanted to ask, for some reason. Infantilism, perhaps. A primordial image.'

The General agreed, cordially.

'You are an introvert, of course,' he said.

'I think undoubtedly.'

'Introverted intuitive type, do you think? I shouldn't wonder.'

'Possibly.'

'Anyway,' said the General, 'keep an eye on not over-compensating. I've been glad to tell that story about Widmerpool to someone who can appreciate the circumstances. Haven't made up my own mind about it yet. I've got a slow reactive rapidity. No doubt about that. Just as well to recognise your own limitations. Can't help wondering about the inhibiting action of the incest barrier though—among other things.'

He moved his leg once more, at the same time shifting the weight of his body, as he pondered this riddle. The angle of his knee and ankle emphasised the beauty of his patent leather boots.

'Well, I mustn't keep you up here away from the others any longer,' he said. 'Lots of people you ought to be meeting. You are going to be a very lucky young man, I am sure. What do you want for a wedding present?'

The change in his voice announced that our fantasy life together was over. We had returned to the world of everyday things. Perhaps it would be truer to say that our real life together was over, and we returned to the world of fantasy. Who can say? We went down the stairs once more, the General leading. Chips Lovell was talking to Miss Weedon, perhaps tiring of her company, because he slipped away at once when I came up to them, making for the drink-tray. Miss Weedon gave her glacial smile and congratulated me. We began to talk. Before we had progressed very far, Molly Jeavons, whose absence from the room I had not previously noticed, came hurriedly towards us.

'Oh, Tuffy, dear,' she said. 'Do go down and see what is happening in the basement. A policeman has just arrived

236

to interview Smith about a postal-order. I don't think he can have come to arrest him, but it would be saintly of you if you could clear it all up.'

Miss Weedon did not look very anxious to investigate this intrusion, but she went off obediently.

'Smith really is a dreadful nuisance,' said Molly. 'I don't mind him drinking more than he should, because he carries it pretty well, but I don't like some of the people who come to see him. I hope he hasn't got into trouble with one of them.'

Jeavons joined us.

'What's the matter now?' he asked.

'A policeman has come to see Smith.'

'Is Smith off to the Scrubs?'

'Don't be silly,' she said; and to me: 'What on earth were you talking to General Conyers about? I thought you were going to spend the rest of the evening together in my little room. I suppose you have heard your friend Mr. Widmerpool's engagement is off. Just as well, I should think. Mildred really goes too far. I've asked him tonight. I thought it might cheer him up.'

'You have?'

'You speak as if you didn't want to meet him. Have you both had a row? Here he is, in any case.'

After so recently hearing an account of his departure from Dogdene, I almost expected Widmerpool to display, morally, if not physically, the dishevelled state described by the General. On the contrary, as he pushed his way through the people in the room, I thought I had never seen him look more pleased with himself. His spectacles glistened. Wearing a short black coat and striped trousers, his manner suggested that he was unaware that such a thing as failure could exist: certainly not for himself. He came up to me at once.

237

'The door was open and I walked in,' he said. 'I think that is what Lady Molly likes. Various people were talking to a policeman in the hall. I hope nothing has gone wrong.'

'Selling tickets for the police sports, I expect.'

'I expect so,' he said. 'Curious how our situations have been reversed. You are getting married, while Mildred and I decided in the end it would be better not. We talked things over quietly, and came to the same conclusion. I think it was all for the best. She has returned to France. She prefers to live there. That was one of the bones of contention. Then, of course, there was also the disparity in age. Between you and me, I was not anxious to take on those two sons of hers. They sound an unsatisfactory couple.'

Miss Weedon now returned from her scrutiny of Smith and the policeman. With her accustomed efficiency, she appeared to have mastered the essential points of this entanglement. She spoke severely, as if she were once more a governess reporting unsatisfactory behaviour on the part of her charges.

'Smith had his name given as a reference,' she said. 'Some man he knows has been arrested. A small embezzlement. Smith is very upset about it. In tears, as a matter of fact.'

'Oh, bless the man,' said Molly. 'Why did I ever say I would take him on again, when Erridge left England? I swore he should never again enter the house after he broke the Dresden coffee-pot. Do go and see, Teddy.'

'The bloke must have been hard up for a reference, if he had to give Smith's name,' said Jeavons, thoughtfully.

He moved off without undue haste, accompanied by Miss Weedon, whose demeanour was grave. Jeavons's face implied no hope of setting right any moral mishap of Smith's.

'My mother agrees that my decision is for the best,' said Widmerpool.

'She does?'

'She liked Mildred. Thoroughly approved of her from the family point of view, for example,' said Widmerpool. 'At the same time there are sides of Mildred she felt doubtful about. My mother never attempted to hide that from me. You know, Nicholas, it is wise to take good advice about such a thing as marriage. I hope you have done so yourself. I have thought about the subject a good deal, and you are always welcome to my views.'

Casanova's Chinese Restaurant

For Harry and Rosie

1

CROSSING THE ROAD by the bombed-out public
house on the corner and pondering the mystery which
dominates vistas framed by a ruined door, I felt for some
reason glad the place had not yet been rebuilt. A direct hit
had excised even the ground floor, so that the basement
was revealed as a sunken garden, or site of archæological
excavation long abandoned, where great sprays of willow
herb and ragwort flowered through cracked paving stones;
only a few broken milk bottles and a laceless boot recalling
contemporary life. In the midst of this sombre grotto five
or six fractured steps had withstood the explosion and
formed a projecting island of masonry on the summit of
which rose the door. Walls on both sides were shrunk away,
but along its lintel, in niggling copybook handwriting,
could still be distinguished the word *Ladies*. Beyond, on
the far side of the twin pillars and crossbar, nothing whatever remained of that promised retreat, the threshold falling steeply to an abyss of rubble; a triumphal arch erected
laboriously by dwarfs, or the gateway to some unknown,
forbidden domain, the lair of sorcerers.

Then, all at once, as if such luxurious fantasy were not
already enough, there came from this unexplored country
the song, strong and marvellously sweet, of the blonde
woman on crutches, that itinerant prima donna of the
highways whose voice I had not heard since the day, years
before, when Moreland and I had listened in Gerrard
Street, the afternoon he had talked of getting married;

when we had bought the bottle labelled *Tawny Wine (port flavour)* which even Moreland had been later unwilling to drink. Now once more above the rustle of traffic that same note swelled on the grimy air, contriving a transformation scene to recast those purlieus into the vision of an oriental dreamland, artificial, if you like, but still quite alluring under the shifting clouds of a cheerless Soho sky.

'Pale hands I loved beside the Shalimar,
Where are you now? Who lies beneath your spell?'

In the end most things in life – perhaps all things – turn out to be appropriate. So it was now, for here before me lay the vestigial remains of the Mortimer where we had first met, the pub in which our friendship had begun. As an accompaniment to Moreland's memory music was natural, even imperative, but the repetition of a vocal performance so stupendously apt was scarcely to be foreseen. A floorless angle of the wall to which a few lumps of plaster and strips of embossed paper still adhered was all that remained of the alcove where we had sat, a recess which also enclosed the mechanical piano into which, periodically, Moreland would feed a penny to invoke one of those fortissimo tunes belonging to much the same period as the blonde singer's repertoire. She was closer now, herself hardly at all altered by the processes of time – perhaps a shade plumper – working her way down the middle of the empty street, until, framed within the rectangle of the doorway, she seemed to be gliding along under the instrumentality of some occult power and about to sail effortlessly through its enchanted portal:

'Pale hands, pink-tipped, like lotus buds that float
On those cool waters where we used to dwell . . .'

Moreland and I had afterwards discussed the where-abouts of the Shalimar, and why the locality should have been the haunt of pale hands and those addicted to them.

'A nightclub, do you think?' Moreland had said. 'A bordel, perhaps. Certainly an establishment catering for exotic tastes – and I expect not very healthy ones either. How I wish there were somewhere like that where we could spend the afternoon. That woman's singing has un-settled me. What nostalgia. It was really splendid. "Whom do you lead on Rapture's roadway far?" What a pertinent question. But where can we go? I feel I must be amused. Do have a brilliant idea. I am in the depths of gloom to be precise. Let's live for the moment.'

'Tea at Casanova's Chinese Restaurant? That would be suitably oriental after the song.'

'What do you think? I haven't been there for ages. It wasn't very exciting on my last visit. Besides, I never felt quite the same about Casanova's after that business of Barnby and the waitress. It would be cheaper to drink tea at home – and no less Chinese as I have a packet of Lap-sang.'

'As you like.'

'But why did they dwell *on* the cool waters? I can't understand the preposition. Were they in a boat?'

A habit of Moreland's was to persist eternally with any subject that caught his fancy, a characteristic to intensify in him resolute approach to a few things after jettisoning most outward forms of seriousness; a love of repetition sometimes fatiguing to friends, when Moreland would return unmercifully to some trivial matter less amusing to others than to himself.

'Do you think they *were* in a boat?' he went on. 'The poem is called a Kashmiri Love Song. My aunt used to sing

245

it. Houseboats are a feature of Kashmir, aren't they?'

'Kipling characters go up there to spend their leave.'

'When we lived in Fulham my aunt used to sing that song to the accompaniment of the pianoforte.'

He paused in the street and offered there and then a version of the piece as loudly trilled by his aunt, interrupting himself once or twice to emphasise contrast with the rendering we had just heard. Moreland's parents had died when he was a child. This aunt, who played a large part in his personal mythology, had brought him up. Oppressed, no doubt, by her nephew's poor health and by thought of the tubercular complaint that had killed his father (who had some name as teacher of music), she was said to have 'spoiled' Moreland dreadfully. There were undeniable signs of something of the sort. She had probably been awed, too, by juvenile brilliance; for although Moreland had never been, like Carolo, an infant prodigy – that freakish, rather uncomfortable humour of only musical genius – he showed alarming promise as a boy. The aunt was also married to a musician, a man considerably older than herself whose generally impecunious circumstances had not prevented shadowy connexions with a more sublime world than that in which most of his daily life was spent. He had heard Wagner conduct at the Albert Hall; Liszt play at the Crystal Palace, seen the Abbé's black habit and shock of iron-grey hair pass through Sydenham; drunk a glass of wine with Tchaikowsky at Cambridge when the Russian composer had come to receive an honorary degree. These peaks are not to be exaggerated. Moreland had been brought up impecuniously too, but in a tradition of hearing famous men discussed on familiar terms; not merely prodigies read of in books, but also persons having to knock about the world like everyone else. The heredity was not unlike Barnby's, with music taking the place of the graphic arts.

'Perhaps this was a houseboat of ill fame.'

'What an enjoyable idea,' Moreland said. 'At the rapturous moments referred to in the lyric one would hear the water, if I may be so nautical, lapping beneath the keel. An overwhelming desire for something of the sort besets me this afternoon. Active emotional employment – like chasing an attractive person round some wet laurels.'

'Out of the question, I'm afraid.'

'What a pity London has not got a Luna Park. I should like to ride on merry-go-rounds and see freaks. Do you remember when we went on the Ghost Railway – when you dash towards closed doors and tear down hill towards a body across the line?'

In the end we decided against Casanova's Chinese Restaurant that day, instead experimenting, as I have said, with the adventitious vintages of Shaftesbury Avenue, a thoroughfare traversed on the way to Moreland's flat, which lay in an undistinguished alley on the far side of Oxford Street, within range of Mr Deacon's antique shop. Once there, after climbing an interminable staircase, you found an unexpectedly neat room. Unconformist, without discipline in many ways, Moreland had his precise, tidy side, instilled in him perhaps by his aunt; mirrored – so Maclintick used to say – in his musical technique. The walls were hung with framed caricatures of dancers in Diaghilev's early ballets, coloured pictures drawn by the Legat brothers, found by Moreland in a portfolio outside a second-hand book shop; Pavlova; Karsavina; Fokine; others, too, whom I have forgotten. The few books in a small bookcase by the bed included a tattered paper edition of Apollinaire's *Alcools*; one of the Sherlock Holmes volumes; Grinling's *History of the Great Northern Railway*. An upright piano stood against one wall, although Moreland, so he always insisted, was no great performer on that instrument. There were always flowers in the vase on the table when Moreland could afford them, which in those days was not often.

'Do you mind drinking wine from teacups, one of them short of a handle? Rather sordid, I'm afraid. I managed to break my three glasses the other night when I came home from a party and was trying to put them away so that the place might look more habitable when I woke up in the morning.'

Following a preliminary tasting, we poured the residue of the bottle down the lavatory.

'If you were legally allowed three wives,' asked Moreland, as we watched the cascade of amber foam gush noisily away, 'whom would you choose?'

Those were the days when I loved Jean Duport. Moreland knew nothing of her, nor did I propose to tell him. Instead, I offered three names from the group of female acquaintances we enjoyed in common, speaking without undue concern in making this triple decision. To tell the truth, in spite of what I felt for Jean, marriage, although looming up on all sides, still seemed a desperate venture to be postponed almost indefinitely.

'And you?'

Moreland possessed that quality, rather rare among men, of not divulging names. At the same time, the secretiveness he employed where his own love affairs were concerned was not without an element of exhibitionism. He was always willing to arouse a little unsatisfied curiosity.

'I am going to marry,' said Moreland, 'I have decided that. To make up my mind is always a rare thing with me, but the moment for decision has arrived. Otherwise I shall become just another of those depressed and depressing intellectual figures who wander from party to party, finding increasing difficulty in getting off with anyone – and in due course suspected of auto-erotic habits. Besides, Nietzsche advocates living dangerously.'

'If you have decided to base your life on the philosophy of writers of that period, Strindberg considered even the worst marriage better than no marriage at all.'

'And Strindberg earned the right to speak on that subject. As you probably know, his second wife kept a nightclub, within living memory, not a thousand miles from this very spot. Maclintick, of all people, was once taken there.'

'But you haven't told me who your wife – your three wives – will be.'

'There is only one really. I don't know whether she will accept me.'

'Oh, come. You are talking like a Victorian novel.'

'I will tell you when we next meet.'

'This is intolerable after I offered my names.'

'But I am serious.'

I dismissed the notion that Moreland could be contemplating marriage with the heroine of a recent story of Barnby's about one of Mr Cochran's Young Ladies.

'Moreland pawned the gold cigarette case Sir Magnus Donners gave him after writing the music for that film,' Barnby had said, 'just in order to stand her dinner at the Savoy. The girl had a headache that night – curse, too, I expect – and most of the money went on taking her back to Golders Green in a taxi.'

Even if that story were untrue, the toughness of Moreland's innate romanticism in matters of the heart certainly remained unimpaired by gravitating from one hopeless love affair to another. That fact had become clear after knowing him for even a few months. Wit, shrewdness about other aspects of life, grasp of the arts, fundamental good nature, none seemed any help in solving his emotional problems; to some extent these qualities, as displayed by him, were even a hindrance. Women found him amusing, were intrigued by his unusual appearance and untidy clothes, heard thàt he was brilliant, so naturally he had his 'successes'; but these, on the whole, were ladies with too desperate an enthusiasm for music. Moreland did not care for that. He liked wider horizons. His delicacy in coping with such eventualities need not be exaggerated. Undoubtedly, he allowed himself reasonable latitude with girls of that sort. Even so, the fact remained that, although fully aware of the existence, the greater effectiveness, of an attitude quite contrary to his own, he remained a hopeless addict of what he used to call, in the phrase of the day, a *princesse lointaine* complex'. This approach naturally involved him in falling in love with women connected in one way or another with the theatre.

'It doesn't matter whether it is the Leading Lady or Second Slave,' he said, 'I myself am always cast as a stage-door johnny of thirty or forty years back. As a matter of fact the hours I have to keep in my profession compel association with girls who have to stay up late – by which I do not necessarily mean tarts.'

All this was very alien to Barnby, himself enjoying to such a high degree the uncomplicated, direct powers of attack that often accompany a gift for painting or sculpture.

'Barnby never has to be in the mood to work,' Moreland used to say. 'The amount of material he can get through is proportionate to the hour he rises in the morning. In much the same way, if he sees a girl he likes, all he has to do is to ask her to sleep with him. Some do, some don't it is one to him.'

Barnby would not in the least have endorsed this picture of himself. His own version was that of a man chronically overburdened, absolutely borne down by sensitive emotional stresses. All the same, in contrasting the two of them, there was something to be said for Moreland's over-simplification. Their different methods were, as it happened, displayed in high relief on the occasion of my first meeting with Moreland.

The Mortimer (now rebuilt in a displeasingly fashionable style and crowded with second-hand-car salesmen) was even in those days regarded by the enlightened as a haunt of 'bores'; but, although the beer was indifferent and the saloon bar draughty, a sprinkling of those connected with the arts, especially musicians, was usually to be found there. The chief charm of the Mortimer for Moreland, who at that time rather prided himself on living largely outside that professionally musical world which, towards the end of his life, so completely engulfed him, was provided by the mechanical piano. The clientèle was anathema; this Moreland always conceded, using that very phrase, a favourite one of his.

For my own part, I never cared for the place either. I had been introduced there by Barnby (met for the first time only a few weeks before) who was coming on to the Mortimer that evening after consultation with a frame-maker who lived in the neighbourhood. Barnby was preparing for a show in the near future. Those were the days when his studio was above Mr Deacon's antique shop; when he was pursuing Baby Wentworth and about to paint those murals for the Donners-Brebner Building, which were destroyed, like the Mortimer, by a bomb during the war. I had recently returned, I remember, from staying in the country with the Walpole-Wilsons. It must, indeed, have been only a week before Mr Deacon injured himself fatally by slipping on the stair at the Bronze Monkey (disqualified as licensed premises the same month as the result of a police raid), and died in hospital some days later, much regretted by the many elements – some of them less than tolerable –

who made his antique shop their regular port of call.

It was pouring with rain that night and the weather had turned much colder. Barnby had not yet arrived when I came into the bar, which was emptier than usual. Two or three elderly women dressed in black, probably landladies off duty, were drinking Guinness and grumbling in one corner. In the other, where the mechanical piano was situated, sat Mr Deacon himself, hatless as usual, his whitening hair hanging lankly over a woollen muffler, the coarse mesh of which he might himself have knitted. His regular autumn exhalation of eucalyptus, or some other specific against the common cold (to which Mr Deacon was greatly subject), hung over that end of the room. He was always pre-occupied with his health and the Mortimer's temperature was too low for comfort. His long, arthritic fingers curled round half a pint of bitter, making an irregular mould or beading about the glass, recalling a medieval receptacle for setting at rest a drinking horn. The sight of Mr Deacon always made me think of the Middle Ages because of his resemblance to a pilgrim, a mildly sinister pilgrim, with more than a streak of madness in him, but then in every epoch a proportion of pilgrims must have been sinister, some mad as well. I was rather snobbishly glad that the streets had been too wet for his sandals. Instead, his feet were encased in dark blue felt snowboots against the puddles. That evening Barnby and I had planned to see a von Stroheim revival – was it *Foolish Wives*? Possibly Barnby had suggested that Mr Deacon should accompany us to the cinema, although as a rule he could be induced to sit through only Soviet films, and those for purely ideological reasons. Mr Deacon was in the best of form that night. He was surrounded by a group of persons none of whom I knew.

'Good evening, Nicholas,' he said, in his deep, deep, consciously melodious voice, which for some reason always made me feel a trifle uneasy, 'what brings you to this humble hostelry? I thought you frequented marble halls.'

'I am meeting Ralph here. We are going to a film. Neither of us had an invitation to a marble hall tonight.'

'The cinema?' said Mr Deacon, with great contempt. 'I am astonished you young men can waste your time in the cinema. Have you nothing else to do with yourselves? I should have thought better of Barnby. Why, I'd as soon visit the Royal Academy. Sooner, in fact. There would be the chance of a good laugh there.'

Although it was by then many years since he had set brush to canvas, and in spite of his equal disdain for all manifestations of 'modern art', Mr Deacon never tired of expressing contempt for Academicians and their works.

'Are cinemas worse than haunting taverns on your part?'

'A just rebuke,' said Mr Deacon, delighted at this duplication of his own sententious tone, 'infinitely just. But, you see, I have come here to transact a little business. Not only to meet *les jeunes*. True, I would much rather be forwarding the cause of international disarmament tonight by selling *War Never Pays!* outside the Albert Hall, but we must all earn our bread and butter. My poor little broadsheet would bring in nothing to me personally. Just a penny for a noble cause. For my goods I have to make a charge. You seem to forget, Nicholas, that I am just a poor *antiquaire* these days.'

Mr Deacon spoke this last sentence rather unctuously. Inclined to mark his prices high, he was thought to make at least a respectable livelihood from his wares. The fact that a certain air of transgression still attached to his past added attraction in the eyes of some customers. It was a long time since the days when, as an artist of independent means living at Brighton, he had been acquainted with my parents; days before that unfortunate incident in Battersea

253

Park had led to Mr Deacon's prolonged residence abroad. A congenital taste for Greco-Roman themes, which had once found expression in his own paintings, now took the form of a pronounced weakness for buying up statuettes and medallions depicting gods and heroes of classical times. These objects, not always easily saleable, cluttered the shop, the fashion for such ornaments as an adjunct to Empire or Regency furniture having by then scarcely begun. Occasionally he would find on his hands some work of art too pagan in its acceptance of sexual licence to be openly displayed. Such dubious items were kept, according to Barnby, in a box under Mr Deacon's bed. In the underworld through which he now moved, business and pleasure, art and politics, life – as it turned out finally – death itself, all had become a shade disreputable where Mr Deacon was concerned. However, even in these morally reduced circumstances, he preferred to regard himself as not wholly cut off from a loftier society. He still, for example, enjoyed such triumphal contacts as the afternoon when Lady Huntercombe (wearing one of her Mrs Siddons hats) had arrived unexpectedly on his doorstep; after an hour bearing away with her an inlaid tea-caddy in Tunbridge-ware, for which, in spite of creditable haggling on her own part, she had been made to pay almost as much as if purchased in Bond Street. She had promised to return – in a phrase Mr Deacon loved to repeat – 'When my ship comes in.'

'Ridiculous woman,' he used to say delightedly, 'as if we did not all know that the Huntercombes are as rich as Crœsus.'

One of the persons surrounding Mr Deacon at the table in the Mortimer, a young man muffled to the ears in a manner which gave him the appearance of a taxi-driver wearing several overcoats, now broke off the energetic conversation he had been carrying on with his neighbour, a fattish person in gold-rimmed spectacles, and tapped Mr

Deacon lightly on the arm with a rolled-up newspaper.

'I should certainly not go near the Albert Hall if I were you, Edgar,' he said. 'It would be too great a risk. Someone might seize you and compel you to listen to Brahms. In fact, after the way you have been talking this evening, you would probably yield to temptation and enter of your own free will. I would not trust you an inch where Brahms is concerned, Edgar. Not an inch.'

Letting go his glass, Mr Deacon lifted a gnarled hand dramatically, at the same time crooking one of his heavily jointed fingers.

'Moreland,' he said, 'I wish to hear no more of your youthful prejudices – certainly no more of your sentiments regarding the orchestration of the Second Piano Concerto.'

The young man began to laugh derisively. Although giving this impression of wearing several overcoats, he was in fact dressed only in one, a threadbare, badly stained garment, from the pockets of which protruded several more newspapers in addition to that with which he had demanded Mr Deacon's attention.

'As I was remarking, Nicholas,' said Mr Deacon, turning once more in my own direction and giving at the same time a smile to express tolerance for youthful extremism of whatever colour, 'I have come to this gin palace primarily to inspect an object of virtu – a classical group in some unspecified material, to be precise. I shall buy it, if its beauty satisfies me. *Truth Unveiled by Time* – in the Villa Borghese, you remember. I must say in the original marble Bernini has made the wench look as unpalatable as the heartless quality she represents. A reproduction of this work was found at the Caledonian Market by a young person with whom I possess a slight acquaintance. He thought I might profitably dispose of same on his behalf.'

'I hope the young person is an object of virtue himself,'

said Moreland. 'I presume the sex is masculine. We don't want anything in the nature of Youth, rather than Truth, being unveiled by Time. Can we trust you, Edgar?'

Mr Deacon gave one of his deep, rather stagy chuckles. He lightly twitched his shoulders.

'Nothing could be more proper than my relationship with this young gentleman,' he said. 'I met his mother in the summer when we were both reinvigorating ourselves at the same vegetarian communal holiday – she, I think, primarily as a measure of economy rather than on account of any deeply felt anti-carnivorous convictions on her own part. A most agreeable, sensible woman I found her, quite devoted to her boy. She reminded me in some ways of my own dear Mama, laid to rest in Kensal Green this many a long year. Her lad turned up to meet her at Paddington when we travelled back together. That was how he and I first came to know one another. Does that satisfy your rapacious taste for scandal, Moreland? I hope so.'

Mr Deacon spoke archly, rather than angrily. It was clear from his manner that he liked, even admired Moreland, from whom he seemed prepared to accept more teasing than he would ever have allowed to most of his circle.

'Anyway, the lad was not here when I arrived,' he went on, briskly turning once more towards myself, 'so I joined this little party of music-makers sitting by their desolate stream. I have been having some musical differences with Moreland here who becomes very dictatorial about his subject. I expect you know each other already. What? No? Then I must introduce you. This is Mr Jenkins – Mr Moreland, Mr Gossage, Mr Maclintick, Mr Carolo.'

The revolutionary bent of his political opinions had never modified the formality of Mr Deacon's manners. His companions, on the other hand, with the exception of Gossage who gave a smirk, displayed no outward mark of conventional politeness. In fact none of the rest of them showed the smallest wish to meet anyone outside their own apparently charmed circle. All the same, I immediately liked something about Hugh Moreland. Although I had never seen him in Mr Deacon's shop, nor in Barnby's studio, I knew of him already as a figure of some standing in the musical world: composer: conductor: pianist: I was uncertain of his precise activities. Barnby, talking about Moreland, had spoken of incidental music for a semi-private venture (a film version of *Lysistrata* made in France) which Sir Magnus Donners had backed. Since music holds for me none of that hard, cold-blooded, almost mathematical pleasure I take in writing and painting, I could only guess roughly where Moreland's work – enthusiastically received in some circles, heartily disliked in others – stood in relation to the other arts. In those days I had met no professional musicians. Later, when I ran across plenty of these through Moreland himself, I began to notice their special peculiarities, moral and physical. Several representative musical types were present, as it happened, that evening in addition to Moreland himself, Maclintick and Gossage being music critics, Carolo a violinist.

Only since knowing Barnby had I begun to frequent such society as was collected that night in the Mortimer, which, although it soon enough absorbed me, still at that time represented a world of high adventure. The hiatus between coming down from the university and finding a place for myself in London had comprised, with some bright spots, an eternity of boredom. I used to go out with unexciting former undergraduate acquaintances like Short (now a civil servant); less often with more dashing, if by then more remote, people like Peter Templer. Another friend, Charles Stringham, had recently risen from the earth to take me to Mrs Andriadis's party, only to disappear again;

but that night had nevertheless opened the road that led ultimately to the Mortimer: as Mr Deacon used to say of Barnby's social activities, 'the pilgrimage from the sawdust floor to the Aubusson carpet and back again'. At the time, of course, none of this took shape in my mind; no pattern was apparent of the kind eventually to emerge.

Moreland, like myself, was then in his early twenties. He was formed physically in a 'musical' mould, classical in type, with a massive, Beethoven-shaped head, high forehead, temples swelling outwards, eyes and nose somehow bunched together in a way to make him glare at times like a High Court judge about to pass sentence. On the other hand, his short, dark, curly hair recalled a dissipated cherub, a less aggressive, more intellectual version of Folly in Bronzino's picture, rubicund and mischievous, as he threatens with a fusillade of rose petals the embrace of Venus and Cupid; while Time in the background, whiskered like the Emperor Franz-Josef, looms behind a blue curtain as if evasively vacating the bathroom. Moreland's face in repose, in spite of this cherubic, humorous character, was not without melancholy too; his flush suggesting none of that riotously healthy physique enjoyed by Bronzino's – and, I suppose, everyone else's – Folly. Moreland had at first taken little notice of Mr Deacon's introduction; now he suddenly caught my eye, and, laughing loudly, slapped the folded newspaper sharply on the table.

'Tell us more about your young friend, Edgar,' he said, still laughing and looking across at me. 'What does he do for a living? Are we to understand that he wholly supports himself by finding junk at the Caledonian Market and vending it to connoisseurs of beauty like yourself?'

'He has stage connexions, Moreland, since you are so inquisitive,' said Mr Deacon, still speaking with accentuated primness. 'He was trained to dance – as he quaintly puts it – "in panto". Drury Lane was the peg upon which he hung his dreams. Now he dares to nourish wider ambitions. I am told, by the way, that the good old-fashioned harlequinade which I used so much to enjoy as a small boy has become a thing of the past. This lad would have made a charming Harlequin. Another theatrical friend of mine – rather a naughty young man – knows this child and thinks highly of his talent.'

'Why is your other friend naughty?'

'You ask too many questions, Moreland.'

'But I am intrigued to know, Edgar. We all are.'

'I call him naughty for many reasons,' said Mr Deacon, giving a long-drawn sigh, 'not the least of them because some years ago at a party he introduced me to an Italian, a youth whose sole claim to distinction was his alleged profession of gondolier, who turned out merely to have worked for a short time as ticket-collector on the *vaporetto*. A delightfully witty pleasantry, no doubt.'

There was some laughter at this anecdote, in which Maclintick did not join. Indeed, Maclintick had been listening to the course of conversation with unconcealed distaste. It was clear that he approved neither of Mr Deacon himself, nor of the suggestions implicit in Moreland's badinage. Like Moreland, Maclintick belonged to the solidly built musical type, a physical heaviness already threatening obesity in early middle age. Broad-shouldered, yet somehow narrowing towards his lower extremities, his frontal elevation gave the impression of a large triangular kite about to float away into the sky upon the fumes of Irish whiskey, which, even above the endemic odours of the Mortimer and the superimposed insistence of Mr Deacon's eucalyptus, freely emanated from the quarter in which he sat. Maclintick's calculatedly humdrum appearance, although shabby, seemed aimed at concealing bohemian affiliations.

The minute circular lenses of his gold-rimmed spectacles, set across the nose of a pug dog, made one think of caricatures of Thackeray or President Thiers, imposing upon him the air of a bad-tempered doctor. Maclintick, as I discovered in due course, was indeed bad-tempered, his manner habitually grumpy and disapproving, even with Moreland, to whom he was devoted; a congenital lack of amiability he appeared perpetually, though quite unsuccessfully, attempting to combat with copious draughts of Irish whiskey, a drink always lauded by him to the disadvantage of Scotch.

'I should be careful what you handle from the Caledonian Market, Deacon,' Maclintick said, 'I'm told stolen goods often drift up there. I don't expect you want a stiff sentence for receiving.'

He spoke for the first time since I had been sitting at the table, uttering the words in a high, caustic voice.

'Nonsense, Maclintick, nonsense,' said Mr Deacon shortly.

His tone made obvious that any dislike felt by Maclintick for himself – a sentiment not much concealed – was on his own side heartily reciprocated.

'Are you suggesting our friend Deacon is really a "fence"?' asked Gossage giggling, as if coy to admit knowledge of even this comparatively unexotic piece of thieves' jargon. 'I am sure he is nothing of the sort. Why, would you have us take him for a kind of modern Fagin?'

'I wouldn't go as far as that,' said Maclintick speaking more amicably this time, probably not wanting to exacerbate Mr Deacon beyond a certain point. 'Just warning him to take proper care of his reputation which I should not like to see tarnished.'

He smiled a little uneasily at Moreland to show this attack on Mr Deacon (which the victim seemed rather to enjoy) was not intended to include Moreland. I learnt later how much Moreland was the object of admiration, almost of reverence, on the part of Maclintick. This high regard was not only what Maclintick himself – on that rather dreadful subsequent occasion – called 'the proper respect of the poor interpretative hack for the true creative artist', but also because of an affection for Moreland as a friend that surpassed ordinary camaraderie, becoming something protective, almost maternal, if that word could be used of someone who looked like Maclintick. Indeed, under his splenetic exterior Maclintick harboured all kind of violent, imperfectly integrated sentiments. Moreland, for example, impressed him, perhaps rightly, as a young man of matchless talent, ill equipped to face a materialistic world. At the same time, Maclintick's own hag-ridden temperament also punished him for indulging in what he regarded as sentimentality. His tremendous disapproval of sexual inversion, encountered intermittently in circles he chose to frequent, was compensation for his own sense of guilt at this hero-worshipping of Moreland; his severity with Gossage, another effort to right the balance.

'It's nice when you meet someone fresh like that once in a while,' said Gossage.

He was a lean, toothy little man, belonging to another common musical type, whose jerky movements gave him no rest. He toyed nervously with his bow tie, pince-nez and moustache, the last of which carried little conviction of masculinity. Gossage's voice was like that of a ventriloquist's doll. He giggled nervously, no doubt fearing Maclintick's castigation of such a remark.

'Personal charm,' said Mr Deacon trenchantly, 'has unfortunately no connexion with personal altruism. However, I fully expect to be made to wait at my age. Lateness is one of the punishments justly visited by youth upon those who have committed the atrocious crime of coming to riper years. Besides, quite apart from this moral and aesthetic justification, none of the younger generation seem to know the meaning of punctuality even when the practice of that cardinal virtue is in their own interests.'

All this time Carolo, the last member of the party to be introduced, had not opened his mouth. He sat in front of a mixed vermouth with an air of slighted genius. I thought, that evening, Carolo was about the same age as Moreland and myself, but found afterwards he was older than he appeared. His youthful aspect was perhaps in part legacy of his years as a child prodigy.

'Carolo's real name is Wilson or Wilkinson or Parker,' Moreland told me later, 'something rather practical and healthy like that. A surname felt to ring too much of plain common sense. Almost the first public performance of music I remember being taken to by my aunt was to hear Carolo play at the Wigmore Hall. I never thought then that one of these days Carolo and I would rub shoulders in the Mortimer.'

Carolo's face was pale and drawn, his black hair arranged in delicate waves, this consciously 'romantic' appearance and demeanour altogether misrepresenting his character, which was, according to Moreland, far from imaginative.

'Carolo is only interested in making money,' Moreland said, 'and who shall blame him? Unfortunately, he doesn't seem much good at getting it these days. He also likes the girls a bit.'

Daydreams of wealth or women must have given Carolo that faraway look which never left him; sad and silent, he contemplated huge bank balances and voluptuous revels.

'Why, there is my young friend,' said Mr Deacon, rising to his feet. 'If you will forgive me, Nicholas . . . Moreland . . . and the rest of you . . .'

On the whole Mr Deacon was inclined to conceal from his acquaintances such minor indiscretions in which he might still, in this his later life, indulge. He seemed to regret having allowed himself to give the impression that one of his '*petites folies*', as he liked to term them, was on foot that night. The temptation to present matters by implication in such a light had been too much for his vanity. Now, too late, he tried to be more guarded, striding forward hastily and blocking the immediate advance of the young man who had just entered the Mortimer, carrying in his arms, as if it were a baby, a large brown paper parcel.

'Why,' said Moreland, 'after all that, Edgar's mysterious friend turns out to be Norman. Did you ever hear such a thing?'

By suddenly sidestepping with an artificial elegance of movement, the young man bearing the parcel avoided Mr Deacon's attempt to exclude him from our company, and approached the table. He was lightly built, so thin that scarcely any torso seemed to exist under his coat. It was easy to see why Mr Deacon had assigned him the rôle of Harlequin. Sad-eyed and pert, he was an urchin with good looks of that curiously puppet-like formation which designate certain individuals as actors or dancers; anonymity of feature and flexibility of body fitting them from birth to play an assumed part.

'Hullo, my dear,' he said, addressing himself to Moreland. 'I hear you saw the new Stravinsky ballet when you were in Paris.'

His voice came out in a drawl, half cockney, half drawing-room comedy, as he changed the position of his feet, striking a pose that immediately proclaimed a dancer's professional training.

'Speaking choreographically——' Moreland began.

Mr Deacon, put out at finding his 'young friend' already

known to most of the company, once more made an effort to intervene and keep the boy to himself, determined that any negotiations conducted between them should be transacted in at least comparative privacy.

'What?' he said, scarcely trying to hide his annoyance. 'You know each other, do you? How nice we should all be friends. However, Norman and I must discuss business of our own. The sacred rites of bargaining must not be overheard.'

He tittered angrily, and laid one of those gothic hands of his on the shoulder of the young man called Norman, who, as if to indicate that he must bow to the inevitable, waved dramatically to Moreland, as he allowed himself to be shepherded to the far end of the bar. There, he and Mr Deacon untied the parcel between them, at the same time folding the brown paper round it, so that they themselves should be, if possible, the sole persons to observe the contents. Mr Deacon must have felt immediately satisfied that he wanted to buy the cast (which reached his shop, although, as it turned out, only for a brief moment), because, after a muttered conversation, they wrapped up the parcel again and left the Mortimer together. As they went through the door Moreland shouted goodnight, a farewell to which only the young man responded by giving another wave of his hand.

'Who is the juvenile lead?' asked Gossage.

He smiled vigorously, at the same time removing his pince-nez to polish them, as if he did not wish Maclintick to think him unduly interested in Mr Deacon and his friend.

'Don't you know Norman Chandler?' said Moreland. 'I should have thought you would have come across him. He is an actor. Also dances a bit. Rather a hand at the saxophone.'

'A talented young gentleman,' said Gossage.

Moreland took another newspaper from his pocket, flattened it out on the surface of the table, and began to read a re-hash of the Croydon murder. Maclintick's face had expressed the strongest distaste during the conversation with Chandler; now he dismissed his indignation and began to discuss the Albert Hall concert Gossage was attending that night. I caught the phrases 'rhythmic ensemble' and 'dynamic and tonal balance'. Carolo sat in complete silence, from time to time tasting his vermouth without relish. Maclintick and Gossage passed on to the Delius Festival at the Queen's Hall. All this musical 'shop', to which Moreland, without looking up from his paper, would intermittently contribute comment, began to make me feel rather out of it. I wished I had been less punctual. Moreland came to the end of the article and pushed the paper from him.

'Edgar was quite cross at my turning out to know Norman,' he said to me, speaking in a detached, friendly tone. 'Edgar loves to build up mystery about any young man he meets. There was a lot of excitement about an "ex-convict from Devil's Island" he met at a fancy dress party the other day dressed as a French *matelot*.'

He leaned forward and deftly thrust a penny into the slot of the mechanical piano, which took a second or two to digest the coin, then began to play raucously.

'Oh, good,' said Moreland. '*The Missouri Waltz*.'

'Deacon is probably right in assuming some of the persons he associates with are sinister enough,' said Maclintick sourly.

'It is the only pleasure he has left,' said Moreland. 'I can't imagine what Norman was selling. It looked like a bed-pan from the shape of the parcel.'

Gossage sniggered, incurring a frown from Maclintick.

Probably fearing Maclintick might make him a new focus of disapproval, he remarked that he must be 'going soon'.

'Deacon will be getting himself into trouble one of these days,' Maclintick said, shaking his head and speaking as if he hoped the blow would fall speedily. 'Don't you agree, Gossage?'

'Oh, couldn't say, couldn't say at all,' said Gossage hurriedly. 'I hardly know the man, you see. Met him once or twice at the Proms last year. Join him sometimes over a mug of ale.'

Maclintick ignored these efforts to present a more bracing picture of Mr Deacon's activities.

'And it won't be the first time Deacon got into trouble,' he said in his grim, high-pitched voice.

'Well, I shall really have to go,' repeated Gossage, in answer to this further rebuke, speaking as if everyone present had been urging him to stay in the Mortimer for just a few minutes longer.

'You will read my views on Friday. I am keeping an open mind. One has to do that. Goodbye, Moreland, goodbye . . . Maclintick, goodbye . . .'

'I must be going too,' said Carolo unexpectedly.

He had a loud, harsh voice, and a North Country accent like Quiggin's. Tossing back the remains of his vermouth as if to the success of a desperate venture from which he was unlikely to return with his life, he finished the dregs at a gulp, and, inclining his head slightly in farewell to the company with an unconcerned movement in keeping with this devil-may-care mood, he followed Gossage from the saloon bar.

'Carolo wasn't exactly a chatterbox tonight,' said Moreland.

'Never has much to say for himself,' Maclintick agreed.

'Always brooding on the old days when he was playing Sarasate up and down the country clad as Little Lord Fauntleroy.'

'He must have been at least seventeen when he last appeared in his black velvet suit and white lace collar,' said Moreland. 'The coat was so tight he could hardly draw his bow across the fiddle.'

'They say Carolo is having trouble with his girl,' said Maclintick. 'Makes him even gloomier than usual.'

'Who is his girl?' asked Moreland indifferently.

'Quite young, I believe,' said Maclintick. 'Gossage was asking about her. Carolo doesn't find it as easy to get engagements as he used – and he won't teach.'

'Wasn't there talk of Mrs Andriadis helping him?' said Moreland. 'Arranging a performance at her house or something.'

I listened to what was being said without feeling – as I came to feel later – that I was, in one sense, part and parcel of the same community; that when people gossiped about matters like Carolo and his girl, one was listening to a morsel, if only an infinitesimal morsel, of one's own life. However, I heard no more about Carolo at that moment, because Barnby could now be seen standing in the doorway of the saloon bar, slowly apprising himself of the company present, the problem each individual might pose. By that hour the Mortimer had begun to fill. A man with a yellowish beard and black hat was buying drinks for two girls drawn from that indeterminate territory eternally disputed between tarts and art students; three pimply young men were arguing about economics; a couple of taxi-drivers conferred with the barmaid. For several seconds Barnby stared about him, viewing the people in the Mortimer with apparent disapproval. Then, thickset, his topcoat turned up to his ears, he moved slowly forward, at the same time casting an expert, all-embracing glance at the barmaid and the two art girls. Reaching the table at last by these easy stages, he nodded to the rest of us, but did not sit down. Instead, he regarded the party closely. Such evolutions were fairly typical of Barnby's behaviour in public; demeanour effective with most strangers, on whom he seemed ultimately to force friendliness by at first withholding himself. Later he would unfreeze. With women, that apparently negative method almost always achieved good results. It was impossible to say whether this manner of Barnby's was unconscious or deliberate. Moreland, for example, saw in Barnby a consummate actor.

'Ralph is the Garrick of our day,' Moreland used to say, 'or at least the Tree or Irving. Barnby never misses a gesture with women, not an inflection of the voice.'

The two of them, never close friends, used to see each other fairly often in those days. Moreland liked painting and held stronger views about pictures than most musicians.

'I can see Ralph has talent,' he said of Barnby, 'but why use combinations of colour that make you think he is a Frenchman or a Catalan?'

'I know nothing of music,' Barnby had, in turn, once remarked, 'but Hugh Moreland's accompaniment to that film sounded to me like a lot of owls quarrelling in a bicycle factory.'

All the same, in spite of mutual criticism, they were in general pretty well disposed to one another.

'Buy us a drink, Ralph,' said Moreland, as Barnby stood moodily contemplating us.

'I'm not sure I can afford that,' said Barnby. 'I'll have to think about it.'

'Take a generous view,' said Moreland, who liked being stood plenty of drinks.

After a minute or two's meditation Barnby drew some money from his pocket, glanced at the coins in the palm of his hand, and laid some of them on the bar. Then he brought the glasses across to the table.

'Had a look at the London Group this afternoon,' he said.

Barnby sat down. He and Moreland began to talk of English painting. The subject evidently bored Maclintick, who seemed to like Barnby as little as he cared for Mr Deacon. Conversation moved on to painting in Paris. Finally, the idea of going to a film was abandoned. It was getting late in the evening. The programme would be too far advanced. Instead, we agreed to dine together. Maclintick went off upstairs to telephone to his wife and tell her he would not be home until later.

'There will be a row about that,' said Moreland, after Maclintick had disappeared.

'Do they quarrel?'

'Just a bit.'

'Where shall we dine?' said Barnby. 'Foppa's?'

'No, I lunched at Foppa's,' Moreland said. 'I can't stand Foppa's twice in a day. It would be like going back to one's old school. Do you know Casanova's Chinese Restaurant? It hasn't been open long. Let's eat there.'

'I am not sure my stomach is up to Chinese food,' said Barnby. 'I didn't get to bed until three this morning.'

'You can have eggs or something like that.'

'Won't the eggs be several hundred years old? Still, we will go there if you insist. Anything to save a restaurant argument. Where is the place?'

Maclintick returned from telephoning. He bought himself a final Irish whiskey and drank it off. Conversation with his wife had been, as Moreland predicted, acrimonious. When told our destination was Casanova's Chinese Restaurant Maclintick made a face; but he failed to establish any rival claim in favour of somewhere he would prefer to eat, so the decision was confirmed. I asked how such a recklessly hybrid name had ever been invented.

'There used to be the New Casanova,' said Moreland, 'where the cooking was Italian and the decoration French eighteenth century – some way, some considerable way, after Watteau. Further up the street was the Amoy, called by some Sam's Chinese Restaurant. The New Casanova went into liquidation. Sam's bought it up and moved over their pots and pans and chopsticks, so now you can eat eight treasure rice, or bamboo shoots fried with pork ribbons, under panels depicting scenes from the career of the Great Lover.'

'What are prices like?' asked Barnby.

'One might almost say cheap. On Sunday there is an orchestra of three and dainty afternoon tea is served. You can even dance. Maclintick has been there, haven't you, Maclintick?'

'Must it be Chinese food tonight?' said Maclintick peevishly. 'I've a touch of enteritis as it is.'

'Remember some of the waitresses are rather attractive,' said Moreland persuasively.

'Chinese?' I asked.

'No,' said Moreland, 'English.'

He laughed a little self-consciously.

'Bet you've got your eye on one,' said Barnby.

I think Barnby made this remark as a matter of routine, either without bothering to consider the matter at all carefully, or on the safe assumption that no one would take the trouble to mention the fact that any given group of girls was above the average in looks without having singled out at least one of them for himself. That would unquestionably have been Barnby's own procedure. Alternatively, Moreland may have spoken of Casanova's on an earlier occasion, thereby giving Barnby reason to suspect there must be something special that attracted Moreland personally to the place. In any case, the imputation was not surprising, although Barnby's own uninterrupted interest in the subject always made him perceptive where the question of a woman, or women, was concerned. However, Moreland went red at the enquiry. He was in one sense, easily embarrassed about any matter that touched him intimately; although, at the same time, his own mind moved too quickly for him to be placed long at a disadvantage by those who hoped to tease. In such situations he was pretty adept at turning the tables.

'I had my eye on a girl there formerly,' he said, 'I admit that. It wasn't entirely the excellent pig's trotter soup that brought me back to Casanova's. However, I can visit that restaurant now without a tremor – not a concupiscent thought. My pleasure in the place has become purely that of *gourmet* of Cathay. A triumph of self-mastery. I will point the girl out to you, Ralph.'

'What happened?' asked Barnby. 'Did she leave you for the man who played the trombone?'

'One just wasn't a success,' said Moreland, reddening again. 'Anyway, I will show you the problem as it stood – no doubt as it stands. Nothing altered, so far as I know, except my own point of view. But let's be moving. I'm famished.'

The name Casanova's Chinese Restaurant offered one of those unequivocal blendings of disparate elements of the imagination which suggest a whole new state of mind or way of life. The idea of Casanova giving his name to a Chinese restaurant linked not only the East with the West, the present with the past, but also, more parochially, suggested by its own incongruity an immensely suitable place for all of us to have dinner that night. We arrived in two large rooms, in which most of the tables were filled. The clientèle, predominantly male and Asiatic, had a backbone of Chinese businessmen and Indian students. A few Negroes sat with very blonde white girls; a sprinkling of diners belonged to those ethnically indefinable races which colonise Soho and interbreed there. Along the walls frescoes tinted in pastel shades, executed with infinite feebleness of design, appealed to Heaven knows what nadir of aesthetic degradation. Almost as soon as we found a table, I marked down Moreland's waitress. She was tall, very thin, fair-haired and blue-eyed, at that moment carrying a lot of glasses on a tray. The girl was certainly noticeable in her white lace cap and small frilled white apron above a black dress and black cotton stockings, the severity of this uniform, her own pale colouring, lending a curious exoticism to her appearance in these pseudo-oriental surroundings. There was an air of childlike innocence about her that could easily be deceptive. Indeed, when more closely observed, she had some of the look of a very expensive, rather wicked little doll. Moreland's answer to Barnby's almost immediate request to have 'the girl we have come to see' pointed out to him, confirmed the correctness of this guess. Barnby took one of his lingering, professional stares.

'Rather an old man's piece, isn't she?' he said. 'Still, I see your point. Poorish legs, though.'

'You mustn't concentrate on legs if your interest is in waitresses,' said Moreland. 'The same is true of ballet dancers, I'm afraid.'

'She looks as if she might well be a nymphomaniac,' said Maclintick, 'those very fair, innocent-looking girls often are. I think I mentioned that to Moreland when he brought me here before.'

Maclintick had hardly spoken since we left the Mortimer. Now he uttered these words in a tone of deep pessimism,

272

as if, so far, he had resented every moment of the evening. He greatly disapproved of Barnby, whose inclination for women was as irksome to him as Mr Deacon's so downright repudiation of the opposite sex. Maclintick possibly thought Barnby had a bad influence on Moreland.

'She showed no sign of being a nympho,' Moreland said. 'On the contrary. I could have done with a little nymphomania – anyway at the start.'

'What are we going to eat?' said Barnby. 'I can't make head or tail of this menu.'

Maclintick and Barnby ordered something unadventurous from the dishes available; under Moreland's guidance, I embarked upon one of the specialities of the house. Moreland's waitress came to take our order for drinks. Although a restaurant of some size, Casanova's had no licence, so that a member of the staff collected beer from the pub opposite, or wine from the shop round the corner. When she came up to the table the waitress gave Moreland a cold, formal smile of recognition, which freely acknowledged him as a regular customer, but suggested no more affectionate relationship. Close up, she looked, I thought, as hard as nails; I did not feel at all tempted to enter into competition. Barnby eyed her. She took no notice of him whatever, noting our orders in silence and disappearing.

'Too thin for my taste,' said Barnby. 'I like a good armful.'

'This lascivious conversation is very appropriate to the memory of the distinguished Venetian gentleman after whom the restaurant is named,' said Maclintick harshly. 'What a bore he must have been.'

He leant across the table, and, like an angry woodpecker, began to tap out his pipe against the side of a large Schweppes ashtray.

'Do you suppose one would have known Casanova?' I said.

'Oh, but of course,' said Moreland. 'In early life, Casanova played the violin – like Carolo. Casanova played in a band – I doubt if he would have been up to a solo performance. I can just imagine what he would have been like to deal with if one had been the conductor. Besides, he much fancied himself as a figure at the opera and musical parties. One would certainly have met him. At least I am sure I should.'

'Think of having to listen to interminable stories about his girls,' said Maclintick. 'I could never get through Casanova's Memoirs. Why should he be considered a great man just because he had a lot of women? Most men would have ended by being bored to death.'

'That is why he was a great man,' said Moreland. 'It wasn't the number of women he had, it was the fact that he didn't get bored. But there are endless good things there apart from the women. Do you remember when in London he overhears someone remark: "Tommy has committed suicide and he did quite right" – to which another person replies: "On the contrary, he did a very foolish thing, for I am one of his creditors and know that he need not have made away with himself for six months".'

Barnby and I laughed at this anecdote. Maclintick did not smile. At the same time he seemed struck by the story. He was silent for some moments. When he spoke again it was in a manner at once more serious, more friendly, than any tone he had previously employed that evening.

'I see nothing particularly funny in their conversation,' he said. 'That is how I propose to behave myself when the time comes. But I agree that Tommy was a fool to misjudge his term of days. I shall not do that. I give myself at least five more years at the present rate. That should allow me time to finish my book.'

'Still,' said Moreland, 'however bent one may be on the idea of eventual suicide oneself, you must admit, Maclintick, that such sentiments must have sounded odd to a man of Casanova's *joie de vivre*. Anyway, professional seducers never commit suicide. They haven't time.'

'The notable thing about professional seducers,' said Maclintick, now returning to his former carping tone of voice, 'is the rot they talk when they are doing their seducing. There is not a single cliché they leave unsaid.'

'Although by definition the most egotistical of men,' said Moreland, 'they naturally have to develop a certain anonymity of style to make themselves acceptable to all women. It is the case of the lowest common factor – or is it the highest common denominator? If you hope to rise to the top class in seducing, you must appeal to the majority. As the majority are not very intelligent, you must conceal your own intelligence – if you have the misfortune to possess such a thing – in order not to frighten the girls off. There is inevitably something critical, something alarming to personal vanity, in the very suggestion of intelligence in another. That is almost equally true of dealing with men, so don't think I hold it against women. All I say is, that someone like myself ought to restrict themselves to intelligent girls who see my own good points. Unfortunately, they are rarely the sort of girls I like.'

Barnby grunted, no doubt feeling some of these strictures in part applicable to himself.

'What do you expect to do?' he asked. 'Give readings from *The Waste Land*?'

'Not a bad idea,' said Moreland.

'In my experience,' Barnby said, 'women like the obvious.'

'Just what we are complaining about,' said Maclintick, 'the very thing.'

'Seduction is to do and say/The banal thing in the banal way,' said Moreland. 'No one denies that. My own complaint is that people always talk about love affairs as if you spent the whole of your time in bed. I find most of my own emotional energy – not to say physical energy – is exhausted in making efforts to get there. Problems of Time and Space as usual.'

The relation of Time and Space, then rather fashionable, was, I found, a favourite subject of Moreland's.

'Surely we have long agreed the two elements are identical?' said Maclintick. 'This is going over old ground – perhaps I should say old hours.'

'You must differentiate for everyday purposes, don't you?' urged Barnby. 'I don't wonder seduction seems a problem, if you get Time and Space confused.'

'I suppose one might be said to be true to a woman in Time and unfaithful to her in Space,' said Moreland. 'That is what Dowson seems to have thought about Cynara – or is it just the reverse? The metaphysical position is not made wholly clear by the poet. Talking of pale lost lilies, how do you think Edgar and Norman are faring in their deal?'

'Remember Lot's wife,' said Maclintick sententiously. 'Besides, we have a cruet on the table. Here are the drinks at last, thank God. You know Pope says every woman is at heart a rake. I'd be equally prepared to postulate that every rake is at heart a woman. Don Juan – Casanova – Byron – the whole bloody lot of them.'

'But Don Juan was not at all the same as Casanova,' said Moreland. 'The opera makes that quite clear. Ralph here sometimes behaves like Casanova. He isn't in the least like Don Juan – are you, Ralph?'

I was myself not sure this assessment of Barnby's nature

was wholly accurate; but, if distinction were to be drawn between those two legendary seducers, the matter was at least arguable. Barnby himself was now showing signs of becoming rather nettled by this conversation.

'Look here,' he said. 'My good name keeps on being bandied about in a most uncalled for manner. Perhaps you wouldn't mind defining the differences between these various personages with whom I am being so freely compared. I had better be told for certain, otherwise I shall be behaving in a way that is out of character, which would never do.'

'Don Juan merely liked power,' said Moreland. 'He obviously did not know what sensuality was. If he knew it at all, he hated it. Casanova, on the other hand, undoubtedly had his sensual moments, even though they may not have occurred very often. With Henriette, for example, or those threesomes with the nun, M.M. Of course, Casanova was interested in power too. No doubt he ended as a complete Narcissus, when love naturally became intolerable to him, since love involved him with another party emotionally. Every Narcissus dislikes that. None of us regards Ralph as only wanting power where a woman is concerned. We think too highly of you for that, Ralph.'

Barnby did not appear flattered by this analysis of his emotional life.

'Thanks awfully,' he said. 'But, to get down to more immediate matters, how would you feel, Hugh, if I asked that waitress to sit for me? For reasons of trade, rather than power or sensuality. Of course she is bound to think I am trying to get off with her. Nothing could be further from the case – no, I assure you, Maclintick. Anyway, I don't expect she will agree. No harm in trying, though. I just wanted to make sure you had no objection. To show how little of a Casanova I am – or is it a Don Juan?'

'Take any step you think best,' said Moreland laughing, although perhaps not best pleased by what Barnby had asked. 'I have resigned all claims. I don't quite see her in your medium, but that is obviously the painter's own affair. If I have a passion for anyone, I prefer an academic, even pedestrian, naturalism of portraiture. It is a limitation I share with Edgar Deacon. Nothing I'd care for less than to have my girl painted by Lhote or Gleizes, however much I may admire those painters – literally – in the abstract.'

All the same, although he put a good face on it, Moreland looked a little cast down. No more was said on the subject until the time came to make our individual contributions to the bill. The waitress appeared again. She explained that she had omitted at an earlier stage of the meal to collect some of the money due for what we had drunk. She now presented her final account. At this point Barnby took the opportunity to allow himself certain pleasantries – these a trifle on the ponderous side, as he himself admitted later – to the effect that she was demanding money under false pretences. The waitress received these comments in good part, unbending so far as to hint that she had not levied the charge before, because, having taken one look at Barnby, she had been sure he would give a further order for drink; she had accordingly decided to wait until the account was complete. Barnby listened to this explanation gravely, making no attempt to answer in the breezy manner he had employed a few seconds earlier this imputation of possessing a bibulous appearance. Just as the girl was about to withdraw, he spoke.

'Look here,' he said, 'I'm an artist – I paint people's pictures.'

She did not look at him, or answer, but she stopped giggling, while at the same time making no attempt to move away from the table.

'I'd like to paint you.'

She still did not speak. Her expression changed in a very slight degree, registering what might have been embarrassment or cunning.

'Could you come and be painted by me some time?'

Barnby put the question in a quiet, almost exaggeratedly gentle voice; one I had never before heard him use.

'Don't know that I have time,' she said, very coolly.

'What about one week-end?'

'Can't come Sunday. Have to be here.'

'Saturday, then?'

'Saturday isn't any good either.'

'You can't have to work all the week.'

'Might manage a Thursday.'

'All right, let's make it a Thursday then.'

There was a pause. Maclintick, unable to bear the sight and sound of these negotiations, had taken a notebook from his pocket and begun a deep examination of his own affairs; making plans for the future; writing down great thoughts; perhaps even composing music. Moreland, unable to conceal his discomfort at what was taking place, started a conversation with me designed to carry further his Time-Space theories.

'What about next Thursday?' asked Barnby, in his most wheedling tone.

'I don't know.'

'Say you will.'

'I don't know.'

'Come on.'

'I suppose so, then.'

Barnby reached forward and took Maclintick's pencil from his hand – not without protest on Maclintick's part – and wrote something on the back of an envelope. I suppose it was just the address of his studio, but painters form the individual letters of their handwriting so carefully, so separately, that he seemed to be drawing a picture specially for her.

'It's above a shop,' Barnby said.

Then, suddenly, he crumpled the envelope.

'On second thoughts,' he said, 'I will come and pick you up here, if that is all right.'

'As you like.'

She spoke indifferently, as if all had been decided long before and they had been going out together for years.

'What time?'

She told him; the two of them made some mutual arrangement. Then they smiled at each other, again without any sense of surprise or excitement, as if long on familiar terms, and the waitress retired from the table. Barnby handed the stump of pencil back to Maclintick. We vacated the restaurant.

'Like Glendower, Barnby,' said Maclintick, 'you can call spirits from the vasty deep. With Hotspur, I ask you, will they come?'

'That's to be seen,' said Barnby. 'By the way, what is her name? I forgot to ask.'

'Norma,' said Moreland, speaking without apology.

To complete the story, Barnby (whose personal arrangements were often vague) told me that when the day of assignation came, he arrived, owing to bad timing, three-quarters of an hour late for the appointment. The girl was still waiting for him. She came to his studio, where he began a picture of her, subsequently completing at least one oil painting and several drawings. The painting, which was in his more severe manner, he sold to Sir Magnus Donners; Sir Herbert Manasch bought one of the drawings, which were treated naturistically. Eventually, as might have been foretold, Barnby had some sort of a love affair with his model; although he always insisted she was 'not his type', that matters had come to a head one thundery afternoon when an overcast sky made painting impossible. Norma left Casanova's soon after this episode. She took a job which led to her marrying a man who kept a tobacconist's shop in Camden Town. There was no ill feeling after Barnby had done with her; keeping on good terms with his former mistresses was one of his gifts. In fact he used to visit Norma and her husband (who sometimes gave him racing tips) after they were married. Through them he found a studio in that part of London; he may even have been godfather to one of their children. All that is beside the point. The emphasis I lay upon the circumstances of this assignation at Casanova's Chinese Restaurant is to draw attention to the extreme ease with which Barnby conducted the preliminaries of his campaign. Anyone who heard things being fixed up might have supposed Norma to have spent much of her previous life as an artist's model; that she regarded making an engagement for a sitting as a matter of routine regulated only by aspects of her own immediate convenience. Perhaps she had; perhaps she did. In such case Barnby showed scarcely less mastery of the situation in at once assessing her potentialities in that rôle.

'Of course, Ralph is a painter,' said Moreland, afterwards. 'He has a studio. Time, place and a respectable motive for a visit are all at his command. None of these things are to be despised where girls are concerned.'

'Time and Space, as usual.'

'Time and Space,' said Moreland.

The incident was not only an illustration of Barnby's adroitness in that field, but also an example of Moreland's diffidence, a diffidence no doubt in part responsible for the admixture of secretiveness and exhibitionism with which he conducted his love affairs. By exhibitionism, I mean, in Moreland's case, no more than a taste for referring obliquely from time to time to some unrevealed love that possessed him. I supposed that this habit of his explained his talk of marriage the day – five or six years after our first meeting – when we had listened together to the song of the blonde singer; especially when he refused to name the girl – or three girls – he might be considering as a wife. It was therefore a great surprise to me when his words turned out to be spoken seriously. However, I did not at first realise how serious they were; nor even when, some weeks later, more about the girl herself was revealed.

He suggested one day that we should go together to *The Duchess of Malfi*, which was being performed at a small theatre situated somewhat off the beaten track; one of those ventures that attempt, by introducing a few new names and effects, momentarily to dispel the tedium of dramatic routine.

'Webster is always a favourite of mine,' Moreland said. 'Norman Chandler has for the moment abandoned dancing and the saxophone, and is playing Bosola.'

'That should be enjoyable. Has he quite the weight?'

Chandler had moved a long way since the day when I had first seen him at the Mortimer, when Mr Deacon had spoken so archly of having acquired his friendship through a vegetarian holiday. Now Chandler had made some name for himself, not only as a dancer, but also as an actor; not in leading rôles, but specialising in smaller, unusual parts suitable to his accomplished, but always intensely personal, style. I used to run across him occasionally with Moreland, whose passion for mechanical pianos Chandler shared; music for which they would search London.

'I also happen to know the Cardinal's mistress,' said Moreland, speaking very casually.

This remark suddenly struck a chord of memory about something someone had said a few days before about the cast of this very play.

'But wasn't she Sir Magnus Donners's mistress too? I was hearing about that. It is Matilda Wilson, isn't it, who is playing that part – the *jolie laide* Donners used to be seen about with a year or two ago? I have always wanted to have a look at her.'

Moreland turned scarlet. I realised that I had shown colossal lack of tact. This must be his girl. I saw now why he had spoken almost apologetically about going to the play, as if some excuse were required for attending one of Webster's tragedies, even though Moreland himself was known by me to be greatly attached to the Elizabethan dramatists. When he made the suggestion that we should see the play together I had suspected no ulterior motive. Now, it looked as if something were on foot.

'She was mixed up with Donners for a time,' he said, 'that is quite true. But several years ago now. I thought we might go round and see her after the performance. Then we could have a drink – even eat if we felt like it – at the Café Royal or somewhere like that.'

To hold a friend in the background at a certain stage of a love affair is a technique some men like to employ; a method which spreads, as it were, the emotional load, ameliorating risks of dual conflict between the lovers themselves, although at the same time posing a certain hazard in the undue proximity of a third party unencumbered with emotional responsibility – and therefore almost always seen to better advantage than the lover himself. Close friends probably fall in love with the same woman less often in life than in books, though the female spirit of emulation will sometimes fix on a husband or lover's friend out of a mere desire to show that a woman can do even better than her partner in the same sphere. Moreland and I used to agree that, in principle, we liked the same kind of girl; but never, so long as I knew him, did we ever find ourselves in competition.

The news that he was involved with Matilda Wilson, might even be thinking of marrying her – for that was the shape things seemed to be taking – was surprising in a number of ways. I had never seen the girl herself, although often hearing about her during her interlude with Sir Magnus, a person round whom gossip accumulated easily, not only because he was very rich, but also on account of supposedly unconventional tastes in making love. Sir Magnus was said to be reasonably generous with his girls, and, provided he was from time to time indulged in certain respects, not unduly demanding. It was characteristic of the situations in which love lands people that someone as sensitive as Moreland to life's grotesque aspects should find himself handling so delicate an affair, where perhaps even marriage was the goal. When we arrived at the theatre we found Mark Members waiting in the foyer. Members was the kind of person who would know by instinct that Moreland was interested in Matilda Wilson, and might be expected to make some reference to her past with Sir Magnus with the object of teasing Moreland with whom he was on prickly terms. However, the subject did not arise. Members had just finished straightening his tie in a large looking-glass. He was now looking disdainfully round him.

'What a shabby lot of highbrows have turned out tonight,' he said, when he saw us. 'It makes me ashamed to be one.'

'Nobody guesses you are, Mark,' said Moreland. 'Not in that natty new suit. They think you are an actuary or an average adjuster.'

Members laughed his tinny laugh.

'How is sweet music?' he asked. 'How are your pale tunes irresolute, Moreland? When is that opera of yours we hear so much about going to appear?'

'I've knocked off work on the opera for the moment,' said Moreland. 'I'm concentrating on something slighter which

I think should appeal to music-lovers of your temperament. It is to be called *Music for a Maison de Passe: A Suite.*'

We passed on to where Gossage was standing a short way off by the curtain that screened the foyer from the passage leading to the auditorium. Gossage was talking with a great display of respect to a lady dressed rather too exquisitely for the occasion; the audience that night, as Members had truly remarked, being decidedly unkempt. This lady, slight in figure, I recognised at once as Mrs Foxe, mother of my old friend, Charles Stringham. I had not seen Stringham since Widmerpool and I had put him to bed after too much to drink at an Old Boy Dinner. Mrs Foxe herself I had not set eyes on for ten years; the day she and Commander Foxe had lunched with Stringham in his rooms in college to discuss whether or not he should 'go down' before taking a degree.

Mrs Foxe was quite unchanged. Beautiful in early middle age, she remained still untouched by time. She was accompanied by a girl of seventeen or eighteen, and two young men who looked like undergraduates. Evidently she was hostess to this party, whom I supposed to be relations; connexions possibly of her first husband, Lord Warrington, or her third husband, Buster Foxe. Stringham, child of the intermediate marriage of this South African millionaire's daughter, used to boast he had no relations; so they were presumably not cousins of his. Gossage, parting now from Mrs Foxe with many smiles and bows, nodded to Moreland with an air of considerable satisfaction as he hurried past. When we reached our seats I saw that Mrs Foxe and her party were sitting a long way away from us. Since I hardly supposed she would remember me, I decided not to approach her during the *entr'actes*. In any case, she and I had little in common except Stringham himself, of whom I then knew nothing except that his marriage had broken up and he was said to be still drinking too much. He had certainly drunk a lot the night Widmerpool and I had put him to bed. Another reason for taking no step in Mrs Foxe's direction was that a stage in my life had been reached when I felt that to spend even a short time with a party of that kind would be 'boring'. For the moment, I had put such things behind me. Perhaps at some future date I should return to them; for the time being I rather prided myself on preferring forms of social life where white ties were not worn. I was even glad there was no likelihood of chance recognition.

Julia, the Cardinal's mistress in *The Duchess of Malfi*, does not come on to the stage until the fourth scene of the first act. Moreland was uneasy until that moment, fidgeting in his seat, giving deep breaths, a habit of his when inwardly disturbed. At the same time, he showed a great deal of enjoyment in Norman Chandler's earlier speeches as Bosola. Chandler had brought an unexpected solidity to this insidious part. The lightness of his build, and general air of being a dancer rather than an actor, had prepared neither Moreland nor myself for the rendering he presented of 'this fellow seven years in the galleys for a notorious murder'.

'Do you think Norman talked like Bosola the night he was bargaining with Edgar Deacon about that statuette?' said Moreland, in an undertone. 'If so, he must have got the best of it. Did I ever tell you that he hadn't been paid when Edgar died, so Norman nipped round to the shop and took the thing away again? That was in the Bosola tradition.'

When at last Matilda Wilson appeared as Julia, Moreland's face took on a look of intensity, almost of strain, more like worry than love. I had been looking forward to seeing her with the interest one feels in being shown for the first time the woman a close friend proposes to marry; for I now had no doubt from the manner in which the evening had been planned that Matilda must be the girl whom Moreland had in mind when he had spoken of taking a wife. When she first came towards the footlights I was disappointed. I have no talent for guessing what an actress will look like off the stage, but, even allowing for an appearance greatly changed by the removal of make-up and the stiffly angled dress in which she was playing the part, she seemed altogether lacking in conventional prettiness. A minute or two later I began to change my mind. She certainly possessed a forceful, enigmatic personality; none of the film-star looks of the waitress in Casanova's, but something, one of those resemblances impossible to put into words, made me recall that evening. Matilda Wilson moved gracefully. Apart from that, and the effectiveness of her slow, clear voice and sardonic enunciation, she was not a very 'finished' actress. Once or twice I was aware of Moreland glancing in my direction, as if he hoped to discover what I thought of her; but he asked no questions and made no comment when the curtain fell. He shuddered slightly when she replied to Bosola's lines: 'Know you me, I am a blunt soldier', with: 'The better; sure there wants fire where there are no lively sparks of roughness'.

When the play was over, we went round to the stage door, penetrating into regions where the habitually cramped accommodation of theatrical dressing-rooms was more than usually in evidence. For a time we wandered about narrow passages filled with little young men who had danced the Masque of Madmen, now dressing, undressing, chattering, washing, playing noisy games of their own, which gave the impression that the action of the play was continuing its course even though the curtain had come down. We found Matilda Wilson's room at last. She was wearing hardly any clothes, removing her make-up, while Norman Chandler, dressed in a mauve dressing-gown of simulated brocade, sat on a stool beside her, reading a book. I never feel greatly at ease 'backstage', and Moreland himself, although by then certainly used enough to such surroundings, was obviously disturbed by the responsibility of having to display his girl for the first time. He need not have worried; Matilda herself was completely at ease. I saw at once, now she was off the stage, how effortless her conquest of Moreland must have been. He possessed, it was true, a certain taste for rather conventional good looks which had to be overcome in favour of beauty of a less obvious kind; in other respects she seemed to have everything he demanded, yet never could find. Barnby always dismissed the idea of intelligence in a woman as no more than a characteristic to be endured. Moreland held different views.

'I don't want what Rembrandt or Cézanne or Barnby or any other painter may happen to want,' he used to say. 'I simply cling to my own preferences. I don't know what's good, but I know what I like – not a lot of intellectual snobbery about fat peasant women, or technical talk about masses and planes. After all, painters have to contend professionally with pictorial aspects of the eternal feminine which are quite beside the point where a musician like myself is concerned. With women, I can afford to cut out the chiaroscuro. Choosing the type of girl one likes is about the last thing left that one is allowed to approach subjectively. I shall continue to exercise the option.'

Matilda Wilson jumped up from her stool as soon as she saw Moreland. Throwing her arms round his neck, she kissed him on the nose. When a woman is described as a '*jolie laide*', the same particular combination of looks is, for some reason, implied; you expect a brunette, small rather than tall, with a face emphasised by eyebrows and mouth, features which would be too insistent if the eyes did not finally control the general effect – in fact what is also known as *beauté de singe*. Matilda Wilson was not at all like that. Off the stage, she was taller and thinner than I had supposed,

288

her hair fairish, with large, rather sleepy green eyes. The upper half of her face was pretty enough; the lower, forcefully, even rather coarsely modelled. You felt the beauty of her figure was in some manner the consequence of her own self-control; that a less intelligent woman might have 'managed' her body without the same effectiveness.

'Oh, darling,' she said, in a voice that at once suggested her interlude in the world of Sir Magnus Donners, 'I am so glad you have turned up at last. Various awful men have been trying to make me go out with them. But I said you were calling for me. I hoped you would not forget as you did last week.'

'Oh, last week,' said Moreland, looking dreadfully put out, and making a characteristic gesture with his hand, as if about to begin conducting. 'That muddle was insane of me. Will you ever forgive me, Matty? It upset me so much. Do let me off further mention of it. I am so hopelessly forgetful.'

He looked rather wildly round him, as if he expected to find some explanation of the cause of bad memory in the furthest recesses of the dressing-room, finally turning to me for support.

'Nick, don't you find it absolutely impossible nowadays to remember anything?' he began. 'Do you know, I was in the Mortimer the other day——'

Up to that time he had made no attempt to tell Matilda Wilson my name, although no doubt she had been warned that I was probably going to join them at the end of the play. He would certainly have launched into a long train of reminiscence about something or other that had happened to him in the Mortimer, if she had not burst out laughing and kissed him again, this time on the ear. She held out her hand to me, still laughing, and Moreland, now red in the face, insisted that the time had passed for introductory formalities. Meanwhile, Norman Chandler had been finishing his chapter without taking any notice of what was going on round him. Now, he put a marker in his book (which I saw to be *Time and Western Man*), and, drawing the billowing robes of his rather too large dressing-gown more tightly round him, he rose to his feet.

' "A lot of awful men"?' he said, speaking in a voice of old-time melodrama. 'What do you mean, Matilda? I offered you a bite with Max and me, if your boy friend did not arrive. That was only because you said he was so forgetful, and might easily think he had made a date for the day after tomorrow. I never heard such ingratitude.'

Matilda put her arm round Chandler's waist and attempted to smoothe his hair with her brush.

'Oh, I didn't mean you, darling, of course I didn't,' she said. 'I don't call you a man. I love you much too much. I mean an awful man who telephoned – and then another awful man who left a note. How could anyone call you awful, Norman, darling?'

'Oh, I don't know so much about that,' said Chandler, now abandoning the consciously sinister, masculine tones of Bosola, and returning to his more familiar chorus-boy drawl. 'I'm not always adored as much as you might think from looking at me. I don't quite know why that is.'

He put his head on one side, forefinger against cheek, transforming himself to some character of ballet, perhaps the Faun from *L'Après-midi*.

'You are adored by me,' said Matilda, kissing him twice before throwing down the hairbrush on the dressing-table. 'But I really must put a few clothes on.'

Chandler broke away from her, executing a series of little leaps in the air, although there was not much room for these *entrechats*. He whizzed round several times, collapsing at last upon his stool.

'Bravo, bravo,' said Matilda, clapping her hands. 'You will rival Nijinsky yet, Norman, my sweetie.'

'Be careful,' said Chandler. 'Your boy friend will be jealous. I can see him working himself up. He can be very violent when roused.'

Moreland had watched this display of high spirits with enjoyment, except when talk had been of other men taking out Matilda, when his face had clouded. Chandler had probably noticed that. So far from being jealous of Chandler, which would certainly have been absurd in the circumstances, Moreland seemed to welcome these antics as relaxing tension between himself and Matilda. He became more composed in manner. Paradoxically enough, something happened a moment later which paid an obvious tribute to Chandler's status as a ladies' man, however little regarded in that rôle by Moreland and the world at large.

'I will be very quick now,' said Matilda, 'and then we will go. I am dying for a bite.'

She retired behind a small screen calculated to heighten rather than diminish the dramatic effect of her toilet, since her long angular body was scarcely at all concealed, and, in any case, she continually reappeared on the floor of the room to rescue garments belonging to her which lay about there. The scene was a little like those depicted in French eighteenth-century engravings where propriety is archly threatened in the presence of an amorous *abbé* or two – powdered hair would have suited Matilda, I thought; Moreland, perhaps, too. However, the picture's static form was interrupted by the sound of some commotion in the passage which caused Chandler to stroll across the room and stand by the half-open door. Some people were passing who must have recognised him, because he suddenly said: 'Why, hullo, Mrs Foxe,' in a tone rather different from that used by him a moment before; a friendly tone, but one at the same time faintly deferential, possibly even a shade embarrassed. There was the sudden suggestion that Chandler was on his best behaviour.

'We were looking for you,' said a woman's voice, speaking almost appealingly, yet still with a note of command in it. 'We thought you would not mind if we came behind the scenes to see you. Such an adventure for us, you know. In fact we even wondered if there was any chance of persuading you to come to supper with us.'

The people in the passage could not be seen, but this was undoubtedly Stringham's mother. She introduced Chandler to the persons with her, but the names were inaudible.

'It would be so nice if you could come,' she said, quite humbly now. 'Your performance was wonderful. We adored it.'

Chandler had left the dressing-room now and was some way up the passage, but his voice could still be heard.

'It is terribly sweet of you, Mrs Foxe,' he said, with some hesitation. 'It would have been quite lovely. But as a matter of fact I was supposed to be meeting an old friend this evening.'

He seemed undecided whether or not to accept the invitation, to have lost suddenly all the animation he had been showing in the dressing-room a minute or two before. Moreland and Matilda had stopped talking and had also begun to listen, evidently with great enjoyment, to what was taking place outside.

'Oh, but if he is an old friend,' said Mrs Foxe, who seemed to make no doubt whatever of the sex of Chandler's companion for dinner, 'surely he might join us too. It would be so nice. What is his name?'

Although she was almost begging Chandler to accept her invitation, there was also in her voice the imperious note of the beauty of her younger days, the rich woman, well known in the world and used to being obeyed.

'Max Pilgrim.'

Chandler's voice, no less than Mrs Foxe's, suggested conflicting undertones of feeling: gratification at being so keenly desired as a guest; deference, in spite of himself, for the air of luxury and high living that Mrs Foxe bestowed about her; determination not to be jockeyed out of either his *gaminerie* or accustomed manner of ordering his own life by Mrs Foxe or anyone else.

'Not *the* Max Pilgrim?'

'He is at the Café de Madrid now. He sings there.'

'But, of course. "I want to dazzle Lady Sybil . . ." What a funny song that one is. Does he mean it to be about Sybil Huntercombe, do you think? It is so like her. We must certainly have Mr Pilgrim too. But will he come? He has probably planned something much more amusing. Oh, I do hope he will.'

'I think——'

'But how wonderful, if he would. Certainly you must ask him. Do telephone to him at once and beg him to join us.'

The exact words of Chandler's reply could not be heard, but there could be little doubt that he had been persuaded. Perhaps he was afraid of Max Pilgrim's annoyance if the supper party had been refused on behalf of both of them. In dealing with Mrs Foxe, Chandler seemed deprived, if only temporarily, of some of his effervescence of spirit. It looked as if he might be made her prisoner. This was an unguessed aspect of Mrs Foxe's life, a new departure in her career of domination. The party moved off, bearing Chandler with them; their voices died away as they reached the end of the passage. Moreland and Matilda continued to laugh. I asked what it was all about.

'Norman's grand lady,' said Matilda. 'She is someone

called Mrs Foxe. Very smart. She sits on all sorts of committees and she met Norman a week or two ago at some charity performance. It was love at first sight.'

'You don't mean they are having an affair?'

'No, no, of course not,' said Moreland, speaking as if he were quite shocked at the notion, 'how absurd to suggest such a thing. You can have a passion for someone without having an affair with them. That is one of the things no one seems able to understand these days.'

'What is it then?'

'Just one of those fascinating mutual attractions between improbable people that take place from time to time. I should like to write a ballet round it.'

'Norman is interested too? He sounded a bit unwilling to go out to supper.'

'Perhaps not interested in the sense you mean,' said Moreland, 'but everyone likes being fallen in love with. People who pretend they don't are always the ones, beyond all others, to wring the last drop of pleasure – usually sadistic pleasure – out of it. Besides, Norman has begun to live rather a Ritzy life with her, he tells me. Some people like that too.'

'I think Norman is quite keen,' said Matilda, adding some final touches to her face that made completion of her toilet seem promising. 'Did you hear the way he was talking? Not at all like himself. I think the only thing that holds him back is fear of old friends like Max Pilgrim laughing.'

'Norman obviously represents the physical type of the future,' Moreland said, abandoning, as he so often did, the particular aspect of the matter under discussion in favour of a more general aesthetic bearing. 'The great artists have always decided beforehand what form looks are to take in the world, and Norman is pure Picasso – one of those attenuated, androgynous mountebanks of the Blue Period, who haven't had a meal for weeks.'

'Come along, sweetie, and don't talk so much,' said Matilda, closing her bag and getting up from the dressing-table. 'If we don't have something to eat pretty soon we shall become attenuated, androgynous mountebanks ourselves.'

No phrase could have better described what she looked like. She had emerged at last in a purple satin dress and sequin mittens, the ultimate effect almost more exotic than if she had remained in the costume of the play. I found her decidedly impressive. It was evident from the manner in which she had spoken of Mrs Foxe that she was on easy terms with a world which Moreland, in principle, disliked, indeed entered only for professional purposes. A wife who could handle that side of his life would undoubtedly be an advantage to him. Conversationally, too, Matilda was equipped to meet him on his own ground. Moreland's talk when pursuing a girl varied little, if at all, from his conversation at any other time. Some women found this too severe an intellectual burden; others were flattered, even when incapable of keeping pace. With Matilda, this level of dialogue seemed just what was required. She was a clever girl, with a good all-round knowledge of the arts: one who liked being treated as a serious person. This was apparent by the time we reached the restaurant, where Moreland at once began to discuss the play.

' "The lusty spring smells well; but drooping autumn tastes well," ' he said. 'How like:

> *Pauvre automne*
> *Meurs en blancheur et en richesse*
> *De neige et de fruits mûrs*

or: *Je suis soumis au Chef du Signe de l'Automne
Partant j'aime les fruits je déteste les fleurs*

I was thinking the other day one might make an anthology
of the banker poets . . . Guillaume Apollinaire . . . T. S.
Eliot . . . Robert W. Service . . .'

He put down the menu which he had been studying.

'A wonderful idea,' said Matilda, who had been adding
magenta to her lips to emphasise the whiteness of her skin
or offset the colour of her dress, 'but first of all make up
your mind what you are going to eat. I have already decided
on Sole Bonne Femme, but I know we shall have to start all
over again when the waiter comes.'

Clearly she possessed a will of her own, and had already
learnt something of Moreland's habits; for example, that
persuading him to choose a dish at a restaurant was a pro-
tracted affair. When faced with a menu Moreland's first
thought was always to begin some lengthy discussion that
postponed indefinitely the need to make a decision about
food.

'What do you think I should like?' he said.

'Oeufs Meyerbeer,' she said. 'You always enjoy them.'

Moreland took up the menu again irresolutely.

'What do you think?' he said. 'I hate being hurried about
any of my appetites. What are you going to eat, Nick? I
am afraid you may order something that will make me
regret my own choice. You have done that in the past. It is
very disloyal of you. You know I think Gossage – in as much
as he possesses any sexual feelings at all – derives a certain
vicarious satisfaction from contemplating the loves of
Norman Chandler and Mrs Foxe. The situation manages to
embrace within one circumference Gossage's taste for rich
ladies and good-looking young men – together with a faint
spice of musical background.'

'Gossage says there is talk of putting on Marlowe's *Tamburlaine the Great*,' said Matilda.

Moreland once again abandoned the menu.

' "Holla, ye pampered jades of Asia," ' he cried. ' "What, can ye draw but twenty miles a day?" That is rather what I feel about the newspaper criticism of Gossage and Maclintick. I should like them to drag me to concerts, as the kings drew Tamerlaine, in a triumphal coach. They would be far better employed doing that than pouring out all that stuff for their respective periodicals every week. Perhaps that is not fair to Maclintick. It is certainly true of Gossage.'

'I am sure Maclintick would draw you to the Queen's Hall in a rickshaw if you asked him,' said Matilda. 'He admires you so much.'

She turned to the waiter, ordered whatever she and I had agreed to eat, and Oeufs Meyerbeer for Moreland, who, still unable to come to a decision about food, accepted her ruling on this matter without dissent.

'I think there is just a chance I might be cast for Zenocrate,' she said, 'if they did ever do *Tamburlaine*. In any case, the show wouldn't be coming on for ages.'

'I wouldn't limit it to Maclintick and Gossage,' Moreland said. 'I should like to be dragged along by all the music critics, arranged in order of height, tallest in front, midgets at the back. That will give you some clue to what the procession would look like. I have always been interested in Tamerlaine. I found myself thinking of him the other day as part of that cruel, parched, Central Asian feeling one gets hearing *Prince Igor*. I am sure it was his bad leg that made him such a nuisance.'

'You may be interested in Tamerlaine, darling,' said Matilda, 'but you are not in the least interested in my career.'

'Oh, Matty, I am. I'm sorry. I am really. I want you to be the Duse of our time.'

He took her hand.

'I don't believe you, you old brute.'

In spite of saying that she smiled, and did not seem seriously annoyed. On the whole they appeared to understand one another pretty well. When the moment came to pay the bill, I flicked a note across to Moreland to cover my share. Matilda at once took charge of this, at the same extracting another note from Moreland himself – always a great fumbler with money. These she handed over with a request for change. When the waiter returned with some money on a plate, she apportioned the silver equitably between Moreland and myself, leaving the correct tip; a series of operations that would have presented immense problems of manipulation to Moreland. All this enterprise made her appear to possess ideal, even miraculous, qualifications for becoming his wife. They were, indeed, married some months later. The ceremony took place in a registry office, almost secretly, because Moreland hated fuss. Not long after, perhaps a year, almost equally unexpectedly, I found myself married too; married to Isobel Tolland. Life – the sort of life Moreland and I used to live in those days – all became rather changed.

2

S UNDAY L UNCHEON at Katherine, Lady Warminster's, never, as it were, specially dedicated to meetings of the family, had in the course of time grown into an occasion when, at fairly regular intervals, several – sometimes too many – of the Tollands were collected together. Now and then more distant relations were present, once in a way a friend; but on the whole immediate Tollands predominated. Everyone expected to meet their 'in-laws'; and, among other characteristics, these parties provided, at least super-ficially, a kind of parade of different approaches to marriage. There was in common a certain sense of couples being on their best behaviour in Lady Warminster's presence, but, in spite of that limited uniformity, routine at Hyde Park Gardens emphasised any individuality of matrimonial tech-nique. Blanche, Robert, Hugo, and Priscilla Tolland still lived under the same roof as their step-mother, so that the two girls attended the meal more often than not; Robert, his social life always tempered with secrecy, was intermittently present; while Hugo, still tenuously keeping university terms accentuated by violent junctures when to be 'sent down' seemed unavoidable, could be seen there only during the vacation. This accommodation in the house of several younger members of the family had not resulted in much outward gaiety of atmosphere. On the contrary, the note struck as one entered the hall and ascended the staircase was quiet, almost despondent. The lack of exhilaration con-firmed a favourite proposition of Moreland's as to the sad-ness of youth.

'I myself look forward ceaselessly to the irresponsibility of middle-age,' he was fond of stating.

It may, indeed, have been true that 'the children', rather than Lady Warminster herself, were to blame for this distinct air of melancholy. Certainly the environment was very different from the informality, the almost calculated disorder, surrounding the Jeavonses in South Kensington, a household I had scarcely visited since my marriage. Ted Jeavons's health had been even worse than usual; while Molly had given out that she was much occupied with reorganisation of the top floor (where her husband's old, bedridden – and recently deceased – cousin had lived), which was now to be done up as a flat for some friend or dependent. No doubt this reconditioning had reduced the Jeavons house to a depth of untidiness unthinkably greater than that which habitually prevailed there. The interior of Hyde Park Gardens was altogether in contrast with any such circumstance of invincible muddle. Hyde Park Gardens was unexceptional, indeed rather surprisingly ordinary, considering the personalities enclosed within, decorations and furniture expressing almost as profound an anonymity as Uncle Giles's private hotel, the Ufford; although, of course, more luxurious than the Ufford's, and kept just the right side of taste openly to be decried as 'bad', or even aggressively out of fashion.

Appreciably older than her sister Molly Jeavons – and, like her, childless – Lady Warminster had largely withdrawn from the world since her second husband's death in Kashmir eight or nine years before. Lord Warminster, who could claim some name as a sportsman, even as an amateur explorer, had formed the habit of visiting that country from time to time, not, so far as was known, on account of the sensual attractions extolled in the Kashmiri Love Song, but for pleasure in the more general beauty of its valleys, and the shooting of ibex there. On this last occasion, grazing his hand while opening a tin, he had contracted blood poisoning, an infection from which he subsequently died. Grieved in a remote way at her loss, although their comparatively brief married life together had been marked on his part by prolonged travel abroad, Lady Warminster had also been delighted to hand over Thrubworth to her eldest step-son, Erridge; to settle herself permanently in London. She had always hated country life. Erridge had been less pleased to find himself head of the family at the age of eighteen or nineteen, saddled with the responsibilities of a large house and estate. Indeed, from that moment he had contended as little as possible with any but the most pressing duties contingent upon his 'position', devoting himself to his left-wing political interests, which merged into a not too exacting study of sociology.

Chips Lovell (with whom I had formerly been teamed up as a fellow script-writer in the film business), who was inclined to call almost everyone of an older generation than himself either 'Uncle' or 'Aunt', and was always prepared at a moment's notice to provide an *a priori* account of the personal history and problems of all his relations and acquaintances, had said: 'Like every other Ardglass, Aunt Katherine only really enjoys pottering about.' It was certainly true that Lady Warminster, as a widow, divided her time between her own ailments, real or imagined – opinion differed within the family on this point – and the writing of biographical studies devoted to the dominating, Amazonian women of history. Maria-Theresa, at the time of which I speak, had offered a theme sympathetic to the fashion of the moment for things Austrian. Lady Warminster enjoyed the reputation of having 'got on' pretty well with her step-children, even if no outstandingly warm sentiments existed between herself and any individual member of the family, except perhaps Blanche. In the past there had been, of course, occasional rows. Frederica and George found their step-mother's way of life too eccentric to wish to play much part in it themselves; Erridge and Norah, on the other hand, thought her hopelessly conventional. Such divergence of view was only to be expected in a large family, and most of her own contemporaries agreed on the whole that Katherine Warminster, so far as her step-children were concerned, was to be congratulated on having made a fairly good job of it. For my own part, I liked Lady Warminster, although at the same time never wholly at ease in her presence. She was immaculately free from any of the traditional blemishes of a mother-in-law; agreeable always; entertaining; even, in her own way, affectionate; but always a little alarming: an elegant, deeply experienced bird – perhaps a bird of prey – ready to sweep down and attack from the frozen mountain peaks upon which she preferred herself to live apart.

Robert Tolland, seventh child and third son of his parents, was in the drawing-room at Hyde Park Gardens when, rather too early for the appointed time of the meal, I arrived there. He was a tall, cadaverous young man of about twenty-four, with his family's blue eyes and characteristic angularity of frame. Of my wife's brothers, Robert was the one with whom I felt myself generally most at home. He had some of the oddness, some of that complete disregard for public opinion, that distinguished Erridge (as I shall continue to call the eldest of the Tollands, since that was the name by which he was known within the family, rather than 'Alfred', or even 'Alf', preferred by his left-wing cronies like J. G. Quiggin), although at the same time Robert was without Erridge's political enthusiasms. He was not so conformist – 'not so bloody boring', Chips Lovell had said – as his second brother, George Tolland (retired from the Brigade of Guards, now working in the City), although

Robert to some extent haunted George's – to Chips Lovell – rather oppressive social world. In fact, outwardly, Robert was just as 'correct' as George, to use the term Molly Jeavons liked to apply to any of her relations whom she suspected of criticising her own manner of life. All the same, a faint suggestion of dissipation was also to be found in Robert; nothing like that thick sea mist of gossip which at an early age already encompassed his younger brother, Hugo, but something that affirmed to those with an instinct for recognising such things at long range, the existence in the neighbourhood of vaguely irregular behaviour. Chips Lovell, whose stories were always to be accepted with caution, used to hint that Robert, a school contemporary of his, had a taste for night-club hostesses not always in their first youth. The case was non-proven. Robert would take girls out occasionally – girls other than the hypothetical 'peroxide blondes old enough to be his mother', so designated, probably imaginatively, by Lovell – but he never showed much interest in them for more than a week or two. By no means to be described as 'dotty' himself, there was perhaps something in Robert of his 'dotty' sister, Blanche: a side never fully realised, emotionally undeveloped. He sometimes reminded me of Archie Gilbert, that 'dancing man' of my early London days, whose life seemed exclusively lived at balls. Robert was, of course, more 'intelligent' than Archie Gilbert, intelligent at least in the crudest sense of being able to discourse comprehensibly about books he had read, or theatres, concerts and private views he had attended; conversational peaks to which Archie Gilbert had never in the least aspired. Robert, as it happened, was rather a keen concert-goer and frequenter of musical parties. He had a job in an export house trading with the Far East, employment he found perfectly congenial. No one seemed to know whether or not he was any good at the work, but

Robert was thought by his sisters to possess a taste for making money. When I arrived in the drawing-room he was playing *Iberia* on the gramophone.

'How is Isobel?'

He threw the newspaper he had been reading to the ground and jumped to his feet, giving at the same time one of those brilliant smiles that suggested nothing could have come as a more delightful, a less expected, surprise than my own arrival in the room at just that moment. Although I was not exactly taken in by this reception, Robert's habitual exhibition of good manners never failed to charm me.

'Pretty well all right now. She is emerging tomorrow. I am going to see her this afternoon.'

'Do please give her my best love. I ought to have gone to see her in the nursing home myself. Somehow one never gets time for anything. What a bore it has been for you both. I was so sorry to hear about it.'

He spoke with solicitude, at the same time giving the impression that he was still, even at this late stage, unable wholly to conceal his wonder that someone should have chosen Isobel – or any other of his sisters – as a wife; nice girls, no doubt, beings for whom he felt the warmest affection, but creatures to be thought of always in terms of playing shops or putting their dolls to bed.

'Who will be at lunch?'

'I'll tell you. But shall we have the other side of this record first? I am playing them all in the wrong order. I love *Les Parfums de la Nuit*. I think that is really the bit I like best.'

'Do you adapt your music to the foreign news, Robert?'

'Rather suitable, isn't it? Now that the Alcazar has been relieved things seem to have become a bit static. I wonder who will win.'

He closed the lid of the gramophone, which began once more to diffuse the sombre, menacing notes adumbrating their Spanish background: tawny skies: dusty plains: bleak sierras: black marble sarcophagi of dead kings under arabesqued ceilings: *art nouveau* blocks of flats past which the squat trams rattled and clanged: patent-leather cocked hats of the Guardia Civil: leather cushions cast upon the sand under posters promulgating cures for impotence and the pox . . . these and a hundred other ever-changing cubist abstractions, merging their visual elements with the hurdy-gurdy music of the bull-ring . . . now – through this land-scape – baked by the sun, lorries, ramshackle as picadors' horses, crawled uphill in bottom gear and a stink of petrol . . . now, frozen by the wind and hooded like the muffled trio in Goya's *Winter*, Moorish levies convoyed pack-mules through the gorges veiled in snow . . .

'I expect you have heard about Erridge,' said Robert.

'That the Thrubworth woods will have to be sold?'

'Well, that, of course. But I mean his latest.'

'No?'

'He is going out there.'

'Where?'

Robert jerked his head in the direction of the shiny wooden cabinet from which Debussy quavered and tinkled and droned.

'Spain.'

'Indeed?'

'Can you imagine.'

'The International Brigade?'

'I don't know whether he will actually fight. As you know, he holds pacifist views. However, he will certainly be on the opposite side to General Franco. We can at least be sure of that. I can't think that Erry would be any great help to any army he joined, can you?'

The news that Erridge contemplated taking a compara-tively active part in the Spanish civil war came as no great surprise to me. Politically, his sympathies would naturally be engaged with the extreme Left, whether Communist or Anarchist was not known. Possibly Erridge himself had not yet decided. He had been, of course, a supporter of Blum's 'Popular Front', but, within the periphery of 'Leftism', his shifting preferences were unpredictable; nor did he keep his relations informed on such matters. The only fact by then established was that Erridge had contributed relatively large sums of money to several of the organisations recently come into being, designed to assist the Spanish Republican forces. This news came from Quiggin, who like myself, visited from time to time the office of the weekly paper of which Mark Members was now assistant literary editor.

The fortunes of these two friends, Quiggin and Members, seemed to vary inversely. For a time Quiggin had been the more successful, supplanting Members as St John Clarke's secretary, finding congenial odd jobs in the world of letters, running away with the beautiful Mona, battening on Erridge; but ever since Mona had, in turn, deserted Quiggin for Erridge, Quiggin had begun to undergo a period of adversity. From taking a patronising line about Members, he now – like myself – found himself professionally dependent upon his old friend for books to review. The tide, on the other hand, seemed to be flowing in favour of Members. He had secured this presentable employment, not requiring so much work that he was unable to find time to write himself; his travel book, *Baroque Interlude*, had been a notable success; there was talk of his marrying a rich girl, who was also not bad-looking. So far as the affair of Mona was concerned, Quiggin had 'made it up' with Erridge; even declaring in his cups that Erridge had done him a good turn by taking her off his hands.

'After all,' said Quiggin, 'Mona has left him too. Poor Alf has nothing to congratulate himself about. He has just heaped up more guilt to carry round on his own back.'

After Erridge's return from the Far East, he and Quiggin had met at – of all places – a party given by Mrs Andriadis, whose sole interest now, so it appeared, was the Spanish war. Common sympathy in this cause made reconciliation possible without undue abasement on Quiggin's part, but the earlier project of founding a paper together was not revived for the moment, although Quiggin re-entered the sphere of Erridge's patronage.

'I correspond a certain amount with your brother-in-law,' he had remarked when we had last met, speaking, as he sometimes did, with that slight hint of warning in his voice.

'Which one?'

'Alf.'

'What do you correspond with him about?'

'Medical supplies for the Spanish Loyalists,' said Quiggin, pronouncing the words with quiet doggedness, 'Basque children – there is plenty to do for those with a political conscience.'

The whole business of Mona had made some strongly self-assertive action to be expected from Erridge; to be, in fact, all but certain to take place sooner or later. After leaving Quiggin, with whom she had been living during the period immediately prior to my own marriage, and setting sail with Erridge for China (where he planned to investigate the political situation), Mona had returned to England only a few months later by herself. No one had been told the cause of this severed relationship, although various stories – largely circulated by Quiggin himself – were current on the subject of Mona's adventures on the way home. She was the first woman in whom Erridge was known to have taken more than the most casual interest. It was not surprising that they should have found each other mutually incompatible. There was nothing easy-going about Mona's temperament; while Erridge, notwithstanding passionately humane and liberal principles, was used to having his own way in the smallest respect, his high-minded nonconformity of life in general absolving him, where other people were concerned, from even the irksome minor disciplines of everyday convention.

By leaving her husband, Peter Templer, in the first instance, Mona had undeniably shown aims directed to something less banal than mere marriage to a comparatively rich man. She would certainly never have put herself out for Erridge in order to retain him as husband or lover. What she did, in fact, desire from life was less explicable; perhaps, as Templer said after she left him, 'just to raise hell'. She had never, as once had been supposed, got herself married to Quiggin, so no question existed of further divorce proceedings. The Tolland family were less complacent about that fact than might have been expected.

'Personally, I think it was the greatest pity Erry failed to hold on to Minna, or whatever her name was,' Norah said. 'She sounds as if she might have done him a lot of good.'

Only George and Frederica dissented from this view among Erridge's brothers and sisters. More distant relations were probably divided about equally between those who resented, and those who thoroughly enjoyed, the idea of Erridge making a *mésalliance*. Lady Warminster's opinion was unknown. Possibly she too, in secret, considered – like Strindberg – any marriage better than none at all. Erridge himself, since his return from Asia, had remained alone, shut up in Thrubworth, occupying himself with those Spanish activities now to take a more decided form, refusing to attend to other more local matters, however pressing. The question of death duties had recently been reopened by the taxation authorities, the payment of which threatened a considerable sale of land to raise the money required. Only

Norah, in face of opposition, had effected an entry into Thrubworth not long before this, reporting afterwards that her eldest brother had been 'pretty morose'. No one knew whether Erridge had achieved any degree of success in getting to the bottom of Far Eastern problems. Probably China and Japan, like his own estate, were now forgotten in contrast with a more fashionable preoccupation with Spain. To someone of Erridge's views and temperament, finding himself in the position he found himself, the Spanish war clearly offered a solution. Robert agreed in seeing nothing surprising in his brother's decision.

'Like big-game hunting in Edwardian days,' said Robert, 'or going to the Crusades a few years earlier. There will be one or two newspaper paragraphs about "the Red Earl", I suppose. Bound to be. Still, Erry gets remarkably little publicity as a rule, which is just as well. For some reason he has never become news. I hope he doesn't go and get killed. I shouldn't think he would, would you? Very well able to look after himself in his own way. All the same, a man I used to sit next to at school was shot in the street in Jerusalem the other day. In the back, just as he was getting into a taxi to go and have a spot of dinner. But he was a professional soldier and they have to expect that sort of thing. Rather different for someone like Erry who is a pacifist. I can't see the point of being a pacifist if you don't keep out of the way of fighting. Anyway, we can none of us be certain of surviving when the next war comes.'

'What will Erry do?'

'I suppose there will be a lot of the sort of people he likes out there already,' said Robert. 'His beard and those clothes will be all the go. He'll hang about Barcelona, lending a hand with the gardening, or the washing up, to show he isn't a snob. I think it is rather dashing of him to take this step considering his hypochondria. Of course, George would at least make some effort to keep up Thrubworth properly if he inherited. I say, I hope everyone is not going to be late. I am rather hungry this morning.'

'You haven't told me who is coming yet.'

'Nor I have. Well, the guest of honour is St John Clarke, the novelist. I expect you know him of old, as a brother of the pen.'

'As a matter of fact, Robert, I have never met St John Clarke. Who else?'

'Blanche, Priscilla – George and Veronica – Sue and Roddy.'

'But why St John Clarke?'

'I gather he more or less asked himself. His name is held on the books, you know. He used to turn up occasionally at Aunt Molly's. I remember Hugo being sick over him as a child. Probably St John Clarke sheered off the place after that. Of course he may be going to lend a hand with the Maria-Theresa book. I have only just thought of that possibility.'

Lady Warminster used sometimes to announce that she was receiving 'help' with one or another of her biographies from some fairly well-known figure – usually a distinguished politician or civil servant – although it was never explained what form this help took. Probably they adjusted the grammar.

'They tell me about punctuation,' she used to say.

This intermittent publication of an historical biography had in no way brought Lady Warminster into the literary world, nor could her house be said to present any of the features of a '*salon*'. A well-known author like St John Clarke was therefore an unexpected guest. At the Jeavonses' everything was possible. There was no one on earth who could occasion surprise there. Lady Warminster, on the contrary, living a very different sort of life, saw only relations and a few old friends. Even minor celebrities were rare, and, when they appeared, tended to be submerged by the family.

Blanche and Priscilla entered the room at that moment, bearing between them on a tray a jigsaw puzzle, newly completed and brought downstairs to be admired.

When people called Blanche 'dotty', no question of incipient madness was implied, nor even mild imbecility. Indeed, after a first meeting it was possible to part company from her without suspicion that something might be slightly amiss. However, few who knew her well doubted that something, somewhere, had unquestionably gone a little wrong. Quieter than the rest of her sisters, good-looking, always friendly, always prepared to take on tedious tasks, Blanche would rarely initiate a conversation. She would answer with a perfectly appropriate phrase if herself addressed, but she never seemed to feel the need to comment on any but the most trivial topics. The world, the people amongst whom she moved, appeared to make no impression on her. Life was a dream that scarcely even purported to hold within its promise any semblance of reality. The cumulative effect of this chronic sleep-walking through her days – which far surpassed that vagueness of manner often to be found in persons well equipped to look after their own interest – together with her own acceptance of the fact that she was not quite like other people, did not care at all that she was different, had finally established Blanche's reputation for 'dottiness'. That was all. The impression of being undeveloped, unawakened, which perhaps in some degree Robert shared, may have caused both to prefer rather secret lives. Publicly, Blanche was almost always occupied with good works: girls' clubs in the East End; charities in which her uncle, Alfred Tolland, was concerned for which he sought her help. Blanche's practical activities were usually very successful so far as the end in view, although she herself never troubled to take much credit for them. Nor did she show any interest in getting married, though in her time not without admirers.

'We've finished it at last,' she said, indicating the puzzle. 'It took five months in all – with everyone who came to the house having a go. Then one afternoon the cats broke most of it up. The last few pieces were due to Priscilla's brilliance.'

She showed a huge representation of Venice, a blue-grey Santa Maria della Salute, reflected in blue-grey waters of the canal, against a blue-grey sky. Priscilla, six or seven years younger than her sister, longer-legged, with fairer, untidy hair, was then about twenty. In spite of his own good resolutions to marry an heiress, Chips Lovell had shown interest in her for a time; apparently without things coming to much. Priscilla had at present several beaux, successfully concealing her own feelings about them. She was not at all like her sister, Norah, in disparaging the whole male sex, but the young men she met at dances never seemed quite what she required. There was talk of her taking a job. A fund was being organised for the promotion of opera, and Robert, who knew some of the members of the board, thought he could find her a place in its office.

'How is Isobel?' Priscilla asked rather truculently, as if she had not yet forgiven her immediately elder sister, even after two years, for getting married before herself.

'Pretty well all right now. I am going to see her this afternoon.'

'I looked in the day before yesterday,' said Priscilla. 'It is a grimmish place, isn't it. I say, have you heard about Erry?'

'Robert told me this moment.'

'Erry is mad, of course. Do you know, I realised that for the first time when I was seven years old and he was grown up. Something about the way he was eating his pudding. I knew I must be growing up myself when I grasped that. Hullo, Veronica, hullo, George.'

The manner in which he wore his immensely discreet suit,

rather than a slight, fair, fluffy moustache, caused George Tolland to retain the flavour of his service with the Brigade of Guards. Years before, when still a schoolboy, I had travelled to London with Sunny Farebrother, that business friend of Peter Templer's father, and he had remarked in the train: 'It helps to look like a soldier in the City. Fellows think they can get the better of you even before they start. That is always an advantage in doing a deal.' Perhaps George Tolland held the same theory. Certainly he had done nothing to modify this air of having just come off parade. Whether assumed consciously or not, the style rather suited him, and was quite unlike Ted Jeavons's down-at-heel look of being a wartime ex-officer. George was said to work like a slave in the City and seemed quite content with a social life offered chiefly by his own relations.

However, George had astonished everyone about eighteen months earlier by making an unexpected marriage. In some ways even Erridge's adventure with Mona had surprised his family less. Erridge was a recognised eccentric. He made a virtue of behaving oddly. In taking Mona abroad he had even, in a sense, improved his reputation for normality by showing himself capable of such an act. George, on the other hand, was fond of drawing attention – especially in contrasting himself with Erridge – to the exemplary, even, as he insisted, deliberately snobbish lines upon which his own life was run. 'I can never see the objection to being a snob,' George used to say. 'It seems far the most sensible thing to be.' Apparent simplicity of outlook is always suspicious. This remark should have put everyone on their guard. It was a sign that something was taking place under the surface of George's immaculate façade. However, since the vast majority accept at face value the personality any given individual puts forward as his own, no one in the least expected George to marry the woman he did. Veronica was the former wife of a businessman called Collins, whose job took him to Lagos for most of the year. She had two children by her first husband ('Native women,' said Chips Lovell, 'also some trouble about a cheque,') whom she had divorced a year or two before meeting George at some party given by City friends. A big brunette, not pretty, but with plenty of 'attack', Veronica was popular with her 'in-laws', especially Lady Warminster. She was older than George, now to all appearances completely under her thumb.

'How is Isobel, Nick?' Veronica asked. 'I went to see her last week. She was looking a bit washed out. I'd have gone again, but one of the kids was running a temperature and I got stuck in the house for a day or two. I hear St John Clarke is coming to lunch. Isn't that exciting? I used to love *Fields of Amaranth* when I was a girl. I never seem to get any time for reading now.'

George and Veronica were almost immediately followed into the room by Susan and her husband, Roddy Cutts, also in the City, now an M.P. Tall, sandy-haired, bland, Roddy smiled ceaselessly. The House of Commons had, if anything, increased a tendency, probably congenital, to behave with a shade more assiduity than ordinary politeness required; a trait that gave Roddy some of the bearing of a clergyman at a school-treat. Always smiling, his eyes roved for ever round the room, while he offered his hosts their own food, and made a point of talking chiefly to people he did not know, as if he felt these could not be altogether comfortable if still unacquainted with himself. In spite of accepting, indeed courting, this duty of putting young and old at their ease, he lacked the powerful memory – perhaps also the interest in individual differences of character – required to retain in the mind names and personal attributes; a weakness that sometimes impaired this eternal campaign of universal good-will. All the same, Roddy was able, ambitious, quite a formidable figure.

George and Roddy did not exactly dislike one another, but a certain faint sense of tension existed between them. Roddy, who came of a long line of bankers on his father's side, while his mother, Lady Augusta's, family could claim an almost equal tradition of shrewd business grasp, undoubtedly regarded George as an amateur where money matters were concerned. George, on the other hand, was clearly made impatient when Roddy, speaking as a professional politician, explained in simple language the trend of public affairs, particularly the military implications of world strategy in relation to the growing strength of Germany. Besides, Susan was George's favourite sister, so there may have been a touch of jealousy about her too. Susan was a pretty girl, not a beauty, but lively and, like her husband, ambitious; possessing plenty of that taste for 'occasion' so necessary to the wife of a man committed to public life.

Lady Warminster now appeared in the room. She had probably mastered her habitual unpunctuality at meals in honour of St John Clarke. Slighter in build than her sister, Molly Jeavons, she looked as usual like a very patrician sibyl about to announce a calamitous disaster of which she had personally given due and disregarded warning. This Cassandra-like air of being closely in touch with sacred mysteries, even with the Black Arts themselves, was not entirely misleading. Lady Warminster was prone to fortune-tellers and those connected with divination. She was fond of retailing their startling predictions. I found that, in her day, she had even consulted Uncle Giles's fortune-telling friend, Mrs Erdleigh, whom she rated high as an oracle, although the two of them had long been out of touch, and had not 'put the cards out' together for years.

'I asked Mr Clarke for half-past one,' said Lady Warminster. 'You know I had not seen him since one of those rum parties Aunt Molly used to give, when I noticed him at Bumpus's last week, browsing about among the books. I think he only goes there to read the new ones, because he showed no sign of wanting to buy anything. When he caught sight of me, he immediately followed me out into Oxford Street and began to talk about Shelley. He told me a long story of how he wanted to see me again, how people no longer liked him on account of his political opinions. He is rather an old humbug, but I remember enjoying the first part of *Fields of Amaranth* when it came out. I always think one ought to be grateful to an author if one has liked even a small bit of a book.'

I had heard little of St John Clarke since the days when Mark Members and J. G. Quiggin had been, one after another in quick succession, his secretary; to be followed by the 'Trotskyist' German boy, Werner Guggenbühl; Guggenbühl, so Quiggin hinted, had been sacked as a result of political pressure, but did not mind leaving as he had found a better job. By this time, so many people of relative eminence were writing, speaking, or marching in one or another form of militant political expression that St John Clarke's adhesion to the Left was a matter of little general interest. He was said to have become at times resentful of a brand of politics he felt to lay a burden on his social life.

'The man has got it in him to be a traitor to any cause,' Quiggin said, when he reported this. 'We shall never see Clarke manning a machine-gun.'

This supposed backsliding on the part of St John Clarke was certainly not because any potential hostess objected to his being a 'Communist'. On the contrary, as an elderly, no longer very highly esteemed writer, such views may even have done something to re-establish his name. The younger people approved, while in rich, stuffy houses, where he was still sometimes to be seen on the strength of earlier reputation as a novelist, a left-wing standpoint was regarded as suitable to a man of letters, even creditable in a widely known, well-to-do author, who might at his age perfectly well have avoided the controversies of politics. However, St John Clarke himself apparently felt less and less capable, in practice, of taking part in the discussion of Marxist dialectic, with its ever-changing bearings. As a consequence of this laxity in 'keeping up', he had lost ground in the more exacting circles of the intellectual Left. His name was rarely seen except in alphabetical order among a score of nonentities signing at the foot of some letter to the press. St John Clarke, according to Members (himself suspected by Quiggin of 'political cynicism') yearned for his former unregenerate life. If so, he must have felt himself too deeply committed, perhaps too old, to make a reversal of programme – which, at that period, would in any case have entailed swimming against a stream that brought to a writer certain advantages. Lady Warminster was probably better informed about St John Clarke than he supposed. Her phrase 'rather an old humbug' established within the family her own, as it were, official attitude. She now made some enquiry about the colds from which Veronica's two children, Angus and Iris, had been suffering.

'Oh, Angus is all right at last,' said George, speaking before his wife could reply. 'We have been looking about for a school for him. I am going down to see another next week.'

'They are both off to their Granny's on Friday,' said Veronica, 'where they will get fussed over a lot and probably catch colds all over again. But there it is. They have to go. The rest of the year will be spent getting them out of bad habits.'

'Talking of grandparents,' said George, who, although reputed to be very 'good' about Veronica's children, probably preferred relations on their father's side to be kept, in so far as possible, out of sight and out of mind, 'I was wondering whether I ought to try and reopen with Erry the question of getting the stained glass window put up to our own grandfather. I saw Uncle Alfred the other day – he has not been at all well, he tells me – who complained the matter had been allowed to drift for a number of years. I thought I would leave it for a time until Erry had settled down after his Chinese trip, then tackle him about it. There are always a mass of things to do after one has come home from abroad, especially after a long tour like that. I don't know what state of mind he is in at the moment. Do you happen to have seen anything of him lately?'

George's line about Erridge was pity rather than blame. That was the tone in which these words had been spoken. Lady Warminster smiled to herself. She was known to regard the whole question of the stained glass window not only as at best a potential waste of money (out-of-date sentiment, threatening active production of ugliness) but also, no doubt correctly, as a matter to which Erridge would in no circumstances ever turn his attention; one, therefore, which was an even greater waste of time to discuss. She may have smiled for that reason alone. In addition, she was going to enjoy communicating to George news so highly charged with novelty as Erridge's latest project.

'You will have to be quick, George, if you want to get hold of Erry,' she said gently.

'Why?'

'He is going abroad again.'

'Where is he off to this time?'

'Spain.'

'What – to join in the war?'

'So he says.'

George took the information pretty well. He was by no

means a fool, even if people like Chips Lovell did not find
him a specially amusing companion. Like others who knew
Erridge well, George had probably observed a cloud of
that particular shape already forming on the horizon. Roddy
Cutts, on the other hand, who, in the course of a couple of
years of marriage to Susan, had only managed to meet her
eldest brother once, was more surprised. Indeed, the whole
Erridge legend, whenever it cropped up, always disturbed
Roddy. He had clear-cut, practical ideas how people behaved. Erridge did not at all fit in with these.

'But surely Erridge isn't going to fight?' Roddy said. 'I
suppose he has gone into the legal status of a British national
taking part in a continental civil war. It is a most anomalous
position – not to mention a great embarrassment to His
Majesty's Government, whatever the party in power. I presume he will be anti-Franco, holding the views he does.'

'Of course he will be anti-Franco,' said George. 'But I
agree with you, Roddy, that I should not have thought actual
fighting would have been in his line.'

All this talk was going on outside Lady Warminster's
immediate orbit. Now she turned towards us to give one of
her semi-official warnings.

'I believe Mr Clarke has something he wants to tell me
about Erridge,' she said. 'It might entail a more or less
private talk with him after luncheon. Don't any of you feel
you have got to stay, if he decides to tell me some long
rigmarole.'

She did not say, perhaps did not know, whether St John
Clarke wanted to discuss Erridge's latest move or some
more general matter that concerned Erridge's affairs. I had
not heard that Erridge had been seeing more of St John
Clarke recently. This indicated that their previous casual
acquaintance must have grown in intimacy. The escapade
with Mona, the decision to take part in the Spanish war,

such things showed Erridge's more picturesque side, the aspect at which his beard and tattered clothes freely hinted. There were other, less dramatic matters to cause his family concern. The chief of these was the reopening of the question of death duties; but, in addition, the Thrubworth agent had died while Erridge was in China, revealing by vacation of office a situation often suspected by the rest of the family, that is to say gross, perhaps disastrous, mismanagement of the estate, which had been taking place over a long period. The account was seriously overdrawn at the bank. Thrubworth woods would probably have to be sold to meet the deficit. At least, selling the woods was Erridge's idea of the easiest way out; the trustees, too, were thought to be amenable to this solution. It was possible that Erridge, having no taste for meeting his step-mother to discuss business, had entrusted St John Clarke with some message on the subject, before he himself set off for Spain, where he could forget the trivialities of estate management in the turmoil of revolution. Perhaps Lady Warminster's last aside was intended to convey that, if business affairs were to be discussed at all, they were not to be interrupted. If so, she made her announcement just in time, because a second later St John Clarke himself was announced. He came hurriedly into the room, a hand held out in front of him as if to grasp the handle of a railway carriage door before the already moving train gathered speed and left the platform.

'Lady Warminster, I am indeed ashamed of myself,' he said in a high, rich, breathless, mincing voice, like that of an experienced actor trying to get the best out of a minor part in Restoration comedy. 'I must crave the forgiveness of you and your guests.'

He gave a rapid glance round the room to discover whom he had been asked to meet, at the same time diffusing about

him a considerable air of social discomfort. Lady Warminster accepted St John Clarke's hand carefully, almost
with surprise, immediately relinquishing it, as if the texture
or temperature of the flesh dissatisfied her.

'I hope you were not expecting a grand luncheon party,
Mr Clarke,' she said. 'There are only a few of the family
here, I am afraid.'

Plainly, that was only too true. There could be no doubt
from St John Clarke's face, flushed with running up the
stairs, that he had hoped for something better than what he
found; perhaps even a *tête-à-tête* with his hostess, rather
than this unwieldy domestic affair, offering neither intimacy
nor splendour. However, if disappointed at first sight, he
was an old campaigner in the ups and downs of luncheon
parties; he knew how to make the best of a bad job.

'Much, *much* pleasanter,' he murmured, still gazing sus-
piciously round the room. 'And I am sure you will agree
with me, Lady Warminster, in thinking, so far as company
is concerned, enough is as bad as a feast, and half a loaf in
many ways preferable to the alternative of a whole one or
the traditional no bread. How enjoyable, therefore, to be just
as we are.'

Although his strongly outlined features were familiar from
photographs in the papers, I had never before met this well-
known author. Something about St John Clarke put him in
the category – of which Widmerpool was another example
– of persons at once absurd and threatening. St John Clarke's
head recalled Blake's, a resemblance no doubt deliberately
cultivated, because the folds and crannies of his face insistently suggested a self-applauding interior activity, a desire
to let everyone know about his own 'mental strife'. I had
seen him in person on a couple of occasions, though never
before closely: once, five or six years earlier, walking up
Bond Street with his then secretary Mark Members; a

second time, on that misty afternoon in Hyde Park, propelled in a wheeled chair by Mona and Quiggin (who had replaced Members), while the three of them marched in procession as part of a political demonstration. Although he still carried himself with some degree of professional panache, St John Clarke did not look well. He might have been thought older than his years; his colour was not that of a man in good health. Once tall and gaunt in appearance, he had grown fat and flabby, a physical state which increased for some reason his air of being a dignitary of the Church temporarily passing, for some not very edifying reason, as a layman. Longish grey hair and sunken, haunted eyes recalled Mr Deacon's appearance, probably because both belonged to the same generation, rather than on account of much similarity about the way their lives had been lived. Certainly St John Clarke had never indulged himself in Mr Deacon's incurable leanings towards the openly disreputable. On the contrary, St John Clarke had been straitlaced, as much from inclination as from policy, during his decades of existence as a writer taken reasonably seriously. Even now, forgotten by the critics but remembered fairly faithfully by the circulating libraries, he had remained a minor public figure, occasionally asked to broadcast on some non-literary, non-political subject like the problem of litter or the abatement of smoke, talks into which he would always inject – so Members alleged – some small admixture of Marxist lore.

'And how is your sister, Lady Molly?' he asked, when we had moved into the dining-room and taken our places. 'It is many a year since I had the pleasure. Why, I scarcely seem to have seen her since she was châtelaine of Dogdene. How long ago seem those Edwardian summer afternoons.'

Lady Warminster, who was in one of her more playful moods, received the enquiry with kindly amusement, offering at once some formal statement which suggested no words of hers could do justice to conditions prevailing in the Jeavons house during redecoration. Lady Warminster had few illusions as to St John Clarke's preference for her sister as Marchioness of Sleaford, rich and presiding over a famous mansion, rather than married to Ted Jeavons and living in disorder and no great affluence in South Kensington. St John Clarke recalled that he had visited the Jeavons house, too, but also a long time ago. A minute or two later I heard her ask him whether he had read any of the two or three books I had written; a question calculated to produce more entertainment for Lady Warminster herself than gratification to St John Clarke or me. Aware, certainly, that I knew Members and Quiggin, he had given me a stiff, distrustful bow when introduced. Memories of his own dealings with that couple must have been unwelcome. Besides, Lady Warminster's buoyant manner was not of a kind to bring reassurance.

'Certainly, certainly,' said St John Clarke guardedly. 'I remember praising one of them. A laudable piece of work.'

He took a sip of the sickly white Bordeaux poured out for us. Lady Warminster possessed a horror of 'drink'. As a rule barely enough appeared at her table to satisfy the most modest requirements. This was perhaps her sole characteristic shared with Erridge. St John Clarke was abstemious too. Members, during his secretaryship, had tried to encourage in his master a taste for food and wine, but complained later that the only result had been a lot of talk about rare vintages and little known recipes, while the meals at St John Clarke's table grew worse than ever.

'Yes,' said St John Clarke, wiping his mouth and refolding the napkin on his knee, 'yes.'

It was true he had spoken favourably of my first book in a New York paper, when discoursing in general terms of younger English writers. That, so far as I was concerned, had been the first indication that St John Clarke – in the hands of Members – was undergoing some sort of aesthetic conversion. Kind words from him only a short time before would have been unthinkable. However, mention of a first novel at the safe remove of an American newspaper's book-page is one thing: to be brought face to face with its author five or six years later, quite another. So, at least, St John Clarke must have keenly felt. Mutual relationship between writers, whatever their age, is always delicate, not so much – as commonly supposed – on account of jealousy, but because of the intensely personal nature of a writer's stock in trade. For example, St John Clarke seemed to me a 'bad' writer, that is to say a person to be treated (in those days) with reserve, if not thinly veiled hostility. Later, that question – the relationship of writers of different sorts – seemed, like so many others, less easily solved; in fact infinitely complicated. St John Clarke himself had made a living, indeed collected a small fortune, while giving pleasure to many by writing his books (pleasure even to myself when a boy, if it came to that), yet now was become an object of disapproval to me because his novels did not rise to a certain standard demanded by myself. Briefly, they seemed to me trivial, un-real, vulgar, badly put together, odiously phrased and 'insin-cere'. Yet, even allowing for these failings, was not St John Clarke still a person more like myself than anyone else sitting round the table? That was a sobering thought. He, too, for longer years, had existed in the imagination, even though this imagination led him (in my eyes) to a world ludicrously contrived, socially misleading, professionally nauseous. On top of that, had he not on this earlier occasion gone out of his way to speak a word of carefully hedged praise for my own work? Was that, therefore, an aspect of his critical faculty for which he should be given credit, or was it an even stronger reason for guarding against the possibility of corruption at the hands of one whose own writings could not be approved? Fortunately these speculations, heavily burdened with the idealistic sentiments of one's younger days, were put to no practical test; not only because St John Clarke was sitting at some distance from me, but also on account of the steps he himself immediately took to change a subject likely to be unfruitful to both of us. He quickly commented on the flowers in the vases, which were arranged with great skill, and turned out to be the work of Blanche.

'Flowers mean more to us in a city than in a garden,' said St John Clarke.

Lady Warminster nodded. She was determined not to abandon the subject of literature without a struggle.

'I expect you are writing a new book yourself, Mr Clarke,' she said. 'We have not had one from you for a long time.'

'Nor from you, Lady Warminster.'

'But I am not a famous writer,' she said. 'I just amuse myself with people like Maria-Theresa who take my fancy. For you, it is quite another matter.'

St John Clarke shook his head energetically, like a dog emerging from a pond. It was ten or fifteen years since he had published anything but occasional pieces.

'Sometimes I add a paragraph to my memoirs, Lady Warminster,' he said. 'There is little about the critics of the present day to encourage an author of my age and experience to expose his goods in the market place. To tell the truth, Lady Warminster, I get more pleasure from watching the confabulation of sparrows in their parliament on the roof-tops opposite my study window, or from seeing the clouds scudding over the Serpentine in windy weather, than I do from covering sheets of foolscap with spidery script that only a few sympathetic souls, some now passed on to the Great Unknown, would even care to read.

No sparrow on any roof was ever lonely
As I am, nor any animal untamed.

Doesn't Petrarch say that somewhere? He is a great stay
me. Childish pleasures, you may tell me, Lady Warminste
but I answer you that growing old consists abundantly
growing young.'

Lady Warminster was about to reply, whether in agre
ment or not with this paradox was never revealed, becau
St John Clarke suddenly realised that his words belonged
an outdated, even decadent state of mind, wholly inconsi
tent with political regeneration. He could hardly have bee
carried away by the white wine. Probably it was some tin
since he had attended a luncheon party of this sort, tl
comparative unfamiliarity of which must have made hi:
feel for a minute or two back in some much earlier sequen
of his social career.

'Of course I was speaking of when the errant mind stray
he added in a different, firmer tone, 'as I fear the mind
that unreliable fellow, the intellectual, does from time
time. I meant to imply that, when there are so many caus
to claim one's attention, it seems a waste of time to wri
about the trivial encounters of an individual like myse
who has spent so much of his time pursuing selfish, and,
fear, often frivolous aims. We shall have to learn to live mo
collectively, Lady Warminster. There is no doubt about i

'That was just what a fellow in the City was saying to n
the other day,' said George. 'We were talking about tho
trials for treason in Russia. I can't make head or tail of ther
He seemed full of information about Zinoviev and Kamen
and the rest of them. He was quite well disposed to Russi
A bill-broker named Widmerpool. You probably rememb
him at school, Nick. Some story about an overcoat, wasi
there?'

'I've met him,' said Roddy. 'Used to be with Donners-Brebner. Heavy-looking chap with thick spectacles. As a matter of fact, he was always regarded as rather a joke in our family at the time when my sister, Mercy, was going to dances. He was the absolute last resort when a man had dropped out for a dinner party. Didn't some girl pour sugar over his head once at a ball?'

'What's happened to Widmerpool?' I asked. 'I haven't seen him for a year or two. Not since Isobel and I were married, as a matter of fact. I've known him for ages.'

'Fettiplace-Jones was giving him dinner at the House,' said Roddy, 'the night of the India debate.'

'Is he thinking of standing?' George asked. 'He is rather the type.'

'Not as a Tory,' Roddy said. 'Widmerpool is far from being a Tory.'

Roddy looked a shade resentful at George's probably quite artless judgment that Widmerpool was the sort of man likely to make an M.P.

'I ran across him somewhere,' said George. 'Then he was sitting at the next table one day at Sweeting's. He struck me as a knowledgeable chap. We had him to dinner as a matter of fact. Now I come to think of it, he said he knew you, Nick. My firm does a certain amount of business with Donners-Brebner, where Widmerpool used to be. He may be going back there in an advisory capacity, anyway temporarily, he told me.'

'I didn't at all take to Mr Widmerpool,' said Veronica, breaking off conversation with Susan on the subject of the best place to buy curtain material. 'He could talk of nothing but Mrs Simpson the night he came to us. You couldn't get him off the subject.'

St John Clarke, who had begun to look a little petulant at all this chatter about persons in general unknown to him, brightened at that name. He seemed about to speak; then some inner prompting must have caused him to think better of expressing any reflections stirring within his mind, because finally he remained silent, crumbling his bread thoughtfully.

'I met Mr Widmerpool once at Aunt Molly's,' said Susan. 'There was that business of his engagement being broken off, wasn't there – with that rather dreadful lady, one of the Vowchurches?'

'I hear poor Uncle Ted is a little better,' said Lady Warminster.

She referred to the war wound from which Jeavons intermittently suffered, at the same time managing to convey also a sense of moral or social improvement in Jeavons's condition which appeared for some reason to forbid further discussion of Widmerpool's unsuccessful attempt of a year or two before to marry Mrs Haycock.

'Roddy and I were at the Jeavonses' last week,' said Susan. 'The worst of the redecorating is over now, although one still falls over ladders and pails of whitewash. Aunt Molly's friend Miss Weedon – whom I can't stand – has moved in permanently now. She has a kind of flat on the top floor. And do you know who is living there too? Charles Stringham of all people. Do you remember him? Miss Weedon is said to be "looking after him".'

'Was that the Stringham we were at school with?' George asked me, but with no idea of what amazement I felt at this news, 'He was another contemporary of Widmerpool's.'

'I used to think Charles Stringham so attractive when he occasionally turned up at dances,' said Susan reminiscently, speaking as if at least half a century had passed since she herself had been seen on a dance floor. 'Then he absolutely disappeared from the scene. What happened to him? Why does he need "looking after"?'

'Charles Stringham isn't exactly a teetotaller, darling,' said Roddy, showing slight resentment at the expression by his own wife of such unqualified praise of another man's charms.

Lady Warminster shuddered visibly at the thought of what that understatement about Stringham's habits must comprehend. I asked Susan how this indeed extraordinary situation had come about: that Miss Weedon and Stringham should be living under the same roof at the Jeavonses'.

'Charles Stringham went to see Miss Weedon there one evening – she was his mother's secretary once, and has always been friends with Charles. He was in an awful state apparently, with 'flu coming on, practically delirious. So Miss Weedon kept him there until he recovered. In fact he has been there ever since. That is Aunt Molly's story.'

'Molly mentioned something about it to me,' said Lady Warminster.

She spoke very calmly, as if in reassuring confirmation that there was really nothing whatever for anyone to worry about. Having once registered her own illimitable horror of alcohol, Lady Warminster was fully prepared to discuss Stringham's predicament, about which, as usual, she probably knew a great deal more than her own family supposed. The information about Stringham was not only entirely new to me, but full of all kind of implications of other things deep rooted in the past; far more surprising, far more dramatic, for example, than Erridge's setting off for Spain.

'Charles is Amy Foxe's son by her second husband,' said Lady Warminster. 'There was a daughter, too – divorced from that not very nice man with one arm – who is married to an American called Wisebite. Amy has had trouble with both her children.'

Stringham's mother was an old friend of Lady Warminster's, although the two of them now saw each other rarely. That was chiefly because Mrs Foxe's unrelenting social activities allowed little time for visits to the drowsy, unruffled backwater in which the barque of Lady Warminster's widowhood had come to rest; unruffled, that is to say, in the eyes of someone like Mrs Foxe. In fact, life at Hyde Park Gardens could not always be so described, although its tenor was very different from the constant rotaion of parties, committee meetings, visits, through which Mrs Foxe untiringly moved. Perhaps this description of Mrs Foxe's existence was less exact since she had become so taken up with Norman Chandler; but, although she might now frequent a less formal social world (her charity organising remained unabated), she had been, on the other hand, correspondingly drawn into Chandler's own milieu of the theatre and music.

'It is really very good of Miss Weedon to look after Charles Stringham,' Lady Warminster continued. 'His mother, what with her hospitals and those terrible wars over them with Lady Bridgnorth, is always so dreadfully busy. Miss Weedon – Tuffy, everyone used to call her – was Flavia Stringham's governess before she became her mother's secretary. Such a nice, capable woman. I don't know why you should not like her, Sue.'

This speech did not make absolutely clear whether Lady Warminster cared as little as Susan for Mrs Foxe's former secretary, or whether, as the words outwardly indicated, she indeed approved of Miss Weedon and liked meeting her. Lady Warminster's pronouncements in such fields were often enigmatic. Possibly we were all intended to infer from her tone a shade of doubt as to whether Miss Weedon should have been allowed to take such absolute control over Stringham as now seemed to prevail. I felt uncertainty on that subject myself. This new situation might be good; it might be bad. I remembered Miss Weedon's unconcealed adoration for him when still a boy; the signs she had shown later at the Jeavonses' of hoping to play some authoritarian rôle in Stringham's life.

'I am doing what I can to help,' Miss Weedon had said, when we had met at the Jeavons house not long before my marriage.

Then, I had wondered what she meant. Now I saw that restraint, even actual physical restraint, might have been in her mind. Perhaps nothing short of physical restraint would meet Stringham's case. It was at least arguable. Miss Weedon seemed to be providing something of the sort.

'Molly will be glad of the additional rent,' said Lady Warminster, who seemed to be warming to the subject, now that its alcoholic aspects had faded into the background. 'She has been complaining a lot lately about being hard up. I tremble to think what Ted's doctor's bill must be like at any time. What difficulties he has with his inside. However, he is off slops again, I hear.'

'Have the Stringhams any money?' George asked.

'Oh, I don't think so,' said Lady Warminster, speaking as if the mere suggestion of anyone, let alone the Stringhams, having any money was in itself a whimsical enough notion. 'But I believe Amy was considered quite an heiress when she first appeared in London and old Lady Amesbury took her about a lot. She was South African, you know. Most of it spent now, I should think. Amy has always been quite thoughtless about money. She is very wilful. People said she was brought up in a very silly way. I suppose she probably lives now on what her first husband, Lord Warrington, left in trust. I don't think Charles's father – "Boffles", as he used to be called – had a halfpenny to bless himself with. He used to be very handsome, and so amusing. He looked wonderful on a horse. He is married now to a Frenchwoman he met at a tennis tournament in Cannes, and he farms in

Kenya. Poor Amy, she has some rather odd friends.'

In making this last comment, Lady Warminster was no doubt thinking of Norman Chandler; although no one could say how much, or how little, she knew of this association, nor what she thought about it. Robert caught my eye across the table. Within the family, he was regarded as the chief authority on their step-mother's obliquity of speech. Robert, strangely enough, had turned out to be one of the young men I had seen with Mrs Foxe at that performance of *The Duchess of Malfi* three or four years before. Mrs Foxe's other two guests had been John Mountfichet, the Bridgnorths' eldest son, and Venetia Penistone, one of the Huntercombes' daughters. After we had become brothers-in-law, and later talked of this occasion, Robert had described to me the excitement shown by Mrs Foxe that night at the prospect of seeing Chandler after the play was over. It was only a week or two since they had met for the first time.

'You know Mrs Foxe is rather daunting in her way,' Robert had said. 'At least she always rather daunts me. Well, she was trembling that night like a leaf. I think she was absolutely mad about that young actor we eventually took out to supper. She didn't get much opportunity to talk to him, because Max Pilgrim came too and spent the whole evening giving imitations of elderly ladies.

This companionship between Mrs Foxe and Chandler still flourished. She was said to give him 'wonderful' presents, expecting nothing in return but the pleasure of seeing him when he had the time to spare. That one of the most exigent of women should find satisfaction in playing this humble rôle was certainly remarkable. Chandler, lively and easy-going, was quite willing to fall in with her whim. They were continually seen about together, linked in a relationship somewhere between lover with mistress and mother to son.

'I could understand it if Norman were a sadist,' Moreland used to say. 'A mental one, I mean, who cut her dates and suchlike. On the contrary, he is always charming to her. Yet it still goes on. Women are inexplicable.'

During all this talk about Stringham and his parents, St John Clarke had once more dropped out of the conversation. His face was beginning to show that, although aware a self-invited guest must submit to certain periods of inattention on the part of his hostess, these had been allowed to become too frequent to be tolerated by a man of his position. He began to shift about in his chair as if he had something on his mind, perhaps wondering if he would finally be given a chance of being alone with Lady Warminster, or whether he had better say whatever he had to say in public. He must have decided that a *tête-à-tête* was unlikely, because he now spoke to her in a low confidential tone.

'There was a matter I wanted to put to you, Lady Warminster, which, in the hurried circumstances of our meeting at Bumpus's, I hardly liked to bring up. That was why I invited myself so incontinently to your house, to which you so graciously replied with an invitation to this charming lunch party. Lord Warminster – your eldest stepson – Alfred, I have begun to call him.'

St John Clarke paused, laughed a little coyly, and put his head on one side.

'*We* call him Erridge,' said Lady Warminster kindly, 'I never quite know why. It was not the custom in my own family, but then we were different from the Tollands in many ways. The Tollands have always called their eldest son by the second title. I suppose he could perfectly well be called Alfred. And yet, somehow, Erridge is not quite an Alfred.'

She considered a moment, her face clouding, as if the problem of why Erridge was not quite an Alfred worried

333

her more than a little, even made her momentarily sad.

'Lady Priscilla mentioned her brother's political sympathies just now,' said St John Clarke, smiling gently in return, as if to express the ease with which he could cope with social fences of the kind Lady Warminster set in his way. 'I expect you may know he is leaving for Spain almost immediately.'

'He told me so himself,' said Lady Warminster.

'The fact is,' said St John Clarke, getting rather red in the face and losing some of his courtliness of manner, 'the fact is, Lady Warminster, your stepson has asked me to look after his business affairs while he is away. Of course I do not mean his estate, nothing like that. His interests of a politico-literary kind——'

He took up his glass, but it was empty.

'Lord Warminster and I have been seeing a good deal of each other since his return from the East,' he said, stifling a sigh probably caused by thought of Mona.

'At Thrubworth?' asked Lady Warminster.

She showed sudden interest. In fact everyone at the table pricked up their ears at the supposition that St John Clarke had been received at Thrubworth. Guests at Thrubworth were rare. A new name in the visitors' book would be a significant matter.

'At Thrubworth,' said St John Clarke reverently. 'We talked there until the wee, small hours. During the past few years both of us have undergone strains and stresses, Lady Warminster. Alfred has been very good to me.'

He stared glassily down the table, as if he thought I myself might well be largely to blame for Members and Quiggin; for the disturbances the two of them must have evoked in his personal life.

'No one can tell what may happen to Lord Warminster in Spain,' St John Clarke said, speaking now more dramatically. 'He knows me to be a strong supporter of the democratically elected Spanish Government. He knows I feel an equally strong admiration for himself.'

'Yes, of course,' said Lady Warminster encouragingly.

'At the same time, Lady Warminster, I am an author, a man of letters, not a man of affairs. I thought it only right you should know the position. I want to do nothing behind your back. Besides that, Alfred has occasional dealings with persons known to me in the past with whom I should be unwilling . . . I do not mean of course . . .'

These phrases, which seemed to appeal to Lady Warminster's better feelings, certainly referred in the main to Quiggin.

'Oh, I am sure he does,' said Lady Warminster fervently. 'I do so much sympathise with you in feeling that.'

She plainly accepted St John Clarke's halting sentences as reprobating every friend Erridge possessed.

'In short I wondered if I could from time to time ask your advice, Lady Warminster – might get in touch with you if necessary, perhaps even rely on you to speak with acquaintances of your stepson's with whom – for purely personal reasons, nothing worse I assure you – I should find it distasteful to deal.'

St John Clarke made a gesture to show that he was throwing himself on Lady Warminster's mercy. She, on her part, did not appear at all unwilling to learn something of Erridge's affairs in this manner, although she can have had no very clear picture of St John Clarke's aims, which were certainly not easy to clarify. No doubt he himself liked the idea of interfering in Erridge's business, but at the same time did not wish to be brought once more in contact with Quiggin. Lady Warminster must have found it flattering to be offered the position of St John Clarke's confidante, which would at once satisfy curiosity and be in the best interests of

335

the family. If Erridge never came back from Spain – an eventuality which had to be considered – there was no knowing what messes might have to be cleared up. Besides, Erridge's plans often changed. His doings had to be coped with empirically. Like less idealistic persons, he was primarily interested in pleasing himself, even though his pleasures took unusual form. Little could be guessed from an outward examination of these enthusiasms at any given moment.

'Write to me, Mr Clarke, or telephone,' said Lady Warminster, 'whenever you think I can be of help. Should my health not allow me to see you at that moment, we will arrange something later.'

I had by then seen too much of Lady Warminster and her stepchildren to be surprised by the calm with which news of this sort was accepted. My own temper was in sympathy with such an attitude of mind. I looked forward to hearing Quiggin's account of the current Erridge situation. Possibly Quiggin himself might decide to go to Spain. Such a move was not to be ruled out. No doubt he too intended to keep an eye on Erridge's affairs; the best way to do that might be to attach himself to Erridge's person. The development of St John Clarke as a close friend of Erridge must be very unsympathetic to Quiggin. St John Clarke's appeal to Lady Warminster was unexpected. He had managed to get most of it said without attracting much attention from the rest of the party, who were discussing their own affairs, but the general drift of his muttered words probably caused the turn conversation took when it became general once more.

'Do you hold any view on what the outcome in Spain will be, Mr Clarke?' asked George.

St John Clarke made a gesture with his fingers to be interpreted as a much watered-down version of the Popular Front's clenched fist. Now that he had had his word with Lady Warminster about Erridge, he seemed more cheerful, although I was again struck by the worn, unhealthy texture of his skin. He still possessed plenty of nervous energy, but had lost his earlier flush. His cheeks were grey and pasty in tone. He looked a sick man.

'Franco cannot win,' he said.

'What about the Germans and Italians?' said George. 'It doesn't look as if non-intervention will work. It has been a failure from the start.'

'In that case,' said St John Clarke, evidently glad to find an opportunity to pronounce this sentence, 'can you blame Caballero for looking elsewhere for assistance.'

'Russia?'

'In support of Spain's elected government.'

'Personally, I am inclined to think Franco will win,' said George.

'Is that to your taste?' asked St John Clarke mildly.

'Not particularly,' George said. 'Especially if that has got to include Hitler and Mussolini. But then Russia isn't to my taste either. It is hard to feel much enthusiasm for the way the Government side go on, or, for that matter, the way they were going before the war broke out.'

'People like myself look forward to a social revolution in a country that has remained feudal far too long,' said St John Clarke, speaking now almost benignly, as if the war in Spain was being carried on just to please him personally, and he himself could not help being flattered by the fact. 'We cannot always be living in the past.'

This expressed preference for upheaval for its own sake roused Roddy Cutts. He began to move forward his knives and forks so that they made a pattern on the table, evidently a preliminary to some sort of a speech. St John Clarke was about to expand his view on revolution, when Roddy cut him short in measured, moderate, parliamentary tones.

'The question is,' Roddy said, 'whether the breakdown

of the internal administration of Spain – and nobody seriously denies the existence of a breakdown – justified a military *coup d'état*. Some people think it did, others disagree entirely. My own view is that we should not put ourselves in the position of seeming to encourage a political adventurer of admittedly Fascist stamp, while at the same time expressing in no uncertain terms our complete lack of sympathy for any party or parties which allow the country's rapid disintegration into a state of lawlessness, which can only lead, through Soviet intrigue, to the establishment of a Communist régime.'

'I think both sides are odious,' said Priscilla. 'Norah backs the Reds, like Erry. She and Eleanor Walpole-Wilson have got a picture of La Pasionaria stuck up on the mantelpiece of their sitting-room. I asked them if they approved of shooting nuns.'

St John Clarke's expression suggested absolute neutrality on that point.

'The tradition of anti-clericalism in Spain goes back a long way, Lady Priscilla,' he said, 'especially in Catalonia.'

Roddy Cutts had no doubt been studying Spanish history too, because he said: 'You will find an almost equally unbroken record of Royalism in Navarre, Mr Clarke.'

'I haven't been in Spain for years,' said Lady Warminster, in her low, musical voice, speaking scarcely above a whisper. 'I liked the women better than the men. Of course they all have English nannies.'

Luncheon at an end, St John Clarke established himself with Blanche in a corner of the drawing-room, where he discoursed of the humour of Dickens in a rich, sonorous voice, quite unlike the almost falsetto social diction he had employed on arrival. Blanche smiled gently, while with many gestures and grimaces St John Clarke spoke of Mr Micawber and Mrs Nickleby. They were still there, just beginning on

Great Expectations, when I set out for the nursing home, carrying messages of good-will to Isobel from the rest of the family.

A future marriage, or a past one, may be investigated and explained in terms of writing by one of its parties, but it is doubtful whether an existing marriage can ever be described directly in the first person and convey a sense of reality. Even those writers who suggest some of the substance of married life best, stylise heavily, losing the subtlety of the relationship at the price of a few accurately recorded, but isolated, aspects. To think at all objectively about one's own marriage is impossible, while a balanced view of other people's marriage is almost equally hard to achieve with so much information available, so little to be believed. Objectivity is not, of course, everything in writing; but, even after one has cast objectivity aside, the difficulties of presenting marriage are inordinate. Its forms are at once so varied, yet so constant, providing a kaleidoscope, the colours of which are always changing, always the same. The moods of a love affair, the contradictions of friendship, the jealousy of business partners, the fellow feeling of opposed commanders in total war, these are all in their way to be charted. Marriage, partaking of such – and a thousand more – dual antagonisms and participations, finally defies definition. I thought of some of these things on the way to the nursing home.

'How were they all?' asked Isobel.

We went over the luncheon party in detail; discussed the news about Erridge. Isobel was returning the following day, so that there were domestic arrangements to be rehearsed, mysteries of the labyrinth of married life fallen into abeyance with her imprisonment, now to be renewed with her release.

'I shan't be sorry to come home.'

'I shan't be sorry for you to be home again.'

Late in the afternoon I left the place. Its passages somewhat like those of Uncle Giles's *pied-à-terre*, the Ufford, were additionally laden with the odour of disinfectant, more haunted with human kind. As in the Ufford, it was easy to lose your way. Turning a corner that led to the stairs, I suddenly saw in front of me, of all people, Moreland, talking to a tall, grey-haired man, evidently a doctor, because he carried in his hand, like a stage property in a farce, a small black bag. Moreland looked hopelessly out of place in these surroundings, so that the two of them had some of the appearance of taking part in a play. The doctor was talking earnestly, Moreland fidgeting about on his feet, evidently trying to get away without too great a display of bad manners. We had not met for over a year – although occasionally exchanging picture postcards – because Moreland had taken a job at a seaside resort known for pride in its musical activities. Sooner or later to be a conductor in the provinces was a destiny Moreland had often predicted for himself in moods of despondency. I knew little or nothing about his life there, nor how his marriage was going. The postcards dealt usually with some esoteric matter that had caught his attention – a peculiar bathing dress on the beach, peepshows on the pier, the performance of pierrots – rather than the material of daily life. In the earlier stages of marriage, Matilda was keeping pace pretty well with circumstances not always easy from shortage of money. When he caught sight of me, Moreland looked quite cross, as if I had surprised him in some situation of which he was almost ashamed.

'What on earth are you doing here?' he asked brusquely.

'Visiting my wife.'

'Like me.'

'Is Matilda in this awful place too?'

'But of course.'

He, too, had seemed in the depths of gloom when I first

saw him; now, delighted at encountering a friend in these unpromising surroundings, he began to laugh and slap a rolled-up newspaper against his leg. Matilda had made him buy a new suit, in general cleaned up his appearance.

'So you have come back to London.'

'Inevitably.'

'For good?'

'I had to. I couldn't stand the seaside any longer. Matilda is about to have a baby, as a matter of fact. That is why I am haunting these portals.'

'Isobel has just had a miscarriage.'

'Oh, Lord,' said Moreland, 'I am always hearing about miscarriages. I used to think such things were quite out of date, and took place only in Victorian times when ladies – as Sir Magnus Donners would say – laced themselves up "a teeny, teeny little bit too tight". Rather one of Sir Magnus's subjects. I may add I shall be quite bankrupt unless Matilda makes up her mind fairly soon. She keeps on having false alarms. It is costing a fortune.'

He began to look desperately worried. The man with the black bag took a step forward.

'Both you gentlemen might be surprised if I told you incidence of abortion,' he said in a thin rasping voice, 'recently quoted in medical journals.'

'Oh, sorry,' said Moreland. 'This is Dr Brandreth.'

I saw the man to be the Brandreth who had been at school with me. Four or five years older, he had probably been unaware of my existence at that time, but I had seen him again at least once in later life, notably at that Old Boy Dinner at which our former housemaster, Le Bas, had fainted, an occasion when Brandreth, as a doctor, had taken charge of the situation. Tall and bony, with hair like the locks of a youngish actor who has dusted over his skull to play a more aged part in the last act, Brandreth possessed those desiccated good looks which also suggest the theatre. I began to explain that I knew him already, that we had been schoolboys together, but he brushed the words aside with a severe 'Yes, yes, yes . . .' at the same time taking my hand in a firm, smooth, interrogatory, medical grip, no doubt intended to give confidence to a patient, but in fact striking at once a disturbing interior dread at the possibilities of swift and devastating diagnosis.

'Another of my woman patients,' he went on, 'happens to be in here. Rather a difficult case for the gynaecologist. I've been giving him a hand with the after-treatment – from the temperamental point of view.'

Brandreth continued to hold Moreland with his eye, as if to make sure his attention did not wander too far afield. At the same time he took up a position closer to myself that seemed to imply appeal to me, as one probably familiar with Moreland's straying mind, to help if necessary in preventing his escape before the time was ripe. Penning us both in, Brandreth was evidently determined to obstruct with all the forces at his command further conversation between us which, by its personal nature, might exclude himself. However, at the critical moment, just as Brandreth was beginning to speak, he was interrupted by the competition of a new, impelling force. A stoutly built man, wearing a Jaeger dressing-gown, pushed past us without ceremony, making towards a door of frosted glass in front of which we were grouped. In his manner of moving, this person gave the impression that he thought we were taking up too much room in the passage – which may have been true – and that he himself was determined to convey, if necessary by calculated discourtesy, demonstrated by his own aggressive, jerky progress, a sense of strong moral disapproval towards those who had time to waste gossiping. Brandreth had already opened his mouth, probably to make some further pronouncement about obstetrics, but now he closed it quickly, catching the man in the dressing-gown by the sleeve.

'Widmerpool, my dear fellow,' he said, 'I want you to meet another patient of mine – one of England's most promising young musicians.'

Widmerpool, whose well-worn dressing-gown covered a suit of grubby pyjamas in grey and blue stripe, stopped unwillingly. Without friendliness, he rotated his body towards us. Brandreth he disregarded, staring first at Moreland, then myself, frowning hard through his thick spectacles, relaxing this severe regard a little when he recognised in me a person he knew.

'Why, Nicholas,' he said, 'what are you doing here?'

Like Moreland, Widmerpool too seemed aggrieved at finding me within the precincts of the nursing home.

'Ha!' said Brandreth. 'Of course you know one another. Fellow pupils of Le Bas. Strange coincidence. I could tell you some stranger ones. We were speaking of the high incidence of abortion, my dear Widmerpool.'

Widmerpool started violently.

'Not abortion, Dr Brandreth,' said Moreland, laughing. 'Miscarriage – nothing against the law.'

'I'm using the word,' said Brandreth, treating our ignorance with genial amusement, 'in the strictly medical sense that doesn't necessarily connote anything illegal. I had been talking to Mr Moreland,' he added, 'about Wagner, a chronic sufferer, I understand, from some form of dermatitis, though he finally succumbed, I believe, to a cardiac lesion – unlike Schubert with his abdominal trouble. They were both, I imagine, temperamental men.'

The fact that Widmerpool and I knew each other at least as well as Brandreth knew Widmerpool, prevented Brandreth from dominating the situation so completely as he had intended before Widmerpool's arrival. His tone in addressing Widmerpool was at once hearty and obsequious, almost servile in its unconcealed desire to make a good impression by play with Moreland's musical celebrity. Brandreth obviously considered Widmerpool a person of greater importance than Moreland, but also one who might be interested to come in contact with sides of life different from his own. In supposing this, Brandreth showed his acquaintance with Widmerpool to be superficial. Widmerpool remained totally unimpressed by the arts. He was even accustomed to show an open contempt for them in *tête-à-tête* conversation. In public, for social reasons, he had acquired the merest working knowledge to carry him through a dinner party, content with St John Clarke as a writer, Isbister as a painter.

'I don't know about those things,' he had once said to me. 'If I don't know about things, they do not interest me. Even if artistic matters attracted me – which they do not – I should not allow myself to dissipate my energies on them.'

Now, he stood staring at me as if my presence in the nursing home was an insoluble, an irritating, mystery. I explained once more that I had been visiting Isobel.

'Oh, yes,' said Widmerpool. 'You married one of the Tollands, did you not, Nicholas? I was sorry not to have come to your wedding. That was some time ago . . . nearly . . . as a matter of fact, I was far too busy. I should like to give you a wedding present. You must tell me something you want, even though I was not able to turn up at the ceremony. After all, we have known each other a long time now. A little piece of silver perhaps. I will consult my mother who arranges such things. Your wife is not suffering from anything serious, I hope. I believe I once met her at her aunt's, Lady Molly Jeavons. Perhaps it was one of her sisters.'

The meeting had, indeed, taken place. Isobel had mentioned it. She had not cared for Widmerpool. That was one of the reasons why I had made no effort to keep in touch with him. In any case I should never have gone out of my way to seek him, knowing, as one does with certain people, that the rhythm of life would sooner or later be bound to bring us together again. However, I remembered that I owed him a meal. Guilt as to this unfulfilled obligation was strengthened by awareness that he was capable of complaining publicly that I had never invited him in return. Preferring to avoid this possibility, I decided on the spot to ask Widmerpool, before we parted company, to lunch at my club; in fact while Isobel's convalescence gave an excuse for not bringing him to our flat.

'I have been enjoying a brief rest here,' he said. 'An opportunity to put right a slight mischief with boils. Some tests have been made. I leave tomorrow, agog for work again.'

'Isobel goes tomorrow, too. She will keep rather quiet for a week or two.'

'Quite so, quite so,' said Widmerpool, dismissing the subject.

He turned abruptly on his heel, muttering something about 'arranging a meeting in the near future', at the same time making a rapid movement towards the door of frosted glass at which he had been aiming when first accosted by Brandreth.

'Can you lunch with me next Tuesday – at my club?'

Widmerpool paused for a second to give thought to this question, once more began to frown.

'Tuesday? Tuesday? Let me think. I have something on Tuesday. I must have. No, perhaps I haven't. Wait a minute. Let me look at my book. Yes . . . Yes. As it happens, I can lunch with you on Tuesday. But not before half-past one. Certainly not before one-thirty. More likely one-thirty-five.'

Quickening his step, drawing his dressing-gown round

him as if to keep himself more separate from us, he passed through the door almost at a run. His displacement immediately readjusted in Moreland's favour Brandreth's social posture.

'To return to Wagner,' Brandreth said, 'you remember *Wanderlust*, Mr Moreland, of course you do, when Siegfried sings: "From the wood forth I wander, never to return!" – how does it go? –"*Aus dem Wald fort in die Welt zieh'n: nimmer kehr'ich zurück!*" Now, it always seems to me the greatest pity that in none of the productions of *The Ring* I have ever heard, has the deeper pessimism of these words been given full weight . . .'

Brandreth began to make movements with his hands as if he were climbing an invisible rope. Moreland disengaged us brutally from him. We descended the stairs.

'Who was the man in the dressing-gown with spectacles?' Moreland asked, when we had reached the street.

'He is called Kenneth Widmerpool. In the City. I have known him a long time.'

'I can't say I took to him,' Moreland said. 'But, look here, what a business married life is. I hope to goodness Matilda will be all right. There are various worrying aspects. I sometimes think I shall go off my head. Perhaps I am off it already. That would explain a lot. What are you doing tonight? I am on my way to the Maclinticks. Why not come too?'

Without waiting for an answer, he began to recount all that had been happening to Matilda and himself since we had last met; various absurd experiences they had shared; how they sometimes got on each other's nerves; why they had returned to London; where they were going to live. There had been some sort of a row with the municipal authorities at the seaside resort. Moreland held decided professional opinions; he could be obstinate. Some people, usually not the most intelligent, found working with him difficult. I heard some of his story, telling him in return how the film company for which I had been script-writing had decided against renewing my contract; that I was now appearing on the book page of a daily paper; also reviewing from time to time for the weekly of which Mark Members was assistant literary editor.

'Mark recommended Dr Brandreth to us,' Moreland said. 'A typical piece of malice on his part. Brandreth is St John Clarke's doctor – or was when Mark was St John Clarke's secretary. Gossip is the passion of his life, his only true emotion – but he can also put you on the rack about music.'

'Is he looking after Matilda?'

'A gynaecologist does that. He is not a music-lover, thank God. Of course, a lot of women have babies. One must admit that. No doubt it will be all right. It just makes one a bit jumpy. Look here, Nick, you must come to the Maclinticks'. It would be more cheerful if there were two of us.'

'Should I be welcome?'

'Why not? Have you developed undesirable habits since we last met?'

'I never think Maclintick much likes me.'

'Likes you?' said Moreland. 'What egotism on your part. Of course he doesn't like you. Maclintick doesn't like anybody.'

'He likes you.'

'We have professional ties. As a matter of fact, Maclintick doesn't really hate everyone as much as he pretends. I was being heavily humorous.'

'All the same, he shows small visible pleasure in meeting most people.'

'One must rise above that. It is a kindness to do so. Maclintick does not get on too well with his wife. The occasional company of friends eases the situation.'

'You do make this social call sound tempting.'

'If nobody ever goes there, I am afraid Maclintick will jump into the river one of these days, or hang himself with his braces after a more than usually gruelling domestic difference. You must come.'

'All right. Since you present it as a matter of life and death.'

We took a bus to Victoria, then passed on foot into a vast, desolate region of stucco streets and squares upon which a doom seemed to have fallen. The gloom was cosmic. We traversed these pavements for some distance, proceeding from haunts of seedy, grudging gentility into an area of indeterminate, but on the whole increasingly unsavoury, complexion.

'Maclintick is devoted to this part of London,' Moreland said. 'I am not sure that I agree with him. He says his mood is for ever Pimlico. I grant that a sympathetic atmosphere is an important point in choosing a residence. It helps one's work. All the same, tastes differ. Maclintick is always to be found in this neighbourhood, though never for long in the same place.'

'He never seems very cheerful when I meet him.'

I had run across Maclintick only a few times with Moreland since our first meeting in the Mortimer.

'He is a very melancholy man,' Moreland agreed. 'Maclintick is very melancholy. He is disappointed, of course.'

'About himself as a musician?'

'That – and other things. He is always hard up. Then he has an aptitude for quarrelling with anyone who might be of use to him professionally. He is writing a great tome on musical theory which never seems to get finished.'

'What is his wife like?'

'Like a wife.'

'Is that how you feel about marriage?'

348

'Well, not exactly,' said Moreland laughing. 'But you know one does begin to understand all the music-hall jokes and comic-strips about matrimony after you have tried a spell of it yourself. Don't you agree?'

'And Mrs Maclintick is a good example?'

'You will see what I mean.'

'What is Maclintick's form about women? I can never quite make out.'

'I think he hates them really – only likes whores.'

'Ah.'

'At least that is what Gossage used to say.'

'That's a known type.'

'All the same, Maclintick is also full of deeply romantic, hidden away sentiments about *Wein, Weib und Gesang*. That is his passionate, carefully concealed side. The gruffness is intended to cover all that. Maclintick is terrified of being thought sentimental. I suppose all his bottled-up feelings came to the surface when he met Audrey.'

'And the prostitutes?'

'He told Gossage he found them easier to converse with than respectable ladies. Of course, Gossage – you can imagine how he jumped about telling me this – was speaking of a period before Maclintick's marriage. No reason to suppose that sort of thing takes place now.'

'But if he hates women, why do you say he is so passionate?'

'It just seems to have worked out that way. Audrey is one of the answers, I suppose.'

The house, when we reached it, turned out to be a small, infinitely decayed two-storey dwelling that had seen better days; now threatened by a row of mean shops advancing from one end of the street and a fearful slum crowding up from the other. Moreland's loyalty to his friends – in a quiet way considerable – prevented me from being fully prepared

349

for Mrs Maclintick. That she should have come as a surprise was largely my own fault. Knowing Moreland, I ought to have gathered more from his disjointed, though on the whole decidedly cautionary, account of the Maclintick household. Besides, from the first time of meeting Maclintick – when he had gone to the telephone in the Mortimer – the matrimonial rows of the Maclinticks had been an accepted legend. However much one hears about individuals, the picture formed in the mind rarely approximates to the reality. So it was with Mrs Maclintick. I was not prepared for her in the flesh. When she opened the door to us, her formidable discontent with life swept across the threshold in scorching, blasting waves. She was a small dark woman with a touch of gipsy about her, this last possibility suggested by sallow skin and bright black eyes. Her black hair was worn in a fringe. Some men might have found her attractive. I was not among them, although at the same time not blind to the fact that she might be capable of causing trouble where men were concerned. Mrs Maclintick said nothing at the sight of us, only shrugging her shoulders. Then, standing starkly aside, as if resigned to our entry in spite of an overpowering distaste she felt for the two of us, she held the door open wide. We passed within the Maclintick threshold.

'It's Moreland – and another man.'

Mrs Maclintick shouted, almost shrieked these words, while at the same time she twisted her head sideways and upwards towards a flight of stairs leading to a floor above, where Maclintick might be presumed to sit at work. We followed her into a sitting-room in which a purposeful banality of style had been observed; only a glass-fronted bookcase full of composers' biographies and works of musical reference giving some indication of Maclintick's profession.

350

'Find somewhere to sit,' said Mrs Maclintick, speaking as if the day, bad enough before, had been finally ruined by our arrival. '*He* will be down soon.'

Moreland seemed no more at ease in face of this reception than myself. At the same time he was evidently used to such welcomes in that house. Apart from reddening slightly, he showed no sign of expecting anything different in the way of reception. After telling Mrs Maclintick my name, he spoke a few desultory words about the weather, then made for the bookcase. I had the impression this was his accustomed gambit on arrival in that room. Opening its glass doors, he began to examine the contents of the shelves, as if – a most unlikely proposition – he had never before had time to consider Maclintick's library. After a minute or two, during which we all sat in silence, he extracted a volume and began to turn over its pages. At this firm treatment, which plainly showed he was not going to allow his hostess's ill humour to perturb him, Mrs Maclintick unbent a little.

'How is your wife, Moreland?' she asked, after picking up and rearranging some sewing upon which she must have been engaged on our arrival. 'She is having a baby, isn't she?'

'Any day now,' said Moreland.

Either he scarcely took in what she said, or did not consider her a person before whom he was prepared to display the anxiety he had earlier expressed to me on that subject, because he did not raise his eyes from the book, and, a second after she had spoken, gave one of his sudden loud bursts of laughter. This amusement was obviously caused by something he had just read. For a minute or two he continued to turn the pages, laughing to himself.

'This life of Chabrier is enjoyable,' he said, still without looking up. 'How wonderful he must have been dressed as a bull-fighter at the fancy dress ball at Granada. What fun it all was in those days. Much gayer than we are now. Why

351

wasn't one a nineteenth-century composer living in Paris and hobnobbing with the Impressionist painters?'

Mrs Maclintick made no reply to this rhetorical question, which appeared in no way to fire within her nostalgic day-dreams. She was about to turn her attention, as if unwillingly, towards myself, with the air of a woman who had given Moreland a fair chance and found him wanting, when Maclintick came into the room. He was moving unhurriedly, as if he had arrived downstairs to search for something he had forgotten, and was surprised to find his wife entertaining guests. Despondency, as usual, seemed to have laid an icy grip on him. He wore bedroom slippers and was pulling at a pipe. However, he brightened a little when he saw Moreland, screwing up his eyes behind the small spectacles and beginning to nod his head as if humming gently to himself. I offered some explanation of my presence in the house, to which Maclintick muttered a brief, comparatively affirmative acknowledgement. Without saying more, he made straight for a cupboard from which he took bottles and glasses.

'What have you been up to all day?' asked Mrs Maclintick. 'I thought you were going to get the man to see about the gas fire. You haven't moved from the house as far as I know. I wish you'd stick to what you say. I could have got hold of him myself, if I'd known you weren't going to do it.'

Maclintick did not answer. He removed the cork from a bottle, the slight 'pop' of its emergence appearing to embody the material of a reply to his wife, at least all the reply he intended to give.

'I've been looking at this book on Chabrier,' said Moreland. 'What an enjoyable time he had in Spain.'

Maclintick grunted. He hummed a little. Chabrier did not appear to interest him. He poured out liberal drinks for everyone and handed them round. Then he sat down.

'Have you become a father yet, Moreland?' he asked.

He spoke as if he grudged having to make so formal an enquiry of so close a friend.

'Not yet,' said Moreland. 'I find it rather a trial waiting. Like the minute or two before the lights go out when you are going to conduct.'

Maclintick continued to hum.

'Can't imagine why people want a row of kids,' he said. 'Life is bad enough without adding that worry to the rest of one's other troubles.'

Being given a drink must have improved Mrs Maclintick's temper for the moment, because she asked me if I too were married. I told her about Isobel being about to leave a nursing home.

'Everyone seems to want babies nowadays,' said Mrs Maclintick. 'It's extraordinary. Maclintick and I never cared for the idea.'

She was about to enlarge on this subject when the bell rang, at the sound of which she went off to open the front door.

'How are you finding things now that you are back in London?' Maclintick asked.

'So-so,' said Moreland. 'Having to do a lot of hack work to keep alive.'

From the passage came sounds of disconnected talk. It was a man's voice. Whomever Mrs Maclintick had admitted to the house, instead of joining us in the sitting-room continued downstairs to the basement, making a lot of noise with his boots on the uncarpeted stairs. Mrs Maclintick returned to her chair and the knickers she was mending. Maclintick raised his eyebrows.

'Carolo?' he asked.

'Yes.'

'What's happened to his key?'

'He lost it.'

'Again?'

'Yes.'

'Carolo is always losing keys,' said Maclintick. 'He'll have to pay for a new one himself this time. It costs a fortune keeping him in keys. I can't remember whether I told you Carolo has come to us as a lodger, Moreland.'

'No,' said Moreland, 'you didn't. How did that happen?' Moreland seemed surprised, for some reason not best pleased at this piece of information.

'He was in low water,' Maclintick said, speaking as if he were himself not specially anxious to go into detailed explanations. 'So were we. It seemed a good idea at the time. I'm not so sure now. In fact I've been thinking of getting rid of him.'

'How is he doing?' asked Moreland. 'Carolo is always very particular about what jobs he will take on. All that business about teaching being beneath his dignity.'

'He says he likes time for that work of his he is always tinkering about with,' said Maclintick. 'I shall be very surprised if anything ever comes of it.'

'I like Carolo here,' said Mrs Maclintick. 'He gives very little trouble. I don't want to die of melancholia, never seeing a soul.'

'What do you mean?' said Maclintick. 'Look at the company we have got tonight. What I can't stick is having Carolo scratching away at the other end of the room when I am eating. Why can't he keep the same hours as other people?'

'You are always saying artists ought to be judged by different standards from other people,' said Mrs Maclintick fiercely. 'Why shouldn't Carolo keep the hours he likes? He is an artist, isn't he?'

'Carolo may be an artist,' said Maclintick, puffing out a long jet of smoke from his mouth, 'but he is a bloody unsuc-

354

cessful one nowadays. One of those talents that have dried up, in my opinion. I certainly don't see him blossoming out as a composer. Look here, you two had better stay to supper. As Audrey says, we don't often have company. You can see Carolo then. Judge for yourselves. It is going to be one of his nights in. I can tell from the way he went down the stairs.'

'He has got to work somewhere, hasn't he?' said Mrs Maclintick, whose anger appeared to be rising again after a period of relative calm. 'His bedroom is much too cold in this weather. You use the room with a gas fire in it yourself, the only room where you can keep warm. Even then you can't be bothered to get it repaired. Do you want Carolo to freeze to death?'

'It's my house, isn't it?'

'You say you don't want him in the sitting-room. Why did you tell him he could work in the room off the kitchen if you don't want him there?'

'I am not grumbling,' said Maclintick, 'I am just warning these two gentlemen what to expect – that is to say Carolo scribbling away at a sheet of music at one end of the room, and some cold beef and pickles at the other.'

'Mutton,' said Mrs Maclintick.

'Mutton, then. We can get some beer in a jug from the local.'

'Doesn't Carolo ever eat himself?' Moreland asked.

'He often meals with us as a matter of fact,' said Mrs Maclintick. 'I don't know why Maclintick should make all this fuss suddenly. It is just when Carolo has other plans that he works while we are having supper. Then he eats out later. He likes living on snacks. I tell him it's bad for him, but he doesn't care. What is so very extraordinary about all that?'

Her husband disregarded her.

'Then you are both going to stay,' he said, almost anxiously. 'That is fixed. Where is the big jug, Audrey? I'll get some beer. What does everyone like? Bitter? Mild-and-bitter?'

Moreland had probably been expecting this invitation from the start, but the Maclinticks' bickering about Carolo seemed to have put him out, so that, giving a hasty glance in my direction as if to learn whether or not I was prepared to fall in with this suggestion, he made some rambling, inconclusive answer which left the whole question in the air. Moreland was subject to fits of jumpiness of that sort; certainly the Maclinticks, between them, were enough to make anyone ill at ease. However, Maclintick now obviously regarded the matter as settled. The prospect of enjoying Moreland's company for the rest of the evening evidently cheered him. His tone in suggesting different brews of beer sounded like a gesture of conciliation towards his wife and the world in general. I did not much look forward to supper at the Maclinticks, but there seemed no easy way out. Moreland's earlier remarks about Maclintick's need for occasional companionship were certainly borne out by this visit. The Maclinticks, indeed, as a married couple, gave the impression of being near the end of their tether. When, for example, Mona and Peter Templer had quarrelled – or, later, when Mona's interlude with Quiggin had been punctuated with bad temper and sulkiness – the horror had been less acute, more amenable to adjustment, than the bleak despair of the Maclinticks' union. Mrs Maclintick's hatred of everything and everybody – except, apparently, Carolo, praise of whom was in any case apparently little more than a stick with which to beat Maclintick – caused mere existence in the same room with her to be disturbing. She now made for the basement, telling us she would shout in due course an invitation to descend. Simultaneously, Maclintick set off for the pub at the end of the street, taking with him a large, badly chipped china jug to hold the beer.

'I am afraid I've rather let you in for this,' said Moreland, when we were alone.

His face displayed that helpless, worried look which it would sometimes take on; occasions when Matilda, nowadays, probably took charge of the situation. No doubt he found life both worrying and irksome, waiting for her to give birth, himself by this time out of the habit of living on his own.

'Is it usually like this here?'

'Rather tougher than usual.'

We waited for some minutes in the sitting-room, Moreland returning to the life of Chabrier, while I turned over the pages of an illustrated book about opera, chiefly looking at the pictures, but thinking, too, of the curious, special humour of musicians, and also of the manner in which they write; ideas, words and phrases gushing out like water from a fountain, so utterly unlike the stiff formality of painters' prose. After a time, Mrs Maclintick yelled from the depths that we were to join her. Almost at the same moment, Maclintick returned with the beer. We followed him downstairs to the basement. There, in a room next to the kitchen, a table was laid. We settled ourselves round it. Maclintick filled some tumblers; Mrs Maclintick began to carve the mutton. Carolo was immediately manifest. Although, architecturally speaking, divided into separate parts, the Maclinticks' dining-room was not a large one, the table taking up most of one end. Maclintick's objection to their lodger working while he and his wife were making a meal seemed valid enough when the circumstances revealed themselves. Carolo sat, his face to the wall, engrossed with a pile of music. He looked round when Moreland and I entered the room, at the same time giving some sort of a hurried greeting, but he did not rise, or pause from his work, for more

357

than a second. Mrs Maclintick's temper had improved again; now she appeared almost glad that Moreland and I had stayed.

'Have some beetroot,' she said. 'It is fresh today.'

Moreland and Maclintick did not take long to penetrate into a region of musical technicality from which I was excluded by ignorance; so that while they talked, and Carolo scratched away in the corner, just as Maclintick had described, I found Mrs Maclintick thrown on my hands. In her latest mood, she turned out to have a side to her no less tense than her temper displayed on arrival, but more loquacious. In fact a flow of words began to stem from her which seemed to have been dammed up for months. No doubt Maclintick was as silent in the home as out of it, and his wife was glad of an outlet for her reflections. Indeed, her desire to talk was now so great that it was hard to understand why we had been received in the first instance with so little warmth. Mrs Maclintick's dissatisfaction with life had probably reached so advanced a stage that she was unable to approach any new event amiably, even when proffered temporary alleviation of her own chronic spleen. Possibly Moreland's friendship with her husband irked her, suggesting a mental intimacy from which she was excluded, more galling in its disinterested companionship than any pursuit of other women on Maclintick's part. She began to review her married life aloud.

'I can't think why Maclintick goes about looking as he does. He just won't buy a new suit. He could easily afford one. Of course, Maclintick doesn't care what he looks like. He takes no notice of anything I say. I suppose he is right in one way. It doesn't matter what he looks like the way we live. I don't know what he does care about except Irish whiskey and the Russian composers and writing that book of his. Do you think it will ever get finished? You know he has been at it for seven years. That's as long as we've been married. No, I'm wrong. He told me he started it before he met me. Eight or nine years, then. I tell him no one will read it when it is finished. Who wants to read a book about the theory of music, I should like to know? He says himself there is too much of that sort of thing published as it is. It is not that the man hasn't got ability. He is bright enough in his way. It is just that he doesn't know how to go about things. Then all these friends of his, like Moreland and you, encourage him, tell him he's a genius, and the book will sell in thousands. What do you do? Are you a musician? A critic, I expect. I suppose you are writing a book yourself.'

'I am not a music critic. I am writing a book.'

'Musical?'

'No – a novel.'

'A novel?' said Mrs Maclintick.

The idea of writing a novel seemed to displease her only a little less than the production of a work on musical theory.

'What is it to be called?'

'I don't know yet.'

'Have you written any other novels?'

I told her. She shook her head, no more in the mood for literature than music. All the time she treated Maclintick as if he were not present in the flesh; and, since he and Moreland were deeply engaged with questions of pitch and rhythm, both were probably unaware of these reflections on her domestic situation.

'And then this house. You can see for yourself it is like a pig-sty. I slave sixteen hours a day to keep it clean. No good. Might as well not attempt it. Maclintick isn't interested in whether his house is clean or not. What I say is, why can't we go and live in Putney? Where *I* want to live is never considered, of course. Maclintick likes Pimlico, so Pimlico it has to be. The place gives me the pip. Well, don't you agree yourself? Even if we move, it has to be somewhere else in Pimlico, and the packing up is more trouble than it is worth. I should like a bit of garden. Can't have that here. Not even a window-box. Of course Maclintick hates the sight of a flower.'

I quoted St John Clarke's opinion that the beauty of flowers is enhanced by metropolitan surroundings. Mrs Maclintick did not reply. Her attention had been distracted by Carolo, who had begun to pile his sheets of music together and stow them away in a portfolio.

'Come and have a drink with us, Carolo, before you go,' she said, with greater warmth than she had shown until that moment. 'Maclintick will get some more beer. We could all do with another drop. Here is the jug, Maclintick. Don't take all the cheese, Moreland. Leave a little for the rest of us.'

Maclintick did not look specially pleased at this suggestion of Carolo joining us at the table, but he too welcomed the idea of more beer, immediately picking up the chipped jug and once more setting off with it to the pub. A chair was drawn up for Carolo, who accepted the invitation with no more than mumbled, ungracious agreement; to which he added the statement that he would not be able to stay long. I had not set eyes on him since that night in the Mortimer. Carolo looked just the same: pale; unromantic; black wavy hair a shade longer and greasier than before. Mrs Maclintick gave him a glance that was almost affectionate.

'Have you got to go out tonight, Carolo?' she said. 'There is a little mutton left.'

Carolo shook his head, looking wearily at the residue of the joint, the remains of which were not specially tempting. He seemed in a thoughtful mood, but, when Maclintick reappeared with the jug and poured him out a glass, he drank a deep draught of the beer with apparent gratification. After wiping his mouth with a handkerchief, he spoke in his harsh, North Country voice.

'How have you been, Moreland?' he asked.

'Much as usual,' said Moreland. 'And you?'

'Pretty middling. How's Matilda?'

'Having a baby,' said Moreland flushing; and, as if he preferred to speak no more for the moment about that particular subject, went on: 'You know, in that book I was reading upstairs, Chabrier says that the Spanish fleas have their own national song – a three-four tune in F major that Berlioz introduces into the *Damnation of Faust*.'

'The Spanish fleas must be having a splendid time nowadays,' said Maclintick, 'biting both sides indiscriminately.'

'The International Brigade could certainly make a tasty dish,' said Moreland, 'not to mention the German and Italian "volunteers". As a matter of fact the fleas probably prefer the Germans. More blonds.'

'I hope to God Franco doesn't win,' said Mrs Maclintick, as if that possibility had at this moment just struck her.

'Who do you want to win?' said Maclintick gruffly. 'The Communists?'

Up till then Maclintick had been on the whole in a better temper than usual. The arrival at the table of Carolo had unsettled him. He now showed signs of wanting to pick a quarrel with someone. His wife was clearly the easiest person present with whom to come into conflict. Biting and sucking noisily at his pipe he glared at her. It looked as if the Spanish war might be a matter of controversy of some standing between them; a source of contention as a married couple, rather than a political difference. Maclintick's views on politics could never be foretold. Violent, changeable, unorthodox, he tended to dislike the Left as much as the Right. He had spoken very bitterly.

'I would rather have the Communists than the Fascists,' said Mrs Maclintick, compressing her lips.

361

'Only because you think it is the done thing to be on the Left,' said Maclintick, with an enraging smile. 'There isn't a middle-brow in the country who isn't expressing the same sentiment. They should try a little practical Communism and see how they like it. You are no exception, I assure you.'

He removed his pipe from his mouth and swallowed hard. Moreland was obviously becoming uneasy at the turn things were taking. He began kicking his foot against the side of his chair.

'I am Pinkish myself,' he said laughing.

'And you want the Communists?' asked Maclintick.

'Not necessarily.'

'And Marxist music?'

'I long to hear some.'

'Shostakovitch, Russia's only reputable post-Revolution composer, not allowed to have his opera performed because the dictatorship of the proletariat finds that work musically decadent, bourgeois, formalist?'

'I'm not defending the Soviet régime,' said Moreland, still laughing. 'I'm all for *Lady Macbeth of the Mtsensk District* – my favourite title. Wasn't there a period in the Middle Ages when the Pope forbade certain chords under pain of excommunication? All I said – apropos of the war in Spain – I am Pinkish. No more, no less.'

This attempt to lighten the tension was not very successful. Maclintick leaned down and tapped his pipe against his heel. Mrs Maclintick, though silent, was white with anger.

'What about Toscanini?' she demanded suddenly.

'What about him?' said Maclintick.

'The Fascists slapped his face.'

'Well?'

'I suppose you approve of that.'

'I don't like the Fascists any more than you do,' said Maclintick. 'You know that perfectly well. It was me that

Blackshirt insisted on taking to the police station in Florence, not you. You tried to truckle to him.'

'Anyway,' said Mrs Maclintick, 'I want the Government in Spain to win – not the Communists.'

'How are you going to arrange that, if they do defeat Franco? As it is, the extremists have taken over on the side of "the Government", as you call it. How are you going to arrange that the nice, liberal ones come out on top?'

'What do you know about it?' said his wife, speaking now with real hatred. 'What do you know about politics?'

'More than you.'

'I doubt it.'

'Doubt it, then.'

There was a moment during the pause that followed this exchange of opinion when I thought she might pick up one of the battered table knives and stick it into him. All this time, Carolo had remained absolutely silent, as if unaware that anything unusual was going on round him, unaware of Spain, unaware of civil war there, unaware of Communists, unaware of Fascists, his expression registering no more than its accustomed air of endurance of the triviality of those who inhabited the world in which he unhappily found himself. Now he finished the beer, wiped his mouth again with the pocket handkerchief, and rose from the table.

'Got to remove myself,' he said in his North Country burr.

'What time will you be back?' asked Maclintick.

'Don't know.'

'I suppose someone will have to let you in.'

'Suppose they will.'

'Oh, shut up,' burst out Mrs Maclintick. 'I'll let him in, you fool. What does it matter to you? You never open a door for anyone, not even your precious friends. It's me that does all the drudgery in this house. You never do a hand's turn, except sitting upstairs messing about with a lot of stuff that is really out of your reach – that you are not quite up to.'

By this time everyone was standing up.

'I think probably Nick and I ought to be going too,' said Moreland, the extent of his own discomposure making him sound more formal than usual. 'I've got to get up early tomorrow . . . go and see Matilda . . . one thing and another . . .'

He succeeded in suggesting no more than the fact that the Maclinticks' house had become unbearable to him. Maclintick showed no sign of surprise at this sudden truncation of our visit, although he smiled to himself rather grimly.

'Do you want to take the book about Chabrier?' he asked. 'Borrow it by all means if you would like to read the rest of it.'

'Not at the moment, thanks,' said Moreland. 'I have got too much on hand.'

Carolo had already left the house by the time we reached the front door. Without bidding us farewell, Mrs Maclintick had retired in silence to the kitchen, where she could be heard clattering pots and pans and crockery. Maclintick stood on the doorstep biting his pipe.

'Come again,' he said, 'if you can stand it. I'm not sure how long I shall be able to.'

'It won't be till after Matilda has given birth,' Moreland said.

'Oh, I forgot about that,' said Maclintick. 'You're going to become a father. Well, good night to you both. Pleasant dreams.'

He shut the door. We set off up the street.

'Let's walk by the river for a bit to recover,' Moreland said. 'I'm sorry to have let you in for all that.'

'Was it a representative Maclintick evening?'

'Not one of their best. But they understand each other in an odd way. Of course, that is the sort of thing people say just before murder takes place. Still, you grasp what I mean when I insist it is good for Maclintick to see friends occasionally. But what on earth can Carolo be doing there? Everyone must be pretty short of cash for Carolo to live with the Maclinticks as a lodger. I should not have thought either party would have chosen that. All the pubs are shut by now in this area, aren't they?'

Cutting down to the Embankment, we walked for a time beside the moonlit, sparkling river, towards Vauxhall Bridge and along Millbank, past the Donners-Brebner Building dominating the far shore like a vast penitentiary, where I had called for Stringham one night years before, when he had been working there.

'Married life is unquestionably difficult,' Moreland said. 'One may make a slightly better shot at it than the Maclinticks, but that doesn't mean one has no problems. I shall be glad when this baby is born. Matilda has not been at all easy to deal with since it started. Of course, I know that is in the best possible tradition. All the same, it makes one wonder, with Maclintick, how long one will be able to remain married. No, I don't mean that exactly. It is not that I am any less fond of Matilda, so much as that marriage – this quite separate entity – somehow comes between us. However, I expect things will be all right as soon as the baby arrives. Forgive these morbid reflections. I should really write them for the Sunday papers, get paid a huge fortune for it and receive an enormous fan-mail. The fact is, I am going through one of those awful periods when I cannot work. You know what hell that is.'

Moreland and I parted company, making arrangements to meet soon. The subject of marriage cropped up again, although in a different manner, when Widmerpool lunched with me the following week.

'We will not take too long over our meal, if you do not

mind,' he said, speaking only after he had hung his hat, topcoat and umbrella on a peg in the hall. 'I am, as usual, very busy. That is why I am a minute or two after time. There is a lot of work on hand as a matter of fact. You probably know that I have accepted the commitment of advising Donners-Brebner regarding the investment of funds for their pension scheme. Sir Magnus, in general an excellent man of business for immediate negotiation, is sometimes surprisingly hesitant in matters of policy. Unexpectedly changeable, too. In short Sir Magnus doesn't always know his own mind. Above all, he is difficult to get hold of. He will think nothing of altering the hour of appointment three or four times. I have had to point out to his secretary more than once that I must make a schedule of my day just as much as Sir Magnus must plan his.'

All the same, in spite of petty annoyances like Sir Magnus's lack of decision, Widmerpool was in far better form than at our last luncheon together, two or three years before, a time when he had himself been thinking of marriage. He ate more than on that occasion, although for drink he still restricted himself to a glass of water, swallowing pills both before and after the meal.

'Brandreth recommended these tablets,' he said. 'He says they are soothing. I find him on the whole a satisfactory medical adviser. He is rather too fond of the sound of his own voice, but he has a sensible attitude towards things. Brandreth is by no means a fool. Nothing narrow about him like so many doctors.'

'Did you go to him because you knew him at school?'

'No, no,' said Widmerpool. 'What an idea. For a man to have shared one's education is, in my eyes, no special recommendation to my good graces. I suppose I could have formed some early impression of his character and efficiency. I regret to say that few, if any, of my school contemporaries struck

366

me sufficiently favourably for me to go out of my way to employ their services. In any case, Brandreth was that amount older than myself to make it difficult to judge his capabilities – certainly his capabilities as a medical man. At the same time, it is true to say that our connexion has something to do with the fact we were at school together. Do you remember that Old Boy Dinner at which Le Bas fainted? I was impressed by the manner in which Brandreth handled that situation – told the rest of the party to go about their business and leave Le Bas to him. I liked that. It is one of my principles in life to surround myself with persons whose conduct has satisfied me. Usually the people themselves are quite unaware that they have benefited by the fact that, at one time or another, they made a good impression on me. Brandreth is a case in point.'

'The opposite process to entertaining angels unawares?'

'I don't quite know what you mean,' said Widmerpool. 'But tell me about yourself, your married life, Nicholas. Where are you living? I dined with your brother-in-law, George Tolland, not long ago. I am never sure that it is a wise thing for soldiers to go into business. If fellows enter the army, let them stay in the army. That is true of most professions. However, he gave me some acceptable advice regarding raising money for my Territorials. The mess fund balance always seems low.'

Widmerpool rarely showed great interest in other people's affairs, but his good humour that day was such that he listened with more attention than usual when subjects unconnected with himself were ventilated. I wondered if some business deal had put him in such a genial mood. Conversation drifted to such matters.

'Things are looking up a little in the City,' he said, when luncheon was over. 'I foresee that the rhythm of the trade circle is moving towards improvement. I have been doing some small calculations on my own account to verify how matters stand. It will interest you to hear my findings. As you know, the general level of dividends is the major determinant of general stock values and market prices over a long period of time. Over shorter periods stock prices fluctuate more widely than dividends. That is obvious, of course. I worked out, for example, that since the Slump, stock prices have risen between 217⅜ per cent and 218½ per cent. So far as I could ascertain, dividends have not exceeded 62¾ per cent to 64⅝ per cent. Those are my own figures. I do not put them forward as conclusive. You follow me?'

'Perfectly.'

'Setting aside a European war,' said Widmerpool, 'which I do not consider a strong probability in spite of certain disturbing features, I favour a reasoned optimism. I hold views, as it happens, on the interplay of motions and emotions of the Stock Exchange, which, in my opinion, are far more amenable to appraisement than may be supposed by the tyro. My method could not be simpler. I periodically divide the market price of stocks – as expressed by some reliable index – by the dividend paid on the index. What could be easier than that. You agree?'

'Of course.'

'But lest I should seem to pontificate upon my own subject, to be over-occupied with the sordid details of commerce, let me tell you, Nicholas, that I have been allowing myself certain relaxations.'

'You have?'

'As you know, my mother has always urged me to spend more time seeking amusement. She thinks I work too hard.'

'I remember your telling me.'

I did not know what he was aiming at. There was no doubt he was pleased about something. He seemed uncertain whether or not to reveal the reason for that. Then, suddenly, his gratification was explained.

'I have been moving in rather exalted circles lately,' he said, giving a very satisfied smile.

'Indeed?'

'Not exactly royal – that is hardly the word yet . . . You understand me . . . ?'

'I think so.'

'It was an interesting experience.'

'Have you actually met . . .'

Widmerpool bowed his head, suggesting by this movement the knowledge of enviable secrets. At the same time he would allow no admission that might be thought compromising either to himself or those in high places whose reputation must rightly be shielded. I tried to extort more from him without any success.

'When did this happen?'

'Please do not press me for details.'

He was now on his dignity. There was a moment of silence. Widmerpool took a deep breath, as if drawing into his lungs all the health-giving breezes of the open sea of an elevated social life.

'I think we are going to see some great changes, Nicholas,' he said, 'and welcome ones. There is much – as I have often said before – to be swept away. I feel sure the things I speak of will be swept away. A new broom will soon get to work. I venture to hope that I may even myself participate in this healthier society to which we may look forward.'

'And you think we shall avoid war?'

'Certainly, I do. But I was speaking for once of society in its narrower sense – the fashionable world. There is much in the prospect before us that attracts me.'

I wondered if he were again planning to marry. Widmerpool, as I had noticed in the past, possessed certain telepathic powers, sometimes to be found in persons insensitive to the processes of thought of other people except in so far as they concern themselves; that is to say he seemed to know immediately that some idea about him was germinating in a given person's mind – in this case that I was recalling his fiasco with Mrs Haycock.

'I expect you remember that the last time you were lunching with me I was planning matrimony myself,' he said. 'How fortunate that nothing came of it. That would have been a great mistake. Mildred would not have made at all a suitable wife for me. Her subsequent conduct has caused that to become very plain. It was in the end a relief to my mother that things fell out as they did.'

'How is your mother?'

'As usual, she is positively growing younger,' said Widmerpool, pleased by this enquiry. 'And together with her always keen appreciation of youth, she tries, as I have said, to persuade me to venture more often into a social world. She is right. I know she is right. I made an effort to follow her advice – with the satisfactory consequence that I have more than half imparted to you.'

It was no good hoping to hear any more. Like Moreland dropping hints about his love affairs, Widmerpool hoped only to whet my curiosity. He seemed anxious to convince me that, although his own engagement had been broken off in embarrassing circumstances, he had been left without any feeling of bitterness.

'I hear Mildred Haycock has returned to the South of France,' he said. 'Really the best place for her. I won't repeat to you a story I was told about her the other day. For my own part, I see no reason to hurry into marriage. Perhaps, after all, forty is the age at which to find a mate. I believe Léon Blum says so in his book. He is a shrewd man, Monsieur Blum.'

3

PEOPLE TALKED as if it were a kind of phenomenon
that Matilda should ever have given birth to a child at all:
the unwillingness of the world to believe that anyone –
especially a girl who has lived fairly adventurously – might
exist for a time in one manner, then at a later date choose
quite another way of life. The baby, a daughter, survived
only a few hours. Matilda herself was very ill. Even when
she recovered, Moreland remained in the deepest dejection.
He had worried so much about his wife's condition before
the child was born that he seemed almost to have foreseen
what would happen. That made things no better. About that
time, too, there was a return of trouble with his lung: money
difficulties obtruded: everything went wrong: depression
reigned. Then, after some disagreeable weeks, two unexpected jobs turned up. Almost from one day to the next
Moreland recovered his spirits. There was, after all, no
reason why they should not in due course have another child.
The financial crisis was over: the rent paid: things began to
look better. All the same, it had to be admitted the Morelands did not live very domestically. The routine into which
married life is designed inexorably to fall was still largely
avoided by them. They kept rigorously late hours. They were
always about together. A child would not have fitted easily
into the circumstances of their small, rather bleak flat (no
longer what Moreland had begun to call 'my former apo-
laustic bachelor quarters') where they were, in fact, rarely
to be found.

We used to see a good deal of the Morelands in those days, dining together sometimes at Foppa's, sometimes at the Strasbourg, afterwards going to a film, or, as Moreland really preferred, sitting in a pub and talking. He would develop a passion for one particular drinking place – never the Mortimer after marriage – then tire of it, inclination turning to active aversion. Isobel and Matilda got on well together. They were about the same age; they had the nursing home in common. Matilda had recovered quickly, after an unpromising start. She found apparent relief in describing the discomfort she had suffered, although speaking always in a manner to cast a veil of unreality over the experience. Lively, violent, generous, she was subject, like Moreland himself, to bouts of deep depression. On the whole the life they lived together – so wholly together – seemed to suit her. Perhaps, after all, people were right to think of her as intended by nature for a man's mistress and companion, rather than as cast for the rôle of mother.

'Matilda's father was a chemist,' Moreland once remarked, when we were alone together, 'but he is dead now – so one cannot get special terms for purges and sleeping pills.'

'And her mother?'

'Married again. They were never on very good terms. Matty left home very young. I think everyone was rather glad when she struck out on her own.'

Two of my sisters-in-law, as it happened, had come across Matilda in pre-Moreland days. These were Veronica, George Tolland's wife, and Norah, who shared a flat with Eleanor Walpole-Wilson. Veronica, whose father was an auctioneer in a country town not far from Stourwater Castle, was one of the few people to know something of Matilda's early life. They had, indeed, been at school together.

'I was much older, of course,' Veronica said. 'I just remember her right down at the bottom of the junior school, a little girl you couldn't help noticing. She was called Betty Updike then.'

'How did you ever discover Matilda was the same girl?'

'When I was living at home and divorcing Fred, I met a local girl in the High Street who'd got a job on the *Daily Mail*. She began to talk about Sir Magnus Donners and said: "Do you know the piece called Matilda Wilson he is always seen around with is really Betty Updike".'

There was nothing particularly surprising about Matilda having taken a new name for the stage. Many people did that. It was something to be expected. The manner in which Matilda had first met Sir Magnus was more interesting.

'This girl told me Matilda Wilson came down one term to help the school dramatic society do *A Midsummer Night's Dream*,' said Veronica. 'They had got permission to act the play at Stourwater. Sir Magnus, wandering round, came across Matilda Wilson dressing up a lot of little girls as elves. That went pretty well.'

It seemed as credible a story as any other. Once involved with Sir Magnus, Matilda had, of course, been 'seen everywhere'; within the limitations of the fact that Sir Magnus preferred to keep his girl of the moment as much as possible to himself, allowing her to meet no more of his own friends than strictly necessary for his own entertainment when the two of them could not be alone together. Certainly that had been true of the time when Sir Magnus was associated with Baby Wentworth, alleged by Barnby to have 'given notice' on this very account. There had been a lot of gossip about Matilda when she was 'with' Sir Magnus. When, not long before my own marriage, I had stayed with Quiggin and Mona in the cottage lent them by Erridge, Quiggin had even talked too much about Matilda for Mona's taste.

'Oh, yes,' Mona had said, in her irritated drawl, 'Matilda Wilson – one of those plain girls men for some extraordinary

373

reason like running after. Because they are not much trouble, I suppose.'

Norah Tolland had encountered Matilda in quite different circumstances; in fact having drinks with Heather Hopkins, the pianist, who had formerly inhabited one of the lower floors of the house in Chelsea where Norah and Eleanor Walpole-Wilson occupied the attics. At the period of which I am speaking – about two years after my own marriage – Norah and Eleanor had both found themselves jobs and become very 'serious', talking a lot about politics and economics and how best to put the world right. They were now rather ashamed of their Heather Hopkins days.

'Poor old Hopkins,' Norah said, when I mentioned her once. 'Such a pity she goes round looking and talking like the most boring kind of man. Her flat might be the bar in a golf club. She is a good-hearted creature in her own way.'

'You get tired of all that clumping about,' said Eleanor, kicking some bedroom slippers out of sight under the sofa. 'And besides, Heather isn't in the least interested in world affairs. One does ask a little sense of responsibility in people.'

However, things had been very different some years before. Then, Hopkins had thrilled Norah and Eleanor with her eyeglass and her dinner-jacket and her barrack-room phrases. Matilda had been brought to the Hopkins flat by a young actress at that time much admired by the hostess. The gathering was, of course, predominantly female, and Matilda, often found attractive by her own sex, but herself preferring men even in an unaggressively masculine form, had spent most of the evening talking to Norman Chandler. She met him for the first time at this Hopkins party. Through Chandler, Matilda had subsequently obtained a foothold in that branch of the theatre which had led in due course to her part in *The Duchess of Malfi*. Norah, usually sparing of praise, had been impressed by Matilda, to whom, as it happened, she only managed to speak a couple of words in the course of the evening.

'I thought she was rather wonderful,' said Norah.

Moreland himself had first met his future wife at a time when Matilda's connexion with Sir Magnus, if not completely severed, had been at least considerably relaxed. Moreland's behaviour on this occasion had been characteristic. He had fallen deeply in love, immediately overwhelming Matilda with that combination of attention and forgetfulness which most women found so disconcerting in his addresses. For once, however, that approach worked very well. Matilda was won. There had already been some ups and downs in their relationship by the time I was allowed to meet her, but, in principle, they were satisfied enough with each other before marriage; they still seemed satisfied when we used to meet them and dine together at Foppa's or the Strasbourg. I discounted Moreland's casual outbursts against marriage as an institution; indeed, took his word for it that, as he used to explain, these complaints were a sign of living in a world of reality, not a palace of dreams.

'People always treat me as if I was a kind of 1880 bohemian,' he used to say. 'On the contrary, I am the sane Englishman with his pipe.'

It was one one of these evenings at the Strasbourg that he announced his symphony was finished and about to be performed. Although Moreland never talked much about his own compositions, I knew he had been working on the symphony for a long time.

'Norman's friend, Mrs Foxe, is going to give a party for it,' he said.

'But how lovely,' said Isobel. 'Will Mrs Foxe and Norman stand at the top of the stairs, side by side, receiving the guests?'

'I hope so,' said Moreland. 'An example to all of us. A fidelity extremely rare among one's friends.'

'Does Mrs Foxe still live in a house somewhere off Berkeley Square?' I asked.

'That's it,' said Moreland. 'With objects like mammoth ice-cream cornets on either side of the front door for putting out the torches after you have paid off your sedan chair.'

'I am not sure that I like parties at that house,' said Matilda. 'We have been there once or twice. I can stand grand parties less and less anyway.'

She was having one of her moods that night, but it was on the whole true to say that since marriage Moreland had increasingly enjoyed going to parties, especially parties like that offered by Mrs Foxe; Matilda, less and less.

'You talk as if we spent our life in a whirl of champagne and diamonds,' Moreland said. 'Anyway, it won't be as grand as all that. Mrs Foxe has promised just to ask our own sordid friends.'

'Who,' asked Isobel, 'apart from us?'

'I'd far rather go off quietly by ourselves somewhere after the thing is over and have supper with Isobel and Nick,' Matilda said. 'That would be much more fun.'

'It *is* rather an occasion, darling,' said Moreland, vexed at these objections. 'After all, I am noted among composers for the smallness of my output. I don't turn out a symphony every week like some people. A new work by me ought to be celebrated with a certain flourish – if only to encourage the composer himself.'

'I just hate parties nowadays.'

'There are only going to be about twenty or thirty people,' Moreland said. 'I know Edgar Deacon used to assure us that "the saloon, rather than the *salon*, is the true artist's milieu", but his own pictures were no great advertisement for that principle. Personally, I feel neither subservience nor resentment at the prospect of being entertained by Mrs Foxe in luxurious style.'

'Have you ever talked to her naval husband?' I asked.

'There is a smooth, hearty fellow about the house sometimes,' Moreland said. 'A well-fed air, and likes a good mahogany-coloured whisky. I once heard him give an anguished cry when the footman began to splash in too much soda. I never knew he was her husband. He doesn't look in the least like a husband.'

'Of course he is her husband,' said Matilda. 'What an ass you are. He pinched my leg the night we were having supper with them after *Turandot*. That is one of the reasons I turned against the house.'

'Darling, I'm sure he didn't. Just your swank.'

'I told you when we got home. I even showed you the bruise. You must have been too tight to see it.'

'He always seems scrupulously well behaved to me,' Moreland said. 'Rather afraid of Mrs Foxe, as a matter of fact. I understand why, now she turns out to be his wife.'

Soon after this meeting with the Morelands came the period of crisis leading up to the Abdication, one of those public events which occupied the minds not only of those dedicated by temperament to eternal discussion of what they read about in the newspapers, but of everyone else in the country of whatever age, sex, or social class. The constitutional and emotional issues were left threadbare by debate. Barnby would give his views on the controversy in his most down-to-earth manner; Roddy Cutts treated it with antiseptic discretion; Frederica's connexion with the Court caused her to show herself in public as little as possible, but she did not wholly avoid persecution at the hands of friends and relations vainly hoping for some unreleased titbit.

'I shall have a nervous breakdown if they don't settle

things soon,' said Robert Tolland. 'I don't expect you hear any news, Frederica?'

'I can assure you, Robert, my own position is equally nerve-racking,' said Frederica. 'And I hear no news.'

She certainly looked dreadfully worried. I found Members and Quiggin discussing the ineluctable topic when I went to collect a book for review.

'I am of course opposed in principle to monarchy, like all other feudal survivals,' Quiggin was saying. 'But if the country must have a king, I consider it desirable, indeed essential that he should marry a divorcée. Two divorces – double as good. I am no friend of the civilisation of Big Business, but at least an American marriage is better than affiliation with our own so-called aristocracy.'

Members laughed dryly.

'Have you taken part in a procession of protest yet, J.G.?' he asked, now in a sufficiently strong economic position vis-à-vis his old friend to treat Quiggin's indignation with amused irony. 'I believe all kinds of distinguished people from the intellectual world have been parading the streets with sandwich boards expressing outraged royalist sentiments.'

'I regard the whole matter as utterly trivial in any case,' said Quiggin, irritably shoving a handful of recently published novels back into the shelf behind Members's desk, tearing the paper wrappers of two of them by the violence of his action. 'You asked me my views, Mark, and I've told you what they are. Like Gibbon, I dismiss the subject with impatience. Perhaps you will produce a book of some interest this week, a change from these interminable autobiographies of minor criminals which flow so freely from the press and to which I am for ever condemned by you.'

I met Moreland in the street just after the story had broken in the newspapers.

'Isn't this just my luck?' he said. 'Now nobody is going to listen to music, look at a picture, or read a book, for months on end. We can all settle down happily to discussions every evening about Love and Duty.'

'Fascinating subjects.'

'They are in one's own life. Less so, where others are concerned.'

'You speak with feeling.'

'Do I? Just my naturally vehement way of expressing myself.'

As it turned out, once the step had been taken, the Abdication become a matter of history, everything resumed an accustomed routine with much greater ease than popularly foreseen. There appeared no reason to suppose the box office for Moreland's symphony would suffer. Priscilla (who had eventually taken the job in the organisation raising money for the promotion of opera) reported, for example, that the cross-section of the public seen through this particular microscope seemed to have settled down, after some weeks of upheaval, to its normal condition. Priscilla was not particularly interested in music – less so than Robert – but naturally this employment had brought her in touch to some degree with the musical world. At the same time, I was surprised when, the day before Moreland's work was to be performed, Priscilla rang up and asked if she could come with us the following evening. Isobel answered the telephone.

'I didn't know you often went to concerts,' she said.

'I don't unless I have a free ticket,' said Priscilla.

'Did you get a free ticket for this one?'

'Yes.'

'Who gave it you?'

'One of the persons whose music is going to be played.'

'I thought they were all dead, or living abroad, except Hugh Moreland.'

'Hugh Moreland gave me the ticket.'

'I didn't know you knew him.'

'Of course I do.'

'Oh, yes. You met him with us, didn't you?'

'And other times too. I meet him in my office.'

'You never mentioned it.'

'Look here, can I come with you and Nick, or can't I?' said Priscilla. 'I am just asking. If you think being seen in my company will get you a bad name, I'll go alone and pretend I don't know either of you if we meet in the bar. Nothing easier.'

This conversation was reported later by Isobel, with the information that Priscilla was dining with us the following night.

'Typical of Hugh to present a ticket to Priscilla, who is not in the least interested in music,' I said, 'when all sorts of people who might be useful to him would have been delighted to be remembered in that way.'

The statement was true, at the same time disingenuous. I was a little aware of that at the time. It was a priggish remark; not even genuinely priggish. There seemed no point in adding that it was obviously more fun to give a ticket to a pretty girl like Priscilla, rather than to some uncouth musical hanger-on whose gratification might ultimately pay a doubtful dividend. I felt it one of those occasions when a show of worldliness might be used as a smoke-screen. But why should a smoke-screen be required?

'I suppose Hugh had a few drinks at some party,' I said, 'and distributed tickets broadcast.'

In the end I convinced myself of the probability of this surmise. Isobel did not express any views on the subject. However, when she arrived at the flat, Priscilla explained that Moreland, the day before, had visited, in some professional capacity, the place where the Opera fund was administered. There, 'rummaging about in his pocket for his cigarettes', he found this spare ticket 'crumpled up among a lot of newspaper cuttings, bits of string, and paper-clips'. He had given the ticket to Priscilla, suggesting at the same time that she should come on to Mrs Foxe's party after the concert. That was a convincing story. It had all the mark of Moreland's behaviour. We talked of other things; of Erridge, who had cabled for thicker underclothes to be sent him in Barcelona, indicating in this manner that he was not, as some prophesied, likely to return immediately. We discussed Erridge's prospects in Spain. By the time we reached the concert hall, Priscilla seemed to have come with us that evening by long previous arrangement.

Moreland was fond of insisting that whatever the critics say, good or bad, all works of art must go through a maturing process before taking their allotted place in the scheme of things. There is nothing particularly original in that opinion, but those who hold firmly to it are on the whole less likely to be spoiled by praise or cast down by blame than others – not necessarily worse artists – who find heaven or hell in each individual press notice. The symphony was, in fact, greeted as a success, but not as an overwhelming success; a solid piece of work that would add to Moreland's reputation, rather than a detonation of unexampled brilliance. Gossage, fiddling about with the mustard pot at some restaurant, had once remarked (when Moreland was out of the room) that he would be wise to build up his name with a work of just that sort. In the concert hall, there had been a lot of applause; at the same time a faint sense of anti-climax. Even for the most self-disciplined of artists, a public taken by surprise is more stimulating than a public relieved to find that what is offered can be swallowed without the least sharpness on the palate. This was especially true of Moreland, who possessed his healthy share of liking to startle, in spite of his own innate antagonism to professional startlers. However, if the symphony turned out to be a little disappointing to those who may have hoped for something more barbed, the reception was warm enough to cast no suggestion of shadow over a party of celebration.

'That went all right, didn't it?' said Isobel.

'It seemed to.'

'I thought it absolutely wonderful,' said Priscilla.

I felt great curiosity at the prospect of seeing Mrs Foxe's house again, not entered since the day when, still a schoolboy, I had lunched there with Stringham and his mother. Nothing had changed in the pillared entrance hall. There was, of course, absolutely no reason why anything should have changed, but I had an odd feeling of incongruity about reappearing there as a married man. The transition against this same backcloth was too abrupt. Some interim state, like steps in the gradations of freemasonry, seemed to have been omitted. We were shown up to a crimson damask drawing-room on the first floor, at one end of which sliding doors were open, revealing the room at right angles to be the 'library – with its huge malachite urn, Romney portrait, Regency bookcases – into which Stringham had brought me on that earlier visit. There I had first encountered the chilly elegance of Commander Foxe; also witnessed Stringham's method of dealing with his mother's 'current husband'.

Commander Foxe, as it happened, was the first person I saw when we came through the door. He was talking to Lady Huntercombe. From a certain bravado in his manner of addressing her, I suspected he had probably let himself off attending the concert. Mrs Foxe came forward to meet us as we were announced, looking just as she looked at *The Duchess of Malfi*, changeless, dazzling, dominating. As an old friend of Lady Warminster's, she had, of course, known Isobel and Priscilla as children. She spoke to them for a moment about their stepmother's health, then turned to me. I was about to recall to her the circumstances in which we had formerly met in what was now so dim a past, wondering at the same time what on earth I was going to say about Stringham, mention of whose name was clearly unavoidable, when Mrs Foxe herself forestalled me.

'How well I remember when Charles brought you to luncheon here. Do you remember that too? It was just before he sailed for Kenya. We all went to the Russian Ballet that night. Such a pity you could not have come with us. What fun it was in those days . . . Poor Charles . . . He has had such a lot of trouble . . . You know, of course . . . But he is happier now. Tuffy looks after him – Miss Weedon; you met her too when you came here, didn't you? – and Charles has taken to painting. It has done wonders.'

'I remember his caricatures.'

Stringham could not draw at all in the technical sense, but he was a master of his own particular form of graphic representation, executed in a convention of blobs and spidery lines, very effective for producing likenesses of Le Bas or the other masters at school. I could not imagine what Stringham's 'painting' could be. This terminology put the activity into quite another setting.

'Charles uses gouache now,' said Mrs Foxe, speaking with that bright firmness of manner people apply especially to close relations attempting to recover from more or less disastrous mismanagement of their own lives, 'designing theatrical costumes and that sort of thing. Norman says they are really quite good. Of course, Charles has had no training, so it is probably too late for him to do anything professionally. But the designs have originality, Norman thinks. You know Norman talks a lot about you and Isobel. He adores you both. Norman made me read one of your books. I liked it very much.'

She looked a bit pathetic when she said that, making me feel in this respect perhaps Chandler had gone too far in his exercise of power. However, other guests coming up the stairs at our heels compelled a forward movement. Moreland, red in the face, appeared in Mrs Foxe's immediate background. We offered our congratulations. He muttered a word or two about the horror of having a new work performed; seemed very happy about everything. We left him talking to Priscilla, herself rather pink, too, with the excitement of arrival. The party began to take more coherent shape. Mrs Foxe had, on the whole, most dutifully followed Moreland's wishes in collecting together his old friends, rather than arranging a smart affair of her own picking and choosing. Indeed, the far end of the crimson drawing-room could almost have been a corner of the Mortimer on one of its better nights; the group collected there making one feel that at any moment the strains of the mechanical piano would suddenly burst forth. The Maclinticks, Carolo, Gossage, with several other musicians and critics known to me only by sight, were present, including a famous conductor of a generation older than Moreland's, invited probably through acquaintance with Mrs Foxe in a social way rather than because of occasional professional contacts between Moreland and himself. This distinguished person was conversing a little loudly and self-consciously, with a great deal of gesticulation, to show there was no question of condescension from himself towards his less successful colleagues. Near this knot of musicians stood Chandler's old friend, Max Pilgrim, trying to get a word or two out of Rupert Wise, another of Chandler's friends – indeed, a great admiration of Chandler's – a male dancer known for his strict morals and lack of small talk. Wise's engagement to an equally respectable female member of the *corps de ballet* had recently been announced. Mrs Foxe had promised to give them a refrigerator as a wedding present.

'Not colder than Rupe's heart,' Chandler had commented. 'It was my suggestion. He may have a profile like Apollo, but he's got a mind like Hampstead Garden Suburb.'

The Huntercombes, as well as the celebrated conductor, were certainly contributed to the party by Mrs Foxe rather than by Moreland. Once – as I knew from remarks let fall by Stringham in the past – Mrs Foxe would have regarded Lady Huntercombe as dreadfully 'slow', and laughed at her clothes, which were usually more dramatic than fashionable. However, now that Mrs Foxe's energies were so largely directed towards seeking ways of benefiting Chandler and his friends, Lord Huntercombe's many activities in the art world had to be taken into account. In his capacity as trustee of more than one public gallery, Lord Huntercombe was, it was true, concerned with pictures rather than with music or the theatre. At the same time, his well recognised abilities in his own field had brought him a seat on several committees connected with other branches of the arts or activities of a generally 'cultural' sort. Lord Huntercombe, small and immensely neat, was indeed a man to be reckoned with. He had caught napping one of the best known Bond Street dealers in the matter of a Virgin and Child by Benozzo Gozzoli (acquired from the gallery as the work of a lesser master, later resoundingly identified), also so nicely chosen the moment to dispose of his father's collection of English pastels that he obtained nearly twice their market value.

Lady Huntercombe, as usual majestically dressed in a black velvet gown, wore a black ribbon round her neck clipped with an elaborate ornament in diamonds. She took a keen interest in music, more so than her husband, who liked to be able himself to excel in his own spheres of patronage, and was not musically inclined. I remembered Lady Huntercombe expressing her disappointment after Stringham's wedding at the manner in which the choir had sung the anthem. 'Dreadfully sharp,' I heard her say at the reception. 'It set my teeth on edge.' Now she was talking to Matilda, to the accompaniment of animated and delighted shakings of her forefinger, no doubt indicative of some special pleasure she had taken in Moreland's symphony; apparently at the same time trying to persuade Matilda – who seemed disposed to resist these advances – to accept some invitation or other similar commitment.

Moving towards the inner room, I observed that Chandler's small bronze of *Truth Unveiled by Time*, long ago bought from the Caledonian Market and rescued from Mr Deacon's shop after his death, had now come finally to rest on the console table under the Romney. Chandler himself was standing beside the table, stirring a glass of champagne with a gold swizzle-stick borrowed from Commander Foxe. Although Chandler might hold Mrs Foxe under his sway, she, on her part, had in some degree tamed him too. His demeanour had been modified by prolonged association with her. He was no longer quite the *gamin* of the Mortimer.

'Hullo, my dear,' he said. 'Fizz always gives me terrible hiccups, unless I take the bubbles away. You know Buster, of course.'

Commander Foxe, greyer now, a shade bulkier than when I had last seen him, was at the same time, if possible, more dignified as a result of these outward marks of maturity. He retained in his dress that utter perfection of turn-out that stopped so brilliantly short of seeming no more than the trappings of a tailor's dummy. His manner, on the other hand, had greatly changed. He had become chastened, almost humble. I could not imagine how I had ever found him alarming; although, even with this later development of geniality, there still existed a suggestion that below the surface he knew how to make himself disagreeable if need be. I mentioned where we had last met. He at once recollected, or pretended to recollect, the occasion; the essence of good manners and friendliness, almost obsequious in his desire to please.

'Poor old Charles,' he said. 'Of course I remember you were a friend of his. Do you ever see him these days? Well, of course, nobody does much, do they? All the same, it hasn't worked out too badly. Do you remember Miss Weedon, Amy's secretary? Rather a formidable lady. Oh, you know all about that, do you? Yes, Molly Jeavons is an aunt of your wife's, of course. Quite a solution for Charles in a way. It gives him the opportunity to live a quiet life for a time. Norman goes round and sees Charles sometimes, don't you, Norman?'

'I simply adore Charles,' said Chandler, 'but I'm rather afraid of that gorgon who looks after him – I believe you are too, Buster.'

Buster laughed, almost achieving his savage sneer of former times. He did not like Miss Weedon. I remembered that. He was no doubt glad to have ridded the house of Stringham too. They had never got on well together.

'At least Tuffy keeps Charles in order,' Buster said. 'If one hasn't any self-discipline, something of the sort unfortunately has to be applied from the outside. It is a hard thing to say, but there it is. Are you in this musical racket yourself? I hear Hugh Moreland's symphony was very fine. I couldn't manage to get there myself, much to my regret.'

I felt a pang of horror at the way his family now talked of Stringham: as if he had been put away from view like a person suffering from a horrible, unmentionable disease, or become some terrifying legendary figure, fearful as the Glamis monster, about whom it was appropriate to joke as dreadful to behold, but at the same time a being past serious credence. All the same, it was hard to know what else they could do about him, how better behave towards him. Stringham, after all, was their problem, not mine. I myself could offer no better solution than Miss Weedon; was in no position to disparage his own relations so far as their conduct towards Stringham was concerned.

'They were a bit hurried in seeing our former King off the premises, weren't they?' said Buster, changing the subject to public events, possibly because he feared his last words might provoke musical conversation. 'Some of one's friends have been caught on the wrong foot about it all. Still, I expect he will have a much better time on his own in the long run. His later job was not one I should care to take on.'

'My dear, you'd do it superbly,' said Chandler. 'I always think that when I look at that photograph of you in tropical uniform.'

'No, no, nonsense, Norman,' said Buster, not displeased at this attribution to himself of potentially royal aptitudes. 'I should be bored to death. I can't in the least imagine myself opening Parliament and all that sort of thing.'

Chandler signified his absolute disagreement.

'I must go off and have a word with Auntie Gossage now,' he said, 'or the old witch will fly off on a broomstick and complain about being cut. See you both later.'

'What a wonderful chap Norman is,' said Buster, speaking with unaccustomed warmth. 'You know I sometimes wonder what Amy would do without him. Or me, either, for that matter. He runs the whole of our lives. He can do anything from arranging the flowers to mixing the best Tom Collins I have ever drunk. So talented in other ways too. Ever seen him act? Then, as for dancing and playing the saxophone . . . Well, I've never met a man like him.'

There seemed no end to Buster's admiration for Chandler. I did not disagree, although surprised, rather impressed, by

Buster's complete freedom from jealousy. It was not that anyone supposed that Chandler was 'having an affair' with Mrs Foxe – although no one can speak with certainty, as Barnby used to insist, about any two people in that connexion – but, apart from any question of physical relationship, she obviously loved Chandler, even if this might not be love of quite the usual sort. A husband, even a husband as unprejudiced as Buster, might have felt objection on personal, or merely general, grounds. Many men who outwardly resembled Buster would, on principle, have disliked a young man of Chandler's appearance and demeanour; certainly disliked for ever seeing someone like that about the house. Either natural tolerance had developed in Buster as he had grown older, or there were other reasons why his wife's infatuation with Chandler satisfied him; after all Matilda had alleged the pinching of her leg. Possibly Chandler kept Mrs Foxe from disturbing Buster in his own amusements. If that was the reason, Buster showed a good grace in the manner in which he followed his convenience; in itself a virtue not universally practised. Perhaps he was a little aware that he had displayed himself to me in an unexpected light.

'Amy needs a good deal of looking after,' he said. 'I am sometimes rather busy. Get caught up in things. Business engagements and so on. Most husbands are like that, I suppose. Can't give a wife all the attention she requires. Know what I mean?'

This self-revelation was so unlike the Buster I remembered, that I was not sure whether to attribute the marked alteration in his bearing in some degree to changes in myself. Perhaps development in both of us had made a mutually new attitude possible. However, before Buster could particularise further on the subject of married life, a subject about which I should have liked to hear more from him, Maclintick, moving with the accustomed lurching walk he employed drunk or sober, at that moment approached us.

'Any hope of getting Irish in a house like this?' he asked me in an undertone. 'Champagne always gives me diarrhoea. It would be just like the rich only to keep Scotch. Do you think it would be all right if I accosted one of the flunkeys? I don't want to let Moreland down in front of his grand friends.'

I referred to Buster this demand for Irish whiskey on Maclintick's part.

'Irish?' said Buster briskly. 'I believe you've got us there. I can't think why we shouldn't have any in the cellar, because I rather like the stuff myself. Plenty of Scotch, of course. I expect they told you that. Wait here. I'll go and make some investigations.'

'Who is that kind and beautiful gentleman?' asked Maclintick acidly, not showing the least gratitude at Buster's prompt effort to satisfy his need for Irish whiskey. 'Is he part of the management?'

'Commander Foxe.'

'I am no wiser.'

'Our hostess's husband.'

'I thought she was married to Chandler. He is the man I always see her with at the ballet – if you can call him a man. I suppose I have shown my usual bad manners again. I ought never to have come to a place like this. Quite against my principles. All the same, I hope Baron Scarpia will unearth a drop of Irish. Must be an unenviable position to be married to a woman like his wife.'

His own matrimonial state seemed to me so greatly worse than Commander Foxe's that I was surprised to find Maclintick deploring any other marriage whatever. Gossage – 'that old witch', as Chandler had called him – joined us before I could answer. He seemed to be enjoying the party, clasping together his fingers and agitating his hands up and down in the air.

'What did you think of Moreland's work, Maclintick?' he asked. 'A splendid affair, splendidly received. Simply wonderful. I rarely saw such enthusiasm. Didn't you think so, Maclintick?'

'No, I didn't,' said Maclintick, speaking with finality. 'So far as reception was concerned, I thought it just missed being a disaster. The work itself was all right. I liked it.'

Gossage was not in the least put out by the acerbity of Maclintick's disagreement. He stood on his toes, placing the tips of his fingers together in front of him like a wedge.

'You judged that, did you, Maclintick?' he said thoughtfully, as if a whole new panorama had been set in front of him. 'You judged that. Well, perhaps there is something in what you say. All the same, I considered it a great personal triumph for Moreland, a great triumph.'

'You know as well as I do, Gossage, that it was not a triumph,' said Maclintick, whose temper had risen suddenly. 'We are all friends of Moreland's – we shouldn't have come to this bloody awful party tonight, dressed up in these clothes, if we weren't – but it is no help to Moreland to go round saying his symphony was received as a triumph, that it is the greatest piece of music ever written, when we all know it wasn't and it isn't. It is a very respectable piece of work. I enjoyed it. But it wasn't a triumph.'

Gossage looked as if he did not at all agree with Maclintick's strictures on Mrs Foxe's party and the burden of wearing evening clothes, but was prepared at the same time to allow these complaints to pass, as well as any views on Moreland as a composer, in the light of his colleague's notorious reputation for being cantankerous.

'There may be opposition from some quarters,' Gossage said. 'I recognise that. Some of the Old Gang may get on their hind legs. A piece of music is none the worse for causing that to happen.'

'I don't see why there should be opposition,' said Maclintick, as if he found actual physical relief in contradicting Gossage on all counts. 'A certain amount of brick-throwing might even be a good thing. There comes a moment in the career of most artists, if they are any good, when attacks on their work take a form almost more acceptable than praise. That happens at different moments in different careers. This may turn out to be the moment with Moreland. I don't know. I doubt it. All I know is that going round pretending the symphony is a lot of things it isn't, does Moreland more harm than good.'

'Ah, well,' said Gossage, speaking now with conscious resignation, 'we shall see what everyone says by the weekend. I liked the thing myself. It seemed to have a lot of life in it. Obvious failings, of course. All the same, I fully appreciate the points you make, Maclintick. But here is Mrs Maclintick. And how is Mrs Maclintick this evening?'

Mrs Maclintick had the air of being about to make trouble. She was wearing a fluffy, pale pink dress covered with rosettes and small bows, from which her arms and neck emerged surrounded by concentric circles of frills. On her head was set a cap, medieval or pre-Raphaelite in conception, which, above dark elfin locks, swarthy skin and angry black eyes, gave her the appearance of having come to the party in fancy dress.

'Do take your hands out of your pockets, Maclintick,' she said at once. 'You always stand about everywhere as if you were in a public bar. I don't know what the people here must think of you. We are are not in the Nag's Head now, you know. Try to remember not to knock your pipe out on the carpet.'

Maclintick took no notice of his wife whatsoever. Instead,

he addressed to Gossage some casual remarks about Smetana which seemed to have occurred to him at that moment. Mrs Maclintick turned to me.

'I don't expect you are any more used to this sort of party than I am,' she said. 'As for Maclintick, he wouldn't have been here at all if it hadn't been for me. I got him into those evening trousers somehow. Of course he never wants to wear evening clothes. He couldn't find a black bow-tie at the last moment. Had to borrow a made-up one Carolo used to wear. He is tramping about in his ordinary clodhopping black shoes too.'

Maclintick continued to ignore his wife, although he must have heard all this.

'What did you think of Moreland's symphony?' she continued. 'Not much of a success, Maclintick thinks. I agree with him for once.'

Maclintick caught her words. He swung round in such a rage that for a moment I thought he was going to strike her; just as I had thought she might stick a dinner knife into him when I had been to their house. There was certainly something about her manner this evening which would almost have excused physical violence even in the circumstances of Mrs Foxe's party.

'I didn't say anything of the sort, you bloody bitch,' Maclintick said, 'so keep your foul mouth shut and don't go round repeating that I did, unless you want to get hurt. It is just like your spite to misrepresent me in that manner. You are always trying to make trouble between Moreland and myself, aren't you? What I said was that the music was "not Moreland's most adventurous" – that the critics had got used to him as an *enfant terrible* and therefore might underestimate the symphony's true value. That was all. That was what I said. You know yourself that was all. You know yourself that was what I said.'

Maclintick was hoarse with fury. His hands were shaking. His anger made him quite alarming.

'Yes, Maclintick was just saying that very thing, wasn't he?' agreed Gossage, sniggering nervously at this display of uncontrolled rage. 'The words were scarcely out of his mouth, Mrs Maclintick. That is exactly what he thinks.'

'Don't ask me what he thinks,' said Mrs Maclintick calmly, not in the least put out of countenance by the force of her husband's abuse. 'He says one thing at one moment, another at another. Doesn't know his own mind in the least. I told him he was standing about as if he was in the Nag's Head. That is the pub near us where all the tarts go. I suppose that is where he thinks he is. It's the place where he is most at home. Besides, if the symphony was such a success, why wasn't Moreland better pleased? Or Matilda, for that matter? Matilda doesn't seem at all at her best tonight. I expect these grand surroundings remind her of better days.'

'I didn't say the symphony was "a great success" either,' said Maclintick, speaking now wearily, as if his outburst of anger had left him weak. 'Anyway, what do you mean? Moreland looks all right to me. What is wrong with him? Of course, it was insane of me to express any opinion in front of a woman like you.'

'Go on,' said Mrs Maclintick. 'Just go on.'

'And what reason have you for saying Matilda isn't pleased?' said Maclintick. 'I only wish I had a wife with half Matilda's sense.'

'Matilda didn't seem to be showing all that sense when I was talking to her just now,' said Mrs Maclintick, still quite undisturbed by this unpleasant interchange, indeed appearing if anything stimulated by its brutality. 'Or to be at all pleased either. Not that I care how she speaks to me. I bet she has done things in her life I wouldn't do for a million pounds. Let her speak to me how she likes. I'm not going to bring up her past. All I say is that she and Moreland were having words during the interval. Perhaps it was what they were talking about upset them, not the way the symphony was received. It is not for me to say.'

Further recrimination was terminated for the moment by the butler bringing a decanter for Maclintick with Buster's apology that no Irish whiskey was to be found in the house. Buster himself appeared a moment later, adding his own regrets for this inadequacy. I withdrew from the group, and went over to speak to Robert Tolland, who had just come into the room. Robert knew Moreland only slightly, as a notable musical figure rather than as a friend. He had probably been asked to the party at the instigation of Mrs Foxe, had perhaps dined with her to make numbers even. I had not seen him in the concert hall.

'I expected to find you and Isobel here,' he said. 'I was asked at the last moment, I hardly know why. One of those curious afterthoughts which are such a feature of Amy Foxe's entertaining. I see Priscilla is here. Did you bring her?'

'Priscilla dined with us. You could have come to dinner too, if we had known you were on your way to this party.'

Robert gave one of his quiet smiles.

'Nice of you to suggest it,' he said, 'but there were things I had to do earlier in the evening as a matter of fact. How very attractive Mrs Moreland is. I always think so whenever I see her. What a relief that one no longer has to talk about the Abdication. Frederica is looking a lot better now that everything is settled.'

He smiled and moved away, exhaling his usual air of mild mystery. Lady Huntercombe, taking leave of Matilda with a profusion of complimentary phrases, swept after Robert. Matilda beckoned me to come and talk to her. She looked pale, seemed rather agitated, either on account of her long session with Lady Huntercombe, or perhaps because she was still feeling shaken by the strain of hearing the symphony performed.

'Give me some more champagne, Nick,' she said, clasping my arm. 'It is wonderful stuff for the nerves. Are you enjoying yourself at this smart party? I hope so.'

This manner was not at all her usual one. I thought she was probably a little drunk.

'Of course – and the symphony was a great success.'

'Did you think so?'

'Very much.'

'Are you sure?'

'Didn't you?'

'I suppose so.'

'Oh, yes.'

'You are certain, Nick?'

'Of course I am. Everything went all right. There was lots of applause. What else do you expect?'

'Yes, it was all right, I think. Somehow I hoped for more real enthusiasm. It is a wonderful work, you know. It really is.'

'I am sure it is.'

'It is wonderful. But people are going to be disappointed.'

'Does Hugh himself think that?'

'I don't think it worries him,' said Matilda. 'Not in his present state of mind.'

For some reason – from the note in her voice, a sense of trouble in the air, perhaps just from natural caution – I felt safer in not enquiring what she regarded as Moreland's 'present state of mind'.

'I see your little sister-in-law, Lady Priscilla, is here,' said Matilda.

She smiled rather in Robert's manner, as if at some secret inner pleasure that was also a little bitter to contemplate.

'You've met her with us, haven't you?'

'Yes.'

'She dined with us tonight.'

'I met her once at your flat,' said Matilda, speaking slowly, as if that were an extraordinary thing to have happened. 'She is very attractive. But I don't know her as well as Hugh does.'

I suddenly felt horribly uncomfortable, as if ice-cold water were dripping very gently, very slowly down my spine, but as if, at the same time, some special circumstance prevented admission of this unaccountable fact and also forbade any attempt on my own part to suspend the process; a sensation to be recognised, I knew well, as an extension of that earlier refusal to face facts about Moreland giving Priscilla the concert ticket. That odd feeling of excitement began to stir within me always provoked by news of other people's adventures in love; accompanied as ever by a sense of sadness, of regret, almost jealousy, inward emotions that express, like nothing else in life, life's irrational dissatisfactions. On the one hand, that Moreland might have fallen in love with Priscilla (and she with him) seemed immensely interesting; on the other – to speak only callously of the Morelands' marriage and Priscilla's inexperience (if she was inexperienced) – any such situation threatened complications of a most disturbing kind on two separate fronts of one's own daily existence. As to immediate action, a necessary minimum was obviously represented by refraining from any mention to Matilda of the complimentary ticket. Silence on that point offered at least a solid foundation upon which to build; the simple principle that a friend's actions, however colourless, vis-à-vis another woman, are always better unrepeated to his wife. Contemplation of this banal maxim increased the depression that had suddenly descended on me. The proposition that Moreland was having some sort of a flirtation with Priscilla sufficiently tangible to cause Matilda – even if

397

she had had too much champagne – to draw my attention to such goings-on appeared at once ridiculous and irritating. Probably Matilda's speculations were unco-ordinated. Quite likely Moreland and Priscilla were indeed behaving foolishly. Why draw attention to that? The matter would blow over. All three persons concerned fell in my estimation. In any case, Matilda's speculations might be wholly unfounded. Priscilla, physically speaking – socially speaking, if it came to that – was not the sort of girl Moreland usually liked. 'Nothing is more disturbing,' he used to say himself, 'than one's friends showing unexpected sexual tastes.' Priscilla, for her part, was not in general inclined towards the life Moreland lived; had never shown any sign of liking married men, a taste some girls acquire at an early age. I thought it best to change the subject.

'I see you asked Carolo,' I said.

Moreland, although always perfectly friendly – indeed, making more effort with Carolo than he usually did with gloomy, silent geniuses – never gave the impression of caring much for his company. I supposed Carolo's invitation due to some inflexion of musical politics of which I was myself ignorant, and about which, to tell the truth, I felt very little interest. However, this comment seemed to sober Matilda, or at least to change her mood.

'We had to ask him,' she said. 'No choice of mine, I can assure you. It was all on account of the Maclinticks. As Carolo lives in the same house as the Maclinticks, Hugh thought it would be awkward if he didn't get an invitation. Hugh was very anxious for Maclintick to come – in fact wouldn't hear of his not coming. Hugh and Maclintick are really great friends, you know.'

'The Maclinticks were having a full-dress row when I left them a short time ago.'

'They always are.'

'They should lay off for an hour or two on occasions like this. A short rest would renew their energies for starting again when they return home.'

'That is just married life.'

'To be married to either of the Maclinticks cannot be much fun.'

'Is it fun to be married to anyone?'

'That is rather a big question. If you admit that fun exists at all – perhaps you don't – you cannot lay it down categorically that no married people get any fun from the state of being married.'

'But I mean *married* to someone,' said Matilda, speaking quite passionately. 'Not to sleep with them, or talk to them, or go about with them. To be *married* to them. I have been married a couple of times and I sometimes begin to doubt it.'

We were now in the midst of dangerous abstractions which might once more threaten further embarrassments of the kind I hoped to avoid. Generalisations about married life could easily turn to particularisation about Moreland and Priscilla, a relationship I should prefer to investigate later, in my own way and time, rather than have handed to me on a plate by Matilda; the latter method almost certainly calling for decisions and agreements undesirable, so it seemed to me, at this stage of the story. I was also very surprised by this last piece of information: that Matilda had had a husband previous to Moreland.

'You have been married twice, Matilda?'

'Didn't you know?'

'Not the least idea.'

I wondered for a moment whether Sir Magnus Donners could possibly have married her clandestinely. If so – and that was very unlikely – an equally clandestine divorce was scarcely conceivable. That notion could be dismissed at once.

'I was married to Carolo,' she said.

'My dear Matilda.'

'That surprises you?'

'Immensely.'

She laughed shrilly.

'I thought Hugh might have told you.'

'Never a word.'

'There is no particular secret about it. The marriage lasted a very short time. It was when I was quite young. In fact pretty soon after I left home. Carolo is not a bad old thing in his way. Just not very bright. Not a bit like Hugh. We used to quarrel a good deal. Then we didn't really get on in bed. Besides, I got tired of him talking about himself all the time.'

'Understandably.'

'After I left Carolo, as you know, I was kept by Donners for a time. At least people are all aware of *that*. It is such a relief not to have to explain everything about oneself to everyone. We met just about the time when Donners was getting restive about the way Baby Wentworth was treating him. He was taking Lady Ardglass out quite often too, but she never really liked being seen with him. I think she found him terribly unsmart. So did Baby Wentworth, I believe, if it comes to that. I did not mind that drab side of him. I got tired of him for other reasons, although he can be nice in his own particular way. He is awful, of course, at times. Really awful. But he can be generous – I mean morally generous – too. I am not interested in money. One thing about Donners, he does not know what jealousy means. When Baby was running round with Ralph Barnby, he did not mind at all. That did not affect me in one way, because unlike so many women, I prefer only one man at a time. But it is nice not to be bothered about where you went last night, or where you are going to tomorrow afternoon. Don't you agree?'

'Certainly I do. Was Carolo like that – jealous in that way?'

'A bit. But Carolo's chief interest is in making conquests. He doesn't much mind who it is. I shouldn't wonder if he doesn't run after Audrey Maclintick. Probably Maclintick would be glad of someone to keep her quiet and take her off his hands. What a bitch she is.'

'All the same, there is a difference between being fed up with your wife and wanting another man to take her off your hands.'

'There wasn't in Carolo's case. He was thankful when I fixed myself up. That is part of his simple nature, which is his chief charm. I had really left Donners by the time I met Hugh. What do you think about Hugh?'

'I should guess that he was not particularly jealous as men go.'

'Oh, I don't mean that. He isn't. I mean what do you think of him as a man?'

'You know quite well, Matilda, that he is a great friend of mine.'

'But his work . . . I do think he is . . . frightfully intelligent . . . a great man . . . whatever you like. Everything one says of that sort always sounds silly about someone you know – certainly someone you are married to. I had quite enough of being told my husband was a genius when I was Carolo's wife. But you do agree about Hugh, don't you, Nick?'

'Yes, I do, as a matter of fact.'

'That is why I am so worried about the symphony. You see, I am sure it will not be properly appreciated. People are so stupid.'

I longed to hear more about Sir Magnus Donners; whether some of the very circumstantial, very highly coloured stories that circulated about the elaboration of his idiosyncrasies, were at all near the truth. However, the moment to acquire such information, the moment for such frivolities, if it had ever existed, was now past. The tone had become too serious. I could not imagine what the next revelation would be; certainly nothing so light-hearted as a first-hand account of a millionaire's sexual fantasies.

'Then there is this business of both of us having a career.'

'That is always difficult.'

'I don't want never to act again.'

'Of course not.'

'After all, if Hugh wanted to marry a squaw, he could easily have found a squaw. They abound in musical circles. It is the answer for lots of artists.'

'Hugh has always been against squaws. Rightly, I think. In the long run, in my opinion, a squaw is even more nuisance than her antithesis – and often cooks worse too.'

'Then why do Hugh and I find it so difficult to get on together?'

'But you always seem to get on a treat.'

'That's what you think.'

'Well, don't you – when you look at the Maclinticks, for example?'

'And then . . .'

I thought for a moment she was going to speak of the child's death, which I now saw had dislocated their marriage more seriously than anyone had supposed from the outside. Instead, she returned to her earlier theme.

'And now he has gone and fallen in love with your sister-in-law, Priscilla.'

'But——'

Matilda laughed at the way in which I failed to find any answer. There was really nothing for me to say. If it was true, it was true. From one point of view, I felt it unjust that I should be visited in this manner with Matilda's mortification; from another, well deserved, in that I had not already acquainted myself with what was going on round me.

'Of course it is all quite innocent,' said Matilda. 'That is the worst thing about it from my point of view. It would be much easier if he had fallen for some old tart like myself he could sleep with for a spell, then leave when he was bored.'

'When did all this start up?'

In asking the question, I committed myself in some degree to acceptance of her premises about Moreland and Priscilla. There seemed no alternative.

'Oh, I don't know. A month or two ago. They met at that office where she works. I knew something of the sort had happened when he came home that day.'

'But they met first at our flat.'

'They'd met before you produced her at your flat. They kept quiet about knowing each other when they met there.'

I spared a passing thought for the slyness of Priscilla; also for Matilda's all-embracing information service. Before more could be said about this uncomfortable subject, two things happened to break up our conversation. First of all the distinguished conductor – rather specially noted for his appreciation of feminine attractions – presented himself with a great deal of flourish to pay his respects to Matilda. He was known to admire her, but until that moment had been unable to escape from persons who wanted to take this opportunity of chatting with a celebrity of his calibre, finally being pinned down by Lady Huntercombe, who had descended upon him after failing to capture Robert. He had already made some opening remarks of a complimentary kind to Matilda, consciously recalling by their form of expression the elaborate courtesies of an earlier age – and I was preparing to leave Matilda to him – when my attention was diverted to something that had taken place at the far end of the room.

This was nothing less than the arrival of Stringham. At first I could hardly believe my eyes. There he was standing by the door talking to Buster. The scene was only made credible by the fact that Buster looked extremely put out. After what had been said that evening, Stringham was certainly the last person to be expected to turn up at his mother's party. He was not wearing evening clothes, being dressed, in fact, in a very old tweed suit and woollen jumper. As usual he looked rather distinguished in these ancient garments, which could not have less fitted the occasion, but somehow at the same time seemed purposely designed to make Buster appear overdressed. Stringham himself was, as formerly, perfectly at ease, laughing a lot at something he had just remarked to Buster, who, with wrinkled forehead and raised eyebrows, had for once lost all his air of lazy indifference to life, and seemed positively to be miming the part of a man who has suddenly received a disagreeable surprise. Stringham finished what he had to say, clapped Buster on the back, and turned towards his mother who came up at that moment. I was too far away to hear Mrs Foxe's words, but, as she kissed her son affectionately, she was clearly welcoming him in the manner appropriate to one returned unexpectedly from a voyage round the world. At the same time, unlike her husband, she showed no surprise or discomposure at Stringham's arrival. They spoke together for a second or two, then she returned to her conversation with Lord Huntercombe. Stringham turned away from her and strolled across the room, gazing about him with a smile. Catching sight of me suddenly, he drew back with a movement of feigned horror, then made towards the place where I was standing. I went to meet him.

'My dear Nick.'

'Charles.'

'I had no idea you had musical tastes, Nick. Why did you keep them from me all these years? Because I never asked, I suppose. One always finds the answer to everything in one's own egotism. But how nice to meet again. I am a recluse now. I see nobody. I expect you already knew that. Everybody seems to know by now. It is just a bit like being a leper, only I don't actually have to carry a bell. They decided to let me off that. Thought I should make too much of a row, I suppose. You can't imagine what a pleasure it is to come unexpectedly upon an old friend one knew several million years ago.'

There could be no doubt that he was drunk, but, within the vast area comprised by that term, among the immensely varied states of mind and body which intoxication confers, Stringham's at this moment was that controlled exhilaration of spirit more akin to madness than carousal, which some addicts can achieve after a single glass. He looked rather ghastly when you were close to him, his skin pale and mottled, his eyes sunken and bloodshot. Even so, there was plenty of the old dash about his manner.

'I had no idea my mother would be giving a party tonight,' he said. 'Just thought I would drop in and have a word with her by the fireside as I haven't seen her for some time. What do I find but a whirl of gaiety. I really came along to tease Buster. I like doing that from time to time. It cheers me up for some reason. You know I now live in a flat at the top of a house owned by a relation of your wife's – Molly Jeavons, one of the most delightful and charming of people. I sometimes hear about you both from her or from Ted. I dote on Ted. He hasn't been very well lately, you know, and he gives wonderful descriptions of what is going on in his lower intestine – that war wound of his. One need never be bored when Ted gets on to that subject. He and I sometimes go out for the quickest of quick drinks. I am not supposed to have much in the way of drink these days. Neither is Ted. I am trying to knock off, really – but it seems such a bore to be a total abstainer, as I believe such people are called. I can have just one drink still, you know. I don't have to keep off it utterly.'

He said these words in such an appealing tone that I felt torn inwardly to think of the condition he must be in, of the circumstances in which he must live. His awareness of his own state seemed almost worse than total abandonment to the bottle. It looked very much as if he might just have come on to his mother's house that night from one of those 'very quick drinks' with Jeavons; perhaps felt unable to bring himself to return to Miss Weedon's flat and paint in gouache – if it was really with painting that he thera-peutically ordered his spare time. His life with Miss Weedon was impossible to contemplate.

'Do you know this fellow Moreland?' he went on. 'I gather from Buster that the party is being given in More-land's honour – that he is a famous musician apparently. It just shows how right it is that I should have to live as a hermit, not to know that Moreland is a famous musician – and have to be told by Buster. All the same, it cuts both ways. If you are a hermit, you can't be expected to keep up with all the latest celebrities. Buster, of course, was quite in-capable of giving any real information about Moreland, the party, the guests, or anything else. He is awfully stupid, poor old Buster. An absolute ape. You know a fact that strikes one very forcibly as one grows older is that some people are intelligent and some are stupid. I don't set up as an intellectual myself – even though I am a great hand with the paintbrush, did they tell you that, Nick? – but if I were as ill-informed as Buster, I should take steps to educate myself. Go to a night-school or hire a well-read under-graduate to teach me a few things in the long vac. The person I shall have to get hold of is Norman. He will tell me all about everything. Have you met Norman yet? He is simply charming. He is – well, I don't want to labour the point, and I can see from your face you have guessed what I was going to say, and you are quite right. All the same, my mother has taken him up in a big way. You must meet Norman, Nick.'

'But I know him well. I have known him for years.'

'I am surprised at the company you must have been keeping, Nick. Known him for years, indeed. I shouldn't have thought it of you. And a married man too. But you do agree, don't you, that Norman is a delightful fellow?'

'Absolutely.'

'I knew you would. I can't tell you how good Norman has been for my mother. Brilliant ideas and helpful comment don't exactly gush from Buster, with all his manly qualities. Besides, when it comes to doing odd jobs about the house, Buster is no good with his hands. What, you say, a sailor and no good with his hands? I don't believe you. It's the perfect truth. I sometimes tease him about it. He doesn't always take that in good part. Now, at last there is someone in the house who can turn to when it comes to hanging a picture or altering the place of a piece of furniture without smashing the thing to a thousand fragments. Not only that, but Norman decides what detective stories ought to come from the Times Book Club, settles what plays must be seen, gives good advice to my mother about hats – in fact excels at all the things poor old Buster fails at so lamentably. On top of that, Norman won't be bullied. He gets his own way. He is just about the only person who deals with my mother who does get his own way.'

'Jolly good.'

'Look here, Nick, you are not being serious. I want to be serious. People are always charging me with not being sufficiently serious. There is something serious I want to ask you. You know the Abdication?'

'I heard something about it.'

'Well, I thought it was a good thing. A frightfully good thing. The only possible thing. I wish to goodness Buster would abdicate one of these days.'

'Not a hope.'

'You're right. Not a hope. I say, Nick, it is awfully nice meeting you again after all these years. Let me get you another drink. You see the extraordinary thing is that I don't feel the smallest need for drink myself. I rise above it. That shows an advance, doesn't it? Not everyone we know can make that boast with truth. I must mention to you that there are some awfully strange people at this party tonight. Not at all like the people my mother usually collects. I suppose it is them, and not me. You agree? Yes, I thought I was right. They remind me more of the days when I used to know Milly Andriadis. Poor old Milly. I wonder what has happened to her. Perhaps they have put her away too.'

While he was speaking his eyes were on Mrs Maclintick, who was now making her way towards us.

'This lady, for example,' said Stringham. 'What could have induced her to dress like that?'

'She is coming to talk to us.'

'My God, I believe you're right.'

Mrs Maclintick arrived within range. Cold rage still possessed her. She addressed herself to me.

'That was a nice way to be spoken to by your husband,' she said. 'Did you ever hear anything like it?'

Before I could reply, Stringham caught her by the arm.

'Hullo, Little Bo-Peep,' he said. 'What have you done with your shepherdess's crook? You will never find your sheep at this rate. Don't look so cross and pout at me like that, or I shall ruffle up all those dainty little frills of yours – and then where will you be?'

The effect on Mrs Maclintick of this unconventional approach was electric. She flushed with pleasure, contorting her body into an attitude of increased provocation. I saw at once that this must be the right way to treat her; that a deficiency of horseplay on the part of her husband and his friends was probably the cause of her endemic sulkiness. No doubt something in Stringham's manner, the impression he gave that evening of having cut himself off from all normal restraints, played a part in Mrs Maclintick's submission. He was in a mood to carry all before him. Even so, she made an effort to fight back.

'What an extraordinary thing to say,' she remarked. 'And who are you, I should like to know?'

I introduced them, but neither was inclined to pay much attention to names or explanations. Stringham, for some reason, seemed set on pursuing the course he had begun. Mrs Maclintick showed no sign of discouraging him, beyond a refusal entirely to abandon her own traditional acerbity of demeanour.

'Fancy a little girl like you being allowed to come to a grown-up party like this one,' said Stringham. 'You ought to be in bed by now I'm sure.'

'If you think I don't know most of the people here,' said Mrs Maclintick, uncertain whether to be pleased or offended at this comment, 'you are quite wrong. I have met nearly all of them.'

'Then you have the advantage of me in that respect,' said Stringham, 'and so you must tell me who everyone is. For example, what is the name of the fat man wearing a dinner jacket a size too small for him – the one drinking something from a tumbler?'

If there was any doubt about the good impression Stringham had already made on Mrs Maclintick, this enquiry set him immediately at the topmost peak of her estimation.

'That's my husband,' she said, speaking at once with

delight and all the hatred of which she was capable. 'He has just been vilely rude to me. He hates wearing evening clothes. The state they were in – even though he never gets into them – you wouldn't have believed. I had to tack the seam of the trousers before he could be seen in them. He isn't properly shaved either. I told him so. He said he had run out of new blades. He looks a fright, doesn't he?'

'He does indeed,' said Stringham. 'You have put the matter in a nutshell.'

'If you had heard some of the things he has been shouting at me in this very room,' said Mrs Maclintick, 'you would not have credited your hearing. The man has not a spark of gratitude.'

'What do you expect with a thick neck like that?' said Stringham. 'Not gratitude, surely?'

'Language of the gutter,' said Mrs Maclintick, as if relishing her husband's phrases in retrospect. 'Filthy words.'

'Think no more of his trivial invective,' said Stringham. 'Come with me and forget the ineptitudes of married life – with which I was once myself only too familiar – in a glass of wine. Let me persuade you to drown your sorrows.

While the Rose blows along the River Brink
With old Stringhám the Ruby Vintage drink . . .

It isn't ruby in this case, but none the worse for that. Buster's taste in champagne is not too bad. It is one of his redeeming features.'

Mrs Maclintick was about to reply, no doubt favourably, but, before she could speak, Stringham, smiling in my direction, led her away. Why he wished to involve himself with Mrs Maclintick I could not imagine: drink; love of odd situations; even attraction to a woman he found wholly unusual; any of those might have been the reason. Mrs Maclintick was tamed, almost docile, under his treatment. I was

410

still reflecting on the eccentricity of Stringham's behaviour when brought suddenly within the orbit of Lord Hunter-combe, who was moving round the room in a leisurely way, examining the pictures and ornaments there. He had just taken up *Truth Unveiled by Time*, removed his spectacles, and closely examined the group's base. He now replaced the cast on its console table, at the same time smiling wryly in my direction and shaking his head, as if to imply that such worthless bric-à-brac should not be allowed to detain great connoisseurs like ourselves. Smethyck (a museum official, whom I had known as an undergraduate) had intro-duced us not long before at an exhibition of seventeenth-century pictures and furniture Smethyck himself had helped to organise, to which Lord Huntercombe had lent some of his collection.

'Have you seen your friend Smethyck lately?' asked Lord Huntercombe, still smiling.

'Not since we talked about picture-cleaning at that exhibi-tion.'

'Before the exhibition opened,' said Lord Huntercombe, 'Smethyck showed himself anxious to point out that *Prince Rupert Conversing with a Herald* was painted by Dobson, rather than Van Dyck. Fortunately I had long ago come to the same conclusion and had recently caused its label to be altered. I was even able to carry the war into Smethyck's country by enquiring whether he felt absolutely confident of the authenticity of that supposed portrait of Judge Jeffreys, attributed to Lely, on loan from his own gallery. What nice china there is in this house. It looks to me as if there were some Vienna porcelain mixed up with the Meissen in this cabinet. I believe Warrington knew some-thing of china. That was why Kitchener liked him. You know, I think I shall have to inspect these a little more thoroughly.'

Lord Huntercombe tried the door of the cabinet. Although the key turned, the door refused to open. He steadied the top of the cabinet with his hand, then tried again. Still the door remained firmly closed. Lord Huntercombe shook his head. He brought out a small penknife from his pocket, opened the shorter blade, and inserted this in the crevice.

'How is Erridge?' he asked.

He spoke with that note almost of yearning in his voice, which peers are inclined to employ when speaking of other peers, especially of those younger than themselves of whom they disapprove.

'He is still in Spain.'

'I hope he will try to persuade his friends not to burn *all* the churches,' said Lord Huntercombe, without looking up, as he moved the blade of the knife gently backwards and forwards.

He had crouched on his haunches to facilitate the operation, and in this position gave the impression of an old craftsman practising a trade at which he was immensely skilled, his extreme neatness and the quick movement of his fingers adding to this illusion. However, these efforts remained ineffective. The door refused to open. I had some idea of trying to find Isobel to arrange a meeting between herself and Stringham. However, I was still watching Lord Huntercombe's exertions when Chandler now reappeared.

'Nick,' he said, 'come and talk to Amy.'

'Just hold this cabinet steady for a moment, both of you,' said Lord Huntercombe. 'There . . . it's coming . . . that's done it. Thank you very much.'

'I say, Lord Huntercombe,' said Chandler, 'I did simply worship those cut-glass candelabra you lent to that exhibition the other day. I am going to suggest to the producer of the show I'm in rehearsal for that we try and get the effect of something of that sort in the Second Act – instead of the dreary old pewter candlesticks we are now using.'

'I do not think the Victoria and Albert would mind possessing those candelabra,' said Lord Huntercombe with complacency, at the same time abstracting some of the pieces from the cabinet. 'Ah, the Marcolini Period. I thought as much. And here are some *Indianische Blumen.*'

We moved politely away from Lord Huntercombe's immediate area, leaving him in peace to pursue further researches.

'My dear,' said Chandler, speaking in a lower voice, 'Amy is rather worried about Charles turning up like this. She thought that, as an old friend of his, you might be able to persuade him to go quietly home after a time. He is a sweet boy, but in the state he is in you never know what he is going to do next.'

'It is ages since I saw Charles. We met tonight for the first time for years. I doubt if he would take the slightest notice of anything I said. As a matter of fact he has just gone off with Mrs Maclintick to whom he is paying what used to be called marked attentions.'

'That is one of the things Amy is worried about. Amy has an eye like a hawk, you know.'

I was certainly surprised to hear that Mrs Foxe had taken in the circumstances of the party so thoroughly as even to have included Mrs Maclintick in her survey. As a hostess, she gave no impression of observing the room meticulously (at least not with the implication of fear pedantic use of that term implies), nor did she seem in the smallest degree disturbed when we came up to her.

'Oh, Mr Jenkins,' she said, 'dear Charles has arrived, as you know since you have been talking to him. I thought you would not mind if I asked you to keep the smallest eye on him. His nerves are so bad nowadays. You have known him for such a long time. He is much more likely to agree to anything you suggest than to fall in with what I want him to do. He really ought not to stay up too late. It is not good for him.'

She said no more than that; gave no hint she required Stringham's immediate removal. That was just as well, because I should have had no idea how to set about any such dislodgement. I remembered suddenly that the last time a woman had appealed to me for help in managing Stringham was when, at her own party years before, Mrs Andriadis had said: 'Will you persuade him to stay?' Then it was his mistress; now, his mother. Mrs Foxe had been too discreet to say outright: 'Will you persuade him to go?' None the less, that was what she must have desired. Her discrimination in expressing this wish, her manner of putting herself into my hands, made her as successful as Mrs Andriadis in enlisting my sympathy; but no more effective as an ally. It was hard to see what could be done about Stringham. Besides, I had by then begun to learn – what I had no idea of at Mrs Andriadis's party – that to people like Stringham there is really no answer.

'Don't worry, Amy, darling,' said Chandler. 'Charles is perfectly all right for the time being. Don't feel anxious. Nick and I will keep an eye on him.'

'Will you? It would be so awful if something did go wrong. I should feel so guilty if the Morelands' party were spoiled for them.'

'It won't be.'

'I shall rely on you both.'

She gazed at Chandler with deep affection. They might have been married for years from the manner in which they talked to one another. Some people came up to say good-bye. I saw Isobel, and was about to suggest that we should look for Stringham, when Mrs Foxe turned from the couple to whom she had been talking.

'Isobel, my dear,' she said, 'I haven't seen you all the evening. Come and sit on the sofa. There are some things I want to ask you about.'

'Odd scenes in the next room,' Isobel said to me, before she joined Mrs Foxe.

I felt sure from her tone the scenes must be odd enough. I found Isobel had spoken without exaggeration. Stringham, Mrs Maclintick, Priscilla, and Moreland were sitting together in a semi-circle. The rest of the party had withdrawn from that corner of the room, so that this group was quite cut off from the other guests. They were laughing a great deal and talking about marriage, Stringham chiefly directing the flow of conversation, with frequent interruptions from Moreland and Mrs Maclintick. Stringham was resting his elbow on his knee in an attitude of burlesqued formality, from time to time inclining his head towards Mrs Maclintick, as he addressed her in the manner of a drawing-room comedy by Wilde or Pinero. These fulsome compliments and epigrammatic phrases may have been largely incomprehensible to Mrs Maclintick, but she looked thoroughly pleased with herself; indeed, seemed satisfied that she was half-teasing, half-alluring Stringham. Priscilla appeared enormously happy in spite of not knowing quite what was going on round her. Moreland was almost hysterical with laughter which he continually tried to repress by stuffing a handkerchief into his mouth. If he had fallen in love with Priscilla – the evidence for something of the sort having taken place had to be admitted – it was, I thought, just like him to prefer listening to this performance to keeping his girl to himself in some remote part of the room. This judgment was superficial, because, as I have said, Moreland could be secretive enough about his girls when he chose; while politeness and discretion called for some show of outwardly casual behaviour at this party. Even so, his behaviour that night could hardly be called discreet in general purport. It was obvious he was very taken with Priscilla from the way he was sitting beside her. He was clearly delighted by Stringham, of whose identity I felt sure he had no idea. When I approached, Mrs Maclintick was apparently describing the matrimonial troubles of some friends of hers.

'. . . and then,' she was saying, 'this first husband of hers used to come back at four o'clock in the morning and turn on the gramophone. As a regular thing. She told me herself.'

'Some women think one has nothing better to do than to lie awake listening to anecdotes about their first husband,' said Stringham. 'Milly Andriadis was like that – no doubt still is – and I must say, if one were prepared to forgo one's beauty sleep, one used to hear some remarkable things from her. Playing the gramophone is another matter. Your friend had a right to complain.'

'That was what the judge thought,' said Mrs Maclintick.

'What used he to play?' asked Priscilla.

'Military marches,' said Mrs Maclintick, 'night after night. Not surprising the poor woman had to go into a home after getting her divorce.'

'My mother would have liked that,' said Stringham. 'She adores watching troops march past. She always says going to reviews was the best part of being married to Piers Warrington.'

'Not in the middle of the night,' said Priscilla. 'He might have chosen something quieter. *Tales from Hoffmann* or Handel's *Cradle Song*.'

'Nonsense,' said Moreland. '*Aut Sousa aut Nihil* has always been my motto in cases of that sort. Think if the man had played Hindemith. At least he wasn't a highbrow.'

'He was just another musical husband,' said Mrs Maclintick fiercely. 'I am not saying he was any worse than Maclintick, I am not saying he was any better. I am just telling you the way musicians treat their wives. Telling you the sort of husband I have to put up with.'

'My own complaint about marriage is a very different one,' said Stringham. 'I admit my former wife was not musical. That might have made things worse. All the same, you never know. If she had been, she could have talked all the time about music while her sister, Anne, was chattering away about Braque and Dufy. It would have formed a counter-irritant. Poor Anne. Marrying Dicky Umfraville was a dreadful judgment on her. Still, a party is no place for vain regrets – certainly not vain regrets about one's ex-sister-in-law.'

'You should have seen Maclintick's sister,' said Mrs Maclintick, 'if you are going to grumble about your sister-in-law.'

'We will visit her, if necessary, dear lady, later in the evening,' said Stringham. 'The night is still young.'

'You can't,' said Mrs Maclintick. 'She's dead.'

'My condolences,' said Stringham. 'But, as I was saying, my former wife was not musical. Music did not run in the family. Mountfichet was not a house to stimulate music. You might compose a few dirges there, I suppose. Even they would have cheered the place up – the morning-room especially.'

'I was going to stay at Mountfichet once,' said Priscilla. 'Then Hugo got chicken-pox and we were all in quarantine.'

'You had a narrow escape, Lady Priscilla,' said Stringham. 'You are unaware of your good fortune. No, what I object to about marriage is not the active bad behaviour – like your musical friend playing the gramophone in the small hours. I could have stood that. I sleep abominably anyway. The gramophone would while away time in bed when one lies awake thinking about love. What broke me was the passive resistance. That was what got me down.'

Moreland began to laugh unrestrainedly again, thrusting the handkerchief in his mouth until it nearly choked him. He too had had a good deal to drink. Mrs Maclintick clenched her teeth in obvious approval of what Stringham had said. Stringham went on uninterrupted.

'It is a beautiful morning,' he said. 'For some reason you feel relatively well that day. You make some conciliatory remark. No answer. You think she hasn't heard. Still asleep perhaps. You speak again. A strangled sigh. What's wrong? You begin to go through in your mind all the awful things you might have done.'

'Maclintick never dreams of going through the awful things he has done,' said Mrs Maclintick. 'It would take far too long for one thing. Anyway, he never thinks about them at all. If you so much as mention one or two of them, he gets out of bed and sleeps on the sofa in his work-room.'

'Look here,' said Moreland, still laughing convulsively, 'I really cannot have my old friend Maclintick maligned in this manner without a word of protest. I know you are married to him, and marriage gives everyone all sorts of special rights where complaining is concerned——'

'You begin adding up your sins of commission and omission,' Stringham continued inexorably. 'Did one get tight? It seems months and months since one was tight, so it can't be that. Did one say something silly the night before? Much more likely. Not that remark about the colour of her father's face at breakfast? It couldn't have been that. She enjoyed that – even laughed a little. I don't know whether any of you ever met my former father-in-law, Major the Earl of Bridgnorth, late the Royal Horse Guards, by the way? His is a name to conjure with on the Turf. When I was married to his elder daughter, the beautiful Peggy, I was often to be seen conjuring with it on the course at Epsom, and elsewhere, but with little success, all among the bookies and Prince Monolulu and the tipster who wears an Old Harrovian tie and has never given a loser.'

'You are getting off the point, my dear sir,' said Moreland. 'We are discussing marriage, not racing. Matrimony is the point at issue.'

Stringham made a gesture to silence him. I had never before seen Moreland conversationally so completely mastered. It was hard to imagine what the two of them would have made of each other in more sober circumstances. They were very different. Stringham had none of Moreland's passionate self-identification with the arts; Moreland was without Stringham's bitter grasp of social circumstance. At the same time they had something in common. There was also much potential antipathy. Each would probably have found the other unsympathetic over a long period.

'And then,' said Stringham, lowering his voice and raising his eyebrows slightly, 'one wonders about making love . . . counts up on one's fingers . . . No . . . It can't be that . . .'

Mrs Maclintick gave a raucous laugh.

'I know!' Stringham now almost shouted, as if in sudden enlightenment. 'I've got it. It was going on about what a charming girl Rosie Manasch is. That was a bloody silly thing to do, when I know Peggy hates Rosie like poison. But I'm wandering . . . talking of years ago . . . of the days before Rosie married Jock Udall . . .'

'Heavens,' said Moreland. 'Do you know the Manasches? I once conducted at a charity concert in their house.'

Stringham ignored him.

'But then, on the other hand,' he went on, in a slower, much quieter voice, 'Rosie may have nothing whatever to do with it. One's wife may be ill. Sickening for some terrible

419

disease. Something to which one has never given a thought. She is sinking. Wasting away under one's eyes. It is just one's own callousness about her state. That is all that's wrong. You begin to get really worried. Should you get up and summon a doctor right away?'

'The doctor always tells Maclintick to drink less,' said Mrs Maclintick. 'Always the same story. "Put a drop more water in it," he says, "then you will feel better." You might just as well talk to a brick wall. Maclintick is not going to drink less because a doctor tells him to. If he won't stop after what I've said to him, is it likely he will knock off for a doctor? Why should he?'

'Why, indeed, you little rogue?' said Stringham, tapping Mrs Maclintick's knee with a folded copy of the concert programme, which had somehow found its way into his hand. 'Well, of course, in the end you discover that all this ill humour is nothing to do with yourself at all. In fact your wife is hardly aware that she is living in the same house with you. It was something that somebody said about her to someone who gossiped to somebody she knew when that somebody was having her hair done. Neither less nor more than that. All the same, it is you, her husband, who has to bear the brunt of those ill-chosen remarks by somebody about something. I've talked it all over with Ted Jeavons and he quite agrees.'

'I adore Uncle Ted,' said Priscilla, anxious to show that she herself had perfectly followed this dissertation.

'And you, Black-eyed Susan,' said Stringham, turning again in the direction of Mrs Maclintick, at the same time raising the programme interrogatively, 'do you too suffer in your domestic life – of which you speak with such a wealth of disillusionment – from the particular malaise I describe: the judgment of terrible silences?'

That was a subject upon which Mrs Maclintick felt herself in a position to speak authoritatively; the discussion, if uninterrupted, might have proceeded for a long time. Moreland was showing some signs of restlessness, although he and the others sitting there seemed to be finding some release from themselves, and their individual lives, in what was being said. The remainder of Mrs Foxe's guests, although in fact just round the corner, appeared for some reason infinitely far away. Then, all at once, I became aware that a new personality, an additional force, had been added to our group. This was a woman. She was standing beside me. How long she had been there, where she came from, I did not know.

It was Miss Weedon. She had probably avoided having herself announced in order to make quietly for the place where Stringham was to be found. In any case, her long association with the house as one of its inmates made such a formality almost inappropriate. As usual, she managed to look both businesslike and rather elegant, her large sharp nose and severe expression adding to her air of efficiency, suggesting on the whole a successful, fairly chic career woman. Enclosed in black, her dress committed her neither to night nor day; suitable for Mrs Foxe's party, it would have done equally well for some lesser occasion. She did not look at all like the former governess of Stringham's sister, Flavia, although there remained something dominating and controlling about Miss Weedon, hinting that she was used to exercising some form of professional authority. Undoubtedly her intention was to take Stringham home. No other objective could have brought her out at this hour of the night. Priscilla, who had probably met Miss Weedon more than once at the Jeavonses' – where Miss Weedon was a frequent guest before moving in as an occupant of the house itself – was the first to notice her.

'Hullo, Miss Weedon,' she said blushing.

Priscilla moved, probably involuntarily, further from Moreland, who was sitting rather close to her on the sofa. Miss Weedon smiled coldly. She advanced a little deeper into the room, her mysterious, equivocal presence casting a long, dark shadow over the scene.

'Why, hullo, Tuffy,' said Stringham, suddenly seeing Miss Weedon too. 'I am so glad you have turned up. I wondered if I should see you. I just dropped in to say good evening to Mamma, whom I hadn't set eyes on for ages, only to find the gayest of gay parties in progress. Let me introduce everyone. Lady Priscilla Tolland – you know Tuffy, of course. How silly of me. Now this is Mrs Maclintick, who has been telling me some really hair-raising stories about musical people. I shall never listen to an orchestra again without the most painful speculations about the home life of the players. Nick, of course, you've often met. I'm afraid I don't know your name, Mr——?'

'Moreland,' said Moreland, absolutely enchanted by Stringham's complete ignorance of his identity.

'Moreland!' said Stringham. 'This is Mr Moreland, Tuffy. Mr Moreland for whom the whole party is being given. What a superb *faux pas* on my part. A really exquisite blunder. How right it is that I should emerge but rarely. Well, there we are – and this, I nearly forgot to add, Mr Moreland, is Miss Weedon.'

He was still perfectly at ease. There was not the smallest sign to inform a casual observer that Stringham was now looked upon by his own family, by most of his friends, as a person scarcely responsible for his own actions; that he was about to be removed from his mother's house by a former secretary who had taken upon herself to look after him, because – I suppose – she loved him. All the same, although nothing outward indicated that something dramatic was taking place, Stringham himself, after he had performed these introductions, had risen from his chair with one of his random, easy movements, so that to me it was clear he knew the game was up. He knew that he must be borne away by Miss Weedon within the next few minutes to whatever prison-house now enclosed him. Moreland and Priscilla glanced at each other, recognising a break in the rhythm of the party, probably wanting to make a move themselves, but unaware quite what was happening. Mrs Maclintick, on the other hand, showed herself not at all willing to have the group disposed of in so arbitrary a manner. She turned a most unfriendly stare on Miss Weedon, which seemed by its contemptuous expression to recognise in her, by some unaccountable feminine intuition, a figure formerly subordinate in Mrs Foxe's household.

'We have been talking about marriage,' said Mrs Maclintick aggressively.

She addressed herself to Miss Weedon, who in return gave her a smile that cut like a knife.

'Indeed?' she said.

'This gentleman and I have been comparing notes,' said Mrs Maclintick, indicating Stringham.

'We have, indeed,' said Stringham laughing. 'And found a lot to agree about.'

He had dropped his former air of burlesque, now appeared completely sober.

'It sounds a very interesting discussion,' said Miss Weedon.

She spoke in a tone damaging to Mrs Maclintick's self-esteem. Miss Weedon was undoubtedly prepared to take anybody on; Mrs Maclintick; anybody. I admired her for that.

'Why don't you tell us what you think about marriage yourself?' asked Mrs Maclintick, who had drunk more champagne than I had at first supposed. 'They say the on-looker sees most of the game.'

'Not now,' said Miss Weedon, in the cosmically terminating voice of one who holds authority to decide when the toys must be returned to the toy-cupboard. 'I have my little car outside, Charles. I thought you might like a lift home.'

'But he is going to take me to a night-club,' said Mrs Maclintick, her voice rising in rage. 'He said that after we had settled a few points about marriage we would go to a very amusing place he knew of.'

Miss Weedon looked at Stringham without a trace of surprise or disapproval; just a request for confirmation.

'That was the suggestion, Tuffy.'

He laughed again. He must have known by experience that in the end Miss Weedon would turn out to hold all the cards, but he showed no sign yet of capitulation.

'The doctor begged you not to stay up too late, Charles,' said Miss Weedon, also smiling.

She was in no degree behind Stringham where keeping one's head was concerned.

'My medical adviser did indeed prescribe early hours,' said Stringham. 'You are right there, Tuffy. I distinctly recollect his words. But I was turning over in my mind the possibility of disregarding such advice. Ted Jeavons was speaking recently of some night haunt he once visited where he had all kind of unusual adventures. A place run by one, Dicky Umfraville, a bad character whom I used to see in my Kenya days and have probably spoken of. Something about the sound of the joint attracted me. I offered to take Mrs Maclintick there. I can hardly go back on my promise. Of course, the club has no doubt closed down by now. Nothing Dicky Umfraville puts his hand to lasts very long. Besides, Ted was a little vague about the year his adventure happened – it might have been during the war, when he was a gallant soldier on leave from the trenches. That all came in when he told the story. However, if defunct, we could always visit the Bag of Nails.'

Mrs Maclintick snatched facetiously at him.

'You know perfectly well I should hate any of those places,' she said gaily, 'and I believe you are only trying to get me there to make me feel uncomfortable.'

Miss Weedon remained unruffled.

'I had no idea you were planning anything like that, Charles.'

'It wasn't exactly planned,' said Stringham. 'Just one of those brilliant improvisations that come to me of a sudden. My career has been built up on them. One of them brought me here tonight.'

'But I haven't agreed to come with you yet,' said Mrs Maclintick, with some archness. 'Don't be too sure of that.'

'I recognise, Madam, I can have no guarantee of such an honour,' said Stringham, momentarily returning to his former tone. 'I was not so presumptuous as to take your company for granted. It may even be that I shall venture forth into the night – by no means for the first time in my chequered career – on a lonely search for pleasure.'

'Wouldn't it really be easier to accept my offer of a lift?' said Miss Weedon.

She spoke so lightly, so indifferently, that no one could possibly have guessed that in uttering those words she was issuing an order. There was no display of power. Even Stringham must have been aware that Miss Weedon was showing a respect for his own situation that was impeccable.

'Much, much easier, Tuffy,' he said. 'But who am I to be given a life of ease?

> Not for ever by still waters
> Would we idly rest and stay . . .

I feel just like the hymn. Tonight I must take the hard road that leads to pleasure.'

'We could give this lady a lift home too, if she liked,' said Miss Weedon.

She glanced at Mrs Maclintick as if prepared to accept the conveyance of her body at whatever the cost. It was a handsome offer on Miss Weedon's part, a very handsome offer. No just person could have denied that.

'But I am not much in the mood for going home, Tuffy,' said Stringham, 'and I am not sure that Mrs Maclintick is either, in spite of her protests to the contrary. We are young. We want to see life. We feel we ought not to limit our experience to musical parties, however edifying.'

There was a short pause.

'If only I had known this, Charles,' said Miss Weedon.

She spoke sadly, almost as if she were deprecating her own powers of dominion, trying to minimise them because their very hugeness embarrassed her; like the dictator of some absolutist state who assures journalists that his most imperative decrees have to take an outwardly parliamentary form.

'If only I had known,' she said, 'I could have brought your notecase. It was lying on the table in your room.'

Stringham laughed outright.

'Correct, as usual, Tuffy,' he said.

'I happened to notice it.'

'Money,' said Stringham. 'It is always the answer.'

'But even if I had brought it, you would have been much wiser not to stay up late.'

'Even if you had brought it, Tuffy,' said Stringham, 'the situation would remain unaltered, because there is no money in it.'

He turned to Mrs Maclintick.

'Little Bo-Peep,' he said, 'I fear our jaunt is off. We shall have to visit Dicky Umfraville's club, or the Bag of Nails, some other night.'

He made a movement to show he was ready to follow Miss Weedon.

'I didn't want to drag you away,' she said, 'but I thought it might save trouble as I happen to have the car with me.'

'Certainly it would,' said Stringham. 'Save a lot of trouble. Limitless trouble. Untold trouble. I will bid you all good night.'

After that, Miss Weedon had him out of the house in a matter of seconds. There was the faintest suspicion of a reel as he followed her through the door. Apart from that scarcely perceptible lurch, Stringham's physical removal was in general accomplished by her with such speed and efficiency that probably no one but myself recognised this trifling display of unsteadiness on his feet. The moral tactics were concealed almost equally successfully until the following day, when they became plain to me. The fact was, of course, that Stringham was kept without money; or at least on that particular evening Miss Weedon had seen to it that he had no more money on him than enabled buying the number of drinks that had brought him to his mother's house. He must have lost his nerve as to the efficacy of his powers of cashing a cheque; perhaps no longer possessed a cheque-book. Otherwise, he would undoubtedly have proceeded with the enterprise set on foot. Possibly fatigue, too, stimulated by the sight of Miss Weedon, had played a part in evaporating desire to paint the town red in the company of Mrs Maclintick; perhaps in the end Stringham was inwardly willing to 'go quietly'. That was the most likely of all. While these things had been happening, Moreland and Priscilla slipped away. I found myself alone with Mrs Maclintick.

'Who was she, I should like to know,' said Mrs Maclintick. 'Not that I wanted all that to go wherever it was he wanted to take me. Not in the least. It was just that he was so pressing. But what a funny sort of fellow he is. I didn't see why

427

that old girl should butt in. Is she one of his aunts?'

I was absolved from need to explain about Miss Weedon to Mrs Maclintick, no easy matter to embark upon, by seeing Carolo drifting towards us. A dinner jacket made him look more melancholy than ever.

'Coming?' he enquired.

'Where's Maclintick?'

'Gone home.'

'Full of whisky, I bet.'

'You bet.'

'All right.'

Stringham had made no great impression on her. She must have seen him as one of those eccentric figures naturally to be encountered in rich houses of this kind. That was probably the most judicious view of Stringham for her to take. Certainly there was no way for Mrs Maclintick to guess that a small, violent drama had been played out in front of her; nor would she have been greatly interested if some explanation of the circumstances could have been revealed. Now – in her tone to Carolo – she re-entered, body and soul, the world in which she normally lived. The two of them went off together. I began to look once more for Isobel. By the door Commander Foxe was saying goodbye to Max Pilgrim.

'Well,' said Commander Foxe, when he saw me, 'that was neatly arranged, wasn't it?'

'What was?'

'Persuading Charles to go home.'

'Lucky Miss Weedon happened to look in, you mean?'

'There was a good reason for that.'

'Oh?'

'I rang her up and told her to come along,' said Commander Foxe briefly.

That answer was such a simple one that I could not imagine why I had not guessed it without having to be told.

Those very obvious tactical victories are always the victories least foreseen by the onlooker, still less the opponent. Mrs Foxe herself might feel lack of dignity in summoning Miss Weedon to remove her own son from the house; for Buster, no such delicacy obstructed the way. Indeed, this action could be seen as a beautiful revenge for much owed to Stringham in the past; the occasion, for example, when Buster and I had first met in the room next door, and Stringham, still a boy, had seemed to order Buster from the house. No doubt other old scores were to be paid off. The relationship between Commander Foxe and Miss Weedon herself was also to be considered. Like two rival powers – something about Miss Weedon lent itself to political metaphor – who temporarily abandon their covert belligerency to combine against a third, there was a brief alliance; but also, for Miss Weedon, diplomatically speaking, an element of face-losing. She had been forced to allow her rival to invoke the treaty which demanded that in certain circumstances she should invest with troops her own supposedly pacific protectorate or mandated territory. In fact there had been a victory for Commander Foxe all round. He was not disposed to minimise his triumph.

'Pity about poor old Charles,' he said.

'I'll have to say good night.'

'Come again soon.'

'That would be nice.'

A general movement to leave was taking place among the guests. Mrs Maclintick and Carolo had already disappeared. Gossage still remained deep in conversation with Lady Huntercombe. There was no sign of the Morelands, or of Priscilla. Isobel was talking to Chandler. We went to find our hostess and say goodbye. Mrs Foxe was listening to the famous conductor, like Gossage, unable to tear himself away from the party.

'I do hope the Morelands enjoyed themselves,' said Mrs Foxe. 'It was so sad Matilda should have had a headache and had to go home. I am sure she was right to slip away. She is such a wonderful wife for someone like him. As soon as he heard she had gone, he said he must go too. Such a strain for a musician to have a new work performed. Like a first night – and Norman tells me first nights are agony.'

Mrs Foxe spoke the last word with all the feeling Chandler had put into it when he told her that. Robert joined us in taking leave.

'It was rather sweet of Charles to look in, wasn't it?' said Mrs Foxe. 'I would have asked him, of course, if I hadn't known parties were bad for him. I saw you talking to him. How did you think he was?'

'I hadn't seen him for ages. He seemed just the same. We had a long talk.'

'And you were glad to see him again?'

'Yes, of course.'

'I think he was right to go back with Tuffy. He can be rather difficult sometimes, you know.'

'Well, yes.'

'I do hope everyone enjoyed themselves,' said Mrs Foxe. 'There was a Mr Maclintick who had had rather a lot to drink by the time he left. I think he is a music critic. He was so sweet when he came to say goodbye to me. He said: "Thank you very much for asking me, Mrs Foxe. I don't like grand parties like this one and I am not coming to another, but I appreciate your kindness in supporting More-land as a composer." I said I so much agreed with him about grand parties – which I *simply* hate – but I couldn't imagine why he should think this was one. All the same, I said, I should arrange it quite differently if I ever gave another, and I hoped he would change his mind and come. "Well, I shan't come," he said. I told him I knew he would because I should ask him so nicely. He said: "I suppose you are right, and I shall." Then he slipped down two or three steps. I do hope he gets home all right. Such a relief when people speak their minds.'

'What's happened to Priscilla?' Isobel asked Robert.

'Somebody gave her a lift.'

At that moment Lord Huntercombe broke in between us. Carrying a piece of china in his hand, he was delighted by some discovery he had just made. Mrs Foxe turned towards him.

'Amy,' he said, 'are you aware that this quatrefoil cup is a forgery?'

4

IF SO TORTUOUS a comparison of mediocre talent could ever be resolved, St John Clarke was probably to be judged a 'better' writer than Isbister was painter. However, when St John Clarke died in the early spring, he was less well served than his contemporary in respect of obituaries. Only a few years before, Isbister had managed to capture, perhaps helped finally to expend, what was left of an older, more sententious tradition of newspaper panegyric. There were more reasons for this than the inevitably changing taste in mediocrity. The world was moving into a harassed era. At the time of St John Clarke's last illness, the National Socialist Party of Danzig was in the headlines; foreign news more and more often causing domestic events to be passed over almost unnoticed. St John Clarke was one of these casualties. If Mark Members was to be believed, St John Clarke himself would have seen this unfair distribution of success, even posthumous success, as something in the nature of things. In what Members called 'one of St J.'s breakfast table agonies of self-pity', the novelist had quite openly ex-pressed the mortification he felt in contrasting his old friend's lot with his own.

'Isbister was beloved of the gods, Mark,' he had cried aloud, looking up with a haggard face from *The Times* of New Year's Day and its list of awards, 'R.A. before he was forty-five – Gold Medallist of the Paris Salon – Diploma of Honour at the International Exhibition at Amsterdam – Commander of the Papal Order of Pius IX – refused a knighthood. Think of it, Mark, a man the King would have delighted to honour. What recognition have I had compared with these?'

'Why did Isbister refuse a knighthood?' Members had asked.

'To spite his wife.'

'That was it, was it?'

'Those photographs the Press resurrected of Morwenna standing beside him looking out to sea,' said St John Clarke, 'they were antediluvian – diluvian possibly. It was the Flood they were looking at, I expect. They'd been living apart for years when he died. Of course Isbister himself said he had decided worldly honours were unbefitting an artist. That didn't prevent him from telling everyone of the offer. Absolutely everyone. He had it both ways.'

In those days Members was still anxious to soothe his employer.

'Well, you've had a lot of enjoyable parties and country house visits to look back on, St J.,' he said. 'Rather a different life from Isbister's, but a richer one in my eyes.'

'One week-end at Dogdene twenty years ago,' St John Clarke had answered bitterly. 'Forced to play croquet with Lord Lonsdale . . . Two dinners at the Huntercombes', both times asked the same night as Sir Horrocks Rusby . . .'

This was certainly inadequate assessment of St John Clarke's social triumphs, which, for a man of letters, had been less fruitless than at that moment his despair presented them. Members, knowing what was expected of him, brushed away with a smile such melancholy reminiscences.

'But it will come . . .' he said.

'It will come, Mark. As I sit here, the Nobel Prize will come.'

'Alas,' said Members, concluding the story, 'it never does.'

As things fell out, the two most alert articles to deal with

St John Clarke were written, ironically enough, by Members and Quiggin respectively, both of whom spared a few crumbs of praise for their former master, treating him at no great length as a 'personality' rather than a writer: Members, in the weekly of which he was assistant literary editor, referring to 'an ephemeral, if almost painfully sincere, digression into what was for him the wonderland of *fauviste* painting'; Quiggin, in a similar, rather less eminent publication to which he contributed when hard up, guardedly emphasising the deceased's 'underlying, even when patently bewildered, sympathy with the Workers' Cause'. No other journal took sufficient interest in the later stages of St John Clarke's career to keep up to date about these conflicting aspects of his final decade. They spoke only of his deep love for the Peter Pan statue in Kensington Gardens and his contributions to Queen Mary's Gift Book. Appraisal of his work unhesitatingly placed *Fields of Amaranth* as the peak of his achievement, with *E'en the Longest River* or *The Heart is Highland* – opinion varied – as a poor second. *The Times Literary Supplement* found 'the romances of Renaissance Italy and the French Revolution smacked of Wardour Street, the scenes from fashionable life in the other novels tempered with artificiality, the delineations of poverty less realistic than Gissing's'.

I was surprised by an odd feeling of regret that St John Clarke was gone. Even if an indifferent writer, his removal from the literary scene was like the final crumbling of a well-known landmark; unpleasing perhaps, at the same time possessed of a deserved renown for having withstood demolition for so long. The anecdotes Members and Quiggin put round about him had given St John Clarke a certain solidity in my mind; more, in a way, than his own momentary emergence at Lady Warminster's. This glimpse of him, then total physical removal, brought home, too, the blunt postscript of death. St John Clarke had merely looked ill at Hyde Park Gardens; now, like John Peel, he had gone far, far away, with his pen and his press-cuttings in the morning; become one of those names to which the date of birth and death may be added in parentheses, as their owners speed to oblivion from out of reference books and 'literary pages' of the newspapers.

As an indirect result of Mrs Foxe's party, relations with the Morelands were complicated by uncertainty and a little embarrassment. No one really knew what was happening between Moreland and Priscilla. They were never seen together, but it was very generally supposed some sort of a love affair was in progress between them. Rather more than usual Priscilla conveyed the impression that she did not want to be bothered with her relations; while an air of discomfort, faint but decided, pervaded the Moreland flat, indicating something was amiss there. Moreland himself had plunged into a flood of work. He took the line now that his symphony had fallen flat – to some extent, he said, deservedly – and he must repair the situation by producing something better. For the first time since the early days when I had known him, he seemed interested only in professionally musical affairs. We heard at second-hand that Matilda was to be tried out for the part of Zenocrate in Marlowe's *Tamburlaine*. This was confirmed by Moreland himself when I met him by chance somewhere. The extent of the gossip about Moreland and Priscilla was revealed to me one day by running into Chips Lovell travelling by Underground. Lovell had by now achieved his former ambition of getting a job on a newspaper, where he helped to write the gossip column, one of a relatively respectable order. He was in the best of form, dressed with the greatest care, retaining that boyish, innocent look that made him in different ways a success with both sexes.

435

'How is Priscilla?' he asked.

'All right, so far as I know.'

'I heard something about her and Hugh Moreland.'

'What sort of thing?'

'That they were having a walk-out together.'

'Who said so?'

'I can't remember.'

'I didn't know you knew Moreland.'

'I don't. Only by name.'

'It doesn't sound very probable, does it?'

'I have no idea. People do these things.'

Although I liked Lovell, I saw no reason to offer help so far as his investigation of the situation of Moreland and Priscilla. As a matter of fact I had not much help to offer. In any case, Lovell, inhabiting by vocation a world of garbled rumour, was to be treated with discretion where the passing of information was concerned. I was surprised at the outspokenness with which he had mentioned the matter. His enquiry seemed stimulated by personal interest, rather than love of gossip for its own sake. I supposed he still felt faint dissatisfaction at having failed to make the mark to which he felt his good looks entitled him.

'I always liked Priscilla,' he said, using a rather consciously abstracted manner. 'I must see her again one of these days.'

'What has been happening to you, Chips?'

'Do you remember that fellow Widmerpool you used to tell me about when we were at the film studio? His name always stuck in my mind because he managed to stay at Dogdene. I took my hat off to him for getting there. Uncle Geoffrey is by no means keen on handing out invitations. You told me there was some talk of Widmerpool marrying somebody. A Vowchurch, was it? Anyway, I ran into Widmerpool the other day and he talked about you.'

'What did he say?'

'Just mentioned that he knew you. Said it was sensible of you to get married. Thought it a pity you couldn't find a regular job.'

'But I've got a regular job.'

'Not in his eyes, you haven't. He said he feared you were a bit of a drifter with the stream.'

'How was he otherwise?'

'I never saw a man so put out by the Abdication,' said Lovell. 'It might have been Widmerpool himself who'd had to abdicate. My goodness, he had taken it to heart.'

'What specially upset him?'

'So far as I could gather, he had cast himself for a brilliant social career if things had worked out differently.'

'The Beau Brummell of the new reign?'

'Not far short of that.'

'Where did you run across him?'

'Widmerpool came to see me in my office. He wanted me to slip in a paragraph about certain semi-business activities of his. One of those quiet little puffs, you know, which don't cost the advertising department anything, but warm the heart of the sales manager.'

'Did you oblige?'

'Not me,' said Lovell.

By no means without a healthy touch of malice, Lovell had also a fine appreciation of the power-wielding side of his job.

'I hear your brother-in-law, Erry Warminster, is on his way home from Spain,' he said.

'First I've heard of it.'

'Erry's own family are always the last to hear about his goings-on.'

'What's your source?'

'The office, as usual.'

'Is he bored with the Spanish war?'

'He is ill – also had some sort of row with his own side.'

'What is wrong with him?'

'Touch of dysentery, someone said.'

'Serious?'

'I don't think so.'

We parted company after arranging that Lovell should come and have a drink with us at the flat in the near future. The following day, I met Quiggin in Members's office. He was in a sulky mood. I told him I had enjoyed his piece about St John Clarke. Praise was usually as acceptable to Quiggin as to most people. That day the remark seemed to increase his ill humour. However, he confirmed the news about Erridge.

'Yes, yes,' he said impatiently. 'Of course it is true that Alfred is coming back. Don't his family take any interest in him? They might at least have discovered that.'

'Is he bad?'

'It is a disagreeable complaint to have.'

'But a whole skin otherwise. That is always something if there is a war on.'

'Alfred is too simple a man to embroil himself in practical affairs like fighting an ideological war,' said Quiggin severely. 'A typical aristocratic idealist, I'm afraid. Perhaps it is just as well his health has broken down. He has never been strong, of course. He is the first to admit it. In fact he is too fond of talking about his health. As I have said before, Alf is rather like Prince Myshkin in *The Idiot*.'

I was surprised at Quiggin's attitude towards Erridge's illness. I tried to work out who Quiggin himself would be in Dostoevsky's novel if Erridge was Prince Myshkin and Mona – presumably – Nastasya Filippovna. It was all too complicated. I could not remember the story with sufficient clarity. Quiggin spoke again.

'I have been hearing something of Alf's difficulties from one of our own agents just back from Barcelona,' he said. 'Alf seems to have shown a good deal of political obtuseness – perhaps I should say childlike innocence. He appears to have treated POUM, FAI, CNT, and UGT, as if they were all the same left-wing extension of the Labour Party. I was not surprised to hear that he was going to be arrested at the time he decided to leave Spain. If you can't tell the difference between a Trotskyite-Communist, an Anarcho-Syndicalist, and a properly paid-up Party Member, you had better keep away from the barricades.'

'You had, indeed.'

'It is not fair on the workers.'

'Certainly not.'

'Alfred's place was to organise in England.'

'Why doesn't he go back to his idea of starting a magazine?'

'I don't know,' said Quiggin, in a voice that closed the subject.

Erridge was in Quiggin's bad books; a friend who had disappointed Quiggin to a degree impossible to conceal; a man who had failed to rise to an historic occasion. I supposed that Quiggin regarded Erridge's imminent return, however involuntary, from the Spanish war in the light of a betrayal. This seemed unreasonable on Quiggin's part, since Erridge's breakdown in health was, after all, occasioned by an attempt to further the cause Quiggin himself had so energetically propagated by word of mouth. Even if Erridge had not fought in the field (where Howard Cragg's nephew had already been killed), he had taken other risks in putting his principles into practice. If it was true that he was marked down for arrest, he might have been executed behind the lines. Quiggin had staked less on his enthusiasms. However, as things turned out there was probably a different reason that afternoon for Quiggin's displeasure on Erridge's account.

Erridge himself arrived in London a day or two later. He was not at all well, and went straight into a nursing home; the nursing home, as it happened, in the passages of which I had encountered Moreland, Brandreth, and Widmerpool. This accommodation was found for her brother by Frederica, ideologically perhaps the furthest removed from Erridge, in certain other respects the closest of the Tollands to him, both from nearness in age and a shared rigidity of individual opinion. The two of them might disagree; they understood each other's obstinacies. When Erridge had settled down at the nursing home, his brothers and sisters visited him there. They were given a lukewarm welcome. Erridge was one of those egotists unable effectively to organise to good effect his own egotism, to make a public profit out of it. He had no doubt enjoyed unusual experiences. These he was unable, or unwilling, to share with others. Isobel brought back a description of a ragged beard protruding over the edge of sheets entirely covered by what appeared to be a patchwork quilt of Boggis & Stone publications dealing with different aspects of the Spanish predicament. Norah, who shared to some extent Erridge's political standpoint, was openly contemptuous.

'Erry always regards himself as the only person in the world who has ever been ill,' she said. 'His time in Spain seems to have been a total flop. He didn't get up to the front and he never met Hemingway.'

Erridge, as Norah – and Quiggin before her – had remarked, was keenly interested in his own health; in general not good. Now that he was ill enough for his condition to be recognised as more than troublesome, this physical state was not unsympathetic to him. The sickness gave his existence an increased reality, a deeper seriousness, elements

Erridge felt denied him by his family. Certainly he could now claim to have returned from an area of action. Although he might prefer to receive his relations coldly, he was at least assured of being the centre of Tolland attention. However, as it turned out, he enjoyed this position only for a short time, when his status was all at once prejudiced by his brother Hugo's motor accident.

Hugo Tolland had 'come down' from the university not long before this period, where, in face of continual pressure of a threatening kind from the authorities, he had contrived to stay the course for three years; even managing, to everyone's surprise, to scrape some sort of degree. The youngest of the male Tollands, Hugo was showing signs of becoming from the family's point of view the least satisfactory. Erridge, it was true, even before his father died, had been written off as incurably odd; but Erridge was an 'eldest son'. Even persons of an older generation – like his uncle, Alfred Tolland – who preferred the conventions to be strictly observed, would display their own disciplined acceptance of convention by recognising the fact that Erridge's behaviour, however regrettable, was his own affair. An eldest son, by no means beyond the reach of criticism, was at the same time excluded from the utter and absolute public disapproval which might encompass younger sons. Besides, no one could tell how an eldest son might turn out after he 'succeeded'. This was a favourite theme of Chips Lovell's, who used to talk of 'the classic case of Henry V and Falstaff'. Erridge might be peculiar; the fact remained he would be – now was – head of the family. Hugo was quite another matter. Hugo would inherit between three and four hundred a year when twenty-one and have to make his own way in the world.

While still at the university, Hugo showed no sign of wishing to prepare himself for that fate. Outwardly, he was a fairly intelligent, not very good-looking, unhappy, rather amusing young man, who kept himself going by wearing unusual clothes and doing perverse things. Because his own generation of undergraduates tended to be interested in politics and economics, both approached from a 'leftish' angle, Hugo liked to 'pose' – his own word – as an 'aesthete'. He used to burn joss-sticks in his rooms. He had bought a half-bottle of Green Chartreuse, a liqueur he 'sipped' from time to time, which, like the Widow's cruse, seemed to last for ever; for only during outbreaks of consciously bad behaviour was Hugo much of a drinker. At first Sillery had taken him up, no doubt hoping Hugo might prove an asset in the field where Sillery struggled for power with other dons. Hugo had turned out altogether intractable. Even Sillery, past master at dealing with undergraduates of all complexions and turning their fallibilities to his own advantage, had been embarrassed by Hugo's arrival at one of his tea parties laden with a stack of pro-Franco pamphlets, which he had distributed among the assembled guests. The company had included a Labour M.P. – a Catholic, as it happened – upon whom Sillery, for his own purposes, was particularly anxious to make a good impression. The story had been greatly enjoyed by Sillery's old enemy, Brightman, who used to repeat it night after night – *ad nauseam*, his colleagues complained, so Short told me – at High Table.

'Hugo will never find a place for himself in the contemporary world,' his sister Norah had declared.

Norah's conclusion, reached after an argument with Hugo about Spain, was not much at variance with the opinion of the rest of the family. However, this judgment turned out to be a mistaken one. Unlike many outwardly more promising young men, Hugo found a job without apparent difficulty. He placed himself with Baldwyn Hodges Ltd, antique dealers, a business which undertook a certain amount of interior decorating as a sideline. Although far from being the sort of firm Molly Jeavons would – or, financially speaking, could – employ for renovating her own house, its managing director, Mrs Baldwyn Hodges herself, like so many other unlikely people, had fetched up at the Jeavonses' one evening when Hugo was there. Very expert at handling rich people, Mrs Baldwyn Hodges was a middle-aged, capable, leathery woman, of a type Mr Deacon would particularly have loathed had he lived to see the rise of her shop, which had had small beginnings, to fashionable success. Hugo and Mrs Baldwyn Hodges got on well together at the Jeavonses'. They met again at the Surrealist Exhibition. Whatever the reason – probably, in fact, Hugo's own basic, though not then generally recognised, toughness – Mrs Baldwyn Hodges showed her liking for Hugo in a practical manner by taking him into her business as a learner. He did not earn much money at first; he may even have paid some sort of fee at the start; but he made something on commission from time to time and the job suited him. In fact Hugo had shown signs of becoming rather good at selling people furniture and advising them about their drawing-room walls. Chips Lovell (who had recently been told about Freud) explained that Hugo was 'looking for a mother'. Perhaps he was right. Mrs Baldwyn Hodges certainly taught Hugo a great deal.

All the same, Hugo's employment did not prevent him from frequenting the society of what Mr Deacon used to call 'naughty young men'. When out on an excursion with companions of this sort, a car was overturned and Hugo's leg was broken. As a result of this accident, Hugo was confined to bed for some weeks at Hyde Park Gardens, where he set up what he himself designated 'a rival *salon*' to Erridge's room at the nursing home. This situation, absurd as the reason may sound, had, I think, a substantial effect upon the speed of Erridge's recovery. Hugo even attempted to present his own indisposition as a kind of travesty of Erridge's case, pretending that the accident to the car had been the result of political sabotage organised by his sister Norah and Eleanor Walpole-Wilson. It was all very silly, typical of Hugo. At the same time, visiting Hugo in these circumstances was agreed to be more amusing than visiting Erridge. However, even if Erridge made no show of enjoying visitors, and was unwilling to reveal much of his Spanish experiences, he tolerated the interest of other people in what had happened to him in Spain. It was another matter if his relations came to his bedside only to retail the antics of his youngest brother, who represented to Erridge the manner of life of which he most disapproved. The consequence was that Erridge returned to Thrubworth sooner than expected. There he met with a lot of worry on arrival, because his butler, Smith, immediately went down with bronchitis.

At about the same time that Erridge left London, Moreland rang me up. Without anything being said on either side, our meetings had somehow lapsed. We had spoken together only at parties or on such occasions when other people had been around us. It was ages since we had had one of those long talks about life, or the arts, which had been such a predominant aspect of knowing Moreland in the past. On the telephone his voice sounded restrained, practical, colourless; as he himself would have said 'the sane Englishman with his pipe'.

'How is Matilda?'

'Spending a good deal of time out on her own with rehearsals and so on. She is going out with some of her theatre people tonight as a matter of fact.'

'Come and dine.'

'I can't. I'm involved in musical business until about ten. I said I would drop in on Maclintick then. I thought you might feel like coming too.'

'Why?'

'The suggestion was made to help myself out really. I agree it isn't a very inviting prospect.'

'Less inviting than usual? Do you remember our last visit?'

'Well, you know what has happened?'

'No.'

'Maclintick's wife has walked out on him.'

'I hadn't heard.'

'With Carolo.'

'How rash.'

'On top of that Maclintick has lost his job.'

'I never thought of him as having a job.'

'He did, all the same. Now he hasn't.'

'Did a paper sack him?'

'Yes. I thought we might meet at a pub, then go on to see Maclintick at his house. He just sits there working all the time. I have been talking to Gossage about Maclintick. We are a bit worried. A visit might cheer him up.'

'I am sure he would much rather see you alone.'

'That is just what I want to avoid.'

'Why not take Gossage?'

'Gossage is busy tonight. Anyway, he is too old a friend. He gets on Maclintick's nerves.'

'But so do I.'

'In a different way. Besides, you don't know anything about music. It is musical people Maclintick can't stand.'

'I only see Maclintick once every two years. We never hit it off particularly well even spaced out at those intervals.'

'It is because Maclintick never sees you that I want you to

445

come. I don't want an embarrassing time with him *tête-à-tête*. I am not up to it these days. I have troubles of my own.'

'All right. Where shall we meet?'

Moreland, from his extensive knowledge of London drinking places, named a pub in the Maclintick neighbourhood. I told Isobel what had been arranged.

'Try and find out what is happening about Priscilla,' she said. 'For all we know, they may be planning to run away together too. One must look ahead.'

The Nag's Head, the pub named by Moreland, was a place of no great attraction. I recalled it as the establishment brought to Mrs Maclintick's mind by her husband's uncouth behaviour at Mrs Foxe's party. Moreland looked tired when he arrived. He said he had been trudging round London all day. I asked for further details about the Maclintick situation.

'There are none to speak of,' Moreland said. 'Audrey and Carolo left together one afternoon last week. Maclintick had gone round to have a talk with his doctor about some trouble he was having with his kidneys. Not flushing out properly or something. He found a note when he returned home saying she had gone for good.'

'And then he lost his job on top of it?'

'He had written rather an astringent article about a concert he was covering. The paper didn't put it in. Maclintick made a fuss. The editor suggested Maclintick might be happier writing for a periodical aiming at a narrower public. Maclintick agreed that he himself had been feeling that for some time. So they parted company.'

'He is absolutely broke?'

'Probably a few minor irons in the fire. I don't know. Maclintick is not a chap who manages his business affairs very well.'

'Is he looking for another job?'

'He has either been working at his book or knocking them back pretty hard since all this happened – and who shall blame him?'

We set off for Maclintick's house.

'When is Matilda's play coming on?'

'They don't seem to know exactly.'

Moreland showed no sign of wishing to pursue the subject of Matilda's stage career. I did not press the question. I wondered whether he knew that Matilda had told me of her former marriage to Carolo. We passed once more through those shadowy, desolate squares from which darkness had driven even that small remnant of life that haunted them by day. Moreland was depressed and hardly spoke at all. The evening before us offered no prospect to stimulate cheerfulness. At last we reached Maclintick's horrible little dwelling. There was a light upstairs. I felt at low ebb. However, when Maclintick opened the front door he appeared in better condition than I had been led to expect. He wore no collar and had not shaved for several days, but these omissions seemed deliberate badges of emancipation from the servitudes of marriage and journalism, rather than neglect provoked by grief or despair. On the contrary, the nervous tensions to which he had been subjected during the previous few days had to some extent galvanised his normally crabbed manner into a show of geniality.

'Come in,' he said. 'You'll need a drink.'

There was a really colossal reek of whiskey as we crossed the threshold.

'How are things?' said Moreland, sounding not very sure of himself.

'Getting the sack keeps you young,' said Maclintick. 'You ought to try it, both of you. I have been able to settle down to some real work at last, now that I am quit of that bloody rag – and freer in other respects too, I might add.'

In spite of this rather aggressive equanimity displayed by Maclintick himself, an awful air of gloom hung over the house. The sitting-room was unspeakably filthy, dirty tea cups along the top of the glass-fronted bookcase, tumblers stained with beer dregs among the hideous ornaments of the mantelpiece. In the background, an atmosphere of un-made beds and unwashed dishes was dominated by an abominable, indefinable smell. As people do when landed in a position of that sort, Maclintick began at once to discuss his own predicament; quite objectively, as if the experience was remote from himself, as if – which in a sense was true – there was no earthly point in our talking of anything else but Maclintick's personal affairs.

'When I realised she had gone,' he said, 'I heaved a great sigh of relief. That was my first reaction. Later, I grasped the fact that I had to get my own supper. Found something I liked for a change – sardines and plenty of red pepper – and a stiff drink with them. Then I started turning things over in my mind. I began to think of Carolo.'

Moreland laughed uneasily. He was a person not well equipped to deal with human troubles. His temperament was without that easy, unthinking sympathy which reacts in a simple manner, indicating instinctively the right thing to say to someone desperately unhappy. He also lacked that subjective, ruthless love of presiding over other people's affairs which often makes basically heartless people adept at offering effective consolation. 'I never know the right moment to squeeze the bereaved's arm at a funeral,' he had once said. 'Some people can judge it to a nicety.' In short, nothing but true compassion for Maclintick's circumstances could have brought Moreland to the house that night. It was an act of friendship of some magnitude.

'Is Carolo in a job?' Moreland asked.

'Carolo taking a job seems to have touched off matters,'

said Maclintick, 'or perhaps *vice versa*. He has at last decided that his genius will allow him to teach. Somewhere in the North-Midlands, I was told, his own part of the world. I can't remember now. He spoke about it a short time before they went off together. Left without paying his rent, need I say? I wonder how he and Audrey will hit it off. I spent yesterday with a solicitor.'

'You are getting a divorce?'

Maclintick nodded.

'Why not,' he said, 'when you've got the chance? She might change her mind. Let me fill your glasses.'

All this talk was decidedly uncomfortable. I did not think Moreland, any more than myself, knew whether Maclintick was in fact glad to have ridded himself of his wife, or, on the contrary, was shattered by her leaving him. Either state was credible. To presume that, because they were always quarrelling, Maclintick necessarily wished to be parted from her, could be wholly mistaken. In the same way, it was equally difficult to know whether Maclintick was genuinely relieved at ceasing to work for the paper that had employed him until the previous week, or was, on the contrary, desperately worried at the prospect of having to look for another job. So far as the job was concerned, both states of mind probably existed simultaneously; perhaps so far as the wife was concerned too. Moreland clearly felt uncertain what line to take in his replies to Maclintick, who himself appeared to enjoy keeping secret his true feelings while he discussed the implications of his own position.

'Did I ever tell you how I met Audrey?' he asked suddenly.

We had been talking for a time about jobs on papers. Moreland had been pronouncing on the subject of musical journalism in particular; but sooner or later Maclintick abandoned the subject in hand, always returning to the matter of his wife. The question did not make Moreland look any happier.

'Never,' he said.

'It was through Gossage,' Maclintick said.

'How very unexpected.'

'There was a clerk in Gossage's bank who was keen on Sibelius,' said Maclintick. 'They used to talk about music together whenever Gossage went to the bank to cash a cheque or have a word about his overdraft – if Gossage ever has anything so irregular as an overdraft, which I doubt.'

'When Gossage went there to bank the bribes given him by corrupt musicians who wanted good notices,' suggested Moreland.

'Possibly,' said Maclintick. 'I wish some of them offered an occasional bribe to me. Well, Gossage invited this young man, Stanley by name, to come with him to a private performance of some chamber music.'

Moreland laughed loudly at this, much louder than the story demanded at this stage. That was from nerves. I found myself laughing a lot too.

'Stanley asked if he might bring his sister along,' said Maclintick. 'I too had to go to the chamber music for my sins. The sister turned out to be Audrey.'

Moreland seemed as much surprised by this narration as I was myself. To produce such autobiographical details was altogether unlike Maclintick. The upheaval in his life had changed his whole demeanour.

'I took a fancy to her as soon as I set eyes on her,' Maclintick said. 'Funny that, because she hasn't much in the way of looks. That was a bad day for me – a bad day for both of us, I suppose.'

'What happened?' asked Moreland.

His curiosity had been aroused. Even Moreland, who knew Maclintick so much better than myself, found these

450

revelations surprising.

'Do you know,' said Maclintick, speaking slowly as if still marvelling at his own ineptitude in such matters, 'do you know I did not exchange a word with her the whole evening. We were just introduced. I couldn't think of anything to say. She drifted off somewhere. I went home early.'

'What did you do next?'

'I had to make Gossage arrange another meeting. It took the hell of a lot of doing. Gossage didn't care for the idea at all. He liked Stanley, but he didn't want to get mixed up with his sister.'

'And then?'

'I didn't know anything about the machinery for taking women out, even when Gossage brought us together again.'

'How did you manage to get married then?'

'God knows,' said Maclintick. 'I often wonder.'

'There must have been a moment when some agreement was reached.'

'There was never much agreement about it,' said Maclintick. 'We started having rows straight away. But one thing is interesting. Gossage told me afterwards that on the night of the chamber music Audrey only opened her lips once – that was to ask him to tell her my name again and enquire what I did for a living.'

'No use fighting against fate,' said Moreland laughing. 'I've always said it.'

'Gossage told her I was a musician,' said Maclintick. 'Her comment was "Oh, God".'

'I find that a very natural one to make,' said Moreland.

'She isn't absolutely tone-deaf,' said Maclintick, speaking as if he had given the matter deep thought. 'She has her likes and dislikes. Quite good at remembering facts and contradicting you about them later. She'd been dragged by her brother to the chamber music. I never quite know why.'

'Brought her as a chaperone,' said Moreland.

'All the music in the family went into Stanley,' said Maclintick. 'I shall miss seeing Stanley once in a while. We used to have beer evenings together twice a year. Stanley can't drink Irish whiskey. But you know, it's astonishing what technical jargon women will pick up. Audrey would argue about music with me – with anyone. I've heard her make Gossage contradict himself about his views on *Les Six*. Odd the way music comes out in a family. I get it through my mother who was half Jewish. My father and grandfather were in the linen trade. They may have gone to a concert occasionally. That was about the extent of it.'

Moreland took this opportunity to guide conversation back into general channels.

'You can't tell what families are going to throw up,' he said. 'Look at Lortzing whose family were hereditary hangmen in Thuringia for two hundred years. Then suddenly the Lortzings cease to be hangmen and produce a composer.'

'You could be a musical hangman, I suppose,' said Maclintick. 'Hum tunes while you worked.'

'I could well imagine some of the musicians one knows becoming hangmen,' said Moreland.

'Surprising Lortzing didn't become a critic with an ancestry like that,' said Maclintick. 'Had it in his blood to execute people when need be – would also know the right knot to tie when it came to his own turn to shuffle off this mortal coil. Lortzing wrote an opera about your friend Casanova, didn't he? Do you remember that night at Casanova's Chinese Restaurant years ago? We talked about seducers and Don Juan and that sort of thing. That painter, Barnby, was there. I believe you were with us too, weren't you, Jenkins? For some reason I have often thought of that evening. I was thinking of it again last night, wondering if Carolo was one of the types.'

Moreland winced slightly. I did not know whether or not Maclintick was aware that Carolo had once been married to Matilda. Probably did not know that, I decided. Maclintick was a man who normally took little interest in the past history of other people. It was even surprising to find him showing such comparative interest in his own past history.

'Carolo doesn't come into the Casanova-Don Juan category,' said Moreland. 'He hasn't the vitality. Too passive. Passivity is not a bad method, all the same. Carolo just sits about until some woman either marries him, or runs away with him, from sheer desperation at finding nothing whatever to talk about.'

Maclintick nodded his head several times, showing ponderous enjoyment at this view of Carolo's technique in seduction. He filled the glasses.

'I suppose one of the tests of a man is the sort of woman he wants to marry,' he said. 'You showed some sense, Moreland, and guessed right. I should have stayed out of the marriage market altogether.'

'Marriage is quite a problem for a lot of people,' Moreland said.

'You know Audrey was my ideal in a sort of way,' said Maclintick, who after drinking all day – probably several days – was becoming thick in his speech and not always absolutely coherent. 'I've no doubt that was a mistake to start off with. There is probably something wrong about thinking you've realised your ideal – in art or anywhere else. It is a conception that should remain in the mind.'

'It wasn't for nothing that Petrarch's Laura was one of the de Sade family,' said Moreland.

'My God, I bet it wasn't,' said Maclintick. 'She'd have put him through it if they'd married. I shall always think of her being a de Sade whenever I see that picture of them again. You know the one. It is always to be found on the walls of boarding houses.'

'The picture you are thinking of, Maclintick, represents Dante and Beatrice,' Moreland said, 'not Petrarch and Laura. But I know the one you mean – and I expect the scene in question was no less unlike what actually happened than if depicting the other couple.'

'You are absolutely right, Moreland,' said Maclintick, now shaking with laughter. 'Dante and Beatrice – and a bloody bad picture, as you say. As a matter of fact, it's the sort of picture I rather like. Pictures play no part in my life. Music fulfils my needs, with perhaps a little poetry, a little German philosophy. You can keep the pictures, whether they tell a story or not.'

'Nowadays you can have both,' said Moreland, cheered by the drink and at last recovering his spirits. 'The literary content of some Picassos makes *The Long Engagement* or *A Hopeless Dawn* seem dry, pedantic studies in pure abstraction.'

'You might as well argue that *Ulysses* has more "story" than *Uncle Tom's Cabin* or *The Rosary*,' said Maclintick. 'I suppose it has in a way. I find all novels lacking in probability.'

'Probability is the bane of the age,' said Moreland, now warming up. 'Every Tom, Dick, and Harry thinks he knows what is probable. The fact is most people have not the smallest idea what is going on round them. Their conclusions about life are based on utterly irrelevant – and usually inaccurate – premises.'

'That is certainly true about women,' said Maclintick. 'But anyway it takes a bit of time to realise that all the odds and ends milling about round one are the process of living. I used to feel with Audrey: "this can't be marriage" – and now it isn't.'

Suddenly upstairs the telephone bell began to ring. The noise came from the room where Maclintick worked. The sound was shrill, alarming, like a deliberate warning. Maclintick did not move immediately. He looked greatly disturbed. Then, without saying anything, he took a gulp from his glass and went off up the stairs. Moreland looked at me. He made a face.

'Audrey coming back?' he said.

'We ought to go soon.'

'We will.'

We could faintly hear Maclintick's voice; the words inaudible. It sounded as if Maclintick were unable to understand what he was being asked. That was likely enough considering the amount he had drunk. A minute later he returned to the sitting-room.

'Someone for you, Moreland,' he said.

Moreland looked very disturbed.

'It can't be for me,' he said. 'No one knows I'm here.'

'Some woman,' said Maclintick.

'Who on earth can it be?'

'She kept on telling me I knew her,' said Maclintick, 'but I couldn't get hold of the name. It was a bloody awful line. My head is buzzing about too.'

Moreland went to the stairs. Maclintick heaved himself on to the sofa. Closing his eyes, he began to breathe heavily. I felt I had had a lot to drink without much to show for it. We remained in silence. Moreland seemed to be away for centuries. When he returned to the room he was laughing.

'It was Matilda,' he said.

'Didn't sound a bit like Matilda,' said Maclintick, without opening his eyes.

'She said she didn't know it was you. You sounded quite different.'

455

'I'm never much good at getting a name on the bloody telephone,' said Maclintick. 'She said something about her being your wife now I come to think of it.'

'Matilda forgot her key. I shall have to go back at once. She is on the doorstep.'

'Just like a woman, that,' said Maclintick. 'There was always trouble about Carolo's key.'

'We'll have to go.'

'You don't expect me to see you out, do you? Kind of you to come.'

'You had better go to bed, Maclintick,' said Moreland. 'You don't want to spend the night on the sofa.'

'Why not?'

'Too cold. The fire will be out soon.'

'I'll be all right.'

'Do move, Maclintick,' said Moreland.

He stood looking down with hesitation at Maclintick. Moreland could be assertive about his own views, was said to be good at controlling an orchestra; he was entirely without the power of assuming authority over a friend who needed 'managing' after too much to drink. I remembered the scene when Widmerpool and I had put Stringham to bed after the Old Boy Dinner, and wondered whether an even odder version of that operation was to be re-enacted here. However, Maclintick rolled himself over into a sitting position, removed his spectacles, and began to rub his eyes just in the manner of my former housemaster, Le Bas, when he could not make up his mind whether or not one of his pupils was telling the truth.

'Perhaps you are right, Moreland,' Maclintick said.

'Certainly I am right.'

'I will move if you insist.'

'I do insist.'

Then Maclintick made that harrowing remark that established throughout all eternity his relationship with Moreland.

'I obey you, Moreland,' he said, 'with the proper respect of the poor interpretative hack for the true creative artist.'

Moreland and I both laughed a lot, but it was a horrible moment. Maclintick had spoken with that strange, unearthly dignity that a drunk man can suddenly assume. We left him making his way unsteadily upstairs. By a miracle there was a taxi at the other end of the street.

'I hope Maclintick will be all right,' said Moreland, as we drove away.

'He is in rather a mess.'

'I am in a mess myself,' Moreland said. 'You probably know about that. I won't bore you with the complications of my own life. I hope Matty will not be in too much of a fret when I get there. What can she be thinking of, forgetting her key? Something Freudian, I suppose. I am glad we went to see Maclintick. What did you think about him?'

'I thought he was in a bad way.'

'You did?'

'Yes.'

'Maclintick is in a bad way,' said Moreland. 'It is no good pretending he isn't. I don't know where it will end, I don't know where anything will end. It was strange Maclintick bringing up Casanova's Chinese Restaurant.'

'Dragging up your past.'

'Barnby went straight to the point,' said Moreland. 'I was struck by that. One ought to make decisions where women are concerned.'

'What are your plans – roughly?'

'I have none, as usual. You are already familiar with my doctrine that every man should have three wives. I accept the verdict that under the existing social order such an arrangement is not viable. That is why so many men are in such a quandary.'

We drove on to where I lived. Moreland continued in the taxi on his way to find Matilda. Isobel was asleep. She woke up at one moment and asked: 'Did you hear anything interesting?' I told her, 'No'. She went to sleep again. I went to sleep for an hour or two, then woke up with a start, and lay there thinking how grim the visit to Maclintick had been; not only grim, but curiously out of focus; a pocket in time; an evening that pertained in character to life some years before. Marriage reduced in number interludes of that kind. They belonged by their nature to an earlier period: the days of the Mortimer and Casanova's Chinese Restaurant. Maclintick's situation was infinitely depressing; yet people found their way out of depressing situations. Nothing was more surprising than man's capacity for survival. Before one could look round, Maclintick would be in a better job, married to a more tolerable wife. All the same, I felt doubtful about that happening. Thinking uneasy thoughts, I fell once more into a restless, disenchanted sleep.

The atmosphere of doom that hung over Maclintick's house, indeed over the whole quarter in which he lived – or so it seemed the night Moreland and I had called on him – proved categorical enough. Two or three days later a paragraph appeared in the evening paper stating that Maclintick's body had been found 'in a gas-filled room': no doubt the room in which he worked designated by his wife as the 'only one where you can keep warm in the house'. The escape of gas had been noticed; the police broke in. The paper described Maclintick as a 'writer on musical subjects'. As with the passing of St John Clarke, new disturbing developments of the European situation prevented Maclintick's case from gaining the attention that a music critic's suicide might attract in more peaceful times. The news was

458

horrifying, yet there was no shock about it. It was cold, slow-motion horror, the shaping of a story recognisably unfinished. I tried to get in touch with Moreland. There was no reply to the telephone. The Morelands' flat seemed always empty. Then one day when I tried again, Matilda answered. She began talking about Moreland at once.

'The poor boy has been having an awful time about Maclintick,' she said. 'You know how he hates even the mildest business talks. Now he is landed with inquests and goodness knows what.'

Matilda had always got on well with Maclintick. He was one of those uncomfortably poised men whom she handled to perfection. There was every reason to suppose that Maclintick's death would distress her. At the same time, I was immediately aware from the sound of her voice on the line that she was pleased about something; the fact of Maclintick's suicide had eased her life for one reason or another. We talked for a time about Maclintick and his affairs.

'Poor old Carolo,' she said.

'You think he is in for it?'

'He has caught something this time.'

'And your play?'

'Coming on soon. I think it will be a success.'

I arranged to see Moreland. The meeting took place a day or two later. He looked as if he had been having a disagreeable time. I asked about Maclintick.

'Gossage and I had to do all the clearing up,' Moreland said. 'It was pretty good hell.'

'Why you two?'

'There did not seem to be anyone else. I can't tell you what we were let in for. It was an awful thing to happen. Of course, one saw it coming. Nothing more certain. That didn't make it any better. Maclintick was a great friend of mine in a way. He could be tiresome. He had some very

459

good points too. It was nice of him not to have done himself in, for example, the night we left him there. That would have been even more awkward.'

'It certainly would.'

'I've no reason to suppose he didn't feel just as much like taking the jump then as three days later.'

'Do you remember when he talked of suicide in Casanova's?'

'Suicide was always one of Maclintick's favourite subjects.

'It was?'

'Of course.'

'He said then that he gave himself five years.'

'He lasted about eight or nine. Gossage has been very good about sorting the musical stuff. There is a mass of it to deal with.'

'Any good?'

Moreland shook his head.

'The smell in the house was appalling,' he said. 'Absolutely frightful. Gossage had to go and stand in the street for a time to recover.'

'Anything been heard of Mrs Maclintick?'

'I had a line from her asking me to deal with certain things. I think Carolo wants to keep out of it as much as possible for professional reasons – rather naturally.'

'Do you think Maclintick just could not get on without that woman?'

'Maclintick always had his fair share of melancholia, quite apart from anything brought on by marriage or the lack of it.'

'But his wife clearing out brought matters to a head?'

'Possibly. It must be appalling to commit suicide, even though one sometimes feels a trifle like it. Anyway, the whole Maclintick business has made certain things clearer to me.'

'As for example?'

'Do you remember when we used to talk about the Ghost Railway and say how like everyday life it was – or at least one's own everyday life?'

'You mean rushing downhill in total darkness and crashing through closed doors?'

'Yes – and the body lying across the line. The Maclintick affair has reminded me of the disagreeable possibilities of the world one inhabits – the fact that the fewer persons one involves in it the better.'

'How do you mean? However you live there are always elements of that sort.'

'I know, but you get familiar with the material you yourself have to cope with. You may have heard that I have been somewhat entangled with a person not far removed from your own family circle.'

'Rumours percolate.'

'So I supposed.'

'But you would be surprised to learn my own ignorance of detail.'

'Glad to hear it. Need I say more? You must surely appreciate the contrast between the sort of thing I have been engaged upon in connexion with poor old Maclintick's mortal remains during the last few days, and the kind of atmosphere one prefers when attempting to conduct an idyllic love affair.'

'I can see that.'

'I do not suggest my daily routine comes within several million light-years of an idyll – but it normally rises a few degrees above what life has been recently.'

I began to understand the reason why Matilda had sounded relieved when we had spoken on the telephone a day or two before.

'The fact is,' said Moreland, 'very few people can deal

461

with more than a limited number of emotional problems at any given moment. At least I can't. Up to a point, I can walk a tightrope held at one end by Matilda, and at the other by the person of whom you tell me you are already apprised. But I can't carry Maclintick on my back. Maclintick gassing himself was just a bit too much.'

'But what are you explaining to me?'

'That any rumours you hear in future can be given an unqualified denial.'

'I see.'

'Forgive my bluntness.'

'It suits you.'

'I hope I have made myself clear.'

'You haven't, really. There is still a lot I should like to know. For example, did you really contemplate terminating your present marriage?'

'It looked like that at one moment.'

'With the agreement of the third party?'

'Yes.'

'And now she knows you think differently?'

'She sees what I mean.'

'And thinks the same?'

'Yes.'

I too could see what he meant. At least I thought I could. Moreland meant that Maclintick, in doing away with himself, had drawn attention, indeed heavily underlined, the conditions of life to which Moreland himself was inexorably committed; a world to which Priscilla did not yet belong, even if she were on her way to belonging there. I do not think Moreland intended this juxtaposition of lot to be taken in its crudest aspect; that is to say in the sense that Priscilla was too young, too delicate a flower by birth and upbringing to be associated with poverty, unfaithfulness, despair, and death. If he supposed that – which I doubt –

Moreland made a big mistake. Priscilla, like the rest of her family, had a great deal of resilience. I think Moreland's realisation was in the fact of Maclintick's desperate condition; Maclintick's inability to regulate his own emotional life; Maclintick's lack of success as a musician; in short the mess of things Maclintick had made, or perhaps had had visited upon him. Moreland was probably the only human being Maclintick had whole-heartedly liked. In return, Moreland had liked Maclintick; liked his intelligence; liked talking and drinking with him. By taking his own life, Maclintick had brought about a crisis in Moreland's life too. He had ended the triangular relationship between Moreland, Priscilla, and Matilda. Precisely in what that relationship consisted remained unrevealed. What Matilda thought, what Priscilla thought, remained a mystery. All sides of such a situation are seldom shown at once, even if they are shown at all. Only one thing was certain. Love had received one of those shattering jolts to which it is peculiarly vulnerable from extraneous circumstance.

'This Maclintick business must have held up all work.'

'As you can imagine, I have not done a stroke. I think Matilda and I may try and go away for a week or two, if I can raise the money.'

'Where will you go?'

'France, I suppose.'

The Morelands went abroad the following week. That Sunday, Isobel's eldest sister, Frederica, rang up and asked if she could come to tea. This suggestion, on the whole a little outside the ordinary routine of things with Frederica, who was inclined to make plans some way ahead, suggested she had something special to say. As it happened, Robert, too, had announced he would look in that afternoon; so the day took on a distinctly family aspect. Frederica and Robert could be received at close quarters, be relied upon to be reasonably cordial to one another. That would not have been true of Frederica and Norah. Hugo was another dangerous element, preferably to be entertained without the presence of his other brothers and sisters. With Frederica and Robert there was nothing to worry about.

As soon as Frederica arrived, it was evident she had recently learnt something that had surprised her a great deal. She was a person of controlled, some – Chips Lovell, for example – thought even rather forbidding exterior; a widow who showed no sign of wanting to remarry and found her interests, her work and entertainment, in her tours of duty as Lady-in-Waiting. However, that afternoon she was freely allowing herself to indulge in the comparatively undisciplined relaxation of arousing her relations' curiosity.

'I expect you have heard of a writer called St John Clarke,' she said, almost as soon as she had sat down.

This supposition, expressed by some of my friends, would have been a method of introducing St John Clarke's name within a form of words intended to indicate that in their eyes, no doubt equally in my own, St John Clarke did not grade as a sufficiently eminent literary figure for serious persons like ourselves ever to have heard of him. The phrase would convey no sense of enquiry; merely a scarcely perceptible compliment, a very minor demonstration of mutual self-esteem. With Frederica, however, one could not be sure. She had received a perfectly adequate education, indeed rather a good one, to fit her for her position in life, but she did not pretend to 'know' about writing. Indeed, she was inclined to pride herself on rising above the need to discuss the ways and means of art in which some of her relations and friends interminably indulged.

'I like reading books and going to plays,' she had once remarked, 'but I do not want to talk about them all the time.'

If Frederica had, in practice, wholly avoided an unin-structed predisposition to lay down the law on aesthetic matters, there would have been much to be said for this pre-ference. Unhappily, you could never be certain of her adherence to such a rule of conduct. She seemed often to hold just as strong views on such matters as those who felt themselves most keenly engaged. Besides, her disinclination to discuss these subjects in general, left an area of uncer-tainty as to how far her taste, for example, in books and plays, had taken her; her self-esteem could be easily, disas-trously, impaired by interpreting too literally her disavowal of all intellectual interests. In the same way, Frederica lumped together in one incongruous, not particularly accept-able agglomeration, all persons connected with painting, writing and music. I think she suspected them, in that time-honoured, rather engaging habit of thought, of possessing morals somehow worse than other people's. Her mention of St John Clarke's name was for these reasons unexpected.

'Certainly I have heard of St John Clarke,' I said. 'He has just died. Isobel and I met him lunching at Hyde Park Gardens not long before he was taken ill.'

'Not me,' said Isobel, 'I was being ill myself.'

'St John Clarke used to lunch at Hyde Park Gardens?' said Frederica. 'I did not know that. Was he often there?'

'He used to turn up at Aunt Molly's too,' said Isobel. 'You must remember the story of Hugo and the raspberries——'

'Yes, yes,' said Frederica, showing no sign of wishing to hear that anecdote again, 'I had forgotten it was St John Clarke. But what about him?'

'Surely you read *Fields of Amaranth* secretly when you were growing up?' said Isobel. 'There was a copy without the binding in that cupboard in the schoolroom at Thrub-worth.'

'Oh, yes,' said Frederica, brushing off this literary

approach as equally irrelevant. 'But what sort of a man was St John Clarke?'

That was a subject upon which I felt myself something of an expert. I began to give an exhaustive, perhaps too exhaustive, account of St John Clarke's life and character. No doubt this searching analysis of the novelist was less interesting to others – certainly less interesting to Frederica – than to myself, because she broke in almost immediately with a request that I should stop.

'It really does not matter about all that,' she said. 'Just tell me what he was like.'

'That was what I was trying to tell you.'

I felt annoyed at being found so inadequate at describing St John Clarke. No doubt it would have been better to have contained him in one single brief, brilliant epigram; I could not think of one at that moment. Besides, that was not the kind of conversational technique Frederica approved. I was attempting to approach St John Clarke from another angle, when Robert arrived. Whatever Frederica had been leading up to was for the moment abandoned. Robert, in his curiously muted manner, showed signs of animation.

'I have got a piece of news,' he said.

'What?' said Frederica. 'Have you heard too, Robert?'

'I don't know what you mean,' said Robert. 'So far as I am aware, I am the sole possessor of this particular item.'

'What is it?'

'You will all know pretty soon anyway,' said Robert, in a leisurely way, 'but one likes to get in first. We are going to have a new brother-in-law.'

'Do you mean Priscilla is engaged?'

'Yes,' said Robert. 'Priscilla – not Blanche.'

'Who to?'

'Who do you think?'

A few names were put forward.

'Come on,' said Isobel. 'Tell us.'

'Chips Lovell.'

'When did this happen?'

'This afternoon.'

'How did you find out?'

'Chips had just been accepted when I arrived back at the house.'

'He was almost a relation before,' said Frederica.

On the whole she sounded well disposed, at least looking on the bright side; because there must have been much about Chips Lovell which did not recommend itself to Frederica. She may have feared worse. Moreland's name was unlikely to have reached her, but she could have heard vague, unsubstantiated gossip stemming ultimately from the same source.

'I guessed something must be in the air when Priscilla told me she was leaving that opera job of hers,' said Robert. 'At one moment she thought of nothing else.'

We talked about Chips Lovell for a time.

'Now,' said Frederica, 'after that bit of news, I shall get back to my own story.'

'What is your story?' asked Robert. 'I arrived in the middle.'

'I was talking about St John Clarke.'

'What about him?'

'Whom do you think St John Clarke would leave his money to?' said Frederica.

'That is a big question, Frederica,' I said.

Revelation coming from Frederica on the subject of St John Clarke's last will and testament would be utterly unexpected. I had certainly wondered, at the time of St John Clarke's death, who would get his money. Then the matter had gone out of my head. The beneficiary was unlikely to be anyone I knew. Now, at Frederica's words, I began to speculate again about what surprising bequest, or bequests, might have been made. St John Clarke was known to possess no close relations. Members and Quiggin had often remarked on that fact after they left his employment, when it was clear that neither of them could hope for anything but a small legacy for old times' sake; and even that was to the greatest degree improbable. There was the German secretary, Guggenbühl. He had moved on from St John Clarke without a quarrel, although with some encouragement, so Quiggin said, because of St John Clarke's growing nervousness about the orthodoxy of Guggenbühl's Marxism. The choice was on this account unlikely to have fallen on Guggenbühl. There remained the possibility of some forgotten soul from that earlier dynasty of secretaries – back before the days of Members and Quiggin – who might have been remembered in St John Clarke's last months; a line whose names, like those of prehistoric kings, had not survived, or at best were to be met with only in the garbled forms of popular legend, in this case emanating from the accumulated conflux of St John Clarke myth propagated by Members and Quiggin. Again, the Communist Party was a possible legatee; St John Clarke seeking amends for his days of bourgeois licence, like a robber baron endowing the Church with his lands.

Even if St John Clarke had left his worldly goods to 'the Party', Frederica would scarcely bother about that, finally though such a bequest might confirm her distrust for men of letters. I was at a loss to know what had happened. Frederica saw she had said enough to command attention. To hold the key to information belonging by its essential nature to a sphere quite other than one's own gives peculiar satisfaction. Frederica was well aware of that. She paused for a second or two. The ransoming of our curiosity was gratifying to her.

'Who?' I asked.

'Whom do you think?'

'We can't spend the afternoon guessing things,' said Isobel. 'Our invention has been exhausted by Priscilla's possible fiancés.'

Robert, who probably saw no reason to concern himself with St John Clarke's affairs, and was no doubt more interested in speculating on the prospect of Chips Lovell as a brother-in-law, began to show loss of interest. He strolled across the room to examine a picture. Frederica saw that to hold her audience, she must come to the point.

'Erridge,' she said.

That was certainly an eye-opener.

'How did you discover this?'

'Erry told me himself.'

'When?'

'I stayed a night at Thrubworth. There were some legal papers of mine Erry had to sign. Taking them there seemed the only way of running him to earth. He just let out this piece of information quite casually as he put his pen down.'

'How much is it?' asked Robert, brought to heel by the nature of this disclosure.

'That wasn't so easy to find out.'

'Roughly?'

'St John Clarke seems to have bought an annuity of some sort that no one knew about,' said Frederica. 'So far as I can gather, there is about sixteen or seventeen thousand above that. It will be in the papers, of course, when the will is proved.'

'Which Erry will get?'

'Yes.'

'He will hand it over to his Spanish friends,' said Robert tranquilly.

'Oh, no, he won't,' said Frederica, with some show of bravado.

'Don't be too sure.'

'One can't be sure,' said Frederica, speaking this time more soberly. 'But it sounded as if Erry were not going to do that.'

'Why not?'

'He didn't leave Spain on very good terms with anyone.'

'The money would pay off the overdraft on the estate account,' said Isobel.

'Exactly.'

'And the woods would not have to be sold.'

'In fact,' said Robert, 'this windfall might turn out to be most opportune.'

'I don't want to speak too soon,' said Frederica, 'especially where Erry is concerned. All the same, so far as I could see, there seemed hope of his showing some sense for once.'

'But will his conscience allow him to show sense?' said Robert.

I understood now why Quiggin had been so irritable when we had last met. He must already have known of St John Clarke's legacy to Erridge. By that time Quiggin could scarcely have hoped himself for anything from St John Clarke, but that this golden apple should have fallen at Erridge's feet was another matter. To feel complete unconcern towards the fact of an already rich friend unexpectedly inheriting so comparatively large a capital sum would require an indifference to money that Quiggin never claimed to possess. Apart from that was the patron-protégé relationship existing between Erridge and Quiggin, complicated by the memory of Mona's elopement. Quiggin's ill humour was not surprising in the circumstances. It was, indeed, pretty reasonable. If St John Clarke had been often provoked by Members and Quiggin during his life, the last laugh had to some extent fallen to St John Clarke after death. At the same time, it was not easy to see what motives had led St John Clarke to appoint Erridge his heir. He may have felt that Erridge was the most likely among the people he knew to use the money in some manner sympathetic to his own final fancies. On the other hand, he may have reverted on his death-bed to a simpler, more old-world snobbery of his early years, or to that deep-rooted, time honoured tradition that money should go to money. It was impossible to say. These, and many other theories, were laid open to speculation by this piece of news, absurd in its way; if anything to do with money can, in truth, be said to be absurd.

'Did Chips mention when he and Priscilla are going to be married?' asked Isobel.

The question reminded me that Moreland, at least in a negative manner, had taken another decisive step. I thought of his recent remark about the Ghost Railway. He loved these almost as much as he loved mechanical pianos. Once, at least, we had been on a Ghost Railway together at some fun fair or on a seaside pier; slowly climbing sheer gradients, sweeping with frenzied speed into inky depths, turning blind corners from which black, gibbering bogeys leapt to attack, rushing headlong towards iron-studded doors, threatened by imminent collision, fingered by spectral hands, moving at last with dreadful, ever increasing momentum towards a shape that lay across the line.

The Kindly Ones

For R.W.K.C.

1

ALBERT, FLESHY, SALLOW, BLUE CHINNED,
breathing hard, sweating a little, fitted an iron bar into
sockets on either side of the wooden shutters he had just
closed across the final window of the stable-block. Rolled
shirt-sleeves, green baize apron, conferred a misleadingly
businesslike appearance, instantly dispelled by carpet-slippers
of untold shabbiness which encased his large, chronically
tender feet. All work except cooking abhorrent to him, he
went through the required movements with an air of weariness, almost of despair. In those days he must have been
in his middle to late thirties. We were on good terms,
although he possessed no special liking for children. Indeed,
I was supposedly helping him lock up these outbuildings
for the night, a task in principle all but completely accomplished, for some unknown reason, in late afternoon. Up to
that moment, it is true, I had done no more than examine
a coloured picture, fastened to the wall by four rusting drawing-pins, of Mr Lloyd George, fancifully conceived as
extending from his mouth an enormous scarlet tongue, on
the liquescent surface of which a female domestic servant
in cap and apron, laughing heartily as if she much enjoyed
the contact, was portrayed vigorously moistening the gum
of a Health Insurance stamp. I was still contemplating this
lively image of state-aided social service – which appeared
in some manner to hint at behaviour unseemly, even downright improper – when night, as if arbitrarily induced at
that too early hour by Albert's lethargic exertions, fell

abruptly in the shuttered room, blurring all at once the outlines of the anonymous artist's political allegory. Albert withdrew ponderously from the dusk now surrounding us. I followed him into the broad daylight of the yard, where tall pine trees respired on the summer air a resinous, somehow alien odour, gently disinfectant like the gardens of a sanatorium in another country than England.

'Don't want any of them Virgin Marys busting in and burning the place down,' Albert said.

Aware of a faint sense of horror at the prospect of so monstrous a contingency – enigmatic, no less than unhallowed, in its heretical insistence on plurality – I asked explanation.

'Suffragettes.'

'But they won't come here?'

'Never know.'

'Do you think they will?'

'Can't tell what those hussies will do next.'

I felt in agreement with Albert that the precariousness of life was infinite. I pondered his earlier phrase. It was disconcerting. Why had he called suffragettes 'Virgin Marys'? Then I remembered a fact that might throw light on obscurity. At lessons that morning – the subject classical mythology – Miss Orchard had spoken of the manner in which the Greeks, because they so greatly feared the Furies, had named them the Eumenides – the Kindly Ones – flattery intended to appease their terrible wrath. Albert's figure of speech was no doubt employed with a similar end in view towards suffragettes. He was by nature an apprehensive man; fond, too, of speaking in riddles. I recalled Miss Orchard's account of the Furies. They inflicted the vengeance of the gods by bringing in their train war, pestilence, dissension on earth; torturing, too, by the stings of conscience. That last characteristic alone, I could plainly see,

476

made them sufficiently unwelcome guests. So feared were they, Miss Orchard said, that no man mentioned their names, nor fixed his eyes upon their temples. In that respect, at least, the Furies differed from the suffragettes, whose malevolence was perpetually discussed by persons like Edith and Mrs Gullick, the former of whom had even seen suffragette processions on the march under their mauve-and-green banners. At the same time, the nature of suffragette aggression seemed to bear, in other respects, worthy comparison with that of the Furies, feminine, too, so far as could be judged, equally the precursors of fire and destruction. Thought of them turned my mind to other no less awe-inspiring, in some ways even more fascinating, local terrors with which we might have to contend during the hours of darkness.

'Has Billson seen the ghost again?'

Albert shook his head, giving the impression that the subject of spectres, generally speaking, appealed to him less than to myself. He occupied one of the two or three small rooms beyond the loose-boxes, where he slept far away from the rest of the household. The occasional intrusion of Bracey into another of the stable rooms offered small support where ghosts were concerned. Bracey's presence was intermittent, and, in any case, there was not sufficient fellow-feeling between the two of them to create a solid resistance to such visitations. It was, therefore, reasonable enough, since he inhabited such lonely quarters, for Albert to prefer no undue emphasis to be laid on the possibilities of supernatural appearance even in the house itself. To tell the truth, there was always something a little frightening about the stable-block in daytime too. The wooden bareness of its interior enjoyably reconstructed – in my own unrestricted imagination – a log cabin or palisade, loop-holed and bullet-scarred, to be defended against Zulus or Red

Indians. In such a place, after nightfall, the bravest might give way to nameless dread of the occult world; more to be feared, indeed, than any crude physical onslaught from suffragettes, whose most far-fetched manifestations of spite and perversity would scarcely extend to an incendiary attack on the Stonehurst stables.

The 'ghosts' of Stonehurst, on the other hand, were a recognised feature of the place, almost an amenity in my own eyes, something far more real than suffragettes. Billson, the parlourmaid, had waked at an early hour only a week or two before to find a white shape of immense height standing beside her bed, disappearing immediately before she had time to come fully to her senses. That, in itself, might have been dismissed as a wholly imaginary experience, something calling for banter rather than sympathy or interest. Billson, however, confessed she had also on an earlier occasion found herself confronted with this or another very similar apparition, a spectre unfortunately reported in much the same terms by Billson's immediate predecessor. In short, it looked very much as if the house was undeniably 'haunted'. Maids were, in any case, disinclined to stay in so out-of-the-way a place as Stonehurst. Ghosts were likely to be no encouragement. Perhaps it was a coincidence that two unusually 'highly strung' persons had followed each other in that particular maid's bedroom. Neither Albert himself, nor Mercy, the housemaid, had at present been subjected to such an ordeal. On the other hand, my nurse, Edith (herself, before my own day, a housemaid), had from time to time heard mysterious rappings in the night-nursery, noises which could not – as first supposed – be attributed to myself. What was more, my mother admitted to a recurrent sense, sometimes even in the day, of an uncomfortable presence in her bedroom. At night, there, she had waked once or twice overwhelmed with an inexplicable feeling of doom and horror. I record these things merely as a then accepted situation. Such circumstances might have been disregarded in a more rationalistic family; in one less metaphysically flexible, they could have caused agitation. In my own, they were received without scepticism, at the same time without undue trepidation. Any discussion on the subject took place usually behind closed doors, simply in order that the house should not acquire a reputation which might dry up entirely the sources of domestic staff. No effort was made to keep such talk from my own ears. My mother – together with her sisters in their unmarried days – had always indulged a taste for investigation of the Unseen World, which even the threatened inconveniences of the Stonehurst 'ghosts' could not entirely quench. My father, not equally on terms with such hidden forces, was at the same time no less imbued with belief. In short, the 'ghosts' were an integral, an essential part of the house; indeed, its salient feature.

All the same, hauntings were scarcely to be expected in this red-tiled bungalow, which was almost capacious, or so it seemed in those days, on account of its extreme, unnatural elongation. It had been built only thirteen or fourteen years before – about 1900, in fact – by some retired soldier, anxious to preserve in his final seclusion tangible reminder of service in India, at the same time requiring nothing of architecture likely to hint too disturbingly of the exotic splendours of Eastern fable. Stonehurst, it was true, might be thought a trifle menacing in appearance, even ill-omened, but not in the least exotic. Its configuration suggested a long, low Noah's Ark, come uncomfortably to rest on a heather-grown, coniferous spur of Mount Ararat; a Noah's Ark, the opened lid of which would reveal myself, my parents, Edith, Albert, Billson, Mercy, several dogs and cats, and, at certain seasons, Bracey and Mrs Gullick.

'Tell her to give over,' said Albert, adverting to the subject of Billson and her 'ghost'. 'Too much cold pork and pickles. That's all the matter. Got into trouble with the indigestion merchants, or off her nut, one or the other. She'll find herself locked up with the loonies if she takes on so.'

'Billson said she'd give notice if it happened again.'

'Give notice, I don't think.'

'Won't she, then?'

'Not while I'm here she won't give notice. Don't you believe it.'

Albert shook off one of his ancient bedroom slippers, adjusting the thick black woollen sock at the apex of the foot, where, not over clean, the nail of a big toe protruded from a hole at the end. Albert was an oddity, an exceptional member of the household, not only in himself and his office, but in relation to the whole character of my parents' establishment. He had started life as hall-boy – later promoted footman – in my mother's home before her marriage. After my grandmother's death – the dissolution, as it always seemed in Albert's reminiscence, of an epoch – he had drifted about from place to place, for the most part unhappily. Sometimes he quarrelled with the butler; sometimes his employers made too heavy demands on his time; sometimes, worst of all, the cook, or one of the maids, fell in love with him. Love, of course, in such cases, meant marriage. Albert was not, I think, at all interested in love affairs of an irregular kind; nor, for that matter, did he in the least wish to take a wife. On that subject, he felt himself chronically persecuted by women, especially by the most determined of his tormentors (given to writing him long, threatening letters), whom he used to call 'the girl from Bristol'. This preoccupation with the molestations of the opposite sex probably explained his fears that evening of suffragette attack.

In the end, after moving from London to the country, from the country back to London, up to Cumberland, down to Cardigan, Albert had written to my mother – habitually in touch with almost everyone who had ever worked for her – suggesting that, as she was soon to lose a cook, he himself should exchange to that profession, which had always appealed to him, the art of cooking running in his blood through both parents. He was, indeed, known, even in his days as footman, for proficiency in cooking, which had come to him almost by the light of nature. His offer. was, therefore, at once accepted, though not without a few privately expressed reservations as to the possibility of Albert's turning out a 'handful'. 'Handful' to some extent he was. Certainly his cooking was no disappointment. That was soon clear. The question why he should prefer employment with a family who lived on so unpretentious a scale, when he might have found little or no difficulty in obtaining a situation as chef in much grander circumstances, with more money and greater prestige, is not easily resolved. Lack of enterprise, physical indolence, liking for the routine of a small domestic community, all no doubt played a part; as also, perhaps, did the residue from a long-forgotten past, some feudal secretion, dormant, yet never entirely defunct within his bones, which predisposed him towards a family with whom he had been associated in his early days of service. That might have been. At the same time, such sentiments, even if they existed, were certainly not to be romantically exaggerated. Albert had few, if any, illusions. For example, he was not at all keen on Stonehurst as a place of residence. The house was little to his taste. He often said so. In this opinion there was no violent dissent from other quarters. Indeed, all concerned agreed in thinking it just as well we should not have to live at Stonehurst for ever, the bungalow being rented 'furnished' on a short renewable lease, while my father's battalion was stationed in the Aldershot Command.

The property stood in country partaking in general feature of the surroundings of that uniquely detestable town, although wilder, more deserted, than its own immediate outskirts. The house, built at the summit of a steep hill, was reached by a stony road – the uneven, treacherous surface of pebbles probably accounting for the name – which turned at a right-angle halfway up the slope, running between a waste of gorse and bracken, from out of which emerged an occasional ivy-strangled holly tree or withered fir: landscape of seemingly purposeful irresponsibility, intentional rejection of all scenic design. In winter, torrents of water gushed over the pebbles and down the ruts of this slippery route (perilous to those who, like General Conyers, attempted the journey in the cars of those days) which continued for two or three hundred yards at the top of the hill, passing the Stonehurst gate. The road then bifurcated, aiming in one direction towards a few barely visible roofs, clustered together on the distant horizon; in the other, entering a small plantation of pine trees, where Gullick, the Stonehurst gardener (fascinatingly described once by Edith in my unobserved presence as 'born out of wedlock'), lived in his cottage with Mrs Gullick. Here, the way dwindled to a track, then became a mere footpath, leading across a vast expanse of heather, its greyish, pinkish tones stained all the year round with great gamboge patches of broom: country taking fire easily in hot summers.

The final limits of the Stonehurst estate, an extensive wired-in tract of desert given over to the devastations of a vast brood of much interbred chickens, bordered the heath, which stretched away into the dim distance, the heather rippling in waves like an inland sea overgrown with weed. Between the chickens and the house lay about ten acres of garden, flower beds, woodland, a couple of tennis courts. The bungalow itself was set away from the road among tall pines. Behind it, below a bank of laurel and Irish yews, espaliered roses sloped towards a kitchen-garden, where Gullick, as if gloomily contemplating the accident of his birth, was usually to be found pottering among the vegetables, foretelling a bad season for whichever crop he stood among. Beyond the white-currant bushes, wild country began again, separated from Stonehurst civilisation by only a low embankment of turf. This was the frontier of a region more than a little captivating – like the stables – on account of its promise of adventure. Dark, brooding plantations of trees; steep, sandy slopes; soft, velvet expanses of green moss, across which rabbits and weasels incessantly hurried on their urgent business: a terrain created for the eternal campaign of warring armies, whose unceasing operations justified recognition of Albert's sleeping-quarters as the outworks of a barbican, or stockade, to be kept in a permanent state of defence. Here, among these woods and clearings, sand and fern, silence and the smell of pine brought a kind of release to the heart, together with a deep-down wish for something, something more than battles, perhaps not battles at all; something realised, even then, as nebulous, blissful, all but unattainable: a feeling of uneasiness, profound and oppressive, yet oddly pleasurable at times, at other times so painful as to be almost impossible to bear.

'General and Mrs Conyers are coming next week,' I said.

'It was me told you that,' said Albert.

'Will you cook something special for them?'

'You bet.'

'Something *very* special?'

'A mousse, I 'spect.'

'Will they like it?'

'Course they will.'

'What did Mrs Conyers's father do to you?'

'I told you.'

'Tell me again.'

'All years ago, when I was with the Alfords.'

'When you helped him on with his overcoat——'

'Put a mouse down the sleeve.'

'A real one?'

'Course not – clockwork.'

'What did you do?'

'Let out a yell.'

'Did they all laugh?'

'Not half, they did.'

'Why did he do it?'

'Used to tell me, joking like, "I've got a grudge against you, Albert, you don't treat me right, always telling me her Ladyship's not at home when I want most to see her. I'm going to pay you out" – so that's what he did one day.'

'Perhaps General Conyers will play a trick on Bracey.'

'Not him.'

'Why not?'

'Wasn't General Conyers put the mouse down the sleeve, it were Lord Vowchurch. No one's going to do a thing like that to Bracey – let alone General Conyers.'

'When does Bracey come back from leave?'

'Day-after-tomorrow.'

'Where did he go?'

'Luton.'

'What did he do there?'

'Stay with his sister-in-law.'

'Bracey said he was glad to get back after his last leave.'

'Won't be this time if the Captain has something to say to him about that second-best full-dress tunic put away in the wrong place.'

Bracey was the soldier-servant, a man unparalleled in smartness of turn-out. His appearance suggested a fox-terrier, a clockwork fox-terrier perhaps (like Lord Vowchurch's clockwork mouse), since there was much of the automaton about him, especially when he arrived on a bicycle. Sometimes, as I have said, he was quartered in the stables with Albert. Bracey and Albert were not on the best of terms. That was only to be expected. Indeed, it was a 'miracle' – so I had heard my parents agree – that the two of them collaborated even so well as they did, 'which wasn't saying much'. Antagonism between soldier-servant and other males of the establishment was, of course, traditional. In the case of female members of the staff, association might, still worse, become amorous. Indeed, this last situation existed to some extent at Stonehurst, where the endemic difficulties of a remote location were increased by the burden of Bracey's temperament, moody as Albert's, though in an utterly different manner.

Looking back, I take Bracey to have been younger than Albert, although, at Stonehurst, a large moustache and face shiny with frenzied scrubbing and shaving made Bracey seem the more time-worn. Unmarried, he was one of those old-fashioned regular soldiers with little or no education – scarcely able to read or write, and on that account debarred from promotion – whose years of spotless turn-out and absolute reliability in minor matters had won him a certain status, indeed, wide indulgence where his own idiosyncrasies were concerned. These idiosyncrasies could be fairly troublesome at times. Bracey was the victim of melancholia. No one seemed to know the precise origin of this affliction: some early emotional mishap; heredity; self-love allowed to get out of hand – any of these could have caused his condition. He came of a large family, greatly dispersed, most of them earning a respectable living; although I once heard Edith and Billson muttering together about a sister of Bracey's said to have been found drowned in the Thames estuary. One brother was a bricklayer in Cardiff; another, a cabman in Liverpool. Bracey liked neither of these brothers. He told me that himself. He greatly preferred the sister-in-law at Luton, who was, I think, a widow. That was why he spent his leave there.

Bracey's periodic vexation of spirit took the form of his 'funny days'. Sometimes he would have a 'funny day' when on duty in the house. These always caused dismay. A 'funny day' in barracks, however trying to his comrades, could not have been equally provoking in that less intimate, more spacious accommodation. Perhaps Bracey had decided to become an officer's servant in order that his 'funny days' should enjoy their full force. On one of these occasions at Stonehurst, he would sit on a kitchen chair, facing the wall, speaking to no one, motionless as a man fallen into a state of catalepsy. This would take place, of course, only after he had completed all work deputed to him, since he was by nature unyieldingly industrious. The burden of his melancholy was visited on his colleagues, rather than my parents, who had to put up with no more than a general air of incurable glumness diffused about the house, concentrated only whenever Bracey himself was addressed by one or other of them. My father would sometimes rebel against this aggressive, even contagious, depression – to which he was himself no stranger – and then there would be a row. That was rare. In the kitchen, on the other hand, they had to bear with Bracey. On such occasions, when mealtimes approached, Bracey would be asked, usually by Billson, if he wanted anything to eat. There would be silence. Bracey would not turn his head.

'Albert has made an Irish stew,' Billson – as reported by Edith – might say. 'It's a nice stew. Won't you have a taste, Private Bracey?'

At first Bracey would not answer. Billson might then repeat the question, together with an inquiry as to whether Bracey would accept a helping of the stew, or whatever other dish was available, from her own hand. This ritual might continue for several minutes, Billson giggling, though with increased nervousness, because of the personal element involved in Bracey's sadness. This was the fact that he was known to be 'sweet on' Billson herself, who refused to accept him as a suitor. Flattered by Bracey's attentions, she was probably alarmed at the same time by his melancholic fits, especially since her own temperament was a nervous one. In any case, she was always very self-conscious about 'men'.

'I'll have it, if it is my right,' Bracey would at last answer in a voice not much above a whisper.

'Shall I help you to a plate then, Private Bracey?'

'If it's my right, I'll have a plate.'

'Then I'll give you some stew?'

'If it's my right.'

'Shall I?'

'Only if it's my right.'

So long as the 'funny day' lasted, Bracey would commit himself to no more gracious acknowledgment than those words, spoken as if reiterating some charm or magical formula. No wonder the kitchen was disturbed. Behaviour of this sort was very different from Albert's sardonic, worldly dissatisfaction with life, his chronic complaint of persecution at the hands of women.

'I haven't had one of my funny days for a long time,'

Bracey, pondering his own condition, would sometimes remark.

There was usually another 'funny day' pretty soon after self-examination had revealed that fact. Indeed, the observation in itself could be regarded as a very positive warning that a 'funny day' was on the way. He was a great favourite with my father, who may have recognised in Bracey some of his own uncalm, incurious nature. From time to time, as I have said, there was an explosion: dire occasions when Bracey would be ordered back to the regiment at twenty-four hours' notice, usually after a succession of 'funny days' had made kitchen society so unendurable that life in the world at large had also become seriously contaminated with nervous strain. In the end, he was always forgiven. Afterwards, for several weeks, every object upon which a lustre could possibly be imposed that fell into Bracey's hands would be burnished brighter than ever before, reduced almost to nothingness by energetic scouring.

'Good old Bracey,' my father would say. 'He has his faults, of course, but he does know the meaning of elbow-grease. I've never met a man who could make top-boots shine like Bracey. They positively glitter.'

'I'm sure he would do anything for *you*,' my mother would say.

She held her own, never voiced, less enthusiastic, views on Bracey.

'He worships you,' she would add.

'Oh, nonsense.'

'He does.'

'Of course not.'

'I say he does.'

'Don't be silly.'

This apparently contrary opinion of my father's – the sequence of the sentences never varied – conveyed no strong sense of disagreement with the opinion my mother had expressed. Indeed, she probably put the case pretty justly. Bracey certainly had a high regard for my father. Verbal description of everything, however, must remain infinitely distant from the thing itself, overstatement and understatement sometimes hitting off the truth better than a flat assertion of bare fact. Bearing in mind, therefore, the all but hopeless task of attempting to express accurately the devious involutions of human character and emotions, you might equally have said with some authenticity that Billson was loved by Bracey, while Billson herself loved Albert. Albert, for his part, possessed that touch of narcissism to be found in some artists whatever their medium – for Albert was certainly an artist in cooking – and apparently loved no one but himself. To make these clumsy statements about an immensely tenuous complex of relationships without hedging them in with every kind of limitation of meaning would be to give a very wrong impression of the kitchen at Stonehurst. At the same time, the situation must basically have resolved itself to something very like these uncompromising terms: a triangular connexion which, by its own awful, eternal infelicity, could almost be regarded by those most concerned as absolutely in the nature of things. Its implications confirmed, so to speak, their worst fears, the individual inner repinings of those three, Billson, Bracey and Albert: Albert believing, with some excuse, that 'the women were after him again'; Bracey, in his own unrequited affections, finding excuse for additional 'funny days'; Billson, in Albert's indifference and Bracey's aspirations, establishing corroboration of her burning, her undying, contempt for men and their lamentable goings-on.

'Just like a man,' Billson used to say, in her simile for human behaviour at its lowest, most despicable.

In spite of her rapid accumulation of experience, both

emotional and supernatural, while living at Stonehurst, Billson had not been with us long, two or three months perhaps. Like Albert, she must have been in her late thirties, though my mother used to say Billson looked 'very young for her age'. Like Bracey, Billson, too, came of a large family, to whom, unlike Bracey, she was devoted. She talked without end about her relations, who lived, most of them, in Suffolk. Billson was fond of telling Edith that her people 'thought a lot of themselves'. Fair, not bad-looking, there was something ageless about Billson. Even as a child, I was aware of that. She had been employed at a number of 'good' houses in London: the only reason, so Albert used to imply, why he was himself so indulgent of her vagaries. A 'disappointment' – said to have been a butler – was known to have upset her in early life, made her 'nervy', too much inclined to worry about her health. One of the many doctors consulted at one time or another had advised a 'situation' in the country, where, so the physician told her, she would be less subject to periodical attacks of nausea, feelings of faintness. London air, Billson often used to complain, did not suit her. This condition of poorish health, especially her 'nerves', explained Billson's presence at Stonehurst, where maids of her experience were hard to acquire.

Behind her back (with reference to the supposed poverty of intellectual resource to be found in the county of her origin), Albert used to call Billson 'Silly Suffolk', and complain of her clumsiness, which was certainly notable. To her face, he was more respectful, not, I think, from chivalrous feelings, but because he feared too much badinage on his own part might be turned against himself, offering Billson indirect means of increasing their intimacy. Billson, in spite – perhaps because – of her often expressed disdain for men (even with Albert her love took a distinctly derisive shape), rated high her own capacity for raising desire in them. She would never, for example, mount a step-ladder (for some such purpose as to re-hang the drawing-room curtains) if my father, Albert or Bracey happened to be in the room. She always took care to explain afterwards that modesty – risk of exposing to a male eye even a minute area of female leg – was her reason for avoiding this physical elevation. I never learnt the precise form taken by her 'chasing after' Albert, about which even Edith – on the whole pretty discreet – was at times prepared to joke, nor, for that matter, the method – equally accepted by Edith – by which Bracey courted Billson. Bracey, it is true, would sometimes offer to clean the silver for her, a job he certainly performed better than she did. It was also true that Billson would sometimes tease Albert by subjecting him to her invariable, her all-embracing pessimism. She could also, of course, show pessimism about Bracey's affairs, but in a far less interested tone.

'Pity it's going to rain now your afternoon off's come round, Albert,' she would say. 'Not that you can want to go into Aldershot much after losing the money on that horse. Why, you must be stony broke. If you're not quick you'll miss the carrier again.'

To Bracey she would be more formal.

'I expect you'll have to go on one of those route-marches, Private Bracey, now the hot weather's come on.'

Billson would upset Albert fairly regularly every few weeks by her fearful forebodings of ill. Once, when she saw the local constable plodding up the drive, she had rushed into the kitchen in a state of uncontrolled agitation.

'Albert!' she had cried, 'what have you done? There's a policeman coming to the door.'

Albert, as I have said, was easily frightened himself. On this occasion, so Edith reported, he 'went as white as a sheet'. It was a relief to everyone when the subject of inquiry turned out to be nothing worse than a dog-licence. I did not, of course, know all these things at the time, certainly not the relative strength of the emotions imprisoned under the surface of passing events at Stonehurst. Even now, much remains conjectural. Edith and I, naturally, enjoyed a rather separate existence, segregated within the confines of night- and day-nursery. There was also, to take up one's time, Miss Orchard, who – teaching all children of the neighbourhood – visited the house regularly. Edith, reasonably enough, felt the boundaries of her own domain were not to be too far exceeded by intrusion on my part into kitchen routine; while Miss Orchard's 'lessons' occupied important expanses of the day. All the same, I did not propose to allow myself to be excluded utterly from a society in which life was lived with such intensity. Edith used to suffer from terrible 'sick headaches' every three or four weeks (not unlike Billson's bouts of nausea), and from what she herself called 'small aches and pains few people die of', so that, with Edith laid low in this manner, my parents away from home, Miss Orchard teaching elsewhere, the veil would be lifted for a short space from many things usually hidden. As a child you are in some ways more acutely aware of what people feel about one another than you are when childhood has come to an end.

For that reason, I always suspected that Billson would – to use her favourite phrase – 'get her own back' on Albert for calling her 'Silly Suffolk', even though I was at the same time unaware, of course, that her aggressiveness had its roots in love. Indeed, so far was I from guessing the true situation that, with some idea of arranging the world, as then known to me, in a neat pattern, I once suggested to Billson that she should marry Bracey. She laughed so heartily (like the maid damping the Insurance stamp on Mr Lloyd George's tongue) at this certainly very presumptuous suggestion, while assuring me with such absolute candour of her own determination to remain for ever single, that – not for the last time within similar terms of reference – I was completely taken in.

'Anyway,' said Billson, 'I wouldn't have a soldier. None of my family would ever look at a *soldier*. Why, they'd disown me.'

This absolute disallowance of the profession of arms as the calling of a potential husband could not have been more explicitly expressed. Indeed, Billson's words on that occasion gave substantial grounds for the defiant shape taken by Bracey's bouts of gloom. There was good reason to feel depression if this was what women felt about his situation. A parallel prejudice against even military companionship, much less marriage, was shared by Edith.

'Nice girls don't walk out with soldiers,' she said.

'Why not?'

'They don't.'

'Who says not?'

'Everybody says not.'

'But why not?'

'Ask anybody.'

'Not even the Life Guards?'

'No.'

'Nor the Blues?'

'Tommies are all the same.'

That seemed to settle matters finally so far as Bracey was concerned. There appeared to be no hope. There was Mercy, the housemaid, but even my own reckless projects for adjusting everyone else's personal affairs according to my whim did not include such a fate for Bracey. I could see that was not a rational proposition. In fact, it was out of the question. There were several reasons. In the first place, Mercy herself played little or no part in the complex of personalities who inhabited the Stonehurst kitchen – no emotional

493

part, at least. Certainly Mercy herself had no desire to do so. She was a quite young girl from one of the villages in the neighbourhood, found for my mother by Mrs Gullick. Together with her parents, Mercy belonged to a local religious sect, so small that it embraced only about twenty individuals, all related to one another.

'They don't believe anyone else is going to Heaven,' Edith said of this communion.

'No one at all?'

'Not a single soul.'

'Why not?'

'They say they're the only ones saved.'

'Why?'

'Call themselves the Elect.'

'They aren't the only people going to Heaven.'

'I should just about think not.'

'They are silly to say that.'

'Silly, no error.'

Billson went still further than Edith on the same theological issue.

'That girl won't be saved herself,' she said. 'Not if she goes about repeating such things of her neighbours. God won't want her.'

The positivist character of Mercy's religious beliefs, more especially in relation to the categorical damnation of the rest of mankind, was expressed outwardly in a taciturn demeanour, defined by Edith as 'downright disobliging', her creed no doubt discouraging frivolous graces of manner. In personal appearance, she was equally severe, almost deliberately unprepossessing.

'*Her* face will never be her fortune,' Albert once remarked, when Mercy had left the kitchen in a huff after some difference about washing up.

Even Bracey, with all his unvoiced disapproval of Albert,

was forced to laugh at the wit, the aptness of this observation. Bracey was, in any case, cheerful enough between his 'funny days'. If his spirits, at the lowest, were very low indeed, they also rose, at other moments, to heights never attained by Albert's. On such occasions, when he felt all comparatively well with the world, Bracey would softly hum under his breath:

'Monday, Tuesday, Wednesday, Thursday,
May be merry and bright.
But I'm going to be married on Sunday;
Oh, I wish it was Sunday night.'

Earlier in the year, during one of these bursts of cheerfulness, Bracey had offered to take me to see a football match. This was an unexpected, a highly acceptable invitation. It always seemed to me a matter of complaint that, although my father was a soldier, we saw at Stonehurst, in practice, little or nothing of the army, that is to say, the army as such. We lived on this distant hilltop, miles away from the daily activities of troops, who were to be sighted only very occasionally on some local exercise to which summer manœuvres had fortunately brought them. Even so much as the solitary outline of a Military Policeman was rare, jogging his horse across the heather, a heavy brushstroke of dark blue, surmounted by a tiny blob of crimson, moving in the sun through a Vuillard landscape of pinkish greys streaked with yellow and silver. I had mentioned to Bracey the sight of one of these lonely riders. He showed no warmth.

'Them Redcaps ain't loved all that.'
'Aren't they?'
'Not likely.'
'What do they do?'

'Run a bloke in soon as look at him.'

'What for?'

'They'll find somethink.'

'What happens to him?'

'Does a spell of clink.'

'What's that?'

'Put behind bars.'

'But they let him out sometime?'

'Twenty-eight days, might be, if he's lucky.'

'In prison?'

'Some blokes want to get even when they comes out.'

'How?'

'Waits behind a hedge on a dark night.'

'And then——'

'Takes the Redcap unawares like. Makes an ambush like. Give him a hiding.'

I accepted this picture of relaxed discipline in the spirit offered by Bracey, that is to say, without expression of praise or blame. Clearly he had described one of those aspects of army life kept, generally speaking, in the background, a world of violent action from which Stonehurst seemed for ever excluded.

Nor was our separation from the army only geographical. Military contacts were further lessened by my mother's distaste – her morbid horror, almost – of officers' wives who were 'regimental' – ladies who speculated on the Battalion's chances of winning the Cup, or discussed with too exact knowledge the domestic crises in the life of Mrs Colour-Sergeant Jones. My mother did not, in fact, enjoy any form of 'going out', military or civilian. Before marriage, she had been keen enough on parties and balls, but, my father having little or no taste for such amusements, she forgot about them herself, then developed greater dislike than his own. Even in those distant days my parents had begun to live a life entirely enclosed by their own domestic interests. There was a certain amount of routine 'calling', of course; subalterns came to tennis-parties; children to nursery-tea.

Bracey's invitation to the football match was therefore welcome, not so much because I was greatly interested in football but more on account of the closer contact the jaunt offered with army life. Permission was asked for the projected excursion. It was accorded by authority. Bracey and I set off together in a dog-cart, Bracey wearing blue walking-out dress, with slight screws of wax at each end of his moustache, a small vanity affected by him on important occasions. I had hoped he would be armed with a bayonet, but was disappointed. It seemed just worthwhile asking if he had merely forgotten it.

'Only sergeants carries sidearms, walking out.'

'Why?'

'Regulation.'

'Don't you ever?'

'On parade.'

'Never else?'

'Reckon we will when the Germans comes.'

The humorous possibilities of a German invasion I had often heard adumbrated. Sometimes my father – in spite of my mother's extreme dislike of the subject, even in jest – would refer to this ludicrous, if at the same time rather sinister – certainly grossly insulting – incursion as something inevitable in the future, like a visit to the dentist or ultimately going to school.

'You'll carry a bayonet always if the Germans come?'

'You bet.'

'You'll need it.'

'Bayonet's a man's best friend in time of war,' said Bracey.

'And a rifle?'

'And a rifle,' Bracey conceded. 'Rifle and bayonet's a

497

man's best friend when he goes to battle.'

I thought a lot about that remark afterwards. Clearly its implications raised important moral issues, if not, indeed, conflicting judgments. I used to ponder, for example, what appeared to be its basic scepticism, so different from the supreme confidence in the claims of heroic companionship put forward in all the adventure stories one read. (Thirty years later, Sunny Farebrother – in contrast with Bracey – told me that, even though he cared little for most books, he sometimes re-read *For Name and Fame; or Through Khyber Passes*, simply because Henty's narrative recalled to him so vividly the comradeship he had himself always enjoyed under arms.) Bracey shared none of the uplifting sentiments of the adventure stories. That was plain. Even within my own then strictly limited experience, I could see, unwillingly, that there might be something to be said for Bracey's point of view. All the same, I knew Bracey had himself seen no active service. His opinion on such subjects must be purely theoretical. In short, the door was not irretrievably closed on the romantic approach. I felt glad of that. During the rest of our journey to the Barracks, however, Bracey did not enlarge further upon the theme of weapons *versus* friendship.

We had a brief conversation at the gate with the Orderly Corporal, stabled the pony, set off across the parade-ground. The asphalt square was deserted except for three figures pacing its far side, moving briskly and close together, as if attempting to keep warm in the sharp weather of early spring. This trio marched up and down continually, always turning about at the same point in their beat. The two outside soldiers wore equipment; the central file was beltless, his right hand done up in a white bandage.

'Who are they?'

'Prisoner and escort.'

'What are they doing?'

'Exercising a bloke under arrest.'

'What's he done?'

'Chopped off his trigger finger.'

'By accident?'

'Course not.'

'How, then?'

'With a bill.'

'On purpose?'

'You bet.'

'Whatever for?'

'Saw his name in Orders on the draft for India.'

'Why didn't he like that?'

'Thought the climate wouldn't suit him, I reckon.'

'But he won't have any finger.'

'Won't have to go to India neither.'

'Were you surprised?'

'Not particular.'

'Why not?'

'Nothing those young blokes won't do.'

Once again Bracey expressed no judgment on the subject of this violent action, but I was aware on this occasion of a sense of disapproval stronger than any he had allowed to take shape in relation to assaulting Military Policemen. Here, certainly, was another story to make one ponder. I saw that the private soldier under arrest must have felt a very active dislike for the thought of army life in the East to have taken so extreme a step to avoid service there: a contrast with the builder of Stonehurst, deliberately reminding himself by the contents and architecture of his house of former Indian days. Like Bracey's picture of ambushed Redcaps, the three khaki figures, sharply advancing and retiring across the far side of the square, demonstrated a seamy, menacing side of army life, one which perhaps explained to some extent the reprobation in which Edith and Billson held soldiers as husbands. These haphazard – indeed, decidedly disreputable – aspects of the military career by no means entirely repelled me; on the contrary, they provided an additional touch of uneasy excitement. At the same time I saw that such episodes must have encouraged Bracey to form his own strong views as to the ultimate unreliability of human nature, his reliance on bayonets rather than comrades. In fact his unspoken attitude towards this painful, infinitely disagreeable, occurrence fitted perfectly with that philosophy. What use, Bracey seemed by implication to argue, would this bandaged soldier be as a companion in arms, if he preferred the loss of a forefinger to the completion of his military engagements when their circumstances threatened to be uncongenial to himself? That was Bracey's manner of looking at things, his inner world, perhaps to some extent the cause of his 'funny days'. A bugle, shrill, yet desperately sad, sounded far away down the lines.

'What is he blowing?'

'Defaulters.'

We passed through hutted cantonments towards the football field.

'Albert cut his finger the other day,' I said. 'There was a lot of blood.'

'Lot of fuss too,' said Bracey.

That was true. Albert's world of feeling was a very different one from Bracey's. A nervous man, he disliked violence, blood, suffragettes, anything of that kind. He was always for keeping the peace in the kitchen, even when his own scathing comments had started the trouble.

'I should not wish to cross the Captain in any of his appetites,' he had once remarked to my mother, when discussing with her what the savoury was to be on the menu for dinner that night.

Accordingly, Albert had been dreadfully alarmed when my father, on a day taken from duty to follow the local hounds, a rare occurrence (heaven knows what fox-hunting must have been like in that neighbourhood), having cut himself shaving that morning, managed in the course of breakfast, the wound reopening, to get blood all over his white breeches. Certainly the to-do made during the next half-hour justified perturbation on a cosmic scale. For my father all tragedies were major tragedies, this being especially his conviction if he were himself in any way concerned. On this occasion, he was beside himself. Bracey, on the other hand, showed calmness in the face of the appalling dooms fate seemed to have decreed on the bungalow and all its inhabitants. While my mother, distressed as ever by the absolutely unredeemed state of misery and rage that misfortune always provoked in my father's spirit, attempted to prepare infinitesimal morsels of cotton-wool to stem the equally small, no less obstinate, flux of blood, Bracey found another pair of riding-breeches, assembled the equipment for extracting my father from his boots, fitted the new breeches, slid him into his boots again. Finally, all this in a quite remarkably short space of time for the completion of so formidable, so complicated, so ultimately thankless a series of operations, Bracey gave my father a leg into the saddle. The worst was over; too much time had not been lost. Later, when horse and rider had disappeared from sight on the way to the meet, the nervous strain he had been through caused Bracey to remain standing at attention, on and off, for several minutes together before he retired to the kitchen. I think the day turned out, in any case, no great success: rain fell; hounds streamed in full cry through a tangle of wire; my father was thrown, retaining his eyeglass in his eye, but hurting his back and ruining his hat for ever. In short, evil influences – possibly the demons of Stonehurst or even the

Furies themselves – seemed malignantly at work. However, that was no fault of Bracey's.

'Why did you think it wrong of Billson to give the little boy a slice of cake?' I asked.

We were still looking at the match, which, to tell the truth, did not entirely hold my attention, since I have never had any taste for watching games.

'Not hers to give,' said Bracey, very sternly.

I can see now, looking back, that the question was hopelessly, criminally, lacking in tact on my own part. I knew perfectly well that Bracey and Albert did not get on well together, that they differed never more absolutely than on this particular issue. I had often, as I have said, heard my parents speak of the delicacy of the Albert–Bracey mutual relationship. There was really no excuse for asking something so stupid, a question to which, in any case, I had frequently heard the answer from other sources. All the same, the incident to which my inquiry referred had for some reason caught my imagination. In fact everything to do with 'Dr Trelawney's place', as it was called locally, always gave me an excited, uneasy feeling, almost comparable to that brought into play by the story of the bandaged soldier. Sometimes, when out for a walk with Edith or my mother, we would pass Dr Trelawney's house, a pebble-dashed, gabled, red-tiled residence, a mile or two away, somewhere beyond the roofs on the horizon faced by the Stonehurst gate.

Dr Trelawney conducted a centre for his own peculiar religious, philosophical – some said magical – tenets, a cult of which he was high priest, if not actually messiah. This establishment was one of those fairly common strongholds of unsorted ideas that played such a part in the decade ended by the war. Simple-lifers, utopian socialists, spiritualists, occultists, theosophists, quietists, pacifists, futurists, cubists, zealots of all sorts in their approach to life and art, later to be relentlessly classified into their respective religious, political, aesthetic or psychological categories, were then thought of by the unenlightened as scarcely distinguishable one from another: a collection of visionaries who hoped to build a New Heaven and a New Earth through the agency of their particular crackpot activities, sinister or comic, according to the way you looked at such things. Dr Trelawney was a case in point. In the judgment of his neighbours there remained an unbridgable margin of doubt as to whether he was a holy man – at least a very simple and virtuous one – whose unconventional behaviour was to be tolerated, even applauded, or a charlatan – perhaps a dangerous rogue – to be discouraged by all right-thinking people.

When out with his disciples, running through the heather in a short white robe or tunic, his long silky beard and equally long hair caught by the breeze, Dr Trelawney had an uncomfortably biblical air. His speed was always well maintained for a man approaching middle years. The disciples were of both sexes, most of them young. They, too, wore their hair long, and were dressed in 'artistic' clothes of rough material in pastel shades. They would trot breathlessly by, Dr Trelawney leading with long, loping strides, apparently making for nowhere in particular. I used to play with the idea that something awful had happened to me – my parents had died suddenly, for example – and ill chance forced me to become a member of Dr Trelawney's juvenile community. Casual mention of his name in conversation would even cause me an uneasy thrill. Once, we saw Dr Trelawney and his flock roaming through the scrub at the same moment as the Military Policeman on his patrol was riding back from the opposite direction. The sun was setting. This meeting and merging of two elements – two ways of life – made a striking contrast in physical appearance, moral ideas and visual tone-values.

My mother had once dropped in to the post office and general shop of a neighbouring village to buy stamps (perhaps the Health Insurance stamps commemorated in Albert's picture of Mr Lloyd George) and found Dr Trelawney already at the counter. The shop, kept by a deaf old woman, sold groceries, sweets, papers, almost everything, in fact, only a small corner behind a kind of iron hutch being devoted to postal business. Dr Trelawney was negotiating the registration of a parcel, a package no doubt too valuable – too sacred perhaps – to be entrusted to the hand of a neophyte. My mother had to wait while this laborious matter was contrived.

'He looked as if he was wearing his nightshirt,' she said afterwards, 'and a very short one at that.'

When the complicated process of registration had at last been completed, Dr Trelawney made a slight pass with his right hand, as if to convey benediction on the old woman who had served him.

'The Essence of the All is the Godhead of the True,' he said in a low, but clear and resonant voice.

Then he left the shop, making a great clatter – my mother said – with his sandals. We heard later that these words were his invariable greeting, first and last, to all with whom he came in contact.

'Horrid fellow,' said my mother. 'He gave me a creepy feeling. I am sure Mr Deacon would know him. To tell the truth, when we used to visit Mr Deacon in Brighton, he used to give me just the same creepy feeling too.'

In saying this, my mother was certainly expressing her true sentiments, although perhaps not all of them. As I have said before, she had herself rather a taste for the occult (she loved delving into the obscurities of biblical history and prophecy), so that, however much Dr Trelawney may have repelled her, there can be no doubt that she also felt some curiosity, even if concealed, about his goings-on. She was right in supposing Mr Deacon would know about him. When I myself ran across Mr Deacon in later life and questioned him on the subject, he at once admitted that he had known Dr Trelawney slightly at some early point in their careers.

'Not a person with whom I ever wanted my name to be too closely associated,' said Mr Deacon, giving one of his deep, sceptical laughs. 'Too much abracadabra about Trelawney. He started with interests of a genuinely scientific and humane kind – full of idealism, you know – then gradually involved himself with all sorts of mystical nonsense, transcendental magic, goodness knows what rubbish. Made quite a good thing out of it, I believe. Contributions from the Faithful, women especially. Human beings are sad dupes, I fear. The priesthood would have a thin time of it were that not so. Now, I don't expect Trelawney has read a line of economics – probably never heard of Marx. "The Essence of the All is the Godhead of the True," forsooth. Then you were expected to answer: "The Vision of Visions heals the Blindness of Sight." I was too free a spirit for Trelawney in spite of his denial of the World. Still, some of his early views on diet were on the right track.'

More than that, Mr Deacon would not say. He had given himself to many enthusiasms at one time or another, too many, he sometimes owned. By the time I met him, when Pacifism and Communism occupied most of the time he could spare from his antique shop, he was inclined to deride his earlier, now cast-down altars. All the same, he never wholly lost interest in Vegetarianism and Hygienic Clothing, even after he had come to look upon such causes as largely frivolous adjuncts to World Revolution.

As it happened, the Trelawney teaching on diet brought the Trelawney establishment more particularly to Stone-

505

hurst notice. These nutritional views played a part in local legend, simply because the younger disciples, several of whom were mere children, would from time to time call at the door of some house in the neighbourhood and ask for a glass of milk or a snack. Probably the fare at Dr Trelawney's, carefully thought out, was also unsubstantial, especially when it came to long, energetic rambles over the countryside, which stimulated hunger. In my own fantasies of being forced to become one of their number, semi-starvation played a macabre part. On one such occasion – it was a first visit by one of Dr Trelawney's flock to Stonehurst – Billson, answering the door, had, on request, dispensed a slice of rather stale seed-cake. She had done this unwillingly, only after much discussion with Albert. It was a moment when Bracey was having one of his 'funny days', therefore, by definition, unable to take part in any consultation regarding this benefaction. When the 'funny day' was over, however, and Bracey was, as it were, officially notified of the incident, he expressed the gravest disapproval. The cake, Bracey said, should never have been given. Billson asserted that she had Albert's support in making the donation. Always inclined to hysteria, she was thoroughly upset by Bracey's strictures, no doubt all the more severe on account of his own warm feelings for her. Albert, at first lukewarm on the subject, was driven into more energetic support of Billson by Bracey's now opening the attack on two fronts. In the end, the slice of seed-cake became a matter of bitter controversy in the kitchen, Bracey upholding the view that the dispensation of all charity should be referred to my parents; Billson sometimes defending, sometimes excusing her action; Albert of the opinion that the cake did not fall within the sphere of charity, because Dr Trelawney, whatever his eccentricities, was a neighbour, to whom, with his household, such small acts of hospitality were appropriate.

No doubt Albert's experience of a wider world gave him a certain breadth and generosity of view, not in the least sentimental, but founded on a fundamental belief in a traditional civilisation. Whether or not that was at the root of his conclusions, the argument became so heated that at last Billson, in tears, appealed to my mother. That was before the 'ghost' appeared to Billson. Indeed, it was the first serious indication of her highly-strung nerves. She explained how much it upset her to be forced to make decisions, repeated over and over again how she had never wanted to deal with the 'young person from Dr Trelawney's'. My mother, unwilling to be drawn into the controversy, gave judgment that dispensation of cake was 'all right, if it did not happen too often'. There the matter rested. Even so, Billson had to retire to bed for a day. She felt distraught. In the same way, my mother's ruling made no difference whatever to Bracey's view of the matter; nor was Bracey to be moved by Albert's emphasis on the undeniable staleness of the cake. It did not matter that Edith and Mrs Gullick supported my mother, or that Mercy did not care, since in her eyes donor and beneficiary were equally marked out for damnation. Bracey maintained his position. From this conflict, I lived to some extent apart, observing mainly through the eyes of Edith, a medium which left certain facts obscure. Getting Bracey alone was therefore an opportunity to learn more, even if an opportunity better disregarded. The fact was, I wanted to hear Bracey's opinion from his own lips.

'She didn't ought to have done it,' Bracey said.

'But Albert thought it was all right.'

'Course he thought it was all right. What's it matter to him?'

'Billson said the little boy was very grateful.'

Bracey did not even bother to comment on this last aspect of the transaction. He only sniffed, one of his habits when displeased. Billson's statement must have struck him as beneath discussion. In fact that foolish question of mine came near to ruining the afternoon. The match ended. There was some ragged cheering. We passed once more across the barrack-square, from which prisoner and escort had withdrawn to some other sphere of penal activity. Bracey was silent all the way home. I knew instinctively that a 'funny day' – almost certainly provoked by myself – could not be far off. This presentiment proved correct. Total spleen was delayed, though stormily, until the following Friday, when a sequence of 'funny days' of the most gruelling kind took immediate shape. These endured for the best part of a week, causing much provocation to Albert, who used to complain that Bracey's 'funny days' affected his own culinary powers, for example, in the mixing of mayonnaise, which – making mayonnaise being a tricky business – could well have been true.

Billson's tactics to entrap Albert matrimonially no doubt took place to some considerable extent in his own imagination, but, as I have said, even Edith accepted the fact that there was a substratum of truth in his firm belief that 'she had her eye on him', hoped to make him 'hang up his hat'. Billson may have refused to admit even to herself the strength of her passion, which certainly showed itself finally in an extreme, decidedly inconvenient form. Anxiety about her own health no doubt amplified a tendency in her to abandon all self-control when difficult situations arose: the loneliness of Stonehurst, its 'ghosts', also working adversely on her nerves. For the occasion of her breakdown Billson could not, in some ways, have picked a worse day; in others, she could not have found a better one. It was the Sunday when General and Mrs Conyers came to luncheon.

Visitors were rare at Stonehurst. No one but a relation or very, very old friend would ever have been invited to spend the night under its roof, any such bivouac (sudden descent of Uncle Giles, for example) being regarded as both exceptional and burdensome. This was in part due to the limited accommodation there, which naturally forbade large-scale entertaining. It was also the consequence of the isolated life my parents elected to live. Neither of them was lacking in a spirit of hospitality as such, my father especially, when in the right mood, liking to 'do well' anyone allowed past the barrier of his threshold. Even so, guests were not often brought in to meals. That was one of Albert's grievances. If he cooked, he liked to cook on as grand a scale as possible. There was little opportunity at Stonehurst. Indeed, Albert's art was in general largely wasted on my parents: my mother's taste for food being simple, verging on the ascetic; my father – again in certain moods – liking sometimes to dwell on the delights of the gourmet, more often crotchety about what was set before him, dyspeptic in its assimilation.

General Conyers, however, was regarded as 'different', not only as a remote cousin of my mother's – although very much, as my brother-in-law, Chips Lovell, would have said, a cousin *à la mode de Bretagne* – but also for his countless years as an old, if never particularly close, friend of the family. Even at the date of which I speak, Aylmer Conyers was long retired from the army (in the rank of brigadier-general), having brought to a close, soon after he married, a career that might have turned out a brilliant one. Mrs Conyers, quite twenty years younger than her husband, was also on good terms with my mother – they would usually exchange letters if more than a year passed without meeting – although, again, their friendship could never have been called intimate. Bertha Conyers, rather sad and apologetic in appearance, had acquired, so people said, a persecuted manner in girlhood from her father's delight in practical jokes (like the clockwork mouse he had launched on Albert), and also from his harrying of his daughters for failing to be born boys. In spite of this air of having spent a lifetime being bullied, Mrs Conyers was believed to exercise a firm influence over her husband, to some extent keeping his eccentricities in check.

'Aylmer Conyers used to have rather a roving eye,' my father would say. 'That's all changed since his marriage. Wouldn't look at another woman.'

'He's devoted to Bertha, certainly,' my mother would agree, perhaps unwilling to commit her opinion in that respect too definitely.

For my father, the Conyers visit presented, like so many other elements of life, a sharp diffusion of sentiment. By introducing my father a short time earlier in the guise, so to speak, of a fox-hunter wearing an eyeglass, I risk the conveyance of a false impression, indeed, a totally erroneous one. The eyeglass was on account of extreme short sight, for, although he had his own brand of dandyism, that dandyism was not at all of the eyeglass variety. Nor was hunting his favourite pastime. He rode fairly well ('blooded' at the age of nine out with the Belvoir, his own father being an unappeasable fox-hunter), but he took little pleasure in horses, or any outdoor occupation. It is true that he liked to speak of hunting in a tone of expertise, just as he liked to talk of wine without greatly caring to drink it. He had little natural aptitude for sport of any sort and his health was not good. What did he like? That is less easy to say. Consecrated, in one sense, to his profession, he possessed at the same time none of that absolute indifference to his own surroundings essential to the ambitious soldier. He was saddled with the equally serious military – indeed, also civilian – handicap of chronic inability to be obsequious to superiors in rank, particularly when he found them uncongenial. He was attracted by the Law, like his brother Martin; allured by the stock-market, like his brother Giles. One of the least 'intellectual' of men, he took intermittent pleasure in pictures and books, especially in such aspects of 'collecting' as rare 'states' of prints, which took his fancy, or 'first editions' of comparatively esoteric authors: items to be safely classified in their own market, without excessive reference, critically speaking, to their standing as works of art or literature. In these fields, although by no means a reactionary in aesthetic taste, he would recognise no later changes of fashion after coming to his own decision on any picture or school of painting. After a bout of buying things, he would almost immediately forget about them, often, a year or two later purchasing another copy (sometimes several copies) of the same volume or engraving; so that when, from time to time, our possessions were taken out of store, duplicates of most of his favourite works always came to light. He used to read in the evenings, never with much enjoyment or concentration.

'I like to rest my mind after work,' he would say. 'I don't like books that make me think.'

That was perfectly true. In due course, as he grew older, my father became increasingly committed to this exclusion of what made him think, so that finally he disliked not only books, but also people – even places – that threatened to induce this disturbing mental effect. Perhaps that attitude of mind – one could almost say process of decay – is among many persons more general than might be supposed. In my father's case, this dislike for thought seemed to stem from a basic conviction that his childhood had been an unhappy one. His melancholy was comparable, even though less eccentrically expressed, with Bracey's, no doubt contributing to their mutual understanding. Much the youngest of his family, his claim to have been neglected was probably true. Happy marriage did not cure him. Painfully sensitive to criticism, he was never (though he might not show this) greatly at ease with other men; in that last characteristic resembling not a few of those soldiers, who, paradoxically, reach high rank, positively assisted by their capacity for avoiding friendship, too close personal ties which can handicap freedom of ascent.

'These senior officers are like a lot of ballerinas,' said my friend Pennistone, when, years later, we were in the army together.

Certainly the tense nerves of men of action – less notorious than those of imaginative men – are not to be minimised. This was true of my father, who, like many persons who believe primarily in the will – although his own will was in no way remarkable – hid in his heart a hatred of constituted authority. He did his best to conceal this antipathy, because the one thing he hated, more than constituted authority itself, was to hear constituted authority questioned by anyone but himself. This is perhaps an endemic trait in all who love power, and my father had an absolute passion for power, although he was never in a position to wield it on a notable scale. In his own house, only he himself was allowed to criticise – to use a favourite phrase of his – 'the powers that be'. In private, he would, for example, curse the Army Council (then only recently come into existence); in the presence of others, even those 'in the Service' with whom he was on the best of terms, he would defend to the last ditch official policy of which in his heart he disapproved.

These contradictory veins of feeling placed my father in a complex position *vis-à-vis* General Conyers, whom Uncle Giles, on the other hand, made no secret of finding 'a bit too pleased with himself'. As a much older man, universally recognised as a first-rate soldier, the General presented a figure to whom deference on my father's part was obviously due. At the same time, the General held revolutionary views on army reform, which he spared no opportunity of voicing in terms utterly uncomplimentary to 'the powers that be', military or civil. My father, of course, possessed his own especial likes and dislikes throughout the hierarchy of the army, both individual and general, but deplored too plain speaking even when he was to some considerable extent in agreement.

'Aylmer Conyers is fond of putting everyone right,' he used to complain. 'If he'd stayed in the Service a few years longer, instead of devoting his life to training poodles as gun-dogs, and scraping away at that 'cello of his, he might have discovered that the army has changed a little since the Esher Report.'

Uncle Giles would immediately have been reproved for making so open a criticism of a senior officer, but my father must have felt that to criticise General Conyers was the only method of avoiding apparent collusion in an attack on the whole Army Council. In any case, Uncle Giles's unsatisfactory mode of life, not to mention his dubious political opinions, radical to the point of anarchism, put him out of court in most family discussions. He was at this period employed in a concern fascinatingly designated a 'bucket-shop'. My father had, in truth, never forgiven his brother for transferring himself, years before – after some tiff with his commanding officer – to the Army Service Corps.

'It's not just snobbishness on my part,' my father used to say, long after Uncle Giles had left that, and every other, branch of the army. 'I know they win a lot of riding events at gymkhanas, but I can't stick 'em. They're such an unco-operative lot of beggars when you have to deal with 'em about stores. I date all Giles's troubles from leaving his regiment.'

However, I mention Uncle Giles at this point only to emphasise the manner in which the Conyers visit was regarded for a number of reasons with mixed feelings by my parents. There were good aspects; there were less good ones. Albert, for instance, would be put into an excellent humour for several weeks by this rare opportunity for displaying his talents. He would make his mousse. He would recall Lord Vowchurch's famous practical joke with the clockwork mouse, one of the great adventures of Albert's life, not only exciting but refreshingly free from the artifices of women – although Mrs Conyers herself was allowed some reflected glory from her father's act.

Mrs Conyers was one of the few people with whom my mother liked to chat of 'old times': the days before she set out on the nomadic existence of a soldier's wife. Mrs Conyers's gossip, well informed, gently expressed, was perfectly adapted to recital at length. This mild manner of telling sometimes hair-raising stories was very much to the taste of my mother, never at ease with people she thought to be 'worldly', at the same time not unwilling to enjoy an occasional glimpse of 'the world', viewed through the window briefly opened by Mrs Conyers. The General had become a Gentleman-at-Arms after leaving the army, so that her stories included, with a touch of racing at its most respectable, some glimpse of the outskirts of Court life.

'Bertha Conyers has such an amusing way of putting things,' my mother would say. 'But I really don't believe all her stories, especially the one about Mrs Asquith and the man who asked her if she danced the tango.'

The fact that General Conyers was occasionally on duty at palaces rather irked my father, not so much because the General took this side of his life too seriously – to which my father would have been quite capable of objecting – but because he apparently did not take his court duties seriously enough.

'If I were the King and I heard Aylmer Conyers talking like that, I'd sack him,' he once said in a moment of irritation.

514

The General and his wife were coming to Stonehurst after staying with one of Mrs Conyers's sisters, whose husband commanded a Lancer regiment in the area. Rather adventurously for that period, they were undertaking the journey by motor-car, a vehicle recently acquired by the General, which he drove himself. Indeed, the object of the visit was largely to display this machine, to compare it with the car my father had himself bought only a few months before. There was a good deal of excitement at the prospect of seeing a friend's 'motor', although I think my father a little resented the fact that a man so much older than himself should be equally prepared to face such grave risks, physical and financial. As a matter of fact, General Conyers, who always prided himself on being up-to-date, was even rumoured to have been 'up' in a flying machine. This story was dismissed by my parents as being unworthy of serious credence.

'Aylmer Conyers will never get to the top of that damned hill,' said my father more than once during the week before their arrival.

'Did you tell him about it?' said my mother.

'I warned him in my letter. He is a man who never takes advice. I'm told he was just the same at Pretoria. Just a bit of luck that things turned out as well as they did for him – due mostly to Boer stupidity, I believe. Obstinate as a mule. Was up before Bobs himself once for disobeying an order. Talked himself out of it, even got promotion a short time after. Wonderful fellow. Well, so much the worse for him if he gets stuck – slip backwards more likely. That may be a lesson to him. Bad luck on Bertha Conyers if there's an accident. It's her I feel sorry for. I've worried a lot about it. He's a selfish fellow in some ways, is old Aylmer.'

'Do you think I ought to write to Bertha again myself?' asked my mother, anxious to avoid the awful mishaps envis-

515

aged by my father.

'No, no.'

'But I will if you think I should.'

'No, no. Let him stew in his own juice.'

The day of the Conyers' luncheon came. I woke up that morning with a feeling of foreboding, a sensation to which I was much subject as a child. It was Sunday. Presentiments of ill were soon shown to have good foundation. For one thing, Billson turned out to have seen the 'ghost' again on the previous night; to be precise, in the early hours of that morning. The phantom had taken its accustomed shape of an elongated white figure reaching almost to the ceiling of the room. It disappeared, as usual, before she could rub her eyes. Soon after breakfast, I heard Billson delivering a first-hand account of this psychical experience to Mrs Gullick, who used to lend a hand in the kitchen, a small, elderly, red-faced woman, said to 'give Gullick a time', because she considered she had married beneath her. Mrs Gullick, although a staunch friend of Billson's, was not prepared to accept psychic phenomena at any price.

'Don't go saying such ignorant things, dear,' was her comment. 'You need a tonic. You're run down like. I thought you was pale when you was drinking your cup of tea yesterday. See the doctor. That's what you want to do. Don't worry about that ghost stuff. I never heard such a thing in all my days. You're sickly, that's what you are.'

Billson seemed partially disposed to accept this display of incredulity, either because it must have been reassuring to think she had been mistaken about the 'ghost', or because any appeal to her own poor state of health was always sympathetic to her. At that early stage of the day, she was in any case less agitated than might have been expected in the light of the supernatural appearance she claimed to have witnessed. She was excited, not more than that. It was true she muttered something about 'giving notice', but the phrase was spoken without force, obviously making no impression whatever on Mrs Gullick. For me, it was painful to find people existed who did not 'believe' in the Stonehurst ghosts, whose uneasy shades provided an exciting element of local life with which I did not at all wish to dispense. My opinion of Mrs Gullick fell immediately, even though she was said by Edith to be the only person in the house who could 'get any work out of' Mercy. I found her scepticism insipid. However, a much more disturbing incident took place a little later in the morning. My mother had just announced that she was about to put on her hat for church, when Albert appeared at the door. He looked very upset. In his hand was a letter.

'May I have a word with you, Madam?'

I was sent off to get ready for church. When I returned, my mother and Albert were still talking. I was told to wait outside. After a minute or two, Albert came out. My mother followed him to the door.

'I do quite understand, Albert,' she said. 'Of course we shall all be very, very sorry.'

Albert nodded heavily several times. He was too moved to speak.

'Very sorry, indeed. It has been a long time . . .'

'I thought I'd better tell you first, ma'am,' said Albert, 'so you could explain to the Captain. Didn't want it to come to him as a shock. He takes on so. I've had this letter since yesterday. Couldn't bring myself to show you at first. Haven't slept for thinking of it.'

'Yes, Albert.'

My father was out that morning, as it happened. He had to look in at the Orderly Room that Sunday, for some reason, and was not expected home until midday. Albert swallowed several times. He looked quite haggard. The flesh of his face was pouched. I could see the situation was upsetting my mother too. Albert's voice shook when he spoke at last.

'Madam,' he said, 'I've been goaded to this.'

He shuffled off to the kitchen. There were tears in his eyes. I was aware that I had witnessed a painful scene, although, as so often happens in childhood, I could not analyse the circumstances. I felt unhappy myself. I knew now why I had foreseen something would go wrong as soon as I had woken that morning.

'Come along,' said my mother, turning quickly and giving her own eyes a dab, 'we shall be late for church. Is Edith ready?'

'What did Albert want?'

'Promise to keep a secret, if I tell you?'

'I promise.'

'Albert is going to get married.'

'To Billson?'

My mother laughed aloud.

'No,' she said, 'to someone he knows who lives at Bristol.'

'Will he go away?'

'I'm afraid he will.'

'Soon?'

'Not for a month or two, he says. But you really must not say anything about it. I ought not to have told you, I suppose. Run along at once for Edith. We are going to be dreadfully late.'

My mother was greatly given to stating matters openly. In this particular case, she was probably well aware that Albert himself would not be slow to reveal his future plans to the rest of the household. No very grave risk was therefore run in telling me the secret. At the same time, such news would never have been disclosed by my father, a confirmed maker of mysteries, who disliked imparting information of any but a didactic kind. If forced to offer an exposé of any given situation, he was always in favour of presenting the substance of what he had to say in terms more or less oracular. Nothing in life – such was his view – must ever be thought of as easy of access. There is something to be said for that approach. Certainly few enough things in life are easy. On the other hand, human affairs can become even additionally clouded with obscurity if the most complicated forms of definition are always deliberately sought. My father really hated clarity. This was a habit of mind that sometimes led him into trouble with others, when, unable to appreciate his delight in complicated metaphor and ironic allusion, they had not the faintest idea what he was talking about. It was, therefore, by the merest chance that I was immediately put in possession of the information that Albert was leaving. I should never have learnt that so early if my father had been at home. We went off to church, my mother, Edith and I. The morning service took about an hour. We arrived home just as my father drove up in the car on his return from barracks. Edith disappeared towards the day-nursery.

'It's happened,' said my mother.

'What?'

My father's face immediately became very grave.

'Albert.'

'Going?'

'Getting married at last.'

'Oh, lord.'

'We thought it was coming, didn't we?'

'Oh, lord, how awful.'

'We'll get someone else.'

'Never another cook like Albert.'

'We may find someone quite good.'

'They won't live up here.'

'Don't worry. I'll find somebody. I'll start on Monday.'

'I knew this was going to happen.'

'We both did.'

'That doesn't help.'

'Never mind.'

'But today, of all days, oh, lord.'

Their reception of the news showed my parents were already to some extent prepared for this blow to fall, anyway accepted, more or less philosophically, that Albert's withdrawal into married life was bound to come sooner or later. Nevertheless, it was a disturbing state of affairs: the termination of a long and close relationship. No more was said at that moment because – a very rare occurrence – the telegraph-boy pedalled up on his bicycle. My parents were still standing on the doorstep.

'Name of Jenkins?'

My father took the telegram with an air of authority. His face had lightened a little now that he was resigned to Albert's departure, but the features became overcast again as he tore open the envelope, as if the news it brought must inevitably be bad.

'Who can it be?' said my mother, no less disturbed.

My father studied the message. He went suddenly red with annoyance.

'Wait a moment,' he said to the boy, in a voice of command.

My mother followed him into the hall. I hung about in the background.

'For goodness' sake say what's happened,' begged my mother, in an agony of fearing the worst.

My father read aloud the words, his voice shaking with irritation:

'Can you house me Sunday night talk business arrive tea-time Giles.'

He held the telegram away from him as if fear of some awful taint threatened him by its contact. There was a long pause. Disturbing situations were certainly arising.

'Really too bad of him,' said my mother at last.

'Damn Giles.'

'Inconsiderate, too, to leave it so late.'

'He can't come.'

'We must think it over.'

'There is no time. I won't have him.'

'Where is he?'

'It's sent from Aldershot.'

'Quite close then.'

'What *the devil* is Giles doing in Aldershot?'

My parents looked at each other without speaking. Things could not be worse. Uncle Giles was not much more than a dozen miles away.

'We heard there was some trouble, didn't we?'

'Of course there is trouble,' said my father. 'Was there ever a moment when Giles was not in trouble? Don't be silly.'

There was another long pause.

'The telegram was reply-paid,' said my mother at last, not able to bear the thought that the boy might be bored or inconvenienced by this delay in drafting an answer. 'The boy is still waiting.'

'Damn the boy.'

My father was in despair. As I have said, all tragedies for him were major tragedies, and here was one following close on the heels of another.

'With the Conyerses coming too.'

'Can't we put Giles off?'

'He may really need help.'

'Of course he needs help. He always needs help.'

'Difficult to say he can't come.'

'Just *like* Giles to choose this day of all days.'

'Besides, I never think Giles and Aylmer Conyers get on very well together.'

'Get on well together,' said my father. 'They can't stand each other.'

The thought of this deep mutual antipathy existing between his brother and General Conyers cheered my father a little. He even laughed.

'I suppose Giles will have to come,' he admitted.

'No way out.'

'The Conyerses will leave before he arrives.'

'They won't stay late if they are motoring home.'

'Shall I tell Giles he can come?'

'We must, I think.'

'It may be just as well to know what he is up to. I hope it is not a serious mess this time. I wouldn't trust that fellow an inch who got him the bucket-shop job.'

Uncle Giles did not at all mind annoying his relations. That was all part of his policy of making war on society. In fact, up to a point, the more he annoyed his relations, the better he was pleased. At the same time, his interests were to some extent bound up with remaining on reasonably good terms with my father. Since he had quarrelled irretrievably with his other brother, my father – also on poorish terms with Uncle Martin, whom we never saw – represented one of the few stable elements in the vicissitudes of Uncle Giles's life. He and my father irritated, without actually disliking, each other. Uncle Giles, the older; my father, the more firmly established; the honours were fairly even, when it came to conflict. For example, my father disapproved, probably rightly, of the form taken by his brother's 'outside broking', although I do not know how much the firm for which Uncle Giles worked deserved the imputation of sharp practice. Certainly my father questioned its bona fides and was never tired of declaring that he would advise no friend of his to do business there. At the same time, his own interest in the stock market prevented him from refraining entirely from all financial discussion with Uncle Giles, with whom he was in any case indissolubly linked, financially speaking, by the terms of a will. Their argument would often become acrimonious, but I suspect my father sometimes took 'Uncle Giles's advice about investments, especially if a 'bit of a gamble' was in the air.

'Shall I say *Expect you teatime today*?'

'How is Giles going to get here?'

'I won't fetch him. It can't be done. The Conyerses may not leave in time.'

My mother looked uncertain.

'Do you think I should?'

'You can't. Not with other guests coming.'

'Giles will find his way.'

'We can be sure of that.'

My mother was right in supposing Uncle Giles perfectly capable of finding his way to any place recommended by his own interests. She was also right in thinking that Albert, after confiding his marriage plans to herself, would immediately reveal them in the kitchen. Edith described the scene later. She was having a cup of tea before church when Albert made the official announcement of his engagement. Billson had at once burst into tears. Bracey was having a 'funny day' – though a mild one – brought on either by regret at the necessity of resuming his duties, or, more probably, as a consequence of nervous strain after a spell in the house of his Luton sister-in-law. Accordingly, he showed no interest in the prospect of being left, as it were, in possession of the field so far as Billson was concerned. After issuing his pronouncement, Albert turned his attention to the mousse, the cooking of which always caused him great anxiety. Billson moved silently from kitchen to dining-room, and back again, laying the table miserably, red-eyed, white-faced, looking as much like a ghost as any she had described. She had taken badly Albert's surrender to the 'girl from Bristol'. The house had an uneasy air. I retired to my own places of resort in the garden.

The Conyers party was scheduled to arrive about one o'clock, but the notorious uncertainty of motor-cars had given rise to much head-shaking on the probability of their lateness. However, I was loitering about the outskirts of the house, not long after the telegraph-boy had disappeared on his bicycle over the horizon, when a car began painfully to climb the lower slopes of the hill. It could only contain General and Mrs Conyers. This was an unexpected excitement. I watched their slow ascent, which was jerky, like the upward movement of a funicular, but, contrary to my father's gloomy forecast, the steep incline was negotiated without undue difficulty. I was even able to open the Stonehurst gate to admit the vehicle. There could be no doubt now of the identity of driver and passenger. By that period, of course, motorists no longer wore the peaked cap and goggles of their pioneering days, but, all the same, the General's long check ulster and deerstalker seemed assumed to some extent ritualistically.

'It is always cold motoring,' my mother used to say.

The car drew up by the front door. The General, leaping from it with boundless energy, came to meet me, leaving his wife to extract herself as best she could from a pile of wraps and rugs, sufficient in number to perform a version of the Dance of the Seven Veils. Tall, distinguished, with grey moustache and flashing eyes, he held out his hand.

'How do you do, Nicholas?'

He spoke gravely, in a tone no different from that to be used with a contemporary. There was about him a kind of fierceness, combined with a deep sense of understanding.

'We are a little earlier than I expected,' he said. 'I hope your father and mother will not mind. I drove rather fast, as your mother said you lived at the back of beyond, and I am always uncertain of my own map-reading. I see now what she meant. How are they educating you up here? Do you go to school?'

'Not yet. I have lessons with Miss Orchard.'

'Oh, yes. Miss Orchard is the governess who teaches all the children round here. I know her well by name. What children are they?'

'The Fenwicks, Mary Barber, Richard Vaughan, the Westmacott twins.'

'Fenwick in the Gloucesters?'

'Yes, I think so – the regiment that wears a badge at the back of their cap.'

'And Mary Barber's father?'

'He's in the Queen's. Richard Vaughan's is in the "Twenty-Fourth" -- the South Wales Borderers.'

'What about the father of the Westmacott twins?'

'A Gunner.'

'What sort of a Gunner?'

'Field, but Thomas and Henry Westmacott say their father is going to get his "jacket" soon, so he may be Royal Horse Artillery by now.'

'An exceedingly well-informed report,' said the General. 'You have given yourself the trouble to go into matters thoroughly, I see. That is one of the secrets of success in life. Now take us to your parents.'

This early arrival resulted in my seeing rather more of General and Mrs Conyers than I should have done had they turned up at their appointed hour. First of all there was a brief examination of the Conyers car, a decidedly grander affair than that owned by my father, a fact which possibly curtailed the period spent over it. Since there was still time to kill before luncheon, the guests were shown round the garden. Permitted to accompany the party, I walked beside my mother and Mrs Conyers, the General and my father strolling behind.

'Has your ghost appeared again?' asked Mrs Conyers. 'Aylmer was fascinated when I told him your parlourmaid had seen one. He is very keen on haunted houses.'

Her husband was famous for the variety of his interests. In this particular connection – the occult one – there was some story, probably mythical, about General Conyers having taken advantage of his appointment to the Body Guard to investigate on the spot some allegedly ghostly visitation at Windsor or another of the royal palaces. This intellectually inquisitive side of the General's character specially irked Uncle Giles, who liked to classify irreparably everyone he knew, hating to be forced to alter the pigeon-hole in which he had himself already placed any given individual.

'Aylmer Conyers may be a good tactician,' he used to say, 'at least that is what he is always telling everyone – never knew such a fellow for blowing his own trumpet – but I can't for the life of me see why he wants to lay down the law about all sorts of other matters that don't concern him in the least. The last thing I heard was that he had taken up "psychical research", whatever that may be.'

My father, although he would never have admitted as much to Uncle Giles, was inclined to agree with his brother in the view that General Conyers would be a more dignified figure if he accepted for himself a less universal scope of interests; so that when the General began to make inquiries about the Stonehurst 'ghost', my father tried to dismiss the subject out of hand.

'A lot of nonsense, General,' he said, 'I assure you.'

General Conyers would have none of that.

'External agency,' he said, 'that's the point. Find it hard
to believe in actual entities myself. Ought to be looked into
more. One heard some strange stories when one was in
India. The East is full of that sort of thing – a lot pure invention, of course.'

'I believe ghosts are thought-forms,' said Mrs Conyers, as
if that settled the whole matter.

'If you are experiencing hallucination,' said her husband,
'then something must cause the hallucination. Telepathic
side, too, of course. I've never had the opportunity to cross-
question first-hand someone who'd seen a ghost. What sort
of a girl is this parlourmaid of yours?'

'Oh, please don't cross-question her,' said my mother.
'We have such dreadful difficulties in getting servants here,
and we are losing Albert as it is. She is not by any means a
girl. You will see her waiting at table. Very hysterical. All
the same, the maid we had before used to tell the same
story.'

'Indeed? Did she? Did she?'

'I must say I think there is something peculiar about the
house myself,' said my mother. 'I shall not be altogether sorry
when the time comes to leave it.'

'What about the people who let it to you?'

'The fellow who built the place is dead,' said my father,
now determined to change the subject, come what may. 'The
lease was arranged through executors. We got it rather cheap
on that account. He was in the Indian Army – Madras
cavalry, I believe. What do you think about the reorganisa-
tions in India, by the way, General? Some people say the
latest concentrations of command are not working too well.'

'We want mobility, mobility, and yet more mobility,' said
General Conyers, 'in India and everywhere else, more especially since the Baghdad Agreement. If the Germans continue
the railway to Basra, that amounts to our recognising the

northern area of Mesopotamia as a German sphere of influence.'

'How much does Mesopotamia matter?' enquired my father, unaware that he would soon be wounded there.

'Depends on when and where Germany decides to attack.'

'That will be soon, you think?'

'Between the Scylla of her banking system, and the Charybdis of her Socialist Party, Germany has no alternative.'

My father nodded respectfully, at the same time a trifle ironically. Although, in principle, he certainly agreed that war must come sooner or later – indeed, he was often saying it would come sooner – I am not sure that he truly believed his own words. He did not, indeed, much care for talking politics, national or international, unless in the harmless form of execration of causes disliked by himself. Certainly he had no wish to hear strategic situations expressed in classical metaphor, with which he was not greatly at ease. He had merely spoken of the Indian Army as a preferable alternative to discussing the Stonehurst 'ghosts'. The General, however, showed no sign of wishing to abandon this new subject.

'One of these fine mornings the Germans will arrive over here,' he said, 'or walk into France. Can't blame them if they do. Everyone is asking for it. We shall be squabbling with the Irish, or having a coal strike, or watching cricket. In France, Cabinet Ministers will be calling each other out to duels, while their wives discharge pistols at newspaper editors. And when the Germans come, it will be a big show – Clausewitz's Nation in Arms.'

'Able fellow, Clausewitz,' my father conceded.

'You remember he said that war was in the province of chance?'

'I do, General.'

'We are a great deal too fond of accepting that principle in this country,' said General Conyers. 'All the same, I thank God for the mess we made in South Africa. That brought a few people to their senses. Even the Treasury.'

My father, equally unwilling to admit the Boer War to have been prosecuted without notable brilliance, or that the light of reason or patriotism could penetrate, in however humble a degree, into the treasonable madhouse of the Treasury, did not answer. He gave a kind of half-sneer, half-grunt. I think my mother must have thought there had been enough talk of war for the time being, because she suggested a return to the house. The hour of luncheon was in any case approaching. I departed to the nursery.

'Everyone's in a taking today,' said Edith, herself rather ruffled when I arrived at table. 'I don't know what has come over the house. It's all your Uncle Giles coming to stay without warning, I suppose. Albert says it's just like him. Now, don't begin making a fuss because the gravy is too thick. I haven't given you much of it.'

In the subsequent rather sensational events of the afternoon, I played no direct part. They were told to me later, piecemeal; most of the detail revealed by my mother only many years after. She herself could never repeat the story without her eyes filling with tears, caused partly by laughter, perhaps partly by other memories of that time. All the same, my mother always used to insist that there had been nothing to laugh about at the moment when the incident took place. Then her emotion had been shock, even fear. The disturbing scene in question was enacted while Edith and I were out for our traditional Sunday 'walk', which took its usual form that afternoon of crossing the Common. We were away from home about an hour and a half, perhaps two hours. Meanwhile, my parents and their guests had moved from dining-room to drawing-room, after what was agreed later to rank as one of the best meals Albert had ever cooked.

'Aylmer Conyers does love his food,' my mother used to say.

When announcing that fact, she would speak as if kindly laughter were the only possible manner of passing off lightly so distressing a frailty in friend or relation. Indeed, the General's pride in his own appreciation of the pleasures of the table was regarded by people like my parents, in the fashion of that day, as a tendency to talk rather more than was decent of eating and drinking. On this occasion he had certainly been full of praise for Albert. Possibly his eulogies continued too long entirely to please my father, who grew easily tired of hearing another man, even his own cook, too protractedly commended. Besides, apart from anything he might feel about the General, the impending arrival of Uncle Giles had justifiably set my father's nerves on edge, in fact thoroughly upset him. As a result he was very fretful by the middle of the afternoon. He freely admitted that afterwards; feeling, indeed, always rather proud of being easily irritated. Mrs Conyers and my mother, come to the end of their gossip, had begun to discuss knitting techniques. Conversation between the two men must have dragged, because the General returned to Near Eastern affairs.

'We haven't heard the last of Enver and his Young Turks,' he said.

'Not by a long chalk,' agreed my father.

'You remember Skobeloff's dictum?'

'Quite so, General, quite so.'

My father rarely, if ever, admitted to ignorance. He could, in any case, be pretty certain of the calibre of any such quotation offered in the circumstances. However, the General was determined there should be no misunderstanding.

'The road to Constantinople leads through the Brandenburger Tor.'

My father had visited Munich, never Berlin. He was, therefore, possibly unaware of the precise locality of the monument to which Skobeloff referred. However, he could obviously grasp the gist of such an assertion in the mouth of one he rightly judged to be a Russian general, linking the aphorism immediately in his own mind with the recent Turkish request for a German officer of high rank to reorganise the Ottoman forces.

'If Liman von Sanders——' began my father.

He never finished the sentence. The name of that militarily celebrated, endlessly discussed, internationally disputed, Britannically unacceptable, German General-Inspector of the Turkish Army was caught, held, crystallised in mid-air. Just as the words left my father's lips, the door of the drawing-room opened quietly. Billson stood on the threshold for a split second. Then she entered the room. She was naked.

'It's always easy to be wise after the event.' My mother used invariably to repeat that saying when the incident was related – and it was to be related pretty often in years to come – implying thereby criticism of herself. Her way was habitually to accept responsibilities which she considered by their nature to be her own, her firm belief being that most difficulties in life could be negotiated by tactful handling. In this case, she ever afterwards regarded herself to blame in having failed to notice earlier that morning that things were far from well with Billson. My mother had, it was true, suspected during luncheon that something was amiss, but by then such suspicion was too late. Billson's waiting at table that day had been perceptibly below – a mere parody of – her accustomed standard. Indeed, her shortcomings in that field had even threatened to mar the good impression otherwise produced on the guests by Albert's cooking. Not only had she proffered vegetables to the General in a manner so entirely lacking in style that he had let fall a potato on the carpet, but she had also caused Mrs Conyers to 'jump' painfully – no doubt in unconscious memory of her father's hoaxes – by dropping a large silver ladle on a Sheffield plate dish-cover. Later, when she brought in the coffee, Billson 'banged down' the tray as if it were red-hot, 'scuttling' from the room.

'I made up my mind to speak to her afterwards about it,' my mother said. 'I thought she wasn't looking at all well. I knew she was a great *malade imaginaire*, but, after all, she had seen the ghost, and her nerves are not at all good. It really is not fair on servants to expect them to sleep in a haunted room, although I have to myself. Where else could we put her? She can't be more frightened than I am sometimes. Then Aylmer Conyers stared at her so dreadfully with those very bright blue eyes of his. I was not at all surprised that she was nervous. I was terrified myself that he was going to begin asking her about the ghost, especially after she had made him drop the potatoes on the floor.'

In short, Billson's maladroitness had been judged to be no more than a kind of minor derangement to be expected from her for at least twenty-four hours after her 'experience', although, as I have said, listening in the first instance to the story about the 'ghost', my mother had been pleased, surprised even, by the calm with which Billson had spoken of the apparition.

'I really thought familiarity was breeding contempt,' said my mother. 'I certainly hoped so, with parlourmaids so terribly hard to come by.'

Albert's announcement of impending marriage was scarcely taken into account. Probably Billson's passion for him had never been accepted very seriously – as, indeed, few passions are by those not personally suffering from them. Possibly I myself knew more of it, from hints dropped by Edith, than did my mother. On top of everything, the prospective arrival of Uncle Giles had distracted attention from whatever else was happening in the house. However, even if the extent of Billson's distress at Albert's decision to marry had been adequately gauged – added, as it were morally speaking, to the probable effect of seeing a ghost that morning – no one could have foreseen so complete, so deplorable, a breakdown.

'I thought it was the end of the world,' my mother said.

I do not know to what extent she intended this phrase, so far as her own amazement was concerned, to be taken literally. My mother's transcendental beliefs were direct, yet imaginative, practical, though possessing the simplicity of complete acceptance. She may have meant to imply, no more, no less, that for a second of time she herself truly believed the Last Trump (unheard in the drawing-room) had sounded in the kitchen, instantly metamorphosing Billson into one of those figures – risen from the tomb, given up by the sea, swept in from the ends of the earth – depicted in primitive paintings of the Day of Judgment. If, indeed, my mother thought that, she must also have supposed some awful, cataclysmic division from on High just to have taken place, violently separating Sheep from Goats, depriving Billson of her raiment. No doubt my mother used only a figure of speech, but circumstances gave a certain aptness to the metaphor.

'Joking apart,' my mother used to say, 'it was a dreadful moment.'

There can be no doubt whatever that the scene was disturbing, terrifying, saddening, a moment that summarised, in the unclothed figure of Billson, human lack of co-ordination and abandonment of self-control in the face of emotional misery. Was she determined, in the habit of neurotics, to try to make things as bad for others as for herself? In that, she largely succeeded. There seemed no solution for the people in the room, no way out of the problem so violently posed by Billson in the shape of her own nude person. My father always confessed afterwards that he himself had been utterly at a loss. He could throw no light whatever on the reason why such a thing should suddenly have happened in his drawing-room, see no way of cutting short this unspeakable crisis. In telling – and re-telling – the highlights of the story, he contributed only one notable phrase.

'She was stark,' he used to say, '*absolutely stark.*'

This was a relatively small descriptive ornament to the really vast saga that accumulated round the incident; at the same time, it was for some reason not without a certain narrative force.

'I've come to give notice, m'm,' Billson said. 'I don't want to stay if Albert is leaving your service, and besides, m'm, I can't stand the ghosts no longer.'

Stonehurst, as I have said, was a 'furnished' house, the furniture, together with pictures, carpets, curtains, all distinctly on the seedy side, all part of the former home of people not much interested in what the rooms they lived in looked like. However, India, one way and another, provided a recurrent theme that gave a certain cohesion to an otherwise undistinguished, even anarchic style of decoration. In the hall, the brass gong was suspended from the horn or tusk of some animal; in the dining-room hung water-colours of the Ganges at Benares, the Old Fort at Calcutta, the Taj Mahal; in the smoking-room, a small revolving bookcase contained only four books: Marie Corelli's *Sorrows of Satan*, St John Clarke's *Never to the Philistines*, an illustrated volume of light verse called *Lays of Ind*, a volume of coloured pictures of Sepoy uniforms; in the drawing-room, the piano was covered with a Kashmir shawl of some size and fine texture, upon which, in silver frames, photographs of the former owner of Stonehurst (wearing a pith helmet surmounted with a spike) and his family (flanked by Indian servants) had stood before being stowed away in a drawer.

In human life, the individual ultimately dominates every situation, however disordered, sometimes for better, sometimes for worse. On this occasion, as usual, all was not lost. There was a place for action, a display of will. General Conyers took in the situation at a glance. He saw this to be no time to dilate further upon Turkish subjection to German intrigue. He rose – so the story went – quite slowly from his chair, made two steps across the room, picked up the Kashmir shawl from where it lay across the surface of the piano. Then, suddenly changing his tempo and turning quickly towards Billson, he wrapped the shawl protectively round her.

'Where is her room?' he quietly asked.

No one afterwards was ever very well able to describe how he transported her along the passage, partly leading, partly carrying, the shawl always decently draped round Billson like a robe. The point, I repeat, was that action had been taken, will-power brought into play. The spell cast by Billson's nakedness was broken. Life was normal again. Other people crowded round, eventually took charge. Mrs Gullick and Mercy appeared from somewhere. The doctor was summoned. It was probably just as well that Albert was having a nap in his room over at the stables, where Bracey, too, surrounded by saddlery, was prolonging his 'funny day'. By the time these two reappeared, the crisis was long at an end. Having taken the first, the essential step, General Conyers, like a military dictator, who, at the close of a successful *coup d'état*, freely transfers his power to the civil authority, now moved voluntarily into the background. His mission was over, the situation mastered. He could return to private life, no more than the guest who happened to have been fortunate enough to find the opportunity of doing his host and hostess a trifling good turn. That was the line the General took about himself when all was over. He would accept neither praise nor thanks.

'She made no trouble at all,' he said. 'More or less walked beside me – just as if we were going to sit out the next one in the conservatory.'

In fact he dismissed as laughable the notion that any difficulty at all attached to the management of Billson in her 'state'. To what extent this modest assessment of his own agency truly represented his experience at the time is hard to estimate. He may have merely preferred to speak of it in that careless manner from dandyism, an unwillingness to admit that anything is difficult. I have sometimes speculated as to how much the General's so successful dislodgement of Billson was due to an accustomed habit of command over 'personnel', how much to a natural aptitude for handling 'women'. He was, after all, known to possess some little dexterity in the latter sphere before marriage circumscribed him.

'Aylmer Conyers couldn't keep away from the women as a young man,' Uncle Giles once remarked. 'They say some fellow chaffed him about it at a big viceregal bun-fight at Delhi – Henry Wilson or another of those talkative beggars who later became generals – "Aylmer, my boy," this fellow, whoever he was, said, "you're digging your grave in bed with Mrs Roxborough-Brown and the rest of them," he said. Conyers didn't give a dam. Not a dam. Went on just the same.'

Whether or not General Conyers would have done well to have heeded that warning, there can be little doubt that some touch of magic in his hand provided Billson with a particle of what she sought, a small substitute for Albert's love, making her docile when led to her room, calming her later into sleep. Certainly he had shown complete disregard for the risk of making a fool of himself in public. That is a merit women are perhaps quicker to appreciate than men. Not that Billson herself can be supposed to have sat in judgment on such subtleties at that uncomfortable moment; yet even Billson's disturbed spirit must have been in some manner aware of a compelling force that bound her to submit without protest to its arbitration.

'I'll just smoke another cigarette, if I may,' said the General, when everything had been accomplished, 'then Bertha and I really must set off in our motor-car. I've got to think about getting down that hill.'

Edith and I returned from the 'walk' just at the moment when General and Mrs Conyers were leaving. Their car had paused at the gate. My parents had come to the end of the drive to see the guests safely down the hill, my father full of advice about gears and brakes. Naturally enough, there was still a certain air of disturbance about the whole party. Even the General looked flushed. When Edith and I appeared, nothing of course was said, there and then, about what had taken place, but I could tell from my mother's face that something very out of the way had happened. The rather forced laughter, the apologies to be heard, confirmed that. The events of the day were by no means at an end, however. My father opened the gate. The Conyers car began to move slowly forward. As it entered the road over a hump in the ground, making rather a jerk, an unexpected impediment was suddenly put in the General's way. This was caused by a group of persons, unusually dressed, who were approaching from the left. They were running towards us. It was Dr Trelawney, followed by a pack of his disciples. They must suddenly have appeared over the brow of the hill. Without pausing to get breath they were now advancing up the road at a sharp pace, Dr Trelawney as usual leading. General Conyers, accelerating through the Stonehurst gate – an awkward one to negotiate – wheeled left, taking the corner in a wide arc, possibly owing to imperfect control of the steering. He had to apply his brakes sharply to avoid collision

537

Dr Trelawney leapt nimbly aside. He was not hit. The car came to a standstill in the middle of the road. General Conyers opened the door and jumped out with all his habitual energy of movement. At first it might have been thought that he intended to call Dr Trelawney to order for obstructing the highway in this manner, strike him, kill him even, like a dog. Some tremendous altercation seemed about to take place. In due course, violence was shown to be far from the General's intention, although for a second or two, while he and Dr Trelawney stood facing each other, anything appeared possible. The same vivid contrast might have been expected, graphically speaking, as when the Military Policeman had ridden through Dr Trelawney's flock, like a hornet flying slowly through a swarm of moths. On the contrary, this pair, so far from being brought into vivid physical and moral opposition, had the air of being linked together quite strongly by some element possessed in common. The General's long, light ulster and helmet-like deerstalker, Dr Trelawney's white draperies and sandals, equally suggested temple ceremonial. The two of them might have met on that high place deliberately for public celebration of some rite or sacrifice. At first neither said a word. That seemed an age. At last Dr Trelawney took the initiative. Raising his right arm slightly, he spoke in a low clear voice, almost in the accents of one whose very perfect enunciation indicates that English is not his native tongue.

'The Essence of the All is the Godhead of the True.'

Then a very surprising thing happened. General Conyers gave an almost imperceptible nod, at the same time removing his hands from the pockets of his ulster.

'The Vision of Visions,' he said, 'heals the Blindness of Sight.'

By that time most of Dr Trelawney's disciples had caught up with their master. They now clustered in the background, whispering together and staring at the car. Through its wind-screen, Mrs Conyers gazed back at them a little nervously, perhaps again fearing that some elaborate practical joke was being staged for her benefit. From the gate my parents watched the scene without approval.

'Well, Trelawney,' said the General, 'I heard you had come to live in this part of the world, but I never thought we should have the luck to run across each other in this way.'

'If you journey towards the Great Gate, you encounter the same wayfarers on the road.'

'True enough, Trelawney, true enough.'

'You are approaching the Sublime Threshold.'

'Do you think so?'

'You should make good your promise to spend a rhythmical month under instruction, General. We have a vacancy in the house. There is no time like the present. You would be subjected to none but probationary exercises at first. Disciplines of the Adept would not be expected of you in the early days.'

'Look here, Trelawney,' said General Conyers, 'I'm a busy man at the moment. Besides, I have a strong convic-tion I should not commit myself too deeply for the rest of the year. Just one of those feelings you have in your bones. I want to be absolutely mobile at the moment.'

'Such instincts should be obeyed. I have heard others say the same recently. The portents are unfavourable. There is no doubt of that.'

'I will write to you one of these days. Nothing I'd like to see more than you and your people at work.'

'At Play, General. Truth is Play.'

'Give me a change of routine. Sort of thing I'm always meaning to do. Got very interested in such things in India. *Bodhisattvas* and such like, *Mahasatipatthana* and all that reflection. However, we shall have to wait. Sure I'm right to wait. Too much business on hand, anyway.'

'Business?' said Dr Trelawney. 'I think you need meditation, General, more than business. You must free the mind from external influences. You must pursue Oneness – the Larger Life.'

'Sure you're right about that too,' said the General. 'Absolutely certain you are right. All the same, something tells me to let Oneness wait for the time being. That doesn't mean I am not going to think Oneness over. Not in the least.'

'Think it over, you must, General. We know we are right. But first you must gain Spiritual Mastery of the Body.'

How long this unusual conversation would have continued in front of the Stonehurst gate, if interruption had not taken place, is hard to say. It was brought to a close by a new arrival, wearing a straw hat and flannel suit, who pushed his way unceremoniously between a group of long-haired boys in short Grecian tunics, who were eyeing the car as if they would very much like to open the bonnet. This person had a small fair moustache. He carried a rolled umbrella and Gladstone bag. The strangeness of Dr Trelawney's disciples clearly made no impression on him. He looked neither to the right nor to the left. The beings round him might just as well have been a herd of cows come to a stop in their amblings along the road. Instead of regarding them, he made straight for my parents, who at once offered signs of recognition. Here was Uncle Giles.

'Hope you did not mind my inviting myself at such short notice,' he said, as soon as he had greeted my mother. 'I wanted to have a word with *him* about the Trust.'

'You know we are always delighted to see you, Giles,' she said, probably even believing that true at the moment of speaking, because she always felt warmly towards hopeless characters like Uncle Giles when they were in difficulties. 'We live so far away from everything and everybody nowadays that it is quite an exception for you to have found Aylmer and Bertha Conyers lunching with us. They were driving away in their motor when——'

She pointed to the road, unable to put into words what was taking place.

'I see Aylmer standing there,' said Uncle Giles, who still found nothing at all unusual in the presence or costume of the Trelawney community. 'I must have a word with him before he leaves. Got a bit of news that might interest him. He is always very keen on what is happening on the Continent. Interest you, too, I expect. I had quite a good journey here. Was lucky enough to catch the carrier. Took me almost to the foot of the hill. Bit of a climb, but here I am.'

He turned to my father.

'How are you?'

Uncle Giles spoke as if he were surprised not to find my father in hospital, indeed, in his coffin.

'Pretty well, Giles,' said my father, with a certain rasp in his voice, 'pretty well. How has the world been wagging with you, Giles?'

That was a phrase my father tended to use when he was not best pleased; in any case his tone graded low as a welcoming manner.

'I wanted to have a talk about business matters,' said Uncle Giles, not at all put out by this reception. 'Mexican Eagles, among other things. Also the Limpopo Development Scheme. There has been rather a crisis in my own affairs. I'd like to ask your opinion. I value it. By the way, did I mention I heard a serious piece of news in Aldershot?'

'What on earth were you doing in Aldershot?' asked my father, speaking without alleviating the irony of his tone.

He must have seen that he was in for a bad time with his brother.

'Had to meet a fellow there. Soldiered together years ago.

Knowledgeable chap. I'll just go across now and have a brief word with Aylmer Conyers.'

Uncle Giles had set down his Gladstone bag by the gate. With characteristic inability to carry through any plan of campaign, he was deflected from reaching the General by the sight of Mrs Conyers sitting in the car. She still looked rather nervous. Uncle Giles stopped and began talking to her. By this time General Conyers himself must have noticed Uncle Giles's arrival. He brought to an end his conversation with Dr Trelawney.

'Well, Trelawney,' he said, 'I mustn't keep you any longer. You will be wanting to lead your people on. Mustn't take up all your day.'

'On the contrary, General, the day – with its antithesis, night – is but an artificial apportionment of what we artlessly call Time.'

'Nevertheless, Trelawney, Time has value, even if artificially apportioned.'

'Then I shall expect to hear from you, General, when you wish to free yourself from bonds of Time and Space.'

'You will, Trelawney, you will. Off you go now – at the double.'

Dr Trelawney drew himself up.

'The Essence of the All is the Godhead of the True.'

The General replied with a jerk of his head.

'The Vision of Visions heals the Blindness of Sight.'

The words were scarcely finished before Dr Trelawney had again begun to hasten along the road, his flock trailing after him. A moment or two later, they were among the trees that concealed Gullick's cottage, where the road became a track. Then the last of them, a very small, pathetic child with a huge head, was finally lost to sight. No doubt they had reached the Common, were pursuing Oneness through the heather. Oneness perhaps also engaged the attention of

General Conyers himself, because, deep in thought, he turned towards the car. He stood there for a second or two, staring at the bonnet. Uncle Giles terminated his conversation with Mrs Conyers.

'I was admiring your new motor-car, General,' he said. 'Hope it is not bringing you as much trouble as most of them seem to cause their owners.'

Now that Dr Trelawney was out of the way, my parents moved towards the car themselves, perhaps partly to keep an eye on Uncle Giles in his relations with the General, still lost in reflection.

'Thought I'd better not introduce you,' said General Conyers, straightening himself as they came up to him. 'One never knows how people may feel about a fellow like Trelawney – especially if he lives in the neighbourhood. Not everybody cares for him. You hear some funny stories. I find him interesting myself. Nasty habits, some people say. Can't believe a word he says, of course. We met him years ago with a fellow I used to know in the Buffs who'd taken up yoga.'

The General lifted the starting-handle from the floor of the car.

'Are you an expert in these machines, Giles?' he asked.

He used the tone of one speaking to a child, not at all the manner of an equal in which he had addressed me earlier in the day. Knowing all about Uncle Giles, he was clearly determined not to allow himself to be irritated by him.

'Never driven one in my life,' said Uncle Giles. 'Not too keen on 'em. Always in accidents. Some royalty in a motor-car have been involved in a nasty affair today. Heard the news in Aldershot. Fellow I went to see was told on the telephone. Amazing, isn't it, hearing so soon. They've just assassinated an Austrian archduke down in Bosnia. Did it today. Only happened a few hours ago.'

Uncle Giles muttered, almost whispered these facts, speaking as if he were talking to himself, not at all in the voice of a man announcing to the world in general the close of an epoch; the outbreak of Armageddon; the birth of a new, uneasy age. He did not look in the least like the harbinger of the Furies.

'Franz-Ferdinand?' asked General Conyers sharply.

'And his morganatic wife. Shot 'em both.'

'When did you say this happened?'

'This afternoon.'

'And they're both dead?'

'Both of them.'

'There will be trouble about this,' said the General.

He inserted the starting-handle and gave several terrific turns.

'Bad trouble,' he said. 'They'll have to postpone tomorrow night's State Ball. Not a doubt of it. This was a Servian, I suppose.'

'They think so.'

'Was he an anarchist?' asked Mrs Conyers.

'One of those fellows,' said Uncle Giles.

'Mark my words,' said General Conyers, 'this is a disaster. Well, the engine has started. We'd better be off in case it stops again. Good-bye to you both, thank you again enormously. No, no, not another word. I only hope the whole matter settles down all right. Good-bye, Giles. Good-bye, Nicholas. I don't at all like the news.'

They went off down the hill. We all waved. My mother looked worried.

'I don't like the news either,' she said.

'Let me carry your bag, Giles,' said my father. 'You'll find things in a bit of a muddle in the house. One of the maids had an hysterical attack this afternoon.'

'I don't expect it's too easy to get staff up here,' said Uncle Giles. 'Is Bracey still your servant? Albert still cooking for you? You're lucky to have them both. Hope I see something of them. Very difficult to get yourself properly looked after these days. Several things I want to talk about. Rather an awkward situation. I think you may be able to help.'

The whole party was moving towards the house. Edith, who had been standing in the background, now detached me from the grown-ups. We diverged to the nursery. I suppose my father, in the course of the evening, helped to sort out the awkward situation, because Uncle Giles left the following day. No one yet realised that the Mute with the Bow-string stood at the threshold of the door, that, if they wanted to get anything done in time of peace, they must be quick about it. Already, the sands had almost run out. The doctor, for example, ordered a 'complete holiday' for Billson. Inquiries revealed that she had gone to rest in her room that afternoon, where, contemplating her troubles, she had fallen asleep to awaken later in a 'state', greatly disturbed, but about which she could otherwise remember little or nothing. No doubt one of those nervous shifts of control had taken place within herself, later to be closely studied, then generally regardéd as a sudden display of 'dottiness'. It was, of course, agreed that she must go. Billson herself was insistent on that point. That decision on both sides was to be expected. Although the story passed immediately into legend, surprisingly little fuss was made about it at the time. A few days later – while the chancelleries of Europe entered into a ferment of activity – Billson, escorted by Edith, quietly travelled to Suffolk, where her family could take care of her for a time. Left alone with my mother during Edith's absence from home on that occasion, I first heard a fairly full and reliable account of the story, fragments of which had, of course, already reached me in more or less garbled versions, from other sources. A long time passed before all the refinements of the saga were recorded and classified.

I do not know for certain what happened to Billson. Even my mother, with all her instinct for not losing touch with the unfortunate, lost sight of her during the war. More than thirty years later, however, what may have been a clue took shape. When Rosie Manasch – or Rosie Udall, as she had then become – used to hold a kind of salon in her house in Regent's Park, she often told stories of a 'daily' she had employed during or just after the war, a former parlourmaid of the old-fashioned kind, who liked to talk about the people for whom she had worked. By then she was called 'Doreen', and said she was nearly seventy.

'She looked years younger,' Rosie said, 'perhaps in her fifties. A man behaved badly to her. I could never make out if he was a butler or a chef. She also had some rather good ghost-stories when she was on form.'

It was all too complicated to explain to Rosie, but this legendary lost love might well have been Albert incorporated – in the way myths are formed – with Billson's earlier 'disappointment'. Albert himself, as might be expected, was greatly outraged by Billson's behaviour that Sunday afternoon, even though he himself had suffered no inconvenience from the immediate circumstances of her 'breakdown'.

'I told you that girl would go off her crumpet,' he said more than once afterwards.

No doubt a series of 'funny days' would normally have been induced in Bracey, but, as things turned out, neither he nor Albert had much time to brood over Billson's surprising conduct. International events took their swift, their ominous, course, Bracey, characteristically, being swept into a world of action, Albert, firm as ever in his fight for the quiet life, merely changing the locality of his cooking-pots. To my mother, Mrs Conyers wrote:

'. . . I was *so glad* Aylmer did not make you meet that

very rum friend of his with the beard. He would have been quite capable of introducing you! I do not encourage him to see *too much* of that person. I think between you and me there is something *very odd* about the man. I would rather you did not mention to anyone – unless you know them *very well* – that Aylmer sometimes talks of staying with *him*. Nothing would induce *me* to go! I do not think that Aylmer will ever pay the visit because he feels sure the house will be *very uncomfortable*. No bathroom! What a *dreadful* thing this murder in Austria-Hungary is. Aylmer is very much afraid it may lead to war. . . .'

General Conyers was right. Not many weeks later – by that time my father and Bracey had been shipped to France with the Expeditionary Force – squads of recruits began to appear on the Common, their evolutions in the heather performed in scarlet or dark blue, for in those early days of the war there were not enough khaki uniforms to go round. Some wore their own cloth caps over full-dress tunics or marched along in column of fours dressed in subfusc civilian suits, so that once more the colour values of the heath were transformed. These exercises of 'Kitchener's Army' greatly perturbed Albert, although his 'feet' precluded any serious suggestion of military service. He used to discuss with Gullick, the gardener, the advisability of offering himself, 'feet' or no 'feet', in the service of his country.

'If you don't volunteer, they'll come and take you,' he would say, 'they're going to put the blokes who haven't volunteered at the head of the column and march 'em along in their shame without any buttons to their uniforms – just to show they had to be forced to join.'

Gullick, silent, elderly, wizened, himself too old to be called to the colours except in the direst need, nodded grimly, showing no disposition to dissent from the menacing possibilities put forward.

'And I'll soon be a married man too,' said Albert, groaning aloud.

However, like my father, Uncle Giles and General Conyers, Albert survived the war. He spent melancholy years cooking in some large canteen, where there was no alternative to producing food at a level painful to his own standards. When peace came at last, he felt, perhaps justly, that he had suffered as much as many who had performed, at least outwardly, more onerous acts of service and sacrifice. He used to write to my mother every Christmas. The dreaded marriage turned out – as Albert himself put it – 'no worse than most'. It appeared, indeed, better than many. Others were less fortunate. Bracey's 'funny days' came to an end when he was killed in the retreat – or, as we should now say, the withdrawal – from Mons. The Fenwicks' father was killed; Mary Barber's father was killed; Richard Vaughan's father was killed; the Westmacott twins' father was killed. Was the Military Policeman who used to jog across the heather killed? Perhaps his duties kept him away from the line. Did the soldier who chopped off his trigger-finger save his own life by doing so? It is an interesting question. Dr Trelawney gave up his house. Edith was told by Mrs Gullick that she had heard as a fact that he had been shot as a spy at the Tower of London. We left Stonehurst and its 'ghosts', inexplicably mysterious bungalow, presaging other inexplicable mysteries of life and death. I never heard whether subsequent occupants were troubled, as Billson and others had been troubled, by tall white spectres, uncomfortable invisible presences. Childhood was brought suddenly, even rather brutally, to a close. Albert's shutters may have kept out the suffragettes: they did not effectively exclude the Furies.

2

IT IS ODD TO THINK THAT ONLY FOURTEEN
or fifteen years after leaving Stonehurst, essentially a haunt of
childhood, I should have been sitting with Moreland in the
Hay Loft, essentially a haunt of maturity: odd, in that such
an appalling volume of unavoidable experience had to be
packed into the intervening period before that historical
necessity could be enacted. Perhaps maturity is not quite the
word; anyway, childhood had been left behind. It was early
one Sunday morning in the days when Moreland and I first
knew each other. We were discussing the roots and aims of
action. The Hay Loft – now no more – was an establishment
off the Tottenham Court Road, where those kept up late by
business or pleasure could enjoy rather especially good bacon-
and-eggs at any hour of the night. Rarely full at night-time,
the place remained closed, I think, during the day. Certainly
I never heard of anyone's eating there except in the small
hours. The waiter, white-haired and magisterial, a stage
butler more convincing than any to be found in private
service, would serve the bacon-and-eggs with a flourish to
sulky prostitutes, who, nocturnal liabilities at an end, in-
filtrated the supper-room towards dawn. Moreland and I had
come from some party in the neighbourhood, displeasing, yet
for some reason hard to vacate earlier. Moreland had been
talking incessantly – by then a trifle incoherently – on the
theme that action, stemming from sluggish, invisible sources,
moves towards destinations no less indefinable.

'If action is to be one's aim,' he was saying, 'then is it

action to write a symphony satisfactory to oneself, which no one else wants to perform, or a comic song every errand-boy whistles? A bad example – a comic song, obviously. Nothing I should like to do better, if I had the talent. Say some ghastly, pretentious half-baked imitation of Stravinsky that makes a hit and is hailed as genius. We know it's bad art. That is not the point. Is it action? Or *is* that the point? Is art action, an alternative to action, the enemy of action, or nothing whatever to do with action? I have no objection to action. I merely find it impossible to locate.'

'Ask the Surrealists. They are keen on action. Their magazine had a photograph on the cover the other day with the caption: *One of our contributors insulting a priest.*'

'Exactly,' said Moreland. 'Violence – revolt – sweep away the past. Abandon bourgeois values. Don't be a prisoner of outworn dogmas. I'm told on all sides that's how one should behave, that I must live intensely. Besides, the abominable question of musical interpretation eternally bedevils a composer's life. What could make one brood on action more than a lot of other people taking over when it comes to performance, giving the rendering of the work least sympathetic to yourself?'

'You might say that happens in love, too, when the other person takes charge of the performance in a manner unsympathetic to yourself.'

'All right,' said Moreland, 'love, then. Is it better to love somebody and not have them, or have somebody and not love them? I mean from the point of view of action – living intensely. Does action consist in having or loving? In having – naturally – it might first appear. Loving is just emotion, not action at all. But is that correct? I'm not sure.'

'It is a question Barnby would consider absurd.'

'Nevertheless, I put it to you. Can the mere haver be said to live more intensely than the least successful lover? That is, if action *is* to live with intensity. Or is action only when you bring off both – loving and having – leaving your money on, so to speak, like a double-event in racing. Speaking for myself, I get the worst of all worlds, failing to have the people I love, wasting time over the others, whom I equally fail to have.'

'You should commit a *crime passionnel* to liven things up.'

'When I read about *crimes passionnels* in the papers,' said Moreland, scraping his plate from which the last vestige of egg had already been long removed, 'I am struck not by the richness of the emotions, but by their desperate poverty. On the surface, the people concerned may seem to live with intensity. Underneath, is an abject egotism and lack of imagination.'

'Stendhal did not think so. He said he would rather his wife tried to stab him twice a year than greeted him every evening with a sour face.'

'Still, he remained unmarried. I've no doubt my own wife will do both. Besides, Stendhal was equally keen on the glance, the kiss, the squeeze of the hand. He was not really taken in by the tyranny of action.'

'But surely some *crimes passionnels* are fascinating. Suppose one of his girls murdered Sir Magnus Donners in fantastic circumstances – I leave the setting to your own fevered imagination.'

'Now, Sir Magnus Donners,' said Moreland. 'Is he a man of action? In the eyes of the world, certainly. But does he, in fact, live intensely?'

'Like Stendhal, he has never married.'

'Hardly a *sine qua non* of action,' said Moreland, now rubbing the plate with a lump of bread.

'But a testing experience, surely. The baronet's wife's subsequent married life with the gamekeeper opens up more interesting possibilities than any of their adulterous frolics.'

'D. H. Lawrence's ideas about sexual stimulation,' said Moreland, 'strike me as no less unreal – no less artificial, if you prefer – than any attributed to Sir Magnus Donners. Suburban, narcissistic daydreams, a phallic never-never-land for middle-aged women. However, that is beside the point, which is that I grant, within the sphere of marriage and family life, Sir Magnus has not lived intensely. Setting marriage aside, on the other hand, he has built up a huge fortune, risen to all but the highest peaks in politics, appreciates the arts in a coarse but perfectly genuine manner, always has a succession of pretty girls in tow. Is he to be styled no man of action because he has never married? The proposition is absurd. After all, we are not married ourselves.'

'And, what's more, must cease to live intensely. It's nearly three o'clock.'

'So it is. How time flies.'

'Raining, too.'

'And the buses have stopped.'

'We will return to action on another occasion.'

'Certainly, we will.'

The interest of this conversation, characteristic of Moreland in a discursive mood, lay, of course, in the fact that he subsequently married Matilda Wilson, one of Sir Magnus's 'girls'. The modest account he gave during this discussion at the Hay Loft of his own exploits at that period probably did Moreland less than justice. He was not unattractive to women. At the same time, his own romantic approach to emotional relationships had already caused him to take some hard knocks in that very knockabout sphere. At the moment when we were eating bacon-and-eggs, neither Moreland nor I had yet heard of Matilda. In those days, I think, she had not even come the way of Sir Magnus himself. In fact, that was about the stage in her life when she was married to Carolo, the violinist, a marriage undertaken when she was very young, lasting only about eighteen months. However, 'the great industrialist' – as Barnby used to call Sir Magnus – was already by then one of Moreland's patrons, having commissioned him not long before to write the incidental music for a highbrow film which had Donners backing. Barnby, too, was beginning to sell his pictures to Sir Magnus at about that date. Barnby often talked about 'the great industrialist', who was, therefore, a familiar figure to me – at least in song and story – although I had myself only seen Sir Magnus twice: once at a party of Mrs Andriadis, which I had attended quite fortuitously; a second time, spending a week-end with the Walpole-Wilsons, when I had been taken over to Stourwater. Later on, one heard gossip about a *jolie laide* (in contrast with the 'pretty girls' Moreland had adumbrated at the Hay Loft) with whom Sir Magnus used occasionally to appear. She was called Matilda Wilson, said to be an actress. Sir Magnus and Matilda had parted company – at least were no longer seen together in public – by the time Moreland first met her. Afterwards, when Matilda became Moreland's wife, I used sometimes to wonder whether Moreland himself ever recalled that Hay Loft conversation. If so, rather naturally, he never returned to the subject.

I think it would be true to say of Moreland that, up to a point, he did live with intensity. He worked hard at seasons, at others, concentrated whole-heartedly on amusing himself. This was within the limitations of the diffidence that enclosed him in dealings with women. There could be no doubt that Matilda herself had taken the decision that they should marry. Barnby used to say that women always take that decision. In any case, Matilda liked taking decisions. This taste of hers suited them both at the beginning of their married life, because Moreland was wholly without it, except where his own work was concerned.

'The arts derive entirely from taking decisions,' he used to say. 'That is why they make such unspeakably burdensome demands on all who practise them. Having taken the decisions music requires, I want to be free of all others.'

Moreland's childhood – since I have spoken at some length of childhood – had been a very different affair from my own. In the first place, music, rather than military matters, had been regarded as the normal preoccupation of those round him in the house of his aunt who brought him up. I mean music was looked upon there not only as an art, but also as the familiar means of earning a livelihood. In my own home, the arts, to some very considerable extent respected, were not at all regarded in that essentially matter-of-fact, no-nonsense, down-to-earth manner. When my father was attached to a cavalry regiment at Brighton before we moved to Stonehurst, my parents might attend an occasional concert at the Pavilion; meet Mr Deacon there, afterwards visit his flat. They would even be aware that Mr Deacon was a 'bad' painter. At the same time, painting, 'good' or 'bad' – like music, sculpture, writing and, of course, acting – would immutably remain for them an unusual, not wholly desirable, profession for an acquaintance. Indeed, a 'good' painter, certainly a well-known 'modern' painter (even though 'modernism' in the arts was by no means frowned upon by my father), would be considered even more of a freak than Mr Deacon himself, since being 'well-known' was, by its very nature, something of a social aberration. It was in Mr Deacon's Brighton flat that he produced those huge pictures that might have been illustrations to Miss Orchard's lessons about the gods of Olympus. Mr Deacon, in the words of his great hero, Walt Whitman, used to describe them as 'the rhythmic myths of the Greeks, and the strong legends of the Romans'. The Furies were prob-

ably never represented by his brush, because Mr Deacon
shunned what Dicky Umfraville used always to call 'the
female form divine'.

In the household of Moreland's aunt, on the other hand,
although there might be no money to spare – keeping sol-
vent in itself rather a struggle – relatively celebrated persons
flourished, so to speak, just round the corner. Moreland
himself rather reluctantly agreed that some of the musicians
who turned up there were 'quite famous', even if the
writers and painters 'showed an abysmal lack of talent'.
'Modernism' in the arts, if not much practised, was freely
discussed. Life was seedy; it was also conducted on a plane
in general more grown-up, certainly more easygoing, than
existence at Stonehurst; for that matter at any of the other
ever changing residences I had known as a child. For
Moreland, the war had been no more than a mysterious, disturbing inconvenience in the background, the disagreeable
cause to which indifferent or inadequate food was always
attributed. It was not the sudden conversion into action of
an idea already to a great extent familiar – even though the
stupendous explosion of that idea, rendered into action, had
never wholly ceased to ring in one's ears. These were not the
only dissimilarities of upbringing. From an early age, Moreland was looked upon by his aunt, and everyone else in their
circle, as a boy destined to make a brilliant career in music.
Even his childhood had been geared to that assumption. My
own more modest ambition – not, as it happened, particularly
encouraged by my parents – was to become a soldier. That
obviously entailed a divergent manner of regarding oneself.
In so far as we ever compared notes about our respective
environments in early life, Moreland always maintained that
mine sounded the stranger of the two.

'Ours was, after all, a very bourgeois bohemianism,' he
used to say. 'Attending the Chelsea Arts Ball in absolutely

historically correct Renaissance costume was regarded as the height of dissipation by most of the artists we knew. Your own surroundings were far more bizarre.'

Perhaps he was right. What Moreland and I possessed unexpectedly in common, however, was on the whole more remarkable than these obvious contrasts. With only a month or two between our ages, some accumulation of shared experience was natural enough: the dog following Edward VII's coffin, the Earls Court Exhibition, tents in Hyde Park for George V's coronation – those all found a place. There were, however, in addition to these public spectacles, certain unaccountable products of the *Zeitgeist* belonging to both childhoods, contributing some particle to each personal myth, so abundant in their way that Moreland and I sometimes seemed to have known each other long before meeting for the first time one evening in the saloon bar of the Mortimer.

For example, in the face of energetic protest at the time, neither, on grounds that the theme was too horrific for the eyes of young persons, had been allowed to attend that primitive of cinematographic art, the film version of Dante's *Inferno*. Later, less explicably, both had taken a passionate interest in the American Civil War and the Dreyfus Case, poring over pictures of those two very dissimilar historical events wherever their scenes and characters could be found illustrated. There were also aesthetic prejudices in common: animosity towards R. M. Ballantyne's *The Coral Island*, capricious distaste for framed reproductions of Raphael's *La Madonna della Sedia*.

One of these altogether unwarrantable items in this eccentric scrapbook of faded mementoes that Moreland and I seemed to have pasted up together in the nursery (though Moreland always denied having had a nursery, certainly a nurse) was a precocious awareness of Dr Trelawney, for 'the Doctor' – as Moreland liked to call him – had never, in fact, suffered the fate, attributed to him by Mrs Gullick, of being shot in the Tower. Moreland's Trelawney experiences had been acquired earlier than my own, though still young enough to experience the same uneasy thrill, alarming, yet enjoyable, at the thought of his menacing shadow.

'I used to hear about Trelawney long before I saw him,' Moreland said. 'One of the down-at-heel poets we knew was a friend of his – indeed, the two of them were said to have enjoyed the favours of succubi together out on the Astral Plane. I first set eyes on him when we were living in rooms at Putney. The time is fixed in my mind because of a bit of trouble with the landlady. The fact was my aunt had bought tickets for a concert with money that ought to have gone in paying the rent. Trelawney was pointed out to me that afternoon in the Queen's Hall. He has musical interests, you know – I may add, of the most banal kind. I remember the wonderfully fraudulent look on his face as he sat listening to Strauss' *Death and Transfiguration*, dressed in a black cape, hair down to his shoulders, rather like photographs of Rasputin.'

'He must have changed his style since my day. Then he was a more outdoor type, with classical Greek overtones.'

'Trelawney was always changing his style – even his name, too, I believe, which is, of course, no more Trelawney than my own is. Nor does anyone know why he should be addressed as Doctor. What was more exciting, my aunt knew a girl who – to use her own phrase – fell into his clutches. She was said to be a promising pianist. That must have been before I went to the Royal College, because I remember being more impressed by the idea of a female pianist who was promising, than I should have been after emerging from that famous conservatoire.'

'What happened to the girl?'

'Rather dreadful. She cast herself from a Welsh mountain-top – Trelawney had a kind of temple at that time in a remote farmhouse in North Wales. There was quite a scandal. He was attacked in one of the Sunday papers. It passed off, as such attacks do.'

'What had he done to the girl?'

'Oh, the usual things, I suppose – no doubt less usual ones, too, since Trelawney is an unusual man. In any case, possibilities are so limited even for a thaumaturge. The point was her subsequent suicide. There was talk of nameless rites, drugs, disagreeable forms of discipline – the sort of thing that might rather appeal to Sir Magnus Donners.'

'Did you ever meet Trelawney yourself?'

'When I first knew Maclintick, who numbered among his acquaintances some of the most unlikely people, he offered to take me to see the Doctor, then living in Shepherd's Bush. In principle, Maclintick disapproved of persons like that, but he and Trelawney used to talk German philosophy together. They had been educated at the same German university – Bonn, I think – and it was a type of conversation hard to obtain elsewhere.'

'Did you go?'

'Somehow, I never found myself in the mood. I felt it might be embarrassing.

> *Oisive jeunesse*
> *A tout asservie*
> *Par délicatesse*
> *J'ai perdu ma vie.*

That was me in those days.'

'I shouldn't have thought much delicacy was required where Dr Trelawney was concerned.'

'My own occult interests are so sketchy. I've just thumbed over *Dogme et Rituel de la Haute Magie*. Never participated in a Black Mass in my life, or as much as received an invitation to a witches' Sabbath.'

'But I thought Dr Trelawney was more for the Simple Life, with a touch of yoga thrown in. I did not realise he was committed to all this sorcery.'

'After you knew him, he must have moved further to the Left – or would it be to the Right? Extremes of policy have such a tendency to merge.'

'Trelawney must be getting on in age now – Cagliostro in his latter days, though he has avoided incarceration up to date.'

'What will happen to people like him as the world plods on to standardisation? Will they cease to be born, or find jobs in other professions? I suppose there will always be a position for a man with first-class magical qualifications.'

That conversation, too, had taken place long before either of us was married. I recalled it, years later, reading in a weekly paper a letter from Dr Trelawney protesting that some reviewer (Mark Members, as a matter of fact), in noticing a recently published work on prophecy and sortilege in which the author approached the subject in the light of psychiatry and telepathy, had confused the sayings of Paracelsus and Nostradamus. This letter (provoking a lively reply from Members) was composed in Dr Trelawney's most florid manner. I wondered if Moreland would see it. It was a long time since we had met. When we were first married, Moreland and Matilda, Isobel and I, used often to see one another. Now those dinners at Foppa's or the Strasbourg took place no longer. They seemed to form an historic period, distinct and definable, even though less remote in time, as the infinitely distant days when Moreland and I had loitered about Soho together.

To explain why you see less of a friend, though there has been no quarrel, no gradual feeling of coldness, is not always easy. In this case, the drawing apart seemed to date from the time when something had been 'on' between Moreland and Isobel's sister, Priscilla. During that period, with Moreland's own marriage in the balance, we had seen little or nothing of him, because the situation was inevitably an awkward one. Now, the Morelands seemed to have settled down again pretty well; Priscilla was married to Chips Lovell. However, married life must always be a little different after an upheaval of that kind. With the Morelands, certain changes were observable from the outside; within, no doubt even more radical adjustments had taken place. Now, as a matter of course, Matilda accepted such parts as she could obtain as an actress. She had made some success in the role of Zenocrate in Marlowe's *Tamburlaine the Great*. She was often away from home for weeks at a time. Moreland himself, moving inexorably into a world exclusively musical in its interests, spent increasing periods working in his room. That was at first the reason why we saw less of him than ever, even after the business with Priscilla had come to an end. By that time, as easily happens, the habit of regular meetings had already passed. We would sometimes talk on the telephone or run across each other casually. Then a further barrier was raised, when, to the surprise of his friends, Moreland announced that he had decided to leave London.

'I'm not going to settle in the country for ever,' he said, 'just retreat for a time from the telephone.'

Moreland, dependent for most of his social life on restaurants and bars, had never been a great hand at entertaining in his own house. Accordingly, after the move, contact ceased almost entirely. That was, in any case, a decidedly eerie period in which to be living. Unlike the Stonehurst epoch, when, whatever jocular references to a German invasion might be made by persons like Bracey, war had come for most people utterly without warning – like being pushed suddenly on a winter's day into a swirling whirlpool of ice-cold water by an acquaintance, unpredictable perhaps, but not actively homicidal – war was now materialising in slow motion. Like one of the Stonehurst 'ghosts', war towered by the bed when you awoke in the morning; unlike those more transient, more accommodating spectres, its tall form, so far from dissolving immediately, remained, on the contrary, a looming, menacing shape of ever greater height, ever thickening density. The grey, flickering sequences of the screen showed with increased persistence close-ups of stocky demagogues, fuming, gesticulating, stamping; oceans of raised forearms; steel-helmeted men tramping in column; armoured vehicles rumbling over the *pavé* of broad boulevards. Crisis was unremitting, cataclysm not long to be delayed.

Such an atmosphere was not at all favourable to writing novels, the activity which chiefly occupied my own thoughts, one that may require from time to time some more or less powerful outside stimulus in the life of a writer, but needs, in between any such disturbances, long periods of comparative calm. Besides, the ancillaries of a writer's profession, the odd jobs that make such an existence financially surmountable, were at that period in by no means a flourishing condition. I was myself in lowish water and, what was worse, found it difficult, almost impossible, to work on a book while waiting for the starting pistol. Even Chips Lovell, who possessed relatively well-paid employment on a newspaper (contributing to a column of innocuous, almost self-respecting 'gossip'), lived, like others in Fleet Street, in recurrent fear of being told his services were redundant.

Since Chips had married Priscilla, he had shown signs of turning into a model husband. Some people regarded him as an incurably raffish young man, but now the interest he had always taken in the affairs of his many relations became redoubled, growing almost feverish in its intensity. He attended marriages, christenings, funerals as if his life depended on it, as, indeed, to some extent it did, since he would usually introduce later into his column discreet reference to such ceremonies. The trifles Chips offered the public were on the whole inoffensive enough, sometimes even of general interest. All the same, not everyone approved of them: Isobel's eldest sister, Frederica Budd, who, since the recent death of the Tollands' stepmother, Lady Warminster, more than ever felt herself custodian of the family's moral and social standards, found Chips's 'paragraphs' particularly vexatious. In any case, Frederica did not much care for Chips, although she, and everyone else, had to admit that his marriage to Priscilla must be reckoned a success. The Lovells had a baby; Priscilla had become quieter, some complained a little sadder, but at the same time her looks had improved, so that now she could almost be called a 'beauty'. Since Moreland had long since removed himself almost entirely from the kind of society in which Chips Lovell liked to move – was to some extent even professionally committed – the two couples never met. Such a meeting would certainly not have embarrassed Chips, who neither minded nor was in a position to mind about such refinements of sensibility where love affairs were concerned. Moreland on the other hand, once things were broken off with Priscilla, certainly preferred to keep out of her and her husband's way.

Then one day, not long after 'Munich', when everyone's nerves were in a thoroughly disordered state, some relieved, some more apprehensive than ever, Isobel ran across Matilda in the hairdresser's. There was a great reunion. The end of it was that a week-end visit was arranged immediately to the Morelands' cottage. Life was humdrum enough at that moment, even though we were living in so unstable, so harassing a period. I mean the events that took place while we were staying with the Morelands formed not only something of a landmark when looked back upon, but were also rather different from the material of which daily life was in general composed.

'Matilda is dying for company,' Isobel said, when she told me of their meeting.

'How is she?'

'Not bad. Out of a job. She says she has decided she is a terrible actress. She is going to give up the stage and take to petit point.'

'Where exactly are they living?'

'A few miles from Stourwater.'

'I had no idea of that. Was it deliberate?'

'Matilda knows the district. She was brought up there. At first I was too delicate to ask how near they were to the castle. Then Matty said Sir Magnus had actually found the cottage for them. Matty rather likes talking of her days with Sir Magnus if one is *tête-à-tête*. They represent, I think, the most restful moment of her life.'

'Life with Hugh can't be very restful.'

'Hugh doesn't seem to mind about being near Stourwater. Matilda said he was delighted to find a cottage so easily.'

I was not sure that I agreed in believing Moreland so indifferent to the proximity of Sir Magnus Donners. It is true that men vary in attitude towards previous husbands and lovers of their wife or mistress. As it happened, that was a favourite theme of Moreland's. Some, at least outwardly, are to all appearance completely unconcerned with what experiences a woman may have had – and with whom – before they took her on; others never become reconciled to their forerunners. I remembered Moreland saying that Matilda's father had kept a chemist's shop in that part of the world. There was a story about her first having met Sir Magnus when she was organising a school play in the precincts of the castle. One side of Moreland was certainly squeamish about the matter of his wife's former connexion with Sir Magnus, the other, tolerant, sceptical, indolent about his own life – even his emotional life – welcomed any easy solution when it came to finding somewhere to live. The cottage might be in the shadow of Stourwater, or anywhere else. It was the characteristic split personality that the arts seem specially to require, even to augment in those who practise them. Matilda, of course, knew very well the easygoing, inactive side of her husband; her grasp of that side of his character was perhaps her chief power over him. She could judge to a hair's breadth just how much to make a convenience of having been Sir Magnus's mistress, while stopping short of seriously upsetting Moreland's susceptibilities on that score. Such at least, were the terms in which I myself assessed the situation. That was the background I expected to find when we stayed at the cottage. I thought that half-humorous, half-masochistic shame on Moreland's part at thus allowing his wife to make use of a rich man who had formerly 'kept' her would express itself in banter, partly designed to punish himself for allowing such circumstances to arise.

As it happened, conversation had turned on Sir Magnus Donners a night or two before we were invited to the Morelands'. We were dining (at short notice, because a more 'political' couple had dropped out) with Isobel's sister, Susan, married to Roddy Cutts, a Tory back-bencher. Susan greatly enjoyed giving small political dinner-parties. Roddy, hardly drinking anything himself, saw no reason to encourage the habit in others, so that wine did not exactly flow. Current affairs, however, were unrestrainedly discussed. They inhabited a hideous little mansion flat in Westminster, equipped with a 'division bell' for giving warning when Roddy's vote was required in 'the House'. Said to be rather a 'coming man' in the Conservative Party, he was in some disgrace with its leaders at that moment, having thrown in his lot with Churchill, Eden and the group who had abstained from voting in the 'Munich' division. That evening another MP, Fettiplace-Jones, was present with his wife. Fettiplace-Jones, a supporter of the Government's policy, was at the same time too wary to cut himself off entirely from dissident members of the party. Like Roddy, his contemporary in age, he represented a northern constituency. Tall, handsome, moon-faced, with a lock of hair trained across his high forehead for the caricaturist, he seemed to require only side-whiskers and a high collar to complete the picture of a distinguished politician of the nineteenth century. His untiring professional geniality rivalled even Roddy's remorseless charm of manner. His wife, an eager little woman with the features of the Red Queen in *Alice in Wonderland* – possibly advised by her husband not to be controversial about Czechoslovakia – spoke sagely of public health and housing. Fettiplace-Jones himself seemed to be exploring avenues of thought that suggested no basic disagreement between himself and Roddy; in short, he himself acknowledged that we must continue to prepare for the worst. When the men were left alone, Fettiplace-Jones, rightly deciding no cigars would be available, took one from his pocket and smelled it.

'The sole survivor,' he said apologetically, as he made an incision. 'Were you in the House when Attlee said that "armaments were not a policy"?'

'Bobetty was scathing,' said Roddy. 'By the same token, I was talking to Duff about anti-aircraft shortages the other night.'

'This continued opposition to conscription is going to do Labour harm in the long run,' said Fettiplace-Jones, who no doubt wanted to avoid anything like a head-on clash, 'even if things let up, as I hope they will.'

'I hope you're right,' said Roddy, who was being more brusque than usual. 'All the same, you'll probably agree we ought to tackle problems of civil evacuation and food control.'

'Do you know Magnus Donners?'

'Never met him.'

'I remember being greatly impressed by him as a boy,' said Fettiplace-Jones. 'I was taken to the House to hear a debate.'

He placed his hand on his forehead, grasping the errant lock, leaning back and smiling to himself, perhaps enjoyably contemplating the young Fettiplace-Jones's first sight of the scene of his own future triumphs.

'Not his delivery,' he said quietly. 'That was nothing. It was the mastery of detail. Now Donners is the sort of man to handle some of those administrative problems.'

'Not too old?'

'He knows the unions and gets on well with them.'

'What does he think about the Czechs?'

'Convinced nothing could be done short of war – at the same time not at all keen on the present situation. More of your view than mine.'

'Is he, indeed?' said Roddy. 'It looked at one moment as if Donners would go to the Lords.'

'I doubt if he ever wanted a peerage,' said Fettiplace-Jones. 'He has no children. My impression is that Donners is gearing his various concerns to the probability of war in spite of the settlement.'

'Is he?' said Roddy.

He had evidently no wish for argument with Fettiplace-Jones at that moment. The subject changed to the more general question of international guarantees.

I knew less of the political and industrial activities of Sir Magnus, than of his steady, if at times capricious, patronage of the arts. Like most rich patrons, his interests leant towards painting and music, rather than literature. Moreland described him as knowing the name of the book to be fashionably discussed at any given moment, being familiar with most of the standard authors. There Sir Magnus's literary appreciation stopped, according to Moreland. He took no pleasure in reading. No doubt that was a wise precaution for a man of action, whose imagination must be rigorously disciplined, if the will is to remain unsapped by daydreams, painting and music being, for some reason, less deleterious than writing in that respect. I listened to Roddy and Fettiplace-Jones talking about Sir Magnus, without supposing for a moment that I should meet him again in the near future. He existed in my mind as one of those figures, dominating, no doubt, in their own remote sphere, but slightly ridiculous when seen casually at close quarters.

We had no car, so reached the Morelands' by train.

'It must be generations since anyone but highbrows lived in this cottage,' said Moreland, when we arrived there. 'I imagine most of the agricultural labourers round here commute from London.'

'Baby Wentworth had it at one moment,' said Matilda, a little maliciously. 'She hated it and moved out almost at once.'

'I've installed a piano in the studio,' said Moreland. 'I get some work done when I'm not feeling too much like hell, which hasn't been often, lately.'

The cottage was a small, redbrick, oak-beamed affair, of some antiquity, though much restored, with a studio-room built out at the back. That was where Moreland had put his piano. He was not looking particularly well. When they were first married, Matilda had cleaned him up considerably. Now, his dark-blue suit – Moreland never made any concession to the sartorial conception of 'country clothes' –

looked as if he had spent a restless night wearing it in bed. He had not shaved.

'What's been wrong?'

'That lung of mine has been rather a bore.'

'What are you working on?'

'My ballet.'

'How is it going?'

'Stuck.'

'It's impossible to write with Hitler about.'

'Utterly.'

He was in low spirits. His tangled, uncut hair emphasised the look his face sometimes assumed of belonging to a fractious, disappointed child. Matilda, on the other hand, so far from being depressed, as Isobel had represented her, now seemed lively and restless. She was wearing trousers that revealed each bone of her angular figure. Her greenish eyes, rather too large mouth, for some reason always made one think she would make a more powerful, more talented actress than her stage capabilities in fact justified. These immediately noticeable features, arresting rather than beautiful, also suggested, in some indirect manner, her practical abilities, her gift for organisation. Matilda's present exhilaration might be explained, I thought, by the fact that these abilities were put to more use now than when the Morelands had lived in London. There, except late at night, or when they lay in bed late in the morning, they were rarely to be found in their flat. Here, they must be alone together most of the day, although no doubt much of the time Moreland was shut away in the studio at work. Matilda, when not acting, had sometimes complained in London that time hung on her hands, even though she was – or had formerly been to some extent – a kind of agent for Moreland, arranging much of his professional life, advising as to what jobs he accepted, what interviews he gave, when he must be left in peace. All the same, as I have said, it was chiefly matters outside the musical world that caused him pain and grief. In the business sphere, Matilda no doubt took a burden from him; in his musical life, as such, he may sometimes even have resented too much interference. Since the baby had died, they had had no other child.

'You are eating sausages tonight,' said Matilda, 'and half-a-crown Barbera. As you know, I'm not a great cook. However, you'll have a square meal tomorrow, as we're going over to Stourwater for dinner.'

'Can you bear it?' said Moreland. 'I'm not sure I can.'

'Do cheer up, darling,' said Matilda. 'You know you'll like it when we get there.'

'Not so sure.'

'Anyway, it's got to be faced.'

Things had certainly changed. Formerly, Moreland had been the one who liked going to parties, staying up late, drinking a lot; Matilda, bored by people, especially some of Moreland's musical friends, wanted as a rule to go home. Now the situation seemed reversed: Matilda anxious for company, Moreland immersed in work. Matilda's tone, her immediate manner of bringing up the subject of Stourwater, was no doubt intended to show in the plainest terms that she herself felt completely at ease so far as visiting Sir Magnus was concerned. Although she had never attempted to conceal her former association with him – which would certainly not have been easy – she seemed to feel that present circumstances required her specially to emphasise her complete freedom from embarrassment. This demeanour was obviously intended to cover Moreland in that respect, as well as herself. She was announcing their policy as a married couple. Possibly she did not altogether carry Moreland with her. He was rebellious about something, even if not about the visit to Stourwater.

'Have you seen the place before?' he asked. 'You realise we are going to conduct you to a Wagnerian castle, a palace where Ludwig of Bavaria wouldn't have been ashamed to disport himself.'

'I was there about ten years ago. Some people called Walpole-Wilson took me over. They live twenty or thirty miles away.'

'I've heard Donners speak of them,' said Matilda.

She always referred to Sir Magnus by his surname. Isobel and I used to discuss whether Matilda had so addressed him in their moments of closest intimacy.

'After all,' Isobel had said, 'she can only have liked him for his money. To call him "Donners" suggests capital appreciation much more than a pet-name. Besides, "Magnus" – if one could bring oneself to call him that – is almost more formal than "Donners", without the advantage of conjuring up visions of dividends and allotment letters.'

'Do you think Matilda only liked him for his money? She never attempted to get any out of him.'

'It's not a question of *getting* the money. It's the money itself. Money is a charm like any other charm.'

'As a symbol of power?'

'Partly, perhaps. After all, men and women both like power in the opposite sex. Why not take it in the form of money?'

'Do you really think Matilda liked nothing else about poor Sir Magnus?'

'I didn't think him very attractive myself the only time I saw him.'

'Perhaps Matilda was won by his unconventional ways.'

'Perhaps.'

'You don't think so?'

'I don't express an opinion.'

'Still, I must agree, she left him in the end.'

'I think Matilda is quite ambitious,' said Isobel.

'Then why did she leave Sir Magnus? She might have made him marry her.'

'Because she took a fancy to Hugh.'

That was no doubt the answer. I had been struck, at the time she said this, by Isobel's opinion that Matilda was ambitious.

'Who are the Walpole-Wilsons?' asked Moreland.

'Sir Gavin Walpole-Wilson is a retired diplomat. His daughter, Eleanor, has shared a flat for years with Isobel's sister, Norah. But, of course, you know Norah and Eleanor of old.'

Moreland reddened at the mention of Isobel's sisters. Thought of them must still have called Priscilla uneasily to his mind. The subject of sisters-in-law was obviously one to be avoided. However, Matilda showed some inclination to continue to talk of them. She had rescued her husband from Priscilla, whom she could consider to have suffered a defeat. She may have wanted to emphasise that.

'How are Norah and Eleanor?' she asked.

'Eleanor is trying to make up her mind again whether she will become a Catholic convert,' said Isobel. 'Heather Hopkins became an RC the other day. Hugo says that puts Eleanor in a dilemma. She wants to annoy Norah, but doesn't want to please Hopkins.'

'I practically never go to Stourwater,' Moreland said, determined to change the subject from one that could possibly lead back to Priscilla. 'Matty pops over there once in a way to see some high life. I recognise that Donners has his points – has in the past even been very obliging to me personally. The fact remains that when I did the incidental music for that film of his, I saw enough of him to last a lifetime.'

If Matilda had wanted to make clear her sentiments about

571

Stourwater, Moreland had now been equally explicit about his own. The question of the proximity of Sir Magnus perhaps irked him more than he would admit to himself, certainly more than I expected. On inquiry, it appeared that even Matilda's visits to Stourwater were rare. I thought Moreland was just in a bad mood, exaggerating his own dislike for 'going out'. He was not by any means without a taste for occasional forays into rich life. This taste could hardly have been removed entirely by transferring himself to the country. Even in London, he had suffered periods of acute boredom. As the week-end took shape, it became clear that these fits of ennui were by no means a thing of the past. He would sit for hours without speaking, nursing a large tabby cat called Farinelli.

'Do you think this sell-out is going to prevent a war?' he said, when we were reading the papers on Sunday morning.

'No.'

'You think we ought to have fought this time?'

'I don't know. The one thing everybody agrees about is that we aren't ready for it There's no point in going to war if we are not going to win it. Losing's not going to help anybody.'

'What are you going to do when it comes?'

'My name is on one of those various army reserves.'

'How did you manage that?'

'Offered myself, and was accepted, before all this last business started.'

'I can only do ladylike things such as playing the piano,' said Moreland gloomily. 'I suppose I shall go on doing that if there's a show-down. One wonders what the hell will happen. How are we getting to this place tonight?'

'Donners rang up and said one of his guests is picking us up in a car,' said Matilda.

'When did he ring up?'

'When you were all at the pub this morning.'

'Why not tell us?'

'I forgot,' said Matilda. 'I told Donners when we were asked he must arrange something. Finding transport is the least the rich can do, if they hope to enjoy one's company. You must shave, sweetie, before we start.'

'All right, all right,' said Moreland, 'I won't let you all down by my tramp-like appearance. Do we know the name of our chauffeur?'

'Somebody called Peter Templer,' said Matilda. 'Anybody ever heard of him?'

'Certainly I've heard of Peter Templer,' I said. 'He's one of my oldest friends. I haven't seen him for years.'

'Who is he? What's he like?'

'A stockbroker. Fast sports car, loud checks, blondes, golf, all that sort of thing. We were at school together.'

'Wasn't he the brother of that girl you used to know?' said Isobel.

She spoke as if finally confirming a fact of which she had always been a little uncertain, at the same time smiling as if she hardly thought the pretence worth keeping up.

'He was.'

'Which girl?' asked Moreland, without interest.

'A woman called Jean Duport, whom I haven't seen for years.'

'Never heard of her,' said Moreland.

I thought what a long time it seemed since I had visited Stourwater on that earlier occasion, when the luncheon party had been given for Prince Theodoric. Prince Theodoric's name, as a pro-British element in a country ominously threatened from without by German political pressure, had been in the papers recently. Stringham, just engaged to Peggy Stepney, had still been one of Sir Magnus's secretaries. Jean Duport, Peter Templer's sister, had been there and I had wondered whether I was not perhaps in love with her. Now, I did not know where she was, was ignorant of the very hemisphere she inhabited. When last seen – parting infinitely painful – she had been on her way to South America, reunited with her awful husband. Baby Wentworth was still – though not long to remain – Sir Magnus's 'girl'. Matilda must have taken on the job soon after that visit of mine. If mere arrival in the neighbourhood had imparted, of itself, a strong sense of having slipped back into the past, that sensation was certainly intensified by the prospect of meeting Peter Templer again. He had passed from my life as completely as his sister. There was nothing at all surprising about his staying at Stourwater, when I came to examine the question, except his own dislike for houses of that sort. Business affairs might perfectly well have brought him within the orbit of Sir Magnus. One of the odd things about Templer was that, although pretty well equipped for social life of any kind, he found places like Stourwater in general too pretentious for his taste. He preferred circles where there was less competition, where he could safely be tipped as the man most likely to appeal to all the women present, most popular with the men. It was not that Templer was in any way ill-adapted to a larger sort of life, so much as the fact that he himself was unwilling to tolerate that larger life's social disciplines, of which the chief was the ever-present danger of finding himself regarded as less important than someone else. That makes him sound intolerable. Templer was, on the contrary, one of the most easygoing, good-natured of men, but he liked being first in the field. He liked, especially, to be first in the field with women. After Mona left him, I imagined he had returned to this former pursuit.

'I have rather suburban taste in ladies, like everything else,' Templer used to say. 'Golf, bridge, an occasional spot of

574

crumpet, they are all I require to savour my seasonal financial flutter.'

The fact that he could analyse his tastes in this way made Templer a little unusual, considering what those tastes were. I felt pleasure in the thought that I was going to see him again, tempered by that faint uneasiness about meeting a friend who may have changed too much during the interval of absence to make practicable any renewal of former ties.

'We haven't brought any evening clothes,' I said.

'Good God,' said Moreland, 'we're not changing for Donners.'

It was a warm autumnal evening, so that we were all in the garden when Templer's car drew up at the gate. The vehicle was of just the kind I had predicted. Templer, too, as he jumped out, seemed scarcely to have changed at all. The car was shaped like a torpedo; Templer's clothes gave the familiar impression – as Stringham used to say – that he was 'about to dance backwards and forwards in front of a chorus of naked ladies'. That outward appearance was the old Templer, just as he had looked at Dicky Umfraville's night-club four or five years before. Now, as he strode up the path with the same swagger, I saw there was a change in him. This was more than the fact that he was distinctly fatter. A coarseness of texture had always coloured his elegance. Now, that coarseness had become more than ever marked. He looked hard, even rather savage, as if he had made up his mind to endure life rather than, as formerly, to enjoy it. From the first impression that he had changed hardly at all, I reversed judgment, deciding he had changed a great deal. When he saw me he stepped back melodramatically.

'Is it really you, Nick?'

'What's left.'

I introduced him to the Morelands and to Isobel.

'I believe you invited me to your wedding, Nick,' said

Templer. 'Somehow I never manage to get to weddings – it's an effort even to reach my own.'

'Have you been having many weddings lately, Peter?'

'Oh, well, not for a year or two,' said Templer, suddenly becoming more serious. 'You knew I married again after Mona?'

'I didn't, as a matter of fact.'

'Yes, indeed.'

'How shameful that we should have missed the announcement.'

'I'm not sure that we made one,' Templer said. 'It was all very quiet. Hardly asked a soul. Since then – I don't know – we've been living in the country. Just see a few neighbours. Betty doesn't like going out much. She has come to Stourwater this week-end, as a matter of fact, but that's rather exceptional. She felt jumpy for some reason about staying at home. She gets these jumpy fits from time to time. Thinks war's going to break out all the time.'

He smiled rather uncomfortably. I felt suddenly certain that Templer's new wife must be responsible for the change that had come over him. At the same time, I tried, quite unsuccessfully, to rationalise in my own mind what exactly this change was. Now that we were face to face and I was talking to him, it was more than ever apparent, almost horrifying. He had slowed up, become more 'serious', at the same time lost that understanding, sympathetic manner formerly characteristic of him, so unexpected in a person of his sort. That was my first thought. Then I wondered whether, in fact, he was even less 'serious' – if that were possible – determined to ʒet as much fun out of living as he could, whatever the obstacles, whatever the cost. These dissections on my own part were rather absurd; yet there was something not far away from Templer that generated a sense of horror.

'What a nice colour your car is,' said Moreland.

I could see he had at once placed Templer in the category of persons he found unsympathetic. That was to be expected. Just as most of the world find it on the whole unusual that anyone should be professionally occupied with the arts, Moreland could never get used to the fact that most people – in this particular case, Templer – lead lives in which the arts play no part whatsoever. That is perhaps an exaggeration of Moreland's attitude. All the same, he always found difficulty in accustoming himself to complete aesthetic indifference. This narrowness of vision sometimes led Moreland, with all his subtlety in some matters, to complete misunderstanding of others, especially to underestimate some of the people who came his way. On Templer's side, the meeting had been equally lacking in fellow feeling. He had no doubt been prepared for the Morelands to look – from his point of view – a pretty extraordinary couple. From Templer's point of view, it had to be admitted, the Morelands did look pretty extraordinary. Matilda was still wearing trousers, bright emerald green in colour, her feet in immensely thick cork-soled sandals, her hair done up on the top of her head, in the fashion of the moment, like a bird's nest. Moreland had shaved, otherwise made no effort to tidy himself, a carelessly knotted tie slipping away from the buttonless collar of his blue shirt. Templer began to laugh, partly, I supposed, at the thought of our having met again after so long, partly, too, I felt sure, at the strange picture the Morelands presented to one unaccustomed to people like them. Templer must also have known of Matilda's former relationship with Sir Magnus. Perhaps that was what made him laugh.

'Come on,' he said, 'all aboard for Stourwater and the picturesque ruins.'

We climbed into the car. The Morelands were rather silent, because there is always something a shade embarrassing about an old friend suddenly encountering another old friend, quite unknown to you. They were perhaps meditating on their own differences of opinion regarding the desirability of accepting the hospitality of Sir Magnus. Templer himself kept up a running fire of questions, as if anxious to delay the moment when he had to speak of his own life.

'It is really too extraordinary our meeting again in this way, Nick,' he said. 'Though it's just like a millionaire to make one of the persons staying with him fetch the guests for dinner, instead of using his own chauffeur, but now I'm glad Magnus was running true to form. Do you live in London?'

'Yes – and you?'

'We're at Sunningdale.'

'Isn't that where Stringham's mother, Mrs Foxe, has a house?'

'Charles Stringham – I haven't thought of him for years.'

'Does she still live there?'

'She does, as a matter of fact. We don't know them. Rather too grand for us. Odd you should mention Stringham. It wasn't quite true when I said I hadn't thought of him for years, because, as it happened, I ran across Mrs Foxe's naval-officer husband at a golf tournament handicap not so long ago who said something about him.'

'Stringham was knocking it back pretty hard when I last saw him. What did Buster Foxe say? They don't much care for each other.'

'Don't they? I gathered from Commander Foxe they were great pals. Now, what did he say? Gone right out of my head. No, I know – Stringham is living at Glimber, the house Mrs Foxe inherited from her first husband. It's huge, uninhabitable, entailed, nobody wants to rent it. Stringham looks after it apparently. He has a former secretary of his mother's to help him. It's like being an agent, I suppose.'

'Sounds rather grim.'

'Oh, I don't know. Stately home, and all that. Commander Foxe said Charles liked it. Now you come to mention it, he did say something, too, about giving up the bottle. I hadn't realised Stringham's drinking had reached the headline category.'

'He used to hit it fairly hard. The secretary you mention is called Miss Weedon – Tuffy to her intimates. Rather a frightening lady. She has always taken a great hand in arranging Charles's life. In fact, she had more or less undertaken to stop his drinking at one moment. They even lived in the same flat.'

'Wasn't she the Medusa-like figure who appeared at that party Mrs Foxe gave for my symphony?' said Moreland.

'She was. Charles Stringham is Mrs Foxe's son.'

'It was Miss Weedon who hauled him off home when he was so tight.'

'It wasn't a very enjoyable party, anyway,' said Matilda.

I remembered that it had ended by Moreland's disappearing with Isobel's sister, Priscilla. Templer showed no interest at all in these reminiscences. They were not, perhaps, very absorbing in themselves, but he might have been expected to have given them more attention inasmuch as they referred to so old a friend as Stringham.

'Talking of people we knew at school,' he said, 'Kenneth will be at Stourwater this evening.'

'Kenneth who?'

'Kenneth Widmerpool.'

'Oh, yes.'

'You're a friend of his, aren't you?' said Templer, evidently surprised at my not grasping immediately whom he meant. 'I've heard him speak of you. His mother has a cottage near here.'

I saw that it was no longer a question of Stringham and Widmerpool having drawn level as friends in Templer's mind; the fact was that Widmerpool was now miles ahead. That was clear from Templer's tone. There was not a flicker of laughter or irony in his employment of Widmerpool's Christian name, as there had certainly been when I had last seen them together at Dicky Umfraville's night-club. There was, of course, absolutely no reason why Templer should adopt a satirical tone towards Widmerpool, who had as much right as anyone else to make friends with – if necessary, even to dominate – persons like Templer, who had made fun of him as a schoolboy. It was the juxtaposition of his complete acceptance of Widmerpool with Templer's equally complete indifference to his old crony, Stringham, that gave the two things an emphasis that certainly jarred a little. Templer had probably not set eyes on him since the day when he had arrived in Stringham's college room, later driven us all into the ditch in his newly bought car. If it came to that, I never saw Stringham these days myself, while Templer, doing business with Widmerpool for a long time now, had naturally come to regard him as a personal friend. By that time we were entering the park of Stourwater.

'Look, the castle,' said Isobel. 'Nobody warned me it was made of cardboard.'

Cardboard was certainly the material of which walls and keep seemed to be built, as we rounded the final sweep of the drive, coming within sight of a large castellated pile, standing with absurd unreality against a background of oaks, tortured by their antiquity into elephantine and grotesque shapes. From the higher ground at the back, grass, close-cropped by sheep, rolled down towards the greenish pools of the moat. All was veiled in the faint haze of autumn.

'I told you it was Wagnerian,' said Moreland.

'When we wind the horn at the gate, will a sullen dwarf

usher us in,' said Isobel, 'like Beckford's at Fonthill or the Castle of Joyous Gard in the *Morte d'Arthur*?'

'A female dwarf, perhaps,' said Moreland, rather maliciously.

'Don't miss the black swans,' said Matilda, disregarding him.

'An anachronism, I fear,' said Moreland. 'Sir Magnus admitted as much to me in an unguarded moment. They come from Australia. Doesn't it all look as if the safety curtain would descend any moment amid bursts of applause?'

Stourwater was certainly dramatic; yet how unhaunted, how much less ghost-ridden than Stonehurst; though perhaps Sir Magnus himself might leave a spectre behind him. In my memory, the place had been larger, more forbidding, not so elaborately restored. In fact, I was far less impressed than formerly, even experiencing a certain feeling of disappointment. Memory, imagination, time, all building up on that brief visit, had left a magician's castle (brought into being by some loftier Dr Trelawney), weird and prodigious, peopled by beings impossible to relate to everyday life. Now, Stourwater seemed nearer to being an architectural abortion, a piece of monumental vulgarity, a house where something had gone very seriously wrong. We crossed the glittering water by a causeway, drove under the portcullis and through the outer courtyard, entering the inner court, where a fountain stood in the centre of a sunken garden surrounded by a stone balustrade. Here, in the days when he had been first ingratiating himself with Sir Magnus, Widmerpool had backed his car into one of the ornamental urns filled with flowers.

'Is Kenneth Widmerpool staying in the house?' I asked, thinking of that incident.

'Just driving over after dinner,' said Templer. 'Some sort of business to clear up. I'm involved to a small extent, because it's about my ex-brother-in-law, Bob Duport. Between you and me, I think I've been asked partly because Magnus wants me to know what is going on for his own purposes.'

'What are his own purposes?'

'I don't know for certain. Perhaps he wants this particular scheme given a little discreet publicity.'

We had drawn up by the wing of the castle that was used for residence. The girls and Moreland had left the car by then, and were making their way up the steps to the front door. Templer had paused for a moment to fiddle with one of the knobs of the dashboard which for some reason seemed to dissatisfy him. This seemed a good opportunity for learning privately what had happened to Jean; for although by then I no longer thought about her, there is always a morbid interest in following the subsequent career of a woman with whom one has once been in love. That I should have been in this position *vis-à-vis* his sister, Templer himself, I felt pretty sure, had no idea.

'Duport is an *ex*-brother-in-law now?'

'Jean finally got a divorce from him. They lived apart for quite a time when Bob was running round with Bijou Ardglass. Then they joined up again and went to South America together. However, it didn't last. You never really knew Jean, did you?'

'I met her when I stayed with your family years ago – a few times later. What's happened to her now?'

'She married a South American – an army officer.'

'And Bob Duport?'

'There is some question of his going to Turkey for Magnus. Kenneth has been fixing it.'

'On business?'

'Magnus is interested in chromite.'

'What's that?'

'Used for hardening steel.'

By that time we were half-way up the steps, at the top of which the others were waiting.

'Shall I lead the way?' said Templer. 'Magnus was in the Bailiff's Room when last seen.'

If the outside of Stourwater made a less favourable impression than when I had come there with the Walpole-Wilsons, improvements within were undeniable. Ten years before, the exuberance of the armour, tapestries, pictures, china, furniture, had been altogether too much for the austere aesthetic ideals to which I then subscribed. Time had no doubt modified the uninstructed severity of my own early twenties. Less ascetic, intellectually speaking, more corrupt, perhaps, I could now recognise that individuals live in different ways. They must be taken as they come, Sir Magnus Donners, everyone else. If Sir Magnus liked to make his house like a museum, that was his affair; one must treat it as a museum. In any case, there could be no doubt that protégés like Moreland and Barnby, mistresses like Baby Wentworth and Matilda, had played their part in the castle's redecoration. Certainly it was now arranged in a manner more in keeping with contemporary fashion. Sir Magnus had cleared out some of the more cumbersome of his belongings, although much remained that was unviable enough.

'It's all rather wonderful, Nick, isn't it?' said Matilda in a whisper, as we passed through the main hall. 'Whatever Hugh may say about the Donners taste. How would you like to own it all?'

'How would you?'

'I nearly did.'

I laughed, surprised by her directness, always attractive in women. Entering a panelled gallery, Templer opened a door and indicated we were to go in. The room overlooked the garden. Between bookshelves hung drawings: Conder, Steer, John, a couple of Sickerts. Barnby's nude of Norma, the waitress from Casanova's Chinese Restaurant, was beside the fireplace, above which stood a florid china statuette of *Cupid Chastised*. Just as the last of our party crossed the threshold, one of the bookcases on the far side of the room swung forward, revealing itself as an additional door covered with the spines of dummy volumes, through which Sir Magnus Donners himself appeared to greet his guests at exactly the same moment. I wondered whether he had been watching at a peephole. It was like the stage entrance of a famous actor, the conscious modesty of which is designed, by its absolute ease and lack of emphasis, both to prevent the performance from being disturbed at some anti-climax of the play by too deafening a round of applause, at the same time to confirm – what everyone in the theatre knows already – the complete mastery he possesses of his art. The manner in which Sir Magnus held out his hand also suggested brilliant miming of a distinguished man feeling a little uncomfortable about something.

'You did not tell me I was to collect one of my oldest friends, Magnus,' said Templer, addressing his host as if he were on the most familiar terms with him, in spite of any differences between them of age and eminence. 'Nick and I were at school together.'

Sir Magnus did not answer. He only raised his eyebrows and smiled. Introductions began. While he was shaking hands with Isobel, I observed, from out of the corner of my eye, a woman – whom I assumed to be Templer's wife – sitting in an armchair with its back towards us in the corner of the room. She was reading a newspaper, which she did not lower at our entry. Sir Magnus shook hands all round, behaving as if he had never before met the Morelands, giving, when he reached me, that curious pump-handle motion to his handshake, terminated by a sudden upward jerk (as if suddenly shutting off from the main a valuable current of good will, of which not a volt too much must be expended), a form of greeting common to many persons with a long habit of public life. Ten years left little mark on him. Possibly the neat grey hair receded a trifle more; the line on one side of the mouth might have been a shade deeper; the eyes – greenish, like Matilda's – were clear and very cold. Sir Magnus's mouth was his least comfortable feature. Tall, holding himself squarely, he still possessed the air, conveyed to me when I first set eyes on him, of an athletic bishop or clerical headmaster. This impression was dispelled when he spoke, because he had none of the urbane manner usual to such persons. Unlike Roddy Cutts or Fettiplace-Jones, he was entirely without the patter of the professional politician, even appearing to find difficulty in making 'small talk' of any kind whatsoever. When he spoke, it was as if he had forced himself by sheer effort of will into manufacturing a few stereotyped sentences to tide over the trackless wilderness of social life. Such colourless phrases as he achieved were produced with a difficulty, a hesitancy, simulated perhaps, but decidedly effective in their unconcealed ineptness. While he uttered these verbal formalities, the side of his mouth twitched slightly. Like most successful men, he had turned this apparent disadvantage into a powerful weapon of offence and defence, in the way that the sledge-hammer impact of his comment left, by its banality, every other speaker at a standstill, giving him as a rule complete mastery of the conversational field. A vast capacity for imposing boredom, a sense of immensely powerful stuffiness, emanated from him, sapping every drop of vitality from weaker spirits.

'So you were at school together,' he said slowly.

He regarded Templer and myself as if the fact we had been at school together was an important piece of evidence in assessing our capabilities, both as individuals and as a team.

He paused. There was an awkward silence.

'Well, I suppose you sometimes think of those days with regret,' Sir Magnus continued at last. 'I know I do. Only in later life does one learn what a jewel is youth.'

He smiled apologetically at having been compelled to use such a high-flown phrase. Matilda, laughing, took his arm. 'Dear Donners,' she said, 'what a thing to tell us. You don't suppose we believe you for a moment. Of course you much prefer living in your lovely castle to being back at school.'

Sir Magnus smiled. However, he was not to be jockeyed so easily from his serious mood.

'Believe me,' he said, 'I would at least give what I have to live again my time at the Sorbonne. One is not a student twice in a lifetime.'

'One is never a student at all in England,' said Moreland, in a tone that showed he was still in no mood to be tractable, 'except possibly a medical student or an art student. I suppose you might say I was myself a student, in one sense, when I was at the Royal College of Music. I never felt in the least like one. Besides, with that sort of student, you enter an area of specialisation, which hardly counts for what I mean. Undergraduates in this country are quite different from students. Not that I was ever even an undergraduate myself, but my observation shows me that undergraduates have nothing in common with what is understood abroad by the word student – young men for ever rioting, undertaking political assassination, overturning governments.'

Sir Magnus smiled a little uncertainly, as if only too familiar with these dissertations of Moreland's on fugitive subjects; as if aware, too, that it was no good hoping to introduce any other matter unless such aimless ramblings had been brought by Moreland himself to a close. Moreland stopped speaking and laughed, seeing what was in Sir Magnus's mind. Sir Magnus began a sentence, but, before he could get the words out, the woman sitting in the corner of the room threw down her newspaper and jumped to her feet. She came hurriedly towards us. She was quite pretty, very untidy, with reddish hair and elaborately blued eyelids. Far from being Templer's wife – unless, by some extraordinary freak, they had married and the news had never come my way – this was Lady Anne Stepney, sister of Peggy Stepney (now divorced and remarried) who had been Stringham's former wife. Anne Stepney was also a *divorcée* – in fact, she was Anne Umfraville, having married that raffish figure, Dicky Umfraville, at least twenty years older than herself, as his third or fourth wife. That marriage, too, had broken up. There had been a time, just before meeting Dicky Umfraville, when Anne had been closely associated with Barnby. Now her manner suggested that she regarded Sir Magnus as her own property.

'I really do agree with you about students,' she said, speaking in a torrent of words addressed to Moreland. 'Why is it we don't have any in England? It would liven things up so. I wish the students would do something to prevent all the awful things that have been happening in Czechoslovakia. I do apologise for my rudeness in not coming to talk to you before now. I was so utterly engrossed in what I was reading, I really had to finish the article. It's by J. G. Quiggin. He says we ought to have fought. I can't think about *anything* but Czechoslovakia. Why can't one of the Germans do in Hitler? Those German students, who are so proud of the duelling scars on their faces, take it like lambs when it comes to being bossed about by a man like that.'

'*The Times* says that the Lord Mayor's Fund for the relief of the Czechs has evoked a wide response,' said Sir Magnus mildly.

Lady Anne made an angry movement.

'But you must all be longing for a drink,' she said, as if

in despair. 'I didn't know you were going to sit in here, Magnus. I told them to put the drink tray in the Chinese Room. Shall I ring and have it transferred here?'

It was clear that she regarded herself as holding an established position at Stourwater. Sir Magnus continued to look embarrassed, but whether on account of this outburst, the distressing situation in Central Europe, or the problem of where to consume our drinks, was not apparent. He was probably far from anxious to embark, there and then, on the rights and wrongs of Munich, the practical issues of which were certainly at that time occupying the foremost place in his mind. Roddy Cutts had indicated that when we had talked of Sir Magnus again, after Fettiplace-Jones and his wife had gone home.

'Donners is in close touch with some of the seedy business-men one or two of the Cabinet think worth cultivating,' said Roddy, who appeared to have kept his own artillery masked while speaking with Fettiplace-Jones, 'but he is alleged to be absolutely out of sympathy with the Chamberlain policy. He is playing a waiting game, perhaps a wise one from his point of view.'

The explosive undertones introduced by Anne Umfraville were deadened at that moment by the entry of another woman, whose arrival immediately altered the atmosphere of the room, without greatly relieving its tensions. She, too, was pretty, with the looks sometimes described as 'porcelain', fragile and delicate, slim and blonde. She gave the impression of being not so much an actress, as the sort of girl an actress often tries to portray on the stage in some play making few demands on the mind: the 'nice' girl in a farce or detective story. A typical Templer girl, I thought, feeling sure she must be Peter's wife, then remembering she was the woman with him at Dicky Umfraville's night-club.

'A Mrs Taylor or Porter,' he had said, 'I can't remember

which. Rather a peach, isn't she?'

Presumably Templer had removed her from Mr Taylor or Porter. As she came through the door, Templer's own expression altered slightly. It was as if his features contracted for a brief instant with a sudden spasm of toothache, an agony over almost as soon as felt. The woman moved slowly, shyly, towards us. Sir Magnus stopped looking at Anne Umfraville, following this new arrival with his eyes, as if she were walking a tight-rope and he feared she might at any moment make a false step, fall into the net below, ruin the act, possibly break her neck. Templer watched her too. She came to a standstill.

'This is Betty,' Templer said.

He spoke as if long past despair. Sir Magnus nodded in resigned, though ever hopeful, agreement that this was indeed Betty. Betty stood for a moment gazing round the room in a dazed, almost terrified, manner, suggesting sudden emergence into the light of day after long hours spent behind drawn curtains. I suddenly thought of the tour of Stourwater's 'dungeons' (strenuously asserted by Miss Janet Walpole-Wilson, on my previous visit, to be mere granaries), when Sir Magnus had remarked with sensuous ogreishness, *I sometimes think that is where we should put the girls who don't behave.* Could it be that Betty Templer, with her husband's connivance – an explanation of Templer's uneasy air – had been imprisoned in the course of some partly high-spirited, partly sadistic, rompings to gratify their host's strange whims? Of course, I did not seriously suppose such a thing, but for a split second the grotesque notion presented itself. However, setting fantasy aside, I saw at once that something was 'wrong' with Betty Templer, not realising, until I came to shake hands with her, how badly 'wrong' things were. It was like trying to shake hands with Ophelia while she was strewing flowers. Betty Templer was 'dotty'.

She was as 'dotty' as my sister-in-law, Blanche Tolland – far 'dottier', because people met Blanche, talked with her at parties, had dealings with her about her charities, without ever guessing about her 'dottiness'. Indeed, in the world of 'good works' she was a rather well known, certainly a respected, figure. Blanche's strangeness, when examined, mainly took the shape of lacking any desire to engage herself in life, to have friends, to marry, to bear children, to go out into the world. Within, so to speak, her chosen alcove, she appeared perfectly happy, at least not actively unhappy. The same could certainly not be said for Betty Templer. Betty Templer, on the contrary, was painfully disorientated, at her wits' end, not happy at all. It was dreadful. I saw that the situation required reassessment. After my failure at shaking hands with her, I made some remark about the weather. She looked at me without speaking, as if horrified at my words.

'Perhaps it would be better to go to the Chinese Room,' said Sir Magnus, 'if the drinks are really there.'

He spoke in that curiously despondent, even threatening, manner sometimes adopted by very rich people towards their guests, especially where food and drink are concerned, a tone suggesting considerable danger that drinks would not be found in the Chinese Room or, indeed, anywhere else at Stourwater Castle; that we should be lucky if we were given anything to drink at all – or to eat, too, if it came to that – during the evening that lay ahead of us.

'Will you lead the way, Anne?' he said, with determined cheerfulness. 'I shall have to speak to you later about trying to keep us from our drinks. Deliberate naughtiness on your part, I fear. Have you heard the New Hungarian String Quartet, Hugh? I haven't been myself. I was at *Faust* the other night, and a little disappointed at some of the singing.'

We followed through the door, crossing the hall again,

while I wondered what on earth had happened to Templer's wife to give her this air of having been struck by lightning. Contact between us was broken for the moment, because, while drinks were being dispensed in the Chinese Room, I found myself talking to Anne Umfraville. By the fireplace there, as if left by some visiting photographer, was a camera on a tripod, beside which stood two adjustable lamps.

'What's all this, Donners?' asked Matilda. 'Have you taken up photography?'

'It is my new hobby,' said Sir Magnus, speaking apologetically, as if this time, at least, he agreed with other people in thinking his own habits a shade undesirable. 'I find it impossible to persuade professionals to take pictures of my collections in the way I want them taken. That was why I decided to do it myself. The results, although I say it, are as good, if not better. I have been photographing some of the Nymphenburg. That is why the apparatus is in here.'

'Do you ever photograph people?' asked Moreland.

'I had not thought of that,' said Sir Magnus, smiling rather wolfishly. 'I suppose I might rise to people.'

'Happy snaps,' said Matilda.

'Or unhappy ones,' said Moreland, 'just for a change.'

Dinner was announced. We found ourselves among those scenes in blue, yellow and crimson, the tapestries illustrating the Seven Deadly Sins, which surrounded the dining-room, remembered so well from my earlier visit. Then, I had sat next to Jean Duport. We had talked about the imagery of the incidents depicted in the tapestries. Suitably enough our place had been just below the sequences of *Luxuria*.

'Of course they are newly married . . .' she had said.

That all seemed a long time ago. I glanced round the room. If the rest of Stourwater had proved disappointing – certainly less overpowering in ornate magnificence – these fantastic tapestries, on the other hand, had gained in magnitude. More gorgeous, more extravagant than ever, they engulfed my imagination again in their enchanting colours, grotesque episodes, symbolic moods, making me forget once more the persons on either side of me, just as I had been unaware of Jean when she had spoken on that day, telling me we had met before. Thinking of that, I indulged in a brief moment of sentimentality permissible before social duties intervened. Then, I collected myself. I was between Matilda and Betty Templer – we were sitting at a table greatly reduced in size from that in use on the day when Prince Theodoric had been entertained at Stourwater – and, abandoning the tapestries, I became aware that Templer was chatting in his easy way to Matilda, while I myself had made no effort to engage his wife in conversation. Beyond Betty Templer, Moreland was already administering a tremendous scolding to Anne Umfraville, who, as soon as they sat down, had ventured to express some musical opinion which outraged him, an easy enough thing to do. Sir Magnus, on the other side, had begun to recount to Isobel the history of the castle.

'Have you been to Stourwater before?' I asked Betty Templer.

She stared at me with big, frightened eyes.

'No.'

'It's rather a wonderful house, isn't it?'

'How – how do you mean?'

That question brought me up short. To like Stourwater, to disapprove, were both tenable opinions, but, as residence, the castle could hardly be regarded as anything except unusual. If Betty Templer had noticed none of its uncommon characteristics, pictures and furniture were not a subject to embark upon.

'Do you know this part of the world at all?'

'No,' she said, after some hesitation.

'Peter told me you lived at Sunningdale.'

'Yes.'

'Have you been there long?'

'Since we married.'

'Good for getting up and down to London.'

'I don't go to London much.'

'I suppose Peter gets back for dinner.'

'Sometimes.'

She looked as if she might begin to cry. It was an imbecile remark on my part, the worst possible subject to bring up, talking to the wife of a man like Templer.

'I expect it is all rather nice there, anyway,' I said.

I knew that I was losing my head, that she would soon reduce me to as desperate a state, conversationally speaking, as herself.

'Yes,' she admitted.

'It was extraordinary Peter's bringing us over in the car this evening. I hadn't seen him for ages. We used to know each other so well at school.'

'He knows such a lot of people,' she said.

Her eyes filled with tears. There could be no doubt of it. I wondered what was going to happen next, fearing the worst. However, she made a tremendous effort.

'Do you live in London?' she asked.

'Yes, we——'

'I used to live in London when I was married to my first husband.'

'Oh, yes.'

'He was in – in jute.'

'Was he?'

For the moment I saw no way of utilising this opening.

'Are you a stockbroker?' she asked.

'No . . . I . . .'

I suddenly felt unable to explain what I did, what I was.

The difficulties seemed, for some reason, insuperable. Fortunately no explanation was necessary. She required of me no alternative profession.

'Most of Peter's friends are stockbrokers,' she said, speaking rather more calmly, as if that thought brought some small balm to her soul, adding, a moment later, 'Some of them live at Sunningdale.'

The situation was relieved at that moment by Matilda's causing conversation to become general by returning to the subject of Sir Magnus and his photography.

'You were talking about photographing people, Donners,' she said. 'Why don't you begin on us after dinner? What could be nicer to photograph than the present company?'

'What a good idea,' said Anne Umfraville. 'Do let's do that, Magnus. It would be fun.'

She was greatly improved, far less truculent, than in the days when I had first met her. If Dicky Umfraville could not be said exactly to have knocked the nonsense out of her, marriage to him had certainly effected a change. At least the nonsense was, so to speak, rearranged in a manner less irksome to those with whom she came in contact. She no longer contradicted, as a matter of principle, every word spoken to her; her demeanour was friendly, rather than the reverse. Soon after our arrival at Stourwater, she had reminded Isobel that they were distant cousins; her musical blunder with Moreland was due to ignorance, not desire to exacerbate him; she was well disposed even to Matilda, who, as a former 'girl' of Sir Magnus's, might well have incurred her antagonism. I thought she had obviously taken a fancy to Templer, and he to her. That might explain her excellent humour. It might also explain, at least in part, his wife's 'state'.

'Oh, are we going to be photographed?' Betty Templer whispered at that moment in an agonised voice.

I concluded she had been reduced to her unhappy condition largely by Templer's goings-on. Her own prettiness, silliness, adoration of himself must have brought Templer to the point of deciding to remove her from the husband who 'bored her by talking of money all the time'. At a period when Templer was no doubt still smarting from his own abandonment by Mona, Betty had re-established his confidence by accepting him so absolutely. In marrying her, Templer had shown himself determined to make no such mistake a second time, to choose a wife unquestionably devoted to him, one possessing, besides, not too much life of her own. Mona, by the time she came Templer's way, had had too many adventures. In Betty, he had certainly found adoration (throughout dinner, she continually cast tortured glances in his direction), but the price had been a high one. In short, Templer had picked a girl probably not quite 'all there' even at the beginning of their married life; then, by his rackety conduct, he had sent her never very stable faculties off their balance. Betty Templer was simply not equipped to cope with her husband, to stand up to Templer's armour-plated egotism as a 'ladies' man'. The qualities that had bowled her over before marriage – that bowled her over, so far as that went, still – had also driven her to the borders of sanity. Never very bright in the head, she had been shattered by the unequal battle. The exercise of powerful 'charm' is, in any case, more appreciated in public than in private life, exacting, as it does, almost as heavy demands on the receiver as the transmitter, demands often too onerous to be weighed satisfactorily against the many other, all too delicate, requirements of married life. No doubt affairs with other women played their part as well. In the circumstances, it was inconceivable that Templer did not have affairs with other women. That, at least, was my own reading of the situation. Anyway, whatever the cause,

595

there could be no doubt Betty Templer's spirit was broken, that she was near the end of her tether. Templer must have been aware of that himself. In fact, his perpetual awareness of it explained my own consciousness of some horror in the background when he had stepped from his car that evening. He was always kind, I noticed, when he spoke to Betty, would probably have done anything in his power – short of altering his own way of life, which perhaps no one can truly do – to alleviate this painful situation. It was a gruesome predicament. I thought how ironic that Templer, my first friend to speak with assurance of 'women' and their ways, should have been caught up in this dire matrimonial trap. These impressions shot across the mind, disquieting, evanescent, like forked lightning. Sir Magnus, who had been silent for a minute or two, now leaned forward over the dinner-table, as if to carry us all with him at some all important board meeting – at a Cabinet itself – in the pursuance of an onerous project he had in mind.

'By all means let us take some photographs after dinner,' he said. 'What a good idea.'

Highlights showed on his greenish eyes. No doubt he saw escape from dishing up 'Munich' for the thousandth time, not only with Anne Umfraville, but also with a handful of guests whose views he could not reasonably be expected to take seriously. Like so many men who have made a successful career through the will, it was hard to guess how much, or how little, Sir Magnus took in of what was going on immediately round him. Did he know that his own sexual habits were a source of constant speculation and jocularity; that Moreland was tortured by the thought of Matilda's former status in the house; that Betty Templer made the party a very uncomfortable one; or was he indifferent to these things, and many others as well? It was impossible to say. Perhaps Sir Magnus, through his antennae, was even more keenly apprised of surrounding circumstances than the rest of us; perhaps, on the other hand, he was able to dismiss them completely from his consciousness as absolutely unessential elements in his own tranquil progress through life.

'Let's pose some tableaux,' said Matilda. 'Donners can photograph us in groups.'

'Historical events or something of that sort,' said Anne Umfraville. 'The history of the castle? We could use some of the armour. Ladies watching a tournament?'

Moreland had shown signs of being dreadfully bored until that moment, expressing his own lack of enjoyment by yawns and occasional tart remarks. Now he began to cheer up. The latest proposal not only pointed to the kind of evening he liked, it also opened up new possibilities of teasing Sir Magnus, a project certainly uppermost at that moment in his mind. Anne Umfraville seemed to some extent to share this wish to torment her host.

'Let's do scenes from the career of Sir Magnus,' said Moreland. 'His eventual rise to being dictator of the world.'

'No, no,' said Sir Magnus, laughing. 'That I cannot allow. It would have a bad effect on my photography. You must remember I am only a beginner. Myself as a subject would make me nervous.'

'Hitler and Chamberlain at Godesberg?' suggested Templer.

That proposal, certainly banal enough, was at once dismissed, not only as introducing too sinister, too depressing a note, but also as a scene devoid of attractive and colourful characters of both sexes.

'What about some mythological incident?' said Moreland. 'Andromeda chained to her rock, or the flaying of Marsyas?'

'Or famous pictures?' said Anne Umfraville. 'A man once told me I looked like Mona Lisa. I admit he'd drunk a lot of

Martinis. We want something that will bring everyone in.'

'Rubens's *Rape of the Sabine Women*,' said Moreland, 'or *The Garden of Earthly Delights* by Hieronymus Bosch. We might even be highbrows, while we're about it, and do *Les Demoiselles d'Avignon*. What's against a little practical cubism?'

Sir Magnus nodded approvingly.

'We girls don't want to die of cold,' said Anne Umfraville. 'Nothing too rough, either. I'm not feeling particularly cubistic tonight.'

'Or too highbrow,' said Templer. 'Nick will get out of hand. I know him of old. Let's stick to good straightforward stuff, don't you agree, Magnus – Anne doing a strip-tease, for instance.'

'Nothing sordid,' said Anne Umfraville, her attention distinctly engaged by this last suggestion. 'It must all be at a high intellectual level, or I shan't play.'

'Well-known verses, then,' said Moreland,

> I was a king in Babylon,
> And you were a Christian slave. . . .

– not that I can ever see how the couple in question managed to be those utterly disparate things at the same moment in history – or, to change the mood entirely:

> Now all strange hours and all strange loves are over,
> Dreams and desires and sombre songs and sweet . . .

There is good material in both of those. The last would be convenient for including everyone.'

My own mind was still on the tapestries. What could be better than variations on the spectacle these already offered?

'Why not the Seven Deadly Sins?'

'Oh, yes,' said Anne Umfraville.

'Modern version,' said Moreland.

598

'A good idea,' agreed Sir Magnus. 'A very good idea indeed.'

He nodded his head in support of the Board's – the Cabinet's – proposal. That was the tone of his words. He glanced round to talk. There was no dissentient voice.

'I shall look forward to seeing some first-rate acting after dinner,' he said.

He nodded his head again. Everything he did had about it heavy, sonorous overtones. He was entirely free from gaiety. Nothing of that kind could ever have troubled him. There was suddenly a tremendous gasp from Betty Templer, who had been quite silent while all this discussion was taking place.

'Oh, we haven't got to act, have we?' she now cried out in a voice of despair. 'I can't act. I never was able to. Need we really?'

'Oh, don't be so silly, darling,' said Templer, addressing her for the first time that evening rather sharply. 'It's only a game. Nothing much will be expected of you. Don't try and wreck everything from the start.'

'But I *can't* act.'

'It will be all right.'

'Oh, I wish I hadn't come.'

'Pull yourself together, Betty.'

This call to order made her lips tremble. Again, I thought there were going to be tears. However, once more she recovered herself. She was more determined than one might suppose.

'Yes, you must certainly play your part, Betty,' said Sir Magnus, with just a hint, just the smallest suggestion, of conscious cruelty. 'We are exactly seven, so everyone must do his or her bit.'

'We're eight,' said Moreland. 'Surely you yourself are not going to be sinless?'

'I shall only be the photographer,' said Sir Magnus, smiling firmly.

'What are the Seven Deadly Sins, anyway?' said Anne Umfraville. 'I can never remember. Lust, of course – we all know that one – but the others, Pride——'

'Anger – Avarice – Envy – Sloth – Gluttony,' said Isobel.

'They are represented all round us,' said Sir Magnus, making a gesture towards the walls, at the same time wiping his lips very carefully with a napkin, as if in fear of contamination, 'sometimes pictured rather whimsically.'

He seemed cheered as Moreland by what lay ahead. He must also have decided either that a little more drink would improve the tableaux, or that the measure of wine up to then provided was insufficient to clear him unequivocally of the sin of Avarice, because he said in an aside to the butler: 'I think we shall need some more of that claret.'

'How are we to decide what everyone is going to do?' said Anne Umfraville. 'Obviously Lust is the star part.'

'Do you think so, Anne?' said Sir Magnus, feigning ponderous reproof. 'Then to prevent argument, I must decide for you all. It will be my privilege as host. I shall allot everyone a Sin. Then they will be allowed their own team to act it. Peter, I think we can rely on you to take charge of Lust – which for some reason Anne seems to suppose so acceptable to everyone – for I don't think we can offer such a sin to a lady. Perhaps, Anne, you would yourself undertake Anger – no, no, not a word. I must insist. Matilda – Envy. Not suit you? Certainly I think it would suit you. Lady Isobel, no one could object to Pride. Betty, I am going to ask you to portray Avarice. It is a very easy one, making no demand on your powers as an actress. Nonsense, Betty, you will do it very well. We will all help you. Hugh, don't be offended if I ask you to present Gluttony. I have often heard you praise the pleasures of the table above all others. Mr Jenkins,

I fear there is nothing left for you but Sloth. There are, of course, no personal implications. I am sure it is quite inappropriate, but like Avarice, it makes no great demands on the actor.'

If the administrative capacity of Sir Magnus Donners had ever been at all in question before that moment, his ability to make decisions – and have them obeyed – was now amply demonstrated. Naturally, a certain amount of grumbling took place about the allotment of Sins, but only superficial. No vital objection was raised. In the end everyone bowed to the Donners ruling. Even Betty Templer made only a feeble repetition of the statement that she could not act at all. It was brushed aside for the last time. Moreland was especially delighted with the idea of portraying Gluttony.

'Can we do them in here?' he asked, 'everyone in front of his or her appropriate Sin?'

'Certainly,' said Sir Magnus, 'certainly. We will return after coffee.'

He had become more than ever like an energetic, dominating headmaster, organising extempore indoor exercise for his pupils on an afternoon too wet for outdoor games. A faint suggestion of repressed, slightly feverish excitement under his calm, added to this air, like some pedagogue confronted with aspects of his duties that gratify him almost to the point of aberration. The rest of dinner passed with much argument as to how best the Sins were to be depicted. All of us drank a lot, especially Moreland, Templer and Anne Umfraville, only Sir Magnus showing his usual moderation. The extravagance of the project offered temporary relief from personal problems, from the European scene. I had not expected the evening to turn out this way. There could be no doubt that Sir Magnus, genuinely exhilarated, was, as much as anyone, casting aside his worries. While the table was cleared, we had coffee in the Chinese Room, drawing lots as to the order in which the Sins should be presented. Camera and arc lamps were moved into the dining-room.

'Do you want any companions, Hugh?' asked Sir Magnus.

'Gluttony at its most enjoyable dispenses with companionship,' said Moreland, who was to lead off.

He had surrounded himself with dishes of fruit and liqueur bottles, from both of which he was helping himself liberally.

'Be prepared for the flash,' said Sir Magnus.

Moreland, not prepared, upset a glass of Kümmel. He must have been photographed half-sprawled across the table. It was agreed to have been a good performance.

'I shall continue to act the Sin for the rest of the evening,' he said, pouring out more Kümmel, this time into a tumbler.

Isobel was next as Pride. She chose Anne Umfraville as her 'feed'. With these two a different note was struck. Moreland's 'turn' was something individual to himself, an artist – in this case a musician – displaying considerable attainment in a medium not his own. With Isobel and Anne Umfraville, on the other hand, the performance was of quite another order. The two of them had gone off together to find suitable 'properties', returning with a metal receptacle for fire irons, more or less golden in material, the legs of which, when inverted, formed the spikes of a crown. They had also amassed a collection of necklaces and beads, rugs and capes of fur. With the crown on her head, loaded with jewels, fur hanging in a triangular pattern from her sleeves, Isobel looked the personification of Pride. Anne Umfraville, having removed her dress, wore over her underclothes a tattered motor rug, pinned across with a huge brooch that might have come from a sporran. She had partially blacked her face; her hair hung in rats' tails over her forehead; her feet were bare, enamelled toenails the only visible remnant of a more ornamented form of existence. Here, before us, in these two, was displayed the nursery and playroom life of generations of 'great houses': the abounding physical vitality of big aristocratic families, their absolute disregard for personal dignity in uninhibited delight in 'dressing up', that passionate return to childhood, never released so fully in any other country, or, even in this country, so completely by any other class. Sir Magnus was enchanted.

'You are a naughty girl, Anne,' he said, with warm approval. 'You've made yourself look an absolute little scamp, a bundle of mischief. I congratulate you, too, Lady Isobel. You should always wear fur. Fur really becomes you.'

'My turn next,' said Anne Umfraville now breathless with excitement. 'Isobel and I can do Anger just as we are. It fits perfectly. Wait a second.'

She went off to the hall, returning a moment later with a long two-handed sword, snatched from the wall, or from one of the figures in armour. With this, as Anger provoked by Pride, she cut Isobel down in her finery.

'That should make a splendid picture,' said Sir Magnus, from behind the camera.

My own enactment of Sloth required no histrionic ability beyond lying on the table supported by piles of cushions. It was quickly over.

'Leave the cushions there, Nick,' said Templer, 'I shall need them all for Lust.'

Matilda's turn, good as it was in some ways, noticeably lowered the temperature of the entertainment. Once again the whole tone of the miming changed. I had the impression that, if Anne Umfraville was unexpectedly tolerant of Matilda, Matilda was less prepared to accept Anne Umfraville. Certainly Matilda was determined to show that she, as a professional actress, had a reputation to sustain. She had draped herself in a long green robe – possibly one of Sir Magnus's dressing gowns, since Matilda's familiarity with the castle rooms had been of help in collecting costumes and 'props' – a dress that entirely concealed her trousers. In this she stood, with no supporting cast, against the panel of the tapestry representing Envy. Everything was to be done by expression of the features. She stood absolutely upright, her face contorted. The glance, inasmuch as it was canalised, seemed aimed in the direction of Anne Umfraville. So far as it went, the performance was good; it might even be said to show considerable talent. On the other hand, the professional note, the contrast with what had gone before, somewhat chilled the party. There was some clapping. There appeared to be no other way of bringing Matilda back to earth.

'Jolly good, Matty,' said Moreland. 'I shall know now what's happened when I next see you looking like that.'

There was still Betty Templer to be hustled through Avarice, before her husband sustained the role of Lust, the final Sin, which, it was agreed, would make a cheerful termination to the spectacle. I was interested to see what would happen when Betty Templer's turn came: whether Sir Magnus would take charge, or Templer. It was Templer.

'Come on, Betty,' he said in a soothing voice. 'I can be a beggar by the side of the road and you can be walking past with your nose in the air.'

That was obviously a simple, kindly solution to Betty Templer's diffidence about acting, to which no objection could possibly be taken. There was assistance from Anne Umfraville and Isobel in providing a suitably rich-looking bag, and various garments, to increase the contrast between riches and poverty. Templer himself had by then removed some of his clothes, so that only a few touches were required to turn him into an all but naked beggar seeking alms. His wife stood smiling unhappily for a second or two, taut and miserable, but carried through, in spite of everything, by her looks. She was undeniably very pretty indeed. In the unpropitious circumstances, she might be said to have acquitted herself well. Now that the ordeal was over, she would no doubt feel better. I thought that the danger of a total breakdown on her part – by no means to be disregarded until that moment – could now be dismissed from the mind. Indeed, having been forced against her will to 'act', Betty Templer would probably discover that she was quite pleased with herself after carrying things off with such comparative success.

'Good, Betty,' said Sir Magnus, perhaps himself a little relieved. 'Now Lust, Peter. Do you want any help?'

'Yes, of course, I do, old boy,' said Templer, now rather tight. 'Really, that is a most insulting remark, Magnus. I shouldn't have thought it of you. I want all the girls I'm not married to. Married Lust isn't decent. I'd like to do some different forms of Lust. You can photograph the one you think best.'

'No reason not to photograph them all,' said Sir Magnus. 'There is plenty of film.'

'Why not do the three ages of Lust?' said Moreland, 'Young, Middle-aged, Elderly?'

'A splendid idea,' said Templer. 'Perhaps Lady Isobel and Mrs Moreland would assist me in the first two, and Anne in the last.'

He began to prepare a corner of the table, upon which the cushions of Sloth still remained. Templer had now entirely thrown off the distant, almost formal air he had shown earlier in the day. He was more like himself when I had known him years before. His first scene, Youthful Lust, as he saw it – an old-fashioned conception, very typical of Templer himself – was to take place in the private room of a restaurant, where a debutante had been lured by a lustful undergraduate: Isobel, in long white gloves (which Sir

Magnus produced, as if by magic), with three ostrich feathers in her hair; Templer, in vaguely sporting attire, shorts and a scarf playing some part. Then, Middle-aged Lust; Matilda for some reason wearing sun-spectacles, was a married woman repelling the advances of a lustful clergyman, Templer in this role wearing an evening collar back-to-front. Neither of these two tableaux was specially memorable. For the third scene, Elderly Lust, a lustful octogenarian entertained to dinner a ballet girl – another typically nineteenth-century Templer concept – an opera-hat being produced from somewhere, white blotting-paper from the writing-table in the morning-room providing a stiff shirt. Anne Umfraville had constructed some sort of a ballet skirt, but was wearing by then little else. In his presentation of senile lust, Templer excelled himself, a theatrical performance he could never have achieved in the past. His acting might almost be regarded as one of those cases where unhappiness and frustration seem to force something like art from persons normally concerned only with the material side of life. Anne Umfraville, as the ballet girl, fell not far short of him in excellence.

'Give me that fly-whisk,' said Templer.

At the height of the act, amid much laughter from the audience, I suddenly heard next to me a muffled howl. It was the noise a dog makes when accidentally trodden on. I turned to see what had happened. The sound came from Betty Templer. Tears were coursing down her cheeks. Up to that moment she had been sitting silent on one of the dining-room chairs, watching the show, apparently fairly happy now that her own turn was passed. I thought she was even finding these antics a little amusing. Now, as I looked at her, she jumped up and rushed from the room. The door slammed. Templer and Anne Umfraville, both by then more or less recumbent on the cushions littering the table, in a dramatic and convincing representation of impotent desire, now separated one from the other. Templer slid to his feet. Sir Magnus looked up from the camera.

'Oh, dear,' he said mildly, 'I'm afraid Betty is not feeling well again. Perhaps she should not have sat up so late.'

For some reason my mind was carried back at that moment to Stonehurst and the Billson incident. This was all the same kind of thing. Betty wanted Templer's love, just as Billson wanted Albert's; Albert's marriage had precipitated a breakdown in just the same way as Templer's extravagances with Anne Umfraville. Here, unfortunately, was no General Conyers to take charge of the situation, to quieten Betty Templer. Certainly her husband showed no immediate sign of wanting to accept that job. However, before an extreme moral discomfort could further immerse all of us, a diversion took pace. The door of the dining-room, so recently slammed, opened again. A man stood on the threshold. He was in uniform. He appeared to be standing at attention, a sinister, threatening figure, calling the world to arms. It was Widmerpool.

'Good evening,' he said.

Sir Magnus, who had been fiddling with the camera, smiling quietly to himself, as if he had not entirely failed to extract a passing thrill of pleasure from Betty Templer's *crise*, looked up. Then he advanced across the room, his hand outstretched.

'Kenneth,' he said, 'I did not expect to see you at this late hour. I thought you must have decided to drive straight to London. We have been taking some photographs.'

By that date, when the country had lived for some time under the threat of war, the traditional, the almost complete professional anonymity of the army in England had been already abrogated. Orders enacting that officers were never to be seen in London wearing uniform – certainly on no social occasion, nor, as a rule, even when there on duty – being to some extent relaxed, it was now not unknown for a Territorial, for example, to appear in khaki in unmilitary surroundings because he was on his way to or from a brief period of training. Something of the sort must have caused Widmerpool's form of dress. His arrival at this hour was, in any case, surprising enough. The sight of him in uniform struck a chill through my bones. Nothing, up to that date, had so much brought home to me the imminence, the certitude, of war. That was not because Widmerpool himself looked innately military. On the contrary, he had almost the air of being about to perform a music-hall turn, sing a patriotic song or burlesque, with 'patter', an army officer. Perhaps that was only because the rest of the party were more or less in fancy dress. Even so, uniform, for some reason, brings out character, physique, class, even sex, in a curious manner. I had never before thought of Widmerpool as possessing physical characteristics at all feminine in disposition, but now his bulky, awkward shape, buttoned up and held together by a Sam Browne belt, recalled Heather Hopkins got up as an admiral in some act at the Merry Thought. Widmerpool was evidently at a loss, hopelessly at a loss, to know what was happening. He put his cap, leather gloves and a swagger stick bound in leather on the sideboard, having for some reason brought all these with him, instead of leaving them in the hall; possibly to make a more dramatic appearance. Sir Magnus introduced the Morelands. Widmerpool began to assert himself.

'I have heard my medical man, Brandreth, speak of you, Mr Moreland,' he said. 'Don't you play the piano? I think so. Now I recall, I believe, that we met in a nursing home where I was confined for a time with those vexatious boils.

I found you in the passage one day, talking to Nicholas here. I believe you are one of Brandreth's patients, too. He is an able fellow, Brandreth, if something of a gossip.'

'I say, Kenneth, old boy,' said Templer, who, in surprise at seeing Widmerpool at this moment in such an outfit, seemed to have forgotten, at least dismissed from his mind, his wife's hysterical outburst, 'are you going to make us all form fours?'

'You are not very up to date, Peter,' said Widmerpool, smiling at such a pitiful error. 'The army no longer forms fours. You should surely know that. We have not done so for several years now. I cannot name the precise date of the Army Council Regulation. It is certainly by no means recent.'

'Sorry,' said Templer. 'You must give us some squad drill later.'

'You are very fortunate not to be faced with squad drill in any case,' said Widmerpool severely, 'it was touch and go. You may count yourself lucky that the recent formula was reached.'

Templer brought his heels together with a click. Widmerpool ignored this facetiousness. He turned to me.

'Well, Nicholas,' he said, 'I did not know you were a Stourwater visitor. Can you explain to me why everyone is clad – or unclad – in this extraordinary manner?'

Sir Magnus took charge of him.

'I am glad you were able to look in, Kenneth,' he said. 'We were taking a few photographs after dinner. Just the Seven Deadly Sins, you know. Like yourself, I am a believer in relaxation in these troublous times. It is absolutely necessary. You look very military, my dear fellow.'

'I have been staying at my mother's cottage,' said Widmerpool, evidently gratified by Sir Magnus's conciliatory tone. 'I spent most of the afternoon with one of the other units in my Territorial division. I was doing a rather special job for our CO. There seemed no point in changing back into mufti. I find, too, that uniform makes a good impression these days. A sign of the times. However, I merely looked in to tell you, Magnus, that arrangements about the Swiss company are all but completed. There were no complications.'

'This is old Bob's affair, is it?' said Templer. 'I saw him last week. He was complaining about the markets. God knows, they're awful.'

Templer, at that moment, was sitting on the edge of the dining-room table, with the opera-hat tipped to the back of his head. Having removed most of his clothes, he had wrapped a heavy rug around him, so that he might have been wearing some garment like an Inverness cape. He looked like a contemporary picture of a Victorian businessman on a journey.

'Steel made a modest recovery,' said Widmerpool, apparently mesmerised by this semi-professional garb of Templer's into talking general business. 'Then Copper has been receiving a fair amount of support. Also the Zinc-Lead group, with certain specific Tin shares. Still, it's a sorry state of affairs. I'm keeping an eye on this calling-in of funds by non-clearing lenders.'

Even Sir Magnus himself was unable to resist this sudden switch to money-matters at Widmerpool's entrance.

'The discount houses are getting sixty-nine per cent of their applications for bills dated any day next week except Saturday at a price equal to a discount rate of practically twenty-five thirty-seconds per cent,' he said.

'What do you think about the rumours of Roosevelt devaluing the dollar, Magnus?' asked Templer. 'You don't mind if I put a few more clothes on, here and now? It's getting a shade chilly.'

'I see the flight of funds to Wall Street as continuing,' said Sir Magnus, speaking very quietly, 'even though we have avoided war for the time being.'

That was an opinion I should have been prepared to hazard myself without laying claim to financial wizardry. Sir Magnus must have been unwilling to commit himself in front of Widmerpool. His words also carried the unmistakable note of implication that we should all go home.

'Well, we have avoided war,' said Widmerpool. 'That is the important point. I myself think we are safe for five years at least. But – to get back to Duport – everything is going through the subsidiary company, as agreed. Duport will collect the material from the Turkish sellers on his own responsibility, and wire the Swiss company when he has enough ores for shipment.'

'This ought to keep old Bob quiet for a bit,' said Templer. 'He does a job well when he's at it, but goes to pieces if unemployed. He brought off some smart deals in manganese when he was in South America, so he is always telling me. Chromite is the main source of manganese, isn't it? I'm no expert.'

'Chromite——' began Widmerpool.

'And payments?' asked Sir Magnus, not without emphasis.

'I've opened an account for him through a local bank,' said Widmerpool, 'since you asked me to handle the credit formalities. That is agreeable to you, I hope. Duport can thereby undertake down-payments. We shall have to keep an eye on the European situation. In my opinion, as I said just now, it is going to steady up.'

'Very good, Kenneth,' said Sir Magnus, in a voice that closed the matter.

He began to fold up the stand of the flash lamp. The evening, for Sir Magnus's visitors, was at an end. The girls, who had already gone off to clean themselves up, were now returning. There was some muttering between Templer and Anne Umfraville. Then she said good night all round, and retired from the dining-room.

'I think I'd better go up too,' said Templer. 'See how Betty is getting on.'

He too said good night. There was a sound of laughter from the stairs, suggesting that Anne Umfraville had not yet reached her room.

'Kenneth,' said Sir Magnus, 'I am going to ask you to take these friends of mine back in your car. It is not out of your way.'

'Where do they live?' asked Widmerpool, without bothering to assume even the most superficial veneer of pleasure, even resignation, at this prospect. 'I was intending to take the short cut through the park.'

'Peter kindly fetched them,' said Sir Magnus, 'but Betty is not feeling well this evening. Naturally he wants to attend to her.'

He was absolutely firm.

'Come on, then,' said Widmerpool, without geniality.

We thanked Sir Magnus profusely. He bowed us out. There was not much room in Widmerpool's car. We charged insecurely through murky lanes.

'What happened to Peter's wife?' asked Widmerpool. 'She is rather delicate, isn't she? I have hardly met her.'

We gave him some account of the Stourwater evening.

'You seem all to have behaved in an extraordinary manner,' said Widmerpool. 'There is a side of Magnus of which I cannot altogether approve, his taste for buffoonery of that kind. I don't like it myself, and you would be surprised at the stories such goings-on give rise to. Disgusting stories. Totally untrue, of course, but mud sticks. You know Magnus will sit up working now until two or three in the morning. I know his habits.'

'What is wrong with Betty Templer?' I asked.

'I have been told that Peter neglects her,' said Widmer-pool. 'I understand she has always been rather a silly girl. Someone should have thought of that before she became involved in your ragging. It was her husband's place to look after her.'

We arrived at the Morelands' cottage.

'Come in and have a drink,' said Moreland.

'I never touch alcohol when I'm driving,' said Widmer-pool, 'more especially when in uniform.'

'A soft drink?'

'Thanks, no.'

'I'll make you a cup of tea,' said Matilda.

'No, Mrs Moreland, I will push on.'

The car's headlights illuminated a stretch of road; then the glare disappeared from sight. We moved into the house.

'Who was that awful man?' said Moreland.

'You met him with me once in a nursing home.'

'No recollection.'

'What a party,' said Isobel. 'Some of it was rather enjoy-able, all the same.'

'What do you think of Stourwater?' asked Matilda. 'I find it really rather wonderful, in spite of everything.'

'*Eldorado banal de tous les vieux garçons,*' said Moreland.

'But that was Cythera,' said Isobel, 'the island of love. Do you think love flourishes at Stourwater?'

'I don't know,' said Moreland. 'Love means such different things to different people.'

3

EVERY CHRISTMAS, AS I HAVE SAID, ALBERT used to send my mother a letter drafted in a bold, sloping, dowager's hand, the mauve ink of the broad nib-strokes sinking deep, spreading, into the porous surface of the thick, creamy writing paper with scalloped edge. He had kept that up for years. This missive, composed in the tone of a dispatch from a distant outpost of empire, would contain a detailed account of his recent life, state of health, plans for the future. Albert expressed himself well on paper, with careful formality. In addition to these annual letters, he would, every three or four years, pay my mother a visit on his 'day off'. These visits became rarer as he grew older. During the twenty-five years or so after we left Stonehurst, I saw him on such occasions twice, perhaps three times; one of these meetings was soon after the war, when I was still a schoolboy; another, just before 'coming down' from the university. Perhaps there was a third. I cannot be sure. Certainly, at our last encounter, I remember thinking Albert remarkably unchanged from Stonehurst days: fatter, undeniably, though on the whole additional flesh suited him. He had now settled down to be a fat man, with the professional fat man's privileges and far from negligible status in life. He still supported a chronic weariness of spirit with an irony quite brutal in its unvarnished view of things. His dark-blue suit, assumed ceremonially for the call, gave him a rather distinguished appearance, brown canvas, rubber-soled shoes temporarily substituted for the traditional felt slippers (which one pictured as never renovated or renewed), adding a seedy, nearly sinister touch. He could have passed for a depressed, incurably indolent member of some royal house (there was a look of Prince Theodoric) in hopeless exile. The 'girl from Bristol' had taken him in hand, no doubt bullied him a bit, at the same time arranged a life in general tolerable for both of them. She had caused him to find employment in hotels where good wages were paid, good cooking relatively appreciated. There were two children, a boy and a girl. Albert himself was never greatly interested in either of them, while admitting they 'meant a lot' to his wife. It had been largely with a view to the children's health and education that she had at last decided on moving to a seaside town (the resort, as it happened, where Moreland had once conducted the municipal orchestra), when opportunity was offered there to undertake the management of a small 'private hotel'. Albert was, in principle, to do the cooking, his wife look after the housekeeping. It was a species of retirement, reflecting the 'girl from Bristol's' energetic spirit.

To this establishment – which was called the Bellevue – Uncle Giles inevitably gravitated. Even if he had never heard of Albert, Uncle Giles would probably have turned up there sooner or later. His life was spent in such places – the Ufford, his *pied-à-terre* in Bayswater, the prototype – a phenomenal number of which must have housed him at one time or another throughout different parts of the United Kingdom.

'Battered caravanserais,' Uncle Giles used to say. 'That's what a fellow I met on board ship used to call the pubs he stayed in. From Omar Khayyám, you know. Not a bad name for 'em. Well-read man in his way. Wrote for the papers. Bit of a bounder. Stingy, too. Won the ship's sweep and nobody saw a halfpenny back in hospitality.'

The position of Albert at the Bellevue offered a family connexion not to be disregarded, one to support a reasonable demand for that special treatment always felt by Uncle Giles to be unjustly denied him by fate and the malign efforts of 'people who want to push themselves to the front'. Besides, the Bellevue offered a precinct where he could grumble to his heart's content about his own family to someone who knew them personally. That was a rare treat. In addition, when Uncle Giles next saw any members of his family, he could equally grumble about Albert, complaining that his cooking had deteriorated, his manners become 'offhand'. Uncle Giles did not visit the Bellevue often. Probably Albert, who had his own vicissitudes of temperament to contend with, did not care – family connexion or no family connexion – to accommodate so cantankerous a client there too frequently. He may have made intermittent excuses that the hotel was full to capacity. Whatever the reason, these occasional sojourns at the Bellevue were spaced out, for the most part, between Uncle Giles's recurrent changes of employment, which grew no less frequent with the years. He continued to enjoy irritating his relations.

'I like the little man they've got in Germany now,' he would remark, quite casually.

This view, apparently so perverse in the light of Uncle Giles's often declared radical principles, was in a measure the logical consequence of them. Dating to some extent from the post-war period, when to support Germany against France was the mark of liberal opinion, it had somehow merged with his approval of all action inimical to established institutions. National Socialism represented revolution; to that extent the movement gained the support, at any rate temporary support, of Uncle Giles. Besides, he shared Hitler's sense of personal persecution, conviction that the world was against him. This was in marked contrast to the feeling of my brother-in-law, Erridge, also a declared enemy of established institutions, who devoted much of his energies to assisting propaganda against current German policies. Erridge, however, in his drift away from orthodox Communism after his own experiences in Spain, had become an increasingly keen 'pacifist', so that he was, in practice, as unwilling to oppose Germany by force of arms as Uncle Giles himself.

'We don't want guns,' Erridge used to say. 'We want to make the League of Nations effective.'

The death of the Tollands' stepmother, Lady Warminster, a year or two before, with the consequent closing down of Hyde Park Gardens as an establishment, caused a re-grouping of the members of the Tolland family who had lived there. This had indirectly affected Erridge, not as a rule greatly concerned with the lives of his brothers and sisters. When Lady Warminster's household came to an end, Blanche, Robert and Hugo Tolland had to find somewhere else to live, a major physical upheaval for them. Even for the rest of the family, Lady Warminster's death snapped a link with the past that set the state of childhood at a further perspective, forced her stepchildren to look at life in rather a different manner. Ties with their stepmother, on the whole affectionate, had never been close in her lifetime. Death emphasised their comparative strength: Norah Tolland, especially, who had never 'got on' very well with Lady Warminster, now losing no opportunity of asserting – with truth – that she had possessed splendid qualities. Although widow of two relatively rich men, Lady Warminster left little or no money of her own. There were some small bequests to relations, friends and servants. Blanche Tolland received the residue. She had always been the favourite of her stepmother, who may have felt that Blanche's 'dottiness' required all financial support available. However, when the point of departure came, Blanche's future posed no problem. Erridge suggested she should keep house for him at Thrubworth. His butler, Smith, had also died at about that moment – 'in rather horrible circumstances', Erridge wrote – and he had decided that he needed a woman's help in running the place.

'Smith is the second butler Erry has killed under him,' said Norah. 'You'd better take care, Blanchie.'

Since his brief adventure with Mona, Erridge had shown no further sign of wanting to marry, even to associate himself with another woman at all intimately. That may have been partly because his health had never wholly recovered from the dysentery incurred in Spain: another reason why his sister's care was required. This poor state of health Erridge – always tending to hypochondria – now seemed to welcome, perhaps feeling that to become as speedily as possible a chronic invalid would be some insurance against the need to take a decision in the insoluble problem of how to behave if hostilities with Germany were to break out.

'I have become a sick man,' he used to say, on the rare occasions when any of his family visited Thrubworth. 'I don't know at all how long I am going to last.'

Robert Tolland had lived in his stepmother's house, partly through laziness, partly from an ingrained taste for economy; at least those were the reasons attributed by his brothers and sisters. At her death, Robert took a series of small flats on his own, accommodation he constantly changed, so that often no one knew in the least where he was to be found. In short, Robert's life became more mysterious than ever. Hitherto, he had been seen from time to time at Hyde Park Gardens Sunday luncheon-parties; now, except for a chance glimpse at a theatre or a picture gallery, he disappeared from sight entirely, personal relationship with him in general reduced to an occasional telephone call. Hugo Tolland, the youngest brother, also passed irretrievably into a world of his own. He continued to be rather successful as assistant to Mrs Baldwyn Hodges in her second-hand furniture and decorating business, where, one afternoon, he sold a set of ormolu candlesticks to Max Pilgrim, the pianist and cabaret entertainer, who was moving into a new flat. When Hyde Park Gardens closed down, Hugo announced that he was going to share this flat. There was even a suggestion – since engagements of the kind in which he had made his name were less available than formerly – that Pilgrim might put some money into Mrs Baldwyn Hodges's firm and himself join the business.

Among her small bequests, Lady Warminster left her sister, Molly Jeavons, the marquetry cabinet in which she kept the material for her books, those rambling, unreviewed, though not entirely unreadable, historical studies of dominating women. The Maria Theresa manuscript, last of these biographies upon which she had worked, remained uncompleted, because Lady Warminster admitted – expressing the matter, of course, in her own impenetrably oblique manner – she had taken a sudden dislike to the Empress on reading for the first time of her heartless treatment of prostitutes. Although they used to see relatively little of each other, Molly Jeavons was greatly distressed at her sister's death. No greater contrast could be imagined than the staid, even rather despondent atmosphere of Hyde Park Gardens, and the devastating muddle and hustle of the Jeavons house in South Kensington, but it was mistaken to suppose these antitheses precisely reproduced the opposing characters of the two sisters. Lady Warminster had a side that took pleasure in the tumbledown aspects of life: journeys to obscure fortune-tellers in the suburbs, visits out of season to dowdy seaside hotels. It was, indeed, remarkable that she had never found her way to the Bellevue. Molly Jeavons, on the other hand, might pass her days happily enough with a husband as broken down, as unemployable, as untailored, as Ted Jeavons, while she ran a kind of free hotel for her relations, a rest-home for cats, dogs and other animals that could impose themselves on her good nature; Molly, too, was capable of enjoying other sides of life. She had had occasional bursts of magnificence as Marchioness of Sleaford, whatever her first marriage may have lacked in other respects.

'The first year they were married,' Chips Lovell said, 'the local Hunt Ball was held at Dogdene. Molly, aged eighteen or nineteen, livened up the proceedings by wearing the Sleaford tiara – which I doubt if Aunt Alice has ever so much as tried on – and the necklace belonging to Tippoo Sahib that Uncle Geoffrey's grandfather bought for his Spanish mistress when he outbid Lord Hertford on that famous occasion.'

For some reason there was a great deal of fuss about moving the marquetry cabinet from Hyde Park Gardens to South Kensington. The reason for these difficulties was obscure, although it was true that not an inch remained in the Jeavons house for the accommodation of an additional piece of furniture.

'Looks as if I shall have to push the thing round myself on a barrow,' said Jeavons, speaking gloomily of this problem.

Then, one day in the summer after 'Munich', when German pressure on Poland was at its height, Uncle Giles died too – quite suddenly of a stroke – while staying at the Bellevue.

'Awkward to the end,' my father said, 'though I suppose one should not speak in that way.'

It was certainly an inconvenient moment to choose. During the year that had almost passed since Isobel and I had stayed with the Morelands, everyday life had become increasingly concerned with preparations for war: expansion of the services, air-raid precautions, the problems of evacuation; no one talked of anything else. My father, in poor health after being invalided out of the army a dozen years before (indirect result of the wound incurred in Mesopotamia), already racked with worry by the well-justified fear that he would be unfit for re-employment if war came, was at that moment in no state to oversee his brother's cremation. I found myself charged with that duty. There was, indeed, no one else to do the job. By universal consent, Uncle Giles was to be cremated, rather than buried. In the first place, no specially apposite spot awaited his coffin; in the second, a crematorium was at hand in the town where he died. Possibly another feeling, too, though unspoken, influenced that decision: a feeling that fire was the element appropriate to his obsequies, the funeral pyre traditional to the nomad.

I travelled down to the seaside town in the afternoon. Isobel was not feeling well. She was starting a baby. Circumstances were not ideal for a pregnancy. Apart from unsettled international conditions, the weather was hot, too hot. I felt jumpy, irritable. In short, to be forced to undertake this journey in order to dispose of the remains of Uncle Giles seemed the last straw in making life tedious, disagreeable, threatening, through no apparent fault of one's own. I had never seen much of Uncle Giles, felt no more than formal regret that he was no longer among us. There seemed no justice in the fact that fate had willed this duty to fall on myself. At the same time, I had to admit things might have been worse. Albert – more probably his wife – had made preliminary arrangements for the funeral, after informing my father of Uncle Giles's death. I should stay at the Bellevue, where I was known; where, far more important, Uncle Giles was known. He probably owed money, but there would be no uneasiness. Albert would have no fears about eventual payment. It was true that some embarrassing fact might be revealed: with Uncle Giles, to be prepared for the unexpected in some more or less disagreeable form was always advisable. Albert, burdened with few illusions on any subject, certainly possessed none about Uncle Giles; he would grasp the situation even if there were complexities. I could do what clearing up was required, attend the funeral, return the following morning. There was no real excuse for grumbling. All the same, I felt a certain faint-heartedness at the prospect of meeting Albert again after all these years, a fear – rather a base one – that he might produce embarrassing reminiscences of my own childhood. That was very contemptible. A moment's serious thought would have shown me that nothing was less likely. Albert was interested in himself, not in other people. That did not then occur to me. My trepidation was increased by the fact that I had never yet set eyes on the 'girl from Bristol', of whom her husband had always painted so alarming a picture. She was called 'Mrs Creech', because Albert, strange as it might seem, was named 'Albert Creech'. The suffix 'Creech' sounded to my ears unreal, incongruous, rather impertinent, like suddenly attaching a surname to one of the mythical figures of Miss Orchard's stories of the gods and goddesses, or Mr Deacon's paintings of the Hellenic scene. Albert, I thought, was like Sisyphus or Charon, one of those beings committed eternally to undesired and burdensome labours. Charon was more appropriate, since Albert had, as it were, recently ferried Uncle Giles over the Styx. I do not attempt to excuse these frivolous, perhaps rather heartless, reflections on my own part as I was carried along in the train.

On arrival, I went straight to the undertaker's to find out what arrangements had already been made. Later, when the Bellevue hove into sight – the nautical phrase is deliberately chosen – I saw at once that, during his visits there, Uncle Giles had irrevocably imposed his own personality upon the hotel. Standing at the corner of a short, bleak, anonymous street some little way from the sea-front, this corner house, although much smaller in size, was otherwise scarcely to be distinguished from the Ufford, his London *pied-à-terre*. Like the Ufford, its exterior was painted battleship-grey, the angle of the building conveying just the same sense of a hopelessly unseaworthy, though less heavily built vessel, resolutely attempting to set out to sea. This foolhardy attempt of the Bellevue to court shipwreck, emphasised by the distant splash of surf, seemed somehow Uncle Giles's fault. It was just the way he behaved himself. Perhaps I attributed too much to his powers of will. The physical surroundings of most individuals, left to their own choice, vary little wherever they happen to live. No doubt that was the explanation. I was in the presence of one of those triumphs of mind over matter, like the photographer's power of imposing his own personal visual demands on the subject photographed. Nevertheless, even though I ought to have been prepared for a house of more or less the same sort, this miniature, shrunken version of the Ufford surprised me by its absolute consistency of type, almost as much as if the Ufford itself had at last shipped anchor and floated on the sluggish Bayswater tide to this quiet roadstead. Had the Ufford done that? Did the altered name, the new cut of jib, hint at mutiny, barratry, piracy, final revolt on the high seas – for clearly the Bellevue was only awaiting a favourable breeze to set sail – of that ship's company of well brought up souls driven to violence at last by their unjustly straitened circumstances?

Here, at any rate, Uncle Giles had died. By the summer sea, death had claimed him, in one of his own palaces, amongst his own people, the proud, anonymous, secretive race that dwell in residential hotels. I went up the steps of the Bellevue. Inside, again on a much smaller scale, resemblance to the Ufford was repeated: the deserted hall; yellowing letters on the criss-cross ribbons of a board; a faint smell of clean sheets. Striking into the inner fastnesses of its precinct, I came suddenly upon Albert himself. He was pulling

623

down the blinds of some windows that looked on to a sort of yard, just as if he were back putting up the shutters at Stonehurst, for it was still daylight.

'Why, Mr Nick . . .'

Albert, dreadfully ashamed at being caught in this act, in case I might suppose him habitually to lend a hand about the house, began to explain at once that he was occupied in that fashion only because, on this particular evening, his wife was in bed with influenza. He did not hide that he considered her succumbing in this way to be an act of disloyalty.

'I don't think she'll be up and about for another day or two,' he said, 'what with the news on the wireless night after night, it isn't a very cheerful prospect.'

It was absurd to have worried about awkward adjustments where Albert was concerned. Talking to him was just as easy, just as natural, as ever. All his old fears and prejudices remained untouched by time, the Germans – scarcely more ominous – taking the place of the suffragettes. He was older, of course, what was left of his hair, grey and grizzled; fat, though not outrageously fatter than when I had last seen him; breathing a shade more heavily, if that were possible. All the same, he had never become an old man. In essential aspects, he was hardly altered at all: the same timorous, self-centred, sceptical artist-cook he had always been, with the same spirit of endurance, battling his way through life in carpet-slippers. Once the humiliation of being caught doing 'housework' was forgotten, he seemed pleased to see me. He launched at once into an elaborate account of Uncle Giles's last hours, making no attempt to minimise the fearful lineaments of death. In the end, with a view to terminating this catalogue of macabre detail, which I did not at all enjoy and seemed to have continued long enough, however much pleasure the narrative might afford Albert himself in the telling, I found myself invoking the past. This seemed the only avenue of escape. I spoke of Uncle Giles's visit to Stonehurst just before the outbreak of war. Albert was hazy about it.

'Do you remember Bracey?'

'Bracey?'

'Bracey – the soldier servant.'

Albert's face was blank for a moment; then he made a great effort of memory.

'Little fellow with a moustache?'

'Yes.'

'Used to come on a bicycle?'

'That was him.'

'Ignorant sort of man?'

'He had his Funny Days.'

Albert looked blank again. The phrase, once so heavy with ominous import at Stonehurst, had been completely erased from his mind.

'Can't recollect.'

'Surely you must remember – when Bracey used to sulk.'

'Did he go out with the Captain – with the Colonel, that is – when the army went abroad?'

'He was killed at Mons.'

'And which of us is going to keep alive, I wonder, when the next one starts?' said Albert, dismissing, without sentiment, the passing of Bracey. 'It won't be long now, the way I see it. If the government takes over the Bellevue, as they looks like doing, we'll be in a fix. Be just as bad, if we stay. They say the big guns they have nowadays will reach this place easy. They've come on a lot from what they was in 1914.'

'And Billson?' I said.

I was now determined to re-create Stonehurst, the very subject I had dreaded in the train on the way to meet Albert again. I suppose by then I had some idea of working up, by

625

easy stages, to the famous Billson episode with General Conyers. I should certainly have liked to hear Albert's considered judgment after all these years. Once again, he showed no sign of recognition.

'Billson?'

'The parlourmaid at Stonehurst.'

'Small girl, was she – always having trouble with her teeth?'

'No, that was another one.'

I recognised that it was no good attempting to rebuild the red tiles, the elongated façade of the bungalow. If Albert supposed Billson to be short and dark, she must have passed from his mind without leaving a trace of her own passion. That was cruel. All the same, I made a final shot.

'You don't remember when she gave the slice of seed-cake to the little boy from Dr Trelawney's?'

The question struck a spark. This concluding bid to unclog the floods of memory had an immediate, a wholly unexpected effect.

'I knew there was something else I wanted to tell you, sir,' said Albert. 'It just went out of my head till you reminded me. That's the very gentleman – Dr Trelawney – been staying here quite a long time. Came through a friend of your uncle's, a lady. I puzzled and puzzled where I'd seen him before. Captain Jenkins said something one day how Dr Trelawney had lived near Stonehurst one time. Then the name came back to me.'

'Does he still wear a beard and take his people out running?'

'Still got a beard,' said Albert, 'but he lives very quiet now. Not so young as he was, like the rest of us. Has a lot of meals in his room. Quite a bit of trouble, he is. I get worried about him now and then. So does the wife. Not too quick at settling the account. Then he does say some queer things.

Not everyone in the hotel likes it. Of course, we have to have all sorts here. Can't pick and choose. Dr Trelawney's health ain't all that good neither. Suffers terrible from asthma. Something awful. I get frightened when he's got the fit on him.'

It was clear that Albert, too well-behaved to say so explicitly, would have been glad to eject Dr Trelawney from the Belle-vue. That was not surprising. I longed to set eyes on the Doctor again. It would be a splendid story to tell Moreland, with whom I had been out of any close contact since we had stayed at the cottage.

'Used my uncle to see much of Dr Trelawney?'

'They'd pass the time of day,' said Albert. 'The lady knew both of them, of course. They'd sometimes all three go out together on the pier and such like. Captain Jenkins used to get riled with some of the Doctor's talk about spirits and that. I've heard him say as much.'

'Was the lady called Mrs Erdleigh?' I asked.

Uncle Giles had once been suspected of being about to marry this fortune-telling friend of his. It was likely that she was the link between himself and Dr Trelawney.

'That's the name,' said Albert. 'Lives in the town here. Tells fortunes, so they say. Used to come here quite a lot. In fact, she rang up and offered to help after Captain Jenkins died, but I thought I'd better wait instructions. As it was, we just put all the clothing from the drawers tidy on the bed, so the things would be easy to pack. We haven't touched the Gladstone bag. Captain Jenkins didn't have much with him at the end. Kept most of his stuff in London, so I believe.'

Albert sniffed. He evidently held a low opinion of the Ufford.

'I'll just give you your uncle's keys, sir,' he said. 'If you'll excuse me, I must see the wife now. She takes on if I don't

keep her informed about veg. Those silly girls never bring
her what she wants neither. One of them's having time off,
extra like, old Mrs Telford persuading her to go to an ambu-
lance class or some such. I don't know what the young
women of today are about. Making sheep's eyes most of the
time, that's what it comes to.'

He moved off laboriously to Mrs Creech's sick-bed. I
thought the best system would be to deal with Uncle Giles's
residue straight away, then dine. The news of Dr Trelawney's
installation at the Bellevue aroused a cloud of memories. That
he had not passed into oblivion like so many others Albert
had met was a tribute to the Doctor's personality. Even he
would have been forgotten, if Uncle Giles had not recalled
him to mind. That was strange because, as a rule, where
others were concerned, Uncle Giles's memory was scarcely
more retentive than Albert's. I wondered what life would
be like lived in this largely memoryless condition. Better?
Worse? Not greatly different? It was an interesting question.
The reappearance of Mrs Erdleigh was also a matter of note.
This fairly well known clairvoyante (whom Lady Warminster had consulted in her day) had once 'put out the cards'
for me at the Ufford, prophesying my love affair with Jean
Duport, for a time occupying so much of my life, now like an
episode in another existence. Later, characteristically, Uncle
Giles had pretended never to have heard of Mrs Erdleigh.
However, rumours persisted at a later date to the effect that
they still saw each other. There must have been a reconciliation. I wondered whether she would turn up at the funeral,
what had been her relations with Uncle Giles, what with
Dr Trelawney.

I had told Albert I would find my own way to the bedroom, which was some floors up. It was small, dingy, facing
inland. The sea was in any case visible from the Bellevue –
in spite of its name – only from the attic windows, glimpsed

through a gap between two larger hotels, though the waves could be heard clattering against the shingle. Laid out on the bed were a couple of well-worn suits; three or four shirts, frayed at the cuff; half a dozen discreet, often-knotted ties; darned socks (who had darned them?); handkerchiefs embroidered with the initials GDJ (who had embroidered them?); thick woollen underclothes; two pairs of pyjamas of unattractive pattern; two pairs of shoes, black and brown; bedroom slippers worthy of Albert; a raglan overcoat; a hat; an unrolled umbrella; several small boxes containing equipment such as studs and razor blades. This was what Uncle Giles had left behind him. No doubt there was more of the same sort of thing at the Ufford. The display was a shade depressing. Dust was returning to dust with dreadful speed. I looked under the bed. There lay the suitcase into which these things were to be packed, beside it, the Gladstone bag to which Albert had referred, a large example of its kind, infinitely ancient, perhaps the very one with which Uncle Giles had arrived at Stonehurst on the day of the Archduke's assassination. I dragged these two pieces out. One of the keys on the ring committed to me by Albert fitted this primitive, shapeless survival of antique luggage, suitable for a conjuror or comedian.

At first examination, the Gladstone bag appeared to be filled with nothing but company reports. I began to go through the papers. Endless financial projects were adumbrated; gratifying prospects; inevitable losses; hopeful figures, in spite of past disappointments. The whole panorama of the money-market lay before one – as it must once have burgeoned under the eyes of Uncle Giles – like the kingdoms of the world and the glory of them. Hardly a venture quoted on the Stock Exchange seemed omitted; several that were not. There were two or three share certificates marked 'valueless' that might have been stock from the South

Sea Bubble. Uncle Giles's financial investigations had been extensive. Then a smaller envelope turned out to be something different. One of the sheets of paper contained there showed a circle with figures and symbols noted within its circumference. It was a horoscope, presumably that of Uncle Giles himself.

He had been born under Aries – the Ram – making him ambitious, impulsive, often irritable. He had secret enemies, because Saturn was in the Twelfth House. I remembered Mrs Erdleigh remarking that handicap when I met her with Uncle Giles at the Ufford. Mars and Venus were in bad aspect so far as dealings with money were concerned. However, Uncle Giles was drawn to hazards such as the company reports revealed by the conjunction of Jupiter. Moreover Jupiter, afflicting Mercury, caused people to find 'the native' – Uncle Giles – unreliable. That could not be denied. Certainly none of his own family would contradict the judgment. Unusual experiences with the opposite sex (I thought of Sir Magnus Donners) were given by Uranus in the Seventh House, a position at the same time unfavourable to marriage. It had to be admitted that all this gave a pretty good, if rough-and-ready, account of my uncle and his habits.

Underneath the envelope containing the horoscope was correspondence, held together by a paper-clip, with a firm of stockbrokers. Then came Uncle Giles's pass-book. The bank statements of the previous year showed him to have been overdrawn, though somewhat better off than was commonly supposed. The whole question of Uncle Giles's money affairs was a mysterious one, far more mysterious than anything revealed about him astrologically. Speculation as to the extent of his capital took place from time to time, speculation even as to whether he possessed any capital at all. The stockbroker's letters and bank statements came to an end. The next item in the Gladstone bag appeared to be a surgical appliance of some sort. I pulled it out. The piece of tubing was for the administration of an enema. I threw the object into the wastepaper-basket, with the company reports. Below again – the whole business was like research into an excavated tomb – lay a roll of parchment tied in a bow with red tape.

'VICTORIA by the Grace of God, of the United Kingdom of Great Britain and Ireland, Queen, Defender of the Faith, Empress of India &c. To Our Trusty and well-beloved *Giles Delahay Jenkins, Gentleman,* Greeting. We, reposing especial Trust and Confidence in your Loyalty, Courage and good Conduct, do by these Presents Constitute and Appoint you to be an Officer in Our *Land* Forces . . .'

Trusty and wellbeloved were not the terms in which his own kith and kin had thought of Uncle Giles for a long time now. Indeed, the Queen's good-heartedness in herself greeting him so warmly was as touching as her error of judgment was startling. There was something positively ingenuous in singling out Uncle Giles for the repose of confidence, accepting him so wholly at his own valuation. No doubt the Queen had been badly advised in the first instance. She must have been vexed and disappointed.

'. . . You are therefore carefully and diligently to discharge your Duty as such in the Rank of *2nd Lieutenant* or in such higher Rank as we may from time to time hereafter be pleased to promote or appoint you to . . .'

The Queen's faith in human nature appeared boundless for, extraordinary as the royal whim might seem, she had indeed been pleased to appoint Uncle Giles to a higher rank, instead of quietly – and far more wisely – dispensing with his services at the very first available opportunity. Perhaps such an opportunity had not arisen so immediately as might have been expected; perhaps Uncle Giles had assumed the higher rank without reference to the Queen. Certainly he was always styled 'Captain' Jenkins, so that there must have been at least a presumption of a once held captaincy of some sort, however 'temporary', 'acting' or 'local' that rank might in practice have been. No doubt her reliance would have been lessened by the knowledge that Mercury was afflicting Jupiter at the hour of Uncle Giles's birth.

'. . . and you are at all times to exercise and well discipline in Arms both the inferior Officers and Men serving under you and use your best endeavours to keep them in good Order and Discipline. And we do hereby command them to Obey you as their superior Officer . . . according to the Rules and Discipline of War, in pursuance of the Trust hereby reposed in you . . .'

The great rolling phrases, so compelling in their beauty and simplicity, might be thought inadmissible for the most heedless, the most cynical, to disregard, so moderate, so obviously right in the circumstances, were their requirements, so friendly – even to the point of intimacy – the manner in which the Sovereign outlined the principles of her honourable service. Uncle Giles, it must be agreed, had not risen to the occasion. So far as loyalty to herself was concerned, he had been heard on more than one occasion to refer to her as 'that old Tartar at Osborne', to express without restraint his own leanings towards a republican form of government. His Conduct, in the army or out of it, could not possibly be described as Good. In devotion to duty, for example, he could not be compared with Bracey, a man no less pursued, so far as that went, by Furies. There remained Uncle Giles's Courage. That, so far as was known, remained untarnished, although – again so far as was known – never put to any particularly severe test. Certainly it could be urged that he had the Courage of his own opinions; the Queen had to be satisfied with that. In short, the only one of her admonitions Uncle Giles had ever shown the least sign of taking to heart was the charge to command his subordinates to obey him.

Even after his own return to civilian life, Uncle Giles tried his best to carry out this injunction in relation to all who could possibly be regarded as subordinate to him. Being 'a bit of a radical' never prevented that; the Sign of Aries investing him with the will to command, adding that touch of irritability of disposition as an additional spur to obedience.

While I thus considered, rather frivolously, Uncle Giles's actual career in contrast with the ideal one envisaged by the terms of his Commission, I could not help thinking at the same time that facile irony at my uncle's expense could go too far. No doubt irony, facile or otherwise, can often go too far. In this particular instance, for example, it was fitting to wonder what sort of a figure I should myself cut as a soldier. The question was no longer purely hypothetical, a grotesque fantasy, a romantic daydream, the career one had supposed to lie ahead as a child at Stonehurst. There was every reason to think that before long now the tenor of many persons' lives, my own among them, would indeed be regulated by those draconic, ineluctable laws, so mildly, so all embracingly, defined in the Commission as 'the Rules and Discipline of War'. How was it going to feel to be subject to them? My name was on the Emergency Reserve, although no one at that time knew how much, or how little, that might mean when it came to joining the army. At the back of one's mind sounded a haunting resonance, a faint disturbing buzz, that was not far from fear.

By the time these disturbing thoughts had descended on me, I had begun to near the bottom of the Gladstone bag. There was another layer of correspondence, this time in a green cardboard file, on the subject of a taxi-cab's collision with a lorry, an accident with regard to which Uncle Giles had been subpoenaed as witness. It went into the waste-paper-basket, a case – as Moreland would have said – in which there was 'nothing of the spirit'. That brought an end to the contents, except for a book. This was bound in grubby vellum, the letterpress of mauve ink, like that used by Albert in his correspondence. I glanced at the highly decorated capitals of the title page:

*The Perfumed Garden
of the Sheik Nefzaoui*
or
The Arab Art of Love

I had often heard of this work, never, as it happened, come across a copy. Uncle Giles was an unexpected vehicle to bring it to hand. The present edition – 'Cosmopoli: 1886' – was stated to be published 'For Private Circulation Only', the English translation from a French version of the sixteenth-century Arabic manuscript made by a 'Staff Officer in the French Army in Algeria'.

I pictured this French Staff Officer sitting at his desk. The sun was streaming into the room through green latticed windows of Moorish design, an oil sketch by Fromentin or J. F. Lewis. Dressed in a light-blue frogged coatee and scarlet peg-topped trousers buttoning under the boot, he wore a pointed moustache and imperial. Beside him on the table stood his shako, high and narrowing to the plume, the white puggaree falling across the scabbard of his discarded sabre. He was absolutely detached, a man who had tasted the sensual pleasures of the Second Empire and Third Republic to their dregs, indeed, come to North Africa to escape such insistent banalities. Now, he was examining their qualities and defects in absolute calm. Here, with the parched wind blowing in from the desert, he had found a kindred spirit in the Sheik Nefzaoui, to whose sixteenth-century Arabic he was determined to do justice in the language of Racine and Voltaire. Perhaps that picture was totally wide of the mark:

the reality quite another one. The Staff Officer was a family man, snatching a few minutes at his beloved translation between the endearments of his wife, the rompings of a dozen children. . . . Rimbaud's father, perhaps, who had served in North Africa, made translations from the Arabic. . . . The 'Rules and Discipline of War' must in some degree have been relaxed to allow spare time for these literary labours. Possibly he worked only on leave. I turned the pages idly. The Sheik's tone was authoritative, absolutely self-assured – for that reason, a trifle forbidding – the chapter headings enigmatic:

'. . . Concerning Praiseworthy Men . . . Concerning Women who deserve to be Praised . . . Of Matters Injurious to the Act of Generation . . . On the Deceits and Treacheries of Women . . . Concerning Sundry Observations useful to Know for Men and Women . . .'

On the Deceits and Treacheries of Women? The whole subject was obviously very fully covered. Sincere and scholarly, there was also something more than a little oppressive about the investigation, moments when the author seemed to labour the point, to induce a feeling of surfeit in the reader. All the same, I felt rather ashamed of my own lack of appreciation, because I could see that much of the advice was good. Disinclination to continue reading I recognised as a basic unwillingness to face facts, rather than any innate fastidiousness to be regarded as a matter for self-congratulation. I felt greatly inferior to the French Staff Officer, whatever his personal condition, who saw this severely technical sociological study, by its nature aseptic, even chilling in deliberate avoidance of false sentiment and specious charm, as a refreshing antidote to Parisian canons of sensuality.

Uncle Giles's acquisition of this book must have been one of the minor consequences of having Uranus in the Seventh

House; that was the best that could be said for him. It reminded him perhaps of ladies like the garage proprietor's widow, manicurist at Reading, once thought to be under consideration as his future wife; possibly it was used as a handbook in those far off, careless days. In any case, there was no reason to suppose Uncle Giles to have become more straitlaced as he grew older. I put the volume aside to reconsider. There was work to be done. The clothes were packed away at last in the suitcase, the papers spared from the wastepaper basket, returned to the Gladstone bag, the two pieces of luggage placed side by side to await removal. As Albert had remarked, Uncle Giles had not left much behind, even though further items would be found at the Ufford. By that time the gong had sounded for dinner.

I took the Sheik Nefzaoui's treatise with me to the dining-room, which was fairly full, single white-haired ladies predominating, here and there an elderly couple. No doubt the seasons made little difference to the Bellevue, the bulk of its population living there all the year round, winter and summer, solstice to solstice. I was given a table in the corner, near the hatch through which food was thrust by Albert. The table next to mine was laid for one person. Upon it stood a half-consumed bottle of whisky, a room-number pencilled on the label. I wondered whether my neighbour would turn out to be Dr Trelawney. That would provide an excitement. I hoped, in any case, that I should catch a glimpse of the Doctor before leaving the hotel, contrive some anecdote over which Moreland and I could afterwards laugh. I had nearly finished my soup – which recalled only in a muted form Albert's ancient skill – when a tall man, about my own age or a year or two older, entered the dining-room. He strode jauntily through the doorway, looking neither to the right nor left, making straight for the table with the whisky bottle. Hope vanished of enjoying near me Dr Trelawney's mysterious presence. This man was thin, with fair to reddish hair, pink-faced, pale eyebrows raised in an aggressive expression, as if he would welcome a row at the least provocation. He wore a country suit, somehow rather too elegant for the Bellevue's dining-room. I experienced that immediate awareness, which can descend all of a sudden like the sky becoming overcast, of the close proximity of a person I knew and did not like, someone who made me, at the same time, in some way morally uncomfortable. For a second, I thought this impression one of those sensations of dislike as difficult to rationalise as the contrasting feeling of sudden sympathy; a moment later realising that Bob Duport was sitting next to me, that there was excuse for this onset of tingling antipathy.

I had not set eyes on Duport since I was an undergraduate, since the night, in fact, when Templer had driven us all into the ditch in his new car. A whole sequence of memories and sensations, luxuriant, tender, painful, ludicrous, wearisome, rolled up, enveloping like a fog. Moreland, as I have said, liked talking of the variations of sexual jealousy, the different effect produced by men with whom a woman has been 'shared'.

'Some of them hardly matter at all,' he had said. 'Others you can't even bear to think about. Very mention of their name poisons the whole relationship – the whole atmosphere. Again you get to like – almost to love – certain ones, husbands or cast-off lovers, I mean. You feel dreadfully sorry for them, at least, try to make their wives or ex-mistresses behave better to them. It becomes a matter of one's own self-respect.'

Duport, so far as I was concerned, had been a case in point. I had once loved his wife, Jean, and, although I loved her no longer, our relationship had secreted this distasteful residue, an unalterable, if hidden, tie with her ex-husband. It was a kind of retribution. I might not like the way Duport

637

behaved, either to Jean or towards the world in general, but what I had done had made him, at least in some small degree, part of my own life. I was bound to him throughout eternity. Moreover, I was, for the same reason, in no position to be censorious. I had undermined my own critical standing. Duport's emergence in this manner cut a savage incision across Time. Templer's Vauxhall seemed to have crashed into the ditch only yesterday; I could almost feel my nose aching from the blow received by the sudden impact of Ena's knee, hear Templer's fat friend, Brent, swearing, the grinding, ghastly snorts of the expiring engine, Stringham's sardonic comments as we clambered out of the capsized car. It had all seemed rather an adventure at the time. I reflected how dreadfully boring such an experience would be now, the very thought fatiguing. However, an immediate decision had to be taken about Duport. I made up my mind to pretend not to recognise him, although the years I had loved Jean made him horribly, unnaturally familiar to me, as if I had been seeing Duport, too, all the time I had been seeing her. Indeed, he seemed now almost more familiar than repellent.

The thought that Duport had been Jean's husband, that she had had a child by him, that no doubt she had once loved him, had not, for some reason, greatly worried me while she and I had been close to each other. Duport had never – I cannot think why – seemed to be in competition with myself where she was concerned. For Jean to have married him, still, so to speak, to own him, although living apart, was like a bad habit (Uncle Giles poring in secret over *The Perfumed Garden*), no more than that; something one might prefer her to be without, to give up, nothing that could remotely affect our feeling for each other. Anyway, I thought, those days are long past; they can be considered with complete equanimity. Duport and I had met only once, fourteen or fifteen years before. He could safely be regarded as the kind of person to whom the past, certainly such a chance encounter, would mean little or nothing, in fact be completely forgotten. No doubt since then new friends of his had driven him scores of times into the ditch with new cars full of new girls. He was that sort of man. Such were my ill-judged, unfriendly, rather priggish speculations. They turned out to be hopelessly wide of the mark.

Duport's first act on sitting down at the table was to pour out a stiffish whisky, add a splash of soda from the syphon also standing on the table, and gulp the drink down. Then he looked contemptuously round the room. Obviously my own presence had materially altered the background he expected of the dining-room at the Bellevue. He stared hard. Soup was set in front of him. I supposed he would turn to it. Instead, he continued to stare. I pretended to be engrossed with my fish. There was something of the old Albert in the sauce. Then Duport spoke. He had a hard, perfectly assured, absolutely uningratiating voice.

'We've met before,' he said.

'Have we?'

'Somewhere.'

'Where could that have been?'

'Certain of it. I can't remember your name. Mine's Duport – Bob.'

'Nicholas Jenkins.'

'Aren't you a friend of my former brother-in-law, Peter Templer?'

'A very old friend.'

'And he drove us both into the ditch in some bloody fast second-hand car he had just bought. Years ago. A whole row of chaps and a couple of girls. The party included a fat swab called Brent.'

'He did, indeed. That was where we met. Of course I remember you.'

'I thought so. Do you ever see Peter these days?'

'Hadn't for ages. Then we met about a year ago – just after "Munich", as a matter of fact.'

'I've heard him talk about you. I used to be married to his sister, Jean, you know. I believe I've heard her speak of you, too.'

'I met her staying with the Templers.'

'When was that?'

'Years ago – when I had just left school.'

'Ever see her later?'

'Yes, several times.'

'Probably when she and I were living apart. That is when Jean seems to have made most of her friends.'

'When I last saw Peter, he was talking about some new job of yours.'

I judged it best to change the subject of Jean – also remembering the talk about Duport between Sir Magnus Donners and Widmerpool. Up to then, I had thought of Duport only in an earlier incarnation, never considered the possibility of running into him again.

'Was he, indeed? Where did you meet him?'

'Stourwater.'

'Did you, by God? What do you do?'

I tried to give some account, at once brief and intelligible, of the literary profession: writing; editing; reviewing; the miscellaneous odd jobs to which I was subject, never, for some reason, very easy to define to persons not themselves in that world. To my relief, Duport showed no interest whatever in such activities, apparently finding them neither eccentric nor important.

'Shouldn't think it brings in much dough,' he said. 'But how do you come to know Donners?'

'We were taken over by some friends who live in the neighbourhood.'

'You're married?'

'Yes.'

'How do you like being married?'

'Support it all right.'

'You're lucky. I find it a great relief not to be married – though I was quite stuck on Jean when we were first wed. But what on earth are you doing in this dump?'

I explained about Uncle Giles, about Albert.

'So that's the answer,' said Duport. 'Of course I used to see your uncle cruising about here. Bad-tempered old fellow. Didn't know he'd dropped off the hooks. They like to keep death quiet in places like this. Look here, when you were staying with Donners, was an absolute bugger called Widmerpool there too?'

'Widmerpool wasn't staying there. He just looked in. Wanted to say something about your business affairs, I think. I know Widmerpool of old.'

'A hundred per cent bastard – word's too good for him.'

'I know some people think so.'

'Don't you?'

'He and I rub along all right. But why are *you* living at the Bellevue?'

'Keeping out of the immediate view of the more enterprising of my creditors. I only wish my stay here were going to be as brief as yours.'

'How did you find the place?'

'Odd chance, as a matter of fact. I once brought a girl down to the Royal for the week-end – one of those bitches you want to have and get out of your system and never set eyes on again. While we were there I made friends with the barman. He's called Fred and a very decent sort of chap. When I found, not so long ago, that I'd better go into comparative hiding, I decided this town would be as good a place as any other to put myself out of commission for a week or two. I left my bags at the station and dropped in to the Royal bar to ask Fred the best place to make an economical stay. He sent me straight to the Bellevue.'

'How do you like Albert?'

'Get along with Albert, as you call him, like a house on fire – but it's a pretty dead-and-alive hole to live in, I can tell you. It's the sort of town where you feel hellishly randy all the time. I've got quite a bit of work to do in the way of sorting out my own affairs. That keeps me going during the day. But there's nothing whatever to do in the evenings. I go to a flick sometimes. The girls are a nightmare. We'd better go out and get drunk together tonight. Make you forget about your uncle. Has he left you anything?'

'Doubt if he'd anything to leave.'

'Never mind. You'll get over it. I'd like to have a talk with you about Widmerpool.'

This intermittent conversation had taken us through most of dinner. I felt scarcely more drawn to Duport than on the day we first met. He was like Peter Templer, with all sympathetic characteristics removed. There was even a slight physical resemblance between the two of them. I wondered if one of those curious, semi-incestuous instincts of attraction had brought Jean to Duport in the first place, or whether Templer and Duport had become alike by seeing a good deal of each other as brothers-in-law and in the City. Duport, I knew, suffered financial crises from time to time. For a period he would live luxuriously, then all his money would disappear. This capacity for making money, combined with inability to keep it, was mysterious to me. I had once said something of the sort to Templer, when he complained of his brother-in-law's instability.

'Oh, Bob knows he will be able to recoup in quite a short time,' Templer had said. 'Doesn't worry him, any more than it worries you that you will be able to write the review of some book when it appears next year. You'll have something to say, Bob'll find a way of making money. It's only momentary inconvenience, due to his own idiocy. It's not making the money presents the difficulty, it's keeping his schemes in bounds – not landing in jail.'

I could see the force of these words. They probably explained Duport's present situation. From what Templer used to say of him – from what Jean used to say of him – I knew quite a lot of Duport. At the same time, there were other things I should not at all have minded hearing about, which only Duport could tell me. I was aware that to probe in this manner was to play with fire, that it would probably be wiser to remain in ignorance of the kind of thing which I was curious to know. However, I saw, too, there was really no escape. I was fated to spend an evening in Duport's company. While I was about it, I might as well hear what I wanted to hear, no matter what the risk. Like Uncle Giles's failings, all was no doubt written in the stars.

'Where shall we go?'

'The bar of the Royal.'

For a time we walked in silence towards the sea-front, the warm night hinting at more seductive pursuits than drinking with Duport.

'News doesn't look very good,' I said. 'Do you think the Germans are going into Poland?'

There seemed no particular object in avoiding banality from the start, as the evening showed every sign of developing into a banal one.

'There's bloody well going to be a war,' said Duport, 'you can ease your mind about that. If I'd been in South America, I'd have sweated it out there. Might in any case. Still, I suppose currency restrictions would make things difficult. I've always been interested in British Guiana aluminium. That might offer something. I'll recount some of my recent adventures in regard to the international situation when we've had some drinks. Did you meet Peter Templer's wife at Stourwater?'

'Yes.'

'What did you think of her?'

'Something's gone a bit adrift, hasn't it?'

'Peter has driven her off her rocker. Nothing else. Used to be a very pretty little thing married to an oaf of a man who bored her to death.'

'What went wrong?'

'She was mad about Peter – still is – and he got too much of her. He always had various items on the side, of course. Then he started up with Lady Anne Something-or-Other, who is always about with Donners.'

'Anne Umfraville.'

'That's the one.'

'There was rather a scene when we were there.'

I gave a brief account of the Masque of the Seven Deadly Sins. Duport listened without interest.

'Donners never seems to mind about other people getting off with his girls,' he said. 'I've heard it said he is a *voyeur*. No accounting for tastes. I don't think Peter cares what he does now. Something of the sort may have upset Betty – though whether she herself, or Anne, was involved, you can't say.'

'I found Peter quietened down on the whole.'

'Quite right. He is in a way. Used to be more cheerful in the days of the slump, when he was down the drain like the rest of us. Then he turned to, and made it all up. Very successful, I'd say. But he never recovered from it. Slowed him up for good, so far as being a pal for a night on the tiles. Prefers now to read the *Financial Times* over a glass of port. However, that need not apply to his private life – may have developed special tastes, just as Donners has. Very intensive womanising sometimes leads to that kind of thing, and you can't say Peter hasn't been intensive.'

By this time we had reached the Royal. Duport led the way to the bar. It was empty, except for the barman, a beefy, talkative fellow, who evidently knew Duport pretty well.

'Fred will fix you up with a girl, if you want one,' said Duport, while drinks were being poured out. 'I don't recommend it.'

'Come off it, Mr Duport.'

'You know you can, Fred. Don't be so coy about it. Where are we going to sit? How do you feel about availing yourself of Fred's good offices?'

'Not tonight.'

'Why not?'

'Not in the mood.'

'Sure?'

'Certain.'

'Don't make a decision you'll regret later.'

'I won't.'

'Do you play poker?'

'Not a great hand at it.'

'Bores you?'

'Never seem to hold a card.'

'Golf?'

'No.'

I felt I was not cutting a very dashing figure, even if I did not accept all this big talk about women as necessarily giving an exact picture of Duport's own life. No doubt women played a considerable part in his existence, but at the same time he seemed over keen on making an impression on that score. He probably talked about them, I thought, more than concerning himself with incessant action in that direction. He was not at all put out that I should fall so far short of the dissipations suggested by him. All he wanted was a companion with whom to drink. Life at the Bellevue must certainly be boring enough.

'I was going to tell you about that swine Widmerpool,' he said.

This seemed no occasion for an outward display of loyalty to Widmerpool by taking offence at such a description. I had stated earlier that Widmerpool and I were on reasonably good terms. That would have to be sufficient. In any case, I had no illusions about Widmerpool's behaviour. All the same, this abuse sounded ungrateful, for what I knew of their connection indicated that more than once Widmerpool had been instrumental in finding a job for Duport when hard up. It was a Widmerpool job for Duport that had finally severed me from Jean.

'Why do you dislike Widmerpool so much?'

'Listen to this,' said Duport. 'Some years ago, when I was on my uppers, Widmerpool arranged for me to buy metal ores for a firm in South America. When that was fixed, I suggested to my wife, Jean, that we might as well link up again. Rather to my surprise, she agreed. Question of the child and so on. Made things easier.'

Duport paused.

'I'll tell you about Jean later,' he said. 'The Widmerpool story first. I don't expect you've ever heard of chromite?'

'The word was being bandied about at Stourwater.'

'Of course. I'd forgotten you'd been there at the critical moment.'

'What was the critical moment?'

'Donners got into his head that he would be well advised to get a foothold in the Turkish chromite market. He'd already talked to Widmerpool about it, when I arrived in London from South America. I'd left South America for reasons I'll explain later. I found a message from Widmerpool, with

646

whom I was of course in touch, telling me to come and see him. I went along to his office. He suggested I should push off to Turkey and buy chromite. It was for Donners-Brebner, but negotiated through a Swiss subsidiary company. What about a refill?'

We ordered some more drinks.

'Widmerpool opened a credit for me through a Turkish bank,' said Duport. 'I was to buy the ores myself and send a shipment as soon as I had enough. I sent one shipment, was getting to work good and proper on the second shipment, when, a week or two ago, do you know what happened?'

'I'm floored.'

'Widmerpool,' said Duport slowly, 'without informing me, cancelled the credit. He did that on his own responsibility, because he didn't like the look of the European situation.'

'Can't you apply to Donners?'

'He is in France, doing a tour of the Maginot Line or something of the sort – making French contacts and having a bit of a holiday at the same time. I was bloody well left holding the baby. The sellers were looking to me for payments impossible for me to make. Of course I shall see Donners the moment he returns. Even if he re-opens the credit, there's been an irreparable balls-up.'

'And you'd go back?'

'If the international situation allows. It may not. I've no quarrel with Widmerpool about the likelihood of war. I quite agree. That is why Donners wants chromite. Widmerpool seems to have missed that small point.'

'Why does Donners specially want chromite if there's war?'

'Corner the Turkish market. The more there is talk of war, the more Donners-Brebner will need chromite. Donners gives out that it is for some special process he is interested in. That was why Peter Templer was asked to Stourwater – so that he would gossip afterwards about that. Not a word of truth. Donners had quite other reasons. He is not going to give away his plans to a fool like Widmerpool, even when it suits his book to use Widmerpool. Widmerpool talks a lot of balls about "reducing the firm's commitments". He's missed the whole bloody point.'

I was not sure that I saw the point myself. It presumably turned on whether or not there was a war – Sir Magnus thinking there would be, Widmerpool undecided how to act if there were. All that was clear was that Duport had been put into an unenviable position.

'So you see,' he said, 'Widmerpool isn't a great favourite with me at the moment.'

'You were going to tell me why you left South America.'

'I was,' said Duport, speaking as if it were a relief to abandon the subject of Widmerpool and chromite. 'Since you know Peter Templer, did you ever meet another ex-brother-in-law of mine, Jimmy Stripling, who was married to Peter's other sister, Babs? He used to have quite a name as a racing driver.'

'Stripling was at the Templers' when I stayed there years ago. I met him once since.'

'Jimmy and Babs got a divorce. Jimmy – who has always been pretty cracked in some ways – took up with a strange lady called Mrs Erdleigh, who tells fortunes. Incidentally, she sometimes came to the Bellevue to see your uncle. I remembered her. Looks as if she kept a high-class knocking-shop. There is another queer fish living at the Bellevue – old boy with a beard. He and Mrs Erdleigh and your late lamented uncle used sometimes to have tea together.'

'I know about Mrs Erdleigh – and Dr Trelawney too.'

'You do? Trelawney tried to bring off a touch last time we talked. I explained I was as broke as himself. No ill feeling. That's beside the point. Also the fact that Myra Erdleigh milked Jimmy Stripling to quite a tune. All I want to know is: what did you think of Jimmy when you met him?'

'Pretty awful – but I never knew him well. He may be all right.'

'Not a bit of it,' said Duport. 'He is awful. Couldn't be worse. Kept out of the war himself and ran away with Babs when her husband was at the front. Double-dealing, stingy, conceited, bad tempered, half cracked. I went to him to try and get a bit of help during my last pre-South American *débâcle*. Not on your life. Nothing doing with Jimmy. I might have starved in the gutter for all Jimmy cared. Now, you say you knew Jean, my ex-wife?'

'She was at Peter's Maidenhead house once when I went there.'

'Nice girl, didn't you think?'

'Yes, I did.'

'Reasonably attractive?'

'I'd certainly have said so.'

'Wouldn't have any difficulty in getting hold of the right sort of chap?'

'It wouldn't be polite to express doubt on that point, since she married you.'

I did not manage to impart all the jocularity fittingly required to give lively savour to this comment. Duport, in any case, brushed it aside as irrelevant.

'Leave me out of it by all means,' he said. 'Just speaking in general, would you think Jean would have any difficulty in getting hold of a decent sort of chap? Yes or no.'

'No.'

'Neither should I,' said Duport. 'But the fact remains that she slept with Jimmy Stripling.'

I made some suitable acknowledgment, tempered, I hoped, by polite surprise. I well remembered the frightful moment when Jean herself had first informed me, quite

649

gratuitously, of having undergone the experience to which Duport referred. I could recall even now how painful that information had been at the time, as one might remember a physical accident long passed. The matter no longer worried me, primarily because I no longer loved Jean, also because the whole Stripling question had, so to speak, been resolved between Jean and myself at the time. All the same, the incident had been a disagreeable one. That had to be admitted. One does not want to dwell on some racking visit to the dentist, however many years have rolled on since that day. Perhaps I would have preferred to have remained even then unreminded of Jean and Stripling. However, present recital could in no way affect the past. That was history.

'Can you beat it?'

I acknowledged inability to offer a parallel instance.

'Well, I can,' said Duport. 'I don't set up as behaving particularly well myself, but, when it comes to behaving badly, women can give you a point or two every time. I just tell you about Jimmy Stripling by the way. He is not the cream of the jest. As I mentioned before, I thought things would be easier if Jean and I joined up again. I found I was wrong.'

'Why was that?'

'Not surprisingly, Jean had been having a bit of a run around while we were living apart,' said Duport. 'I suppose that was to be expected.'

I began to feel decidedly uncomfortable. So far as I knew, neither Duport, nor anyone else, had the smallest reason to guess anything of what had passed between Jean and myself. All the same, his words suggested he was aware of more than I might suppose.

'The point turned out to be this,' said Duport. 'Jean only wanted to link up with me again to make things easier for herself in carrying on one of her little affairs.'

'But how could joining up with you possibly help? Surely

things were much easier when she was on her own?'

Duport did not answer that question.

'Guess who the chap was?' he said.

'How could I possibly?'

'Somebody known to you.'

'Are you sure?'

'Seen you and him at the same time.'

Duport grinned horribly. At least I guiltily thought his grin horrible, because I supposed him to be teasing me. It was unlikely, most unlikely, that Jean had told him about ourselves, although, since she had told both of us about Stripling, such a confession could not be regarded as out of the question. Perhaps someone else, unknown to us, had passed the story on to Duport. In either case, the situation was odious. I greatly regretted having agreed to come out drinking with him, even more of having encouraged him to speak of his own troubles. My curiosity had put me in this position. I had no one but myself to blame. It was just in Duport's character, I felt, to discompose me in this manner. If he chose to make himself unpleasant about what had happened, I was in no position to object. Things would have to be brazened out. All the same, I could not understand what he meant by saying that Jean had come back to him in order to 'make things more convenient'. Her return to her husband, their journey together to South America, had been the moment when we had been forced finally to say good-bye to each other. Since then, I had neither seen nor heard of her.

'Just have a shot at who it was,' said Duport, 'bearing in mind Jimmy Stripling as the standard of what a lover should be.'

'Did he look like Stripling?'

I felt safe, at least, in the respect that, apart from any difference in age, no two people could look less alike than Stripling and myself.

'Even more of a lout,' said Duport, 'if you can believe that.'

'In what way?'

There was a ghastly fascination in seeing how far he would go.

'Wetter, for one thing.'

'I give it up.'

'Come on.'

'No good.'

I knew I must be red in the face. By this time we had had some more drinks, to which heightened colouring might reasonably be attributed.

'I'll tell you.'

I nerved myself.

'It was another Jimmy,' said Duport. 'Perhaps Jimmy is just a name she likes. Call a man Jimmy and she gets hot pants at once, I shouldn't wonder. Anyway, it was Jimmy Brent.'

'Brent?'

At first the name conveyed nothing to me.

'The fat slob who was in the Vauxhall when Peter drove us all into the hedge. You must remember him.'

'I do remember him now.'

Even in retrospect, this was a frightful piece of information.

'Jimmy Brent – always being ditched by tarts in night-clubs.'

I felt as if someone had suddenly kicked my legs from under me, so that I had landed on the other side of the room, not exactly hurt, but thoroughly ruffled, with all the breath knocked out of me.

'Nice discovery, wasn't it?' said Duport.

'Had this business with Brent been going on long?'

'Quite a month or two. Took the place of something else, I gather. In fact there was a period when she was running both at the same time. That's what I have good reason to believe. The point was that Brent was going to South America too. It suited Jean's book for me to buy her ticket. We all three crossed on the same boat. Then she continued to carry on with him over there.'

'But are you sure this is true? She can't really have been in love with Brent.'

This naïve comment might have caught the attention of someone more interested than Duport in the emotions of other people. It was, in short, a complete give-away. No one was likely to use that phrase about a woman he scarcely knew, as I had allowed Duport to suppose about Jean and myself. As it was, he merely showed justifiable contempt for my lack of grasp, no awareness that the impact of his story had struck a shower of sparks.

'Who's to say when a woman's in love?' he said.

I thought how often I had made that kind of remark myself, when other people were concerned.

'I've no reason to suppose she wasn't speaking the truth when she told me she'd slept with him,' Duport said. 'She informed me in bed, appropriately enough. You're not going to tell me any woman would boast of having slept with Jimmy Brent, if she hadn't. The same applies to Jimmy Stripling. It's one of the characteristics the two Jimmies have in common. Both actions strike me as even odder to admit to than to do, if that was possible.'

'I see.'

'Nothing like facing facts when you've been had for a mug in a big way,' said Duport. 'I was thinking that this morning when I was working out some freight charges. The best one can say is that Jimmy and the third party – if there was a third party – were probably had for mugs too.'

I agreed. There was nothing like facing facts. They blew into the face hard, like a stiff, exhilarating, decidedly gritty breeze, which brought sanity with it, even though sanity might be unwelcome.

'What made you think there was another chap too?' I asked, from sheer lack of self-control.

'Something Jean herself let fall.'

It is always a temptation to tell one's own story. However, I saw that would be only to show oneself, without the least necessity, in a doubly unflattering light to someone I did not like, someone who could not, in the circumstances, reasonably be expected to be in the least sympathetic. I tried to sort out what had happened. Only a short while earlier, I had thought of myself as standing in an uneasy position *vis-à-vis* Duport, although at the same time a somewhat more advantageous one. Now, I saw that I, even more than he, had been made a fool of. At least Duport seemed to have begun the discord in his own married life – although, again, who can state with certainty the cause of such beginnings? – while I had supposed myself finally parting with Jean only in order that her own matrimonial situation might be patched up. That charming love affair, which had formerly seemed to drift to a close through my own ineffectiveness, had, in reality, been terminated by the deliberate manœuvre of Jean herself for her own purposes, certainly to the detriment of my self-esteem. I thought of that grave, gothic beauty that once I had loved so much, which found fulfilment in such men. The remembered moaning in pleasure of someone once loved always haunts the memory, even when love itself is over. Perhaps, I thought, her men are gothic too, beings carved on the niches and corbels of a mediaeval cathedral to arouse at once laughter and horror. In any case, I had been one of them. If her lovers were horrifying, I too had been of their order. That had to be admitted.

'It is no good pontificating,' Mr Deacon used to say, 'about other people's sexual tastes.'

For the moment, angry, yet at the same time half inclined to laugh, I could not make up my mind what I thought. This was yet another example of the tricks that Time can play within its own folds, tricks that emphasise the insecurity of those who trust themselves over much to that treacherous concept. I suddenly found what I had regarded as immutable – the not entirely unsublime past – roughly reshaped by the rude hands of Duport. That was justice, I thought, if you like.

'What happened after?'

'After what?'

'Did she marry Brent?'

Duport's story had made me forget entirely that Templer had already told me his sister had made a second marriage.

'Not she,' said Duport. 'Ditched Brent too. Can't blame her for that. Nobody could stick Jimmy for long – either of them. She married a local Don Juan some years younger than herself – in the army. Nephew of the President. I've just met him. He looks like Rudolph Valentino on an off day. Change from Brent, anyway. It takes all sorts to make a lover. Probably keep her in order, I should think. More than I ever managed.'

He stretched.

'I could do with a woman now,' he said.

'Why not have one of Fred's?'

'Fred hasn't got what I want. Besides, it's too late in the evening. Fred likes about an hour's notice. You know, I'll tell you something else, as I seem to be telling you all about my marital affairs. My wife wasn't really much of a grind. That was why I went elsewhere. All the same, she had something. I wasn't sorry when we started up again.'

I loathed him. I still carried with me *The Perfumed Garden*. Now seemed a suitable moment to seek a home for the Sheik Nefzaoui's study. Room could no doubt be found for it in the Duport library. To present him with the book would be small, secret amends for having had a love affair with his wife, a token of gratitude for having brought home to me in so uncompromising a fashion the transitory nature of love. It would be better not to draw his attention to the chapter on the Deceits and Treacheries of Women. He could find that for himself.

'Ever read this?'

Duport glanced at the title, then turned the pages.

'*The Arab Art of Love*,' he said. 'Are you always armed with this sort of literature? I did not realise you meant that kind of thing when you said you reviewed books.'

'I found it among my uncle's things.'

'The old devil.'

'What do you think of it?'

'They say you're never too old to learn.'

'Would you like it?'

'How much?'

'I'll make a present of it.'

'Might give me a few new ideas,' said Duport. 'I'll accept it as a gift. Not otherwise.'

'It's yours then.'

'Got to draw your attention to the clock, Mr Duport,' said the barman, who was beginning to tidy up in preparation for closing the bar.

'We're being kicked out,' said Duport. 'Just time for a final one.'

The bar closed. We said good night to Fred.

'Nothing for it but go back to the Bellevue,' said Duport. 'I've got a bottle of whisky in my room.'

'What about the pier?'

'Shut by now.'

'Let's walk round by the Front.'

'All right.'

The wind had got up by that time. The sea thudded over

656

the breakwaters in a series of regular, dull explosions, like a cannonade of old-fashioned artillery. I felt thoroughly annoyed. We turned inland and made for the Bellevue. The front door was shut, but not locked. We were crossing the hall, when Albert came hurrying down the stairs. He was evidently dreadfully disturbed about some matter. His movements, comparatively rapid for him, indicated consternation. He was pale and breathless. When he saw us, he showed no surprise that Duport and I should have spent an evening together. Our arrival in each other's company seemed almost expected by him, the very thing he was hoping for at that moment.

'There's been a proper kettle of fish,' he said. 'I'm glad to see you back, Mr Nick – and you too, Mr Duport.'

'What's happened?'

'Dr Trelawney.'

'What's he done?'

'Gone and locked himself in the bathroom. Can't get out. Now he's having one of his asthma attacks. With the wife queer herself, I don't want to get her out of bed at this time of night. I'd be glad of you gentlemen's help. There's no one else in the house that's less than in their seventies and it ain't no good asking those silly girls. I'm all that sorry to trouble you.'

'What,' said Duport, 'the good Dr Trelawney, the bearded one? We'll have him out in a trice. Lead us to him.'

This sudden crisis cheered Duport enormously. Action was what he needed. I thought of Moreland's remarks about men of action, wondering whether Duport would qualify. This was not how I had expected to meet Dr Trelawney again. We hurried along the passages behind Albert, slip-slopping in his ancient felt slippers. There were many stairs to climb. At last we reached the bathroom door. There it became clear that the rescue of Dr Trelawney presented difficulties. In fact it was hard to know how best to set about his release. From within the bathroom, rising and falling like the vibrations of a small but powerful engine, could be heard the alarming pant of the asthma victim. Dr Trelawney sounded in extremity. Something must be done quickly. There was no doubt of that. Albert bent forward and put his mouth to the keyhole.

'Try again, Dr Trelawney,' he shouted.

The awful panting continued for a minute or two; then, very weak and shaky, came Dr Trelawney's thin, insistent voice.

'I am not strong enough,' he said.

Albert turned towards us and shook his head.

'He's done this before,' he said in a lower tone. 'It's my belief he just wants to get attention. He was angry when your uncle died, Mr Nick, and the wife and I had to see about that, and not about him for a change. It can't go on. I won't put up with it. He'll have to go. I've said so before. It's too much. Flesh and blood won't stand it.'

'Shall we bust the door down?' said Duport. 'I could if I took a run at it, but there isn't quite enough space to do that here.'

That was true. The bathroom door stood at an angle by the end of the passage, built in such a way that violent attack of that kind upon it was scarcely possible. Dr Trelawney's hoarse, trembling voice came again.

'Telephone to Mrs Erdleigh,' he said. 'Tell her to bring my pills. I must have my pills.'

This request seemed to bring some relief to Albert.

'I'll do that right away, sir,' he shouted through the keyhole.

'What on earth can Mrs Erdleigh do?' said Duport.

Albert, with an old-fashioned gesture, touched the side of his nose with his forefinger.

'I know what he wants now,' he said. 'One of his special

pills. I might have thought of Mrs Erdleigh before. We'll have him out when she comes. She'll do it.'

'What pills are they?'

'Better not ask, sir,' said Albert.

'Drugs, do you mean?'

'I've never pressed the matter, sir, nor where they come from.'

Duport and I were left alone in the passage.

'I suppose we could smash the panel,' he said. 'Shall I try to find an instrument?'

'Better not break the house up. Anyway, not until Albert returns. Besides, it would wake everybody. We don't want a bevy of old ladies to appear.'

'Try taking the key out, Dr Trelawney,' said Duport in an authoritative voice, 'then put it back again and have another turn. That sometimes works. I know that particular key. I thought I was stuck in the bloody hole myself yesterday, but managed to get out that way.'

At first there was no answer. When at last he replied, Dr Trelawney sounded suspicious.

'Who is that?' he asked. 'Where has Mr Creech gone?'

'It's Duport. You know, we sometimes talk in the lounge. You borrowed my *Financial Times* the other morning. Creech has gone to ring Mrs Erdleigh.'

There was another long silence, during which Dr Trelawney's breathing grew a little less heavy. Evidently he was making a great effort to bring himself under control, now that he found that people, in addition to Albert, were at work on his rescue. Then the ritual sentence sounded through the door:

'The Essence of the All is the Godhead of the True.'

Duport turned to me and shook his head.

'We often get that,' he said.

This seemed the moment, now or never, when the spell

must prove its worth. I leant towards his keyhole and spoke the concordant rejoinder:

'The Vision of Visions heals the Blindness of Sight.'

Duport laughed.

'What on earth are you talking about?' he said.

'That's the right answer.'

'How on earth did you know?'

We heard the sound of Dr Trelawney heaving himself up with difficulty from wherever he was sitting. He must have staggered across the bathroom, for he made a great deal of noise as he came violently into contact with objects obstructive to his passage. Then he reached the door and began to fumble with the key. He removed it from the lock; after a moment or two he tried once more to insert it in the keyhole. Several of these attempts failed. Then, suddenly, quite unexpectedly, came a hard scraping sound; the key could be heard turning slowly; there was a click; the door stood ajar. Dr Trelawney was before us on the threshold.

'I told you that would work,' said Duport.

Except for the beard, hardly a trace remained of the Dr Trelawney I dimly remembered. All was changed. Even the beard, straggling, dirty grey, stained yellow in places like the patches of broom on the common beyond Stonehurst, had lost all resemblance to that worn by the athletic, vigorous prophet of those distant days. Once broad and luxuriant, it was now shrivelled almost to a goatee. He no longer seemed to have stepped down from a stained-glass window or ikon. His skin was dry and blotched. Dark spectacles covered his eyes, his dressing-gown a long blue oriental robe that swept the ground. He really looked rather frightening. Although so altered from the Stonehurst era, he still gave me the same chilly feeling of inner uneasiness that I had known as a child when I watched him and his flock trailing across the heather. I remembered Moreland, when we had once talked of Dr

Trelawney, quoting the lines from *Marmion*, where the king consults the wizard lord:

> 'Dire dealings with the fiendish race
> Had mark'd strange lines upon his face;
> Vigil and fast had worn him grim,
> His eyesight dazzled seem'd and dim . . .'

That just about described Dr Trelawney as he supported himself against the doorpost, seized with another fearful fit of coughing. I do not know what Duport and I would have done with him, if Albert had not reappeared at that moment. Albert was relieved, certainly, but did not seem greatly surprised that we had somehow brought about this liberation.

'Mrs Erdleigh promised she'd be along as quick as possible,' he said, 'but there were a few things she had to do first. I'm glad you was able to get the door open at last, sir. Mrs Creech must have that door seen to. I've spoken to her about it before. Might be better if you used the other bathroom in future, Dr Trelawney, we don't want such a business another night.'

Dr Trelawney did not reply to this suggestion, perhaps because Albert spoke in what was, for him, almost a disrespectful tone, certainly a severe one. Instead, he held out his arms on either side of him, the hands open, as if in preparation for crucifixion.

'I must ask you two gentlemen to assist me to my room,' he said. 'I am too weak to walk unaided. That sounds like the beginning of an evangelical hymn:

> I am too weak to . . . walk unaided . . .

The fact is I must be careful of this shell I call my body, though why I should be, I hardly know. Perhaps from mere courtesy to my medical advisers. There have been warnings – cerebral congestion.'

He laughed rather disagreeably. We supported him along the passage, led by Albert. In his room, not without effort, we established him in the bed. The exertions of Duport and myself brought this about, not much aided by Albert, who, breathing hard, showed little taste for the job. Duport, on the other hand, had been enjoying himself thoroughly since the beginning of this to-do. Action, excitement were what he needed. They showed another side to him. Dr Trelawney, too, was enjoying himself by now. So far from being exhausted by this heaving about of the shell he called his body, he was plainly stimulated by all that had happened. He had mastered his fit of asthma, brought on, no doubt, as Albert had suggested, by boredom and depression. The Bellevue must in any case have represented a low ebb in Dr Trelawney's fortunes. Plenty of attention made him almost well again. He lay back on his pillows, indicating by a movement of the hands that he wished us to stay and talk with him until the arrival of Mrs Erdleigh.

'Bring some glasses, my friend,' he said to Albert. 'We shall need four – a number portending obstacles and opposition in the symbolism of cards – yet necessary for our present purpose, if Myra Erdleigh is soon to be of our party.'

Albert, thankful to have Dr Trelawney out of the bathroom and safely in bed at so small a cost, went off to fetch the glasses without any of the peevishness to be expected of him when odd jobs were in question. Dr Trelawney's request seemed to have reference to a half-bottle of brandy, already opened, that stood on the wash-stand. I had been prepared to find myself in an alchemist's cell, where occult processes matured in retorts and cauldrons, reptiles hung from the ceiling while their venom distilled, homunculi in bottles lined the walls. However, there were no dog-eared volumes of the Cabbala to be seen, no pentagrams or tarot cards. Instead, Dr Trelawney's room was very like that formerly occupied by Uncle Giles, no bigger, just as dingy. A pile of luggage lay in one corner, some suits – certainly ancient enough – hung on coat-hangers suspended from the side of the wardrobe. The only suggestion of the Black Arts was wafted by a faint, sickly smell, not immediately identifiable: incense? hair-tonic? opium? It was hard to say whether the implications were chemical, medicinal, ritualistic; a scent vaguely disturbing, like Dr Trelawney's own personality. Albert returned with the glasses, then said good night, adding a word about latching the front door when Mrs Erdleigh left. He must have been used to her visits at a late hour. Duport and I were left alone with the Doctor. He told us to distribute the brandy – the flask was about a quarter full – allowing a share for Mrs Erdleigh herself when she arrived. Duport took charge, pouring out drink for the three of us.

'Which of you answered me through the door?' asked Dr Trelawney, when he had drunk some brandy.

'I did.'

'You know my teachings then?'

I told him I remembered the formula from Stonehurst. That was not strictly speaking true, because I should never have carried the words in my head all those years, if I had not heard Moreland and others talk of the Doctor in later life. My explanation did not altogether please Dr Trelawney, either because he wished to forget that period of his career, or because it too painfully recalled happier, younger days, when his cult was more flourishing. Possibly he felt disappointment that I should turn out to be no new, hitherto unknown, disciple, full of untapped enthusiasm, admiring from afar, who now at last found dramatic opportunity to disclose himself. He made no comment at all. There was something decidedly unpleasant about him, sinister, at the same time absurd, that combination of the ludicrous and alarming soon to be widely experienced by contact with those set in authority in wartime.

'I may be said to have come from Humiliation into Triumph,' he said, 'the traditional theme of Greek Tragedy. The climate of this salubrious resort does not really suit me. In fact, I cannot think why I stay. Perhaps because I cannot afford to pay my bill and leave. Nor is there much company in the Bellevue calculated to revive failing health and spirits. And you, sir? Why are you enjoying the ozone here, if one may ask? Perhaps for the same reason as Mr Duport, who has confided to me some of the secrets of his own private prison-house.'

Dr Trelawney smiled, showing teeth as yellow and irregular as the stains on his beard. He was, I thought, a tremendously Edwardian figure: an Edwardian figure of fun, one might say. All the same, I remembered that a girl had thrown herself from a Welsh mountain-top on his account. Such things were to be considered in estimating his capacity. His smile was one of the worst things about him. I saw that Duport must be on closer terms with the Doctor than he had pretended. I had certainly not grasped the fact that they already knew each other well enough to have exchanged reasons for residing at the Bellevue. Indeed, Duport, while he had been drinking at the Royal, seemed almost deliberately to have obscured their comparative intimacy. There was nothing very surprising about their confiding in one another. Total strangers in bars and railway carriages will unfold the story of their lives at the least opportunity. It was probably true to say that the hotel contained no more suitable couple to make friends. The details about his married life which Duport had imparted

to me showed that he was a more complicated, more intro-
spective character than I had ever guessed. His connexion
with Jean was now less mysterious to me. No doubt Jimmy
Stripling's esoteric goings-on had familiarised Duport, more
or less, with people of Dr Trelawney's sort. In any case, Dr
Trelawney was probably pretty good at worming information out of other residents. Even during the time we had
been sitting in the room I had become increasingly aware of
his pervasive, quasi-hypnotic powers, possessed to a greater
or lesser degree by all persons – not necessarily connected
with occultism – who form little cults devoted primarily to
veneration of themselves. This awareness was not because
I felt myself in danger of falling under Dr Trelawney's
dominion, though it conveyed an instinctive warning to be
on one's guard. Perhaps the feeling was no more than a
grown-up version of childish fantasies about him, perhaps
a tribute to his will. I was not certain. Duport, on the other
hand, appeared perfectly at ease. He sat in a broken-down
armchair facing the bed, his hands in his pockets. I explained
about my early associations with Albert, about Uncle Giles's
funeral.

'I used to talk with your uncle,' said Dr Trelawney.

'What did you think of him?'

'A thwarted spirit, a restless soul wandering the vast sur-
faces of the earth.'

'He never found a job he liked.'

'Men do not gather grapes from off a thorn.'

'He told you about himself?'

'It was not necessary. Every man bears on his forehead the
story of his days, an open volume to the initiate.'

'From that volume, you knew him well?'

'Who can be said to know well? All men are mysteries.'

'There was no mystery about your uncle's grousing,' said
Duport. 'The only thing he was cheerful about was saying

there would not be a war. What do you think, Dr Trelawney?'

'What will be, must be.'

'Which means war, in my opinion,' said Duport.

'The sword of Mithras, who each year immolates the sacred bull, will ere long now flash from its scabbard.'

'You've said it.'

'The slayer of Osiris once again demands his grievous tribute of blood. The Angel of Death will ride the storm.'

'Could this situation have been avoided?' I asked.

'The god, Mars, approaches the earth to lay waste. Moreover, the future is ever the consequence of the past.'

'And we ought to have knocked Hitler out when he first started making trouble?'

I remembered Ted Jeavons had held that view.

'The Four Horsemen are at the gate. The Kaiser went to war for shame of his withered arm. Hitler will go to war because at official receptions the tails of his evening coat sweep the floor like a clown's.'

'Seems an inadequate reason,' said Duport.

'Such things are a paradox to the uninstructed – to the adept they are clear as morning light.'

'I must be one of the uninstructed,' said Duport.

'You are not alone in that.'

'Just one of the crowd?'

'Reason is given to all men, but all men do not know how to use it. Liberty is offered to each one of us, but few learn to be free. Such gifts are, in any case, a right to be earned, not a privilege for the shiftless.'

'How do you recommend earning it?' asked Duport, stretching out his long legs in front of him, slumping down into the depths of the armchair. 'I've got to rebuild my business connexions. I could do with a few hints.'

'The education of the will is the end of human life.'

'You think so?'

'I know.'

'But can you always apply the will?' said Duport. 'Could I have renewed my severed credits by the will?'

'I am concerned with the absolute.'

'So am I. An absolute balance at the bank.'

'You speak of material trifles. The great Eliphas Lévi, whose precepts I quote to you, said that one who is afraid of fire will never command salamanders.'

'I don't need to command salamanders. I want to shake the metal market.'

'To know, to dare, to will, to keep silence, those are the things required.'

'And what's the bonus for these surplus profits?'

'You have spoken your modest needs.'

'But what else can the magicians offer?'

'To be for ever rich, for ever young, never to die.'

'Do they, indeed?'

'Such was in every age the dream of the alchemist.'

'Not a bad programme – let's have the blue-prints.'

'To attain these things, as I have said, you must emancipate the will from servitude, instruct it in the art of domination.'

'You should meet a mutual friend of ours called Widmerpool,' said Duport. 'He would agree with you. He's very keen on domination. Don't you think so, Jenkins? Anyway, Dr Trelawney, what action do you recommend to make a start?'

'Power does not surrender itself. Like a woman, it must be seized.'

Duport jerked his head in my direction.

'I offered him a woman in the bar of the Royal this evening,' he said, 'but he declined. He wouldn't seize one. I must admit Fred never has much on hand.'

'Cohabitation with antipathetic beings is torment,' said

Dr Trelawney. 'Has that never struck you, my dear friend?'

'Time and again,' said Duport, laughing loudly. 'Perfect hell. I've done quite a bit of it in my day. Would you like to hear some of my experiences?'

'Why should we wish to ruminate on your most secret orgies?' said Dr Trelawney. 'What profit for us to muse on your nights in the lupanar, your diabolical couplings with the brides of debauch, more culpable than those phantasms of the incubi that rack the dreams of young girls, or the libidinous gymnastics of the goat-god whose ice-cold sperm fathers monsters on writhing witches in coven?'

Duport shook with laughter. I saw that one of Dr Trelawney's weapons was flattery, though flattery of no trite kind, in fact the best of all flattery, the sort disguised as disagreement or rebuke.

'So you don't want a sketch of my love life in its less successful moments?' said Duport.

Dr Trelawney shook his head.

'There have been some good moments too,' said Duport. 'Don't get me wrong.'

'He alone can truly possess the pleasures of love,' said Dr Trelawney, 'who has gloriously vanquished the love of pleasure.'

'Is that your technique?'

'If you would possess, do not give.'

'I've known plenty of girls who thought that, my wife among them.'

'Continual caressing begets satiety.'

'She thought that too. You should meet. However, if what you said about a war coming is true – and it's what I think myself – why bother? We shall soon be as dead as Jenkins's uncle.'

Duport had a way of switching from banter to savage melancholy.

'There is no death in Nature,' said Dr Trelawney, 'only transition, blending, synthesis, mutation.'

'All the same,' said Duport, 'to take this uncle of Jenkins's again, you must admit, from his point of view, it was different sitting in the Bellevue lounge, from lying in a coffin at the crematorium, his present whereabouts, as I understand from his nephew.'

'Those who no longer walk beside us on the void expanses of this fleeting empire of created light have no more reached the absolute end of their journey than birth was for them the absolute beginning. They have merely performed their fugitive pilgrimage from embryo to ashes. They are in the world no longer. That is all we can say.'

'But what more can anyone say?' said Duport. 'You're put in a box and stowed away underground, or cremated in the Jenkins manner. In other words, you're dead.'

'Death is a mere phantom of ignorance,' said Dr Trelawney. 'It does not exist. The flesh is the raiment of the soul. When that raiment has grown threadbare or is torn asunder by violent hands, it must be abandoned. There is witness without end. When men know how to live, they will no longer die, no more cry with Faustus:

O lente, lente currite, noctis equi!'

Dr Trelawney and Duport were an odd couple arguing together about the nature of existence, the immortality of the soul, survival after death. The antithetical point of view each represented was emphasised by their personal appearance. This rather bizarre discussion was brought to an end by a knock on the door.

'Enter,' said Dr Trelawney.

He spoke in a voice of command. Mrs Erdleigh came into the room. Dr Trelawney raised himself into a sitting position, leaning back on his elbows.

'The Essence of the All is the Godhead of the True.'

'The Vision of Visions heals the Blindness of Sight.'

While she pronounced the incantation, Mrs Erdleigh smiled in a faintly deprecatory manner, like a grown-up who, out of pure good nature, humours the whim of a child. I remembered the same expression coming into her face when speaking to Uncle Giles. Dr Trelawney made a dramatic gesture of introduction, showing his fangs again in one of those awful grins as he lay back on the pillow.

'Mr Duport, you've met, Myra,' he said. 'This gentleman here is the late Captain Jenkins's nephew, bearing the same name.'

He rolled his eyes in my direction, indicating Mrs Erdleigh.

'*Connaissez-vous la vieille souveraine du monde,*' he said, '*qui marche toujours, et ne se fatigue jamais?* In this incarnation, she passes under the name of Mrs Erdleigh.'

'Mr Jenkins and I know each other already,' she said, with a smile.

'I might have guessed,' said Dr Trelawney. 'She knows all.'

'And your introduction was not very polite,' said Mrs Erdleigh. 'I am not as old as she to whom the Abbé referred.'

'Be not offended, priestess of Isis. You have escaped far beyond the puny fingers of Time.'

She turned from him, holding out her hand to me.

'I knew you were here,' she said.

'Did Albert say I was coming?'

'It was not necessary. I know such things. Your poor uncle passed over peacefully. More peacefully than might have been expected.'

She wore a black coat with a high fur collar, a tricorne hat, also black, riding on the summit of grey curls. These

670

had taken the place of the steep bank of dark-reddish tresses of the time when I had met her at the Ufford with Uncle Giles seven or eight years before. Then, I had imagined her nearing fifty. Lunching with the Templers eighteen months later (when she had arrived with Jimmy Stripling), I decided she was younger. Now, she was not so much aged as an entirely different woman – what my brother-in-law, Hugo Tolland, used to call (apropos of his employer, Mrs Baldwyn Hodges) a 'blue-rinse marquise'. This new method of doing her hair, the tone and texture of which suggested a wig, together with the three-cornered hat, recalled Longhi, the Venetian ridotto. You felt Mrs Erdleigh had just removed her mask before paying this visit to Cagliostro – or, as it turned out with no great difference, to Dr Trelawney.

'Sad that your mother-in-law, Lady Warminster, passed over too,' said Mrs Erdleigh. 'She had not consulted me for some years, but I foretold both her marriages. I warned her that her second husband should beware of the Eagle – symbol of the East, you know – and of the Equinox of Spring. Lord Warminster died in Kashmir at just that season.'

'She is greatly missed in the family.'

'Lady Warminster was a woman among women,' said Mrs Erdleigh. 'I shall never forget her gratitude when I revealed to her that Tuesday was the best day for the operation of revenge.'

Dr Trelawney was becoming restive, either because Mrs Erdleigh had made herself the centre of attention, or because his own 'treatment' had been delayed too long.

'We think we should have our . . . er . . . pill, ha-ha,' he said, trying to laugh, but beginning to twitch dreadfully. 'We do not wish to cut short so pleasurable an evening. I am eternally grateful to you, gentlemen – though to name eternity is redundant, since we all perforce have our being within it – and I hope we shall meet again, if only in the place where the last are said to be first, though, for my own part, I shall not be surprised if the first are first there too.'

'We shall have to turn in as well,' said Duport, rising, 'or I shall have no head for figures tomorrow.'

I thought Duport did not much care for Mrs Erdleigh, certainly disliked the fact that she and I had met before.

'The gods brook no more procrastination,' said Dr Trelawney, his hoarse voice rising sharply in key. 'I am like one of those about to adore the demon under the figure of a serpent, or such as make sorceries with vervain and periwinkle, sage, mint, ash and basil . . .'

Mrs Erdleigh had taken off her coat and hat. She was fumbling in a large black bag she had brought with her. Dr Trelawney's voice now reached an agonised screech.

'. . . votaries of the Furies who use branches of cedar, alder, hawthorn, saffron and juniper in their sacrifices of turtle doves and sheep, who pour upon the ground libations of wine and honey . . .'

Mrs Erdleigh almost hustled us through the door. There was something in her hand, a small instrument that caught the light.

'I shall be with my old friend at the last tomorrow,' she said, opening wide her huge, misty eyes.

The door closed. There was the sound of the key turning in the lock, then, as we moved off down the passage, of water poured into a basin.

'You see what living at the Bellevue is like,' said Duport.

'I'm surprised you find it boring. Have you still got *The Perfumed Garden*?'

'What's that?'

'The book I gave you – *The Arab Art of Love*.'

'Hell,' said Duport, 'I left it in Trelawney's room. Well,

672

I can get it again tomorrow, if he hasn't peddled it by then.'

'Good night.'

'Good night,' said Duport. 'I don't envy you having to turn out for your uncle's funeral in the morning.'

The Bellevue mattress was a hard one. Night was disturbed by dreams. Dr Trelawney – who had shaved his head and wore RAF uniform – preached from the baroquely carved pulpit of a vast cathedral on the text that none should heed Billson's claim to be pregnant by him of a black messiah. These and other aberrant shapes made the coming of day welcome. I rose, beyond question impaired by the drinks consumed with Duport, all the same anxious to get through my duties. Outside, the weather was sunny, all that the seaside required. Nevertheless, I wanted only to return to London. While I dressed, I wondered whether the goings-on of the night before had disturbed other residents of the hotel. When I reached the dining-room, the air of disquiet there made me think we had made more noise than I had supposed. Certainly the murmur of conversation was uneasy at the tables of the old ladies. An atmosphere of tension made itself felt at once. Duport, unexpectedly in his place, was eating a kipper, a pile of disordered newspapers lying on the floor beside him. I made some reference to the unwisdom of terminating an evening of that sort with Dr Trelawney's brandy. Duport made a face. He ignored my comment.

'Nice news,' he said, 'isn't it?'

'What?'

'Germany and Russia.'

'What have they done? I haven't seen a paper.'

'Signed a Non-Aggression Pact with each other.'

He handed me one of the newspapers. I glanced at the headlines.

'Cheerful situation, you will agree,' said Duport.

'Makes a good start to the day.'

I felt a sinking inside me as I read.

'Molotov and Ribbentrop,' said Duport. 'Sound like the names of a pair of performing monkeys. Just the final touch to balls up my affairs.'

'It will be war all right now.'

'And Hitler will be able to buy all the chromite he wants from the Soviet.'

'So what?'

'It's good-bye to my return to Turkey, whatever happens.'

'But if there's war, shan't we want the stuff more than ever?'

'Of course we shall. Even a bloody book-reviewer, or whatever you are, can see that. It doesn't prevent Widmerpool from failing to grasp the point. The probability of war made the pre-empting of the Turkish market essential to this country.'

'Then why not still?'

'Buying chromite to prevent Germany from getting it, and buying it just for our own use, are not the same thing. All the chromite Germany wants will now be available from Russian sources – and a bloody long list of other important items too.'

'I see.'

'Donners will handle matters differently now. I shall drop out automatically. I might get another job out of him, not that one. But can you imagine Widmerpool being such a fool as to suppose the prospect of war would diminish Donners-Brebner requirements. "Cut down our commitments", indeed.'

Duport spat out some kipper-bones on to his plate. He took several deep gulps of coffee.

'Of course in a way Widmerpool turned out to be right,' he said. 'As usual, his crassness brought him luck. As a matter of fact, I wouldn't wonder if he didn't cut off my credits as much from spite as obtuseness.'

'Why should Widmerpool want to spite you?'

'Just to show who's master. I sent him one or two pretty curt telegrams. He didn't like that. Probably decided to get his own back. Anyway, I'm up a gum tree now.'

I saw he had cause to grumble. At that moment, I could not spare much sympathy. In any case, I did not care for Duport, although I had to admit he had his points. He was, in his way, a man of action. Ahead, I thought, lay plenty of opportunity for action of one kind or another. Even now, a thousand things had to be done. Then and there, the only course to follow was to oversee Uncle Giles's cremation, return home, try to make plans in the light of the new international situation.

' 'Spect they'll requisition the place now all right,' said Albert, when I saw him. 'That's if there's anything to requisition in a day or two. Hitler's not one to tell us when he's coming. Just loose a lot of bombs, I reckon. The wife's still poorly and taking on a treat about the blackout in the bedrooms.'

For a man who thoroughly disliked danger, Albert faced the prospect of total war pretty well. At best its circumstances would shatter the props of his daily life at a time when he was no longer young. All the same, the Germans, the Russians, the suffragettes were all one when it came to putting up the shutters. He might be afraid when a police-man walked up the Stonehurst drive; that trepidation was scarcely at all increased by the prospect of bombard-ment from the air. Indeed, his fear was really a sort of courage, fear and courage being close to each other, like love and hate.

'Mr Duport and I sat up with Dr Trelawney for a while after he went to bed last night,' I said.

Albert shook his head.

'Don't know how we're going to get rid of him now,' he said. 'Flesh and blood won't stand it much longer. If there's requisitioning, he'll be requisitioned like the rest of us, I suppose. It won't do no good talking. Well, it's been nice seeing you again, Mr Nick.'

I felt no more wish to adjudicate between Albert and Dr Trelawney than between Duport and Widmerpool. They must settle their own problems. I went on my way. The crematorium was a blaze of sunshine. I had a word with the clergyman. It looked as if I was going to be the only mourner. Then, just as the service was about to begin, Mrs Erdleigh turned up. She was shrouded in black veils that seemed almost widow's weeds. She leant towards me and whispered some greeting, then retired to a seat at the back of the little chapel. The clergyman's voice sounded as if he, too, had sat up drinking the night before, though his appearance put such a surmise out of court.

'. . . For man walketh in a vain shadow, and disquieteth himself in vain; he heapeth up riches and cannot tell who shall gather them . . .'

Uncle Giles's spirit hovered in the air. I could well imagine one of his dissertations on such a theme. The coffin slid through the trap-door with perfect precision: Uncle Giles's remains committed to a nomad's pyre. I turned to meet Mrs Erdleigh. She had already slipped away. Her evasiveness was perhaps due to delicacy, because, when Uncle Giles's will (proved at the unexpectedly large figure of seven thousand, three hundred pounds) came to light, Mrs Erdleigh turned out to be the sole legatee. Uncle Giles could not be said to have heaped up riches, but he had seen to it that his relations did not gather them. It was one of those testamentary surprises, like St John Clarke's leaving his money to Erridge. The bequest gave some offence within the family.

'Giles was always an unreliable fellow,' said my father, 'but we mustn't speak ill of him now.'

4

When the sword of Mithras – to borrow Dr Trelawney's phrase – flashed at last from its scabbard, people supposed London would immediately become the target of bombs. However, the slayer of Osiris did not at first demand his grievous tribute of blood, and a tense, infinitely uneasy over-all stagnation imposed itself upon an equally uncomfortable, equally febrile, over-all activity. Everyone was on the move. The last place to find a friend or relation was the spot where he or she had lived or worked in peacetime. Only a few, here and there, discovered themselves already suitably situated for war conditions. Frederica Budd, for example, Isobel's eldest sister, as a widow with children to bring up, had not long before gone to live in the country within range of their schools. Her small house stood in a village within twenty or thirty miles of Thrubworth, upon which Frederica always liked to keep an eye. Here it was arranged that Isobel should stay, if possible, until she gave birth. Without much in common except their relationship as sisters, the temperaments of Isobel and Frederica – unlike those of Frederica and Norah – were at the same time not in active conflict. Isobel's help in running the house was as convenient to Frederica as this arrangement was acceptable to ourselves.

Thrubworth had been requisitioned as a military headquarters. In principle detesting war in all its manifestations, Erridge was reported, in practice, to enjoy the taking over of his house by the government. This unexpected attitude on his part was not, as might be thought, because of any theoretical approval of state intervention where private property was concerned, so much as on account of the legitimate grievance – indeed, series of legitimate grievances – with which the army's investment of his mansion provided him. Erridge, a rebel whose life had been exasperatingly lacking in persecution, had enjoyed independence of parental control, plenty of money, assured social position, early in life. Since leaving school he had been deprived of all the typical grudges within the grasp of most young men. Some of these grudges, it was true, he had later developed with fair success by artificial means, grudges being, in a measure, part and parcel of his political approach. At first the outbreak of war had threatened more than one of his closest interests by making them commonplace, compulsory, even vulgarly 'patriotic'. The army at Thrubworth, with the boundless inconvenience troops bring in their train, restored Erridge's inner well-being. There was no major upheaval in his own daily existence. He and Blanche, in any case, inhabited only a small corner of the house, so that domestically speaking things remained largely unchanged for him on his own ground. At the same time he was no longer tempted to abandon all his high-minded activities. Provided with a sitting target, he was able to devote himself to an unremitting campaign against militarism as represented in person by the commanding officer and staff of the formation quartered on his property. A succession of skirmishes raged round the use of the billiard-table, the grand piano, the hard tennis-court, against a background of protest, often justifiable enough, about unsightly tracks made by short cuts across lawns, objects in the house broken or defaced by carelessness and vandalism. However, these hostilities could at the same time be unremitting only so far as Erridge's own health allowed, the outbreak of war having quite genuinely transformed him

679

from a congenital sufferer from many vague ailments into a man whose physical state bordered on that of a chronic invalid.

'Erry helped to lose the Spanish war for his own side,' said Norah. 'Thank goodness he is not going to be fit enough to lose this one for the rest of us.'

Norah herself, together with her friend, Eleanor Walpole-Wilson, had already enrolled themselves as drivers in some women's service. They could talk of nothing but the charm of their superior officer, a certain Gwen McReith. Eleanor's father, Sir Gavin Walpole-Wilson, after many years of retirement, had made a public reappearance by writing a 'turn-over' article for *The Times* on German influence in the smaller South American countries. This piece had ended with the words: 'The dogs bark: the caravan moves on.' In fact everyone, one way and another, was becoming absorbed into the leviathan of war. Its inexorable pressures were in some ways more irksome for those outside the machine than those within. I myself, for example, felt lonely and depressed. Isobel was miles away in the country; most of the people I knew had disappeared from London, or were soon to do so. They were in uniform, or some new, unusual civil occupation. In this atmosphere writing was more than ever out of the question; even reading could be attempted only at short stretches. I refused one or two jobs offered, saying I was 'on the Reserve', should soon be 'called up'. However, no calling-up took place; nor, so far as I could discover, was any likely to be enunciated in the near future. There was just the surrounding pressure of uneasy stagnation, uneasy activity.

I was not alone, of course, in this predicament. Indeed, my father, who might have been expected to be of some assistance, was, as it turned out, in worse case even than myself. He was by this time totally immersed in the problem of how to bring about his own re-employment, a preoccupation which, in spite of her very mixed feelings on the subject, equally engrossed my mother, who partly feared he might succeed, partly dreaded his despair if left on the shelf. It was hard, even impossible, for my father to concentrate for even a short time on any other subject. He would talk for hours at a time about possible jobs that he might be offered. His prospects were meagre in the extreme, for his health had certainly not improved since retirement. Now, his days were spent writing letters to contemporaries who had achieved senior rank, hanging about his club trying to buttonhole them in person.

'I managed to have a word with Fat Boy Gort at the Rag yesterday,' he would say, speaking as if in a dream. 'Of course I knew he could do nothing for me himself in his exalted position, but he wasn't at all discouraging. Gave me the name of a fellow in the Adjutant-General's own secretariat who is entering my name on a special file with a few others of much the same category as myself. Something may come of it. Brownrigg's doing his best too. As a member of the Army Council, he ought to bring something off.'

Then it struck me that General Conyers might be worth approaching in my own interests. By that time my parents had almost lost touch with the General, having themselves drifted into a form of life in which they hardly ever 'saw' anybody, certainly a way of life far removed from the General's own restless curiosity about things, an energy that age was said to have done little to abate. At least that was the picture of him to be inferred from their occasional mention of his name. To tell the truth, they rather disapproved of rumours that percolated through to them that General Conyers would sometimes attend meetings of the Society for Psychical Research, or had given a lecture at one of the universities on the subject of Oriental secret societies. My parents preferred to think of General Conyers as living a life of complete retirement and inactivity since the death of his wife four or five years before. At that date he had sold their house in the country, at the same time disposing of such sporting poodles as remained in the kennels there. Now he lived all the year round in the small flat near Sloane Square, where he was still said to play Gounod on his 'cello in the afternoons.

'Poor old Aylmer,' my father would say, since he liked to think of other people existing in an unspectacular, even colourless manner. 'You know he was rather a gay spark in his youth. Never looked at another woman after he married Bertha. It must be a lonely life.'

At first I hesitated to call on General Conyers, not only on account of this forlorn picture of him, but also because great age is, in itself, a little intimidating. I had not set eyes on him since my own wedding. Finally, I decided to telephone. The General sounded immensely vigorous on the line. Like so many of his generation, he always shouted into the mouthpiece with the full force of his lungs, as if no other method would make the instrument work.

'Delighted to hear your voice, Nick. Come along. Of course, of course, of course.'

He was specific about the time I was to call on the following day. I found myself once more under his photograph in the uniform of the Body Guard I had so much admired as a child, when my mother had taken me to see Mrs Conyers not long after we had left Stonehurst. I think the General admired this picture too, because, while we were talking of people we knew in common, he suddenly pointed to this apotheosis of himself in plumed helmet bearing a halberd.

'They made me give all that up,' he said. 'Reached the age limit. Persuaded them to keep me on for quite a while longer than allowed by regulations, as a matter of fact, but they kicked me out in the end. Lot of nonsense. It's not the fellows of my age who feel the strain. We know how to hold ourselves easily on parade. It's the fellow in his fifties who has to go to bed for a week after duty at a court or levée. Tries to stand to attention all the time and be too damned regimental. Won't do at that age. Anyway, I've got plenty to occupy me. Too much, I don't mind telling you. In any case, gallivanting round in scarlet and gold doesn't arise these days.'

He shook his head emphatically, as if I might try to deny that. His face had become more than ever aquiline and ivory, the underlying structure of bone and muscle, accentuated by age, giving him an other-worldliness of expression, a look withdrawn and remote (not unlike that of Lady Warminster's features in the months before she died), as if he now lived in a dream of half-forgotten campaigns, love affairs, heterodox experiences and opinions. At the same time there was a restless strength, a rhythm, about his movements that made one think of the Michelangelo figures in the Sistine Chapel. The Cumæan Sybil with a neat moustache added? All at once he leant forward, turning with one arm over the back of his chair, his head slightly bent, pointing to another picture hanging on the wall. I saw he was an unbearded Jehovah inspiring life into Adam through an extended finger.

'Sold most of the stuff when Bertha died,' he said. 'No good to Charlotte, married to a sailor, never has a home. Thought I'd keep the Troost, though. Troost? Van Troost? Can't remember which he is. Not sure that I was wise to have had it cleaned on the advice of that fellow Smethyck.'

The scene was a guard-room in the Low Countries.

'Undisciplined looking lot,' General Conyers went on. 'No joke soldiering in those days. Must have been most difficult to get your orders out to large bodies of men. Still, that's true today. Immense intricacies even about calling them up in the categories you want them.'

I told him that was the very subject about which I came to speak; in short, how best to convert registration with the Reserve into a commission in the armed forces. Before the war, this metamorphosis had been everywhere regarded as a process to be put automatically in motion by the march of events; now, for those in their thirties, the key seemed inoperative for entry into that charmed circle. The General shook his head at once.

'If Richard Cœur de Lion came back to earth tomorrow,' he said, 'he would be able to tell you more, my dear Nick, than I can about the British Army of today. I am not much further advanced in military knowledge than those fellows Troost painted in the guard-room. Can't your father help?'

'He's trying to solve his own problem of getting back.'

'They'll never have him.'

'You think not?'

'Certainly not. Never heard such a thing.'

'Why not?'

'Health isn't good enough. Too old.'

'He doesn't believe that.'

'Of course he's too old. Much too old. Aren't you getting a shade old yourself to embark on a military career? Wars have to be fought by young men nowadays, you know, my dear Nick, not old buffers like us.'

'Still, I thought I might try.'

'Does you credit. Can't one of your own contemporaries give you a tip? Some of them must be soldiers.'

He stood for a moment to straighten out his rheumatic leg, carefully smoothing the thick dark check of the trouser as far down as the cloth top of his buttoned boot. I felt a little dashed to find suddenly that I was so old, by now good for little, my life virtually over. The General returned to his chair.

'Didn't you once tell me years ago that you knew Hugh Moreland, the composer?' he asked. 'Splendid thing of his I heard on the wireless not long ago. Now, what was it called? *Tone Poem Vieux Port* . . . something of the sort . . . wondered if I could get a record . . .'

He had evidently dismissed the army – the war itself – from his mind for a moment. Quite other thoughts were in his head.

'How are all Isobel's brothers and sisters?' he asked.

I gave some account of them.

'Erridge is a psychosomatic case, of course,' said the General. 'Not a doubt of it. Contradictory exterior demands of contending interior emotions. Great pity he doesn't get married.'

He looked at his watch. I made a movement to leave. As a man of action, General Conyers had failed me. He put out his hand at once.

'No, don't go yet,' he said. 'Stay just a moment more, if you can. There is someone coming I would like you to meet. That was why I asked you at this time. Got a bit of news to tell you, as a matter of fact. You can pass it on to your parents during the next day or two.'

He paused, nodding his head knowingly. He was evidently very pleased about something. I wondered what could have happened. Perhaps he had been given at long last some decoration he specially coveted. It would be late in the day to award him decorations, but such official afterthoughts are not unknown. All the same, it would be unlike General Conyers to care greatly about such things, certainly to speak of them with this enthusiasm, though one can never tell what specialised goals people will set their hearts on attaining.

'I am getting married again,' he said crisply.

I had just enough control not to laugh aloud.

'Some people might think it a mistake,' said the General, speaking now very sternly, as if he well knew how to deal in the most crushing fashion with such persons. 'I perfectly realise that. I have not the smallest doubt that a good many of my friends will say that I am making a mistake. My answer is that I do not care a damn. Not a damn. Don't you agree, Nicholas?'

'Absolutely.'

'After all, it is I who am getting married, not they.'

'Of course.'

'They can mind their own business, what?'

'Certainly.'

'That's a thing no one likes to do.'

General Conyers laughed very heartily at this thought of the horrible destiny pursuing his critics, that they would have to mind their own business, most dreaded of predicaments.

'So I should like you to stay and meet my future wife,' he said.

I wondered what my parents were going to say to this. From their point of view it would be the final nail in the coffin of Aylmer Conyers. There was nothing of which they would more disapprove. At that moment the front-door bell rang.

'Forgive me,' said the General, 'as I explained before, I have no longer any domestic staff.'

He went off to open the door. I heard a woman's voice in the hall; soft laughter, as if at a too violent embrace. I thought how furious Uncle Giles would have been had he lived to hear that General Conyers was contemplating re-marriage. Certainly the news was unexpected enough. I wondered who on earth was going to appear. A succession of possibilities, both ludicrous and conventional, presented themselves to the mind: ash-blondes of seventeen; red-wigged, middle-aged procuresses, on the lines of Mrs Erdleigh; silver-haired, still palely-beautiful widows of defunct soldiers, courtiers, noblemen. I even toyed for a moment with the fantasy that the slight asperity that had always existed between the General and my sister-in-law, Frederica, might really have concealed love, dismissing such a possibility almost as soon as it took shape. Even that last expectation scarcely came up to the reality. I could not have guessed it in a million years. A tall, dark, beaky-nosed lady of about fifty came into the room. I rose. She was distinctly well dressed, with a businesslike, rather than frivolous, air.

'We have often met before,' she said, holding out her hand.

It was Miss Weedon.

'At Lady Molly's,' she said, 'and long before that too.'

The General took my arm between his forefinger and thumb, as if about to break it neatly just above the elbow with one sharp movement of his wrist.

'So you know each other already?' he said, not absolutely sure he was pleased by that fact. 'I might have guessed you would have met with Molly Jeavons. I'd forgotten she was an aunt of Isobel's.'

'But we knew each other in much more distant days as well,' said Miss Weedon, speaking in a gayer tone than I had ever heard her use before.

She looked enormously delighted at what was happening to her.

'I ran into Jeavons the other day in Sloane Street,' said General Conyers. 'Have you seen him lately, Nick?'

'Not for a month or two. There has been such a lot to do about Isobel going to the country and so on. We haven't been to Molly's house for ages. How are they?'

'Jeavons is an air-raid warden,' said the General. 'We had

quite a talk. I like Jeavons. Don't know him well. Hear some people complain he is a bore. I don't think so. He put me on to a first-rate place to buy cheap shirts many years ago. Shopped there ever since.'

'I believe Lady Molly is going back to Dogdene,' said Miss Weedon. 'They have evacuated a girls' school to the house. She may help to run it – not teach, of course. How strange to return after being châtelaine of the place.'

'Of course, she was once married to that pompous fellow, John Sleaford, wasn't she?' said the General. 'One forgets things. Sleaford must be dead these twenty years. How King Edward abominated him.'

'I don't think the present marchioness will be too pleased to find her former sister-in-law in residence at Dogdene again,' said Miss Weedon, with one of those icy, malicious smiles I well remembered. 'Lady Molly has always been so funny about what she calls "the latest Dogdene economy".'

'Poor Alice Sleaford,' said the General. 'You must not be unkind to her, Geraldine.'

I had never before heard Miss Weedon addressed as 'Geraldine'. When secretary to Stringham's·mother, Mrs Foxe, she had always been 'Tuffy'. That was what Molly Jeavons called her, too. I wanted to ask about Stringham, but, in the existing circumstances, hesitated to do so. As bride of General Conyers, Miss Weedon had suddenly become such a very different sort of person, almost girlish in her manner, far from the Medusa she had once been designated by Moreland. At the same time, she still retained some of her secretary's formality in speaking of people. However, she herself must have decided that her present position would be weakened, rather than strengthened, by all avoidance of the subject of Stringham, which, certain to turn up sooner or later, was best put at once on a solid basis. She now raised it herself.

'I expect you want to hear about Charles,' she said, very cheerfully.

'Of course. How is he?'

'Quite all right now.'

'Really?'

'Absolutely.'

'Charles is the fellow you were helping to look after his mother's house, is he?' asked General Conyers, speaking with that small touch of impatience, permissible, even to be applauded, in the light of his own engagement. 'You knew Charles Stringham, did you, Nicholas? At school with him, were you? I hear he drank too much, but has given it up. Good thing.'

'Is he still at Glimber?'

'Glimber has been taken over as an evacuated government office. Charles is in London now, looking for a job. He wants to get into the army. Of course his health isn't very good, even though he has stopped drinking. It isn't going to be easy. There have been money troubles too. His father died in Kenya and left such money as he had to his French wife. Mrs Foxe is not nearly so rich as she was. Commander Foxe is so terribly extravagant. He has gone back to the navy, of course.'

'Good old Buster.'

Miss Weedon laughed. She deeply detested Buster Foxe.

'Nicholas wants to get into the army too,' said General Conyers, anxious to dismiss the subject of Stringham and his relations. 'He is also having difficulties. Didn't you say so, Nicholas? Now, tell me, don't I remember a former servant of your parents manages a hotel somewhere? Some seaside place. Very good cook, wasn't he? I remember his soufflés. Thought we might perhaps honeymoon at his hotel. Not going to make it a long affair. Just a week or ten days. Quite enough.'

'They have probably requisitioned the place. I was down there a month or two ago for Uncle Giles's funeral.'

'Saw his death in the paper. Made rather a mess of his life, didn't he? Don't think I set eyes on him since a week or two before the earlier war broke out.'

'Do you remember Dr Trelawney? He was staying in the hotel.'

'That old scoundrel. Was he, indeed? How is he?'

'He got locked in the bathroom.'

'Did he, did he?' said the General thoughtfully. 'The Essence of the All is the Godhead of the True . . . may be something in it. Always meant to go and have a look at Trelawney on his own ground . . . all that stuff about the Astral Plane . . .'

He pondered; then, with an effort, brought himself back to earth, when I said that I must be going.

'Sorry not to have been more use about your own problem, Nick. Have another talk with your father. Better still, get some young fellow to help you. No good trying too high up. Somebody quite junior, like a lieutenant-colonel. That's the kind of fellow. Very nice to have seen you. You must come and visit us after we get back. Don't know where we shall go yet.'

I left them together, discussing that question, Miss Weedon still looking immensely pleased about everything. As the flat door closed, I heard her laughter, now quite shrill, begin again. She had reason to be pleased. Stringham, so it appeared, had been cured by her of 'drink'; now she had captured General Conyers. The one achievement was as remarkable as the other. They were perhaps not so disparate as might at first sight appear. There was a kind of dash about Stringham comparable with the General's manner of facing the world; at the same time, the General's advanced age, like Stringham's taste for the bottle, gave Miss Weedon something ponderable upon which to exercise her talent for 'looking after' people, her taste, in short, for power. General Conyers had seemed as enchanted with Miss Weedon as she with him. I wondered what other men – in addition to Stringham – had been 'in her life', as Mrs Erdleigh would have said; what, for that matter, had been Miss Weedon's true relationship with Stringham. One passes through the world knowing few, if any, of the important things about even the people with whom one has been from time to time in the closest intimacy.

'Valéry asks why one has been summoned to this carnival,' Moreland once said, 'but it's more like blind man's buff. One reels through the carnival in question, blundering into persons one can't see, and, without much success, trying to keep hold of a few of them.'

There could be no doubt that General Conyers had taken on a formidable woman; equally no doubt that he was a formidable man. If he could handle Billson naked, he could probably handle Miss Weedon clothed – or naked, too, if it came to that. I felt admiration for his energy, his determination to cling to life. There was nothing defeatist about him. However, my parents, as I had expected, were not at all pleased by the news. They had, of course, never heard of Miss Weedon. The engagement was, indeed, quite a shock to them. In fact, the whole affair made my father very cross. Now that Uncle Giles was no more, he may have felt himself permitted a greater freedom of expression in openly criticising General Conyers. He did so in just the terms the General had himself envisaged.

'No fool like an old fool,' my father said. 'I shouldn't have believed it of him, Bertha hardly cold in her grave.'

'I hope he hasn't made a silly mistake,' said my mother. 'I like old Aylmer, with all his funny ways of behaving.'

'Very awkward for his daughter too. Why, some of his

grandchildren must be almost grown up.'

'Oh, no,' said my mother, who loved accuracy in such matters, 'not grown up.'

'Where did he meet this woman?'

'I really don't know.'

It turned out later that General Conyers had sat next to Miss Weedon at a concert some months before the outbreak of war. They had fallen into conversation. Finding they knew many people in common, they had arranged to meet at another concert the following week. That was how their friendship had begun. In short, General Conyers had 'picked up' Miss Weedon. There was no denying it. It was a true romance.

'Adventures only happen to adventurers,' Mr Deacon had said one evening when we were sitting drinking in the saloon bar of the Mortimer.

'That depends on what one calls adventurers,' said Moreland, who was in a hair-splitting mood. 'What you mean, Edgar, is that people to whom adventures happen are never wholly unadventurous. That is not the same thing. It's the latter class who have the real adventures – people like oneself.'

'Don't be pedantic, Moreland,' Mr Deacon had answered.

Certainly General Conyers was not unadventurous. Was he an adventurer? I considered his advice about the army. Then the answer came to me. I must get in touch with Widmerpool. I wondered why I had not thought of that earlier. I telephoned to his office. They put me through to a secretary.

'Captain Widmerpool is embodied,' she said in an unfriendly voice.

I could tell from her tone, efficient, charmless, unimaginative, that she had been given special instructions by Widmerpool himself to use the term 'embodied' in describing his military condition. I asked where he was to be found. It was a secret. At last, not without pressure on my own part, she gave me a telephone number. This turned out to be that of his Territorial battalion's headquarters. I rang him up.

'Come and see me by all means, my boy,' he boomed down the wire in a new, enormously hearty voice, 'but bring your own beer. There won't be much I can do for you. I'm up to my arse in bumph and don't expect I shall be able to spare you more than a minute or two for waffling.'

I was annoyed by the phrase 'bring your own beer', also by being addressed as 'my boy' by Widmerpool. They were terms he had never, so to speak, earned the right to use, certainly not to me. However, I recognised that a world war was going to produce worse situations than Widmerpool's getting above himself and using a coarsely military boisterousness of tone to which his civilian personality could make no claim. I accepted his invitation; he named a time. The following day, after finishing my article for the paper and looking at some books I had to review, I set out for the Territorial headquarters, which was situated in a fairly inaccessible district of London. I reached there at last, feeling in the depths of gloom. Entry into the most arcane recesses of the Secret Service could not have been made more difficult. Finally an NCO admitted me to Widmerpool's presence. He was sitting, surrounded by files, in a small, horribly stuffy office, which was at the same time freezingly cold. I was still unused to the sight of him in uniform. He looked anything but an army officer – a railway official, perhaps, of some obscure country.

'Been left in charge of details consequent on the unit's move to a training area,' he said brusquely, as I entered the room. 'Suppose I shouldn't have told you that. Security – security – and then security. Everyone must learn that. Well, my lad, what can I do for you? You need not stand. Take a pew.'

I sat on a kitchen chair with a broken back, and outlined my situation.

'The fact is,' said Widmerpool, glaring through his spectacles and puffing out his cheeks, as if rehearsing a tremendous blowing up he was going to give some subordinate in the very near future, 'you ought to have joined the Territorials before war broke out.'

'I know.'

'No good just entering your name on the Reserve.'

'There were difficulties about age.'

'Only after you'd left it too late.'

'It was only a matter of months.'

'Never mind. Think how long I've been a Territorial officer. You should have looked ahead.'

'You said there wasn't going to be a war after "Munich".'

'You thought there was, so you were even more foolish.'

There was truth in that.

'I only want to know the best thing to do,' I said.

'You misjudged things, didn't you?'

'I did.'

'No vacancies now.'

'How can I put that right?'

'The eldest of our last intake of commissioned subalterns was twenty-one. The whole lot of them had done at least eighteen months in the ranks – *at least.*'

'Even so, the army will have to expand in due course.'

'Officers will be drawn from the younger fellows coming up.'

'You think there is nothing for me to do at present?'

'You could enlist in the ranks.'

'But the object of joining the Reserve – being accepted for it – was to be dealt with immediately as a potential officer.'

'Then I can't help you.'

'Well, thanks for seeing me.'

'I will keep an eye out for you,' said Widmerpool, rather less severely. 'As a matter of fact, I may be in a position well placed for doing so before many moons have waned.'

'Why?'

'I am probably to be sent to the Staff College.'

'Oh?'

'Again, for security reasons, that should not be mentioned beyond these four walls.'

He began to gather up his multitudinous papers, stowing some away in a safe, transferring others to a brief-case.

'I shall be coming back to this office again after dinner,' he said. 'Lucky if I get away before midnight. It's all got to be cleared up somehow, if the war is to be won. I gave my word to the Brigade-Major. He's a very sharp fellow called Farebrother. City acquaintance of mine.'

'Sunny Farebrother?'

'Have you met him?'

'Years ago.'

Widmerpool gave a semi-circular movement of his arm, as if to convey the crushing responsibility his promise to the Brigade-Major comprehended. He locked the safe. Putting the key in his trouser-pocket after attaching it to a chain hanging from his braces, he spoke again, this time in an entirely changed tone.

'Nicholas,' he said, 'I am going to ask you to do something.'

'Yes?'

'Let me explain very briefly. As you know, my mother lives in a cottage not very far from Stourwater. We call it a cottage, it is really a little house. She has made it very exquisite.'

'I remember your telling me.'

'Since she lives by herself, there has been pressure – rather severe pressure – applied to her by the authorities to have evacuees there.'

'Oh, yes.'

'Now I do not wish my lady mother to be plagued by evacuees.'

That seemed a reasonable enough sentiment. Nobody wanted evacuees, even if they accepted the fact that evacuees must be endured. Why should they? I could not see, however, in Mrs Widmerpool's case, that I could help in preventing such a situation from arising. I realised at the same time that Widmerpool had suddenly effected in himself one of those drastic changes of policy in which, for example, from acting an all-powerful tyrant, he would suddenly become a humble suppliant. I understood very clearly that something was required of me, but could not guess what I was expected to do. Some persons, knowing that they were later going to ask a favour, would have made themselves more agreeable when a favour was being asked of them. That was not Widmerpool's way. I almost admired him for making so little effort to conceal his lack of interest in my own affairs, while waiting his time to demand something of myself.

'The point is this,' he said, 'up to date, my mother has had an old friend – Miss Janet Walpole-Wilson, sister of that ineffective diplomatist, Sir Gavin – staying with her, so the question of evacuees, until now, has not arisen. Now Miss Walpole-Wilson's work with the Women's Voluntary Service takes her elsewhere. The danger of evacuees is acute.'

I thought how Miss Janet Walpole-Wilson's ordinary clothes must have merged imperceptibly into the uniform of her service. It was as if she had been preparing all her life for that particular dress.

'But how can I help?'

'Some relation of Lady Molly Jeavons – a relative of her husband's, to be more precise – wants accommodation in the country. A place not too far from London. Miss Walpole-Wilson heard about this herself. She told us.'

'Why not ring up the Jeavonses?'

'I have done so. In fact, I am meeting my mother at Lady Molly's tonight.'

Widmerpool was still oppressed by some unsolved problem, which he found difficulty about putting into words. He cleared his throat, swallowed several times.

'I wondered whether you would come along to the Jeavonses tonight,' he said. 'It might be easier.'

'What might?'

Widmerpool went red below his temples, under the line made by his spectacles. He began to sweat in spite of the low temperature of the room.

'You remember that rather unfortunate business when I was engaged to Mildred Haycock?'

'Yes.'

'I haven't really seen anything of the Jeavonses since then.'

'You came to the party Molly gave for Isobel just before we were married.'

'I know,' said Widmerpool, 'but there were quite a lot of people there then. It was an occasion. It's rather different going there tonight to discuss something like my mother's cottage. Lady Molly has never seen my mother.'

'I am sure it will be all right. Molly loves making arrangements.'

'All the same, I feel certain embarrassments.'

'No need to with the Jeavonses.'

'I thought that, since Molly Jeavons is an aunt of your wife's, things might be easier if you were to accompany me. Will you do that?'

'All right.'

'You will come?'

'Yes, if you wish.'

I had not visited the Jeavonses for some little time – not since Isobel had gone to stay with Frederica – so that I was quite glad to make this, as it were, an excuse for calling on them. Isobel would certainly enjoy news of the Jeavons household.

'Very well, then,' said Widmerpool, now returning at once to his former peremptory tone, 'we'll move off forthwith. It is five minutes to the bus. Come along. Party, quick march.'

He gave some final instructions in the adjoining room to a gloomy corporal sitting before a typewriter, surrounded, like Widmerpool himself, with huge stacks of documents. We went out into the street, where the afternoon light was beginning to fade. Widmerpool, his leather-bound stick caught tight beneath his armpit, marched along beside me, tramp-tramp-tramp, eventually falling into step, since I had not taken my pace from his.

'I don't know what Jeavons's relative will be like,' he said. 'I don't feel absolutely confident she will be the sort my mother will like.'

I felt more apprehension for the person who had to share a cottage with Mrs Widmerpool.

'I saw Bob Duport just before war broke out.'

I said that partly to see what Widmerpool would answer, partly because I thought he had been unhelpful about the army, tiresome about the Jeavonses. I hoped the information would displease him. The surmise was correct. He stiffened, strutting now so fiercely that he could almost be said to have broken into the goosestep.

'Did you? Where?'

'He was staying in a hotel where an uncle of mine died. I had to see about the funeral and ran across Duport there.'

'Oh.'

'I hadn't seen him for years.'

'He is a bad mannered fellow, Duport. Ungrateful, too.'

'What is he ungrateful about?'

'I got him a job in Turkey. You may remember we were talking about Duport's affairs at Stourwater, when I saw you and your wife there about a year or more ago – just after "Munich".'

'He'd recently come back from Turkey when we met.'

'He had been working for me there.'

'So he said.'

'I had to deal rather summarily with Duport in the end,' said Widmerpool. 'He showed no grasp of the international situation. He is insolent, too. So he mentioned my name?'

'He did.'

'Not very favourably, I expect.'

'Not very.'

'I don't know what will happen to Duport,' said Widmerpool. 'He must be in a difficult position financially, owing to his reckless conduct. However, anybody can earn three pounds a week these days as an air-raid warden. Even Jeavons does. So Duport will not starve.'

He sounded rather sorry that Duport was not threatened with that fate.

'He thought Sir Magnus Donners might find him something.'

'Not if I know it.'

'Do you think Donners will be asked to join the Government, if there is a Cabinet reshuffle?'

'The papers speak of him as likely for office,' said Widmerpool, not without condescension. 'In some ways Magnus would make an excellent minister in time of war. In others, I am not so sure. He has certain undesirable traits for a public man in modern days. As you probably know, people speak of – well, mistresses. I am no prude. Let a man lead his own life, say I – but, if he is a public man, let him be careful. More than these allegedly bad morals, I object in Magnus to something you would never guess if you met him casually. I mean a kind of hidden frivolity. Now, what a lamentable scene that was when I looked in on Stourwater when you were there. Suppose some journalist had got hold of it.'

Widmerpool was about to enlarge on the Masque of the Seven Deadly Sins as played in the Stourwater dining-room, when his attention – and my own – was caught by a small crowd of people loitering in the half-light at the corner of a side street. Some sort of a meeting was in progress. From the traditional soapbox, a haggard middle-aged man in spectacles and a cloth cap was addressing fifteen or twenty persons, including several children. The group was apathetic enough, except for the children, who were playing a game that involved swinging their gas-mask cases at each other by the string, then running quickly away. Two women in trousers were hawking a newspaper or pamphlet. Widmerpool and I paused. The orator, his face gnarled and blotched by a lifetime of haranguing crowds out of doors in all weathers, seemed to be coming to the end of his discourse. He used that peculiarly unctuous, coaxing, almost beseeching manner of address adopted by some political speakers, reminding me a little of my brother-in-law, Roddy Cutts, whose voice would sometimes take on that same pleading note when he made a public appeal for a cause in which he was interested.

'. . . why didn't the so-called British Government of the day clinch the Anglo-Soviet alliance when they had the chance . . . get something done . . . Comrade Stalin's invitation to a round-table conference at Bucharest . . . consistent moral policy . . . effective forces of socialism . . . necessary new alignments . . . USSR prestige first and foremost . . .'

The speech came to an end, the listeners demonstrating

700

neither approval nor the reverse. The haggard man stepped down from the soapbox, wiped his spectacles, loosened the peak of his cap from his forehead, lit a cigarette. The children's gas-mask game reached a pitch of frenzied intensity, so that in their scamperings one of the women selling newspapers almost had the packet knocked from her hand. Widmerpool turned to me. He was about to comment, when our attention was engaged by a new speaker. This was the second newspaper-selling woman, who, having now handed over her papers to the man with the cloth cap, herself jumped on to the soapbox. In a harsh clear voice she opened a tremendous tirade, quite different in approach from the quieter, more reasoned appeal of the spectacled man.

'. . . blooming bloody hypocrisy . . . anybody wants this war except a few crackpots . . . see a chance of seizing world power and grinding the last miserable halfpence from the frozen fingers of stricken mankind . . . lot of Fascist, terroristic, anti-semitic, war-mongering, exploiting White Guards and traitors to the masses . . .'

It was Gypsy Jones. I had not set eyes on her since the days when we used to meet in Mr Deacon's antique shop. She had lost a front tooth, otherwise did not look greatly changed from what she had been in the Mr Deacon period: older, harder, angrier, further than ever from her last bath, but essentially the same. Her hair was still cut short like a boy's, her fists clenched, her legs set wide apart. Over her trousers she wore a man's overcoat, far from new, the aggressive inelegance of the ensemble expressing to perfection her own revolutionary, destructive state of mind. In the old days she had worked for Howard Craggs at the Vox Populi Press, was said to be his mistress. Craggs had moved a long way since the Vox Populi Press. Lately, he had been appointed to a high post in the Ministry of Information. I recalled the night when Gypsy Jones had been dressed as Eve in order to accompany Craggs, as Adam, to the Merry Thought fancy-dress party: the encounter we had had at the back of Mr Deacon's shop. There had been a certain grubby charm about her. I felt no regrets. Love had played no part. There was nothing painful to recall. Then Widmerpool had fallen for her, had pursued her, had paid for her 'operation'. Such things seemed like another incarnation.

'. . . not appealing to a lot of half-baked Bloomsbury intellectuals and Hampstead ideologues . . . bourgeois scabs and parlour-socialist nancy boys . . . scum of weak-kneed Trotskyite flunkeys . . . betraying the workers and anyone else it suits their filthy bloody blackleg book to betray . . . I'm talking about politics – socialism – reality – adaptability . . .'

I felt my arm caught tightly. It was Widmerpool. I turned towards him. He had gone quite pale. His thick lips were trembling a little. The sight of Gypsy Jones, rousing vague memories in myself, had caused him to react far more violently. To Widmerpool, she was not the mere handmaid of memory, she was a spectre of horror, the ghastly reminder of failure, misery, degradation. He dragged at my arm.

'For God's sake, come away,' he said.

We continued our course down the street, over which dusk was falling, Widmerpool walking at a much sharper pace, but without any of his former bravura, the stick now gripped in his hand as if to ward off actual physical attack.

'You realised who it was?' he said, as we hurried along.

'Of course.'

'How soon did you see her?'

'Only after she had begun to speak.'

'Me, too. What an escape. It was a near thing.'

'What was?'

'She might have noticed me.'

702

'Would that have mattered?'

Widmerpool stopped dead.

'What do you mean?' he asked abruptly.

'Supposing she had seen us, even said something to us?'

'I didn't say us, I said *me*.'

'You then?'

'Of course it would have mattered. It would have been disastrous.'

'Why?'

'How can you ask such a question? There are all kind of reasons why it should matter. You know something of my past with that woman. Can't you understand how painful the sight of her is to me? Besides, you heard what she was shouting. She is a Communist. Did you not understand what the words meant? Your denseness is unbelievable. She is attacking the prosecution of the war. Haven't you grasped that Russia is now Hitler's ally? Suppose that woman had suddenly addressed herself to me. That would have been a fine thing. You don't realise what it means to be in an official position. Let me explain. I am not only an army officer, I am a man with heavy responsibilities. I have been left in charge of a headquarters. I have access to all kind of secret documents. You would not guess the nature of some of them. What if she had been seen speaking to me? Have you ever heard of M.I.5? What if its agents had seen us conversing? There may well have been one of them among the crowd. Such meetings are quite rightly kept under supervision by the contre-espionage department.'

I could think of no answer. Although Widmerpool's view of himself as a man handling weighty state secrets was beyond belief in its absurdity, I felt at the same time that I had myself shown lack of feeling in treating so lightly his former love for Gypsy Jones. Love is at once always absurd and never absurd; the more grotesque its form, the more love itself confers a certain dignity on the circumstances of those it torments. No doubt Widmerpool had been through a searing experience with Gypsy Jones, an experience even now by no means forgotten. That could be the only explanation of such an outburst. I had rarely seen him so full of indignation. He had paused for breath. Now, his reproaches began again.

'You come and ask me for advice about getting into the army, Nicholas,' he said, 'and because I spare the time to talk of such things – make time, when my duty lies by rights elsewhere – you think I have nothing more serious to occupy me than your own trivial problems. That is not the case. The General Staff of the Wehrmacht would be only too happy to possess even a tithe of the information I locked away before we quitted the Orderly Room.'

'I don't doubt it. I realise you are busy. It was kind of you to see me.'

Widmerpool was a little placated. Perhaps he also feared that, if he went too far in his reproofs, I might excuse myself from accompanying him to the Jeavonses'. He tapped me with his stick.

'Don't worry further about your remarks,' he said. 'The sight of that woman upset me, especially behaving as she was. Did you hear her language? Besides, I have been over-working as usual. You feel the strain at unexpected moments.'

He made no further comment. We found a bus, which transported us in due course to the neighbourhood of the Jeavons house in South Kensington. The bell was not answered for a long time. We waited outside the faintly Dutch edifice with its over ornamented dark red brick façade.

'I expect Mother has preceded us,' said Widmerpool.

He was better now, though still not wholly recovered from the sight of Gypsy Jones. The door was opened at last by Jeavons himself. His appearance took me by surprise. Instead of the usual ancient grey suit, he was wearing a blue one-piece overall and a beret. Some people – as General Conyers had remarked – considered Jeavons a bore. Such critics had a case, undeniably, when he was sunk in one of his impenetrable silences, or, worse still, was trying, in a momentary burst of energy, to make some money by selling one of those commodities generically described by Chips Lovell as 'an automatic boot-jack or infallible cure for the common cold'. To find Jeavons in the latter state was rare, the former, fairly frequent. Even apart from his war wound, Jeavons was not at all fitted for commercial employments. He had hardly done a stroke of work since marrying Molly. His wife did not mind that. Indeed, she may have preferred Jeavons to be dependent on her. Whatever some of her relations may have thought at the time of her marriage, it had turned out a success – allowing for an occasional 'night out' on Jeavons's part, like the one when he had taken me to Dicky Umfraville's night-club.

'Come in,' he said. 'How's your war going? It's touch and go whether we're winning ours. Stanley's here, and a lady who has come to see about lodging Stanley's missus in the country. Then Molly met a fellow at Sanderson's who was trying to find a home for his cat, and she's gone and asked him to stay. The man, I mean, not the cat.'

'The lady who has come about moving your – is it sister-in-law? – is my mother,' said Widmerpool. 'I spoke to you on the telephone about it. I am Kenneth Widmerpool, you know. We have met in the past.'

'So you did,' said Jeavons, 'and so we have. It went out of my head like most other things. I thought Nick had just come to call and brought a friend. You can talk to Molly about it all when she comes downstairs, but I think your Mum has pretty well fixed everything up as it is.'

Jeavons's voice, hoarse and faint, sounded as usual as if he had a cold in his head or had been up too late the night before. He seemed restive, disorientated, but in good form.

'Who is Stanley?' I asked.

'Who's Stanley?' said Jeavons. 'My brother, of course. Who did you think he was?'

'Never knew you had a brother, Ted.'

'Course I've got a brother.'

'What does he do?'

'Accountant.'

'In London?'

'Nottingham. Given it up now, of course. Back to the army. Staff-Captain at the War House. Fancy your never having heard of Stanley. No reason why you should, I suppose. Still, it strikes me as funny. Rather a great man, Stanley, in his way. Gets things done.'

Among so much that was depressing, the news that Jeavons had a brother was for some reason cheering. It was certainly information to fascinate Isobel, when I next saw her, even to stagger Chips Lovell, who, regarding himself as an authority on his wife's relations, had certainly never heard of this outgrowth. Jeavons was known only to possess two or three vague connexions, sometimes to be found staying in the house, though never precisely placed in their kinship, in any case always hopelessly submerged in number by his wife's cousins, nephews and nieces. He had had, it was true, an old aunt, or great-aunt, to whom Molly was said to have been 'very good', who had lingered on in the house for months suffering from some illness, finally dying in one of the upstairs rooms. A Jeavons brother was quite another matter, a phenomenon of wartime circumstances. Jeavons, his dark, insistently curly hair now faintly speckled with grey, had himself taken on a subtly different personality since the onset of war. After all, war was the element which had, in a sense, made his career. Obviously he reacted strongly to its impacts. Until now his appearance had always suggested a temporary officer of the '14–'18 conflict, who had miraculously survived, without in the least ageing, into a much later epoch. The blue overall changed all that. Jeavons had also allowed his Charlie Chaplin moustache to grow outwards towards the corners of his mouth. With his own curious adaptability and sense of survival, he had effortlessly discarded what was in any case no more than a kind of disguise, now facing the world in the more contemporary role, equally artificial, of the man who had come to clean the windows or mend the boiler. We moved up the stairs.

'Met one of Isobel's uncles at the warden-post the other night,' said Jeavons. 'Alfred Tolland, the one Molly always teases.'

'How was he?'

'We had a talk about how difficult it is for people with daughters to bring 'em out properly in wartime,' Jeavons said.

He spoke without levity. Although he remained always utterly himself, Jeavons, after twenty years of marriage to Molly, had taken on much of his wife's way of looking at things. It would be more true to say the way the world into which she had been born looked at things, for Molly herself would probably have given little thought to how daughters were to be 'brought out' in wartime, even had she any daughters of her own. All the same, she would recognise that, to some people, the matter constituted a problem. Jeavons, who had never made the smallest effort to adopt that world's manner of talking, its way of dressing, its general behaviour, had at the same time, quite objectively, absorbed certain of its traditional opinions, whether his wife held them or not. Alfred Tolland, for example, had probably found in Jeavons an unusually sympathetic listener to his – no doubt antediluvian – views on how young ladies should conduct themselves or be conducted, certainly more sympathetic than he would ever have found in Molly herself. The fact that Jeavons had no daughters, had no children at all, would never have prevented him from holding strong views on the subject.

'Take my advice, don't give up your home-farm,' Chips Lovell had once heard Jeavons say to Lord Amesbury, admittedly a fairly formidable figure to counsel when it came to discussing the economics of estate management. 'Eddie Bridgnorth gave up his and never ceased to regret it.'

To have prefaced this recommendation with the avowal that he himself came from a walk of life where people did not own home-farms would have seemed to Jeavons otiose, wearisome, egotistical. Everything about him, he knew, proclaiming that fact, he would have regarded such personal emphasis as in the worst of taste, as well as being without interest. Marriage to Molly had given him opportunities to see how a lot of hitherto unfamiliar forms of life worked. He had developed certain opinions, was prepared to give evidence. Home-farms fell into that category. The notion that he might be trying to pass himself off as a fellow-owner of a home-farm would have seemed to Jeavons laughable. Whether or not Jeavons's advice tipped the scale was never known, but Chips Lovell reported that Lord Amesbury did not sell, so that he may have been convinced by this objectivity of reasoning. Perhaps it was of such matters that Jeavons was thinking when he would stand for hours in the corner of the drawing-room at one of Molly's parties for young people (when the rugs would be turned back and they would dance to the gramophone), smiling to himself, gently clinking the money in his pocket.

'Do help with the drinks, Teddy, dear,' his wife would say on such occasions. 'Are you feeling all right or is it your inside again?'

Then Jeavons would move like a sleep-walker towards the bottles.

'What's it going to be?' he would mutter, almost beneath his breath. 'Rotten tunes they always play nowadays.'

However, although Widmerpool had shown signs of restiveness at our too long delay in the hall, Jeavons was far from one of those comatose, stagnant moods that evening. There could be no doubt that the war had livened him up. He felt at home within its icy grasp. The house was more untidy than ever, the hall, as usual, full of luggage. I noticed that the marquetry cabinet bequeathed by Lady Warminster had reached no farther than the foot of the stairs. Some of the heavier pictures had been taken from their hooks and rested against the wall. Packing cases and trunks were everywhere.

'People keep on arriving for a night or two,' said Jeavons. 'Place might be a doss-house. Of course, Stanley is only here until he can fix himself up. Then Molly must bring this other fellow to stay. Seems a nice bloke. She had to go and see the vet. No avoiding that. Can't fight a war with quite the number of dogs and cats we normally have in the house. Got to find homes for them.'

'What happened to Maisky, your pet monkey?'

'Rather a sad story,' said Jeavons, but did not enlarge.

The conditions he described were less abnormal here than they would have been in most households. Indeed, war seemed to have accelerated, exaggerated, rather than changed, the Jeavons way of life. The place was always in a mess. Mess there was endemic. People were always coming for a night or two, sometimes for much longer periods. There were always suitcases in the hall, always debris, untidiness, confusion everywhere. That was the way Molly liked to live, possibly her method of recovering from the tedium of married life with John Sleaford. Jeavons, whether he liked it or not, was dragged along in her train. No doubt he liked it, too, otherwise he would have left her, for no one could have stood such an existence unless reasonably sympathetic to him at heart. The sight of Jeavons's brother sitting on the sofa beside Mrs Widmerpool brought home to one the innate eccentricity of Jeavons. This man in uniform, with a captain's pips and three 'First War' ribbons, was recognisable as a brother more from build than any great similarity of feature. He was far more anonymous than Jeavons: older, solider, greyer, quieter, in general more staid. When you saw Stanley Jeavons, you recognised the adventurer in Ted. I thought of Moreland's emendation, the distinction he drew between adventurers and those not wholly unadventurous, to both of which categories adventures happened – to the latter, perhaps, more than the former. Jeavons, although tending to play a passive role, could not be said to have led an entirely unadventurous life; perhaps one could go further, say without qualification that Jeavons was an adventurer. There was no time to think longer of such things at that moment, because Jeavons was making some kind of introduction.

'Stanley's a brass-hat now,' he said. 'God, how we used to hate the staff in our war, Stan, didn't we? Fancy your ending up one of that mob.'

As we came into the room, Mrs Widmerpool had at once bared her teeth in a smile to indicate that we had met before. I was about to speak to her, when she jumped to her feet and seized Widmerpool by the shoulders, unable to allow Jeavons the undivided honour of presenting him to his brother.

'My soldier son,' she said, nodding delightedly like a Japanese doll.

'Oh, don't be absurd, Mother,' said Widmerpool.

He grinned back happily at her through his spectacles, his composure, lately so shattered by Gypsy Jones, now completely restored. Mrs Widmerpool returned to the sofa, continuing to nurse on her knee a cardboard box, which at first I thought might be some sort of present she had brought Widmerpool, but recognised a second later as her gas-mask, carried with her into the drawing-room. She looked, as her son had described her a year earlier, 'younger than ever'. She was squarely built, her heavy, nearly classical nose set between cheeks shining and pink like an apple. She wore a thick tweed suit and a tweed hat with a peak. Stanley Jeavons, who seemed rather glad to be absolved from talking to her further for the time being, turned his attention to Widmerpool.

'What's your outfit?' he asked.

They began to speak of army matters. I was left with Mrs Widmerpool.

'*You* are one of Kenneth's literary friends, I remember,' she said, 'are you not?'

'Well, yes.'

'Kenneth used to be such a reader too,' she said. 'Now, alas, he has no time for books. Indeed, few of us have. But I suppose you continue in the same manner?'

'More or less.'

Before I could enlarge on my own activities, Molly Jeavons came into the room, making all the disturbance that naturally noisy people always bring in their train. Dark, large, still good-looking at fifty, there was something of the barmaid about her, something of the Charles II beauty, although Molly, they said, had never been exactly a 'beauty' when younger, more from lack of temperament to play the part, than want of physical equipment. These two sides she represented, merging in middle age, suited her tomboyish, all enveloping manner. This manner seemed designed by her to dispense with aristocratic frills unsuitable to the style in which the Jeavonses lived, but – caught by Time, as all idiosyncrasies of talk and behaviour can be – the final result was somewhat to emphasise the background she was at pains to understate. She was wearing various rather ill-assorted woollen garments. After greeting Widmerpool and saying something about his mother's cottage, she turned to me.

'We've been having the most awful time, Nick,' she said, 'trying to fix up the rows of animals that always infest the house. Sanderson, the vet, a great friend of mine, has been an angel. I talked to the sweetest man there who was trying to find a home for his cat. His wife had just left him and he'd just been turned out of the furnished flat he was living in because the owner wanted it back. He had nowhere to go and was absolutely at the end of his tether. He seemed so nice, I couldn't leave until we'd arranged the cat's future. The long and the short of it is he's going to stay for a night or two here. He had his bag with him and was going to some awful hotel, because he has very little money. He seems to know a lot of people we all know. You probably know him yourself, Nick.'

'What is he called?'

'I simply can't remember,' she said. 'I've had such a lot of things to do today that I am feeling quite dizzy and the name has completely gone out of my head. He'll be down in a moment. He is just unpacking his things – and now I must hear how the arrangements about the cottage are getting on.'

She joined the conversation taking place between Jeavons's brother, Widmerpool and Widmerpool's mother. Jeavons, who had been listening abstractedly to these negotiations, came and sat beside me.

'What's happening to all the Tollands, Nick?' he asked. 'I haven't heard anything of them, except that your wife,

Isobel, is going to have a baby and is staying in the country with Frederica.'

'George has gone back to his regiment.'

'Ex-Guardsman, isn't he?' said Jeavons. 'He'll be for a holding battalion.'

'Then Hugo has become a Gunner.'

'In the ranks?'

'Yes.'

Hugo, regarded in general by his family as a fairly unsatisfactory figure, in spite of recent achievements in selling antique furniture, had taken the wind out of everyone's sails by his enlistment.

'One will be called up anyway,' Hugo had said. 'Why not have a start of everyone? Get in on the ground floor.'

Such a view from Hugo was unexpected.

'He looks a bit strange in uniform.'

'Must be like that song Billy Bennett used to sing,' said Jeavons:

> 'I'm a trooper, I'm a trooper,
> They call me Gladys Cooper.

Ages since I've been to a music-hall. Aren't what they used to be anyway. Still, it does Hugo credit.'

'Robert has some idea of joining the navy.'

'Plenty of water in the trenches, without going out of your way to look for it,' said Jeavons shuddering. 'Besides, I feel bilious most of the time, even when I'm not rolling about in a boat.'

'Chips Lovell, like me, is thinking things over. Roddy Cutts, being an MP, arranged something – a Yeomanry regiment, I think.'

While we were talking someone came into the room. I had not taken very seriously Molly Jeavons's surmise that I should probably know the man she had picked up at the vet's. She always imagined Isobel and I must know everyone roughly the same age as ourselves. Perhaps she liked to feel that, if necessary, she could draw on our reserves for her own purposes. I thought it most improbable that I should have met this casual acquaintance, certainly never guessed he would turn out to be Moreland. However, Moreland it was. He looked far from well, dazed and unhappy.

'Good God,' he said, catching sight of me.

Molly Jeavons detached herself from the talk about Mrs Widmerpool's lodger.

'So you do know him, Nick.'

'Of course we know each other.'

'I felt sure you would.'

'Why are you here?' said Moreland. 'Did you arrange this?'

'Will you be all right in that room?' Molly asked. 'For goodness sake don't touch the blackout, or the whole thing will come down. It's just fixed temporarily to last the night. Teddy will do something about it in the morning.'

'I really can't thank you enough,' said Moreland. 'Farinelli . . . one thing and another . . . then letting me come here. . . .'

He had probably been drinking earlier in the day, was still overwrought, though not exactly drunk, not far from tears. Molly Jeavons brushed his thanks aside.

'One thing I can't do,' she said, 'is to give either you or Nick dinner here tonight. Nor any of these other people either, except Stanley. We simply haven't got enough food in the house to offer you anything.'

'We'll dine together,' I said. 'Is there anywhere in the neighbourhood?'

'A place halfway up Gloucester Road on the right. It's

called the Scarlet Pimpernel. The food is not as bad as it sounds. They'll send out for drinks.'

'Do you feel equal to the Scarlet Pimpernel, Hugh?'

Moreland, almost past speech, nodded.

'Give him your key, Teddy,' said Molly Jeavons. 'We can find him another in the morning.'

Jeavons fumbled in one of the pockets of his overall and handed a key to Moreland.

'I'll probably be pottering about when you come in,' he said, 'can't get to sleep if I turn in early. Come back with him, Nick. We might be able to find a glass of beer for you.'

I went across the room to take leave of Widmerpool and his mother. When I came up to her, Mrs Widmerpool turned her battery of teeth upon me, smiling fiercely, like the Wolf in Little Red Riding Hood, her shining, ruddy countenance advancing closer as she continued to hold my hand in hers.

'I expect you are still occupied with your literary pursuits,' she said, taking up our conversation at precisely the point at which it had been abandoned.

'Some journalism——'

'This is not a happy time for book-lovers.'

'No, indeed.'

'Still, you are fortunate.'

'Why?'

'With your bookish days, not, like Kenneth, in arms.'

'He seems a Happy Warrior.'

'It is not in his nature to remain in civil life at time of war,' she said.

'I will say good night, then.'

'Good luck to you,' she said, 'wherever you may find yourself in these troublous times.'

She gave me another smile of great malignance, returning immediately to her discussions about rent. Widmerpool half raised his hand in a gesture of farewell. Moreland and I left the house together.

'What the hell were you doing in that place?' he asked, as we walked up the street.

'Molly Jeavons is an aunt of Isobel's. It is a perfectly normal place for me to be. Far stranger that you yourself should turn up there.'

'You're right about that,' Moreland said. 'I can't quite make out how I did. Things have been moving rather quickly with me the last few months. Who was that terrifying woman you said good-bye to?'

'Mother of the man in spectacles called Widmerpool. You met him with me at a nursing home years ago.'

'No recollection,' said Moreland, 'though he seemed familiar. His mother began on Scriabin as soon as I arrived in the house. Told me the *Poème de l'Extase* was her favourite musical work. I say, I'm feeling like hell. Far from *de l'extase*.'

'What's been happening? I didn't even know you'd left the country.'

'The country, as it were, left me,' said Moreland. 'At least Matilda did, which came to much the same thing.'

'How did all this come about?'

'I hardly know myself.'

'Has she gone off with somebody?'

'Gone back to Donners.'

The information was so grotesque that at first I could hardly take it seriously. Then I saw as a possibility that a row might have taken place and Matilda done this from pique. At certain seasons, Matilda, admittedly, had a fairly rough time living with Moreland. She might require a short spell of rich life to put her right, although (as Mrs Widmerpool could have said) wartime was hardly the moment to pursue rich life. Sir Magnus Donners, as a former lover, himself no longer young, would provide a comparatively innocuous vehicle for such a temporary interlude. The Moreland situation, regarded in these cold-blooded terms, might be undesirable certainly, at the same time not beyond hope.

'I'll tell the story when we get to the restaurant,' said Moreland. 'I haven't eaten anything since breakfast. Just had a few doubles.'

We found the Scarlet Pimpernel soon after this. The place was not full. We took a table in the corner at the back of the room. At this early stage of the war, it was still possible to order a bottle of wine without undue difficulty and expense. The food, as Molly Jeavons had said, turned out better than might have been expected from the mob-caps of the waitresses and general tone of the establishment. After some soup and a glass of wine Moreland began to recover himself.

'One always imagines things happen in hot blood,' he said. 'An ill-considered remark starts a row. Hard words follow, misunderstandings. Matters that can be put right in the end. Unfortunately life doesn't work out like that. First of all there is no row, secondly, nothing can be put right.'

'Barnby says he is always on his guard when things are going well with a woman.'

'Still, your wife,' said Moreland, 'it's bloody uncomfortable if things are not going well between yourself and your wife. I speak from experience. All the same, there may be something in Barnby's view. You remember the business about me and – well – your sister-in-law, Priscilla?'

'You conveyed at the time that a situation existed – then ceased to exist, or was stifled in some way.'

I did not see why I should help Moreland out beyond a certain point. If he wanted to tell his story, he must supply the facts, not reveal one half and allow the other to be guessed.

717

He had always been too fond of doing that when extracting sympathy for his emotional tangles. No one had ever known what had happened about himself and Priscilla, only that some close relationship had existed between them, which had caused a great deal of disturbance in his married life. Some explanation was required. The situation could not be pieced together merely from a series of generalisations about matrimony.

'Anything you like,' said Moreland. 'The point is that, during that rather tricky period, Matty could not have behaved better. She was absolutely marvellous – really marvellous. It was the one thing that made the whole awfulness of life possible when . . .'

He did not finish the sentence, but meant, I supposed, when the affair with Priscilla was at an end.

'Why on earth, if Matty was going to leave me, didn't she leave me then? I'll tell you. She enjoyed the emotional strain of it all. Women are like that, the lame girl in Dostoevsky who said she didn't want to be happy.'

'How did it start?'

'Matilda was in a show that opened in the provinces – Brighton or somewhere. She just wrote and said she was not returning home, would I send her things along, such as they were. She had already taken most of her clothes with her, so I presume she had already decided on leaving when she set out.'

'How long ago?'

'Two or three weeks.'

'Is it generally known?'

'Not yet, I think. Matilda is often away acting, so it is quite usual for her to be absent from home.'

'And you had no warning that all was not well?'

'I am the most modest man in the world when it is a question of trying to make a woman fall for me,' said Moreland. 'I never expect I shall bring it off. On the other hand, once she's fallen, I can never really believe she will prefer someone else. These things are just the way vanity happens to take you.'

'But where does Donners come in? She can't have fallen for him.'

'She has been going over to Stourwater fairly often., She made no secret of that. Why should she? There didn't seem any reason to object. What could I do, anyway? You remember we all dined there that rather grim evening when everyone dressed up as the Seven Deadly Sins. I recall now, that was where I saw your friend Widmerpool before. Does he always haunt my worst moments? Anyway, Matilda's visits to Stourwater were of that sort, nothing serious.'

'Is Matilda living at Stourwater at this moment?'

'No – staying in the flat of a girl she knows in London, another actress. The point is this: if I allow Matilda to divorce me, Donners will marry her.'

'No.'

Moreland laughed.

'Indeed, yes,' he said. 'I see I have surprised you.'

'You certainly have.'

'It now turns out that Donners asked her to marry him before – when she was mixed up with him years ago.'

'What are you going to do?'

'What can I do?'

'But will you let yourself be divorced?'

'I've tried every way of getting her back,' said Moreland. 'She is quite firm. I don't want to be just spiteful about it. If she is consumed with a desire to become Lady Donners, Lady Donners let her be.'

'But to want to be Lady Donners is so unlike Matilda – especially as she turned down the offer in the past.'

'You think it unlike her?'

'Don't you?'

'Not entirely. She can be tough, you know. One of the worst things about life is not how nasty the nasty people are. You know that already. It is how nasty the nice people can be.'

'Have you no idea what went wrong?'

'None – except, as I say, the Priscilla business. I thought that was all forgotten. Perhaps it was, and life with me was just too humdrum. Now I'll tell you something else that may surprise you. Nothing ever took place between Priscilla and myself. We never went to bed.'

'Why not?'

'I don't really know,' said Moreland slowly, 'perhaps because there did not seem anywhere to go. That's so often one of the problems. I've thought about the subject a lot. One might write a story about two lovers who have nowhere to go. They are at their wits' end. Then they pretend they are newly married and apply to a different estate-agent every week to inspect unfurnished houses and flats. As often as not they are given the key and manage to have an hour alone together. Inventive, don't you think? I was crazy about Priscilla. Then Maclintick committed suicide and everything was altered. I felt upset, couldn't think about girls and all that. That was when Priscilla herself decided things had better stop. I suppose the whole business shook the boat so far as my own marriage was concerned. It seemed to recover. I thought we were getting on all right. I was wrong.'

I was reminded of Duport telling me about Jean, although no one could have been less like Jean than Matilda, less like Moreland than Duport.

'The fact is,' said Moreland, 'Matilda lost interest in me. With women, that situation is like a vacuum. It must be filled. They begin to look round for someone else. She decided on Donners.'

'She was still pretty interested in you at the party Mrs Foxe gave for your symphony.'

'How do you know?'

'She talked to me about it.'

'While I was getting off with Priscilla?'

'More or less.'

Moreland made a grimace.

'Surely she'll come back in the end?' I said.

'You see, I'm not absolutely certain I want Matilda back,' he said. 'Sometimes I feel I can't live without her, other times, that I can't bear the thought of having her in the house. In real life, things are much worse than as represented in books. In books, you love somebody and want them, win them or lose them. In real life, so often, you love them and don't want them, or want them and don't love them.'

'You make it all sound difficult.'

'I sometimes think all I myself require is a quiet life,' said Moreland. 'For some unaccountable reason it is always imagined that people like oneself want to be rackety. Of course I want some fun occasionally, but so does everyone else.'

'What does Matilda want? A lot of money?'

'Not in the obvious way, diamonds and things. Matilda has wanted for a long time to spread her wings. She knows at last that she will never be any good as an actress. She wants power. Plenty of power. When we were first married she arranged all my life for me. Arranged rather too much. I'm not sure she liked it when I made a small name for myself – if one may be said to have made a small name for oneself.'

'She will have to play second fiddle to Sir Magnus, more even than to yourself.'

'Not second fiddle as an artist – as an actress, in her case. Being an artist – to use old fashioned terminology, but what other can one use? – partakes of certain feminine characteristics, is therefore peculiarly provoking for women to live with. In some way, the more "masculine" an artist is, the worse her predicament. If he is really homosexual, or hopelessly incapable of dealing with everyday life, it is almost easier.'

'I can think of plenty of examples to the contrary.'

'Anyway, there will be compensations with Donners. Matilda will operate on a large scale. She will have her finger in all kind of pies.'

'Still, what pies.'

'Not very intellectual ones, certainly,' said Moreland, 'but then the minds of most women are unamusing, unoriginal, determinedly banal. Matilda is not one of the exceptions. Is it surprising one is always cuckolded by middlebrows?'

'But you talk as if these matters were all concerned with the mind.'

Moreland laughed.

'I once asked Barnby if he did not find most women extraordinarily unsensual,' he said. 'Do you know what he answered?'

'What?'

'He said, "I've never noticed."'

I laughed too.

'I suppose,' said Moreland, 'had you asked Lloyd George, "Don't you think politics rather corrupt?", he might have made the same reply. Minor factors disappear when you are absorbed by any subject. You know, one of the things about being deserted is that it leaves you in a semi-castrated condition. You're incapable of fixing yourself up with an alternative girl. Deserting people, on the other hand, is positively stimulating. I don't mind betting that Matty is surrounded by admirers at this moment. Do you remember when we heard that crippled woman singing in Gerrard Street years ago:

> Whom do you lead on Rapture's roadway, far,
> Before you agonize them in farewell?

That's what it comes to. But look who has just arrived.'

Three people were sitting down at a table near the door of the restaurant. They were Mark Members, J. G. Quiggin and Anne Umfraville.

'I feel better after getting all that off my chest,' said Moreland.

'Shall we go back?'

'Do you think Lady Molly will have forgotten who I am?' said Moreland. 'It's terribly kind of her to put me up like this, but you know what bad memories warm hearted people have.'

I saw from that Moreland had perfectly grasped Molly Jeavons's character. Nothing was more probable than that she would have to be reminded of the whole incident of inviting him to the house when she saw him at breakfast the following morning. Like so many persons who live disordered lives, Moreland had peculiar powers of falling on his feet, an instinctive awareness of where to look for help. That was perhaps the legacy of early poverty. He and Molly Jeavons – although she made no claims whatever to know about the arts – would understand each other. If he overstayed his welcome – with Moreland not inconceivable – she would throw him out without the smallest ill-feeling on either side.

'We might have a word with the literary critics on the way out,' said Moreland.

'What happened to Anne Umfraville in the light of recent developments?'

'I don't know,' said Moreland. 'I thought she was interested in your friend Templer. I understand she was passing out of Donners's life in any case. She must have made some new friends.'

We paid the bill, pausing on the way out at the table by the door.

'Who told you of this restaurant?' said Quiggin. 'I thought it was only known to Anne and myself – you have met, of course?'

His air was somewhat proprietorial.

'Anne has a flat not far from here,' he said. 'Mark and I have been working late there.'

'What at?'

'Proofs,' said Quiggin.

He did not explain what kind of proofs. Neither Moreland nor I inquired.

'How is Matty, Hugh?' asked Members.

'On tour.'

'I do adore Matilda,' said Anne Umfraville. 'Have you been to Stourwater lately? I have rather quarrelled with Magnus. He can be so tiresome. So pompous, you know.'

'I don't live near there any longer,' said Moreland, 'so we haven't met for a month or two. Sir Magnus himself is no longer occupying the castle, of course. It has been taken over by the government, but I can't remember for what purpose. Just as a castle, I suppose.'

'What a ludicrous way this war is being run,' said Quiggin. 'I was talking to Howard Craggs about its inanities last night. Have you got a decent shelter where you live?'

'I'm just going back there,' said Moreland, 'never to emerge.'

'Give my love to Matty when you next see her,' said Members.

'And mine,' said Anne Umfraville.

We said good night.

'I think people know about Matilda,' said Moreland.

We passed through streets lit only by a cold autumnal moon.

'Have you the key?'

Moreland found it at last. We went upstairs to the drawing-room. Jeavons was wandering about restlessly. He had abandoned his beret, now wore a mackintosh over pyjamas. His brother was in an armchair, smoking his pipe and going through a pile of papers beside him on the floor. He would check each document, then place it on a stack the other side of his chair.

'We got rid of them at last,' said Jeavons. 'Molly's gone to bed. They struck a pretty hard bargain with Stanley. Still, the place seems to suit. That's what matters. I'd rather it was Lil than me. What was dinner like?'

'Not bad.'

'How was our blackout as you came up the street?'

'Not a chink of light.'

'Have some beer?'

'I think I'll go straight to bed, if you don't mind,' said Moreland. 'I feel a bit done in.'

I had never heard Moreland refuse a drink before. He must have been utterly exhausted. He had cheered up during dinner. Now he looked like death again.

'I'll come up with you to make sure the blackout won't fall down,' said Jeavons. 'Never do to be fined as a warden.'

'Good night, Nick.'

'Good night.'

They went upstairs. Stanley Jeavons threw down what was apparently the last of his papers. He took the pipe from his mouth and began to knock it out against his heel. He sighed deeply.

'I think I'll have a glass of beer too,' he said.

He helped himself and sat down again.

'It's extraordinary,' he said, 'how you get a hunch from a chap's handwriting if he's done three years for fraudulent conversion.'

'In business?'

'In business, too. I meant in what I'm doing now.'

'What are you doing?'

'Reservists.'

'For the army?'

'Sorting them out. Got a pile of their personal details here. Stacks more at the office. Brought a batch home to work on.'

'Then what happens?'

'Some of them get called up.'

'I'm on some form of the Reserve myself.'

'Which one?'

I told him.

'You'll probably come my way in due course – or one of my colleagues'.'

'Could it be speeded up?'

'What?'

'Finding my name.'

'Would you like that?'

'Yes.'

'Don't see why not.'

'You could?'

'M'm.'

'Fairly soon?'

'How old are you?'

I told him that too.

'Health A.1?'

'I think so.'

'School OTC?'

'Yes.'

'Get a Certificate A there?'

'Yes.'

'What arm is your choice?'

'Infantry.'

'Any particular regiment?'

I made a suggestion.

'You don't want one of the London regiments?'

'Not specially. Why?'

'Everyone seems to want a London regiment,' he said. 'Probably be able to fix you up with an out-of-the-way regiment like that.'

'It would be kind.'

'And you'd like to get cracking?'

'Yes.'

'I'll see what we can do.'

'That's very good of you.'

'Might take a week or two.'

'That's all right.'

'Just let me write your name in my little book.'

Jeavons returned to the room.

'That friend of yours is absolutely cooked,' he said. 'He'd have been happy to sleep on the floor. His blackout is all correct now, if he doesn't interfere with it. Well, Stan, I don't know how much Lil is going to enjoy living in a cottage with Mrs W.'

'Lil will be all right,' said Stanley Jeavons. 'She can get on with all sorts.'

'More than I can,' said Jeavons.

Stanley Jeavons shook his head without smiling. He evidently found his brother's life inexplicable, had no desire whatever to share its extravagances. Jeavons moved towards the table where the beer bottles stood. Suddenly he began to sing in that full, deep, unexpectedly attractive voice, so different from the croaking tones in which he ordinarily conversed:

> 'There's a long, long trail a-winding
> Into the land of . . . my dreams,
> Where the night . . . ingale is singing
> And the white moon beams.
> There's a long, long night of waiting,
> Until my dreams all . . . come true . . .'

He broke off as suddenly as he had begun. Stanley Jeavons began tapping out his pipe again, perhaps to put a stop to this refrain.

'Used to sing that while we were blanco-ing,' said Jeavons. 'God, how fed up I got cleaning that bloody equipment.'

'I shall have to go home, Ted.'

'Don't hurry away.'

'I must.'

'Have some more beer.'

'No.'

'Come and see us soon,' said Jeavons, 'before we all get blown up. I'm still not satisfied with the fold of that curtain. Got the blackout on the brain. You haven't a safety-pin about you, have you, Stan?'

Outside the moon had gone behind a bank of cloud. I went home through the gloom, exhilarated, at the same time rather afraid. Ahead lay the region beyond the white-currant bushes, where the wild country began, where armies for ever campaigned, where the Rules and Discipline of War prevailed. Another stage of life was passed, just as finally, just as irrevocably, as on that day when childhood had come so abruptly to an end at Stonehurst.